The Curator of Broken Things

------ FULL TRILOGY ------

A novel by Corine Gantz

ISBN: 978-0-9834366-9-0

Book 1 - From Smyrna to Paris
Corine Gantz

To David and Nathan

CHAPTER 1

Move-in Day

All around, Cassie saw men. But it seemed that that ship had sailed for her. Fathers or sons, young or old, the percentage who paid her any attention was exactly zero.

It was liberating, this new-found invisibility. These days Cassie dressed strictly for comfort, her black curls had reverted to their natural unruliness, and the money she economized on makeup was spent liberally and without guilt on chocolate.

It was liberating, yes, but also depressing, if she dwelled on the thought too long.

She was sitting on a plastic chair between a pool table and a vending machine and pretending to be immensely occupied with her cellphone. What she was doing, though, was observing without being seen, one of the rare perks of impending middle age.

Freshmen of every race, shape, culture, nationality, and gender – some whose race or gender she could not identify – entered and exited the building carrying suitcases, boxes, rolled-up memory foam mattresses, clothes on hangers, toasters, and computers, while their parents fretted. Move-in Day, Cassie understood, was a flirt-fest on an epic scale. The boys and girls were checking each other out, ready as they were for the parentally orchestrated and financed independence that awaited them.

It should have been a consolation that she wasn't the only one struggling. Around Cassie, other hapless, apologetic-looking parents carried objects up and down stairwells in a heart-wrenching attempt at being relevant one last time. Meanwhile, the freshmen, consciously or not, counted the minutes until that last hug, when the gates would at last close behind their lives as children.

It dawned on her that up until today she had had a function. The function of mother of twins. But Alexander and Jeanne had come in like a tornado, transformed her life into a seventeen-year-long hurricane, and in a matter of hours would be out of the house and into college, both of them on the very same day. In the chaos and excitement of organizing them for college, Cassie had not prepared herself for becoming extraneous to their lives overnight.

Whom would she take care of now?

Who would take care of her?

Move-in Day for both kids being on the same weekend, they had divided the task. Peter, her ex-husband, was in New York with Alex, while Cassie was in Miami with Jeanne. Alexander and Jeanne had come out of her womb with distinct outlooks on life. Jeanne would be studying acting at the University of Miami, the only school willing to overlook her 2.0 GPA. Cassie and Peter had the strong suspicion that Peter's status as the most sought-after screenwriter in Hollywood had weighed heavily on the admission committee's decision. They regardless breathed a huge sigh of relief and Peter gladly signed the exorbitant tuition check. Meanwhile, Alexander, surprising no one, had been accepted to several Ivy Leagues and had opted for the full ride at Columbia.

Cassie tucked herself in a corner of the hall to do what people do when they already feel immensely crappy about their lives and called her ex-husband.

She dialed his cell, almost hoping to land on voicemail but Peter picked up on the first ring.

"What's going on in New York?" she asked.

"I'm at the campus's Starbucks," Peter said, "treating myself to a delicious tres leches iced macchiado. I asked the barista if it was vegan but she did not know."

"Why vegan?"

"Jessica wants me to give it a shot," Peter said.

"Tres leches means three milks in Spanish," Cassie pointed out.

"Oh well, I already syphoned half of it anyway."

"You're with Alex?"

"No, by myself."

Cassie sat back in her plastic chair and rolled her eyes, "Sheesh, Peter."

"What?"

"You won't be seeing your son until Thanksgiving and you're spending those last precious minutes alone at Starbucks?"

Peter had known her for eighteen years and had spent the first twelve married to her. He could tell when she was upset. "How are you feeling?" he asked.

"They still haven't come up with an adjective to describe what I'm feeling," she said.

"Here is what you're feeling," Peter said. "Proud, excited, and a little sad."

"Children pried away from their parents and vice versa. I can't understand what there is to rejoice about."

"French kids go to college too," Peter said. "I'm sure they have Move-in Day there as well. It's all part of life."

Cassie had grown up in France and gone to school there. Her conception of American university life was second-hand or fictionalized: Legally Blonde, Animal House, Peter droning on about his alma mater, brochures depicting intellectually and genetically gifted youth, rape on campus statistics – and what in the world was a sorority rush? "I'll have you know that the rest of the world's schools aren't filled with cheerleaders, marching bands, and keg parties," she said.

Peter did not respond, as was his new technique when she was unjustifiably aggressive. Had he done just that when they were married, had he just waited for the storm to pass as he now did so well, they might still be together today.

Peter was a good guy, great father, and a friend. The worst of Peter, not to mention Cassie's worst, had found free and creative ways to express itself in their marriage. Five years after their separation Peter seemed at last capable of being happily married, although to someone else.

"I hate that I'm not with you and Jeanne today," Peter said. "I hate it every time I need to be two places at once. It just tears me up inside."

What other time was there? Cassie briefly wondered. "Damn. That lump in my throat is back," she said, "I don't want Jeanne to see me in tears when she comes back."

"Where is she?"

"I got sick of following her around like a love-struck puppy. I'm sitting in the reception area while she organizes her room. I don't want to be one of those pathetic mothers who makes her daughter's bed and arranges her closet."

Now, of course, that was precisely what she wanted to do.

"You know this is a sanctioned day for parents to be pathetic," Peter said. "We're all in the same boat. A little humiliation is part of the separation process."

Cassie considered that before replying. "Only my situation is a little shittier than yours." She stopped herself. She didn't want to look any more pitiful than was necessary.

"I know what you mean," Peter said conciliatorily.

"No, you don't."

Peter knew not to go there. After dropping off Alex, he would be returning to Los Angeles; to his crisp, new, shiny life; to Jessica, his young wife whom Cassie called Jessica Rabbit – although never to her face – because of her cartoon-like figure and determination to be with child every eighteen months or so, who was pregnant at the moment with their third boy in five years. Whereas tomorrow Cassie would fly back to Los Angeles and return to an empty house.

Peter knew all too well that tomorrow Cassie was back to square one.

****

Later, in the cafeteria, Cassie and Jeanne were having lunch. Cassie stared at the stringy meat on her plate, the pale mushrooms that floated in industrial-strength gravy. In the cafeteria line, students stood next to their parents, the kids wishing their parents could just disappear, and the parents just as aware of being unwanted. All were piling up bland food on their plastic trays. Cassie wondered what was worse, not to be wanted, or not to be needed?

"What are you going to do now, mom?" Jeanne asked.

Cassie looked at Jeanne. If someone could become a Hollywood star, it was her daughter. Not for the acting – although she was terrific at drama and was, after all, here to learn all about it since they were investing two hundred thousand dollars into it – but for her loveliness, her sleek auburn hair, her eyes a rare shade of green, her porcelain skin, her slender neck, and her long body. The question took Cassie by surprise. It wasn't like Jeanne to corner her like this. "I'll go on living if that is what you're wondering."

"I'm just imagining you being all alone in Los Angeles. I bet Alex is thinking about it too."

"Yet you both spent the last two years planning an East Coast education."

"You could have told us not to apply out of state."

"The last thing you need is to worry about where it leaves me," Cassie said.

Jeanne picked at the lone tomato slice in her salad. "But I do."

Cassie's heart melted. It was hard to remember the hell Jeanne had put her through over the last few years. "Please don't worry about me," she said. "See, you made it to college! Isn't that incredible? You are starting your life, my love. My job here is done." Jeanne's eyes flooded with tears, and the green of her pupils turned gorgeously near-fluorescent. Cassie bit her lip. She too had greenish eyes, although hers were more on the amber side, but all she'd get out of tears would be puffy eyes and a red nose. "I'll be fine, mon ange. I'll garden. You know. I've been looking forward to gardening for years."

"Mom, you know you're never going to garden."

"And there are so many things I look forward to doing now. Reading uninterrupted, going to the movies, spending time with friends, writing for myself for once."

Jeanne shook her head. "First of all, what friends? The only people you spend time with are Dad and us."

"I have friends," Cassie protested. "Friends are overrated. People are, in general."

"I can't picture you working from home with Dad every day. It's kind of creepy."

"Why creepy? Your father and I have been working together for almost two decades."

"I don't know … Alex and I won't be around. It'll be weird, the old home, the ex-husband, no kids. Will Jessica be creeped out by that?"

"Honey, Jessica Rabbit and I are not in competition. You just enjoy school. What your mother does from here on out is none of your beeswax."

Jeanne rolled her eyes. "Oh Mom, stop saying that. You can't even say it right."

"How do you say it?"

"Without a French accent."

"I look forward to my accent not being mocked." Cassie added, "Motherhood is about adapting to your children's needs and changes. Right now, your need is that I get out of the way so that you and your brother can become adults. I left my country and started over with a new language when I was barely older than you are. I think I've demonstrated my capacity to adapt. The whole world is open to you. Your job is to start soaring."

"Hello, Mother! Don't act like you have a foot in the grave. You're 39. Most of my friends' moms are much older than you are. That's the good part of having us when you were twenty."

"The bad part is that I was a child when I had children and did not know myself at all. Don't make the same mistake, I'm begging you."

"My point is, you better find something exciting to do. You know how you are. You get restless. And you have potential too, for soaring and stuff."

"I'm not like you and Alex, honey. I've had a very different set of circumstances."

"French parents, I know."

"That's right."

"That great Potential-Crusher."

"Exactement."

Jeanne bit into a French fry and said, "There are people with worse childhoods than yours that end up doing all kinds of cool stuff."

"And for this I applaud them." Cassie looked at her beautiful daughter and tried to sear this moment into her memory. "Promise me just one thing," she pleaded.

Jeanne looked at her wearily. "What?"

"Call your brother occasionally."

Jeanne twisted her lip. "You know Alex has no desire to speak to me."

"Then email him. You don't have to say personal things. Maybe send him a funny link, or, I don't know, like his Facebook status."

"We're not even friends on social media, mom. He hates me."

"The two of you are just going through a phase."

"He can't stand that I got into a college in the end and that I enjoyed high school. I didn't have to kill myself the way he did."

Cassie did not respond. How could she have responded? This was the truth. She had experienced a similar reaction from Alex when she had made the same request before he left. Her son was more laconic, less inclined to volunteering information, but he was sweet and gentle, except when it came to his sister. "The only reason they admitted her," he had said, "is that they saw Dad's name on her application."

"I'm sure it was a factor," Cassie had to admit.

"Remind me again? How much are you forking out for her acting education?"

"This is the first time your sister is motivated to do something."

"As if she wasn't self-indulgent enough. You realize she'll never make a living that way?"

"What are we going to do, Alex? Disown her because you're a workhorse and a math genius? And had you not gotten the scholarship, we would have paid for your education too."

"But I did get the scholarship. And you won't have to pay for my education."

"Alex, we are so proud of you. And yes, we hope that your sister will rise to the occasion. But parenting is not a meritocracy. We love you both for your strengths, your weaknesses, and everything in between. I know it's hard to comprehend that we can love you for being so accomplished while at the same time love her for –"

"– being a fuck-up?" Alex asked.

"Please just try to call her once in a while."

"She'll be much too busy posting videos of herself applying makeup. And you know she hates me."

"She doesn't. It's just that she might feel a bit insecure around you."

"Same difference."

On the plane back to Los Angeles, Cassie felt numb, as though none of this was happening to her. She told herself that if anything, this was good material. When you're a writer and life kicks you in the jaw, you always have that consolation.

CHAPTER 2

The Ottoman Boy

1912. Smyrna, in the ailing Ottoman Empire. Above, only blue sky. It is the hottest time of the day on the hottest day of the year. Everywhere: dirt, rocks, boulders, some as tall as houses. A half dozen petrified-looking goats stunned into stillness by the terrible heat. The sharp scent of wild sage. The crackling hum of flying insects. And then something peculiar in the distance: a lone dark silhouette is climbing agilely through the barren earth and jagged rocks. On closer observation, it is a boy, perhaps ten years old, dressed entirely in black in the traditional garment of rabbinical students, in a heavy cloak and a wide-brimmed hat. The boy hops from rock to rock, light-footed despite the cumbersome clothes, and suddenly he is gone: disappeared into thin air.

****

For the last two years, Albano never took the same path twice so that his footsteps did not form a trail. He wiped his brow, leaned against the pulsating heat of the stone and, for a minute, took in his deserted surroundings. Satisfied that no one was there who could have seen him, he plunged under the seemingly impenetrable thorny bushes at the base of the rock, into the narrow opening only he knew about. On his hands and feet, he crawled into the pitch-black cavity in the rocks and felt for the matches he had placed there. He sat down on the cool dirt and lit the oil lamp.

When the cave illuminated, Albano was always gripped with the same feeling. A miracle had brought him here.

The cave was a cool and damp world of echoing silence and looked the way all of Earth must have at the beginning of time. A minuscule spring trickled from a crack in the rock and pooled in one corner to disappear a few meters further down a subterranean path. A bit of light found its way through a crack high above, and so things grew there: nothing much, moss and a few tender ferns, but enough to transform the cave into an otherworldly wonder. It was about twenty by fifteen feet wide and tall enough for a man to stand. A palace.

Albano wasted no time in removing his clothes. His cave was furnished with only what he had managed to hide under his clothes, bits of useful objects which might make a person comfortable: an oil lamp, a rug, even a small reserve of food and water. He removed his leather slippers, breeches, and black linen stockings and placed them neatly on a rock.

He wished that he could remain this way eternally, feel the cool air on his bare skin, the freedom of it. The feeling of being undressed transported him to the time when his mother used to let him and his brothers splash around in the sea half naked. He knelt on a rug next to the spring, cupped his hand, and drank the cold water. For a while, he sat by the water, breathed in the dampness, and listened to the bubbling brook that echoed against the smooth stone of the cavern. For a fleeting moment, he experienced a sense of deep connectedness with a beauty and power he could not name.

Two years ago, the cholera pandemic had left absolute loss in its trail. Days after it happened, he was torn away from his village and everything he knew and was brought to Smyrna's Jewish quarter to live with his cousins and Uncle Joshua and Aunt Sadie – the only relatives able to take in an eight-year-old orphan.

He had discovered the cave by accident, on a day when he had hoped to die. But the cave had welcomed him like a loving mother, made him feel protected, made him feel safe. It was in this cave that Albano had taken refuge and cursed Adonai for taking his mother, father, brothers, and sisters and sparing him for no reason he could understand. It was in the cave that he was able to bury his face into his arms and sob in secret. It was in the cave that he had later on resigned himself to his aunt and uncle's decision that he should take on rabbinical studies.

But in the last few days, he had met Uncle Moshe, and then Hagop and Xandra. Now everything had changed, and perhaps his whole life and destiny along with it.

Albano carefully folded his tallis, brought his lips to it, and said a prayer of his composition. Adonai would not approve of what he was about to do. He reached inside a narrow crevice between two rocks and felt for the leather satchel. He opened it. The money was still there.

Albano unfolded the white linen djellaba, the loose breeches, and the sandals his friend Hagop had given him. Hagop. Yes, Albano now had a friend. A friend who was not Jewish!

When he was dressed, Albano slung the satchel over his thin body. He combed his payots behind his ears the way Hagop had taught him, which was no easy feat, and then secured them in place with a red fez. "You don't want to look like a Jew," Hagop had told him. "No one in Smyrna trusts a Jew. Not the Turks, not the Greeks, not the Armenians, not even the Jews themselves." This was not true, of course. Jews did trust Jews. Although Hagop's comment had made Albano angry at the time, he could not deceive himself entirely. Wasn't he, at this very moment, being untrustworthy to his people?

Up on the highest ridge inside the cave, set upright against the stone, in a spot where they caught the best light of the single ray of sun that made its way inside the cave, his family's finials seemed to look down at him with reproach. The two Torah ornaments destined to top a Torah case were shaped like tiny, intricate gold and silver crowns, each only large enough for a squirrel's head. His father, a Kohen descendant of Aaron, brother of Moses, and high priest by birth, had demanded of him, on his deathbed, to hide the finials. They were sacred, although Albano didn't know what made them so. They had belonged to his father and his grandfather, and his great-grandfather before that. Albano only needed to know that, like all things that were ancient, precious, and sacred, they had to be kept a secret. One day, Albano would take on the responsibility of Kohanim, which was an everlasting covenant, although he was unsure what the words Kohanim, everlasting, and covenant meant.

His mother used to love to tell the tale of how, when he was born, the village's rabbi had scrutinized him for disqualifying traits. Albano had been born with both hands and feet; he wasn't blind, his eyebrows weren't too thick, his limbs were in good proportion and his testicles in good order, and therefore the rabbi had proclaimed him suitable. But because he was a Kohen, Albano was not allowed to take part in his family burials. Those were the kinds of rules that God made. Albano carried the weight of that responsibility and also the burden of what they meant regarding his obligation to God.

When he exited the cave later, Albano looked very different. He was dressed in white and wore a fez. He looked just like a Muslim boy. He walked down the rocky sides of Mount Pagus, trying not to think too much about the Kohanim, and kept a nervous hand in his trouser pocket into which he had tucked a portion of yesterday's earnings. This was just enough akçes for today's business. The bulk of his and Hagop's profit would remain hidden in the cave for now. Albano felt great anguish at the responsibility of keeping his new friend's share of their earnings, but Hagop slept with four nosy sisters in a small room above his parent's bakery and so did not possess a good hiding place of his own.

But wasn't Hagop contradicting himself? Hagop had an agile mind, and Albano often became confused when his friend spoke to him a mile a minute in a mixture of Arabic, Armenian, and Hebrew, but this time, Albano had a solid argument. By trusting him to hold on to the money, wasn't Hagop the precise example of an Armenian boy trusting a Jew? Albano smiled at the idea and began to rehearse in his mind their future conversation on the subject.

Albano descended the hill feeling light at last in clothes so much better suited for walking in the sun than the clothes meant to toil over the word of God. He thought of Moshe, the extraordinary uncle he had just met, who had arrived in Smyrna and within a week's time had managed to turn Albano's life upside down. Uncle Moshe was scandalous; that was what the women in the Jewish quarter said. But in what way? This, Albano could not figure out. When he asked, there were eye rolls and giggles, and that was that. Did

Albano's time spent with his new friend Hagop make him scandalous as well, he wondered?

As he reached the main road, deserted mountains turned into the city's suburb. There were many people in the streets. Houses sprouted one after another, and the temperature eased with each step. A faint sea breeze swept lightly through the air, and the arid landscape made way for palm trees and masses of bougainvillea against whitewashed walls. The pungent aroma of wild oregano soon mingled with the scents of jasmine emanating from the houses' courtyards. Albano followed the dirt road where it made its turn around the mountain and, as it happened every time without fail, he was overcome with awe at the beauty before him. There, magnificent, dark blue against the turquoise sky, was the vast expanse of the Aegean Sea cradled by the glorious bay of Smyrna and, further into the horizon, his wide-open future.

CHAPTER 3

Empty Nester

Cassie faced the jungle that was her garden. She and the plants knew that this had nothing to do with gardening. This was war. The bougainvillea, which was tangled into the Italian Cypress almost all the way up, had won the minute it began to grow thorns the size of butcher's knives. She narrowed her eyes at the mass of giant echiums and their foot-long cone-shaped flowers. No, not them either. Their silver leaves stuck to everything like Velcro: hair, clothes, even mysteriously the inside of her bra. And forget about the pampas grass, so feather-like and innocent-looking but mercenary with blades sharp as razors, or the blue trumpet vines, which she had planted fifteen years before: three saucer-size flowers on a strand of vine wrapped daintily around a two-foot tall bamboo. Since then each flower had popped bullet-like seeds that rudely planted themselves and multiplied like the broom in Fantasia. They had overtaken the garden, and Cassie was allergic to them on contact. This much she had learned in her nearly two decades of gardening in Southern California: here a plant either withered and died within a week or became invasive and wanted to kill you.

Cassie threw down her hedge trimmers and went inside the house. Jeanne had been spot-on. Nearly eight months later, Cassie wasn't having such a great time enjoying her new found quiet after all. She had waited from September to Christmas for the twins to come for winter break, but as soon as they were back home, they had resumed their teenage habits and disappeared to hang out with old friends, only coming home to sleep, and did not wake up until noon while she paced. Had she not been a horrible cook she would have fed them delicious meals, but even this was out of her reach. Her microwave chocolate cake in a mug only went so far to lure in her children.

In the last eight months, Peter and Jessica had produced another spawn, Jeanne and Alex had gone through almost two semesters of college, and all Cassie had to show for it were rose thorn scratches and cracked fingernails. Christmas and all its trimmings had been consummated at Peter's house. Jessica Rabbit (who was a won-der-ful! cook) had prepared the whole meal while handling two toddlers and a newborn with Mary Poppins-like magic. Cassie had tried so hard to act relaxed that her body, clenched to the breaking point, had thrown in the towel the next day with the mother of all sciaticas, and she had spent January unable to stand straight.

Inside the house, she placed the last of the boxes of her cleaning spree by the entryway. Her efforts were single-minded, more akin to the Great Purge than to spring cleaning. Everything had to go. Why she wasn't sure. This last box was filled with old shoes, boots, sandals, and that pair of one-size-too-small Christian Louboutin stilettos that Peter had given her on some occasion. That book she had read recently on the evils of a cluttered life had legitimized her craving for something, and she had decided that what she craved was minimalism. It was progress, she told herself, to crave something. But if she was honest with herself, she had made too little progress where it mattered the most: when it came to the one major goal she had set for herself, which was to let go of Peter, Cassie had not made a dent.

She went down the staircase to her bedroom and unearthed from the depth of the closet the last item she had planned to add to the giveaway pile: an old suitcase, monstrous-looking with a green and pink zebra pattern, a rusty zipper, and wobbly wheels. She dragged it up the stairs. The main part of the house stood at street level and was jaw-dropping with glossy wood floors, white walls, and a soaring ceiling. A first impression that blinds you to details that will, down the line, ruin your life – i.e. the two rooms per floor, the laundry room located at the lowest level, and the millions of steps this quirk implies. Because of this oversight, you will spend the next eighteen years climbing and descending steps, which will give you, along with buns and thighs of steel, a major laundry chip on your shoulder. The floor plan that had seemed eccentric and so Los Angeles, not to mention all that Cassie and Peter could afford at the time, had soon turned into a massive annoyance to them both. From day one (maybe to be allowed to argue about something safe), Cassie had made herself the house's staunch advocate and Peter its relentless detractor. He had wanted to move. She had wanted to stay. Everyone had dug in their heels.

She parked the suitcase next to the pile of boxes. She had timed this just right. The Salvation Army truck would be here any moment, and Peter was arriving at one. The boxes had better be gone before he got here or she would never hear the end of it. She looked at the nice pile. Mission accomplished!

But what she heard coming from the street below was not the sounds of the Salvation Army truck making its way up the hill, but the groan of Peter's Porsche.

Merde! She thought.

A minute later Peter was letting himself in. "You're early!" she said as Peter made a beeline for the pile of boxes.

"Jessica's car is at the shop," he said. "She had to drop me off on her way to taking the boys to their Glockenspiel class. What's all this?"

"What in the world is a Glockenspiel class?"

Peter was digging into the boxes already. "Beats me," he said.

"By the way, she better not just let herself in when she picks you up."

Peter shrugged, "Then lock the front door."

"I want her to learn to knock first, and then wait for me to open the door, whether the door is open or not."

"Cassie, I can't tell Jess that. She won't understand. She'll think you're mad at her."

"Well, I am."

"You know she adores you. She looks up to you."

"Oh yes, because I'm what to her? A mother figure?"

"She considers you a friend."

"My friends don't barge in unannounced. They sensibly knock and wait for me to let them in."

"How's gardening treating you?" Peter asked. He was taking things out of the cardboard boxes, examining them.

"Terribly," she admitted.

A handsome, masculine specimen at age forty-five, Peter filled any room with his massive presence. Six-foot-three, 250 pounds, all banter and charm. Peter never shortchanged anyone of his attention, his warmth, even his hugs. Even now, even divorced, if she asked him for a hug, he would take her in his arms and make her feel safe. Now that Jessica groomed him, he wore designer jeans and shirts and pointy shoes that didn't suit him at all. Cassie preferred him in sneakers, cargo shorts, and generic T-shirts, the kind of clothes a man who loves his steak and beer could function in. She liked him all-American, not in that metrosexual look Jessica had cooked up for him.

As he bent down over the cardboard boxes, his too-tight shirt popped out of his too-tight jeans. "What is this?" he yelped, brandishing a framed photo. "You're not giving Alexander's baseball portrait away are you?"

"We already have all those pictures," she mumbled, feeling caught. "Digitally."

"If you don't want a picture, burn it!"

"It felt wrong to destroy it."

"Giving your own children's framed photographs to charity? Who does this?"

"Oh, come on, this was just one picture. Of course, with my luck, that's the first thing you find."

"What else is in there?" Peter started opening more boxes and digging through them.

"This is my stuff! I can do whatever I want with it. Unless you want it all, but I don't imagine our family memorabilia will sit well with Jessica Rabbit."

"Stop calling her that," he said, his head deeper into the box. He came out of it waving a baseball trophy. "You can't throw those things out! You just can't. And what do you have against baseball?" Peter shook his head in disbelief as he handled an old plaid shirt of his, a lampshade, a ping pong racket and then dropped them back into the box and foraged for more damning evidence. He would tire of this and stop, she hoped. Peter had the attention span of a hamster. She hoped he would stop before getting to the bottom boxes where the real sentimental stuff was: posters they had bought together, mixed tapes, letters they had exchanged, lingerie from their honeymoon.

"I'm doing it for the twins," she said. "That way, after I'm dead, they won't have to feel guilty throwing away objects that I was too weak to part with."

"Who's dying? You haven't had a cold in years. You'll be a centenarian, giving everyone a pain in the ass for generations to come."

"I'm facing my mortality, thinking about a future without me."

"While methodically destroying the past!"

You're the one who destroyed the past, buddy, Cassie thought. "If you had it your way, this house would remain a mausoleum to your old life, and I would be the keeper of all the shit you moved on from. This would be the museum of your old family, and I would be its curator."

"I'm talking about the past past. It's your pattern," Peter said, opening an old tin can, finding it empty, sniffing it, and tossing it back into the cardboard box. "Your childhood. Your parents. Trashing all our stuff is more of what you've been doing all along: brushing your somber family antecedents under the rug."

"I'd love to sweep things under the rug, but you keep pulling it from under me."

Peter stopped in mid-dig and lifted his head. "That's good. That's a fun line. Let's use it in the screenplay." He pulled something out and, brandishing it, said, "This is still good! A perfectly usable bathroom mat."

"Take it. You can ask Jessica to weave winter booties out if it."

"What's this?" he asked, holding a small gilded frame. Inside the frame was an old key on display atop black velvet. The glass was cracked in places.

"Some junk from Alex's room."

"Oh yeah, your father gave this to him the last time we went to France as a family," Peter said. "We were at their house, remember?"

"Nope."

"Alex found it in a drawer, and your father said he could have it. That's as close to a gift as our children ever received from that disgruntled geezer." Peter pointed to the zebra suitcase. "This, however, you can trash."

"How about you keep all this. Jessica will be thrilled to find a place for it in that tower of cold metal you call a house."

"She's a minimalist," Peter said.

"You sure compartmentalize. Little shrines all over my house devoted to your old family, while your new house is all about the new wife, the minimalism, the babies."

"I don't have a new and an old family, Cassie," he said. "You are all my family. And don't forget that I'm not the one who threw our life upside down." As expected, Peter lost interest in the boxes and went into the kitchen to inspect the cupboard for Oreos. The indignity was that now that the kids were gone, Cassie bought processed snacks for her ex-husband. There was something reassuring in the act of filling a grocery cart with comfort food her family liked. Peter opened a package and stuffed the whole cookie into his mouth. "You chaid you were micherable," he said, chewing. "You kicked me out and into a hotel room when I had done noching. Noching!" He opened the refrigerator. "Wheh ich my lactoche-free milk?"

She went to the fridge, took out his milk, and set it on the kitchen table, their preferred workplace, in the bright light, within arm's reach of the coffee maker. The kitchen had been the object of an expensive and soul-crushing remodel and, per Peter's modernistic taste, was all open shelves, frosted glass cupboards, polished concrete countertop, and a gleaming six-burner range that remained gleaming due to Cassie's utter incompetence as a cook. Why could everything not be prepared in a microwave, and in a mug? Cassie did not care about food much. As long as she had ketchup to pour on whatever was served, she ate it. "I asked for time to evaluate my life for a few weeks, and you find yourself some chick," she said.

"See how you rewrite history? Six months is not a few weeks. We were separated. And Jessica isn't some chick," Peter said as he set his laptop at the kitchen table. "Stay with the anger, by the way. Your character is supposed to be a bitch."

"Must every strong woman be a bitch?"

"This one is."

"Is that how you see her? That's not how I want the audience to feel about her."

"Don't worry," Peter said, "we're Hollywood. We'll tell them how they're supposed to feel."

As they had done daily for the better part of two decades, Cassie flipped the switch on the coffee maker, and they sat across from each other in front of their respective laptops. As the smell of coffee mingled with the jasmine scent that flowed in through the open window, they dug into their screenplay Women in Black, Before There Was Space, the prequel to Women in Black–An Intergalactic Dramedy, their blockbuster of two summers ago. The film had grossed 250 million dollars internationally and had been hailed by some critics as a wild romp through space, time, and the fear of women, and by others as a wretched film that epitomized everything that's wrong with America and the movie business. Meanwhile, the sequel, Women in Black, Part Two, was about to open on screens worldwide the following week, helped by a stratospheric advertising budget.

Sitting across from each other, a mug of steaming coffee in hand, they began writing, each typing on a shared document. Peter usually wrote one character's lines and Cassie another's, and they went back and forth, analyzing each word, trimming and pumping up the emotional resonance in each scene, crafting dialogues until they gave the illusion of sounding natural. Screenwriting was to words what food photography was to actual, edible food. A lot of artifice, glycerin, and spray paint went into making that burger look juicy and piping hot.

Peter was fresh out of film school when he and Cassie got married. His first job was that of a quasi-slave and whipping boy for the prolific writer of a now-defunct soap opera. Peter's job was to edit the screenplays. The pay was laughable. The screenplays began coming at Peter at ever-increasing speed by courier – this was before the internet – at first one per week, then two, then one or two per day. Cassie and Peter accepted that this was the way the game was played. He had to pay his dues. It was how people entered what is referred to in Los Angeles as The Business. But Peter couldn't cope with the volume of work, so Cassie began to help. English was not her first language, and she had no training, but she caught on fast. They divided the task. The courier would arrive. Cassie would open the envelopes and read the scripts. She would explain the plots to Peter, and they would brainstorm ideas, find ways out of impasses, polish dialogue by acting them out. It was a fun time. Through this process, she absorbed all kinds of writing techniques and at the same time perfected her English. Soon Peter was asked to write for the soap opera, and he was officially in The Business. A year later he was hired to write for a new sitcom. When it came to writing, Cassie turned out to be fast, efficient, indefatigable, and she had one attribute Peter lacked: concentration. Peter was the one who had gone to film school, the one with the TV credit and Emmy under his belt. Also, he was a fantastic salesperson. Hollywood loves a man with both skills and an affable personality.

All this paid very well. When Rescue Hour, their first feature film screenplay, written on specs, was made into a movie and became a box office smash, Peter's career was launched for good.

The divorce papers had come with a work contract stipulating that Peter wanted to continue their work relationship. It even specified how much he would pay Cassie to do what she had previously done for free, and it gave her a writing credit on all the work they would collaborate on in the future, something she never had in the past.

Cassie got a lot out of the divorce. She also stopped being Cassandra Carawell, Peter's last name (when she introduced herself in Los Angeles. people often asked, "Carawell? The one from Women in Black?" and she answered, "No, only his wife") and went back to signing her checks Cassandra Lombard. She now was paid considerable money to do something she enjoyed. She got custody of the children. The house was hers. What else could she ask for? Peter's enveloping hands on her? No, this she could not have anymore.

Peter did well in the deal too. By buying a nearby house, he got to keep the twins close at hand. He kept his work relationship with her and got to start a whole new family with a girl with big boobs. Jessica was sweet. Very sweet. There was nothing for which Cassie could reproach Jessica. Aside from stealing her man and destroying her family.

Peter could afford the wife, the ex-wife, both houses, and all the children. He was, according to Newsweek, the most sought-after screenwriter in Hollywood. And Cassie was the most sought-after screenwriter in

Hollywood's secret weapon. She alone could read Peter's mind and transform it into one hundred and twenty pages of twists, turns, snappy dialogue, wit, and drama. Working together for so many years came with its share of conflicts. They argued the most about which screenplay ideas to pitch. Peter felt that their bread and butter was high concept comedies and thrillers. She said there was never a cliché he didn't embrace, and she was ready to write something more substantial. When the studios bought only his ideas, she accused him of not pitching hers.

"You think you can become an A-list screenwriter because you can write?" Peter had said one day in one of his rants when she had threatened to stop helping him. "Screenwriting isn't about writing, Cassie. It never was about writing. If your ambition is to produce great writing, write a novel. Screenwriting is about timing. It's about connections. It's about your alma mater and how much you can out-drink the boys at parties. It's about golf more than it is about movies. It's about luck."

The best thing about the divorce was an understanding when it came to a contentious point that had polluted their marriage. Cassie now had a credit. Yep, Hollywood couples have something to fight about that is unknown to the general population. A particular disease. A unique form of mutual torture. For years, Cassie and Peter had fought about proprietorship of the screenplays they worked on together over the course of their marriage, including six screenplays optioned, and four made into blockbuster movies. It was not a money thing. It was an ego thing. "So, you really think you can fly solo?" Peter had said. "Go for it. Write a screenplay and try to get someone to read it – anyone. Good luck with that. Without my connections, your beautiful screenplay will languish in some asshole's drawer because he will be too busy meeting with me, reading my screenplays, and having cocktails with me." And the sad truth was that Peter was right.

According to their contract, Cassie could not reveal her contribution to past screenplays. Peter was the one with a mile-long list of credits on IMDb. It would have been a logistic nightmare to go back in time, paperwork, expenses, Peter had explained, and she suspected a bit of humiliation too, so she let it go. For all past work done together, she was a ghostwriter in the strictest of sense. No one would ever know about her involvement. From her standpoint, she had something better. During their entire marriage, Peter had never admitted to anyone, least of all himself, that he needed Cassie to write, and it was finally right there, printed on a legal document. It was sad that when that validation arrived at last, it was via lawyers and for all the wrong reasons.

This was an excellent arrangement for everyone, a symbiotic relationship – hopefully symbiotic and not parasitic, as she had pointed out to him many times.

****

Cassie and Peter were engrossed in their work, giggling and snarling dialogue lines at each other when the telephone rang. They looked at the phone. The rule was not to pick up unless it was family. Peter frowned at the lengthy set of digits displayed, but Cassie recognized the number, pounced out of her chair, her face flushed, and said "Allô?" in French. She did not need to tell Peter why she was picking up. This was a call from France. No other phone call put her in that kind of state.

"Cassandra?" asked a woman's voice.

"Oui," Cassie answered, switching to French. Only four people in the world called her Cassandra, all of them French, all of them related to her. It was Sabine, her younger sister. The fact that Sabine called at all, let alone in the middle of the night in France, was cause for worry. Sabine's speech was always cautious, deliberate, as though she weighed the power of every syllable and was reluctant to use any more words than necessary. "C'est Papa," she said. "Il est à l'hôpital."

"My dad is in the hospital," she responded mezza voce to Peter's interrogative stare. "What happened?" she asked Sabine.

"He went in four days ago to replace a valve in his heart."

"What? No one told me!" Cassie exclaimed. The words came out shriller than she intended. She needed to take it down a notch, or her sister would retract into her shell like a hermit crab. "How is he?"

"I guess we didn't want to worry you," Sabine said.

"That's okay. I'm fine with that," Cassie lied. She mentally thanked Sabine for her tact. Her parents and two sisters kept her out of the loop deliberately. That was how they dealt with her, from small things to major family crises. She thought of what Peter had said: some things were better off swept under the rug.

"The heart surgery went well," Sabine said. "But he contracted an infection at the hospital. Now he is … we don't know. It's harder to recover at his age."

"I had no idea that he needed heart surgery."

"It was elective. He was tired all the time. He could not keep up with mom."

"Why would he need to keep up with her? She's twenty years younger than he is."

"They gave him a new valve, from a pig, or a metal valve; I forget which one."

Oh, but both would be rather fitting, Cassie thought meanly. "Is he in pain?"

"Right now, he can't seem to wake up. It's kind of why I'm calling you."

Cassie felt her knees go soft, "What do you mean?"

"He can't seem to regain consciousness," Sabine said. She sounded exhausted. And distant. "They're pumping his system with antibiotics."

"How are Maman and Odile doing?"

"Hard to tell."

"How are you?"

Sabine answered cryptically, "The same."

The front door opened. It was Jessica. Peter's Jessica. She just walked into Cassie's house, smiling warmly at her. She had this light way of walking, as though her feet were mounted on springs. She was a shade blonder than the week before and very tanned: her summer look. In her yoga pants and a bra, everything about her was enviably tight and smooth, despite her having given birth only six months ago. Jessica gave Cassie a happy wave and went to kiss Peter, who was still in the kitchen, sitting at his computer and eavesdropping on every word of the phone conversation. "How can I help?" Cassie asked Sabine.

"Maybe you should come?" her sister suggested in a small voice.

"Come to France?" The notion was a shock. Almost more shocking than the news that her father was unconscious following a surgery she did not know he was having.

"If you want to," Sabine said.

"To see Papa?" Cassie let the sentence float between them. In the kitchen, Jessica was standing behind Peter's chair and massaging his shoulders. "Is that what they want me to do?"

Sabine paused before answering. "You don't have to. I'm sending you an email with the name of the hospital, d'accord?"

"Oui, bien sûr," Cassie said.

Sabine hung up without goodbyes, as was her habit, and Cassie fell into her chair and glowered at Peter before he could open his mouth. "I'm telling you right now, stop looking at me that way. There is not a chance in hell I'm going."

"Oh, you're going," Peter said.

After Peter and Jessica left, Cassie sat in the kitchen, stunned. Paris? Really?

The windows were open, and the scent of jasmine swooshed through the house like a spring spirit. April, and not a cloud in the sky, only a light haze of Los Angeles smog, the sun fierce at not even mid-morning. Minutes following the phone call, Peter had booked her ticket. In a few hours, he was taking her to the airport. Was she really about to take a plane and fly to Paris to see her family for the first time in five years?

****

There had been no time to fine-tune the concept. It was good that Peter was clearheaded about the whole thing because Cassie's thinking process had turned into a foggy mess. Peter bought the ticket, while she went online looking for a hotel close to her father's hospital. Ten days seemed the right amount of time to spend there, Peter had said. Long enough for her father to recover, not so long as to mess with their writing schedule.

Why was her dad in the hospital, exactly? What had Sabine said? And why was it Sabine who called, rather than Odile, her other sister, or her mother? Could it be that they did not want her to come, or that they did not want her to know? They had not cared to consult her about the surgery. Had things gone according to plan, would she have ever found out about it?

She looked around her. Her house, her beautiful house: that was real! That was what grounded her. Or maybe not. Now that Jeanne and Alex were gone, Cassie faced the real possibility that she had been wrong about the house, and even more wrong to insist on keeping it in the divorce. It was as though she had bet the rest of her life on the concept that the house would be all she needed to be happy. This she had believed and repeated for the last eighteen years: she loved her house! She loved her house! She was a homebody, and she loved her house. It was possible that her stubbornness about the house had, if not ruined her marriage, at least not improved it. As Peter's career took off, his income increased by a hundred-fold. He wanted to move, but Cassie had dug in her heels and refused. She insisted that she was content with this quirky house, this lifestyle, and found ostentatious displays of wealth an embarrassment. "If you have money to burn, give it away to people who need it," she would say. The truth was, she did not like the way fame, money, and the trail of sycophants in his wake were changing him.

Peter wanted something very different from life. He wanted to want things and pursue things. He wanted Hollywood parties. He wanted the good life, the frisson of power, while Cassie wanted – or believed she wanted – things to be simple and remain eternally the same.

From the time the kids were five, Peter had been on a mission to find them a new house. House-hunting became his weekend pastime. He was sure that one day he would present her with a house so wonderful she would have no choice but to succumb. He often took the twins with him and tried to put them on his side. When they visited a particularly awesome house, incidentally one that cost upwards of two million dollars, the three of them would beg her to look at it. But she was pig-headed about it. "I need roots," she would say. "I left my country and my family, and I need stability. This house is my anchor." Since no one could move without Cassie's consent, Peter had been reduced to expressing his longing for exterior signs of success by buying a new luxury car each year, even a boat once, and one time a Harley and the dumb aviator glasses to go with it.

The twins were twelve years old when Cassie and Peter separated. It had been a mutual decision, albeit one precipitated by Cassie kicking him out of the house. Peter had moved into the Beverly Hills Hotel and after a few months had looked for a house to rent. Jessica was a real estate agent. They met at an open house for an ultra-modern structure made of steel, concrete, wood, and glass that he ended up buying. He was finally getting a house he liked, one that was a far better reflection of his success.

Cassie and Peter had an arrangement any divorcée would envy: amicable, equitable, fair, grown up. It was a no-brainer to invite Peter over for dinner several times a week, and then to welcome Jessica into her life as well. Jessica, too, Cassie had to admit, was a better reflection of Peter's success.

There was just that small thing she'd gladly trade the house for. This was not something she'd ever advertise, that harmless fantasy of getting Peter back. She'd never be a home wrecker. It was just a little bout of regression that kept her safe from exploring romantic options. It was just that now that Peter loved someone else, she could love him better. Unrequited love, along with microwave mug cake, was her true specialty.

****

It was a good thing that the Salvation Army truck had not materialized because all the suitcases were at college with the kids and she had to resort to using the ugly zebra one. She sniffed the suitcase's mildewed interior. The zipper looked about to give out, and she didn't like the look of one of the wheels.

In her bedroom closet were nothing but T-shirts and jeans – in other words, clothes for a world that did not include France and her chic mother and sisters. Cassie had no sense of fashion. For a French woman, it was embarrassing. Since the divorce, she felt pressured to look nice, and attractive, and well put together, all definitions she doubted applied to her. She had no idea how to dress in ways that represented who she was supposed to be. It was like trying to dress for an interview when you don't even know what the job is. What was she exactly? Single? A divorcée? A retiree from life? What were ghostwriters supposed to wear? A white shroud with holes for the eyes? In Los Angeles, among the women her age, Cassie had yet to find her niche. She was not one of those women who perfected the extremities: the nails, the hair, the makeup. She had no patience for sitting in salons, and she was afflicted with curls, tons of them, black and unruly better left au naturel. Her nails were permanently chipped, her hands scratched up from gardening. Her entire makeup routine consisted of painfully extracting lipstick remnants with the aid of Q-tips out of a dozen old tubes scattered in various bathroom drawers.

She admired the various breeds of Los Angeles female humans. For example, there were the Jessicas: women driven to physical perfection who dressed in exercise clothes during the day and like movie stars at night. Cassie bought her undies in packs of six. Her sole form of exercise consisted of taking the trash out to the street and going up and down the stairs of her house carrying laundry baskets. There were the Malibu moms, who wore flowing things: hair, dangling earrings, fringed everything, silk, lace. And then there were the women dressed to display exterior signs of a libido Cassie simply didn't possess. She admired women who dove into the dating race with great courage and grit. It's not that she was out of touch with being a woman. An apathetic side of her wished she could feel vibrant and sexy again, but not to the point of doing anything about it. She was in flux, neither able to embrace wrinkles and flab nor involved in a frantic attempt to turn back time or send sexual messages she was not willing to live up to. Her solution was to pretend the whole thing didn't exist. And if this meant that she was taking herself out of the dating game, that she was passing the baton to women of reproductive age (the age that men preferred anyway), then so be it.

Paris could feel like winter in April, but a quick peek online told her that Europe had been enjoying an unseasonable heat wave, with temperatures in the high seventies. She folded into the suitcase two pairs of jeans, a week's worth of underwear and bras, a half dozen T-shirts, three sweatshirts, all the while thinking of Odile. Her sister epitomized French uptightness in her pearls, scarves she knew how to tie just so, and mousy colored clothes to complement her mousy self. Cassie peered at the zebra suitcase with reproach, through Odile's eyes. Already, she was having an argument in her head with her sister. Sabine was ten years younger than she was, and only eight years old when Cassie had left France. In many ways, she and Sabine had never had the opportunity to get to know each other. But self-righteous Odile, just eighteen months her senior, she knew all too well. Cassie added into the suitcase a yellow and orange polka-dot T-shirt Odile would disapprove of and a pair of snazzy sandals. On the plane, she would wear her Uggs.

She pressed her foot on the suitcase for leverage to force the uncooperative zipper closed as she grappled with the notion that her father was sick, sick enough for at least one family member to ask her to come. How did she feel about her father being sick? She did not feel worried. Or upset. Or sad. She felt foggy. Foggy was good. She wasn't going to Paris for herself. She was going because Peter thought she should. She was going because of Sabine. Sabine had been the single neutral relative and had made the most efforts, often acting as the liaison between her and the rest of the family. Sabine had never asked anything of her before, and this time, she seemed to be asking.

Cassie backed up her laptop, activated her cell's international call feature, and placed her chargers in the tote bag that would serve as her carry on. For the next week, electronics would be a lifeline to sanity. Already, she was packed with time to spare. She was more in control of things than she was giving herself credit for. It was only ten days. She had given birth to twins at twenty years old, had started over in a new country, had pushed through a divorce with her soul intact. She could survive ten days in Paris.

****

At the airport, Cassie was making no motion to enter the security line in front of the Air France counter. Peter nudged her in, handing her a plastic bag.

"What's this?"

"Just a little something from Jessica."

Cassie peered into the bag to find four small precious packages in various shapes and sizes and wrapped extravagantly in glistening paper and frilly bows. "What the hell?"

"You know how she is. It's little gifts for your family."

"She bought all this and wrapped it in one hour?"

"She skipped her massage for this. She just wanted to reach out, be nice. You know how she's always trying."

"She's always shopping, that's what she's always doing." It had never occurred to her to bring gifts for her family, and here was Jessica acing it again. "Fine. Thank her for me," she said. Over the loudspeaker, a voice in French informed them that the planes were on time. Just hearing French, Cassie experienced a bout of cold sweat. "I'm not doing this," she said, gripping Peter's sleeve. "Take me back home. Please."

"You can do this. You need to do this," Peter assured her. And with this, he opened his arms.

She sank into his hug, buried her nose in his jacket to inhale the reassuring scent of his after-shave, the one thing Jessica had not been able to change. She felt that sense of safety she could only experience in Peter's arms, even if she knew that his embrace often came with an aftertaste of longing and regrets. "What if I'm captured?" she asked.

"I'll pay the ransom, of course. I've rescued you from them once; I'll rescue you again."

"But what's your incentive now? Your children are raised, and you found someone new to warm your bed?" She meant it as a joke but saying it out loud brought her dangerously near to tears.

"I still need you for the writing," Peter said. The plain honesty of the statement befuddled her so much that she could not think of how to respond and only walked forward in the line, moving away from him. "You've got the adapter for the 220 current?" he asked.

"I packed the old one."

"That thing is antiquated. I've told you before it was crap. They have them everywhere inside the airport. Buy a new one as soon as you pass security."

Cassie rolled her eyes, "Peter, I've got this."

"It's only ten days in Paris," he said, patting her on the arm. "It's the number one item on most bucket lists."

"It's just not a safe country for me."

"Don't drink the water," he responded and with this gave her a gentle push toward the line.

She boarded the plane, anonymous among passengers, and settled into her aisle seat, far in the back near the bathrooms. Peter had remembered her preference. She tried not to read too much into this small kindness. Every time he did something nice for her she ended up, even for a brief moment, imagining they could go back to the way things were.

****

She had not been in France for five years. The last time had been weeks before her separation from Peter. The trip was intended as a family vacation but had been an epic failure. The twins, then twelve years old, had been going through stuff, no doubt acting out the discord in her marriage. They both had been monsters. Or rather they had been normal American pre-teens, but once in France, where children must be seen and not heard, they had appeared barbarous, even to her own eyes. Raymonde Lombard, her mother, then sixty, had been a quiet trap of disapproval. Gustave Lombard, her father, who was eighty-two at the time, hardly acknowledged her or the twins. Odile's children, meanwhile, had been delightful. The then two- and four-year-olds did everything right. Their prowess included the ability to speak French – the only language their grandparents spoke – their exquisite table manners, the ease with which they said bonjour and merci (which her twins, lock-jawed the way only teenagers can be, refused to do), their skill at making eye contact with grownups and at bringing smiles to Grandpapa Lombard's face.

Caught between her parents and her twins, Cassie had felt like a mediator between two countries in the grip of a cold war. She tried to sell her own children's adorableness to her parents just as she was fighting serious doubts about it, and she tried to sell her parents' wonderfulness to the twins against all evidence to the contrary.

Her children were Americans. Her children spoke English exclusively; no, she had not been able to teach them French. Her children were brooding and uncommunicative. Her children could not fit into the French mold of silence and docility. But in Cassie's view, the biggest babies were her parents. They were incapable of the most basic attempt at winning the twins over. With the hubris that characterized them, they believed that children should be the ones to make the effort. She had hated them for that. She had also hated her twins for falling short of expectation. She had hated Odile, Odile's children, and, of course, she had hated Peter.

But she had hated herself the most.

"Your kids are tuning out their grandparents," Odile had had the nerve to say.

"You have no idea what teenagers are like. You just wait and see."

"I doubt very much that I'm raising my children to turn into that kind of teenagers."

"Your kids are afraid of you, just as we were afraid of mom. Do you think their politeness is genuine? It's fear-based. I'm surprised they can sleep at night."

"So what?" Odile said, swallowing the insult with remarkable aplomb. "Life is stressful. They need to learn to handle stress. Your job as a parent is to teach your kids self-control and give them opportunities to experience failure and disappointment. They need to know that in life there are consequences when you can't get along in society."

"What consequences? Their disgruntled grandparents won't approve of them? Big deal."

"You let your kids grow like weeds, and you tiptoe around their feelings," Odile had told her. "You're giving them an unrealistic expectation when it comes to life and their abilities."

"You've only been a parent for four years, and already you're an expert."

"I might not be an expert, but I won't let my children grow up thinking they're little geniuses, and I won't let them act like mini-despots."

"I recognize Maman's rule book. Only one despot allowed. By all means, go for it. It worked for her. Too bad it didn't turn us into happy adults."

"You're not teaching your kids happiness though," Odile had said with condescension. "Everything they experience is artificial. They expect life to be smooth and people to be at their beck and call. Good luck with the rude awakening that's ahead of them."

"How about we resume the conversation when your kids are teenagers," Cassie had suggested.

"I'd be glad to."

The entire trip had been a nightmare. She had used Peter as a punching bag and a buffer. Each night, squeezed together in her too small childhood bed, they'd argued in frantic whisperings about how miserable they were making each other feel, what inept parents they were. They blamed each other for being selfish, emotionally unavailable, lousy at any form of intimacy, unwilling to deal with their respective neuroses. He blamed her for the lack of sex in the marriage while she blamed him for not giving her writing credit.

Upon their return to Los Angeles from Paris, jetlagged and at the end of her rope, she had told Peter she wanted to separate. Yes, this time, I'm sure of this, she had said.

She still hadn't been sure.

Within two years of the family trip to France, Odile's words had turned prophetic. Alex began suffering from extreme anxiety – when high school and normal life stress began to pile up; he had no idea how to cope. As for Jeanne, she chose denial, expecting life to remain one pink and pretty merry-go-round. If that meant taking drugs and booze any time the going got tough, that's what Jeanne did. Alex quieted his stress by overachieving at school, to the detriment of everything else. Jeanne got rid of hers through being promiscuous and flunking every subject. Even P.E. Odile had been right; her kids were indeed unprepared for the vicissitudes of life. In the end, maybe it was Cassie who had been the biggest baby of them all.

Cassie settled into her seat, tucked her bag under the seat in front of hers and breathed. An unmistakably French couple in their forties labored up the plane's aisle and came to sit in her row. The man wore a gray suit and a tie, and the woman stood very straight in a belted green dress, her stomach tucked in as though she was about to step on the red carpet. Neither had felt compelled to wear something comfortable for the transatlantic flight. The woman, especially, reminded her somehow of Odile. Thank goodness there was an empty seat between them.

A flight attendant walked through the cabin, handing travelers headphones, eye masks, and menus printed on small cards. The man looked at his menu and turned to Cassie. "Encore un repas dégeulasse," he said. Another awful meal.

Cassie shook her head as if to say she did not understand French.

The man turned to his wife. "Elle est Américaine," he said, referring to Cassie.

"Of course, she is," the wife responded in French. "Who else would be wearing snowshoes on a plane?"

Snowshoes? Cassie looked down at her Uggs with a sinking feeling. What exactly had she packed for the trip?

An ample woman in her sixties was ambling up the aisle. She stopped in front of Cassie and squinted at the numbers above her head. "I don't mean to bother you," the woman said, "but is it possible that you're in my seat?"

Cassie looked at her boarding pass, and sure enough, hers was not the aisle seat after all but the one in the middle. "I apologize," Cassie said as she moved one seat to her left. "Just as I was mentally thanking my ex-husband for knowing me so well and for reserving the aisle seat."

"You can't trust anyone these days," the woman said cheerfully as she settled in her seat. "Not even ex-husbands." She set a large bag on her lap. "Food," she explained. "If we're going down, at least I'm not going down hungry."

"I know what you mean," Cassie said. "Who would want to tread water for days in the middle of the Atlantic Ocean on an empty stomach?"

"The worst!" the woman laughed. Within minutes, she was digging into her bag and laying out food on her tray: a box of Milano cookies, chocolate covered macadamia nuts. "I detect an accent?" she said.

"I was born in France, but I've lived in the U.S. for the last nineteen years," Cassie said.

"What brought you to the U.S. then?"

"Love. And a burning desire to get the hell away from my family."

"Are you going to France to visit them?"

"My father's ill."

"Sorry to hear. Are you close?"

"We've hardly spoken in the last five years."

"Oh my," the woman said, removing the outer wrapping of a box of chocolate-covered Hawaiian Macadamia nuts and plopping one, two, three in her mouth, then a fourth, a fifth. "What happened?"

Cassie accepted a chocolate from the open box the woman shoved in front of her. "Where to even begin?" she said. "I left the country. I married a foreigner. I'm a pain in the derrière. My children don't speak French. And then a few years ago I had a bit of a meltdown, said the wrong things." Cassie gave a small laugh that was meant to sound joyful and came out pathetic instead. "I put those wrong things in writing, actually, in a letter they did not like very much. After that, they did not take my calls for two years. You know, the usual story."

"That doesn't sound so usual to me," the woman said.

"And since they would not let me tell them how angry I was with them, I divorced my husband instead." Cassie thought for a moment. "You know, I was saying that as a joke, but I'm pretty sure that's precisely what happened."

"Maybe this is a chance to open the lines of communication with your father, talk about your feelings."

"He doesn't do that."

"What?"

"Talk about feelings. He only talks about things."

"Things?"

"In the literal senses. Things. Objects. Architecture, furniture, rugs, cutlery even. He can ramble on about manufacturing techniques of Persian rugs, or the anatomy of a sailboat, or the leg shapes of eighteenth-century chairs. But he has no vocabulary when it comes to emotions."

"On the autism spectrum perhaps?"

"I don't think so. Once, when I was little, I had a whole cabinet fall on me – to be fair I had climbed into it – and I was bleeding from my head, and all my father was worried about was his damn crown."

"He wears a crown?"

Cassie laughed, "It's not an actual crown. The crown is what my sisters and I call it. It's an artifact. His prized possession. It's silver and gold and what not. Ancient. He calls it his finial, whatever that means. It looks exactly like a crown, only tiny. One that could fit a doll's head. Which is just what I intended to do with it when I climbed that cabinet."

"What about your mother. Could you speak to her?"

"I never can tell if she hides behind my father because she doesn't have to have an opinion, or if she is the one pulling his strings."

The woman smiled at her kindly. "Well, it looks like you have your work cut out for you on this trip."

"Me? Oh no! It won't be work at all. It will be a quick in, quick out; nobody gets hurt. I'm not going there to dig deep, believe me. I've been burned before, and I'm over it. I'm going to be on my best behavior, ruffle no feathers, gather no moss, and then come back home safe to California and resume my life."

"Well, good luck then," the woman said.

"What about you?" Cassie asked. "Why are you going to Paris?"

"I'm attending a conference on eating disorders."

Cassie tried not to stare at the candy and cookie wrappers in front of them. "You have to go as far as France for this?"

"Oh yes. It's an international symposium. I'm a professor of psychiatry at UCLA."

Cassie's jaw dropped. "I just told my life story to a psychiatrist?"

"It tends to happen," the psychiatrist said.

The psychiatrist soon fell asleep. If only Peter knew this, ha! He who had begged her to go to therapy, calling her damaged, telling her that she needed therapy more than anyone he'd ever met, and Cassie dismissing it, saying she was too private to air her dirty laundry in front of a stranger. The irony wasn't lost on her.

She fell asleep and woke up from a dream where she walked through rooms where doors fell and disintegrated like wet cardboard between her fingers. Water dripped from the ceiling onto her father's Persian rugs. She called, but no one answered, so she took her father's finial and tried to use it to collect the water falling from the ceiling. But the water ran right through the finial, and she cried and cried.

CHAPTER 4

Children of Smyrna

To gather a sense of what was happening around him, Albano learned to pay attention to what people said. Even more could be learned from what was not said the contained anger of a trembling hand, the nervousness of a sweaty forehead, the complicity in a repressed smile. Aunt Sadie was not the kind of woman who bothered to answer ten-year-old boys' questions, let alone those of a nephew who was an added burden to her, so when she sprang out of bed one morning and, kvetching the entire time, launched into a meticulous house cleaning for no religious reason, Albano knew that something was afoot. Then Uncle Joshua ordered new shoes, leather ones. A visitor was coming, an important one. Important and disliked by Aunt Sadie, which was an intriguing combination.

By the time Uncle Joshua received the letter informing them of the day of his arrival, Uncle Moshe and his merchandise were already on the boat to Smyrna, leaving the family with only a few days to prepare.

"That is just like him," Aunt Sadie said. "Not a care in the world but giving everyone else an attack of nerves."

Who was this mysterious Uncle Moshe everyone worked so hard to please? And why the undercurrent of disdain for a man special enough to precipitate the ordering of new shoes and the slaughter of a goat? Albano overheard Aunt Sadie tell Uncle Joshua that she would not allow Moshe to share a roof with her children. Yet she used her best linen in preparing his bed. She said Moshe was *hadras I baranas*. A boisterous mess. Uncle Joshua, an amicable man who knew that peace at home begins with not mingling in a woman's affairs, got more tense as the day approached and as Aunt Sadie grew more vociferous.

There was to be an expedition to fetch Uncle Moshe and his merchandise when he disembarked at the quay of Smyrna in two days. Relatives and friends were coming over to Uncle Joshua's house that night to plan the whole thing. Albano was studying at the table in the big room with Uri and Zev, who were his cousins and Uncle Joshua and Aunt Sadie's sons. Uncle Joshua nervously arranged and rearranged the chairs while Aunt Sadie busied herself at the stove. The smell of yeast and anise seeds wafted deliciously through the room, giving it a welcoming feel. Each time Aunt Sadie's back was turned, Cousin Uri and Cousin Zev took turns hitting each other hard on the head with their school books, muffling their cries of pain and laughter, which made them want to laugh even more. Aunt Sadie was not a woman you wanted to mess with, but tonight she was too preoccupied to protest. This did not mean she would turn a blind eye on Albano if he misbehaved, so he strained his eyes in the weak light of candles and tried to concentrate on his book. Uri and Zev were twelve and fifteen, older than Albano, yet allowed to be ignorant all they wanted while Albano had to study late into the night. The reason for this was that he was to become a rabbi. Aunt Sadie loved all things rabbinical yet had failed to produce an offspring who could pass the rabbinical school's entrance exam and who could, like Albano, read Hebrew, Latin, and Greek by the age of ten. Albano's father had prized education above all else. He had been a patient tutor to his children, and Albano was from a young age well versed in academic matters. Also, Albano was a Kohen, as his father had been, a priest by blood, descendent from a priest; and there was nothing he could do about that.

The cholera epidemic had also taken the life of Aunt Sadie and Uncle Joshua's only daughter, and ever since Aunt Sadie had become more pious and more afraid. She was the one who had set her mind on the idea that Albano should go to rabbinical school, and Albano had been given no choice in the matter. Uncle Joshua was respected in the community for his practicality and his good judgment, but he let that judgment be superseded by his wife's discretely whispered admonitions at home. So the decision was made. Would his real father and mother want him to become a rabbi had they survived? Albano did not know, but Aunt Sadie seemed to think so.

As Albano squinted at his books, the men entered and were greeted by Uncle Joshua. With each arrival, the room became hotter and smaller. Rabbi Levi arrived last, his long gray beard, somber mood, black cloak, and formidable presence stealing whatever breathable air was left in the room. He sat at the end of the table, and Aunt Sadie fretted over him, bringing him tea in her best cup.

Rabbi Levi peered at Albano from above his round glasses and said, "Aren't you Yoseph's boy, the rabbinical student?"

"I am, Rabbi Levi."

"Are you a diligent student, dear boy?"

"Yes, Rabbi Levi."

Aunt Sadie brought pastries and placed them before Rabbi Levi. "I make sure he is, Rabbi. Surely Adonai must have had a design for him to make me suffer so, putting this boy in my care. Taking my daughter and sparing him."

Rabbi Levi narrowed his eyes. "Lest we forget that the boy suffered as well," he said.

"Ah, yes," Aunt Sadie hurried to say. "We have all suffered very much indeed."

Now everyone was here. Two strong men from the Jewish quarter whose names Albano didn't know, also Selig and Rafael, who were not so strong but were his father's and Uncle Joshua's and Moshe's childhood friends, and thus part of the welcoming committee. The two strong men, Selig, Rafael, Rabbi Levi, Uncle Joshua, Cousin Uri, Cousin Zev, and Albano sat around the table. Albano made himself small and hoped he would be allowed to stay and listen. Aunt Sadie placed on the table pots filled with mint tea and plates of cumin and anise breads, round, golden and warm from the oven and said, "Albano, what are you still doing here? Close your books and leave, hush." Albano gathered his book and got up.

"Albano can stay, why not?" Uncle Joshua suggested.

Albano beamed. He was about to sit back on his chair, but one look at Aunt Sadie made him freeze into place. "He's a child and a rabbinical student. He should not bother himself with men's business," she said, adding briskly, "Albano, go!" Albano, his cheeks bright red, stepped away from the table and tried to look at no one.

Perhaps it was the residue of several days and possibly nights of Aunt Sadie's constant complaining about Moshe's arrival, but Uncle Joshua reacted with uncharacteristic defiance. "This child will be a man soon enough, won't he? Albano. Sit!" Albano folded back onto the chair, hoping to disappear. He did not like to be a source of discord between his uncle and aunt, and Uncle Joshua's sudden display of authority as master of the house was almost comical.

Aunt Sadie camped herself in front of the men. "I made a solemn promise to his mother on her deathbed to raise him as my own!" she said. Her contradicting Uncle Joshua was a common thing, but to do so in front of the men was a tactical mistake. She was giving Uncle Joshua nowhere to go.

"And I," Joshua said, puffing his chest, "I too made a solemn promise to his father, Yoseph, my beloved brother now tragically dead, to raise him as my own." Then realizing that all eyes were on him, he raised his voice in a way that was unnatural to him. "And I decide when a boy can start being part of men's business and when he cannot."

"But I—" Aunt Sadie said.

"Woman, enough!"

Aunt Sadie seemed to shrink upon herself in humiliation, or perhaps anger. There would be hell to pay for Uncle Joshua later on, but for now, he had won. Albano curled back onto his chair, thrilled. Men's business!

Uncle Joshua, his voice made stronger by his own bravery said, "Moshe's merchandise is, I believe, mostly rugs. How many I don't know, the letter said nothing. Neither do I know how heavy those will be. There is a risk that we will have to make several trips, in which case some of us will need to stay behind on the quay overnight to guard what was not loaded onto the wagons."

"Wagons? How about camels?" Rafael asked.

"Camels will not do. Not with rugs. We need to borrow at least two wagons with excellent wheels and equip each with two good horses." The men nodded gravely and lit their pipes. "As I cannot be certain that proper

Kosher food will be available to us in Smyrna, the women will prepare food to bring," Uncle Joshua said. "Finally," he added, the alarm in his voice betraying his concern, "we must be armed." A wave of mixed emotions reverberated around the table: anxiety, worry, excitement, but mostly excitement, Albano could tell, from the gleaming eyes and straightened postures of the men. "How do we know what we might encounter along the way?" Joshua said, looking at each face around the table. "Cholera has brought terrible loss to our community and all throughout the Empire. But now the epidemic is over, and people are back to their misdeeds. We could encounter robbers. Or worse. Each of you must decide if leaving the Jewish quarter is something that you find a risk worth taking." He added, his voice filled with oratory tremors, "Moshe is my brother. As such my sons and I must go. All of you must decide if you want to come down to the quayside."

Smyrna's quayside. The name evoked untold riches and mysteries. At home, Aunt Sadie spoke of decency and tradition and was the enforcer of both. She believed that everything in Smyrna that wasn't the Jewish quarter brimmed with vice and diseases and was a death trap for Jews. But Albano had heard other stories about Smyrna from the men. Smyrna, the City of Infidels, as Muslims called it, was said to be one of the most cosmopolitan places on earth. In Smyrna, every religion had its place of worship, and every language under the sun was spoken. From Mount Pagus and the Jewish quarter, Albano could only glimpse at the mysterious city below, the gulf, the hundreds of boats that circled the bay, moving voyagers and merchandise to and from the Ottoman Empire.

He could only imagine the wealthy Levantine families who were said to live in gilded castles surrounded with servants, and whose days were spent lounging in fragrant gardens filled with roses and fountains, and who employed people in their fields and factories by the hundreds of thousands. He could only dream of Frank Street and its myriads of shops, and of the fabled Greek department stores that sold goods from every corner of the world. He could only yearn to see with his own eyes the legendary Smyrna waterfront, where the architecture was said to resemble that of cities in Europe. But the Jews kept to the Jewish quarter for the most part, especially the children. There were people in Smyrna, and all throughout the Empire, who would kill a man just for being Jewish, or Muslim, or Christian, or for wearing the wrong clothes, or for having too short or too long a beard.

Uncle Joshua's warning seemed to ruffle no one. The danger must not have been that high, or else the men in the room were indeed very brave. In fact, for the next two hours, there was great excitement in the air as arrangements were made in the thickening smoke of pipes and the diminishing light of candles. The men discussed which road would be safest from robbers and which would be easiest for the horses and wagons. Must they bring extra wheels? How long would it take to cover the few miles down to the waterfront? Boats could be delayed, so they needed to prepare for a night or two of sleeping there. They would need to take turns mounting guard at night. How much straw should they bring for the horses? How long would the return trip take once the wagons, heavy with Uncle Moshe's mysterious merchandise, were brought back uphill to the Jewish quarter? Albano listened, transfixed. He wanted nothing more than to accompany them but he was not Uncle Joshua's son, and he wasn't yet a man, so he had neither rights nor expectations. Aunt Sadie was moving about the room with tiny steps bringing more kettles filled with tea and trays of pastries, taking back empty cups and plates, all the while not losing a crumb of what was being said.

The entire time Rabbi Levi sat glumly in his chair and did not speak, and Albano could read nothing in his half-closed eyes and crossed arms. Uncle Joshua turned to him and said with deference, "Rabbi, with all the important things that are your responsibility here in the Jewish quarter, we understand if you prefer not to partake in this arduous journey."

"I prefer not to go," Rabbi Levi said, suddenly irate. "But this crazy brother of yours is coming, so I have no choice. How else can I ensure nothing blasphemous will take place?"

"Rabbi Levi," Uncle Joshua protested. "My brother is beloved by us all."

The rabbi lifted a reproachful finger. "Beloved, yes, that is another alluring embodiment of sin. One can be beloved, as you say, for all kinds of immoral reasons. I must come to ensure that he intends to follow our rules, at least as long as he stays in the Jewish quarter."

"Of course," Uncle Joshua said, pretending to ignore Aunt Sadie's triumphant glare. She must have made her case about Moshe behind her husband's back.

"And what about Albano?" Cousin Zev suddenly asked. "Is he coming with us?" Albano's pulse quickened.

Uncle Joshua scratched his beard, shrugged. "I guess. Why not."

"In what capacity?" Aunt Sadie interjected, unable to contain herself. The men all looked at her, then at Uncle Joshua. Albano held his breath.

Uncle Joshua exploded, "In the capacity that he is Moshe's nephew! The sole surviving child of his dead brother! That's the capacity!"

And so, Albano was to go. And his life would be forever changed.

This much Albano knew about Uncle Moshe: he had left the Jewish quarter, his family, and his roots at age fifteen and only came back on rare occasions for business. Moshe was thirty years old now, a mature man, and he was frowned upon for creating a life that had little to do with the way he had been raised. He was also admired for becoming an intrepid businessman who traveled the world where he picked up precious rugs from around Persia and then went to sell them in Constantinople, Marseille, or Naples. It was said that his rugs even found homes in the high societies of Paris and London. Uncle Moshe did not live in any particular country or any particular place. He had never married and had no children. And he was said to have reneged on God. Uncle Moshe's reputation was something amorphous. He was different and did things differently, but what did different look like? Having never left the Jewish quarter, Albano had no idea.

It was a particularly sweltering summer day when their small group made its way from the Jewish quarter to Smyrna's waterfront. By nine in the morning, they were suffocating in their black clothes. By ten o'clock, their clothes clung to their bodies and their bare feet were coated with the dirt of the road. Only Rabbi Levi and Uncle Joshua wore shoes. "They are hard as metal," Uncle Joshua said, cursing the shoemaker under his breath. At one point, he removed one of the shoes to uncover an impressive row of red-hot blisters. He stoically put the shoe back on and continued down the hill pinching his lips and sweating profusely through the pain, until he finally gave up and went barefoot like everyone else.

Notable along the way had been the conspicuous absence of danger. Walking defensively around the horses and empty wagons, they encountered none of the bandits, brigands, robbers, and fanatics the road to the city was supposed to be filled with.

On the way, they walked past groups of veiled women carrying goods on their heads, men sitting atop moving camels, the animals impassible despite their load, even small children walking alone. The Muslim people were dressed in light-colored clothes well suited for the heat and the landscape, whereas their group in black coats, black pants, and black wide-brimmed hats seemed only suited for sitting around a table and worrying about the outside world. Albano, for his part, floated rather than walked the distance, such was his excitement to be part of the caravan. He did not mind the heat. He was used to climbing up Mount Pagus in his black clothes on the way to and from his cave, and the bare soles of his feet were well callused. At one point, they had to make way for a machine coming from a distance at great speed. They stood by the side of the road and watched in dismay as a black automobile passed them in a flurry of sand and dust. In the automobile, two red-faced men in funny round hats and thick mustaches looked straight ahead.

"Who are these people?" Albano asked his cousin.

"British," Cousin Zev answered with authority.

"How do you know?"

"The round hats. They also wear funny trousers and jackets with many compartments and buttons. And they have cloth squares they take out to dab at their sweat." Cousin Zev laughed at that one. "A cloth just for sweat. And a pocket just for that cloth!"

"Why is their skin so red?"

"Because of the blood that's inside of them. It's redder than ours," Cousin Uri said.

"Redder than our blood?" But Cousin Uri and Cousin Zev exchanged a look, and Albano guessed they were not telling the truth. "What language do they speak?"

"Why, they speak British I guess."

"What does it sound like?"

"French."

"What do they eat?"

"Pig sausages, mainly. Now stop with all your questions."

Pig? Albano swallowed his disgust.

Soon, dirt roads turned to paved ones. There were people everywhere: Muslims, Christians, Europeans. People with normal skin colors, and people with red, pink, white, even black skins. People with normal noses, and people with tiny noses, or flat noses, or enormous noses. People with yellow hair. People with red hair! He saw people whose eyes were as blue as the sky. And more automobiles, and camels, and a breeze at last, but one that brought on unknown scents, strong ones: grilled meat, and spices, and strange, pleasant fragrances, and rotting fish. Leading their horse and cart, they crossed one more street, made another turn, and there they were: the Smyrna waterfront!

How could Albano have imagined the waterfront other than as a large-scale embodiment of what he already knew? He had pictured the Jewish quarter, only larger and on the water, an amalgam of gray stone houses, small alleys where barefoot children played alongside scaly dogs, and men and women dressed in black, careful never to make eye contact with one another. How wrong he had been! Before Albano's astonished eyes lay a massive esplanade surrounded by white buildings several stories tall. At the foot of those buildings were terraces of restaurants and cafés where every table was occupied by people, one stranger-looking than the next. Beyond that, the harbor, filled with hundreds of boats and the most dizzying wall of humanity Albano had ever witnessed. It was like market day in the Jewish quarter, multiplied by a hundred! A thousand! The smells of camels, horses, goats, live chickens, ducks, and rabbits by the cageful, mingled with the scent of spices, ripe and dried figs, fish, and many other things he could not name grabbed his throat, coming in wafts that took his breath away. And the noises! The cacophony of animals in close-quarter was a loud hum covered only in intervals by the strident horns of the many steamboats that crowded the harbor. Men called to one another in dozens of languages. Music mingled. Strange sounds coming from unknown instruments pierced the air without rhyme or reason. Merchant ships spilled their contents onto the dock, littering it with crate after crate of goods from across Europe. There were piles of bags, as tall as men, of dried figs, and apricots, cinnamon, cardamom, pepper, garments, precious wood, oil lamps, and tobacco all awaiting shipment. On the dock, boats were so tightly packed against one another that you could not see the water. Steamboats crisscrossed the harbor and docked noisily to unload passengers who poured onto the quayside like a human tidal wave. Further out, a hundred or more ships crammed into the harbor, majestic three-masted barkentines, massive three-screw transatlantic passenger liners, and a flurry of vessels large and small. Further out at sea, brightly colored sails decorated the horizon like garlands on the Aegean Sea.

Uncle Joshua's shoes were back on his feet, and they all stood, confusion on their faces, their eyes searching the crowd for Uncle Moshe. They must have been an odd sight, huddled as they were around the two empty wagons, the sweat on their faces, the panting horses, the long black coats, the curled payots, the tall hats, the woolen tzitzit dangling from the sides of their bodies, so different from the rest of the crowd, and yet everyone was too busy and purposeful to pay any attention to them.

Albano had never seen so many people in one place. Out on the waterfront, there were Namibian men with skins as dark and smooth as polished stone, Muslim men wrapped in white capes, Greek Orthodox priests, pink-faced European men in funny tight pants and jackets. There were women too. The Muslim women wore headdresses, the Jewish, Armenian, and Greek women wore black, long sleeves and shawls, but the European women were so out of the ordinary, like nothing he had ever seen. They dressed in garments tight at the waist and wore brightly colored dresses and coats, wide-brimmed hats and lacy umbrellas, jewels, and beads. Albano immediately knew what his aunt had meant by "immodest." European women even had ankles, arms, and necks exposed. Some wore fur shawls despite the temperature, their pale skins reddened by the heat. It was all very puzzling, as though the European women wore clothes to make you look at them, instead of making you look away. But what amazed Albano the most was how the European women mingled with men, some even engaged in conversation in plain sight and broad daylight! The European men were just as peculiar-looking as the women in their tailored suits with wide-shouldered jackets and trousers that were tight on the leg and creased in front. And the hats, so many hats! Top hats, bowler hats, fezzes, and turbans all bobbed in harmony all over the quayside. He wondered which of these people were the rich Levantine men and women who owned the city.

Cousin Zev elbowed Cousin Uri, whispering and pointing more or less discreetly. "Look! A harlot!"

Leaning against a wall was a blonde woman of extremely immodest attire. Her dress was red and black and fluffy, and some of her bosom was exposed, and she was laughing at something a man said.

"A harlot?" Albano asked, "What is that?"

"Ask my mother. She'll explain all about it," Cousin Zev said, winking at Cousin Uri.

"A harlot," Cousin Uri began, "is…." He was silenced by Rabbi Levi's striking him quite harshly on the head with a book.

"There he is!" Rafael exclaimed. Albano looked in the direction where Rafael pointed and saw a strange-looking man who stood erect and confident, as though the entire quayside belonged to him. Next to him was a formidable pile of rolled rugs at least two meters high.

If Albano had been in charge of spotting Uncle Moshe, his poor uncle would well have remained standing there until morning. The man standing on the quay bore no resemblance to Uncle Joshua or his father, or any of the bearded men of the Jewish quarter. Whereas Joshua was short and skinny, like his father Yosef had been, Moshe was tall and wide as a boulder, with a prominent belly. To Albano's amazement, Uncle Moshe did not have a beard. Instead, he wore a peculiar, thin moustache above his full, smiling lips, and instead of black, he was dressed in a light blue suit and sported a strange hat Albano had never seen before – he learned later when those began sprouting in the Jewish quarter, in shops and market stalls, no doubt in imitation of Uncle Moshe himself, that this kind of hat was called a French canotier. Uncle Moshe wore his inclined to the front of his face and slightly off center. Over his winged-collared shirt was a button-down vest – a waistcoat, as Albano later learned. A heavy gold chain went from his trouser pocket to a small pocket on his jacket.

Yet this stranger, the most bizarre-looking man Albano had ever seen, had exactly his father's smiling eyes.

Uncle Moshe and Uncle Joshua fell into each other's arms. "Now you come?" Uncle Moshe exclaimed in a thunderous voice, a voice which, Albano would soon notice, remained thunderous even when he was whispering. Tears of joy fell freely from Uncle Moshe's eyes as he admonished his brother, "I could have been robbed and mugged a hundred times!" But Uncle Joshua was too busy dabbing at his own eyes to respond.

Uncle Moshe was introduced to everyone, and he hugged them, all with equal abandon, even a very shocked Rabbi Levi who stiffened at the physical demonstration. Taking his time bantering and reminiscing with each one, Uncle Moshe did not at first notice him. This gave Albano a chance to gawk at him, open-mouthed. However strange his attire, Uncle Moshe did not seem self-conscious in the least. He wore his funny clothes in a way that was so regal that it made you wish you were dressed just as he was. And he had a way of speaking and laughing and firing questions that made even the dullest one of them with their monotonous life suddenly seem more exciting. Moshe's joy was so communicative that even Rabbi Levi had to stop himself from smiling on more than one occasion. Uncle Joshua, overcome with emotion, laughed and cried unrestrainedly. The two had not seen each other in seven years.

"And this?" Uncle Moshe finally bellowed, grabbing Albano's arm and feeling his biceps. "Is this one of the strong men you promised me as an escort?"

"This," Uncle Joshua said, "is Albano."

To this, Uncle Moshe responded by lifting him until Albano was tight against his fat belly and his feet dangled ten inches from the ground. Moshe held him there for a long while. Albano did not know how to react and just tried breathing through the squeeze. But soon he felt that Uncle Moshe's body was shaking with silent sobs, so he stayed very still for what seemed like an eternity. "Your father," Uncle Moshe roared in his ear finally, "was the best man on earth. You hear me? The very best, kindest man on earth." With this, he set Albano down, and Uncle Moshe and Uncle Joshua stood for an instant, not speaking, looking at the ground in sadness.

The men began loading up the wagons. Albano, looking for something he could do, said, "I will fetch water for the horses."

He needed to say no more. In the excitement, everyone had forgotten about the horses. "The horses!" Uncle Joshua murmured. "Yes, they must drink. At once!"

"Good boy," Uncle Moshe hollered. "He is the brain of this family, I can tell, just as his father was. And how did our family produce such a handsome child? Where did he get those gold eyes of his?"

Albano grabbed the two pails and set out to find fresh water on the quay.

Looking for a fountain or a spigot, he walked around the waterfront, his heart beating wildly in his chest through the cacophony of blaring horns, the clanging of pots falling on the stone quays, the yelling of fishmongers who sold their day's catch right out of their boats, the whistling and screeching of docking barges, and the smells of decaying fish, camel droppings, incense, vanilla, and overripe fruit.

He had heard that the architecture of the waterfront was reminiscent of Europe and built to resemble it. Now here it was, right before him on the beautiful waterfront. Who knew when he would be able to get such a close look again, if ever? Blinded by the reflection of the sun on the white façades, he walked closer to the buildings. They were two or three stories high with balconies at each window and had lace-like wrought iron banisters. On some of the balconies, people had placed potted flowers and plants cascaded down. The buildings were the most beautiful, man made things Albano had ever set eyes on.

But even more fascinating were the cafés and restaurants at ground level filled with dozens of tables at which men in their fineries sipped unknown beverages. Each terrace was shaded by colorful awnings: yellow, red, blue, orange. It was so festive, all this color. Each café and restaurant was topped by signs on which were words in languages Albano did not know. He walked closer to the terraces. The tables were set with white dishware over crisp tablecloths. Silver cutlery and etched crystal gleamed in the light. Waiters came to and fro, wearing aprons down to their feet and holding large trays filled with food and drinks in tall glasses in which ice floated. On the plates were strange, delicious smelling foods that made Albano's mouth water: stews, small roasted birds, vegetables in little mounds, grilled fish in sauces, slices of cakes, and to his relief, nothing resembling a pig.

On the quayside closer to the water, men and women strolled arm in arm, umbrellas shading them. The European children accompanying their parents wore little hats and leather shoes. Girls wore ribbons in their hair which was curled and arranged just so. If the quay was a dangerous place, it certainly did not appear to be. Quite the contrary, it was a wonderfully happy place where families could stroll or have a meal in peace, all languages and ethnicities intermingling.

"Go, move," a waiter said in Arabic as he hurried by, carrying a three-tiered dish he then set on a table with a flourish. The diners made excited sounds and spoke to each other in an unknown language. On each level of the dish was a circular tray of crushed ice, filled with mounds of nothing but treif! Shrimp, lobster, crab and shellfish all presented to be eaten as though they were delicacies. The diners, Albano figured to be mostly Levantines, Americans, Europeans, and Greek. Obviously, Christian was the religion to have if you were to eat at any of those restaurants, but if this is what they wanted to eat, they could have it all to themselves. Albano felt thankful he was not born Christian. He would likely have starved to death!

Albano moved away from the building, carrying his pails and looking for water until he saw an old woman carrying an empty bucket and decided to follow her. She led him to a large fountain where Albano stood in line awaiting his turn. The fountain was wide and squat with a single spigot that let out a powerful stream of water. A boy his age dressed in a white djellaba, a red fez camped on his head, sat atop the fountain and turned the spigot on and off, while letting out a continuous high-pitch flow of sentences in Arabic, Greek, Armenian and other languages. Albano saw that as people filled their containers, they gave the boy a coin.

Albano did not have money. He had been gone for fifteen minutes and still did not have water for the horses. He got out of the line and stood there, wondering what to do next.

"Hey, Jew!" the boy called in broken Hebrew.

"Me?" Albano asked in Arabic.

"You're the only Jew here. You speak Arabic?"

"Some."

"You want water?"

"I have no money."

The boy laughed. "So?" He hopped off the fountain and pointed at the spigot. "Then help yourself. The water is for everyone. I only open and close the spigot. What am I to do when fools think they should pay me for it? Refuse their money?"

Albano stepped toward the fountain tentatively, set his pails down, and turned on the water. The water came out so forcefully that he was splashed in the face and the pail overturned.

"Lower, turn it lower. No fool, the other way!" Albano was drenched now, and still the water was coming at him. The boy pounced forward, turned the spigot, and let the water slowly fill the pail. "What are those things for," the boy said, touching Albano's tzitzit that dangled from the side of his trousers.

Albano considered the question. "They bring me closer to God."

The boy was astonished. "How could they?"

Albano shrugged. "They just do, I guess."

The boy roared with laughter. "Those are only bits of thread! If they brought people closer to God, everyone would have them. You Jews are fools indeed."

"Where did you learn to speak Hebrew?"

"You're not the only Jew in Smyrna you know. I've seen others before you."

Albano looked at the boy who smiled a bright smile and watched him intently. "Not Jews like me you haven't," Albano assured him, a twinkle in his eye. "I am studying to become a rabbi."

"Yes," the boy admitted. "You are my first rabbi."

Albano's pails were full. "You are Muslim?" he asked.

"I'm many things," the boy answered cryptically.

"Thank you for the water," Albano said. He lifted the pails and began to turn around. The boy hopped on top of the fountain and was back to jabbering to everyone in line. When Albano was a few meters away, he heard the boy call after him.

"I'm here on the quay every day. Come back soon, Rabbi."

Albano left and turned once or twice and watched in awe as the boy swindled more fools out of their coins.

****

The group found a quiet spot on the quay, gave the horses their water and straw, and sat to eat their meal by the water. Sitting away from the rest of the group on the stone parapet, Uncle Moshe and Uncle Joshua had removed their shoes and rolled up their pant legs. Uncle Moshe had also removed his socks, which were held together with funny little straps around his chubby calves. They had their feet in the water and were catching up with each other, whispering. From his shaded spot under a tree, Albano admired the Aegean Sea and the sailboats in the distance. What would life be like on one of those boats, covering great distances between far away countries, docking in Marseille and Genoa, Constantinople and the great port cities in Greece or Egypt? What did the air feel and smell like there? Did the soft wind now on his skin come from one of those faraway places? The seagulls that danced above had seen more of the world than he had. He had heard of cold countries where ice and snow covered the ground, and of countries where the trees were so dense that you could not see the sky for miles. Could one travel to those by boat? Albano inhaled the salty air. Soon he would return to the Jewish quarter, the rank air, the hours of studying by candlelight, Aunt Sadie's reproachful gaze.

The sea breeze carried gleams of Moshe's loud whispers, and Albano heard foreboding words that carried weight when spoken by such a jovial fellow as Moshe: words such as war, ethnic nationalism, massacres, a group called Young Turks. Uncle Joshua nodded and shook his head and combed his fingers through his beard the way he did when he was perplexed. Albano felt the chill return, the sense of doom that had been with him since the cholera epidemic had taken his family.

The time came to make the trek back to the Jewish quarter. Rabbi Levi hopped on the wagon atop the rugs because he was old and tired. Uncle Joshua posted the men around the wagons and led the caravan. Albano and Moshe walked together in back. His strange new uncle, despite his considerable girth, was bouncing up the hill more than he walked. When they were sufficiently high to see the bay from above, Moshe stopped without warning in the middle of the road. Albano stopped too. The rest of the group did not notice this and continued trudging up. Moshe faced the beautiful bay of Smyrna below and opened his arms wide, gazing at the shimmering Aegean Sea on one side, and the plains and mountains on the other. He sighed deeply, "Ha, Smyrna … the beautiful. How I have missed you." He casually pulled a thin silver box out of a pocket and out of the box a funny little cigarette, long, thin, and perfect. He lit it with great flourish and took several large minty puffs out of it.

"You're not afraid of robbers, Uncle Moshe?" Albano asked with alarm as he saw the space between them and the rest of the group widen.

Uncle Moshe took another puff out of his cigarette and unhurriedly resumed the climb. "Have you ever seen a robber carrying loot such as one of those heavy rugs?" he asked playfully. "Three men would need to lift one, roll it, and what would they do? Scamper away stealthily up Mount Pagus?" The thought made Uncle Moshe howl with laughter, and it was such an infectious laughter that Albano laughed along with him. "Say, chap," Uncle Moshe said, "your Uncle Joshua says that you want to become a rabbi, huh? That is a great honor for our family indeed. I'm sure your father would be proud."

Albano looked at the dirt on the road. "Yes, Uncle Moshe."

"Is it yes, your father would be proud? Or is it yes, you want to become a rabbi?"

"Both," Albano answered. He thought about it and added, "But mostly the part you said about my father." Uncle Moshe laughed, so Albano laughed too, not knowing why. He had now laughed twice in a minute. It was a strange thing, to laugh. He had forgotten how good it felt.

"It's your aunt, isn't it?" Uncle Moshe said. "Why not have one of her sons become a rabbi and leave you to do as you wish?"

Albano shrugged, "It is because I have an aptitude for studying."

Uncle Moshe shook his head. "That woman … A wonderful, pious woman don't get me wrong, but why would she have the final say?"

Albano hesitated and timidly asked, "What else is there to do for a boy like me?"

Uncle Moshe raised his eyebrows, "A boy like you? What kind of boy are you?"

Albano looked away, afraid that Uncle Moshe's piercing gaze might bring on tears of self-pity in him. "A boy with no mother and no father," he said.

To this, Moshe opened his arms wide again, as though he were embracing the entire world. "My boy, this could be the freest you will ever be! Think of it: no parents to disappoint, no wife to tell you what to do, no children to worry about. Why, you could do anything! You could become a sailor, a teacher, a merchant. Once your muscles come in, you could even become one of those dangerous carpet robbers that haunt the flanks of Mount Pagus." Uncle Moshe laughed at his joke and Albano laughed too until tears sprang from his eyes.

"But what about God, Uncle Moshe? Am I not supposed to serve Him. I'm studying the Torah, and then to stop … Wouldn't I disappoint God?"

"So, God takes your entire family, and you're worried about disappointing Him? You should be the one who's disappointed." Albano balked at the sacrilegious words. "Listen," Uncle Moshe continued. "God and I, true, we've had our differences, but for the time being He is leaving me to live life as I wish. In exchange for this, I try to be the man He intends for me to be. God created all kinds of creatures, you see. The giraffe and the starfish, the gazelle and the flea; they each have a purpose on this earth. It is the same thing with men. Some men are supposed to be rabbis, and some are supposed to be robbers. You can be a rabbi if this is what you truly believe it is the purpose for which you were brought forth on this earth, nephew. If not, then find your purpose and do that. Don't you think God would be more disappointed in a rabbi who loathes being a rabbi than in a robber who truly accomplishes his God-given destiny as robber?"

****

That night, dinner at Uncle Joshua and Aunt Sadie's was an unusually joyous affair. Friends and relatives came from all over the Jewish quarter to visit Uncle Moshe, admire his famous rugs, or any other excuse they could conjure up to see the man who was fast becoming a legend.

To everyone who visited, each bringing a delicious dish, Uncle Moshe gave the greeting of a long-lost brother, even to those he didn't know. He had such an infectious, warm air about him that it was impossible for anyone not to be charmed, especially the little children who were fascinated by this man who spoke their language but was loud and colorful as a jester and so different. And he ate and ate, and he drank bottle after bottle of sweet wine. Soon, neighbors were bringing their violins and accordions, the family dinner transformed into a massive celebration of nothing in particular.

Later, Uncle Moshe let his little nephews climb on his lap and crawl all over him. Nothing about him was stern, nothing about him was proper, and everything about him felt generous and open-hearted. Albano camped himself near him and would not budge, hanging on to Uncle Moshe's lips for the extraordinary stories he strung together.

Cousin Toby, who was just five years old, said, "Uncle Moshe, is it true you own a motorcar?"

"Do I own a motorcar? Of course, I don't own a motorcar! I own nothing, my boy. I am a free man, owning nothing, and owned by no one."

"You own rugs."

"I merely move them from one place in the world to another."

"But you are rich. You could buy a motorcar if you wanted to."

"Bah!" Uncle Moshe said. "I usually travel by whale."

"On top of a whale?"

"Inside, there is a special cavity for voyagers."

"Like Jonah?"

"He made it popular. I personally find it quite rank and dark," he added mysteriously. "I much rather travel by air."

"How do you travel by air, Uncle Moshe?" Albano asked.

"Why, I travel by magic carpet!" The little children opened their mouths, transfixed. "Although magic carpets are temperamental, much like donkeys. One day they're in the mood, the next day they are not. You could be sitting on one for hours and nothing, and then suddenly, for no reason at all, they will soar through the sky and take you wherever they wish."

"You fly through the sky?"

"All the time."

"But isn't it windy up there? How do you hang on?" one little girl asked.

"As long as you fly at the precise speed of the wind, which carpets know to do instinctively, you will not feel the wind at all."

"And what about rain?"

"You must make sure there will be no rain. Any little drop of water and the rug plummets to the ground, and you with it."

"And what about clouds? Do you travel through clouds?"

"Ha, clouds are a tricky business. Clouds are the reason I will never again ride a magic carpet to Paris." He scrunched up his eyebrows. "I had an incident once … but I do not want to bore you."

"Tell us!" the kids cried out in unison.

"Have you heard of the Eiffel Tower?"

"No."

"The Eiffel Tower is an immense tower in the center of Paris, which is the most beautiful city in France, and it might well be the most beautiful city in the world outside of Smyrna. This tower is made entirely out of tremendous beams of metal. Yet from a distance it appears to be made of very fine lace." Uncle Moshe drew the shape of the tower in the air with his finger. "It is also the tallest building ever created by man."

"Is it as tall as Mount Pagus?"

"Far taller."

"Can one climb it?"

"You can climb it but it may take many days, and you must do it by foot. I attempted once to climb it by camel, but they refused. And I don't mean the authorities refused; the camel refused to go up those steep metal steps. So, as I was telling you, the tower is so very tall that it reaches all the way up to the clouds, and the stairs get thinner and thinner as it goes up, so much so that the base is as wide as a village, and the very tip is sharp as a needle and twice as long as a sword. This sharp tip I discovered the hard way. I was riding one of my favorite carpets through the clouds of Paris. It is my fault. I blame myself entirely for this, as I had an important business meeting to attend in Vienna, many countries away, and was in a hurry. (Now you must know that it is important to hide in the clouds, and ride at night if possible, especially when you're flying in a foreign country; you do not want to draw attention to yourself.) When suddenly, was it the clouds, was it the moonless night, or a combination of both, I felt a sudden sharp tug and heard a great sound of tearing; my carpet had caught on to the spear at the top of the Eiffel Tower! And just like that, in one instant, the carpet was sliced in half. I barely had time to hang on to the tip of the tower. I dangled there for a while, wondering what I should do next. Then I had no choice but to climb down the side of the tower, meter by meter. And believe me when I tell you that is a lot of meters, and as you can see, I am a man of considerable size. Adonai be thanked, it was dark, so no one saw me. When I finally reached the ground, the clouds had subsided, and it was daybreak. My clothes now hung loosely on my body, as I had sweated off half my weight. When I lifted my eyes, I saw my poor carpet, still caught at the tip and dangling miserably."

"How did they get the carpet down?"

"They dispatched a team of specially trained monkeys. The French are quite organized. They always use monkeys to go up and down the Eiffel Tower and take care of those details."

In bed that night, Albano wondered if Uncle Moshe was the way he was because he had been away when cholera struck. The fact was, the entire Jewish quarter had stopped being happy then. And here was Uncle Moshe, reminding them how it was done.

****

The day Uncle Moshe left, a month later, everyone was crying. Albano felt a deep sense of loss. Who else was there in the entire Jewish quarter who could make the impossible feel possible, who could use tragedy to laugh at himself, and make the threat of war appear like a golden opportunity for much-needed change? Albano had hoped he would be allowed to be part of the escort that brought Uncle Moshe back to the harbor, but this time Aunt Sadie made sure he was busy. Aunt Sadie had never warmed up to Uncle Moshe. "This man, he eats like ten men. You can be sure I am relieved he is gone," she told anyone who would listen.

"Why don't you like him, Ma? Cousin Zev asked. Everyone else does."

"He makes a joke of our traditions. That's why."

"Because he did not marry?"

Aunt Sadie had a small laugh. "Your Uncle Moshe has … other interests," she said mysteriously.

The day of his departure, friends and family congregated at the door of the Jewish quarter, and Uncle Moshe embraced everyone with the same gusto, pinching children's cheeks, flattering the women with compliments on the handsomeness of their children and deliciousness of their food, shaking hands and hugging everyone in sight.

"Where is my rabbi?" Uncle Moshe called out. People made way for Rabbi Levi.

"My boy, I hope that you will soon rethink your sinful ways," Rabbi Levi said, but although he tried to sound stern, it was obvious Rabbi Levi was as much under Uncle Moshe's spell as everyone else.

"Sin, what is sin?" Uncle Moshe laughed. "Everything that is beautiful you call sin, Rabbi. Food is sin, love is sin, traveling the world is sin, dressing this way and that is sin. But tell me then, Rabbi, why did God bother Himself to invent so many sins?" The men laughed. Offended, Rabbi Levi mumbled in his beard.

When it was Albano's turn to be hugged, Uncle Moshe spoke in his ear. "Son, don't let people tell you what sin is or isn't. Fearful people call sin everything they do not understand."

The weeks after Uncle Moshe left, Albano did not feel like himself. He was both more excitable and sadder. Although his days mirrored the days before Uncle Moshe had come to Smyrna, now nothing felt or tasted the same. He was sad in a new way. It was not the old sadness of crying quietly at night for his family. It was a new sadness about the very nature of his days. Now the endless rising before daybreak, studying, and reading did not feel like something he was meant to do, but something he was made to do. Energy brewed inside him. Staying in one place felt painful to the point of screaming. He wanted to escape and run to his cave, but there was never time. His cousins were outside, running, fighting, screaming while he pored over ancient texts. Watching the Hebrew letters blend into each other, he thought the inside of him, his brain, his heart, his muscles, could no longer be contained by the outside of him: his skin, his clothes, even his shoes. At night, he dreamt wildly of monkeys, of flying carpets, of boats, of whales that swallowed him whole. During the day, he longed to return to the harbor and talk to that curious boy who spoke so many languages. In the short hours he had spent on the quayside, Albano had smelled odors he did not know existed, felt the ocean breeze right on his skin. He had seen the European buildings, and the clothes, and the hats, and the boats, and the people. What other sensations and sights were there to experience?

The harbor became his obsession. In those short hours he had been there, he had not felt lonely. How could it be then that here in the Jewish quarter, among his cousins, his blood, placed among his people, he felt forlorn, like an outcast. His trip to the harbor had permanently erased the notion that the city was dangerous. Now it was the thought of never leaving the Jewish quarter that terrified him. He constantly thought about Uncle Moshe's words on life's purpose? How was Albano to discover his if he stayed put?

He began to devise a plan. It was not a smart or well-thought-out plan at all. Aunt Sadie would never let him go back; this much was clear. If he wanted to visit the harbor again he would have to do it without her permission or knowledge. And whatever he did, he simply would have to face the consequences. His plan was just to go. Early one morning he would take the road down to the city instead of the road to shul. His plan was that once he came back, he would be punished. There was no escaping the punishment. A beating he could take, he reasoned. He had been beaten before. He knew what to expect. And whatever punishment and chores were given to him, he could simply do. And that was the whole plan.

He searched in his books, in the Torah, and didn't find any signs that to walk down to a city filled with Muslims and Christians constituted a sin. He would be doing something forbidden, yes, but not by God. There was racial tension everywhere in the Empire, but judging from the mingling of races and religions on the quayside, Smyrna appeared immune to it. He did not fear the Muslims, but he had been taught to mistrust Christians who had persecuted Jews from time immemorial. His own ancestors had been driven away from their Spanish homeland by King Ferdinand and Queen Isabella's edict in 1492. The Christians had given them a few months to take a boat to any country that would have them. This was how his family had ended up in the Ottoman Empire. Sultan Bayezid had welcomed Jews with open arms. According to the story, he had declared the king and queen of Spain fools for chasing away their brightest and most prosperous subjects and letting him have them. The Torah finials were all that remained of that time for his family, who had smuggled them, buried them, hidden them under clothes, and passed them down from one Kohanim to the next for nearly five hundred years, and now they were hidden in Albano's cave.

So, if Albano was not committing a crime against God, and he wasn't endangering his life, then this was simply an act of family disobedience.

Even with all the thinking Albano had done on the subject, when the day to go came at last, he had not planned it. Not exactly. He rose at three in the morning, as usual, went to the kitchen alone to have the bread that Aunt Sadie left out for him for his breakfast, and dressed in his rabbinical school uniform, in black from top to bottom except for the stiff, white buttoned-down shirt. Only, instead of walking south toward shul, he found himself wandering toward the boundaries of the Jewish quarter and, in the dark still, down the hill instead of up.

He walked by the light of the setting moon and under the fading stars and continued downhill in the slowly lightening sky. The silence and aloneness, rather than intimidating him, filled him with a sense of awe and possibilities. Dawn broke just as he arrived at the deserted pier. Having only experienced the waterfront at the busy hour, Albano had eagerly anticipated the same activity and had not imagined it any other way, but to be part of Smyrna's awakening was uniquely mesmerizing. The waterfront seemed longer and wider in its emptiness. Muslim men swept and washed the pavement sleepily. As the sky filled with streaks of pinkish hues and the sea went from black to cobalt blue, the waterfront revealed itself, stretching unhurriedly like a cat. Boats on the docks rocked gently to the low clanking of buoys.

Albano inhaled the delicious moment, the sea air, the merry clinking of bells, the clapping of sails. On the waterfront, cafés were just beginning to open: awnings unfolded, busboys lifted piles of wicker chairs and set them on terraces, white cloths were spread squarely on tables.

Soon, a handful of early-rising, impeccably dressed European and Levantine businessmen were sitting at scattered tables. The businessmen took spectacles out of their coat pockets, pinched them on their noses, and unfolded newspapers as waiters brought them coffee in tiny cups and plates filled with pastries. Albano did not doubt that those men were the kinds of men who, with their money, their work, their importance, their newspapers, shaped the world. He stood transfixed. This is what he wanted to do with his life! He wanted to be one of those men who, in early morning hours, sat in peace and luxury at the terraces of cafés!

Standing alone on the pier, intoxicated by the clean scent of the sea and the aroma of fresh coffee and pastries, Albano felt inexplicably alive.

He sat right on the pier, let his bare feet dangle toward the water, unfolded the cloth in which he had placed his bread and a chunk of goat cheese, and as he watched the sea, began to eat. Surely God would want him to know about His creation. God could not possibly have meant for him to be ignorant of anything that was not the Torah and Jewish affairs. He watched the sailboats and the ever-brightening blue sky and began to imagine with great pleasure what it would be like to ride in one of those boats, what it would be like to explore the strange cities those boats came from, what it would be like to be a sailor moving about the world.

He vaguely heard a high-pitch call, "Rabbi!" but in his reverie, he didn't react. A few seconds later, someone was sitting right beside him. "I thought it was you, Rabbi!" Albano looked in amazement: it was the boy from the fountain! "Did you come here to see me?" the boy was asking in Arabic.

Taken aback, Albano muttered, "I did not." Although in a way it was true.

The boy camped himself in front of him. He wore the traditional dress of Muslim men, a white djellaba, a red fez. Next to him was an extraordinarily large leather satchel filled with newspapers. "I knew you would come back," the boy said. He spoke animatedly, but his eyes remained fixed on the horizon, as though he was looking at something. "In fact, I thought to myself, when will my friend the rabbi pay me another visit?"

Friend? Albano thought. "How did you learn to speak Hebrew?" he asked.

"And how can you speak Arabic? I thought Jews only spoke Hebrew."

"Everyone in the Jewish quarter speaks Arabic. And my family speaks Ladino because we're Jews from Spain."

"There are not too many rabbis your age walking around the pier," the boy noted.

"I'm not yet a rabbi. Only learning."

"What is your name, Rabbi? Mine is Hagop."

"I'm Albano."

"Where is your group from last time? And your horses?"

Albano was surprised that the boy knew so much about his last visit to the pier. "I came alone."

"They let you go?"

"They do not know I'm here," Albano admitted.

Looking at the horizon, Hagop whistled between his teeth appreciatively. "A disobedient rabbi," he said.

"I'm only curious about Smyrna," Albano said defensively.

Hagop nodded in understanding and pointed to the place on the horizon where his gaze had been fixed. "See that Ferry over there? That is the first ferry of the day, and with it comes mayhem. Then it's one after the other. I will not lie to you: this is not easy work. But these people coming on those boats, they are starving for them; they haven't gotten any since they have been at sea. They will pay anything for them."

Albano looked at the boy, dumfounded. "Starving for what?"

Hagop turned to his enormous bag and laid it between them. "News!" he said. "Newspapers: Greek, French, British, even American." He pointed to the horizon again. "See the steamboats arriving? Those are passenger liners that come in each day from all over the world, not just the Empire. People sail here from Genoa, Marseille, Trieste, London. They arrive every hour, and in those boats are men from all those countries. Most of them only speak their own language. They're from America and Africa and Europe and Russia and everywhere. Do you know the single thing they all have in common?"

"They are seasick?" Albano suggested.

"They want news. They want newspapers!" Hagop exclaimed. He continued excitedly, speaking a mile a minute. "They are ravenous for them! They are desperate for them! They want newspapers more than they want food to eat or air to breathe. And now that war is on everyone's lips and in every headline, they need news more than ever. They want to know how the world's affairs will affect their travel, their business, everything. They are so desperate for newspapers that I can set my price; they will pay double, triple! And whatever they pay over cost is my benefit."

"Can they not purchase newspapers at the kiosks over there?" Albano jutted his chin in the direction of the small tent that had sprouted on the quay and where a merchant was busying himself arranging newspapers and periodicals.

Hagop shook his head impatiently. "The key is to present them newspapers right as they disembark. Smyrniots aren't the ones who buy from me. They know that in only a few steps they will purchase it at the regular price. But all the others, especially those who have never set foot in Smyrna, those people are ripe for the picking."

"Isn't this dishonest?" Albano inquired.

"It is called supply and demand."

"What does this mean?"

"They don't know if there will be a supply," the boy said assuredly, "so, they demand. I'll tell you what, Rabbi. Do you want me to show you Smyrna?"

Albano looked at Hagop dubiously, but the boy's wide smile and enthusiasm were contagious. "Maybe."

"I'll make a deal with you. You help me sell the newspapers this morning, and in exchange, I will show you Smyrna."

Albano pointed to the way he was dressed. "Will people buy from someone like me?"

Hagop ignored him. "Here in this satchel, I have newspapers in Greek, Armenian, English, French, and Italian. The minute people dock we can see what nationality they are, and we present that language to them. The two of us can go twice as fast, and then we have the rest of the day to explore."

"I'm not supposed to be here," Albano admitted.

"What, you think I'm supposed to be here?"

"I would not know how to sell. What do I tell people?"

"You tell them nothing, you shove the newspaper right under their noses, they read the headline, and they're hooked. Like a big juicy tuna fish." Hagop considered Albano, tilted his head, assessing him. He reached for Albano's chin with dubiously clean fingers and moved Albano's face this way and that to see it from several angles and nodded knowingly. "You will present the newspapers to the ladies."

Albano widened his eyes in horror. "Why the ladies?"

Hagop laughed. "Have they no mirrors in the Jewish quarter? Just go to well-dressed ladies, the ones with the laces and jewels. They might even give you a tip. But I get to keep all the money, is it clear? You earn a tour of the most cosmopolitan, the most exciting city on earth, by one of the city's top guides."

"You?"

"Me!" The next moment, Hagop was on his feet. He took half the newspapers out of the satchel and thrust them into Albano's arms. "Follow me," he said, and before Albano had any time to think, they both started running toward the docking steamboat, Hagop holding on to the red fez on his head and Albano to his wide-brimmed black hat.

What followed was indeed a whirlwind. The incoming steamboat was filled with French citizens coming from Marseille. Hagop moved French newspapers to the top of his and Albano's piles and, while advancing against the disembarking crowd, began screaming, "Le Figaro! Le Monde! Dernières nouvelles! Achetez Le Figaro, Achetez Le Monde!" Albano was astounded that Hagop, a Turkish boy his age, could know Hebrew and the French language. Mute, his stomach in a knot, the newspapers moistened from the sweat of his gripped fingers, Albano rigidly stood where Hagop had told him to stand. Fancily dressed men and women made their way down the ramp, holding on to handrails and a flurry of Turkish men fretted around them, offering to carry their luggage. The French ladies clutched their bags and held dogs the size of rats. The French gentlemen took out their wallets. Albano went stiffer still. Hagop summoned him in Hebrew, "Closer, Rabbi! Come close to the women!" and then he resumed calling out the names of the newspapers in various languages. "Tribute, Figaro, Corriere de la Serra!" Newspapers were flying out of Hagop's hand while Albano still had not made a single sale. And how could he have? He did not look like a salesman at all. He looked like a child in rabbi clothing, dumb, stiff, and mute, who happened to be standing there gripping a pile of French newspapers.

A beautiful woman, surely the most beautiful woman Albano had ever seen, came down the ramp, all cream lace, silk clothes and pink cheeks. She held on to the arm of a mustachioed man who wore the same funny straw hat Uncle Moshe had worn that first day he arrived. "Là, le journal," the woman said, pointing in the direction of Albano. "Vous avez Le Monde?" the man asked. Albano could not understand them. He looked at his papers as though this was the first time he was laying eyes on them, which is exactly what it was. Unable to read the names of the newspapers written in languages he did not know, he just presented them in a pile and let the man find the one he wanted. "Combien?" the beautiful French lady asked. Albano, unaccustomed to being addressed by a beautiful woman, European or otherwise, blushed violently. "Il est si beau," the woman laughed. "Donne-lui de l'argent, Eugène." The man handed him a coin. Albano looked at the coin dumfounded. "C'est suffisant?" the man asked. Albano only stared, so the man gave him another coin, and a third. Albano must have looked terribly confused because the lady smiled warmly at him and the man just shrugged, exasperated. Albano, frozen, the coins still sitting on his upright palm, watched his first ever customers walk toward the restaurants. He was still watching them when the lady turned back toward him and flashed him a smile so alluring that Albano dropped half the papers onto the pavement.

Hagop gave him a light tap on the cheek, plucked the coins from Albano's hand and announced, "I was right about the ladies."

Albano picked up the newspapers scattered at his feet. "I only sold one."

"You'll get better at it."

The rest of the morning, as the cafés became a sea of hats and open newspapers, Hagop and Albano sold newspapers. This was the most exciting thing Albano had ever done. Once Hagop recognized a docking steamboat and figured out what the nationality of the travelers might be, he showed Albano how to pronounce the title of the papers the travelers would most likely purchase. He also taught him how to pronounce the prices in a number of languages and gave him huge slaps on the back when Albano pronounced correctly.

Hagop was fearless in his approach, but Albano rapidly figured out how to repeat the feat of his first sale. Yes, Hagop was right. For some reason, all Albano had to do was stand there and one lady or another would notice him and nudge her husband in his direction. She would smile at him. Some ladies would speak to him, ask him questions in languages he could not understand, so all he did was repeat the name of the newspaper in their language and tell them the price. Effortlessly, the papers sold themselves. Exclamations of "Muy caro" and "bel ragazzo" and "gentil garçon juif" and an outraged "das ist die Zeitung von gestern," followed them, but he did not know what those meant.

"These European people," Albano asked Hagop once the sun was high in the sky and most of the newspapers were sold, "why do they not haggle?"

Hagop shrugged, "They don't know how."

"Everyone knows how to haggle."

"It is considered rude in Europe."

Albano decided he had much to learn. Either the rest of the world was upside down, or else it was right side up, and it was the Ottoman Empire that did things wrong. It was all so confusing. The one thing Albano tried not to think about was the beating that awaited him when he came home. He also tried not to think too much about sin. Was spending time with a Muslim boy a sin? Was smiling at European ladies a sin? There were no rules against commerce that he knew of, and he hoped this was commerce, not robbery.

When the last steamboat had docked, Hagop held up his hand. "Give me my money, Rabbi. Are you hungry?"

"I have no food. And now," Albano added, dropping his earnings into Hagop's hand, "I have no money either."

Hagop laughed. "You are funny, Rabbi. Come with me. I will feed you and show you Smyrna."

"What do you do with the money you earn selling newspapers?"

"I spend it."

"What do you buy?"

"More newspapers!" Hagop said.

They walked across the quay and away from the sea. "See the road to the Jewish and Turkish quarters are up to the right, south of the quayside. The Armenian quarter begins straight across from the ocean to the east, just past Frank Street. Have you seen Frank Street?"

"Everyone speaks of it."

"Northeast is the Greek quarter. To the north there is the American Consulate and Sporting Club, and after that the European quarter where most of the Levantines live. Now, if you've never seen wealth, you will be amazed. I'll take you to Frank Street, and then to the Turkish Bazaar, and then the Armenian quarter."

As they walked toward Frank Street, Hagop pointed to white marbled façades, minarets, intricate mosaics, stained glass, and stone stairs that lead to massive buildings, naming everything faster than Albano could make sense of it. "This is the French Bank! And this is the Greek Bank!" Each time he seemed as proud as if the establishment belonged to him alone. "And this to the left is the entrance to the Hamman! And this is…? I don't know what this is…. And this is the brothel! And this is the English Consulate! This is the Imperial Ottoman Bank! Over there is the Opera house. This is the Crédit Lyonnais, the French Bank. This is the headquarters of an international insurance company. This is the Catholic Church of Saint Mary, the Greek Orthodox Cathedral. And this is the entrance to Frank Street…."

The narrow street, encased on each side by buildings made of stone and wood tall enough to shade it completely, was long, sinuous, and narrower than Albano had pictured. Frank Street was barely wide enough for the dense crowd, yet all manner of vehicles and people squeezed themselves into it: men atop camels, horse-drawn buggies, barefoot peddlers pushing carts filled with goods who stopped in the middle of the road to sell merchandize to passersby. Every centimeter of the cobblestone pavement was dense with people in all sorts of strange shapes, sizes, and appearance, animals, dead and living, and mounds of merchandise, some of which he could recognize, most of it entirely mysterious to him. In the center of the pavement, you quickly learned to avoid the gutter that carried off soiled water and animal excrements. There were men in kaftans next to men in three-piece suits and top hats, women veiled from head to toe next to women dressed in the latest European fashion. Greek, Jewish, Armenian, Levantine, and European women and children, each wearing the attires of their respective people, pressed themselves into the crowd. At the stores' thresholds, merchants shouted the merits of their goods and switched to honeyed voices to coax shoppers into entering their stores. Everyone was buying or selling. Everyone was yelling and calling. Everyone was eating, cooking, singing, walking, arguing, bartering, or haggling. The street was loud with ethnic music and voices in every language. Periodically, the traffic would come to a standstill, and Albano and Hagop compressed themselves into this sea of humanity.

Above, the buildings on each side had balconies spilling bougainvillea and pink laurel, and clotheslines with drying laundry went from one side of the street to the other like playful banderoles. Painted signs in wood and metal attached to the façades stuck out into the street, and colorful awnings jutted from walls naming the various shops and eating establishments. Albano's head spun to the right and the left as Hagop breathlessly explained things: "This is Xenopoulos, the famous Greek flagship store." Albano knew enough written Greek to recognize some of the words painted on the fancy walls of the shop: silk and wool, dresses, ribbons, lace, umbrellas, blankets.

"This is the French store Au Bon Marché." Hagop continued excitedly, "They carry goods from Europe and the whole world, and that's where the Levantines, the Europeans, and all the rich people shop."

But next to this luxurious establishment, out of which fancy women in corseted dresses walked, followed by servants with arms filled with bags and boxes, there were stores for regular people too. Stores for Muslims, stores for Christians, stores for Jews, more stores than he could imagine existed: hat makers, shoemakers, jewelers, watchmakers and goldsmiths, apothecary shops, shops that sold olives and raisins, oils and dried fruit, tobacco leaves, tea, and coffee. There were grocers, gambling parlors, butchers, fish sellers, coffee shops, horse and wagons for hire, each store with its own stench, or perfume, each with colorful signs written in a dozen languages. In shop fronts were displays of meat – cooked and raw – live goats and poultry, piles of vegetables and fruit, dried goods, spices and grains in open baskets. Everyone had something to sell, and there was something to buy for every budget. The many cafés spilled their customers onto the streets by setting chairs and tables out on the pavement. American sailors, drunk into a stupor, coexisted there with pipe-smoking men donning fezzes, turbaned Bedouins who sat around small tables and drank Turkish coffee in silence, Greek men with long beards who drank ouzo out of metal goblets, and still more red-faced British men and their funny rounded hats. As he spoke nonstop, Hagop carved their way through the dense crowd. Albano kept bumping into people because he was looking up and down, to the left and to the right, trying to keep up with Hagop's tour and at the same time being overwhelmed by the sights, sounds, and scents all around. The smells reminded Albano that he was hungry, but his stomach could wait. He would, in all likelihood, never lay eyes on a more amazing spectacle than Frank Street, never again witness a sight more capable of taking his breath away, and never again feel more excited and alive than he did at this very moment.

Albano followed Hagop who continued to speak in a high-pitched voice. They made their way up a small alley that sprouted off Frank Street and arrived in the heart of the Turkish bazaar. The street was narrower and barely wide enough for three men to stand side by side. Merchandise dangled from walls and spilled onto the street. Everything one could want to purchase was in the bazaar: fabric, mosaics and tiles, metal lamps, crystals, pipes and hookahs, raw meat, fur and cloth, rugs, pottery, hats, tobacco, tea, spices. But this was not a place where Europeans shopped. Gone were the rich people, the banks, the temples and churches. In the bazaar everything was more rugged, the dress and language coarser, and many of the men more dangerous looking.

Hagop did not seem intimidated in the least, and no one was paying attention to them, so Albano began to relax about his surroundings, even though he looked conspicuously Jewish in this predominantly Muslim area. Suddenly the nagging thought he had tried to ignore awakened in him. By now, the people at shul must have noticed he was missing. It should not be too much of an issue as long as he got back to his house on time, which was still a possibility if he left right now. The problem was, he was not about to leave. Not so soon. Not now that he had a friend in Smyrna, a friend who knew the city. The thought of never returning home just to avoid the inescapable beating flickered through his mind.

Hagop, who had ignored every other store they walked past, came to a halt in front of a table piled high with angora blankets, silk garments, cotton clothing, and hats. He began fingering the merchandise, unfolding fabric, trying on this hat and that one. The merchant, a turbaned old man with bushy eyebrows, crossed his arms menacingly the instant he saw Hagop. "Salamalekum, may God be with you," Hagop clamored happily to the man.

"I don't know what you're up to," the man shouted angrily. "But I will call the police on you unless you stop coming here."

"Noble merchant, I don't know what you mean. I have done nothing wrong but admire your merchandise."

The old man raged, "I know you are stealing from me!"

Hagop looked contrite and, holding out his palms said, "Honored merchant, may Allah be with you. But before you accuse me and my Jewish friend of a crime, perhaps you need to see that our hands are empty." Hagop twirled, then made a show of opening his satchel, which was empty now. He bowed deeply. The man showed him his fist and screamed at him some more in Arabic as they walked away.

Albano waited for them to be out of earshot and asked, "Why is this merchant so angry with you? Is it true that you stole from him?" Then he noticed something. "You lost your hat!"

"Quite the contrary," Hagop said. "My hat is not lost; it has found its way home."

"What do you mean?"

"It's simple," Hagop beamed. "Each morning I walk past this foolish man's shop, I borrow a fez and put it on my head. When I come back home, I return it. The man knows that something is happening yet he doesn't know what!"

"But why do you do this?"

"If anyone in my quarter sees me with a fez on my head and tells my parents, I will not live to see another blessed day."

Albano did not understand. "So you steal, then you return?"

"I borrow. It is a business arrangement."

"One where only one person benefits," Albano pointed out.

"Oh, quite the opposite. I am the one who gets the least. I only get a stupid hat, while this man gets a puzzle to exercise his brain."

"Soon he will figure it out."

"Why worry? There are more fez merchants in Smyrna than there are boats in the Smyrna harbor."

"Why would your parents not want you to wear a fez?"

Hagop did not respond. Albano followed him up a narrow, sinuous street, admiring his new friend's self-confidence, his fearlessness. This was how he wanted to be: he wanted to be more like Uncle Moshe or like Hagop. Except that for every action he took, Albano could imagine hundreds of possible outcomes. The possibility of danger, of hurting someone, of being caught did not usually measure up against his curiosity and the thrill of adventure. And yet, here he was, following a reckless boy full of laughter.

"Now I will take you to the finest bakery in the Armenian quarter," Hagop said.

"But Armenians are Christians. Can a Jew and a Muslim be safe there?"

Hagop burst into roaring laughter. "I'm not Muslim! I'm a Christian. Apostolic Armenian, to be exact."

"This is why you can't wear a fez?"

"This is why I can't wear a fez."

"But why pretend to be Muslim?"

"When you dress like a Muslim boy in Smyrna, no one pays attention to you. I can walk around the city however I please."

"Do you not have school?"

Hagop shrugged in a way that expressed his utter disinterest in the matter. "I am a baker's apprentice. By the time the sun rises, I have already done my day's work. So I just head here before others awake, and I'm the first one on the quay."

"When do you sleep?"

"In the afternoon. Such is a baker's life, which is why I hate it so. We are lucky if we see the sun at all."

On Frank Street and in the bazaar, there were many Jews dressed much like him. But as they entered the Armenian quarter, Albano felt aware of his dark coat and tall black hat, the fringes that came down from his pockets, the long hair that spilled from his hat on both sides of his face. Now he knew what Hagop meant. If Hagop could transform into a Muslim simply by donning a fez, then it was possible that the difference between a Muslim, a Christian, or a Jew was even shallower than skin deep. Could he himself remove his clothes, cut his hair, and pass as a Muslim or a Christian boy? Would he want to? His skin was fair, his hair was a light shade of brown, and his eyes were that pale color that everyone noticed and was so unusual in the Jewish quarter. Were he to don short pants and long socks, and wear a European sort of hat, would he ever be mistaken for a French child? The funny thought distressed him. It made him anxious that his deepest sense of identity could be stripped from him simply by taking away his clothes. "Is a boy dressed like me safe in the Armenian quarter?" he asked.

Hagop considered this. "We don't like Jews much." He scratched his now fez-free skull. "But we don't like Greeks and Muslims either. And we don't like the Levantines. Or the Europeans. We just like to sell them things and work in their factories. Do Jews like Armenians?"

"I don't think so," Albano said.

The Armenian quarter was not unlike the Jewish quarter, Albano noticed. The same women's voices clamoring, muted sounds of donkey hoofs on dirt paths, laundry drying at windows, girls carrying jugs of water on their heads, grimy, barefoot boys chasing each other, men getting shaved on chairs set out by barbers in the street, old women gossiping on benches. The greatest difference was the smells. The quayside had smelled of fish and perfume, the bazaar had smelled of tobacco and raz el hanout, the Jewish quarter smelled of yeast and cinnamon, and now, in the Armenian quarter, it smelled of fried oil and honey. Hagop walked proudly through the streets, calling people by their names and laughing. Albano soon became acutely conscious of the many sets of eyes on him. Hagop read his thoughts. "Maybe take off that hat," he said helpfully. "But don't worry, my new Jewish friend, no one will harass you when you are with the son of Yori."

"Is your father a powerful man?"

"Better than that. He is the best baker in the Armenian quarter. No one here would take a chance of being refused his famous dolmas." Hagop rubbed his belly and licked his lips to illustrate. Soon he pointed at a bakery up the street and exclaimed, "This is it!" Inside the bakery it smelled heavenly, of warm bread and honey. The place bustled with activity and animated conversations. There were a dozen wooden tables and chairs where customers sat, drinking coffee and eating pastries. The length of one of the walls was covered in a beautiful fresco depicting men and women working together in a field of golden wheat. Hagop signaled for Albano to follow him toward a small table in back of the store. "That painting you're looking at, it's over one hundred years old. That's how old this bakery is. It belonged to my grandfather, and his father before that." Hagop noticed that many were staring at Albano. "What?" He told a gawking boy and his mother. "Is this the only Jew you have ever seen? This one is extremely holy, as you can judge from his extremely holy clothes. I found him down on the quay." Hagop plopped down heavily on a chair. "Sit," he said with much emphasis and pride. "And wait to feast on the best pastries in the whole Ottoman Empire." He added royally, "You can have anything here you desire." Albano sat, and Hagop began extricating coins out of his many pockets, spreading them on the table and gathering them into little stacks by currency: lira, pounds, French and Swiss francs, American pennies. He began counting, cursing, counting again.

There were perhaps twenty people inside the bakery. Some sat at the tables lined against the whitewashed walls, some stood in line, waiting to be served, pointing at merchandise, while two women who looked like mother and daughter hurried about the room. The two women wore their jet-black hair the Armenian women's way: severely parted in the middle and into one long, thick braid that reached way down their backs. They wore white blouses, long black skirts and a heavy crimson apron that came down to the floor. The mother, a heavyset woman with a kind face, did all the talking and interactions with the customers, taking orders, receiving money, and giving change with authority. The girl, who was about Albano's age, came in and out the back of the store carrying large trays filled with steaming pastries. Long sleeves covered her arms, and the collar of her dress was buttoned up to the nape of her slender neck. She carried her head high, and her eyes were unflinching. Her skin was very pale, her face a perfect oval, her nose small and straight, but it was her grave black eyes that made Albano lose his breath. Her eyes were immense and luminous, her eyebrows finely delineated, her lips crimson and full. Albano opened his mouth and forgot to close it. He was jerked away from his admiration by Hagop's reaching across the table and putting a hand on his collar. "When I tell you that you can have anything you want here, I am only speaking of pastries."

Albano decided Hagop had to be a magician to be able to read all his thoughts. "Wha, What do you mean?" he stuttered.

"If you look at her like this I will have to gouge your eyes out."

"She is your wife?" Albano said, astonished at Hagop's good fortune.

Hagop laughed. "What wife? I'm ten years old! She is my sister." Hagop and his sister looked very much alike: similar eyes with heavy lids, similar mouths, and bright, straight teeth. But Hagop's features were more pronounced and asymmetrical, which gave him the crazy air of a jester. His eyes bulged almost. His mouth was rapacious, whereas Xandra's features were so perfect they seemed painted on the lovely oval of her face. "Xandra!" Hagop called. "Meet my new friend."

"Nooo," came the strangled sound out of Albano's mouth. But already the girl was standing before him, holding a tray of pastries, her gaze amused and inquisitive.

"I found a rabbi on the quay, and now he is my friend," Hagop told her in Arabic so that Albano could understand what he was saying. "He and I are going into business together."

She looked at Albano and spoke in Arabic. "Are you certain? My brother may not be the most reliable of partners. He's never on time." Albano's stomach made 360-degree flips inside his belly. Xandra spoke to him, and the effect this had on him was something new and incredible. He could barely look at her and was unable to utter a word.

"Time, time, time!" Hagop clamored. "All you bakers think of is time. And rising in the dead of night. And shelling nuts by the boatful. And breaking your backs carrying bags of flour. Not me. I am meant for sunshine and adventure! I am meant to be a businessman." Hagop frowned at the narrowness of his dream and revised it. "I am meant to be a banker!"

"My brother the adventurous banker." Xandra laughed, looking at Albano. Albano laughed too, not even knowing why.

Hagop was furious. "One day you will see I will have my own seat on the train with my name on it, just like a rich Levantine."

"You always said you didn't want a partner," Xandra pointed out.

"I'm an ugly fellow, so I need a good-looking partner. You have to see Albano with the ladies. The key to success is who you associate with."

"Are you good with ladies?" Xandra inquired.

Albano could only come up with a strangled, "I … don't—"

"Isn't he handsome?" Hagop said with pride. "I will change his clothes, and he will look just fine."

"What is this for?" Xandra asked, pointing to Albano's sidelocks.

Albano felt his face redden. "Ahem … tradition, I think."

"Can you cut them?"

Albano widened his eyes, "Oh no!"

"Can you tuck them behind your ears?" Hagop asked pragmatically.

"I think so."

"What is your name?" Xandra asked.

"A, Albano."

"Can I give you something to eat, Albano?" she said, nodding to the tray she was still holding which was filled with pastries, some in the shape of crescents topped with powdered sugar and others like well-leavened rounds that glistened with honey.

To hear this beautiful girl pronounce his name, Albano nearly jumped out of his skin. He didn't know what the pastries on her tray were called. "I would like … a pastry?" he said stupidly, his voice barely above a murmur.

Xandra turned her coal-black eyes to her brother. "He isn't that good with the ladies," she said. "But it is true, Hagop, you have found yourself a handsome-looking rabbi."

CHAPTER 5

La Parisienne

Cassie stood by the conveyor belt waiting for her luggage when a chuckle emanated from the crowd. Then another. Then everyone was giggling. She looked for what was so amusing and found it; right there, moving on the conveyor belt, a single white, high-waist cotton panty was traveling alone. She laughed. It was all so incongruous and well, hilarious. It wasn't until a yellow and orange polka-dot shirt was ejected from the bowels of the terminal and began its own rotation of shame that Cassie understood that those were, in fact, her panties and her polka-dot shirt! They were followed by another T-shirt, this one purple, and a bra, an electric toothbrush rolled down, and, finally, the pièce de résistance: her zigzag suitcase, gutted, its innards of clothes and undies disgorging out of it like a cartoon zebra road kill.

She sprang forward waving her arms calling. "C'est à moi!" and began a humiliating scavenger hunt along the conveyor belt, apologizing and fishing out clothes and shoving them, red-faced, into her tote bag. "Merci," she mumbled to the psychiatrist who bent down and retrieved the polka-dotted T-shirt and held it between two fingers. "Merci," she told a beaming five-year-old girl who handed her the toiletry bag. "Merci," she whispered to a large man who waved a pair of socks in her direction. "Pardon. Je suis désolée," she blurted out to two pairs of feet next to which she scooped another T-shirt. "Merc" – recognizing the feet belonged to the French couple, Cassie switched to English – "I mean, sorry!" and she fished a lime green viscose bra from atop a still rotating suitcase.

After a few grunts, head shakes, and clicking of tongues, the Charles de Gaulle Airport baggage authorities washed themselves of any responsibility, pronouncing the gutted suitcase, "très vieille avec une fermeture à glissière en mauvais état." Antiquated, with a broken zipper. Cassie was given the options of a large trash bag or duct tape and agreed to the duct tape.

She exhaled as she exited the terminal and stepped out into the morning air. Then she inhaled and stopped in her tracks. It was freezing! Or perhaps a degree or two above freezing, judging from the pouring rain. There was supposed to be a heat wave! With her two layered, long-sleeved shirts made of ultrathin cotton, a lavender one over a light pink one, she might as well have been wearing tissue paper.

She considered the Frankenstein-looking suitcase sausaged in duct tape at her feet and renounced trying to retrieve her jacket. She eyed the taxi line and decided to make a run for it. Her suitcase, grinding against the wet asphalt, twisted and turned on itself with each step. In the line, a little man with a receding chin camped himself right behind her much too closely and lit a cigarette. Adjust, adjust, she thought. Ahead of her in line was the French couple from the plane. The wife wore a warm coat and seemed quite smug about it. She observed Cassie's unruly hair, the too thin clothes, the mangled suitcase, and the Uggs acting as fast-absorbing sponges on the soaked pavement. When a taxi Parisien whisked the two away, Cassie breathed better. If she could not handle the disapproval of complete strangers, it didn't bode well for the rest of the trip. She could not have been in Paris more than ten minutes, and already she was cold to the core and felt defeated. When it was her turn to enter a cab, her suitcase came off-balance. She turned her head in time to see one of the wheels fall off like a ripe fruit off a tree and go rolling off into the distance.

It was already three in the afternoon in Paris and six in the morning in her brain. She was filled with a strange, hollow, out-of-body energy but decided she better get to the hospital before the hotel. "Hôpital Saint-François. Dans le dixième arrondissement, s'il vous plaît," she told the driver over the blaring radio. The cab driver wore a white prayer hat and drove too fast for comfort, honking rather than slowing down when people or cars got in his way. Outside, it was as though she had never left. The city was familiarly gray, hazy, and wet. People in rain suits and umbrellas jumped over puddles. There were bakeries and cafés, shops with brands she recognized and some new ones. The windshield wipers moved with the rhythm of the music. In the city, the top edges of buildings melted into the thick sky. And then she saw them, the first giant billboard, then a second one, and a third, with smaller versions of them on the bus stops and métro entrances: posters of Women in Black, Part Two, the words in green lettering against black. "Oh God," she moaned. "It's everywhere."

"Comment?" the driver said.

"Where is the heat wave?" she asked in French.

"C'est fini," he responded in his thick North African accent. "L'hiver est revenu," he added. Winter is back. And with this, he laughed.

She leaned against the headrest. "When they throw a hook, don't bite," Peter had said. It was interesting, the use of the pronoun. They. A monolithic block, or so it seemed. "They're horrible people," she had told Peter on her way to the airport. "Even parents of serial killers don't refuse to take their own child's phone calls for two years over one stupid letter."

"They're thick-headed," Peter had said. "Like someone I know."

"What makes it worse is how many heads the beast has – my mother, my father, Odile, and perhaps even Sabine, all united against me."

"Look, you can fix this," Peter said. "You need to fix this. Especially with your dad; the guy is old."

"Not that old."

"Honey, you're in denial."

"Oh, stop it. I forget my dad's age: I'm in denial. I say I don't want to look for a boyfriend: I'm in denial. I say that I'm comfortable being an empty nester: I'm in denial. I'm always in denial with you, and you're always wrong."

"Except when you're in denial."

"It's my prerogative not to dwell on some things."

"That's the definition of denial," Peter had said. "The thing about your dad is, you can't go on for the rest of your life weeping every time you talk about him."

"I'm weepy just thinking about him. I can't help it."

"He's capable of a heart," Peter said. "Look how he adores Odile and her kids."

In the cab, Cassie tried to think of an answer she could have given to Peter. Because that was precisely the thing: when they were little girls, and to this day, her dad had always adored Odile.

****

Cassie stood in front of the austere entrance of Hôpital Saint-François. She was drenched. Her hair, her too thin clothes, her boots, were soaked. Past the gate, the architecture reminded her of the Place des Vosges; there was a rectangular courtyard with a fountain in the center, arcaded walkways, colonnades. She entered the building. As she walked through the corridors, her duct-taped suitcase dragged on the side where the wheel was gone and made a terribly high-pitch screech against the marble floor. People stared at her with a mix of amusement and disapproval as the screech echoed through the vast hallways and bounced off the cathedral ceiling. At least those hideous pterodactyl noises covered the embarrassing squish-squish of her wet footsteps.

She followed the brightly colored signs. Could they really practice cutting-edge medicine in a castle-like building that, according to a sign, had been built in the 1840s?

At the reception desk of the intensive care unit, a thin, morose-looking woman in a greenish smock read Télérama and chewed gum. She had frizzy hair and colorless skin. "Excuse me," Cassie said, "I'm here to visit my –"

The woman pointed a finger toward a sign that said "Vestiaire." Cloakroom. "Change over there," she said without lifting her eyes.

"Into what?" Cassie said, expecting in return the kind of bonhomie that took place between people when one attempted humor.

When the woman looked at her glacially, Cassie said, "I was joking."

"It's all in there," the woman said, not amused in the least.

Adjust … adjust, Cassie thought.

Inside the changing room, she found written instructions. "For reasons of hygiene, all visitors to the intensive care unit must wear a paper gown over their clothes, a paper bonnet over their hair and paper slippers over their shoes, and a surgical mask." She wasn't convinced that those would provide much protection against all the germs she carried from her exposure to the plane, the taxi, or life in general. Nevertheless, she put on the gown, tied the paper belt, and slipped the paper over her boots. Instantly, the paper soaked up the humidity in her hair and boots. She poked her head out of the room. "May I bring my suitcase in the room?" she called.

Rather than say yes, which is what she meant, the frizzy woman said, "Non! C'est complètement interdit! It's strictly forbidden to leave personal belonging in the cloakroom." Complètement and interdit. How French people loved to use those two words together. The woman's tone implied that this was a question of rare idiocy. "The mask too, Madame," she told Cassie as she exited out of the room. Cassie slipped on the mask and looked at herself in a mirror. She looked moronic. This was how her family would see her the first time they laid eyes on her in five years: eyes blood-shot from a night spent on a plane, wrapped in paper from head to toe, and at her side, a suitcase mummified in duct tape. She reminded herself to breathe and pushed open the door that led to the patients' rooms. The bright lobby was strangely quiet. Two dozen people, doctors, nurses, staff, and visitors dressed in paper, moved about in morgue-like silence. The effect sobered her up. This was no joke; her father's condition, foggy and theoretical until now, became real.

She looked for the room number. The door was closed. She turned the knob and opened the door ever so quietly.

In contrast to the lobby, the room was very dark, and she saw nothing at first. There was the smell of bleach and the ominous beeps of machines. Her vision adapted to the low light, and she saw a hospital bed perched up high and, on the bed, an old man whose face was half-hidden by a plastic mask. Briefly, she hesitated, refusing to believe that this was her dad. There was an enormous bandage on his chest. Dark purple bruises covered his bare legs. All manner of clunky apparatus connected to his arms via wires. Tubes went from his body to hanging IV bags and pouches down below. There was a thick tube coming out of his mask, and it made him look like some insect, a fly, a mosquito. His eyes were closed. Overwhelmed with what she was seeing, she did not immediately notice the two motionless human shapes sitting by the bed, dressed in paper outfits and surgical masks identical to hers. They were staring at her soundlessly, the weight of their gazes piercing through her, judging her already.

"Maman? Odile?" Cassie whispered.

One of the human shapes got up and gestured to follow her out of the room.

In the hallway, Odile removed her mask. "With these ridiculous things they make us wear, I wasn't sure it was you. It's all theatrics if you ask me." Odile had aged in the last five years, Cassie noted, and not a little. It wasn't just the wrinkles; Odile now looked a lot like their mother.

"How's Papa? Was that Maman in there?" Cassie asked, but her words came out all muffled.

"You know, you can remove the mask now," Odile said with irritation.

Cassie slipped the mask down to her neck. "Sorry," she said.

"Well, you didn't change one bit," Odile exclaimed, maybe with a hint of envy.

"Neither did you," Cassie lied. "Is Papa feeling any better?"

Odile stiffened. "Doesn't look like it, does it? He's stable, whatever that means. You know they're the ones who put him in this state in the first place."

"They?"

"The hospital. The heart surgery went fine. They had to put him to sleep to intubate him, at some point, I don't know why," Odile said. "Then they removed the endotracheal tube and weaned him off the ventilator, and that's when they realized he had developed an infection in his lungs."

"I've heard that those tubes are tricky. People get pneumonia from them."

Odile shrugged defensively. "We don't know what's at the root of the infection."

"I thought his heart was the problem?"

"Changing the heart valve went fine. I just told you what the problem was."

"Yes, but –" Cassie decided against trying to explain herself. She did not want to slip into the family dynamic that fast. Already she was walking on eggshells. "Is he sleeping now? I mean, can he wake up? Sabine said that—"

"He can wake up when they take down the sedation. But each time they try to he gets agitated and jerks around, and pulls at his IV, which he needs for the antibiotics. And so, they sedate him again."

"How is Maman?"

"A real bitch about the whole thing, as usual. You'd think all this is happening to her."

But it is happening to her, Cassie thought. "I should say hello to Maman," she said. The two of them put their masks back on and reentered the room. Raymonde was still sitting in her chair, looking straight at the door, just as she had been doing minutes ago. Cassie walked toward her, afraid to look in the direction of the bed. "Bonjour Maman." She kissed her mother on both cheeks, over the mask. It was funny how Americans felt that kissing on both cheeks was too intimate, and instead put their entire bodies into a hug. The last thing she could have done at the moment was to hug any of them. Far too much vulnerability and love went into hugs. With their surgical masks, though, the exchange of kisses felt idiotic. "How are you holding up, Maman?" Cassie asked.

"When did you arrive?" Raymonde asked, her voice muffled by the mask. If she was glad to see Cassie, the two inches of face above the mask did not show it. If she was unhappy about it, there was no sign of that either.

The same could be said of Odile. They both seemed intent on showing no emotion. Cassie felt that she had no choice but to mirror their lack of expression. On the bed, her father stirred. They looked in his direction, held their breath. He stopped moving. They turned back to each other.

"I landed two hours ago," Cassie said. "I haven't checked into my hotel yet," she added in case her mother offered for her to stay at the apartment. But Raymonde didn't say anything, and Cassie tried not to read into it. "The instant you're around them you get sucked into the family dynamic," Peter had said, then added, "well that's a misnomer actually – the family apathy is more like it."

Cassie turned toward the bed and dared to take a good look at her father. He was breathing with difficulty through the plastic mask. A pump was rhythmically sending air into the mask. His slack jaw that seemed to gasp for air at intervals was heartbreaking to watch. Cassie stood next to him, not sure what to do next. Should she bend down to kiss his cheek and risk waking him up? But if she did not, would Odile and her mom see her as uncaring? The short gown her father wore did not cover his legs and was wide open at the chest. She had the urge to pull all the tubes and wires out of him, and an even stronger urge to put a warm blanket over his body.

She realized she was shivering from her wet clothes. Was the room warm enough? He only wore a thin hospital gown. If he was chilled, he could not express it. She wanted her dad to be covered but realized it was not only because he might be cold. All his life, he had taken such pride and care in the way he presented himself. He had worn a suit and a tie even on the weekends. In the evenings after dinner, he'd methodically remove tie, trousers, and jacket and put on a long bathrobe over ironed pajamas. She had never seen him any other way than meticulously dressed. She was certain that had her dad been conscious, he would have been sickened to know himself unshaven and in this state of undress. The bruises on his legs were hard to look at. Why so many bruises? Old people bruised easily. Was that the reason? Had she ever seen her father's bare feet before? Probably in her childhood when they went on vacation, but even then, he wore seersucker suits, summer loafers, and a starched, buttoned-down shirt. She brushed the tip of her finger on her father's hand. "Do you think he can hear us?" she asked.

"You were just on an airplane; maybe you should not get too close," Odile suggested.

"I washed my hands," she said apologetically. Odile's comment had the immediate effect of making her feel soiled. "Is Sabine here?" she asked.

Odile shrugged, "Who knows?"

Raymonde's silence was already sending Cassie into mental overdrive. Was this meant as an icy reception or a manifestation of grief? If she suggested the three of them go outside in the hallway to talk, would it be interpreted as bossy? She went to fetch the empty chair in the corner of the room, and recognized, folded over it, one of her father's coats. The presence of this particular coat struck her as incongruous. It was what her mother had always called "the relic," a gray coat made of heavy wool. The cut was oddly outdated, and it hung in the closet. Her dad never wore it but kept it for unknown reasons. Cassie moved the chair next to her mom and sister and, finding no other place to put it, folded the coat over her lap. She instantly felt warmer. There was a yellowing label at the neck, not printed but embroidered. P. Germain, Tailleur. The coat smelled of her father's lavender aftershave, a smell so particular to him, the smell of a childhood where her father was invincible and the most wonderful human being in the world.

They stared at beeping machines in strained silence. Cassie's brain was on overdrive, but her body lagged in dull fatigue down to her bones. Now that she had gained weight, Odile looked so peculiarly like Raymonde. Her mother and her sister had similar small, straight and narrow noses, straight blondish hair, and blue eyes, very Nordic, whereas Cassie and Sabine had black hair, more aquiline noses, and this unusual eye color, a light amber hue that was hard to define. Sabine, who had gotten away with the best of both gene pools, was, unlike her, blessed with straight hair.

Ten interminable minutes passed during which Cassie didn't dare budge. At last, Odile got up from her chair and approached Gustave's bed. She felt his forehead with the back of her hand and sighed. She turned to Cassie and whispered, "Let's go outside."

In the hallway, Cassie was relieved to return to the world of ringing telephones and hurried footsteps. "Maman hasn't said a word to me," she told Odile.

Her sister rolled her eyes. "That one, she's driving me crazy."

Cassie pondered the meaning of this. "It's a weird time in my head. I need to get to my hotel to sleep, at some point."

"You're not staying at Maman's place?"

"Last time I heard I was not on speaking terms with her … or Papa." She omitted to state the obvious, which was that she did not know if she was on speaking terms with Odile either.

"It's time you bury the hatchet, don't you think?" Odile said coldly.

"I have no hatchet," Cassie said, although she knew this to be a lie.

Odile made a small grimace, a familiar, slight, downturn of the lips to mean whatever. The dismissal was not verbalized, but it might as well have been. Cassie fought the urge to confront her. Instead, she managed to say, "How are your kids?"

"I had to leave them with their dad and come here. I can't tell you the nightmare that it is to get here all the way from Poitier. But they're in school. What could I do? Uproot them for an indefinite amount of time until Papa recovers?" The reproach was clear: Odile was sacrificing herself to be here, while Cassie, whose children were grown, was of no help. Forgotten perhaps was the fact that they had not bothered to tell her about the surgery. Although if she was honest with herself, would she have come had she known?

"Are you staying at Maman's?" she asked.

Odile shrugged at the apparent idiocy of Cassie's question. "Where else would I stay?"

"Where is Sabine?"

"That's the million-euro question," she said.

"What do you mean?"

"She was here earlier. Yesterday too. But she won't come into the room. She stays outside in the hallway. Does that make any sense? She works nearby and comes during her lunch hour. But what's the point of showing up if it's to stay in the hallway?" Odile thought, hesitated, and then added, "Oh, and I'm telling you right now since you'll discover it soon enough, she ended the pregnancy."

"Who was pregnant? Sabine was pregnant?"

"You didn't know? Well, it happened, the abortion I mean, after Paul left her."

"Paul left her?"

"She didn't want to be a single mother, understandably."

"When did this all happen?" Cassie said, trying to hide the distress in her voice. But perhaps she didn't do such a good job because Odile clammed up.

"I guess it's her business if she opted not to tell you."

"But still –" Cassie stopped herself; it was when she cared and showed it that she most rubbed the family the wrong way, but she said it anyway, "– it's a pretty momentous decision."

"She's an adult. It's not like she needed our permission."

Was that it? Did the family hide this from her for fear that she would try to talk Sabine out of it? "Did Maman encourage her?"

Odile looked at her with a brewing storm in her eyes. "You really think this is the time and place to criticize Maman?" Odile's act of virtuous daughter was crumbling already, the composure of her face making way for something else.

"I'm not criticizing anyone."

Odile pointed in the direction of the garden, behind the glass door a hundred feet away. "It's still lunchtime for Sabine. She's probably smoking somewhere." Odile put her hand on the door to their father's room. "Oh," Odile added, "actually, I wouldn't mention it to her."

"It?"

"No one talks about it. It makes her upset."

The hospital's garden lay behind a wall of glass. In the center of the garden was a large fountain and stone benches where paths edged with neat rows of boxwood converged. The rain seemed to have stopped. A few convalescents walked on the path or sat in wheelchairs pushed by nurses. Cassie stood by the glass door looking for Sabine and spotted her. Her younger sister was leaning against a wall, her thin frame wrapped in a black coat elegantly tied at the waist, looking as she always did, inscrutable. Odile and Cassie had grown up together. They knew each other the way only sisters close in age could. They knew what made the other one tick; they knew which buttons to push. Sabine, being younger by ten years, was nearly a stranger. Her sister's enviably straight hair was shorter now, cut just above the shoulder. Sabine was the elegant one in the family. Odile and Raymonde looked provincial in comparison. Not that Cassie, who dressed like a Californian slob, was a good judge in the matter.

The glass door opened, and a handsome young doctor came out of the garden and into the hallway. He held the door for her. She did not move. "Dedans ou dehors?" he said. In or out?

"Out," she said in French. "I mean in. This garden should be out but the hospital is built all around it and –" The cute doctor smiled politely and walked away. The moment she stepped outside, the cold air slapped her with big angry hands. She walked toward Sabine. "Well hello!" she said.

Sabine had a faint smile and moved to kiss Cassie on both cheeks. "You'll freeze without a coat," she said.

For no good reason, Cassie exclaimed, "I'm fine! I've missed the cold in fact. I'm sick of perfect weather, you know."

Sabine took out a pack of chewing gum from her purse, "There's no smoking in hospitals any more. Some law they passed, apparently" she said, offering her a piece of gum.

"No thanks, I don't smoke," Cassie said idiotically. Then she laughed just as idiotically. She was nervous as hell. Everything she was not supposed to say wanted to jump out of her mouth. "How are you? Maman and Odile seem shell-shocked."

"You think so?" Sabine let her sentence trail off. She moved her hair away from her face. Sabine was the beautiful sister, but at the moment, her beauty was dulled by sadness.

"Thank you for calling me. About Papa, I mean. I can't think of why Maman and Odile didn't tell me."

"They would have, eventually."

Why had Paul left Sabine, Cassie wondered? They had been together for years. When was this? A week ago? A month? A year? She and Sabine must have spoken on the phone during that time, which meant that Cassie had been left out of the loop deliberately. Peter's assessment would be the same as it had always been. "Don't get emotionally tossed around," he would tell her. "These people are emotionally crippled."

"Where are you staying?" Sabine asked. "You can stay on my couch if you want."

"Oh no, thank you, I made a reservation at a hotel. Oh, hmm, Sabine?"

"Yes?"

"I'm thinking I'm going to die if I don't get next to a heater in the next five seconds."

"That's what I thought," Sabine said.

Inside the hospital, they walked but not in the direction of their father's room. Sabine was silent, which was disconcerting and gave Cassie the urge to talk for two. "Odile says you don't want to go into Papa's room? You don't like to? Is it too depressing?"

Sabine sighed, "I'll go in with you."

In the dressing room, Sabine removed her coat. She looked brittle. It would have been the right moment to say something, but Cassie could not find the words. Sabine was neutral in the conflict, or was she? Maybe it was not the moment to ask questions. Already, Cassie had this reputation of unnecessarily stirring things up.

As they put on their paper gowns, their differences lifted. Now they were two daughters terrified to enter a room.

They entered and were assailed by the smell of bleach, detergent, and lavender aftershave. As though time inside obeyed different laws, Odile and Raymonde still sat in their chairs, wrapped in paper gowns, surgical masks over their lower faces, motionless, expressionless. There was still the ominous beeping of machines in the background. When you live in a paper dress, don't throw stones, Cassie thought absurdly. "Can he wake up?" she whispered.

"Only when they stop the sedation," Raymonde said.

"But when they do, he gets erratic," Odile added.

Cassie looked at her father's bare legs. "When Alex needed surgery for his broken arm a few years ago, they put compression devices on his legs, to prevent blood clots."

"Well, here they must not," Odile said sharply.

"He might like a blanket don't you think?"

"It feels like an oven in here," Odile said.

"Maybe it would be comforting for him to feel tucked in." Cassie began pacing the room, opening cabinets. "Hmm … nope, none here. I'll ask a nurse."

Odile's eyes filled with tears. "Papa's on so many drugs: morphine, antibiotics, sedatives."

"Why morphine? Is he in pain?"

"They can't tell. Papa doesn't talk, as you may have noticed. He's unconscious." She emphasized that last word, as though Cassie was in some way to blame.

"Are we sure he needs all that?"

"If they give it to him there is a reason!" Odile said sharply through her tears.

"Maybe if they cut the sedation, he'll be able to tell us if he is in pain. Or if he is warm, or cold."

"Maman and I have been here for days, and you just show up here and tell us what to do!"

"I would have been here earlier had anyone bothered to tell me that he was about to have heart surgery," Cassie said under her breath.

"I've stopped my life to be here and take care of Papa," Odile cried, "and you just waltz in here knowing nothing about the situation and start telling us we're not giving him the right treatment."

"I'm not telling anyone anything. I'm asking questions." But now both Odile and Raymonde were looking away with pointed purpose. "I'm going outside," Cassie said, "I'll ask for a blanket."

"He does NOT need a blanket!" Odile said with a savagery that made Cassie freeze into place.

"What the hell, Odile?"

"It's always like that with you," Odile said with fury. "You have to create problems. You have to be difficult!"

Sabine made a motion toward the door with her chin, got to her feet, and left the room. After a beat, Cassie ran out behind her.

They walked down the hallway in silence, removing their masks, and sat on a bench a good distance away from the room.

"Oh. My. God," Cassie said, deflating with each syllable.

"She was going to say that no matter what," Sabine said with a shrug.

"Who? Say what?"

"Odile. She was going to call you difficult."

Cassie stared at Sabine. "You can't possibly know how grateful I am that you're acknowledging this."

Sabine pushed her hair away from her face. "That was decided long before your plane landed."

At that moment, the cute doctor walked right past them and surprised Cassie by giving her a nod of recognition and a smile. Cassie beamed, waited for him to be out of earshot, and said, "Did you see how adorable that doctor is?"

"I noticed," Sabine said. "But you can't have him."

"I can't?"

"Oh no, you're much too difficult."

Cassie burst out laughing and Sabine, after a moment, laughed softly.

****

Aside from the modern cars and the cell phones inches away from everyone's nose, the city was nearly identical to when Cassie was eighteen and dreamed of escape. Cigarette smell. Exhaust. Narrow streets. The roar of mopeds. Trashcans rolled into the street by apartment buildings concierges. Old ladies with transparent plastic bonnets over their heads and straw baskets in the crook of their arms. School children in colorful raincoats. Men smelling of wine coming in and out of a Bar-Tabac. People in line outside a charcuterie. The hotel was a few blocks away from the hospital, but in this weather, it might as well have been on the other side of the earth.

She felt smashed from a toxic cocktail of jet lag, hunger, chill, and the rising anger she was trying to suppress. In the rain, Cassie pulled and dragged her suitcase, avoiding cars as she crossed streets. On the narrow sidewalk, she bumped into people. Had she lived in Los Angeles so long that she had forgotten how to walk on crowded streets? She got poked in the head by someone's umbrella – twice. Her hair dripped with rain; her cheeks felt both feverishly hot and cold enough to fall off her face. Were it not for the threat of hypothermia, she would be tempted to curl into a ball at the foot of the first building and wait for Peter to rescue her. Already, she no longer felt like herself. Already, discouragement loomed.

She passed the fantastic aroma coming out of a boulangerie. All she needed was a meal and a bed. She dug deep for the last of her strength and pushed forward. To be here was surreal. It felt as though she had never left, and at the same time, everything felt alien, as though she could have imagined the last twenty years in the United States and awakened suddenly to the life she would have had in Paris, had she stayed.

The day was ending. Streetlights lit up one by one, and the wet cobblestone pavement glistened. The green neon sign above pharmacies crackled and brightened. Plants set outside in the rain in front of a flower shop were taken back indoors. Nothing had changed, and everything had, because she had.

She arrived at her hotel at last. The lobby was ultramodern and impeccably designed, all metal and polished wood. Peter would approve. She liked things to look a bit more organic, but the sleek minimalism of the place reassured her. She had booked it online, had chosen it for the pictures. It was an expensive hotel, an expensive room. But there was a restaurant inside and a spa, and since something resembling mental illness overtook her when she was around her family, this was no time to skimp on material comfort.

Behind the desk, a young French beauty with yellow hair held in a tight ponytail said, "Bienvenue à l'Hôtel de la Seine." Her smile faded when she took in Cassie's soggy Uggs and duct-taped suitcase. In a clipped tone she added, "Puis-je vous aider, Madame?" May I help you? Cassie out of exhaustion gave her name in English. The woman peered at her computer screen, nervously fingered the orange silk scarf tied around her neck and said in a thick accent, "I see not the reservation under that name."

"I booked online," Cassie said.

The woman shook her head, looking at the screen, "I'm apologize, I don't see it."

"I have this!" Cassie produced a printout of her reservation and handed it to her.

The woman frowned at it. "Ah, oui. It happens since many time, Madame," she said, modulating her intonation to one of patient annoyance. "You made a reservation with a different hotel."

"What? Absolutely not!"

The woman hovered a reluctant index finger above the piece of paper, as though touching it might contaminate her. "It say Hôtel Petite Seine, vous voyez? This here is Hôtel de la Seine."

Cassie looked at the paper. "I don't understand."

"Yes, Madame, and the two hotels, they are on the same street. People make a lot that mistake. It's often confused, the both." Cassie opened her mouth, realizing what had happened. Stupidly, she must have clicked on the wrong link when making the reservation! Nearly the same name, and in the same street, how could she have not? It had happened so fast, and she had been in a state. "Never mind," she said, "I would like a room then."

"Impossible, Madame! There is a doctor's symposium at Hôpital Saint-François. We are fully booked."

"Not even a tiny room for one?" Cassie pleaded, "I'm exhausted. I just need one night if that's all you have. Just a pillow and a shower, honestly."

"Non. Impossible. Vraiment." The woman brightened and added in a tone that Cassie did not like, "And besides, this is a four-star establishment. You might find that Hôtel Petite Seine –" she paused, looked at Cassie's soggy boots and gutted suitcase, searching for the right word – "for all budgets."

Cassie was astounded. What had the woman implied? That she was downtrodden? A homeless woman? In all fairness, if she did not get a room immediately, she would be homeless indeed. Heat rose in her. In the most imperious tone she had in her she demanded, in French this time, "What's your name, please?"

The woman gave her a patient smile. "We do not give out our names, évidemment."

"Then give me the name of your supervisor."

The young woman shook her head energetically. "We do not give out names of supervisors."

"Like hell you don't," Cassie said between her teeth. And then she remembered. She was in France. The American way to do business, the concept of customer service, of servility of any kind, did not jive here. In the United States, customers had tantrums and got their way. That's how it worked. But the customer wasn't always right in France, and in this particular case, Cassie wasn't even a customer.

The telephone rang. The woman picked it up and, with the most expert of dismissive looks, proceeded to ignore her. Cassie examined her options: throw herself at the yellow-haired monster and strangle her with her dumb scarf or turn around on her soggy fur heels, tuck her tail under, and find Hôtel Petite Seine.

She walked out into the street followed by the screech of her suitcase. Anger had worked its magic, and she no longer felt cold or tired. A few blocks down the street, she found the street number indicated on the reservation printout. But this could not be right; all she saw was a bakery and – uh-oh! On the door to the right of the bakery was a black plastic plaque no larger than a postcard with an engraved inscription in washed-out gold paint: Hôtel Petite Seine. She lifted her head. A smallish neon sign affixed to the façade of the building blinked on and off weakly. The many small windows sported an assortment of curtains without unity of style. Petite all right. At this point, it would have to do. She'd crash here for the night and look online for a better hotel in the morning. Defeated, Cassie pushed open the unadorned door.

She found herself inside a dark, minuscule reception area. No one was behind the desk. French television commercials blared in the background, and the smell of cabbage soup filled the air. She found a bell and pressed it. Nothing happened. She pushed twice more.

"Ça va! Ça va!" A man well in his eighties with a thick white mane emerged from the back room and looked at her with puzzlement. "Oui Madame?" he said in the baffled tone of someone who finds a stranger has materialized in his living room.

"Good afternoon, sir," she said in French. "This is Hôtel Petite Seine isn't it?"

"I sure hope so," he said jovially, "or else I've just spent the last six hours working here in error." His shirt was open at the neck, as though he had been in the process of putting on his pajamas. He buttoned it all the way up, hiding the abundant white hair that escaped from it like straw out of a scarecrow.

"I have a reservation," she said. She gave her name, but the old man only stared at her. She pointed to the large black book set on the counter. "Maybe it's in here?" she said helpfully.

"Ah, bien sûr!" He felt in his pocket and having found his glasses adjusted them over his nose in slow motion. He traced down the page with a shaky finger.

She read the book upside down and pointed to her name. "Here I am!"

"Ha, oui! Room twenty-three, the fifth floor. My niece will do the paperwork later. She does all those things."

"And the elevator is…?"

The man raised a bushy white eyebrow. "The elevator?"

"You know, to go up."

"Oh no, we most definitely don't have one."

"Do you have a room on a lower floor?"

"Je ne sais pas. My niece, she does all these things. But people seem to like room 23."

"When will your niece be back?"

"Soon."

"How soon?"

"Next week."

"Can anyone help me bring my luggage up to the room?" She rattled the suitcase for further effect. "It's broken, you see."

The man removed his glasses with extreme slowness. "There is only me."

She sighed. "I'll manage." She took the medieval-looking key he handed her. "I assume you don't have internet access?"

The old man took offense. "Mais bien sûr que si, Madame," adding with sarcasm, "as well as running water."

Cassie grabbed the suitcase, lifting it up against her chest, and proceeded up the stairs. The dark stairwell had the scent of old Parisian buildings, slightly rank but not in an unpleasant way, the smell of things ancient but well cared for. Despite her exhaustion, she went up the five sets of steep, uneven, narrow stairs without breaking a sweat. Years of schlepping baskets full of laundry up and down stairs in her house were paying off.

Numéro vingt-trois. She turned the archaic key into a matching wrought iron keyhole.

The room was small but adorable. The bed was perched up high and covered with a cozy-looking comforter and lacy pillows. The wood floor creaked pleasantly underfoot. The high ceiling was ornate with stucco moldings, disproportionate to the size of the room. A crystal chandelier dangled from the center. The wallpaper, a pinkish Toile de Jouy motif, peeled in several places, and the bedside table was a flimsy thing barely sturdy enough to support the heavy lamp where carved cupids supported an ambitious lampshade. But everything was very clean. There was a pretty mantle over a fireplace. Overall, the effect was cozy and shabby, charming in an old-world sort of way.

She turned on the bathroom light and was astonished to find, rather than the standard cheap remodel she expected, a black-and-white-checkered marble floor, an age-blotched mirror, framed and gilded above the ceramic sink, copper pipes running up and down the walls, well-polished faucets, an anachronistic bidet, and underneath the large window, an honest to goodness claw-foot tub.

Back in the bedroom, she opened the glass door and stepped out on the balcony as the last of the sun's rays pierced through the rain clouds. A tiny table and folding chairs filled the entire space. She leaned over the railing. The sky at dusk had taken on a golden pink hue that was reflected on a forest of rooftops and chimneys slick with rain. Beyond that, Paris, its edges softened by haze, with thousands of glass panes reflecting the last of the day's light, glimmered and seemed to float in time and space. Minuscule in the distance, like a beacon, the ghost of the Eiffel Tower sparkled.

Beautiful Paris!

In the same breath, she thought of Peter. This was the most romantic little hotel room, and she had no one to share it with.

She stayed on the balcony and looked at the city for a few more minutes, assailed by images of her father on his hospital bed, the machines, his unshaven jaw. First and foremost, she had to keep in mind that her dad's apparent helplessness did not mean she should put down her guard. He knew how to hurt her even when he did nothing. Especially because he did nothing. Like that time when she had come to Paris with Alex and Jeanne when they were five years old. They were at the perfect darling age. She had convinced herself that her father would fall in love with them. How could he not? But he had hardly given them – or her – a shred of interest. She had come to Paris with lofty hopes and had left with the sense that she and her kids were barely tolerated strangers. At the end of that trip, she had returned to Los Angeles not just sad, as she had in the past, but furiously angry. Suddenly the little things in her childhood that she had fought to ignore became proof of his neglect. What were the clues? What did they mean? How far back could she go to best torture herself? There was the time at the public pool when she had felt awkward and awful in her bathing suit, and her dad had made fun of her lack of breasts. And that time when he had shrugged and walked away after she had shown him a piece of art she had made in school. When Odile said something, he fawned over her. When Cassie did, he seemed annoyed, unresponsive. And there were the excellent report cards he took for granted while he made a fuss about Odile's lower grades.

It could be argued that none of this ever happened. Her sense of not getting the love could have been a projection. If her dad was mean to her, it could be argued that he had not been intentionally mean. If he ignored her, it could be argued that he had other things on his mind. If he did not praise her, it could be argued that she was overly sensitive. It could be argued that she imagined all of this, the sense that she was not getting the love, that she became less visible to him every day, because he had not always been that way with her.

When she was little, he was fabulous. He adored her. They were peas in a pod. And then he seemed to change. As a teenager, she was overwhelmed with powerlessness and incomprehension at her dad's change in attitude towards her. So she tried harder. But the more she fought to be visible, the more she excelled, the funnier and livelier she tried to be, the more deliberate his indifference, the rarer the eye contact. But it was also possible that she was a bitter, paranoid person. She had to stop measuring everything. She had to stop being jealous of Odile. But she was in Paris again, and it was as though the rooftops, the sidewalks, the sky, the smell, made her swing back in time. Her entire life had been spent fighting the profound sense that the problem wasn't her father, but herself, that she should have been somehow different, that there was an entry code to her father's heart that she time after time failed to break. An entry code only Odile could access.

She stepped away from the balcony and returned inside the room, shaking off her resentment, her childish feeling of injustice. She was a grown-up now, and her father was a sick old man in the hospital.

She peeled the duct tape off the suitcase, opened it on the floor, and went through its contents in disbelief. Each item of clothing she had brought was more weather inappropriate than the next. But she was only here for ten days, and it did not make sense to buy a winter wardrobe that she would never use back in Los Angeles Maybe she could email Sabine and ask to borrow a warm jacket or a coat. She looked at her Uggs, pitiful by the room heater. She would have to buy shoes, toot sweet.

She decided to send Peter a quick email to let him know she had arrived. She emptied the contents of her tote bag onto the bed, lined up the sleek, thin laptop, the smartphone, their respective cords and chargers, and the old converter. No matter how hairy things got from here, no matter how out-of-body the experience, she would be connected to the real world: electronics as a lifeline to sanity.

She searched beneath the bedside table, found the electrical outlet and plugged in her converter, which had two prongs so that she could charge both her laptop and her cell phone at the same time. She plugged in her cell phone charger. She plugged in her laptop charger. She then brought her charger cord to her laptop and plugged in that.

She smelled it and heard it before she could see it and instinctively leaped away from the bed. "NO!" she screamed. But already it was over. In one instant, the charge of 220 current buzzed and hissed, and a tremendous heat charged through the electrical outlet, through the chargers and all the way to the depth of her laptop and cell phone. WHOOSH!

Then silence.

Cassie blinked at her laptop. The screen was black. The space between the keys was black too; a faint smoke seemed to emanate from both the laptop and the cell phone. After another long moment, she tentatively brought her finger to the on switch on her laptop and pressed. Nothing. She tried to turn on her cell phone. Nothing. She sniffed them. Both had an ominous smell of burnt plastic.

She looked around the room, her heart in a vise. She now understood with perfect clarity the nagging emotion she had felt all afternoon but failed to pinpoint. Disappointment. Her father was unconscious. She had known he would be; Sabine had warned her. And yet ever since she had bought her ticket, she had let herself dream up something very silly. She had imagined arriving at her father's bedside and him being, at long last, happy to see her.

****

There was a phone booth in the hotel lobby. Cassie entered it, slid the door shut, sat on the single stool, and looked around. It was bizarrely upholstered wall to ceiling in a burgundy-red velvety fabric. Above, a single fixture cast a dim light. It was like sitting inside an upright coffin – one that smelled of cabbage soup. She called Peter collect. "Were you sleeping?" she asked.

"Darling, I have a newborn," Peter said, "I'm never sleeping." He added, "Also, it's ten in the morning here."

Hearing his voice, Cassie felt better. "I haven't slept yet," she said.

"You're going to be cranky. You always get testy when you don't sleep enough."

"I went to the hospital straight from the airport. I only got to the hotel an hour ago."

"How's the old goat? And the rest of that gloomy cast of characters? I swear to you, I could put each member of your family in a screenplay and terrify the world."

"Don't. I'm the one who's earned the right to fictionalize my family's dysfunction. Listen. This is bad. My laptop. Well it, hmm, broke down."

"Did you back up the files?" Peter cried out.

"Relax, your precious screenplays are backed up in half a dozen places."

"But your laptop is brand new!"

"Well, it was. And, hmm – about my cell phone: it kinda stopped working too."

Peter burst into laughter. "You fried them!"

"Of course, I did not fry them!" She waited for Peter to stop guffawing. "You know what I miss the most about you?" she asked. "It's your gift for empathy."

"How in the world did you manage? Phone and laptop? You're a genius at this! It was that lousy converter, wasn't it? Am I right? I bet I'm right. The charger short-circuited, didn't it? You knew this was a piece of obsolete shit. Now, that should have gone to the Salvation Army instead of the kids' baseball trophies."

Cassie realized she could lean and rest against the velvety wall and it felt nice and mushy against her back. "The point is, I can't be reached for the time being. I'll give you the number at the hotel, and you can leave a message, but I'm warning you, they don't speak English."

"In what hotel in the Known Universe do they not speak English?"

She closed her eyes. "I can't get into this right now."

"No way!" Peter exclaimed, gleeful. "You botched the reservation too?"

She did not bother to respond. "I can't be called, or call," she said. "I can't send or receive emails. I'm not sure what the solution is because I can't even go online to search for a repair shop until morning. I'm only here for ten days, so I'm tempted to wait it out. I have warranties."

"Honey, warranties work when the merchandise malfunctions, not when its user does!" Peter laughed at his bon mot. "You won't last in Paris without a phone or laptop. How about you buy new ones and return them before coming back home?"

"You can't buy things and return them for a full refund on a whim here."

"Why not?"

"That's not how businesses work in France."

"Even at Target?"

"There is no Target here."

"No Target?" Peter repeated, dismayed.

"Whatever I buy, I'll be stuck with it. And it would be set on the French system, and then I'd have to use a converter for it at home."

"And repeat this fiasco in reverse," Peter laughed.

"Look, tell Alex and Jeanne that I'm here and I'm okay," Cassie said, although she felt very much not okay. She gave Peter Sabine's cell number and the hotel number and hung up. Now all she could hear was the silence buzzing in her head. She gently poked the soft red velvet of the wall with her index finger. It sank into the fabric, leaving a small dent. Slowly, the wall reverted to shape, and the mark was gone. Mushy walls? This phone booth wasn't a coffin after all, but a giant, cabbage-smelling womb. A 1980s womb, from before the invention of the internet, the worst kind of womb there was. She searched for the doorknob, but there wasn't one. She pushed the door, shook it, immediately feeling trapped, until she remembered that it slid open.

It was almost seven p.m. Her eyelids felt coated with sand, but she was thirsty and hungry. If she did not take care of herself in some basic way, she'd lose her mind very quickly. She decided to brave the cold and find something to eat. At the reception desk, she asked the old man for a place to eat.

"The closest is La Jument Bleue," he said. "It's not fancy, but the food's good." He paused, looked at her and said, "You might need a coat."

"Ha!" she told him, "I'm made of strong stuff."

La Jument Bleue was right around the corner, so she did not have to freeze for too long. As soon as she pushed the glass door of the bistro, she was welcomed by the heat and the smell of coffee and greasy food that every cell of her body craved. This was the kind of place where they sold cigarettes and lottery tickets and served cafés and plat du jour to neighborhood residents. She walked past the zinc counter and found a table in the back, set against the glass window. From there, she could observe the people who stood at the counter and sat at the few occupied tables. The door to the kitchen swung open and closed as a waiter and a woman in her sixties with red cheeks and abundant bosom, who appeared to be La Jument Bleue's owner, came in and out carrying plates of food. From her position by the window, Cassie also had a good view of the street, which was getting dark.

La patronne, the owner, came to her table. "Bonjour Madame, what will it be for you tonight?" she asked.

"Do you have a menu?" Cassie said.

The woman's smile froze. "The kitchen has closed," she answered tersely.

"I was told you served dinner."

"You were told wrong," she said icily.

Cassie briefly wondered what she had done wrong for the woman to go from jovial to antagonistic in two seconds flat and then realized that she had trampled over the most basic rule of French engagement by omitting to say bonjour! When it came to being served anything, by anyone in France, you better remember your manners, and she had blown it. Was that what had happened with that blonde at the hotel? "Je suis désolée," she apologized. "I am jetlagged and exhausted. I'll have … a glass of milk, I guess."

The woman softened, "What would you like to eat?"

"I would not want to be an inconvenience to the chef."

"The chef is my husband, and I decide whether he should be inconvenienced or not."

"In that case, do you have ketchup?"

"Ketchup? That's all?"

"Whatever you want to serve, I will be happy with."

The patronne considered this and seemed to approve of her subservience. "A steak au poivre et frites then? To go with your ketchup."

Unlike Cassie, the average French person did not dip her string beans in ketchup or use it as a pasta sauce. Ketchup was for fries only. Cassie preferred her food well coated with a layer of Americanness. That particular condiment reassured her taste buds. "That would be perfect," Cassie said. "Thank you."

"And one assiette de crudités to start?" the patronne declared more than asked. Cassie dared not decline.

As businesses and offices closed for the day, people who worked in the neighborhood began pouring into La Jument Bleue, filling the tables one by one. Soon, the zinc counter was lined with customers. In the space of fifteen minutes, La Jument Bleue went from sleepy to bustling. The patronne's step quickened; waiters zoomed to and fro, holding large circular trays filled with drinks high in the air as customers continued coming in.

Her crudités arrived: grated carrots and celery roots, delicate pink radishes, sliced hearts of palm and a small vinaigrette dish. At first, Cassie felt a little self-conscious to be eating alone, but no one paid her any attention. She was a fly on the wall. Une mouche sur le mur. She tossed the translation around in her mind. In French, it had no meaning whatsoever.

At the next table, a teenage boy and girl sat holding hands across the table. The waiter walked up and set two tall, foamy beers in front of the young couple, whom Cassie, and any American, would have considered children.

She devoured her crudités and sponged vinaigrette with the best bread she'd ever eaten, watching as three young women entered La Jument Bleue, removed their coats, and placed them on the communal coat hanger. One of them was the mean blonde from the hotel. The three women were dressed in the hotel's uniform: a sky-blue blouse, a tight navy cardigan and matching skirt, and that square of orange silk tied at the neck. They stood at the counter, laughing and talking with animation. And was this not the old man from her hotel, in the funny Cossack fur hat? He saw her and tipped his head. This was what he had meant by "everyone goes there." La Jument Bleue appeared to be the quartier's preferred watering hole. Cassie noted the contrast with her local Starbucks, where patrons were careful not to infringe on others' space. People here knew each other. Those who arrived were greeted with handshakes or a flurry of kisses on cheeks. The noise level rose. There was laughter, and opinions were loudly thrown around. People two tables removed got into a heated political discussion. She overheard a sexual joke. The three women from the hotel sat at a table and were soon joined by two men. There were more kisses on cheeks.

When her dish arrived, Cassie scraped the pepper cream sauce off her steak with the back of her knife, poured ketchup on top and dug in. Best French fries ever, she thought. Best ketchup ever.

Her table had a perfect vantage point to observe without being too obvious about it those who entered, those at the counter, and the passersby on the sidewalk. The blatant flirting that went on around La Jument Bleue fascinated her. The men sweet-talked the women, who responded in kind. Women, even women her age and older, smiled and chatted away, whispering and giggling. The flirtatious energy in the room intensified with the arrival of four men in their early thirties dressed in sweater vests, scarves, and loafers. As they came through the door, cigarettes in mouth, the patronne pushed them back out. They finished their smoking outside in great inhalations, tossed and crushed under heels butts of cigarettes, and returned inside.

Cassie leaned back in her chair. Nothing felt quite real, as though she were watching the scene on TV. She dug a pen out of a purse, removed the paper mat from under the plate, and wrote:

1- Find electronic repair shop
2- Buy cheap cell phone?
3- Ask Sabine for coat tomorrow
4- Think of questions for Papa's doctor

She lifted her pen. Would her father be alarmed by her presence? The fact that she had flown in from the United States to see him might worry him about his own condition. He looked so helpless in that hospital gown. It angered her. It didn't matter considering the situation, that his bare legs and feet were exposed. But what about his dignity? He was proud of his appearance. He always dressed to the nines, even when he took her and Odile to the Zoo de Vincennes, the Jardin d'Acclimatation, or the Musée Grévin when they were little. Back then, she and Odile were dressed identically by their mother, as was the style, in matching plaid dresses, coats, and high socks. She remembered clinging to their dad, fighting with Odile to be the one nearer to him, the one holding his hand. Memories came in, jumbled: the bus and métro rides through Paris, competing to be the one to sit on his lap. Always a competition with Odile. And the endless strolls through Paris's quartiers. Her dad knew Paris comme son mouchoir, like his handkerchief, which in English translated to the back of his hand. He was a Parisian, born and raised. That's about all he ever said of his childhood. Those outings with her dad stopped at some point. Why was her father so intent on taking his daughters out of the house? Was it to escape Raymonde's noxious moods? But if she thought about it, it was not that the outings stopped, it was that she no longer came along. If there were reasons for this, she couldn't remember them. But on second thought, she had begun to feel unwelcome, as though she and her sister had been competing for their father's love all along, and Odile had won.

And where had Sabine been this whole time?

She wrote on the placemat.

5- Ask Papa about his childhood, when he wakes up.

6- Be strong!

Night had settled over the street. Now, the light came from the old lampposts and the neon signs across the street from the pharmacy and the flower shop. She leaned against the glass pane to look outside when the huge roar of a motorcycle startled her. She watched the motorcyclist maneuver his heavy machine expertly onto the curb and park on the sidewalk on the other side of the window, inches from where she sat. The man wore a bomber jacket reminiscent of Indiana Jones. He turned off the engine and, still straddling his motorcycle, removed his thick gloves, and then his helmet. He was in his late forties, with wide shoulders, a thick mane, and piercing blue eyes, and was not a bad-looking guy if you liked them rugged.

His helmet tucked under his elbow, he disappeared as he crouched next to his motorcycle to wrap a chain around a pole. Cassie brought her face closer to the window to watch how he was going about it. The man lifted his face, and all of a sudden, they were eye to eye on opposite sides of the window pane. She continued staring, perhaps because she had accepted the idea of being invisible. But invisible she was not. He knitted his eyebrows into an interrogative frown, and Cassie jumped back in embarrassment. When the man entered the café a minute later, he seemed to look in her direction with reproach, but a moment later she was invisible again, and he was surrounded by the preppy men. Cassie asked for the bill and, bracing herself, asked la patronne. "I'm wondering if it would be possible for me to receive a call here, in the case of an emergency?"

"What kind of emergency?" la patronne asked.

"My cell phone broke. I don't imagine I should need it, but just in case?"

"Alright," la patronne grumbled. "But don't make a habit of it."

Cassie paid, stepped into the night, and, shivering through and through, walked back to her hotel. In her room, she removed her clothes and let herself fall, face first, onto the bed. She was asleep in seconds.

CHAPTER 6

The Baker's Daughter

His payots tucked behind his ears and held in place by an embroidered cap, Albano left his cave and climbed down the flank of Mount Pagus in the direction of Smyrna's quay. Only a year ago he had been frightened to skip shul and leave the Jewish quarter alone for the first time. Now the whirlwinds of Smyrna's streets, the busy quayside, selling newspapers with Hagop, earning money, and disguising himself as a Muslim boy were natural things. He had left the Jewish quarter long before sunrise, had briefly gone up to his cave by the moonlight and changed clothes, and was now walking down the deserted hillside with only the buzz of crickets as companions. It was cold; his ears were cold, and so were his cheeks, but he felt warm inside. The moon was thin, but once his eyes were accustomed to the obscurity, he felt he could see very well. On occasion, he thought he felt near him the breath of mountain lions or coyotes, but he did not feel scared. Under the stars and inside his cave, Albano felt protected by a force he could not name. More than a force, it was a sense of joy, a sense that God was near. It was a peculiar thing that he never felt the divine in his books and prayers, but always when he was alone and in nature.

As he walked down the mountain, he thought of that day when he had returned home after selling his first newspapers with Hagop and meeting Xandra. He had been resigned to the anticipated beating but was astonished to discover that no one had noticed his absence. Even his deep sunburn from being in the sun all day raised no suspicion. At shul, it had been assumed that Albano was sick. At home, it had been assumed he was at shul. Either no one had paid attention, or else no one had cared.

The next week, emboldened, Albano had returned and found Hagop on the quay. "I have something for you," Hagop had said, and out of a burlap bag he had pulled new clothes for Albano and insisted he put them on. "Here. Now you're a good Muslim boy." Hagop had placed a 'borrowed' fez on Albano's head. Then he had adjusted his own and grinned that Hagop grin, full of mischief and bravado with something ferocious under it.

Uncle Moshe had been correct. Having no parents of your own when the adults around you are busy with children, businesses matters, bouts of gout, funerals, tooth abscesses, weddings, and leaky roofs could be a blessing. Especially if what you wanted to do was lead a double life. Now, his teachers frowned at his absences, but Albano was not the only boy to skip shul, others skipped to earn money for their family. This was the excuse he gave his teachers, and that was only a half-truth, since Uncle Jacob and Aunt Sadie knew nothing about his work, and since Albano and Hagop kept the money for themselves, or rather for the enlarging leather satchel hidden inside the cave. His grades remained excellent no matter how much of shul he missed, and when one of his teachers took it upon himself to tell Uncle Joshua about his absence, Uncle Joshua only limply admonished him. Often, though, Albano wished there was a grown-up to rely on for guidance. Someone like Uncle Moshe, whom he hadn't seen in a year. Uncle Moshe had a different way of looking at the world. Perhaps he could help Albano decipher the meanderings of his heart.

****

To Hagop, Albano soon learned, nothing was serious, and nothing was sacred. He laughed at the droll and the tragic with the same affected insouciance. Hagop was the eldest and only boy with four sisters, the oldest of which was Xandra. Their parents, Yori and Ina, relied heavily on them. Xandra helped her mother at the bakery and for deliveries, and Hagop worked nights at the mixes and the baking. Yori presided over the baking, and it was on Hagop that fell the thankless task of shelling nuts by the thousands, a tedious work he abhorred. Hagop's other responsibility was to watch over the family's secret yeast blends. And so Hagop always smelled like uncooked dough and Xandra like a sweet bun fresh out of the oven. Hagop laughed at his father but only when his back was turned, for his dad could turn spiteful, especially when he drank. When Hagop did not work to his liking, Yori would grab a walnut or a hazelnut and throw it hard at Hagop from across the room, so Hagop's body was covered in mean little bruises.

"One day, when he is drunk, I will shove my father into his oven and let him cook like one of his bread loaves."

"But if he is dead, then you inherit the bakery," Albano pointed out. "And you end up becoming what you don't want to become: a baker." This was the kind of verbal jousting he and Hagop enjoyed. It was a game, an exercise, although one that often ended in Hagop sulking if Albano did not let him have the last word.

"My brother will run the bakery," Hagop said.

"You have no brother."

"I will eventually. Why do you think I have so many sisters? My parents keep trying to make a replacement for me." Hagop went on to loudly imitate the sounds his parents made in bed so that Albano, who was according to Hagop a prude rabbi at heart, would have to cover his ears.

****

Rather than meet Hagop at the quay, Albano usually headed out early to the Armenian quarter to eat a fresh pastry from Yori's bakery before they set out for the quay. Pastries weren't the reason Albano awakened at three in the morning, rather than four, and walked all the way from the Jewish to the Armenian quarter in the night, but it was the reason he gave Hagop. After breakfast, Albano and Hagop would then walk down to Frank Street, purchase their stock of international newspapers, and assume their respective spots on the quayside where they sold to arriving travelers for a couple of hours. By late morning, the papers were gone. Albano would hurry back to the Jewish quarter and arrive at shul having missed the morning classes. Learning from rabbis, who hardly ventured past the Jewish quarter or their conservative viewpoint, or from stale texts with no basis in the modern world paled in comparison to what Albano learned on the quay. From reading newspapers and listening to the people, he learned about politics and the world. He learned languages the same way; French and other Latin languages were easy for him. He had also become excellent at counting their earnings. He now was the one who decided which papers to buy and in which quantity, based on past sales and profits.

That day, as he entered the Armenian quarter, and although the seeds of secrecy between Hagop and him had already long sprouted, Albano had no idea he was about to start a triple life.

That morning there was a peculiar, uneasy atmosphere throughout the Armenian quarter. Men talked animatedly. Women cried. The unease grew as he approached the street where Hagop's family lived. There were men on horseback from the Turkish police stopping people and asking questions. Albano had picked up sufficient Armenian to converse, but he wasn't able to understand what people were upset about.

Before entering the bakery, he stopped on the other side of the street and discreetly watched Xandra as she laid trays of freshly baked baklava, birds nest and fig cookies in the window. The scent of yeast and honey wafted through the open door. His heart thumped at the sight of her small, precise hands and the pale skin of her neck. She lifted her face, and their eyes met for just an instant. Usually, that instant was enough to weaken Albano's knees for a good ten minutes. But today, he saw with alarm that she had been crying.

When he entered the bakery, Hagop jumped at him. "Did you hear? Silla, the butcher, was arrested."

"Is that why everyone is crying? For the butcher?"

"He beheaded his eldest daughter, Szophia."

"Beheaded!" Albano had to sit down at this news. "Szophia? The one who served at his shop?"

"Last year she left her husband because he was beating her," Xandra said, her voice breaking. "She had come back to live with her parents above the butcher shop, but then her father thought that she –"

"–There was proof!" Hagop interrupted.

"Proof of what?" Albano asked.

"That she was seeing a man," Hagop said. "She brought dishonor upon her father. Her whole family, shamed."

It was too much for Xandra who burst into tears. "He carried her head by the hair up and down the street."

Albano wished he could comfort her, hold her, but that was impossible. "Will he be put to death?" he asked.

"There will be a judgment," Xandra said, but her expression showed she doubted any harm would come to the butcher.

"She was a whore." Hagop spat.

Xandra's eyes turned to fire, and she yelled, "And what is her father? A hero?"

Hagop shrugged at Xandra's outburst. "Women cannot understand," he explained to Albano. "They think with their heart. A man must protect his honor and the honor of his family, whatever the law says."

Xandra ran to the back of the store and buried her face in her hands. Albano thought of what he could say to soothe her but found nothing. And what could he do? Come near Xandra and speak to her, alone, as he dreamed? No, that was impossible. There were rules for girls and boys. They were twelve years old, and in the last few months, Xandra looked more like a woman, even if he still only looked like a child. If there were people around them, they could speak up, but they could not speak to each other.

Later, as Hagop described the scene vividly with many more details than he cared to hear, Albano thought of what he could tell Xandra if he was able to speak to her in private. As Hagop excitedly described the scene, the butcher's arrest, the blood marks on the pavement, the butcher's wife's wailing with grief, Albano had an idea.

****

Albano and Hagop did their usual route, bought their stacks of newspapers, and waited for the boats to arrive. By noon, their stock was sold. Hagop ran back to the bakery to shell a fresh arrival of almonds, and they parted for the day.

But rather than head back to the Jewish quarter, Albano headed toward the Levantine quarter. Albano loved the Levantine area. He would go there often just to admire it and to dream up an alternate, unlikely future for himself. Despite his poverty, in stark contrast to the Levantine families' wealth, it never occurred to Albano to feel resentment toward them. He admired them, in fact, for having prospered to such extent despite being of mixed blood. Here in Smyrna especially, the Levantines had triumphed. They were crucial to Smyrna's abundance of work. The Levantine families' factories employed hundreds of thousands of Smyrniots, and they did not care which religion the workers were, or which nationality. The Levantine bourgeoisie of Smyrna were like benevolent parents to the population. Had they not existed, hundreds of thousands would have starved. Many believed that as long as the Levantine families maintained their monopoly over commerce and continued to control shipping, textile and rugs, and the exports of all the goods produced, Smyrna would continue to thrive.

Of all the breathtakingly beautiful parts of Smyrna, the Levantine areas were the most breathtaking. Most Levantine families lived a few miles outside of town in communities with names such as Paradise or Boudja, which connected to Smyrna via a steam train with designated seats for its more prominent members. The first time Hagop took him to the European quarter where many Levantines had primary residences, Albano had not wanted to believe that those were mansions for single families. The Levantines homes were palaces with architecture inspired by Italy; sprawling villas with loggias, and fountains, and rooms upon rooms, and dozens of servants hurrying about to make everything perfect. In the gardens and front yards, there were rows of cypress trees, magnolias, and citrus trees, pergolas and glass houses, climbing jasmine, tall hibiscus borders, bougainvillea draped over rooftops and rose gardens tended by meticulous gardeners.

Next week was Christmas, a festive time in the Christian quarters. Everyone in Smyrna loved to live outdoors, and the Levantines were no exception, and so anyone could watch them having meals and enjoying their manicured paths and gardens. The children, girls in summer dresses, boys in shorts and long socks, played croquet on the lawns and chased after pet goats. Men in leisure clothes, canotiers on their heads, light vests and open shirts, smoked on balconies. Women in straw hats and lacy dresses sat on chairs and couches set under pergolas as servants brought refreshments. Albano passed a group of carol singers. The people listening were clapping and having a lovely time.

Albano, his heart racing, found a central spot from which he could survey the street. He waited.

He spotted Xandra as she exited the back door of a Levantine house. She was walking to her next delivery now. She had a large woven basket on her back and one on each arm. She walked fast despite the load and had on her face that determined expression that both intimidated him and made him want to take her in his arms. Because of the horrors of today, she looked sad too, and her eyes were red. This was not Albano's first time observing her as she made her delivery, and yet this was the first time it occurred to him to speak to her. Today, he had an excuse to. He felt nauseous, and his legs were almost paralyzed at the sight of her. But the idea of speaking to her had come to him, and he felt the urgency of carrying it through. Today, at last, he had a reason. The thing had happened with the Butcher, and it would be a natural thing to discuss.

Xandra walked right past him, and then he stepped out of the corner so that she saw him. She stopped in her tracks, either in surprise or fright. Her face was very pale and her hair and eyes so black that they seemed to absorb the light and every bit of Albano's courage. "Why are you here?" she murmured, her eyes cast down, not looking at him.

Albano's heart was beating too fast. He too was afraid to look at her. His plan had gone as far as deciding to come and speak to her, but he had not prepared what he would say. "I sometimes wonder if it is safe for a girl alone in the streets," he said, improvising.

Her eyes shone with angry tears. "Fathers will behead their daughters in the name of honor, but they are not so worried that they won't let them walk alone in the street. As long as it brings money."

"I am here so you will not be bothered by anyone," he said. He was conscious of how preposterous this was: a scrawny boy without a hair on his chest could not do much to protect himself, let alone a girl, but Albano said this with assurance, and as he did, he straightened to make himself look taller.

"You can carry my baskets then if you want to help," she said. She removed the straw basket that weighed heavily on her slender back and helped Albano put it on his own back. Then she put her hand baskets over each of his arms and said, "Come donkey! Come."

Albano pretended to be a donkey for a few steps, and she laughed at that. Then they walked, making sure to remain ten feet from each other, as was the unspoken proper distance between a boy and a girl. As they walked, they did not look at each other; they looked straight ahead. They spoke, but it was as though they spoke to the street in front of them.

"Tell me why you are really here," Xandra said to the street.

"I wanted to tell you something."

"How did you know where I would be?"

Albano could not tell Xandra that he often followed her from afar since she had taken over the task of delivery from her mother who was expecting another child. He had always felt uneasy about her being alone, even in Levantine streets filled with gilded houses and pleasure gardens. He would follow her until he saw her reenter the Armenian quarter and he felt she was safe again because the community watched over its own. Now he was no longer so sure about the community. "I was only hoping you would be here," he lied.

"What is it you wanted to tell me?"

"The man, the butcher," Albano said. "He should be imprisoned. Or put to death for killing his own daughter."

"Why not say this earlier?"

"Hagop is like a brother, but he and I have different minds."

"So?" she asked, defiantly. "Do you not think a man has a right of life and death over his daughters?"

"No one has the right of life and death over another human being. That's what I think."

Xandra did not respond. She continued to walk somberly. But despite the event that had just occurred, Albano could not feel somber. He walked alongside her feeling the soft air on his skin every time they stepped in the shade, and the heat of the sun every time they came back into the light. He felt that this moment was full of grace and perfection, and he was happy.

"Do you not think those are heavier than your newspapers?" she asked. "Hagop says the newspapers are much heavier." The baskets were full of bread and pastries, and they were heavy, but Albano could not feel the baskets at all. Walking with Xandra he was weightless.

"I could help you with your deliveries," he heard himself say. He did not even think this ahead of time, and it just came out of him, and there was nothing he could do to stop himself from speaking. "I would carry the baskets for you, and you can bring the merchandise to each house."

"Albano!" She laughed, her laughter like a bird's song, "you're already doing this!"

"I mean, on other days," he said while looking at the street so their eyes would not meet. He hesitated. "Every day. If you want."

Xandra looked down at her feet as she walked. The silver threads of her embroidered slippers and skirt gleamed in the sun. "And what will Hagop think?" she finally said.

"I'll help him with the newspaper in the morning, and I'll help you with the pastries in the afternoon."

"Will you tell him?"

"I don't need to."

"But I can't pay you. The money I earn is not mine."

Albano smiled. "It's all right," he said.

The next day he met her at the entrance of the Levantine quarter, and he authoritatively took the baskets from her hands. He followed her from house to house and waited in front of each house as she pushed through the gates and went in the back of each house into the servants' quarters to deliver her goods. That week, it was a miracle Albano could manage to sleep at all, such was his happiness.

By the end of the first week, Xandra insisted that Albano come to each door with her and not wait for her in the street. This was how Albano discovered the courtyards of the rambling villas, like personal oases inside the city. There were elaborate water fountains, play areas for the children, gravel paths, bird baths, tiled barns where gleaming motorcars were tended by drivers, mosaic pools. Some of the houses were right on the Aegean Sea with private beaches and floating docks onto which pleasure boats were tied. There were children in white clothes playing badminton or hide and seek between the boxwood hedges of French gardens. As Albano marveled at their surroundings, Xandra entered the kitchens or the servant quarters through back doors and made her deliveries. Then they both walked out of the house and toward the next one.

"Sometimes," Xandra said one day, "I imagine that I live in a beautiful house, with a fountain and a garden. And in the gardens, there are roses and jasmine, and it always smells wonderful."

"How many rooms does your house have?" Albano asked.

Xandra smiled with pleasure that Albano was playing along. "It has seven rooms, and there is one room just for bathing. And water arrives inside the room through a pipe; you do not even need a well."

"Does electricity come to your house?" The Ottoman Electric Company's first coal-fire electricity-generating station was now powering the Sultan's house in Constantinople, and the word electricity was on everyone's lips.

"Of course," she smiled.

"Tell me more about your house."

"It is painted white, with columns. There is a large deck all around overlooking the sea, and there are palm trees and climbing roses everywhere."

"It sounds beautiful."

"Also…."

"What?"

"I have a little dog all to myself."

"Do you have children?"

"Yes," she laughed. "But no more than three."

"And…." Albano paused, then asked tentatively, "Who is your husband?"

She blushed. "I don't know yet."

"Is he Christian?" The question, which came to his lips before he had a chance to think it, changed everything.

Xandra became grave. "My family will want that."

"Will he be Armenian?" Albano dared to ask.

Xandra lifted her eyes toward him. "It is the tradition. I have to." They continued in silence until she entered the last house on her route and took the baked goods out of the basket Albano was carrying. This was his favorite part when she got things out of the basket and for a moment stood centimeters from him. She walked into the house and out of it, and suddenly it was time to say goodbye. This, was Albano's least favorite part.

"There are places in the world where traditions are different," Albano told her as they headed back toward the Armenian quarter. "In France, in Italy."

"What are the traditions there?"

"To Americans and Europeans, we are all the same. Greek, Armenians, Muslims, and Jews. They cannot tell the difference."

She shook her head, "How is that possible?"

"They see us all as inferior. Or else they see themselves as superior. You might not believe this, but they can't tell us apart. Our eyes aren't blue; our hair is not red or yellow. They can't even tell our religion from our clothes. We're just poor people to them."

"How do you know all this?"

"I read the newspapers."

They continued walking for a hundred yards, and Xandra said, "What about you? Will you marry a girl from the Jewish quarter?"

"I only care about what my heart says," he murmured.

"What does your heart say?"

"My heart says. . . ." Albano was bursting with love, and he did not know how to express it, and part of him felt he should not. Xandra had given no indication of how she felt. "My heart says that I want to live in one of those beautiful houses with a garden, with my wife. And give her just the life she wants."

"I think your wife will be very happy with you then," Xandra said.

Day after day they met at the same place. Now she waited for him. He'd hoist the baskets on his back and over his shoulders, and they'd set out on the delivery route. The conversation between them lost its awkwardness; now it was as though they had always been able to speak and laugh together. They'd speak of Hagop and giggle at the crazy things he did and said. She told him about her life at the bakery, and he told her about life in the Jewish quarter. They discussed their religion, injustices, family. But there was a subject they avoided since that first talk they had about marriage. They did not speak about love.

One day, nearly a month later, as delivery ended, rather than go their separate ways, they followed the road past the last house of the European quarter and walked along the beach. The sun was low in the sky on this January afternoon. There was no wind at all, and the sea was as smooth as mercury. They walked on the sand in silence and sat on a large flat rock under the low branches of a dense tree with waxy leaves that had found a way to take root right into the sand.

"Tell me again about the places in the world where traditions are different," Xandra said. They were both acutely aware that the two of them should not be here: a boy and a girl sitting under a tree in the setting sun. And yet they had headed there as though it was the natural thing to do.

"Their traditions are different, but not always better."

"Then tell me about places where people do not kill each other over religion or race."

"In Europe, there are zoos with humans in them," he said.

"I don't believe it."

"At the Jardin d'Acclimatation in Paris, they have enslaved an entire family from the continent of India so that people can buy tickets to look at them. The Indians wear feathered headdresses, and they paint their faces. There also have other kinds of people, from other parts of the world. They have short people from Africa. They are called pigmy, and they are very small. The children are even smaller."

"Like birds?"

"Larger than that. They are in cages. There are signs that say, 'do not feed the indigenous.'"

"Like animals?"

"Exactly, like animals. They call these ethnographic exhibitions."

They were quiet for a few minutes, pondering the meaning of this.

Xandra broke the silence. "Things are changing in the Empire, Albano. I do not like the way men are talking about politics. Everyone is thinking about war. The men want war."

"I do not want war."

"It is as though all the men are turning mad."

"I promise you I will not turn mad."

"But what if everyone else does?"

Albano held his breath and finally said, "Then I will take you away."

She looked at him and beamed. "You will?"

"I will take you to France. I will save the money from newspapers. After a few years, I will have enough. I will take you on a boat to France or Italy where no one is mad."

"But what if they put us in a zoo?" she laughed.

"As long as you and I are … in the same enclosure … I wouldn't mind." Realizing what he had just dared to say, he added quickly, "The sun is setting; you better get back."

"Not yet," Xandra murmured. She raised her face to him, and her face reflected the pink of the sky.

"Your family will worry about you if you do not hurry back," he insisted.

Xandra's eyes filled with tears. "Take me to France, Albano. Take me to a place where an Armenian girl can marry whomever she likes."

"Don't cry," he said, and he took her hand, which rested on her lap. Her face was next to his, and her body was next to his, and the next thing he knew he was taking her in his arms and they were kissing.

CHAPTER 7

Paris in the Rain

Cassie was wide awake, ready to start the day, but when she looked at her watch, she realized it was not daytime at all, but two in the morning. She groaned and pulled the blanket to her chin. There would be at least three more hours before daybreak, three hours without the internet, and she had finished her book on the plane. She got up and peeked out the window at the darkened Parisian skyline, like a Japanese painting, charcoal on charcoal. Even the Eiffel Tower was asleep. It was surreal, being alone in this Parisian hotel room at two in the morning. Surreal, but not unpleasant. She turned on the light. This room, new to her just a few hours ago, now was as familiar as if she'd always lived in it. How strange this was, the hotel room after a single night, the street below, La Jument Bleue bistro filled with patrons, all felt so much more tangible than her life in Los Angeles. Everything that had been so crucial less than twenty-four hours ago, her garden, her habits, her house even, now receding into vagueness. Even the faces of her children were more opaque to her now that they were in college. It was almost as though she had just awakened from a dream where she was an ex-wife, a mother, a writer, an American, only to realize that none of it was real.

What would her life be had she not decided to marry Peter? But was anything that happened in life a decision? It felt more like a series of happenstances, of forks in the road that led to this life. Had she not, for example, met Peter years ago in a Parisian café much like La Jument Bleue, her life would resemble nothing it was today. She would not have the twins. She might not even know how to speak English. Would she even be writing? Despite all evidence to the contrary, she knew herself to be unadventurous by nature. She did not seek this life. Things had happened to her as she had just floated along the river of life.

Now the river was at a standstill, it seemed. Left to her own devices, without Peter to nudge her forward, she was stuck. The thing was, with Peter it had been easier to go along with most things. He was all willpower and certainty. Raising twins, her life with Peter, their working together had made her happy for the most part, but with an undertone of rushed bewilderment. Refusing to move from their house on the hill was an arbitrary line in the sand that gave her the illusion of continuity when in fact life was nothing but grasping at straws.

Without warning, loneliness gripped her, and she spent the next few moments fending off dread. She went to the bathroom and splashed cold water on her face and thought of how awful it was to wake up alone in a strange place. If another fork in the road appeared today, she would steer clear of it this time. She needed predictability in life. She needed the exterior to be predictable because lately her emotions were all over the map. Suddenly, she needed to be out of the room.

Of course, that was what she would do! She would go to the hospital, right now, and be by her father's side. It would be horrible for him to wake up alone in a hospital bed, tangled in a mess of wires and machines.

She layered clothes, and minutes later, she was outside. She gasped at the frigid night air. The sky was like ink. The neon signs in the shop windows had been turned off, and the only light was the yellowing hue of the street lamps. Without the car noises, the humid air muffled all other sounds, and she walked in the direction of the hospital in cottony silence.

At the ICU desk, a bleary-eyed receptionist worked on her Sudoku in the harsh light of incandescent bulbs. "But Madame," she told Cassie. "It is the middle of the night."

"I know," Cassie said, cheerful. "I've just flown here from the US where I live. I'm jet-lagged, and I could not sleep." To the receptionist's look of incomprehension, she said, "No problem. I'll wait here until it opens. At least I see you have medical brochures to read, that's better than in my hotel room."

"But, Madam…." There was a pregnant pause. "Visiting hours are between one and eight in the afternoon."

"What? How about morning visits?"

The receptionist pronounced carefully, as though she were speaking to a simpleton, "Visitors are allowed between the hours of one and eight in the afternoon."

"But, why?"

"That's how it is."

"That's ridiculous; what kind of hospital is this?"

"It's the same in all Parisian hospitals, Madame."

She considered the clerk's glacial tone. The words were beyond reproach, but the intonation and absence of eye contact told a different story. "Ah, I see," Cassie said. Remembering that to demand things would bring her nowhere, she said sweetly, "I apologize. You see, as I mentioned, I live in the United States, and we do things very differently there. I flew in yesterday. And I was hoping to be in the room with my dad. How about just for a few minutes, just to say hello? If he is asleep, I'll come right out."

The woman crossed her arm, not the slightest bit charmed. "C'est absolument impossible."

Cassie's blood turned hot. "In that case, may I please speak to whoever is running the ICU unit?"

The receptionist looked at her. "I don't understand." Her puzzlement was genuine. "What is it you want, and whom do you wish to speak to?"

"I don't know. You tell me. A doctor? An administrator? Whoever has the authority to let me visit my father outside of visiting hours."

The woman looked at her with suspicion. "What's the patient's name?" Cassie gave her dad's name, briefly holding the notion that the woman was changing her mind. It turned out she only wanted to confirm the existence of a real patient to rule out the probability that Cassie was a lunatic who ambled into hospitals at night making ludicrous demands. The woman then dialed an extension. "There is a woman here at the desk," she added mezza voce. "She says she is here to visit a patient." She stopped there, needing to add nothing to convey the strangeness of the request.

A minute later, a lanky doctor in a white coat and balding cranium approached. "Madame, may I help you?"

"I'm American," she said, words rushing out of her mouth all at once. "Although I might not understand how things work vis-à-vis visiting hours, well, I'm here now, and I'm told that I can't see my father."

"That would be correct," the doctor said, scratching his forehead.

"This is the middle of the night, I get that, but they say I won't be able to visit him until one in the afternoon."

The doctor pondered, looked at her not unkindly, and said, "Between one p.m. until eight p.m."

"But that's nonsensical! What could be the reason for this?"

"In order for the staff to do their work without interruption, and so that the patient can rest."

"Rest? They've been resting all night! Listen, I took the first plane from the United States, and you're telling me I won't be able to see my sick, elderly father, whom I haven't seen in five years, for another eleven hours?"

The doctor looked at his watch and said helpfully, "Ten and a half hours."

"They would never treat someone like this in the United States!"

He sighed, as though drained. "Madame, forgive me, but this is not the United States."

"I think that what my father needs right now is his family."

"What he needs right now is rest and capable medical care. And this is what he is receiving."

"Well, let's talk about his medical care, shall we? Why are you pumping so much morphine into his bloodstream that he can't even wake up?"

"I am not at liberty to discuss patients' files."

"I am his daughter."

"Even if you were the president of the United States, Madame, there is such a thing as patient privacy here." He added, "In France."

****

Cassie slumped all the way back to the hotel, the steps up to her room steeper and in greater number than they had seemed before. What was she going to do for the next ten and a half hours? Sabine, her only semi-ally here – and that was not a given – would be working all day. As for old friends in Paris, she had none. She had managed to let that go in her manic effort to put space between her and her childhood. She could not call anyone; she could not email anyone; she could not get any work done.

She undressed, got back into bed, tossed and turned, counted sheep without luck, and resigned herself to an interminable night.

At five in the morning at long last, after checking all night long for signs of street life outside her window, there seemed to be some activity down at La Jument Bleue. She figured this was a reasonable hour to activate the howling of water pipes. She took a shower standing in the tub, got dressed, layered clothes, came down the stairs, and walked a block under the night sky. She entered the café at the very moment it opened and felt swept up by a feeling of everlasting gratitude for the smell of fresh coffee and the sight of another human being. She sat at the same table and ordered a café au lait and a croissant. The coffee arrived, piping hot and smelling like hope itself. The croissants were crumbly, buttery, and all around gorgeous. As dawn lifted, the street became visible from her table. She wasn't the sole early riser in Paris. Soon a dozen people were ordering breakfast: sanitation men on their break, delivery men, two women in fishnet stockings and high heels. The old hotel manager entered and went to stand at the counter. When he saw Cassie, he gave her a friendly wave.

There was a roar outside the window. It was the motorcyclist from the night before as he made his thundering arrival. He parked his motorcycle in the same spot as the evening before. He entered the café and walked in her direction. When he saw her sitting there, he frowned, turned around, and went to sit a few tables away. She heard him order a café crème et baguette on which he slathered butter and confiture. He ate while reading Le Monde, as if this were his private dining room, and paid her no more attention.

In a caffeine-induced rush, Cassie dusted croissant flakes off her placemat and began scribbling. Lists, thoughts, resolutions, recriminations, bits of dialogue, runs at the perfect sentences she might use with her dad the moment he woke up. She wrote on both sides of the placemat and only lifted her face when she ran out of writing space.

When she lifted her head, the people who had been in the café earlier were gone and replaced by new patrons. Indiana Jones – that's what she called him in her mind – had left as well, and she had not even heard his motorcycle. It was seven in the morning. She paid, returned to her hotel, and was overwhelmed by a wave of fatigue. Just a tiny nap, she thought, but immediately fell into a deep, dreamless sleep.

She woke up to bright daylight aiming straight at her face. She looked at her watch for a long time to make sense of what it said. One in the afternoon? How could this be? She had slept for six hours straight, and now she was late for visiting hours.

****

Odile, Sabine, and her mother were already sitting in the waiting room. No matter that Cassie had beaten them to the hospital by ten and a half hours, she now looked like the one who didn't care. Odile's eyes were puffy, her nose red. Raymonde looked exhausted, and Sabine just gave her a look resembling reproach, although she wasn't sure. "Is everything all right?" Cassie asked. Odile shook her head no and disappeared into her tissue. Cassie's heart quickened.

"We tried to reach you on your cell," Sabine said.

"My phone broke, I'm sorry."

"They cut the sedative this morning, and he is waking up. We were worried that you would miss that."

They were ushered into the changing room and hustled into their paper gowns, paper masks, and paper slippers, and took turns tying the flimsy cords behind each other's backs. Cassie was so nervous that her fingers turned rubbery, and she was having trouble making simple knots.

When they were done, they looked at each other. Paper everywhere, above which were four sets of confused eyes. It was unclear who had the first giggle. Cassie noticed that Odile's shoulder shook and that she was trying to stop herself. When she understood that her sister was laughing, she was instantly affected. It was bad and irrepressible, coming from the belly and wanting to burst out. Before she knew it, Sabine was looking away to control the urge, and Raymonde was emitting mousy little chortles from under her mask. It was infectious, but apparently only to her family because the other people in the dressing room did not see the humor in this and looked at them with displeasure. And the guiltier the four of them felt for laughing, the more hilarious and wrong it was.

They managed to calm down at last by refusing to look at each other. They were about to enter Gustave's room when a doctor with gray hair and a plump physique stood between them and the door. The embroidered badge on his coat indicated that his name was Docteur Dumant. Pompously, and with such slowness that Cassie was tempted to push him and enter the room in a stampede, the doctor enunciated:

"We now have the result of the sensitivity … test. We are starting him on a new course of antibiotics more specific to his … particular infection."

"He is better then?" Odile asked.

"There are many factors. The age of the patient adds to … the complexity of the case."

"But is he better?" Cassie asked again.

"We have a long road ahead. But the side … effects of morphine on the elderly vary. As you know from previous … attempts, he was somewhat cognitively impaired to some … extent. He may exhibit signs that resemble delirium and be more excitable … than usual.

"I'm surprised that you are not using compression devices on his legs," she said.

The doctor looked at her askance. "Are you a physician?" he inquired.

"No," Cassie said.

"In that case, I don't see how this would be … hmm … relevant."

Cassie started to say, "But in the United States—" when Odile's hand on her forearm interrupted her.

"Thank you Doctor Dumant," Odile said. The doctor nodded curtly and left. Odile turned to Cassie, her voice muffled by the surgical mask she still wore. "What are you doing questioning Papa's treatment? And yes, we know, Americans do everything better."

"I'm not hurting anything by asking a couple of questions."

"You're antagonizing the doctor, and who knows how it will affect Papa. And us."

"What are you talking about? We have every right to advocate for him. It won't affect him negatively. Quite the opposite!"

"Not in France!" Odile snapped under her surgical mask.

"France or not, he's an ICU doctor, not a disgruntled waiter you're worried might spit in your soup."

"Don't be a child, Cassandra," Odile said.

Cassie clenched her jaw. As they filed into the room, they looked idiotic, like a procession of paper-cloaked clones. Gustave turned his face toward them and stared at them with wide open eyes, showing no other emotion than confusion. They had removed his oxygen mask, but the machine by his side still made rhythmic swooshing Darth Vader sounds. He's so weak, Cassie thought. Can he even recognize us? Dressed like this they might as well be surgeons about to operate on him or candy factory workers straight out of an I Love Lucy episode. They gathered around him in silence and Raymonde said, "Ça va Gustave? We all came here to visit."

He did not respond for a long time, and then he whispered, "I'm making do." Odile bent over him, took his hand, and asked him if he needed anything. "A prettier nurse," he said with great effort. "They all look like horses." Cassie smiled with relief under her mask. Humor! A terrific sign.

"We'll work on it, Papa," Odile said. "Is there anything you want to drink or eat?"

"Chocolate pudding," he said, and closed his eyes from the effort.

In his weakness and confusion, Gustave had not yet registered Cassie's presence, so she stepped forward and said, "I'm here too, Papa, I'm so glad you're feeling better." Gustave opened his eyes and stared at her. He raised his eyebrows perplexedly and said nothing. He was disoriented, clearly. She lived thousands of miles away and had not seen him in such a long time. She pushed her mask away from her face so that he could recognize her. "It's me!" she said. "I came all the way here to see you."

But right then, her father did something peculiar. He closed his eyes shut and shook his head vigorously back and forth on the pillow.

"What is it, Papa?" Odile said.

"No!" Gustave barked. Then he opened his eyes again, looked around the room, flummoxed and angry. He raised a trembling finger in Cassie's direction. "Why is she here?" he said, his voice quivering with something that sounded like rage.

"Papa! I'm here to visit you," Cassie whispered, blinking away tears. "I took a plane. I came yesterday, but you were sleeping." Gustave had shut his eyes tight again, as though looking at her was beyond his strength. He was shaking his head forcefully, his mouth a tight line, like a baby refusing to be spoon-fed.

"Come on." Odile pulled on her sleeve a little. "Step back maybe," she whispered. "I think you're tiring him out."

Cassie wanted to step back. She wanted to run away right this minute, but she planted her feet on the floor while her stomach flopped around in her abdomen. "Jeanne and Alexandre couldn't come. They're in college," she said, knowing full well that her dad had never shown interest in her children. Did he even remember their names? She added, "Peter had to stay in Los Angeles."

The rhythm of her father's heart monitors accelerated. Without warning, Gustave bolted upright, opening his eyes wide and dragging with him all manner of tubes and wires, and pointing at Cassie, roared, "I don't want to see her! Make her go away!"

Dread, bafflement, and shame swept through Cassie like a wave. Suddenly, she could not move had she wanted to. Sabine came between her and Gustave and put a protective arm around Cassie's shoulder.

Cassie turned to her mother, helpless. "He doesn't want to see me?" she asked. Raymonde and Odile looked as confused as she was.

Raymonde shook her head with genuine dismay. "I don't know."

Gustave was shaking now, the heart rate monitor beeping faster still. Cassie had the vague sense that Sabine was tugging at her to make her step away, but she could not move. "It's me!" she told her dad.

"That whore!" Gustave bellowed. "That bitch!" The heart monitor triggered an alarm, and in seconds, the room was filled with a strident beeping. Nurses appeared. Cassie, Sabine, Raymonde, and Odile were kicked out of the room, but Cassie could not make her legs work. She felt Sabine's firm grip on her hand, pulling her. At last, they were all in the hallway, tearing at their masks.

"Merde" was all Cassie could say.

"Are you all right?" Sabine asked.

"What the hell just happened?"

"Don't take it personally," Odile told her.

Raymonde said nothing.

They waited outside the room without speaking. Cassie was too numb with incomprehension to utter a word. After ten minutes, a young doctor came out of Gustave's room. "He got over stimulated, but he is fine now," he said.

"Can we go back in?" Raymonde asked.

"He's asking for chocolate pudding," the physician said.

"I don't know about you," Sabine told Cassie, "but I could use a cigarette first."

"Maybe it's better if Maman and I go first," Odile agreed. "Just in case he is still agitated, you know."

"No! I don't know," Cassie barked. But she did not reenter the room, and Sabine stayed with her.

While Raymonde and Odile returned to Gustave's room, Cassie and Sabine removed their paper clothes and walked in silence out of the hospital and into the street where smokers had taken refuge. In the cold, nicotine-saturated air, and amid the pandemonium of car honks and ambulance sirens, Sabine lit a cigarette and took a long drag. "Are you okay?" she asked Cassie.

"I don't even know my own frigging name right now," Cassie murmured.

"The morphine is making him mean; the doctor told us this might happen."

"Papa could be mean to me before the morphine."

Sabine considered this. "This probably has nothing to do with you."

"I don't know how I'm going to be able to go back in there."

"I don't want to spend another minute in there either," Sabine said. "It reeks of crazy."

They did return, eventually, back into their paper gowns and into the room. Odile was bringing a spoonful of pudding to Gustave's mouth. He lapped it up, his eyes half-closed, like a cat. The moment belonged to Odile. She oversaw it all, capable, efficient, necessary. Raymonde was standing back, useless, and Cassie felt sorry for her.

Gustave was peaceful now, so Cassie stepped closer to the bed. Odile was bringing to his lips another spoonful, which Gustave ate. He watched Cassie as he chewed, his eyes rolling in a bizarre way that did not seem like him. Odile brought another spoonful close to his mouth, but Gustave shut his mouth and turned away. He rolled his head on the pillow toward Cassie, pointed his finger at her again, slowly and measuredly this time. His voice clear and unwavering, he said, "Get that bitch out of here!"

They all froze. Cassie shriveled back and away from him, from the emotional impact. "But Papa," she murmured. "It's just me."

But Gustave growled, "Get Marceline out of here!"

Marceline? "Who's Marceline?" Cassie asked the whole room.

"Get her OUT!" her father shouted, and the heart monitor went beep beep at an ever-accelerating pace. "I DON'T want her here!"

Stunned, Cassie removed her hat and mask, threw them on the floor and left the room.

In the hallway, she placed her forehead against the wall and tried to breathe. What had just happened to her?

Twenty minutes later, Gustave was sleeping again. Sabine, Odile, Cassie, and Raymonde gathered around a hospital cafeteria table. Odile seemed invigorated by the visit. Raymonde was practically catatonic, and Sabine kept looking around, as though scanning the place for an emergency exit.

They ordered espressos, and Cassie stared at the cafeteria menu without understanding what she read. She got up and piled her tray high with everything that looked good, and everything did: salade composée, lapin confit aux pruneaux, camenbert, tarte Tatin. Only in a French hospital, Cassie thought. She was denied ketchup – apparently, they only served it on days that had French fries on the menu. She paid and returned to the table. They all stared at her tray.

"You're going to eat at this hour?" Raymonde asked.

"Why not?" But she knew why not: because her French mother could not conceive of eating a meal outside of the appropriate time range.

"It's almost two in the afternoon," Raymonde said.

"I'm jet-lagged," she reminded her. "It's early morning in L.A."

Between tearful bouts, and with irritating self-importance, Odile detailed Gustave's treatment, the infection in his lungs that refused to be tamed, how it had started somewhere in his throat as he recovered from his heart valve replacement. How the heart surgery had been a success, and how the inexplicable infection, now in his lungs, had nothing to do with the reason he had first entered the hospital. As Cassie wolfed down her food, and as Raymonde and Sabine sat in silence, Odile proceeded with a detailed description of Gustave's medicine. The name and dosage of his antibiotics. The name and dosage of the antibiotics before that. She described his pudding intake, even the state of his bowel movements.

Why did Sabine look so miserable? Her jaw was tense, her eyes absent. Was she also annoyed by Odile, or by her? Raymonde's expression was of dull resentment, but towards whom? Raymonde should have been the one giving updates, listening to doctors. She should have been the one feeding Papa pudding. Maybe she resented that Odile was robbing her of those functions. Cassie asked, "Maman, do you think it's the morphine that made Papa angry?"

Odile was going to answer, but Raymonde said, "The last time he woke up, he shouted racial slurs. He called the nurse a dirty Jew."

Cassie gasped. "What? That's awful."

"We know that Papa isn't like that," Sabine said.

"Drugs can make you feel and say crazy things," Odile said.

"How did the nurse respond?"

Odile laughed. "She was Asian. She said that she had been called many things in her life, but this, never."

"Could Papa be a closeted anti-Semite?" Cassie asked.

"He doesn't think about … anything Israelite," Raymonde said forcefully.

"You mean Jewish?"

"Oh, by God, Cassie. Always stirring the pot."

"I'm only asking."

"It was the morphine," Sabine said, addressing the elephant in the room. "He was not speaking to you. He didn't recognize you."

Cassie sighed. "A man able to make a specific request for chocolate pudding should be able to recognize his own daughter."

"Maybe it was a hallucination," Raymonde offered.

Cassie shrugged, "There's also the possibility that the morphine allowed him to express how much he hates me."

"Oh please," Odile said, rolling her eyes. "Not this again."

"Again?"

"With you, it's always one conspiracy or another."

They all knew what conspiracy theory Odile was referring to: the Letter. Cassie inhaled, braced herself, and said, "Maybe without the drugs, he is better able to disguise his dislike of me as indifference."

"It's not because you repeat something over and over that it makes it true," Odile snapped.

"Well, if you needed proof, what about this latest outburst?"

"It wasn't about you, you, you!" Odile exploded. "The more we tell you that it's not about you, the more you insist. Every time it's the same thing: you disappear, then you barge in, tell lies, and leave me behind to clean up the mess you left."

"What are you referring to? If I disappeared, it's because I was written off. Cast away by all of you!"

Sabine and Raymonde looked down at their food, but Odile was galvanized. "You wrote a letter of insults; Papa and Maman had to defend themselves!"

"Defend from what? From my feelings?"

"From your inventions and your lies."

Cassie had the urge to reach across the table and slap Odile. She tucked her hand between her knees and looked at her mother who showed no expression. She said, "In this family, the minute you share an unpleasant truth you're called a liar."

They all looked down at their empty espresso cups for a long moment, no one knowing what to say next. Sabine broke the thick silence. "Maman, why do you think Papa mentioned this name? Marceline?" She said this with deliberation. It was unlike Sabine to cross-examine anyone. It was as though she was encouraging their mother to speak up about something only she knew about. All three sisters held their breath and looked at Raymonde.

"Me? I— how would I know," Raymonde said, staring at the table.

"Does he know someone with that name, maybe?" Sabine insisted. "Someone from his past?" Sabine was looking at Raymonde fiercely, impelling her to answer.

Raymonde's eyes darted from one daughter to another angrily and finally blurted out, "I can't remember!"

Despite the fight just a moment ago, an invisible current passed between Odile and Cassie. Their mother was lying, it was obvious. The lie floated between them. Something unusual had just happened, but neither of them was ready to cross-examine Raymonde.

"I'm getting a smoke," Sabine said. She got up. "You want one?" she asked, giving Cassie an excuse to leave. Cassie stood up.

Odile and Raymonde returned to Gustave's room, and Cassie and Sabine walked into the street. They leaned against a stone wall to protect themselves from the falling rain. Cassie observed her sister as she took a cigarette out of a pack and brought it to her lips, lighting it, inhaling, and exhaling deeply. She was tense, and her eyes were sad.

"Okay, you're going to say I have too much imagination," Cassie said, "but didn't Maman look embarrassed when we asked about that Marceline person?"

Sabine inhaled and said, "That's clear."

"First, she says Papa hallucinated. Like instead of seeing me he was seeing someone else? And then why would Maman pretend not to know that person unless…."

"Unless Maman is manipulative."

"Well, I was thinking, is it possible that Papa had some kind of affair?"

"No," Sabine said. "It's something else."

"You do know something!"

"I heard things," she said, exhaling smoke through her nose into the cold air.

"What?"

"The expression 'that bitch Marceline.' Papa used it when we were growing up," Sabine said. "I heard it when he and Maman were talking."

"I never heard any of that."

"If some woman named Marceline was his mistress, he would not commiserate with his wife against her."

"You didn't ask who she was?"

Sabine had a small smile. "You know how it goes in this family. We're not supposed to ask questions, and anyway, no one will answer them."

Cassie looked at Sabine wide-eyed. "That's right! That's exactly how it goes! I thought I was crazy to think that. Everyone in this family thinks I'm crazy."

"No one believes that you're crazy," Sabine said, laughing a little. "We just want you to think that you are."

"I'm about to fall to my knees to thank you for this," Cassie said.

Sabine lifted her chin and blew a cloud of smoke up at the sky. "You're welcome," she said.

After Sabine had returned to her work, Cassie paced in the waiting room. She had heard of ICU psychosis. Hallucinations and paranoia were known side effects of heavy sedative use and ventilation. She needed to ask the doctor if that was what he had meant when he had warned them of possible delirium. It would explain everything. Also: she would be innocent.

Behind the front desk, the frizzy desk clerk was looking as glum as ever. "I'd like to speak with my father's doctor," Cassie said.

"He's busy," the woman responded without looking up.

Cassie inhaled, exhaled an already much hotter air. "I'd like to make an appointment, then."

"Doctor Dumant doesn't take appointments." The woman made everything sound as though the person in front of her was stupid, in the wrong, or both. It was oh so subtle, nothing you could pinpoint, but the contempt was there.

"I've never heard of a doctor who doesn't take appointments," Cassie said. "That would be like a teacher who doesn't see students," she explained. "Or a butcher who doesn't handle meat."

The woman stared at her with a vacant expression. "You might be able to see him when he is making his rounds," she said.

"When is that?"

"I don't manage his schedule."

"I've been walking up and down this hospital, and I don't see him. I'm starting to wonder if he is playing frisbee in some deserted hallway instead of treating sick people. Shouldn't the doctor be doctoring?"

The clerk shrugged, uninterested. "He sees the patients who need to be seen when they need to be seen."

At that moment, Cassie spotted him. Doctor Dumant was charging through the hallway, half a dozen interns trotting after him. She thought she recognized one of the young men she had seen at La Jument Bleue that first night. She began to trot along with the group. "Excusez moi, Docteur Dumant! I'm wondering if you would have a minute."

The doctor stopped in front of a patient's door, picked up a file, and put his hand on the doorknob, ignoring her.

"Excuse me!" she said loudly. "I know you aren't deaf, and I'm pretty certain that I'm not invisible, so please speak to me." The interns were stunned into immobility, a collective horrified expression on their faces.

"What is … this?" Doctor Dumant said.

"I need to talk to you about my father's treatment," Cassie said.

The doctor looked at her with impatience. "I am extremely … busy, Madame."

Flustered, Cassie forgot why she wanted to talk to him, so she improvised. "I heard that there is such a thing as taking too strong a course of antibiotics."

The physician was perplexed by this. "And?"

"I heard it could lead to kidney or liver failure."

"Are you suggesting we stop the antibiotics, and let … him fend for himself?" Doctor Dumant asked, inspiring a collective mirth among his entourage.

"No, of course not," Cassie said. "Also, I'm wondering about the degree of inclination of his bed."

"What about it?"

"I heard that feeding tubes can leak into a patient's lungs with the wrong degree of inclination. Are we sure that it won't happen?"

The interns looked at her with bemusement, waiting for Doctor Dumant to react. "Quite certain," the doctor said.

Suddenly Cassie remembered her original question. "My dad shouted at me out of nowhere yesterday. Is it possible that he has ICU psychosis?"

"Possible," the doctor said meanly, "but in your … specific case, unlikely."

What an a-hole! Cassie, anger swelling in her chest, went on the offensive despite herself. "You'll understand my concerns; my father entered here for a heart valve replacement and contracted a nosocomial infection, you know, a hospital-acquired infection?"

"I'm well acquainted with the term," Dumant said icily.

"I bet you are," she said.

"Has the patient authorized you to … speak on his behalf?" Doctor Dumant asked sharply. The interns, attuned to the doctor's emotional temperature, shifted on their heels.

Cassie shrugged. "I imagine my mother, my sisters are. I'm probably as well."

"Either you are, or you are not. Why don't you … find out." With this, he opened the door.

Cassie raised her voice. "If you're unwilling to answer basic questions, I'll speak to your boss." But the doctor and his interns had disappeared into the room.

Cassie scanned the now deserted hallway for something to break. Feeling like ramming her fist into the wall, she headed for the front desk. There were four people in line ahead of her. The frizzy clerk was busy dispensing her non-help to everyone. Cassie waited, furious. When it was her turn, she said in a voice she tried to keep even, "I want to make an appointment with the director of this department."

The frizzy clerk made her repeat, as though the request was beyond the grasp of her understanding. "You want a what?"

"An appointment."

"With the head of the intensive care unit?"

"That's right."

"Madame, c'est impossible! He doesn't deal with patients, let alone the family of patients. He's an administrator."

"Well, I have an administrative issue. What's his name?" Behind her, a half a dozen people stood in line. Sensing they would be made to wait now, the line emitted a collective sigh of annoyance.

"Madame," the clerk responded in a tone of personal outrage, "we obviously don't give out names of the faculty, or administration."

"Why not?"

"But Madame, if people came here and got the names of people on staff, it would violate their privacy. This is a hospital. We have rules."

Behind her, sighs made way for groans of impatience, which Cassie tried to ignore. "This is nothing but obstruction," she said. "Once the director finds out what is going on here, I am quite sure he will find it interesting to learn that this department makes people sick, not better, and that the patients are treated like cattle."

Far from being intimidated, the clerk had an exhausted smile. "Next!" she called.

****

The heavy rain had turned into a mean and windy sort of drizzle. Cassie walked fast, trying to put as much distance between her and the hospital as her soggy boots would allow. She walked down Boulevard de Magenta and crossed Boulevard de Rochechouart toward rue de Clignancourt. She passed graffiti-covered walls, African beauty shops, kosher butchers, porn shop signs, fake leather purses hanging like grapes on the outside walls of discount stores. The sidewalks were as crowded as the street and smelled of exhaust pipes, cannabis, and cooked lamb. The crackling sounds of mopeds faded by the time she reached rue Pierre Picard. Suddenly, there were trees. Pedestrians disappeared, and she found herself alone in the street. A minute later she was at the foot of Montmartre.

The stairs leading up to the Sacré-Coeur were empty save for a few intrepid tourists battling the weather with overturned umbrellas. She climbed, and the street noises became muffled and then disappeared. Montmartre, wet and glistening, was all hers. Below her, stone stairs and trees. Above her, more stairs and trees, many of them starting to show signs of spring. The texture of the air changed. An icy draft bit her hard.

There were no more street noises, only the chirping of a few brave birds, as though she had climbed out of the city and into the countryside. She emerged on the Sacré-Coeur's esplanade. The basilica was massive, so much bigger than it appeared from the bottom of the butte. Above her were the gray sky and the stillness of bare trees and branches. Below, Paris was grey, muted.

She stood by the balustrade. The cold wind slapped her without mercy as immense pangs of sadness and guilt beat down on her. No wonder she usually took a shortcut to anger. It was a readily available emotion, simple, immediately accessible, energizing, an emotion far less painful than the alternatives: sadness, grief, envy, self-loathing. Anger felt good.

Until, of course, it destroyed everything. The Letter to her parents, that irreparable fracture, written in a single day when she had needed to blame someone for her unhappiness, had been the product of anger.

She had penned the Letter the day that followed her return to Los Angeles with Peter, after that disastrous trip to Paris. On that day, they had fought. He had accused her of blaming him for things beyond his control. She had called him a narcissist, he had called her a professional victim, and she had accused him of having an affair, had called him a man-whore and a douchebag. She had shouted that she wanted a divorce, that she wanted him gone. Out of the house right this instant. He took all the writing credit. He was ignoring her. They did not even talk anymore. She had not meant this, at least not the part about wanting him gone.

None of this had been a new argument. Only, to her dismay, Peter had packed a bag this time and spent the night at the Sunset Marquis. A week later, he still had not returned. A month later, he was filing for divorce.

The day Peter had left, she had decided that she was done with lies and compromises, that she wanted to tell the Truth. In the Letter, she told her parents how horrible visiting them had been. She accused her father of playing favorites, her mother of being complacent, and Odile of reveling in the whole mess.

Just like her threat to Peter, she had only meant to vent. The Letter should have been no problem at all – had she not mailed it. A week later, she received a terse response from Odile notifying Cassie that, in return for the calumnious web of lies, her parents no longer wished to speak to her.

She had not expected this. She hadn't expected that her anger could make all of them angry.

Her parents' reaction to her letter had floored her. They had written her off so easily, validating all her suspicions. The heartbreak she experienced was so violent that she knew what the term meant now. She felt it, her heart. She felt the physical shattering of it.

She had scrambled to fix things with Peter. But it was as though she had hit an off-switch with him. He said that he had failed at making her happy for years and that he no longer had it in him to try.

The years that followed the separation were abysmal. The children, as predicted by Odile, began to act out. Jeanne fell in with the wrong crowd. It's always about other children having a bad influence on yours, but what happens when it is your child who is caught selling pot to other middle schoolers? Jeanne was expelled and put on juvenile probation. For the next few years, Cassie had to chase after her daughter to get her to pee in a cup to prove her sobriety to juvenile court. Alex, meanwhile, disappeared into AP classes and Robotics Club until – she was the last one to find out, through Peter – it was revealed that he had been suffering from debilitating bouts of anxiety and was under the care of a psychiatrist who had prescribed heavy-duty psychotropic meds.

When Peter was picked like a ripe plum by Jessica, it was the last straw. A giant sinkhole of pain and guilt swallowed Cassie whole. Peter was her best friend, possibly her soul mate, and she had pushed him away. She had kicked him out, as Peter reminded her, sending him straight into Jessica's arms.

Watching Peter and Jessica together, witnessing their happiness, was torture – Jessica's youth, the pregnancies, the fact that their life together was only picking up steam whereas hers had collapsed, all of it brought her to her knees. She would have agreed to anything in the divorce, as long as she could continue to have Peter in her life. She did not know how to live without him. They agreed to work together, and those were the crumbs on which she fed. And thus, she saw Peter every day, and she starved.

After a year without speaking to her parents, and at Sabine's suggestion, Cassie found the courage to call. She had told her parents about the divorce and apologized to them. Or more to the point, she had grovelled. Cassie had blamed her behavior on the stress of her marriage falling apart and recanted all she had said. The apology hadn't been sincere, but she was at a low point and in desperate need of their love.

But the love didn't come. For the next four years, she made every effort, struggled through perfunctory, strained conversations (as if in a permanent act of contrition, she was the one expected to call; they never did). The relationship with her father stalled to nothing. Her calls seemed an annoyance he avoided. The more Cassie did the talking, with an increasingly manic intensity, the more aloof he seemed. He did not ask questions and went from vague and disinterested to not coming to the phone at all. And on the rare occasions when he picked up the phone, he handed it to Raymonde. When Cassie asked to speak to him, he was always out or napping.

She confronted her mother and Odile about it, but they assured her that nothing was the matter. Once again, she was making things up. Over time, she called less. Every other week, and then once a month. And then only for Christmas and on birthdays. It was no surprise that they did not feel the need to tell her about his heart operation; she was barely part of the family.

Leaning against the parapet, Cassie shivered. It had started to rain again. Her fingers were numb. She walked across the esplanade and stopped in front of an engraved plaque stating that the construction of the Sacré-Coeur was completed in 1914. She looked up at the basilica, so intricate, so ancient, immutable-looking, when in fact it was only about a hundred years old! She could have grandparents that age. She did not. Her mother's parents had passed away, and come to think of it, she had never met her paternal grandparents and did not even know their names. Her dad never spoke of them.

He was so hard to know, her father, so hard to read. He had always been a silent, secret man. She had tried to read him, tried to connect, but he had not let her. Sacré-Coeur, sacred heart. Peter. Her father. This longing for the love of two men who could not give it to her in return was akin to masochism. And yet she continued to want it.

Shouldn't her heart be sacred too? Did it not need protecting?

****

It began to rain hard. Cassie hurried back down the stairs. Her first order of business was not to get hurt. By anyone. What could they do to her that they had not already done? Her dad had clearly lost interest in her a long time ago. This outburst was more of the same. Who cared who Marceline was, or why he had confused her with Cassie? He was out of his mind because of the drugs. It meant nothing. If the rest of the family gave her the cold shoulder, so be it. At least she had showed up in Paris, done the right thing. There was a family narrative, "Cassie est dure," they would say, which might be translated as tough, or harsh, depending on the intention. Cassie was thought to land on her feet. Cassie was not sensitive the way Odile was. She could have perceived this as a compliment but took it as a reproach. It made her feel self-serving, unfeeling. But she could not defend herself from this reproach without appearing dure indeed, so she embraced it. She was tough. She was strong. She had grit. She did not need anyone. Not Peter, not the kids now that they had left for college.

But strength, toughness, and grit implied self-sufficiency. No one thought that people like her needed tender loving care. The needs of tough, strong, gritty people tend to be overlooked, first of all by themselves.

****

Just as she arrived at the hospital, a voice over the loudspeaker informed her that visitation hours had come to an end. Dozens of family members began to file docilely out of patients' rooms, removing their hats, masks, and paper gowns and tossing them into nearby wastebaskets. Cassie ran back into her father's room as Odile and Raymonde were leaving. She peeked inside the room; her dad seemed to be sleeping peacefully. Sabine wasn't there.

"Do you want to have dinner together?" Cassie asked.

Raymonde looked at Odile, signifying that the two had agreed on this. "We're exhausted. Maybe another time if you don't mind," Odile said. She nudged Cassie out of the room before she could get closer to her father's bed. "He's sleeping now; better let him be."

They walked out of the hospital. Rain poured. Odile and her mother, in their warm coats, opened their umbrellas. Cassie stood under her mother's umbrella. The three formed a little tent, steam billowing out of their mouths as they spoke. "Maman?" Cassie said, "I'm wondering about something."

"What?"

"How come we never got to meet Papa's parents?"

Raymonde looked at Odile as if she needed her authorization to respond, but Odile gave her a blank stare. "You ask this now?" she protested. "It's your dad's business."

Odile surprised her by coming to Cassie's aid. "They are our grandparents," she said.

Raymonde shrugged. "Your grandfather died during the war, and your grandmother died when you were little. After that, there was a … falling-out."

Cassie avoided looking at Odile, but she was sure her sister had registered it too. Odile said, "A falling out with whom, if they were both dead?"

Raymonde eyed her with panic, or perhaps anger. "Oh, I don't know!"

"Where were they from?" Odile asked. "Our grandparents, what were their names?"

Raymonde's jaw clenched. "I can't remember! It's too long ago!"

Cassie narrowed her eyes. "You can't remember your mother-in-law's name?"

"I only met her a couple of times!" Raymonde protested. It was one thing to brush Cassie off, and another one to deflect questions when her daughters were united. Tapping her boots on the pavement and gripping her umbrella, Raymonde raised her voice. "I did not meet with her approval! She was all hoity-toity. I was too working-class. I don't know what she imagined for her son, some duchess or something? That's what she was into – status. But I was penniless. A shop girl." She added defensively, "I wasn't after Gustave's money. And his family never gave him a franc. Not that he would have taken it were it offered!"

Cassie and Odile exchanged a furtive look. A current of excitement passed between them. This was a long-taboo subject. The topic of their father's past would not have been allowed had he been present. But now that Raymonde was entangled in her explanations, a little push could result in something interesting. From whom was Gustave estranged? As far as the story went, he had no living relatives.

"Papa was what? Forty years old when he met you?" Cassie said, craftily. "Maybe his mother did not approve of Papa's choice of a twenty-year-old bride?"

Raymonde, reeling from what appeared to be a reopened wound, said, "So what? I was young and pretty, I'll have you know. You saw the pictures of me back then, thin and all. Who wouldn't want this for their son? But not her. Oh, no. Her Majesty never wanted to know me. I could not bear the way she was treating me, in that house of theirs, their castle," she said, pronouncing that last word with a mix of resentment and admiration.

"A castle?" Cassie said.

"Well, not exactly. But the way they had their décor, they would have you think it was Versailles."

"How did she treat you?" Odile asked.

"Like I was dirt," Raymonde spat.

"What did you say Papa's mom's name was again?" Cassie said, knowing full well her mother had claimed not to know.

"Lucienne." Raymonde realized her mistake. "I guess I remember now," she grumbled.

"And then what happened?"

"Then your father wrote a letter and said he wanted to have nothing to do with them." She pinched her lips. "That's all I know."

"How familiar," Cassie said. "I disagreed with Dad, and he wrote me off too."

"We were tired of being insulted!" Raymonde barked, all too happy to bring the conversation back to something she and Odile agreed on. "Your letter was nothing but lies."

Cassie expected Odile to come to her mother's rescue, but she didn't. Instead, she pressed on. "Them?" Odile asked. "His father was dead, so who is 'them?' There was Lucienne, Papa's mother. Who else?"

"Well," Raymonde said evasively, "there was his sister."

In unison, Cassie and Odile exclaimed, "What sister?"

"Papa had a sister?"

"Has. She's still alive as far as I know."

"Did you meet her?"

"Is she younger or older?"

"I met her," Raymonde said, defeated. "You were little. This wasn't her first marriage. She was marrying a count. Not her first count, at that! I imagine that's why we were invited: so that they could rub our noses in it."

"Do we have cousins?" Odile asked, excited.

"Perhaps. I don't know. No. I don't think so. Maybe."

"What was the name of the count?" Cassie asked. She needed to gather as much info as possible before her mother closed up like a clam.

"Some ridiculous aristocratic name."

"Can't you remember?"

"Not really."

Odile and Cassie pondered this. A sister. A living relative. An aunt! "What's her name?" Odile asked with authority.

Raymonde shrugged, as though the answer was obvious, "Well, Marceline."

Cassie and Odile exchanged an excited glance. The name hovered between them, ripe with mystery and speculation. Marceline, the bitch.

"That's who he was ranting about?" Odile said.

Raymonde wasn't listening. The discussion had brought her back to a loop in her thinking, whatever had happened, still undigested. "By marrying me, your father went from the bourgeoisie to working class. A step down. They didn't approve, oh no. He was never good enough for them, and neither was I."

"Why did Papa never tell us about Marceline?" Cassie asked.

"Your father hates his sister. That's why you never met her. He despises her like you have no idea."

"After today, I'd say that we got a pretty good idea actually," Odile said. She turned to Cassie. "As I suspected, this was not about you. He was confused, that's all."

"Why would Papa agree to go to his sister's wedding if he hated her so much?" Cassie asked.

"I guess they wanted us to witness their grand airs. I don't know why he went." Raymonde paused and looked around as if searching for a quick exit route. Outside, the rain was relentless. The umbrella wasn't broad enough, and Cassie felt the cold, wet fabric of her thin jacket against her back. She was cold to the core, but not about to move. She could tell that Odile wasn't budging either, physically or mentally. She was just as curious as Cassie was.

"Why would Papa not tell us any of this?" Odile said. "Why the big secret?"

"That's all I know," Raymonde said, pinching her lips.

"What's Marceline's last name?" Cassie asked.

"Oh, I don't know. A complicated name." Raymonde was getting flustered. "You can ask your father when he wakes up!" She turned to walk away and suddenly said, "Ah, yes! I remember," perhaps because the name had just popped into her mind or because she had burned to pronounce it all along. "Marceline Bécasel D'Alompe! No, Comtesse de Bécasel D'Alompe, believe it or not." With this, she turned away and walked down rue Ambroise Paré. "I'm cold," she told Odile. "Let's go."

Odile looked at Cassie, shrugged, and hurried after her mother.

"I'll see you tomorrow," Cassie called after them.

Now that the umbrella was gone, Cassie was left standing in the rain. She watched them walk toward the metro station. Neither had asked a single question about her life, her children, her divorce, how she fared, or even where she would be staying.

Cassie rushed back inside the hospital and into the intensive care area. At the desk, she asked for a piece of paper, and she jotted down the words Comtesse Marceline de Bécasel D'Alompe before she forgot. The woman at the desk was a new nurse that Cassie had yet to alienate. She decided to take her chance. "Excuse me," she said, trying to appear sweet and obedient, "I realize visitation hours are over, but I forgot my wallet in my father's room."

The woman hesitated. "Hurry then. And don't get near the patient, you know, because of germs."

"He won't even know I was there," Cassie assured as she rushed toward the room.

****

Her father lay on his back, asleep. On his face was the mask to help him breathe, connected to a tube and a machine. The only signs of life were the beeping of the heart monitor and the laborious up and down motion of his chest as he labored to breathe. "Poor Papa," she whispered. "What have they done to you?" She brought the thin blanket up to his chin. She found two other covers and spread those across his body, but when she looked up at him again, his eyes here wide open, unblinking. "Papa?" she said.

Gustave gripped her arm. His eyes rolled around, taking in the room, his expression close to panic. He began to moan, or perhaps to speak. "Are you trying to say something?" Cassie asked urgently. She looked at the door, then down at her hands. Were they clean enough? She lifted his mask off his face. "What is it?"

Her father murmured, "I saw his ghost."

"What?"

"Baba."

"Baba?"

"It wasn't my fault."

"Of course, relax now, just rest."

"You have to find Baba," he muttered. "You'll see. He'll tell you."

An instant later, his eyes were closed. Cassie waited a moment and placed the mask back on his face. She tiptoed to the other side of the room, snatched her father's coat and ran out of the hospital.

****

Wrapped in her dad's coat, and for the first time since she had gotten off the plane Cassie felt warm. The coat was too wide, too long, but she liked how it weighed on her shoulders, how rough it was to the touch, like a coat of armor, one that smelled of her father's lavender aftershave. The coat, or "relic" as her mother had labeled it for some reason, had been a presence in her childhood. It existed in her parent's closet without ever being worn. In fact, the coat did not fit her dad either. It was too wide for his build, and the cut was from another era. Why keep this old thing, she wondered? And why, of all the coats he owned, had her father chosen this one to bring to his heart surgery?

Cassie, looking increasingly less chic and Parisian in the strange coat, walked toward the hotel and clambered into La Jument Bleue.

At the door, she came shoulder to shoulder with Indiana Jones, who appeared intent on beating her to it. He let her in first, with a reluctant, "Après vous."

"Merci," she said. But as soon as she passed the threshold, he walked past her and then did something so rude that she nearly gasped in indignation: Had he actually rushed ahead to steal her table? Yes, he had! He was stealing her table, just like that. Robbery in broad daylight!

The only empty table left was the one across from where he was sitting. Seething, Cassie headed for it, removed her coat and folded it over her chair. She sat down and crossed her arms, intent on not looking in his direction. The waiter arrived to take her order. Unprepared, and feeling Indiana's eyes on her, she fumbled with words and ordered the same steak au poivre she had eaten the day before. "Avec du ketchup," she added. She waited, impatient, pen in hand, for the waiter to set the table. She removed the white paper placemats from the table and began writing, feverishly laying on paper the thoughts that lay in a jumble inside her head.

Something extraordinary had taken place today. Her father had mistaken her for his sister. A living sister! One he kept secret from his daughters. Why? How? And who was this Baba?

She wrote:

1- Look online for relatives, family tree, something

2- Find internet café

3- Tell Sabine the story

4- Find out more about Marceline. Who is she?

6- Do I look like her?

She gazed up to find that Indiana Jones was watching her with keen interest. She put her arms over her placemat, hiding her writing like a school girl, and looked pointedly away. A moment later he opened a book, and it was her turn to observe him. No ring on any of the fingers. Could be gay. Or not. In Paris, it was hard to tell. She cared about none of this, of course. However, a handsome man at the next table was proving himself difficult to ignore.

Her steak-frites arrived and with it a laughably minuscule ramekin filled with about a tablespoon of ketchup. "Pardonnez-moi," she told the waiter, "I'm going to need a whole lot more ketchup." The waiter returned with a bottle. She used the back of her knife to scrape the sauce off her steak and poured ketchup on her plate. She ate, setting her fork down every so often to write on her placemat, and made every effort to ignore Indiana Jones for the rest of the meal.

It was dark when she left La Jument Bleue. As she crossed the street, she stepped down from the curb and into a deep puddle. Instantly and effortlessly, the Uggs absorbed the dirty gutter water like high-efficiency sponges. She stood in shock. Icy water was up to her ankles inside her boots! She dragged her now much heavier feet all the way to the hotel, cursing the rain in French.

****

Inside the hotel's phone booth, she sat on the bench, removed her boots and socks, and called Sabine. The call went straight to voicemail, twice. No point in leaving a message since she could not be called back. The day had been so hard, and she was so tired, and her toes had turned to shriveled little blue things. What she did next was just plain stupid. She dialed Odile's cell phone. "I'm thinking I'd like to get in touch with that Marceline woman," she told her older sister.

"Why?" Odile asked coldly. "What would that accomplish?"

"I'm curious about her, that's all."

"I think you should drop the idea."

"Okay. But I would just need a tiny favor from you though. Could you help me out?"

"Depends."

"Could you go online and look for her address?"

There was a long silence as Odile considered this. "Why can't you do it yourself?" she asked.

"I don't have any access to the internet at the moment. It's just a quick look on google. I wrote down the name."

"Sorry, I can't," Odile said.

"How difficult would it be for you to spend the five seconds it takes to look up a single address?"

"I can't—"

"How hard would it be to give me the time of day for once in your life? How about that?"

"And how about I'm at Maman's, and she doesn't have a computer."

Cassie leaned her forehead on the glass door and bumped it gently a couple of times. "Okay," she said. "You don't want to look on your phone?"

"No, Cassie, I do not want to look on my phone right now."

"Okay."

"Are you going to do it anyway?"

Cassie hesitated. "Probably," she admitted.

Odile's voice changed pitch, something either near tears or explosion. "Do you think that's appropriate?"

"What?"

"Going behind Papa's back?"

How did she do it? Odile had a gift. Between the withholding of emotions, and the reproachful, judgmental undertone of everything she said, Odile could give a master class on how to be passive-aggressive. "I am not going behind his back!" Cassie snapped. And realizing that in fact, she was, she said, "Fine! Don't help me."

She then dialed Peter's cell phone collect. She needed to speak to him. Needed to! Peter was, she was now convinced, her last friend in the world. She was never going to be able to cope without him. In a few sentences, he would calm her down, put things in perspective, make fun of her.

She dialed and dialed again, but each time her call went to voicemail. She had no luck reaching Peter at home either. She tried again, feeling more rejected and alone with each try.

The reason she could not cope with life without Peter is that she had never developed a life of her own. In the marriage, she had remained in a safe, little world. She had never quite learned to function outside of her house and outside of her role as wife and mother. As an expatriate, those roles had felt safer than to attempt to integrate into a new country or a new culture. But really, it was not Peter's fault, even if it had been convenient for him to keep her available to him and ignorant of everything else. Now, for the first time, she accepted the blame for making one man her Everything, and then for pushing him away the way she had. Now she was confused, forgetting digits and fumbling with the phone like in a bad dream. She had lost Peter. He was no longer hers. That was the absolute truth.

What am I doing?

She stopped dialing and hung up. She had spent half her life counting on Peter to solve her problems, but now she needed to fend for herself. I need to move on, she thought, the words resounding in her head like a terrible fatality. She could no longer afford to need Peter or his friendship. It wasn't fair to him, it wasn't fair to Jessica Rabbit, and, ultimately, it wasn't fair to herself. She wasn't giving herself a proper chance at life.

She had been a daughter, and then a wife, and then a mother, and now she was nothing. She burst into tears, alone in her red velvet padded phone booth. She cried for a good long time. And when she was bored with crying and with feeling sorry for herself, she walked up the stairs.

In her room, she brushed her teeth and took off her clothes. She lay on top of the covers, brought her dad's coat to bed, wrapped herself in its coarse wool, and fell asleep protected by the scent of lavender aftershave.

CHAPTER 8

The Armenian Visitor

On a warm October day, Albano watched incoming ferries, his back propped against burlap bags filled with grains awaiting shipment. The 1914 harvest had been spectacular and the succession of hot days and dry nights had made the conditions ideal for the drying process, thus ensuring another year of prosperity for Smyrna.

The Ottoman Empire had bombed Russia's Black Seaport and officially entered the war, and the mood on the quay had turned festive almost overnight. Among the citizens of the Empire, there was a sense of great anticipation and the giddiness of men preparing for heroism. Men who had always worn simple peasant clothes, some who had never worn shoes in their life, looked grand in their fresh uniforms.

Albano did not like the air of authority the uniform gave them. Humble men now turned soldiers seemed drunk on patriotism and pride. In the cafés and restaurants, on the pier and throughout Smyrna, rumors flew, and temperaments ran wild. On the quay, the flurry of activity had doubled in intensity. Few foreigners remained. Those from countries that had allied with the Ottoman Empire and were now part of the Central Powers, Germany, the Austro-Hungarian Empire, and Bulgaria, stayed in Smyrna unless they had been mobilized to fight by their respective governments. Foreigners from the Allied Powers, Great Britain, France, Russia, and Italy, had been repatriated with their families. Other foreign families who had lived in Smyrna longer and had deeper roots here had required more time to liquidate assets and were now hurrying to leave. The loading docks were filled with mounds of luggage and anxious foreigners wringing their hands.

Albano opened the last of his French newspapers and read its content avidly. Of all the languages Albano had learned over the two years since he had first met Hagop, he loved French the best. Learning new languages was easy for him. He would read newspaper articles in Turkish, Arabic, Greek, or Armenian, then look for corresponding subjects in the contents of a French, Italian, or British newspaper and over time would start to make sense of it. When pronunciation eluded him, he listened in on conversations between men from London, Milan, Paris, or Prague and sponged up the accents. Then he practiced to himself out loud as he walked between the Jewish quarter, Mount Pagus, and the quayside. He studied how Europeans dressed, how they greeted one another, trying to decode the subtlety between classes.

Sometimes, when Albano was alone in his cave, he practiced standing and walking the way French people did. France held the most charm in his mind ever since Uncle Moshe had made it so vivid with his tales of monkeys and Eiffel Towers.

With the Europeans being repatriated, a gaping hole was opening in the very fabric of Smyrna. Gone were Danish bankers and Italian insurance men in their silk suits. Gone were English women in large skirts and lace, French women wearing the new fashions from Paris. From the quay's restaurants, the smell of tagine and Greek stew no longer mingled with the aroma of boeuf bourguignon and sauerkraut. The top hats, canotiers, and feathered hats were mostly gone. All that was left were turbans, fezzes, and felt embroidered caps. With the political agitation, he and Hagop had sold out of European newspapers within the hour. Hagop had gone to the store to fetch more, but already he was heading back to Albano empty-handed. "Starting tomorrow it will be illegal to sell anything printed by any country of the Triple Entente," Hagop morosely said as he plopped down next to Albano and leaned against one of the burlap bags.

"This is the end of our prosperity," Albano said.

"We need to think of something else we can sell now," Hagop said bitterly. "Ammunition? Coffins?"

"We could sell your father's pastries just like Xandra does in the Levantine quarter. Sell them here, on the quay."

"Think about it, Albano," Hagop said. "Those baskets are heavy." Albano bit his lip to keep from responding. If Xandra was strong enough to do it, maybe the two of them could do it as well. But Hagop did not find much value in hard work. What he found value in were shortcuts – the least amount of effort for the highest return. Cleverness, to Hagop's way of thinking, not sweat, was what made men rich. "We could take them in a wheelbarrow," Albano suggested.

"We could," Hagop shrugged. Then he thought about it. "It's below us. Men don't go around selling pastries."

They watched in silence as the hundreds of boats covering the marina moved about. Attracted by the fishing boats, seagulls dove madly into the waters, zooming through the sky and dive-bombing. The late October sky now had the soft haze that preceded the arrival of cooler days. A group of soldiers walked by proudly, but judging from suppressed winces of pain and the way they hopped from foot to foot, they were still unused to stiff leather boots. Albano was about to point out how comical they looked when Hagop said, "Why can't we be wearing uniforms too?"

Albano shrugged, "Because we're too young."

Hagop pointed to the French newspaper Albano was holding. "You said you were out of newspapers."

"I want to keep this last one for myself."

"Hide it then. You don't want to be seen reading it, starting today. Besides, you ought to be less in love with France. Everyone in Smyrna seems to want to be French, but there is more pride in being what and who we are."

"What and who are we?"

"Obviously, you and I are not the same," Hagop mused. "You're a Jew. I'm a true Armenian."

"What is a true Armenian?"

"One who only aspires to be Armenian, speak Armenian, eat Armenian, marry Armenian. A true Christian." Saying this, he took out his knife and made a small incision in the burlap bag against which he was leaning. A tickle of sunflower seeds fell into his hands, and he popped a handful in his mouth.

Albano did not like when Hagop did these kinds of things, but he was tired of fighting him about it. Still he pointed out, "Aren't Greeks also Christian?"

Hagop spat out sunflowers shells at a pigeon. "Armenians are the only true Christians," he said.

Albano had heard it all before. Lately, that undertone of nationalistic and religious pride seeped into everything. He shook his head. "Greeks say the same thing. It's nonsense. These days each ethnic group is pulling the blanket toward itself and away from its brothers."

Hagop ignored him. "My father thinks we need to return to our roots, go back to the stricter rules of the Armenian millets. We must remain pure of race. Father says we need to start by forbidding people to intermarry. Then both races lose. The children are forever bastards and communities are weakened."

"Your father says all this?" Albano asked feebly.

"Each ethnic group should separate," Hagop announced. "Those who already have intermarried must not be allowed to have children, and the new cases must be made a punishable offense, with tribunals."

"But … why?"

"So that we can achieve a pure race."

Albano's heart sank. "What is so desirable about a pure race?"

Hagop thought for a moment, "I don't know. I will have to ask Father." He spat sunflower seeds shells on the ground. "I have to go. I'm sick of doing what he wants. I'm a man of action, not destined to live in the basement of a bakery. As soon as I'm old enough to enlist, I will. I'm wasting time here. I want to help my people."

"Soldiers need bread. You can help your people by making it."

Hagop snorted at this preposterous notion, spat out the last of the sunflower seed shells, and left. Albano waited for half an hour before walking across the width of the quayside toward the Levantine quarter.

There, among the white-washed stone walls of beautiful villas, climbing jasmine, fountains, and statues, it was almost possible to forget the war. There were no soldiers in sight, only privilege, and beauty, luxury, peace, and comfort. Between the houses, he glimpsed the private docks where pristine boats bobbed gently. He thought of what it would be like to have a boat that could take him away from shore on a whim. He thought of what it would be like to have enough money to buy safety. With money, he thought, a lot of it, you could even buy invincibility from the war.

He spotted Xandra, who had already started her deliveries. She was dressed entirely in black, with petticoat and layer upon layer of black clothes, an apron, and long sleeves, and she had tied her hair back. When she saw him, she beamed and set down the heavy straw backpack that contained the pastries. Albano approached the bag, which was enormous. "This is far too heavy for you. You will hurt yourself," he said, trying to make it seem effortless for him as he hoisted it up and onto his back.

"Business is good," she said. "We have more orders. Mother says the war makes people crave sweet things."

They set out the way they had now done for over a year: Albano reading the addresses and the items ordered, Xandra retrieving them from the basket, tapping at doors, and handing out the baked goods to servants. If things went smoothly and no one tried to make conversation with her, Xandra and Albano would be able to spend some free time together. Thirty minutes at most. Thirty minutes stolen from a life that conspired to keep them apart. It wasn't enough, but this is what they could have, and they were thankful for it.

Albano was in love with Xandra. And Xandra was in love with Albano. This time was all they had, but it was theirs and theirs alone. Neither mentioned their fear that one day she might be called to another task, that one of her little sisters might be told to take over the route. Neither mentioned Hagop anymore, fiery Hagop, whom they sensed could never be told about their daily meeting in the Levantine quarter, let alone about their love.

When the basket was empty and the deliveries made, they headed toward the beach. As they stepped in the sand, Albano removed his sandals, but Xandra had to remain clothed from head to toe, for modesty. They arrived under their tree, that gnarled thing with wiry black trunk and spotty leaves that had decided to grow in the sand, against nature. The tree provided them with shade and enough privacy so that they could be together mostly unseen and undisturbed. Before them, the Aegean Sea shimmered, and sailboats glided in the distance. They spoke in Armenian, with Xandra gently correcting his diction. They never ran out of things to say because everything either of them said was interesting to the other. In the early days, they had spoken about their families, the war, their apprehensions. But now they were speaking of more dangerous things. The future. A future where a Jewish boy and an Armenian girl could have a life together.

As they spoke, Albano feasted on the sight of her: her large, marvelous eyes and the way she covered her mouth with one hand when she laughed.

"I overheard servants talking," Xandra said. "The Levantines are feeling anxious. Levantine families with French or British ancestry worry they might soon be considered the enemy."

"Most of them have never set foot in Europe."

"It is hard to imagine anyone could be fearful possessing all that wealth."

"I want to be rich one day," Albano said.

"I don't need you to be rich, Albano."

"The rich can marry whoever they want, even in Smyrna."

They watched the sea in silence, dreaming their shared dream. Xandra smiled mysteriously and looked at her hands. "A rich man such as yourself might prefer those fair-haired European ladies with their nice manners."

"I will never marry anyone else but you."

She looked at him eagerly. "If I didn't exist, if you had never met me, would you not rather marry one of those beautiful European ladies, rather than a Jewish peasant girl from a village, even a pretty one?"

Albano smiled and shook his head, sensing the trap. On occasion Xandra needed to hear that she was the only one, the most beautiful one, and that there would never be anyone else in his heart, so he told her so. But later, after they parted and headed back to their respective quarters, Albano had to admit to himself that he was smitten by Europeans. Not by the ladies, but by the entire lifestyle. It was not just about the blissfulness of wealth; it was the idea of being somebody. To be recognized and respected within an upper layer of society was something he would have liked very much. It was clear to him now that the money he and Hagop made, which had seemed like a fortune before, was laughable in comparison to the way the Levantine families lived. As impossible as it may be, these riches, these clothes, these beach houses, and cars, and servants, those were things he wanted now, for himself and for Xandra.

As he made the trek toward the Jewish quarter, remnants of a conversation with Hagop a few days earlier polluted his thoughts. They had been sitting on the dock, facing the water, waiting for the next steamer and Hagop had said, "When the time comes to enlist, we will need to know which side to fight for."

War was on everyone's mind, but he had been making a conscious effort not to think about how it would affect him. "Perhaps war will come and go before we are of age to enlist," Albano had answered. "But I guess we'll have to fight for whatever side the Empire is on."

"The Turks do not speak for the entire Ottoman Empire!" Hagop had snapped, raising his voice. "Why should I enlist into an army that wants to annihilate my people?"

Albano kept his voice low and spoke in Armenian should there be a spy here on the quay. Lately, even he, the foolish optimist, had begun to function in a state of mistrust and suspicion. From the onset of war, everyone could now be a spy. There were so many mingling cultures in Smyrna that it was impossible to be sure where to place your allegiance. "It's hard to tell what is true. The Armenian papers speak of mistreatments by the Turkish nationals, but the Turkish newspapers don't."

"And it is those you choose to believe? They are spreading false rumors that Armenians are on the side of the Russians. Why would we be? We have nothing to gain by that!" Hagop had spoken loudly and in Arabic. He wanted to be heard, to set the record straight. But he switched to speaking Armenian to add, "This is just an excuse to persecute us. The Turks have always hated us."

It would have been easier to agree with his friend, but Albano thought it his duty to reason with him. "Why would they hate you?"

"They hate us because we are Christian."

"The Greeks are Christian. Do the Turks hate them too?"

"The Greeks are powerful and can defend themselves. The Armenians are not."

"You and your family have not suffered," Albano said, his heart in a vise. Hagop, so full of street sense, so able to make light of situations, now held the same incendiary discourse as everyone else. War seemed to galvanize spirits in ways that peace never did. People found reasons to hate when what was needed was calm and reason. Racial and ethnic tensions had always existed. But now it was bubbling up to the surface, and those most strident and hateful awaited, like a pack of wolves concealed in the darkness of the woods, for the moment to pounce.

"Sometimes you want to see nothing and understand nothing, Albano! You want to convince yourself that everyone is good. If you don't believe me, then come to my house. Tonight. There is a meeting. You will hear for yourself."

Albano looked at the many soldiers on the quay and the anxious Europeans who lined up at the dock with their families. He thought of Xandra. A new chill overtook him. "The war cannot come between us, Hagop? It won't, will it?"

Hagop put his arm around Albano's neck. "You and I are brothers. Our bond cannot be broken."

****

The room was filled with men from the Armenian quarter. The grey-skinned Yori, who lived at night by his bakery's furnace, his brother Petrak, close-shaven and fiery-eyed, Emmanuel, the shoemaker and community elder who was permanently hunchbacked from a lifetime bending over his work. There was also Silla, the butcher, who had once killed his own daughter and severed her head. He had spent three months in prison for it and now walked around the quarter like a shining example of fatherly morality. There were ten other men Albano did not know. The men spoke in a low, grave tone, furrowed their brows, and pulled on their pipes. Dinner was served. Albano and Hagop, knowing their place, sat at a corner of the table and did not speak. Ina hurried around, putting down trays of bread, and in the center of the table a large dish of fragrant goat stew with olives. Xandra served wine in every goblet. The men ate as they discussed business, farming, the war, and the price of goods. Albano was careful never to look at Xandra for even a moment.

When the food was eaten, the women served bowls of dates and figs and poured Artsakh into small glasses. It wasn't until they left the room that Yori finally addressed the old man who sat among them and had not said a word thus far. The old man had a terrible time eating. His hands trembled so violently that he could hardly bring his spoon to his lips, which were nearly gray. His entire face was burnt and peeling. His left eye was clouded and opaque. He was emaciated as only the very old, and the very sick, could look. His clothes were too large for him, and his thin neck and wrists protruded from his shirt. It wasn't until he started to speak that Albano realized that the man wasn't old at all. He was so frail and sick that he looked twice his age.

"He came two days ago," Hagop whispered to Albano. "He has done nothing but sleep and eat. At first, when he ate he got terribly sick. He arrived with just shreds of clothing on his body. The community has been taking care of him."

"Tell us what you saw, Toros," Yori told the man with gentle insistence.

Toros gazed up from his plate as if surprised. When he understood what was expected of him, he set down his spoon and with great effort began to speak.

"I saw. I saw everything," he said in a hollowed voice, looking at no one. "Then I escaped. And then I walked. And then I was found." Toros paused as if worn out from the effort of speaking. But perhaps he was hesitating to continue. In the room, there was silence. "It was morning when they came. Men on horses, with guns, screaming and going through the village. There was no warning. It all happened in a few hours.... The Turks come in with their horses and their bayonets, and they tell us we're being relocated. Every Armenian in the village must go. They say we must leave at once or be shot. And then it goes very fast. Everyone is sent into a panic and a frenzy of preparation. We are given less than an hour. All the Armenian families are rounded up. Few can bribe their ways out because we have nothing left, no commerce, no farming, from all the men being gone into the military service."

"But you were still in the village?"

Toros looked up and said fiercely, "When they say that men must report to military service, don't go. We think now that this is how they weakened the village. They tell the men they have to report to military service, and they wait for all the men to be gone to go after the women and old people." He pointed to his face. "I am blind in one eye, so I stayed back in the village when all the men left."

Yori asked, "They said that the Armenian presence creates unrest with Turkish villagers. Was it true in your village?"

Toros shrugged, disgusted. "There was no unrest. We have been living side by side with the Turks, and there was no more unrest now than before." He lifted his glass of wine with a trembling hand and drank avidly, red liquid coming down his chin. And then he began again, as if in a trance. "Fear is in our heart as we leave the village in silence. There is only the cries of children and the shouting of soldiers. Fear is in our heart but also hope. We hope that they are telling the truth. The women hope that they are taking us somewhere where they will be reunited with the men. I feel hopeful because we're all together in a group of one hundred people, and it is reassuring. The Turks order us to bring nothing but what we can carry. So the women pack up only what we can lift. Many have babies in their arms. The children old enough to walk must walk. The old people too old to walk must walk. Some are taken from their beds, and they must walk too, and those who can't walk, we have to carry. As we leave the village, we feel terrible sadness and disbelief that we are being uprooted from our ancestral homeland. The other villagers, the Jews, the Greeks, the Muslims, watch us leave. Some spit and throw stones at us. Others weep for us. We weep too. But deep down, we think we will come back.

"As we walk inland, we pass through many other villages. Here too the Armenian families are made to leave their homes. Our group grows. We wonder where they will take us. Sometimes we see a familiar face from a nearby village, and this brings us some warmth and courage, to be reunited. We act brave, and we try not to upset the children who already are tired and hungry. So, the group is quite large now, perhaps five hundred of us. And the men on horseback are all around us like we are a herd of cattle. We've been walking for hours. Those who slow down or try to rest are threatened by the Turks on horses. And so, adults carry the young ones, the healthy carry the sick, and we go on.

"Later there are many thousands of us walking in silence but for the cries of children. When night comes, we sleep on the dirt without making any fire; anyway, there is no food to cook. Children are asking for food and water, but there is none.

"In the morning, we wake up to the smell of excrement. Everyone asks where the camp is. The Turks now take to whipping us when we ask questions. Now some of us notice that the Turks, unlike us, have food in carts pulled by horses. They have food and water for days, but only for themselves. We are afraid of what this means. There are rumors that we are being taken to Mesopotamia or Syria, but that is much too far away to be believable.

"By mid-day, no encampment has appeared. It is hot, and we are very thirsty. We pass a river. We all rush to collect water into our gourds. A few men throw themselves into the river and begin to swim away. That's when the Turks start shooting. People stop jumping in the water. We watch the bodies of the men float down the river, but now we also see other bodies, coming from upstream. Now we know that more of this is happening upstream to others, and we are terrified.

"That night is bad. We hear the wails of women who are being raped, but we can't do anything without risking being shot, and so we hold the children closer. In the morning, we wake up to see that several have found a way to run away from the group. But those who have children or old people in their care have stayed. Their absence enrages the guards, and now they watch us even more. We realize that the chance to escape is gone. Now there is only desert ahead of us and desert behind us, and those who are seen trying to escape are gunned down. I know that I missed my chance to run, and I hope for another river.

"On the third day, no one has any food and the water collected at the river is gone from our gourds.

"We keep going. When we've been walking for four days, people start to collapse from dehydration. We witness with terrible sadness when one of us falls. Some people are simply too old, too sick, or too young to survive several days of walking in the hot sun with hardly any water or food. We are not allowed to bury the dead. We are threatened with guns and bayonets if we stop. So we leave the bodies behind, and people weep. As we walk past them, we grab rocks, and everyone puts one rock upon the dead bodies, to try to show respect for them as much as we can.

"We are heading deeper into the desert. There are no more rivers. We see a long black line on the horizon. People. At first, we're excited. We think it is the camp. We are about to rest. We will have food and water. But we get closer, and soon we suspect the terrible truth: these are hundreds of thousands of villagers from across Anatolia. This is not a camp: these people are walking just like we are, and we're about to join their ranks. When we meet them, we finally understand everything.

"They are covered in sand and dirt. Sand inside their mouths. Flies all over, and filth. These people are walking skeletons without any light left in their sunken eyes. They don't speak. Many in their group have also died; all the old people are gone. What is left are the few men, the older children, and the mothers. The mothers refuse to give up. They continue going until the last one of her children dies, which is usually the babies because they are fed until their mothers' last drop of milk or their last breath. There is a mother who carries two children in her arms. They are both dead and covered in flies, but she will not let go of them. When the woman falls to her knees, the guards do nothing. I see that the mother has set her babies on the dirt and has covered them with her body. They don't shoot her. They are saving their bullets. There is no need to shoot her because she will die anyway here in the desert as soon as the group has moved on.

"That is the purpose of the walk. There is no relocation. There is no camp. They are just walking and starving us until we all die. And so, we continue walking. The guards aren't as vigilant, only patient. They know that even if we escape, we cannot go back on our tracks, it is too far, and we are all so weak.

"One morning, I don't know how long we have walked, I awaken, and the children aren't crying anymore. All of them have died. And I tell myself it is better to be killed than this. I decide that I will not continue. Before that, I felt a responsibility to stay with the group, but not now that the children are dead. Now I decide I will run away. And if they shoot me, they shoot me. I know that they want my death anyway, and I decide to choose how I will die.

"The guards need water for themselves, and so they steer the group along a river. When we get to the river, thousands of us plunge. They are shooting, and many are killed. But I am not shot. I float with whatever strength I have left. I don't know how long I float, maybe a day. As I float down the river, I think of the mothers with their babies. Then I open my eyes, and it is days later. I am inside a house, in a bed. I'm in a village. People have found me and rescued me."

"So there were still Armenians in some of the villages?" Emmanuel the shoemaker asked the man.

Toros shook his head in disbelief. "I woke up in a Muslim house. They found me and rescued me. And they knew I was Armenian. They helped me at great risk to themselves." The men in the room let this information sink in, drawing on their pipes. "When I could walk again I set out and found my way to Smyrna," Toros concluded.

"Do you think anyone made it to Mesopotamia?" Petrak asked.

"I want to believe that some did," Toros said. "I want to believe that there is a camp in Mesopotamia or elsewhere. But everything I wanted to believe didn't come true. Until their last breath, the people from our village hoped that God would take care of us. Even as we were made to step over the bodies of our family members, we continued praying to God not to forget us."

"Could you have rebelled earlier on?" Silla asked, embarrassed by the insinuation that they were in any way responsible for their fate. But he was right to ask. It was important to know.

"Without weapons?" Toros said, visibly exhausted by the effort of reliving the events. "How can unarmed women and children and the elderly rebel? Most of the men were away at military service."

"What about all the men in military service?" Petrak asked. "Where are they?"

Toros only shook his head to signify that he didn't know.

Petrak exclaimed, "There is no military service for us! It is a ploy to round up Armenian men without raising suspicion. Once we report to service and arrive in camps, they kill us."

"How can you be sure?" Yori asked.

"They walk the helpless women and children to their death," Emmanuel the Shoemaker said, "and you think they are keeping the men alive?"

Silla said, "The villagers were caught by surprise. If they had known the truth like we do, they would have fought. They believed they had a better chance of surviving if they went along. But they did not know of the plan until they were too weak to revolt. Once they understood the plan, it was too late; there was little they could do."

"Still, the Turks had horses and weapons," Petrak said.

"But the villagers had the greater number," Silla insisted. "They could have attacked them with rocks. They could have overtaken them."

"What can we do to prepare?" Emmanuel mumbled as though to himself.

"Believe nothing they say," Petrak said. "When they tell us to turn in our weapons, give them some, and hide the rest. When they say to report to military service, hide in the mountains. When they come to take our women and children, attack."

"Governor Rami Bey won't let any of this happen to the citizens of Smyrna. We're not like those hidden from sight in remote villages—"

"Rami Bey could easily be overthrown, and then we have no defender," Petrak interrupted.

Yori shook his head. "This is a big city. All of Europe has political or business interests here. There is the Red Cross. There are ships of every European country moored in the bay, and the eyes and ears of every government's representatives are on us. They would not let any of this happen here because...." But no one was listening to him.

Silla turned to Petrak and said, "We should take the offensive."

Emmanuel spoke. "What we must do is watch for the signs when they start to imprison or kill our leaders, draft the young men, tell us to hand in our weapons because we're allegedly a threat ... those are all the signs we should watch for. So far, nothing of the sort has taken place here."

"What do you think your family will do?" Albano asked Hagop later on when they had walked to the edge of the Armenian quarter. "Will you hide as Toros said to do? Will you wait? Will you fight?"

"You Jews have it good," Hagop said. "You make alliances; you see where the wind is blowing. Armenians aren't like that. It's not so easy for us. We have pride. We won't just hide. We want revenge for our people."

"The Jews are worried too," Albano said.

Hagop scoffed at the thought. "What is it the Jews ever have to worry about?"

"We are all the same, Hagop. We all have to decide the best course of action to survive."

"All the same, you say? How about the Turks? When they kill our children and rape our women? Are they like us?"

"There are monsters among them, it's true. But also, righteous people, like the Muslims who rescued Toros."

Hagop laughed an angry laugh. "One good Muslim out of a thousand and you think that Muslims and Armenians are the same?"

Albano wanted to mention the butcher and what he had done to his daughter. "Men have a bestial nature. Jews, Muslims, Christians, it does not matter. It is within some of us more than others. As is goodness."

In the months that followed, calm and reason did not prevail. War, which unified in patriotism countries such as Germany, Italy, and France, seemed to tear apart the Empire. The sense of nationalism within the various groups turned from pride to zeal. Religious and ethnic strife between people who had coexisted for centuries reawakened inexplicably over one rumor, one newspaper headline, or one comment from a neighbor of a different ethnicity. It was as though sleepy little sparks of hatred spontaneously ignited everywhere. How long before those sparks turned into uncontrollable blazes?

Albano needed to know what to think of the Armenian man's account. Had he told the truth or was he a crazy man? He wanted to ask Uncle Joshua what he thought, but he did not have the kind of relationship with his uncle in which he felt safe to ask questions.

One morning when he came back from the quay and entered his uncle and aunt's house, a great surprise greeted him. Uncle Moshe was sitting at the kitchen table.

"Uncle Moshe! You are here? No one said you were coming."

"Your Uncle Moshe surprised us all," Uncle Joshua said. He tried to keep his tone light, but his face was tense.

Aunt Sadie was pacing the room, resentful. "I had no time to prepare the house."

Uncle Moshe's mustache was shaved off, and his ample girth ampler than it had been two years before. "I refuse to believe this young man is my child nephew. Impossible!" he said in his booming voice as he squeezed Albano in his arms.

"It is truly me, Uncle Moshe!" Albano laughed. "Are you here to sell rugs? How long will you stay?"

Uncle Moshe looked him up and down and, away from Uncle Joshua's and Aunt Sadie's earshot, said, "I have seen rabbinical students before, and they do not usually look this healthy. The ones I have seen have glabrous, ashen faces and the delicate physiques of those whose sole physical effort is to squint at the Torah." Because of his daily treks from the Jewish quarter to the quay and the heavy lifting of newspapers and pastry baskets, Albano looked healthy indeed. Uncle Moshe raised a suspicious eyebrow. "And you obviously carry the Torah up and down Mount Pagus as well, what with those muscles?" Albano could not suppress a smile.

All, including Cousins Zev and Cousin Uri, sat down for dinner. They learned that Uncle Moshe was only here for a few days to settle some business. He was on his way to Chile and Argentina where he would, as he put it, wait out the war.

"When the war is over, I will return to France and try to obtain citizenship," he said.

"Why would you want to become French, Uncle Moshe?" Cousin Zev asked.

"My nephew, the Ottoman Empire is dying. The millets are deteriorating. The Empire is at risk of becoming a patchwork of disparate countries, and who knows how favorable the area will become to Jews." He turned to Uncle Joshua. "Perhaps you should consider a change of life sometime soon, Brother."

Uncle Joshua sighed. "My business is here. My life is here. At my age, to start over—"

"And find ourselves surrounded with people of your sort?" Aunt Sadie interrupted shrilly. "The problem with you, Moshe, is that you have no attachments. We have a community here; people respect us."

"Well, you can stay here if you wish, and your husband can move to France," Uncle Moshe mused. Aunt Sadie gave Uncle Moshe a murderous look.

"But why France?" Uncle Joshua asked.

"France values artists, intellectuals. There is an openness of minds," he remarked and paused. "People with my … predisposition are left alone for the most part."

"What predisposition is that, Uncle Moshe?" Albano asked.

Uncle Moshe opened his mouth to answer, but an uneasy exchange of glances between Uncle Joshua and Aunt Sadie silenced him. "You must visit someday, Albano. I have many friends in Paris I'd love you to meet." Aunt Sadie scoffed at this and stomped out of the room.

Later, during dinner, the men all agreed that no matter the unrest throughout the Empire, for now, the city was as racially eclectic, energetic, and prosperous as ever. "To imagine Smyrna any other way is impossible," Uncle Joshua said.

Albano, who had been sitting nearby and missed not a beat of the conversation, found the courage to ask his uncles the question that had been torturing him. "Is it true?" he asked, "what is said about the Armenians who are outside Smyrna? That terrible things are happening to them?"

"Why does it matter to you, dear boy?" Uncle Moshe asked.

"I have an Armenian friend now."

Uncle Joshua nodded, unconcerned. "It is probably true." To which he added, "But not in Smyrna,"

"Why not, Uncle?"

"Because our city holds a privileged place in the heart of everyone, including the Turks. Smyrna is a city destined for the enjoyment of life, for trade, a city where people take pleasure in the diversity of cultures."

"I'm afraid that you are naïve about Smyrna, my dear brother," Uncle Moshe said. "There are persecutions against Armenians, it is true, and they are widespread. It is only a matter of time before it reaches this city." He turned to Albano. "You should tell your friend to leave."

Albano felt a terrible chill. "But where should he go?"

"Anywhere outside the Empire."

"But Uncle Moshe, war is everywhere."

"Then your friend is out of luck," Uncle Joshua said.

Uncle Moshe patted Albano on the head. "At the first hint of racial persecutions, there are three things a man can do: fight, run, or hide. It seems that when outnumbered, one would be mad to attempt the first. So I say, run."

"Hide! Hide is better," Uncle Joshua said.

"You don't think it cowardly to run or hide, Uncle Moshe?" Cousin Zev asked.

"For your enemy to win, he must eliminate you. For you to win, you must refuse to be eliminated by any means at your disposal. If fighting decreases your chance of survival and running and hiding increases them, it is mathematical."

"But what of honor?" Cousin Zev pressed.

Uncle Moshe dismissed this with a raised hand. "Warmongers invented the notion of honor and cowardice so that they can put weapons in men's hands and have them do their bidding. It is quite a clever scheme, truly."

"We are Jewish, so we are safe," Uncle Joshua said peremptorily, as though this had been the sole thought on his mind. "When we Jews have a country to call our own, then we'll worry about it."

"I disagree, Uncle Joshua," Uncle Moshe said. "Jews should always worry." To Albano, he said, "Keep your ears and eyes on alert. When people start nationalistic rhetoric, all a Jew needs to hear is the drumbeat of anti-Semitism. It was always the world's favorite form of xenophobia. Anti-Semitism has been developed and perfected over thousands of years."

"What would happen to the millets if there was a dissolution of the Empire?" Albano asked. "Would the Jews be forced to go into exile the way it was after the Spanish Queen chased us away?"

"That is the bad thing about having no land to claim as our own," Uncle Joshua noted somberly.

"If the Ottoman Empire were to decide to turn against its Jews, then we would go elsewhere. As Jews have done for centuries before." Uncle Moshe said gravely. "It has not been pleasant, but it has made us who we are."

"But you said it yourself, Jews have enemies everywhere," Uncle Joshua pointed out.

"We also have settled everywhere, and so we count many friends at every far corner of the earth. In some countries, Jews have even shaped policies. That is why I choose France. It's a country where, since the Dreyfus affair, anti-Semitism is clearly unfashionable."

"Ha! Imagine that," Uncle Joshua said. "All the Jews of the Ottoman Empire taking refuge in France. Anti-Semitism wouldn't be out of fashion for long."

****

Four years later, in 1918, the Great War ended, and as Uncle Moshe predicted, the Ottoman Empire, which had been on the losing side, was partitioned, cut into chunks like a cake. And while Europe got busy rebuilding itself, a new war started in the region, this time between Greece and the Turkish National Movement. Smyrna, placed under Greek control, was for the moment protected.

Albano and Hagop were sixteen years old. As if by magic, their bodies now manifested hair and muscles, and they had grown to the size of men. Hagop was taller than Albano by a head, and he had bulk. Albano was still rail thin, no matter how many Armenian pastries he clandestinely ingested. Yet it was Albano who provoked the admiration of women, whether this was something he wished for or not. Hagop used to find that endlessly funny, but now there was resentment in his voice when he said that Albano was too handsome a friend and that he was hurting his own chances with women.

Hagop didn't know that Albano had no interest in stealing women away from him or anyone. His heart, mind, and blood were so thoroughly occupied by thoughts of Xandra it excluded thoughts of anyone else.

Now that they looked like men and had the steady income from the sale of newspapers, they no longer sat on a rock near the dock, but at the terraces of cafés. That morning, Albano and Hagop were sipping the bitter Italian espressos they had acquired a taste for as they read the headlines of newspapers. The more sensational the headlines, the better the sales for the day. Albano loved that moment in the early morning, reading the paper, sitting at a café terrace. It made him feel cosmopolitan and sophisticated, like the European men around them, or so he hoped. He looked across the pier. Smyrna was back to looking very much the same as it had before the war, with Europeans promptly returning to their commerce and interests in Asia Minor. But something in the mood had changed. The men in uniforms no longer displayed any gaiety unless they were drunk. Those who had returned from the war in one piece had come back humiliated. Their faces were hard, their eyes those of killers. The mistrust between ethnic groups was at a high, each suspecting his neighbor of being a spy, a turncoat, a coward, a fomenter, or a crook.

Hagop, who had been reading quietly across the table from Albano, let out a roar of frustration and crumpled the Turkish newspaper he was reading. "Armenians are not betraying the Empire!" he cried out. Across the terrace, men peered at him from above their opened newspapers.

"Who is betraying who?" Albano said softly, hoping that Hagop would mirror his tone.

"It says it, right here," Hagop said, tapping the printed words violently with his finger. "It says that the Armenians plan to join the Russian forces. Lies! All lies! Just another scheme to unleash the fury of the Turks."

Albano shifted uneasily in his chair. He looked around. Hagop needed to be careful. Why did he refuse to be careful? "None of that has reached Smyrna," he said.

"Smyrna? Who thinks of Smyrna? It is happening all over," Hagop exclaimed. "They arrive in Armenian stores demanding to collect war contributions, and when the merchants refuse, they loot and set the shop on fire!" Hagop was angrier these days. His fiery temperament could barely be contained. He was angry with this father, angry with his community, which he accused of being too passive, angry with the Turks, the Greeks, and the Jews. "And what about the mass deportations of Armenians away from the coast?" Hagop continued. "How can you speak of Smyrna alone when we know that the entire populations of villages are being displaced, or worse." He was referring to the persistent rumors of Armenians being marched to their certain death under the guise of relocation. The story that Toros had told them years ago had been echoed by many more witnesses and was impossible to ignore. Yet such inhuman cruelty toward civilian population was not something Albano wanted to imagine possible.

That afternoon, Albano, as he had continued to do in secret from Hagop for years now, walked to the Levantine quarter to help Xandra with her baskets. The risks of doing this were something he and Xandra never discussed. Perhaps they both had managed to convince themselves that they were doing nothing wrong. But Albano knew better. He knew the contents of his thoughts, which were not innocent thoughts, far from it. Now the way he looked at Xandra was hungrier, more desperate, and nothing felt simple anymore. It was no longer enough to see her or speak to her. He urgently wanted to touch her, and kiss her, and hold her in his arms, but there was no place where this could happen. Eyes were everywhere and a boy and a girl, even from the same ethnicity, especially these days, could get into great trouble being seen as much as holding hands in public. Already this morning, he had twice been stopped for identity checks. Once, Greek soldiers had asked to see his papers. Another time, he was asked to provide proof of residence by Turkish policemen. The racial tension was tremendous, and uniformed men needed no excuse to stop those they wanted to harass. The uniforms themselves appeared to give them license to misbehave as they wished, abusing their power, taking bribes, or threatening populations the instant their superiors had their backs turned. There was so much of this going on that to take on cases of such misdeeds one by one was impossible. No tribunal, civilian or military, had that kind of manpower. Each time he saw Xandra, Albano tried to make her feel safe and at peace. But in truth, time felt as though it was closing in on them. Travel routes out of the country were cut. There was nowhere to go unless by boat, and even that was not safe. In the last few months, to make matters worse, Xandra's parents had begun to discuss whom she should marry. She was, after all, sixteen. With all this on their minds, Albano was surprised to find Xandra happy. He had to wait until the end of their delivery route to find out why. As soon as the two were alone on the beach, she said, "I know what I will do so that they don't marry me!"

"What is it?"

"Someone needs to take care of my parents in old age. I will volunteer to remain unmarried. Mother loves me best. If she agrees, then we could convince my father."

Albano considered this. "They will want to marry you first, not only because you're the oldest, but because you're the most beautiful one."

She grew pale. "So, this is what gets in the way of my happiness?" she asked. "Beauty? If it didn't mean that you would stop loving me, then I would make it so that I am no longer beautiful."

"That is impossible. That cannot be changed."

"There are ways," she said, her teeth clenched. "I could scar myself, cut off my hair. I could break my front teeth."

Her intensity upset him so that he decided to laugh it off. "Oh, that would never work. Even with no teeth, no hair, and missing a leg, you would still be the most beautiful girl in all of Smyrna."

"You would not want me either if I would be ugly and disfigured." She added sadly, "But I can't bear being married to anyone if I can't be with you."

"Men are being drafted every day. People might not think of marrying their daughters to men who might not return. That is what you should tell your family to gain time."

"If men are being drafted, then you could be as well, as soon as next year when you turn of age." She tore at the skin around her fingernails with her teeth. Lately, her hands had become the battle zone of her anxiety. "There is nothing Hagop wants more than to fight."

"Hagop has not been the same," Albano said. "You think he suspects something about us?"

Her back straightened and, looking out at the sea, she said, "If Hagop suspected something about us, he would have long ago killed me with his bare hands."

Albano felt the hair on his skin rise on end. "You cannot mean that."

She shook her head. "My brother is furious at everything and everyone. All he talks about is enlisting, and he would if my father didn't threaten him with bodily harm. Hagop feels powerless about what is happening to our people. We all do. He is angry. And he'll never show if he is afraid or sad. That is his way."

"I had a dream about you," Albano said soothingly. "In my dream, you walked in through a front door with marble columns on each side, and everywhere there was the smell of jasmine and roses. A servant took your shoes and washed your hands. All around, there were beautiful blooming trees, and fountains, and rugs. You were dressed in lace, and silver, and pearls. Servants stood, waiting for your command, one in every room. You sat, and they brought you mint tea and rose-flower flavored pastries." Albano did not mention that it was a daydream more than a dream, that he was in it, and that he had imagined much more afterward.

Xandra, forgetting for a moment about being seen, placed her palm on his cheek and sighed, "Albano, my dreamer. To live this kind of life you would have to be born into it."

Albano shook his head adamantly. "That is not true. There are men who started without a name and family fortune who now live in abundance."

She laughed, "Crooks you mean?"

"My Uncle Moshe was born right here in Smyrna. But he took his chances, traveled the world, and became a rug merchant."

"Your uncle is an exception."

"Xandra, I will do this. I too can be an exception! And you will be my exceptional bride."

Xandra smiled her beautiful smile. "I do not want a castle, or lace and pearls. But I do want to be your bride." Then she added somberly, "But people here will never let us marry. Not for the next hundred years. Things have been the way they are for centuries, and they cannot change."

"After the war, when the sea roads reopen, we could sail to Europe. I think that if I were to ask my uncle, he would let me work for him in France. We would tell no one that I am Jewish and you are not. In fact, my uncle says that no one would ask."

She looked at him. This was not a vision or a dream: this was a plan. This was a possibility. "The two of us, in Paris?" she murmured.

"I can speak Armenian nearly without an accent. We can both say that we're Armenians."

"Let's be Jewish then! It is much safer than being Armenian." She set her hand between them so that her baby finger touched his. Together they watched the sea and the sails of the boats heading, they imagined, toward the beautiful architecture of Paris, the wide boulevards, the many cars, the shops and restaurants, which they imagined as a larger, more magnificent version of Smyrna.

Later that evening Albano walked up to the Armenian quarter, nervous as he was every time he was invited into Hagop and Xandra's house. Their mother, Ina, was a kind woman who did not mind a Jew sharing their food and had taken a liking to him. The three little sisters, Clara, Agda, and Octavia, worshiped him, and the new baby, Tessa, loved pulling on his tassels. Yori wasn't quite as welcoming. He had not shown Albano antipathy, but neither had he quite acknowledged his existence. Albano hoped that if he maintained model behavior and made sure not to look conspicuously Jewish, perhaps one day Yori would, if not warm up to him, at least not act as though he did not exist. One day, Albano would be rich. That day, he would come to Yori and offer him a gold watch like the ones he had seen in the window of the French department store Au Bon Marché over on Frank Street. He would wear a suit and ask him for Xandra's hand in marriage, and Yori would remember that this was the same boy his son trusted, and his wife liked, and he would say yes.

The Armenian community in Smyrna scrambled to secure political allies, but its fate was the last thing on everyone's mind. The Turkish-Greco war raged, rapidly transforming Asia Minor into a battlefield. Tales of horrifying acts perpetrated against Armenians continued to come from every corner of the Empire. But there were also accounts of atrocities against Muslim civilian communities, against Greeks, against Jews. All these terrible things appeared to stop at Smyrna's door, and so they did not see it happen. Was any of this true? The accounts of decimated villages, of mass killings, of beheadings, of rape and torture often conflicted. You would hear the same story from every corner of the city, only depending on who spoke, it had happened to a Muslim community, or a Greek one, or an Armenian one. This inflamed people's spirits and cemented the bitter chasm between the millets.

For the moment, Smyrna remained under Greek control, and in the city reigned a semblance of peace, or rather the sense that everyone was holding their breath. On Smyrna's quay, commerce went on. The sky was still piercingly blue. Restaurants and cafés were once again full of Europeans. On the sea, the same sailboats, pushed by clement winds, glided on the horizon by the hundreds. But what would happen to the non-Muslims if the Turks won the war and the Greeks lost control of the city? No one felt secure. Nothing seemed permanent. Everyone was afraid.

Over the course of the following months, there was an increase of questionings and searches by the Turkish police in the Armenian quarter. And then, in the last weeks, there had been arrests. A few men were accused of plotting a conspiracy. What could Albano possibly say to Xandra now? How could he assure her that her father and Hagop would be safe?

He could not. So he began to prepare.

He did not tell Hagop of his plan. If he did, Hagop might refuse, and if he refused, the way Hagop was these days, thickheaded and angry, he would never go back on his decision. Albano did not tell Xandra either, in part because he thought this would alarm her, and in part because there was no guarantee any of it would work.

Each day, Albano gathered supplies, dried fruit, blankets, firewood, candles, mats, dried meat, and everything he could think of, and he brought everything to his cave. This became the focus of his days, and he no longer even had the pretense of continuing his rabbinical studies, Kohanim or not. It did not matter that Aunt Sadie threatened him, screamed at him, and even beat him at times. In the morning, he would leave. If she didn't want to feed him, he had enough money to feed himself.

Most days he spent in Smyrna. Most nights he spent in the cave, preparing it for Hagop, Xandra, and their family. By now, Uncle Joshua and Aunt Sadie had renounced trying to influence how their sons occupied their time, let alone what Albano did. Cousin Zev was married now and lived with his wife just a few streets away. Cousin Uri had become a shoemaker apprentice and was engaged to the butcher's daughter. As for Albano, they understood that notions of rabbinical studies had long been abandoned and that he preferred to live alone in some cave up on Mount Pagus. People in the Jewish quarter had even taken to calling him the troglodyte.

Through 1919, Xandra's face betrayed her exhaustion and the pressure her family was under. She was pale and too thin in a way that broke Albano's heart. Even so, and even as he prepared in secret, Albano did not seriously believe a day would come when he would have to put his plan into action. And then, in May 1920, that day came.

The instant he saw Xandra arrive at their usual spot in the Levantine quarter, he knew that something bad had happened. "They arrested Emmanuel and his son," she said, her face pale with anguish but her voice steady. "The police came in, and there was nothing they could do."

Albano was stunned by this news. "How is an old shoemaker a risk to them?" he said.

Xandra shook her head. "He has done nothing. Nothing at all!"

"They must see him as a leader of the community," Albano said. "That is what my uncles spoke about. They silence those at risk of speaking their mind first."

"Albano! If that is the case, my father is next on their list."

"You must talk to him. Tell him that perhaps now is the time to hide."

"He doesn't take advice from women, especially not a daughter. And besides, all my father ever wants to do is wake up, and make his bread. You could never tell him to leave his bakery. He is as stubborn as my brother."

Absorbed in their conversation, Albano and Xandra did not see a shadow approaching behind them. When they, at last, noticed him, Hagop was standing a few feet from them, arms crossed over his chest, jaw clenched. "Albano, what are you doing here?" he said icily. His eyes were bloodshot, his skin greenish like a man about to get sick. Albano and Xandra had just been caught speaking to each other, standing inches from each other. The air turned thick. Redness came to Albano's cheeks, and Xandra's face drained of life. They looked at Hagop, finding nothing to say. "Explain to me why you are holding my sister's basket," Hagop said, each of his words pronounced like a threat.

Albano inhaled and said, "I was just in the neighborhood, and I saw Xandra … and I thought I should help her with her heavy load … and—"

Xandra interrupted in a tiny voice. "Hagop, why are you here?"

Hagop's eyes filled with furious tears. "They arrested Father!" he shouted. Albano heard Xandra's quick intake of breath and felt his body drain of strength. "They had a gun to his chest!" Hagop raged. "And not just Father. They arrested about thirty men, Petrak, and Tadeos, and Silla, and Emanuel! They arrested them all!" He lowered his face, his mouth distorted into something that resembled crying, but he stopped himself. "I was just getting home, and I saw them in the distance, so I ran away. They might have taken me too." He lifted his face and looked at Xandra. "This is why I came to get you!" Then with a rage that seemed directed at them, as though they, somehow, were the cause of all this he asked, "What am I supposed to do now?"

Xandra was crying softly, but her voice was steady when she said, "You can't return there."

"I am not a coward!"

"Mother needs you not to be imprisoned. If Father is in jail, it makes you the man of the house. You cannot get arrested. I will go home to Mother while you go into hiding."

"Nowhere is safe, idiot woman," Hagop spat. "They are searching the houses."

"Here is what we need to do, please, Albano," Xandra said. She did not seem like a scared young girl suddenly but like a woman able to think with a cool head. "Beg your aunt and uncle to hide Hagop in the Jewish quarter. The Turks won't be looking for Armenians there."

"I don't belong with Jews!" Hagop roared.

"I will help you," Albano said.

Hagop looked at him with distrust and growled. "Help me? Like you are helping my sister?"

****

This was how Hagop came to live in Albano's cave.

In Smyrna, Armenian men continued to be arrested under pretexts ranging from unpaid taxes to suspicion of treason. Many of the younger men, those most at risk of being sent to labor camps, found their way into hiding. Only the older men were left in the Armenian quarter to haul, make, or sell merchandise. Without supplies and deprived of the men's skills, stores closed one by one. In short succession, Armenian commerce froze, services became paralyzed, finances sank into limbo, and the unprotected women and children became vulnerable to assaults, and soon to hunger. Without Yori to bake goods, and because he had never revealed his techniques to his wife and daughters, there were no bread, cakes, or pastries to sell. Hagop, Xandra, their mother, and four little sisters would soon depend on the money Albano and Hagop had saved up, which was kept safely inside the cave in two leather satchels.

Through winter and spring, Xandra made the long trek up Mount Pagus to bring Hagop the clothes she had washed for him the day before and whatever food she had managed to buy with the money they gave her. She brought with her news of the family and the community. Each day, she would return with a few coins, hidden in the hem of her skirt, which Hagop dispensed parsimoniously, telling her how their mother was to spend it. Yori remained in prison. However, unlike so many of the men, he had not been sent to work camp. They speculated that it was because they needed his baking skills at the prison. Albano continued to sell newspapers in the morning and then rushed back to the cave, in part to distract Hagop, but mostly to keep an eye on him. Confinement did not suit Hagop. He was mad with boredom and frustration. His body was weakened by inactivity, his thoughts circular. During the day, he remained hidden in the cave, pacing and throwing rocks into the stream. At night, when the moon was high, he walked outside, never venturing far from the cave, and threw more rocks. Much of the time he slept, and when he did not sleep, he lamented and raged. One day, after many months of this, Albano was horrified to find Hagop sitting outside the cave in broad daylight. "I need to do something!" Hagop said, seething. "Anything is better than this. Death is better than this!"

They went inside the cave, and Albano rekindled the fire that Hagop had let die. The sun was high, and it was the time of the day when a bit of the sun radiated through the crack between the boulders above, brightening the cave in a way that made the rocks shimmer. This was the most beautiful time of the day inside the cave, but Hagop was immune to the beauty of the cave. The fire grew, basking their skin in a warm orange hue and turning the rough walls to gold. "If you go out during the day, you might reveal yourself and our cave," Albano reminded him softly.

"It will be summer soon. How long can I stay here without losing my mind?"

"If you are seen, someone might report you. Your mother told the police that you had left the country. They would know that she lied. You would put her and yourself at risk."

Hagop crouched and poked at the fire with a stick. Sparks flew. "This mountain is more barren than the moon," he said angrily. "Who will report me? Coyotes? Owls? And why do you come every day? Am I a sick man on his deathbed?"

"I'm only trying to see how you are doing."

"I am a man in jail. I'm every bit as jailed as my father is. This is not freedom you have given me. It is captivity! And you are my jailor."

"But it is better than risking labor camp."

"But I want labor! I need labor. I'm made for action, not for cowering under a rock."

Albano shook his head. This was the same conversation they had every day, with Hagop arguing with him until Albano managed to coax him into staying. Until the next day, when it all started again. "People are not coming back from those camps," he said.

"You and Xandra are making me mad with your help and your kindness. You want to help me? Find me a weapon. Then I would go at night to the jail and I would free the men."

Albano knew better than to tell him that this was madness. With Hagop these days, it was better to say nothing. On the other hand, Albano could see that Hagop never turned his threats to action. He could have left the cave a hundred times, he could have snuck out to the Armenian quarter or anywhere he wished at night, but he had not. Albano took a folded newspaper out of his satchel. "Look, I have a French newspaper left. If you want, I can translate it for you."

Hagop peered at the newspaper with distrust. "Lies. Every written word is a lie, and you are the greatest fool of them all for reading them. And a French newspaper, of course. You and my sister, enamored with France. A couple of fools." Hagop's face hardened. "We need to speak about Xandra," he said, looking at him with suspicious eyes. Albano, disconcerted, poked at the fire. "I've been observing her when she comes here," Hagop continued, "and I have come to a decision." He paused, scrutinizing Albano's face. He got up and began pacing as Albano sat on the mat. "She has too much freedom now that there is no man to watch out for her."

"I will watch out for your whole family," Albano said tentatively.

Hagop was standing behind him, and he felt his stare on the back of his neck. "Tell me, what are my worthless sisters doing these days?"

"They go to school, still. The baby stays with your mother. She and Xandra go to the jail every day with the other women and beg for news of your father. Xandra works very hard, wakes before dawn. She and your mother bake, the best they can to try to make a few sales. You must reconsider how much money you give them. It is not quite enough to make do."

Hagop was not listening. "Men must be looking at Xandra. She needs to marry."

Albano swallowed. Why did he have the impression that Hagop was looking for his reaction? "She is young still," he said, trying to sound unconcerned. He needed to look Hagop in the eyes now. He inhaled, stood up, and faced him.

Hagop had a crooked smile. "But she is not too young for you, heh?"

Albano's mouth went dry. "For me?"

Hagop laughed. "I know you too well. I've seen the way you look at her," he said. "Yes, I know, she is beautiful. And this is why she needs a husband and not a moment too soon. I will choose to whom she should be married. Now that Father is imprisoned, the duty falls to me." He watched Albano's face and added, "And you shall help me look for a suitable husband for her."

Albano felt a sense of dread. Why was Hagop saying all those things now? "Most of the men are gone," he said.

"Not the old ones," Hagop said with a smirk.

"You want Xandra to marry an old man?"

Hagop shrugged, "If that's all that's left. Better an old Armenian than a young Greek." Hagop thought about this and mumbled to himself, "A Greek would be a terrible thing."

Albano decided to try his chance. "You are not worried that a Muslim might court her?" He swallowed and added, "Or a Jew?"

"Even my daft sister wouldn't consider a marriage so far below her," Hagop said with savagery, a bit of spit coming from his mouth. "The point is, I need to safeguard her honor, and the longer we wait, the more we take risks. What if she loses her honor? What use would she be to us then, when no man will marry her? I want you to speak to my mother and ask her to make a list of the men. Bring me the list tomorrow and I will make my choice."

Albano went to the entrance of the cave. He crawled outside to catch his breath and hide his emotion from Hagop. Outside, he leaned against a rock, peering at the horizon. All his thoughts were in a jumble. He felt a sense of mounting panic. Hagop was his friend, and oftentimes he made sense. He was in fact a very smart person. Perhaps he did mean this, in which case Albano could try to talk him out of it. But then why did this feel like a test? Or was it another empty threat, like his threat of leaving the cave, something Albano had to humor for a day or two but was expected to do nothing about?

The day was hot. Judging from the sun, it was about ten in the morning. Xandra would be here soon to bring food. Albano contemplated the arid beauty of the landscape. Long after men were done slaughtering each other, the earth would still stand, and lizards and bushes and seas and clouds would remain, in peace and harmony until the end of time. Animals did not know war. They were not self-aware. Why was it that the only creature God created that could name Him and know Him was the most ferocious, the most mercenary one?

When Xandra appeared at the foot of the hill, his dark thoughts vanished. "Here she is," he murmured to himself. He walked down toward her and around the boulder. From that angle, Hagop could not see them by looking through the crawling space, unless he stepped out of the cave as well. He had to warn her now, about the marriage nonsense, before Hagop saw them.

She should have seen how upset he was, but instead, she jumped at him, nearly taking him off balance. "Albano, I have wonderful news. My father was released! He is back at home!" She laughed a laugh of pure joy.

Albano forgot all about his worries. "How is this possible? This is indeed a great blessing!"

"Some of our Levantine customers you went to see intervened on his behalf. The police had nothing against him. He was no political instigator, just a simple baker. Finally, they let him go. It is thanks to you, Albano! You were the one who spoke to the Levantines. You did this!"

"How is he?"

"He is skin and bones. Mother is delousing him now," she said, laughing. "But you know my father; he said he would start looking for flour and sugar right away and start baking. Oh, Albano, I am so thankful!"

"I am so happy for your family," Albano said, overjoyed. "There is hope now." This would distract Hagop of his notions of marrying Xandra. And it was true that he may have been instrumental in Yori's release. He had written letters and brought them to the Levantine quarter, and had asked the servants to forward them, letters pleading for Yori's most loyal customers to intervene. Even if they had not been reached through their hearts, he made sure to appeal to their stomachs by adding a list of the wonderful pastries which were part of Yori's repertoire, French éclairs, baba au rum, mille-feuilles. And they would have these again when he was released.

"I can't wait to tell Hagop!" she said as they made the turn around the boulder.

"Tell me what?"

Hagop was leaning against the rock at the entrance of the cavern, his arms crossed over his chest. "What news is making both of you smile so much?"

"Father is back, Hagop! He was released."

Instead of his expression changing to a happy one, Hagop looked sourer still. He dangled something white in front of them. "What is this, can you tell me?"

Albano and Xandra looked at what Hagop was holding. It was an embroidered handkerchief. They knew precisely what this was. Xandra had embroidered it herself and given it to Albano on his birthday.

"It is mine. I made it," Xandra mumbled.

Hagop ignored her and only addressed Albano. "Why do you have my sister's handkerchief folded with your things?"

"I … I found it." Albano lied.

"Where? Where did you find it? And why did you keep it, instead of returning it to her?"

"I found it … on the ground."

"You are lying to me," Hagop roared. "Did you take it from her or did she give it to you?"

"I took it," Albano lied again.

"Because she cannot give you something," Hagop said, his voice lowered to a threatening hiss. "This would mean she has feelings for you. She cannot have feelings for you. Don't lie to me."

Albano looked at Xandra apologetically. How could he lie about this? "I have … feelings for her," he admitted.

Hagop threw the piece of cloth to the ground and crushed it with his foot. The beautiful handkerchief became the color of the dirt. "Well, you cannot. She is not for you. She will never be for you."

Albano nodded and looked at his feet. Things made sense now. Hagop's rant about marrying Xandra had indeed been a test. He was planning to confront them all along. "I know this."

Hagop turned to Xandra. "Did you know that our Jewish friend here has this that belongs to you?"

Xandra did not answer. She and Albano looked at each other. Their silence alone was an admission of guilt. Albano felt a terrible uneasiness in the pit of his belly. Hagop advanced toward Xandra and pushed her, making her stumble back. "You have feelings for him too?" he asked menacingly.

Albano took a step toward them, partly to protect Xandra, but mostly to stop her from speaking. If Xandra told her brother the truth, there would be no turning back.

But it was too late, tears sprang from her eyes as she said, shouting almost, "Albano and I are in love!"

The words were not yet out of her mouth when Hagop released like a spring and threw himself at her, pushing her to the ground. It happened so fast that Albano did not have time to stop it. He rushed to Xandra, helped her up, and then stood between her and Hagop.

"Take your hands off her," Hagop screamed, red-faced. "You cannot be in love. You must stop immediately!"

"We did not plan on this," Albano said.

"You have destroyed her honor!" Hagop howled. "How can you betray me, your own brother?"

"Xandra's honor is safe. We have done nothing that…."

"We want to marry one day," Xandra said, defiant now. "It is not for you to stop me. Papa is back. You are not the man of the house now."

Hagop looked at her with disgust. "You can't. You will never. You can't marry a Jew. No one will let you. I won't let you. How long have you two conspired behind my back?" He peered at Albano, his eyes like slits. "I trusted you with my life, and instead you took what was even more precious: my sister's honor."

Albano stood in front of him. "Xandra's honor is intact. We have done nothing. I swear this to you!"

"You think our father will accept this? He will lock her up and never let her out. And he will beat her. He should beat her. In fact, I should beat her myself."

"You will not beat her," Albano said firmly. "Hagop, you must calm down."

"If we can't marry here, then we will go to Europe," Xandra said. "In a place where Armenians and Jews can marry, and where there is nothing you or Papa can do about that!"

Hagop scoffed. "You are a disgrace. You have dishonored yourself and us. You will never find a husband now." He looked at Albano. "Were you going to take my money too?"

"Our money," Albano corrected, "and no, I was not."

To this, Hagop answered nothing and rushed inside the cavern. A minute later he was out again, wearing his sandals. Both money satchels hang over his shoulder.

"Where are you going, Hagop?" Albano cried out. "You know this is the only place where you will be safe."

"I'm taking all the money. This money was never yours, Albano!" Hagop raged. "You were only my tool in amassing it and hiding it."

"The Turkish police are everywhere; you don't have proper papers!" Xandra said.

"Now I know why you wanted me in this cave," Hagop spat. "It was so that you could hide your disgusting secret. You never wanted to protect me! You wanted to keep me in the dark."

"Don't do anything stupid," Albano said.

Hagop turned to Xandra. "You, come," he ordered. But Xandra did not budge. "Come, I say!" he yelled, and seeing she was looking at Albano and not moving, he hurled himself at her. In an instant, he had seized her by her hair. She screamed and he pulled her hair, shook her head hard.

"Hagop, stop!" Albano yelled, but Hagop pulled harder and began to drag Xandra who pinched her lips and remained silent through the pain. "Let go of her; you're hurting her." But Hagop did not let go. Albano lunged at Hagop, all his body forward, his fists forward and put all his weight into a terrible punch to Hagop's stomach. Hagop let go of Xandra's hair and dropped to the ground, doubled over with the pain of the punch as he struggled to breathe.

Xandra rushed to her brother screaming his name, but he lifted himself to his knees and slapped her so hard that she fell to the ground. Before he could make another move, Albano charged Hagop and wrestled him to the ground as Xandra got to her feet. Albano punched Hagop, and Hagop punched him back again and again. "Don't hurt each other, I beg of you!" Xandra cried out.

Albano let go and stepped away from Hagop. He stood, breathing hard, his fists ready for another round. "I'm in love with your sister; it is true. And as long as I am alive, I intend to care for her."

Hagop slowly got up. There was blood coming down his nose, staining his shirt. Instead of charging again, Hagop rushed to the money satchels and grabbed them. "Then you must both die," he said. "And I am the one who will kill you." Hagop's face was distorted into something hideous. There could be no doubt that he meant what he said.

Albano called to Xandra. "Please go in the cave. Now." Xandra stepped back, but she seemed torn between her desire to obey and her fear of leaving him alone to fight her brother. To Hagop, he said, "It is between you and me. One of us will kill the other." Albano's eyes were full of tears, but he was resolute to do whatever it took to protect Xandra.

Hagop looked at Albano in disgust and astonishment. "You called yourself my brother? What brother would betray our whole family like this?"

"I have committed no betrayal. Neither has she. Our love is pure. I will convert to your religion. I will speak only your language. I will learn your customs. Your family might never accept me as one of them, but I will become Armenian. Our children will never know that I once was Jewish."

"You can no more become Armenian than a scorpion can become a hawk," Hagop said, his voice strangled.

Albano knew that behind his friend's murderous rage was sadness and the accumulated losses of an entire people. He shook his head and only said, "I love Xandra with all my heart."

It was as though the words pierced through Hagop, who seemed to deflate. He slumped until he was sitting on the rocky earth with his head in his hands. His shoulders shook violently. "I cannot kill you," Hagop admitted as if to himself.

"I'm sorry," Albano said. "I'm so sorry."

Hagop drew his knees to his chest and, with his face buried in his arms like a child, he sobbed softly, periodically wiping his nose with his sleeve. Albano did not know if he should sit next to his friend and put his arm around him or stand guard and be ready to fight him. But after a few minutes, Hagop stood up. "I cannot stay here," he said. "Not when my brother and sister fornicate before my eyes."

"But we have not! I told you this. You must believe us!"

"I'll go into town," Hagop continued in a hollowed voice. "I will give Father the money so that he can rebuild his bakery. Then I will enlist."

"Take the money," Albano said, thinking that letting go of his share of the money was a small price to pay. "But you cannot return to the Armenian quarter, and you must not enlist. It's a slaughterhouse, throughout the country."

"You give me no choice," Hagop said as he hoisted up the satchels. He began to step down the rocky path. "Tell my whore of a sister that she better not show her face in the Armenian quarter ever again."

Panic and sorrow gripped Albano's heart. "Will you come back for us?" he asked. "Will you tell people about this place?" Hagop pulled the satchels straps tight and walked away without answering.

They watched him walk down the mountain and returned to the cave. Albano shivered despite the heat. Xandra watched him gravely. In the light of the fire, her face was golden and still. Albano slumped on his mat and tried to breathe, but he was overcome with grief. Xandra took both of his hands in hers. They had never been able to face each other, be so close, look at each other in the eyes, and hold hands before. "It's over," she simply said.

"I will speak to your family," he said, mouthing the words but not believing them. "They'll understand."

"I am dead to them now," she said.

"I will go to your house and—"

"They will lynch you, Albano. I know what happens to girls suspected of losing their virginity before marriage. And with you who are not Armenian? Even if my father wanted to forgive me, the community would shun him. He has to reject me. He has no other choice."

"Xandra, it's all my fault."

"It is better this way," she said, adding resolutely, "It is what I wanted. It only came early."

"I will think of a solution," he muttered. "There has to be a solution." Xandra did not respond. Instead, she proceeded to undo Hagop's bed. She lifted the blankets and brought then outside. Albano heard her shake the blankets with vigor. Then she did the same thing with the straw mattress, dragging it outside and tapping it violently with a broom. The entire time, Albano sat on his own mat and watched her come and go out of the cave. The harder he thought about the situation, the fewer ideas came to him and the more despondent he felt. He was heartbroken about Hagop's reaction, and he felt so stupid. Blinded by both his love for Xandra and his friendship for Hagop, he had rehearsed for years the way he would tell Hagop, and how Hagop would understand and accept the notion of Albano and Xandra as husband and wife. Each time he imagined this, it went better in his mind. He had been terribly foolish. Now, any moment, Hagop could come back to the cave and give them away. Or, just as upsetting, he could be intercepted by the Turkish police on his way to the Armenian quarter and be sent to forced labor or to jail. As unimaginable as this was, because of Albano's stupidity, Xandra could risk her life at the hands of her own father and brother, simply for loving him.

When Xandra reentered the cave, her face was grave and resolute. Instead of setting the bedding where Hagop's bed had been, she laid it right next to Albano to form a larger bed.

A bed large enough for two.

Albano watched her in incomprehension. And then he understood. "Xandra!"

"This is our home now," she said, and she gave him a weak smile. She approached him and he stood up. She brought her body close to his, "I am your fiancée now," she said. She took his face in her hands and kissed his mouth.

They kissed, and Albano felt a fire rise in him. He jumped away from her. "I … I cannot," he muttered. "I must continue to respect you … I won't…."

"Hold me," she said.

And for the first time, Albano got to hold Xandra in his arms. He held her for a long time, overwhelmed with sadness and with joy, with fear for Hagop, and love for her.

That night, they lay side by side. He could not sleep at all. His mind was a battleground of sadness, and excitement, and fear, and hope. He was mesmerized by the soft movement of her sleep, up and down with each breath. He tried not to get too close to the warmth her body emanated. Was he, with his love, destroying Xandra's life, and that of Hagop? If anything happened to either of them, it would be entirely because of him. Tomorrow, he decided, he would try to find Hagop on the quayside and he would speak to him. If he let Hagop fight him, perhaps then Hagop would be able to be reasoned with. At that thought, Albano felt guilt and anguish grab him tighter still, and yet, when he finally fell asleep, he was touching Xandra's hair with the tips of his fingers, happy like he had no right to be.

For the next few days, Albano was too worried about Hagop returning, or Xandra being alone in the cave, so he did not look for Hagop in Smyrna. After five days, there was still no sign of Hagop or Yori. If Hagop did not tell Yori about the location of the cave, then they would be safe. After a week, Albano took his chance and went down to the quayside. He looked for Hagop in all their usual spots. Not only was he not there, but no one he asked had seen him. He could not take the risk of looking for him in the Armenian quarter. If anything happened to him there, Xandra would be powerless and alone.

He returned to the cave, and they stayed there for days, wondering what had come of Hagop, and if he had told their family the situation. But after a few days, they ran out of food and walked up to the Jewish quarter to get supplies, food, and candles. When he arrived, Uncle Joshua was waiting for him. "I don't like not knowing where your cave is. What if I must reach you? One day you will break your leg and be stranded, and no one will be able to rescue you. And people will say, 'Where is your foolish nephew, the one who is supposed to be a great rabbi' And I will say, 'Oh, he is a troglodyte now, or perhaps a corpse somewhere on Mount Pagus. He has renounced God for a couple of boulders.' By the way," Uncle Joshua added, "an Armenian woman came yesterday asking for you."

"An Armenian woman?"

"She gave me this note for you." Uncle Joshua handed him a piece of paper, which Albano unfolded. He tried to read, but although he could read some Armenian when it was printed on paper, the letter was handwritten and incomprehensible. "She was walking around the Jewish quarter asking people where you were, and they sent her to me. Why is an Armenian woman looking for you, Albano?" Uncle Joshua asked. But Albano was already running back to the cave.

Xandra was cooking bean soup on the fire. He presented her the note. Xandra stared at it. "It is from my mother," she marveled. "My mother went all the way to the Jewish quarter to give me this note!"

She read in silence, her eyes scanning the letter in disbelief. Then she read it again, and again. "My mother," she said, breathless. "She is imploring me to not come back. She says Father is wounded by my betrayal. No Armenian man, young or old, will have me now, he says. She tells me that I must stay away in hiding and not come back." Xandra should have burst into tears at that point, but to Albano's amazement, she went on. "Mother says that if I come, my life is in danger. They will beat me and might kill me." Xandra read the rest of the note to herself, and her face whitened. "Oh my God," she mumbled.

"What?"

"Hagop! Mother says he was taken! And they stole all the money!"

Albano sat on his mat, his legs suddenly limp. "Taken where?"

"Mother doesn't say." Xandra's chin trembled when she added, "Mother says she loves me and wishes me great happiness."

"I am to blame," Albano muttered. "Everything that has happened is because of me."

Xandra crouched, facing him, and looked into his eyes in the dim light of the cave. "Hagop threw himself into the lion's mouth. You know that."

"He did that because my action left him no other choice."

"His actions were wrong; yours were not."

They sat in silence for a long time, thinking of Hagop and of what the future might bring. Finally, Albano said, "I will ask my uncle for help."

Albano went to the Jewish quarter and told Uncle Joshua everything. "Does Moshe know about this whole fiasco?" Uncle Joshua asked. "It all seems like his kind of meshuggah ideas."

"It was all my own doing. Uncle Moshe knows nothing about it."

Uncle Joshua paced the room. "If you are thinking of asking me to take that girl in, don't. Your Aunt Sadie would never stand for it. But also, my nephew, you must understand. There is a war. Everyone's situation is precarious. The tension between the ethnic groups is too strong. I cannot put my family in the middle of it. If I were to welcome her into our house, I could be accused of all kinds of evil."

"I understand," Albano said.

"Food, clothes, you can have anything you like."

Albano returned to the cave with a heavy load of supplies and food, and thus Xandra and Albano began their life together.

There is something I want to show you, Albano told Xandra one evening as they sat by the light of the fire. He lifted one of the mats and dug up from the ground a wooden box he had hidden there. When he opened the box to reveal the golden finials, the light of the fire shone on them, and Xandra gasped. "What are those?"

For the first time in his life, Albano could show them and reveal how happy and proud he was to possess objects of such beauty. "They are the kele kodesh," he said. "It means sacred vessels. It is all that is left of a very ancient Sefer Torah that once belonged to my family. Here," he said, handing them to her. "You can touch them."

She took one between her fingers and inspected the graceful lace-like engraving, the tiny bells, the polished edges. "What is a Sefer Torah?"

"The Torah is the Jewish people's holy book. It contains the first five Books of Moses."

"Like a bible?"

"Yes, but not in the shape of a book. The Torah is a scroll. It is made of parchment and handwritten by scribes, and then rolled over wooden rolls. We call the rolls the Tree of Life, but I don't know why. After the Torah is read, the rabbis roll it and place it in its case, and then they place the sacred vessels at the top. There is a sort of larger crown in the middle. That was lost too. And then these two smaller ones are set atop the tree of life."

"They are so beautiful."

"I will pass them down to my first-born son. That is the tradition. He will be Kohen too."

"Kohen?"

"A special role. The role of priest."

"Are you a priest?"

"I guess I'm supposed to be."

"Hagop doesn't know about them?"

Albano admitted to Xandra at the same time he admitted to himself, "I feared showing them to him."

For a long time, they admired the finials in the light of the fire.

"They look like little crowns," Xandra noted.

Albano placed one above her head playfully. "And you are my queen."

Xandra placed the other above his head and said, "And you are my king." They looked at each other and laughed.

Albano was reluctant to leave the cave. Every moment he spent away from Xandra seemed fraught with peril. Hagop could return, leading others to them. A woman living alone on the mountain was an aberration. And yet, the very cave that had felt like a jail cell to Hagop was to them as warm, inviting, and full of love as any home he could imagine. He should have been sad and worried, and he was, but not merely that. He was with Xandra, and this filled him with joy. His heart was so light in his chest it was as though a giant balloon lifted him up as he walked. She was his fiancée now. When he would come back to the cave after having picked up supplies for them, there she was, waiting for him, her beautiful smile like a million suns radiating straight to his heart. "You're an excellent troglodyte," he would tell her, mimicking Uncle Joshua.

Xandra had none of her brother's impatience, and she was incapable of the brooding that consumed him. She never ran out of things to occupy herself with, and she was indefatigable, always at work. She sewed and she weaved, she melted bits of candles to make whole ones, she found ways to create a small oven with stones that she hand-picked and that Albano lifted and placed how she instructed him to, and now she even baked. She collected scented plants and hung them around the cave; she managed to make traps to catch prairie dogs that she skinned and rubbed with herbs before roasting them. By her mere presence, Xandra brightened and lightened everything. Her sadness was there, under the surface, but she never complained, never uttered a word of pity for herself. Albano would arrive, and she would rush to see what he had brought, finding a use for everything and marveling at the bit of candle wax, the strip of leather, the chunk of goat cheese, the few marinated olives. She was utterly accepting of her predicament and boundless in her expressions of love. Albano in return did everything for her. One of the things he did for her was one of the hardest to give. They endlessly kissed, but those kisses were chaste. Albano kept the promise he had made to Hagop and to himself to respect her.

For a full month, this was their life. Xandra was tormented with questions about her family. Was her father able to bake and earn a living? How did her mother and sisters fare? What if Yori was arrested again? Didn't her mother need her now more than ever? Because of the folly of men, she and Albano were forbidden to help. Having not heard from Hagop, they feared the worst for him. Hagop had only been in the Armenian quarter long enough to tell his parents about them, but not long enough to make it back to the cave. Had he changed his mind about getting his sister back, or was he arrested before he did?

For two months, Xandra and Albano slept side by side in the cave. At night they were anxious, and sleep was difficult. But during the day, Albano was happy. He had Xandra all to himself, and each minute with her was a gift. Happy, as well as consumed with desire, around Xandra, Albano was a timorous boy. His dreams and thoughts were filled with visions of her. He tried not to look at her lustily and was failing at this. Each time he chased an impure thought away with splashes of water on his face, or a strenuous walk up the mountain, another thought would come, bringing with it a wave of ardor. It was as though his brain had turned to soup and he could think of nothing else. Their near-constant physical proximity, the solitude of the mountain, his youth and energy, and the way they were physical with each other, kissing the way they kissed, did nothing to help. Albano had no idea how long he could go on in such a manner.

One evening, like many others, they were sitting together in the cave, on the mat, their backs propped against pillows set against the coolness of the stone. Albano was reading out loud from an old French newspaper they had kept, translating as he went and helping her with her pronunciation. The fire, still warm, flickered and lit up the walls of the cave. "You see," Xandra suddenly said, "the ground has not opened up from beneath our feet. We are happy. The war will never reach us here. We can stay together here, safe, forever."

"But very soon, we need to be married," he answered urgently. "But how? No priest, no rabbi, will accept to marry us," he added, sounding pathetic.

"When the time is correct, we will be husband and wife," she answered enigmatically.

That same week, she gave him a long list of herbs and minerals to bring back from the city. "What is it for?" he asked.

"A remedy," she answered.

"For what ailment?" She smiled and did not answer. It took him a while to gather the proper herbs from various shops on Frank Street. When she had them all, she made a brew. "Are you sick?" he asked. Again, she did not answer.

That night, instead of simply going to bed, she asked him to add logs to the fire. Then she knelt by the spring and removed her petticoat in front of him. Usually, she washed in private when he was out, but now she was before him only wearing a shirt, her arms and legs bare. She poured water in a bowl and using a cloth washed her face and arms. From his mat he watched, mesmerized, her arms so white, the skin so marvelously smooth. Feeling his gaze on him, she turned and beamed. "Outside, in the night, your face is smooth and white and bright enough to rival the moon," he told her. "But here, with the fire, it is orange and it glows like the sun."

Xandra stood up to face him, and said, "Tonight, we will be married."

"We … will?" Albano stuttered. And then he watched Xandra do something incredible: she let her shirt fall to the floor.

Albano stopped breathing. He remained on the mat as she stood facing him, the dappled light of the fire flickering on her bare body. "You are so beautiful," Albano whispered. He needed to look away. He needed to run out of the cave. He jumped to his feet, "I … I cannot be here. I have to go," he muttered, and yet he did not look away, and he did not run.

"Stay," she said, extending her hand to take his.

Albano knew with every cell in his brain that he mustn't take her hand, just as every cell in his body moved his hand forward toward hers. "I cannot be here next to you like this and still respect—"

"I know," she said, gently, slowly, placing his hand on her bare breast.

"No, no," he murmured, but an instant later he fell to his knees and embraced her bare body in his arms, letting his head rest on her stomach. "I mustn't do this."

She caressed his hair and whispered, "Please, my love, I am ready for you."

Albano took her in his arms and kissed her, but this time, he let himself kiss her the way he had always wanted to kiss her. Overtaken, she began to melt, so Albano gently laid her on the mat. And just like that, they were married.

****

That night, after they had made love for the first time, Xandra consumed her brew. "It is against babies," she explained.

"How do you know how to make it?"

"Women pass down this knowledge."

"Isn't it against your religion?"

"Women have to be practical. If we are taken by force and we are not married, the alternative is death. My mother made me memorize it. It does not always work, so I will have to be careful about cycles of the moon."

"How so?"

Xandra's answer filled him with awe. "The moon decides when a woman is fertile and when she is not," she said.

The next morning felt like the first day of their lives. They made love, again and again, amazed at the big secret that was now theirs. They ate cheese and bread, fresh figs, and dried fruit. When it was night, and no one could see them, they went to a nearby stream and removed all their clothes. They bathed in the cold water and further discovered each other's body and their own. Albano held Xandra in the water as she floated, her body glistening in the light of the moon. "You are my moon lady, weightless in the night."

"When I am in your arms, I feel safe."

"I will hold you forever, and forever keep you safe," he swore.

CHAPTER 9

Cité des Fleurs

Cassie awakened from her second night in her Parisian hotel room to the revelation that she had slept ten hours straight. Outside her window was nothing but gray skies and rooftops sleek with rain. She took a bath and washed her hair. The humidity in the air did not bode well regarding follicle cooperation, but she had not thought of bringing a blow-dryer, of course. She put on her jeans, layered three T-shirts, forced her last two pairs of dry socks on top of each other, brushed on mascara, and applied lipstick. She could almost picture herself acing this day. But when she slid her feet into Uggs that had the feel and consistency of a wet sponge, dampening her last pairs of dry socks all the way through, and when each strand of her hair began curling malevolently upon itself, suddenly she was not so sure. How could she expect cooperation from anyone in her family when her own hair was giving her the finger?

She went down to the deserted lobby. The sound of French cartoons played on a nearby television, and the lobby smelled of freshly brewed coffee and burnt toast. She entered the phone booth and dialed Sabine. In one breathless sentence, she explained to how she had managed to book the wrong hotel, how she had obliterated both her cell phone and her laptop, how she had borrowed their father's coat, and how the only shoes she had brought were turning into festering swamps. "I have moss growing between my toes," she joked.

On the line, there was no laugh, not even a polite one. "What's your shoe size?" Sabine asked. "I'll lend you a pair. I'm a thirty-eight."

"Forty," Cassie said. "That won't work but thanks for the offer. But that's not why I called you. Okay, so here is the scoop: You were right. That Marceline character, she was not Papa's mistress."

"Who was she?"

"Are you sitting down? She is Papa's sister!"

"His what?"

"He has a sister! Isn't it incredible?"

"Has or had?" Sabine asked.

"Apparently, she is still alive. She's two years older than Papa."

"We have an aunt?" Sabine sounded incredulous, but also excited.

"And we knew nothing. Absolutely nothing!"

Sabine was quiet for a beat. Then she said, "When Papa had his weird blow up, he thought you were her?"

"Better than the alternative," Cassie said. "I'm pretty relieved that it wasn't actually me he called all those names."

"That's what Maman meant when she said he was hallucinating," Sabine said. "She knew perfectly well who Marceline was the whole time."

"You'd think she would have volunteered the information to make me feel better."

"She likes it better when she holds all the cards," Sabine said, pragmatic.

"Wouldn't it be incredible to meet relatives we didn't know existed?"

"Considering how well we fare with the ones we already have, I'm not so sure," Sabine said.

"Do you think you could look up her name and see if you find anything? I wrote it down. A name straight out of a Flaubert novel." Cassie unfolded her paper. "Here it is: Marceline de Bécasel D'Alompe."

Cassie heard the swift sound of fingertips on a keyboard. "Comtesse Marceline de Bécasel D'Alompe. 4682 Cité des Fleurs in the seventeenth arrondissement," Sabine said. "Papa's sister is a countess?"

"She's listed?" Cassie marveled. "What kind of miracle is this?"

"It's called the internet."

"She's not even hiding a little bit? Incredible. What do you think I should do?"

"Buy shoes," Sabine said.

"Any telephone number?"

"I don't see one listed."

"Maybe I should go to the address, see what I find. Anyway, I have nothing better to do before visiting hours."

"You're going back to the hospital?" Sabine sounded surprised.

"Well … yes, why?"

"I guess that makes sense. That's why you came here but…."

Cassie waited for the rest of the sentence, which didn't come. "Are you all right?" she asked.

There was a long silence. "I'm alive, I guess," Sabine said.

Alarm bells rang in Cassie's ears. "We should get together just the two of us," she hurried to say. "Talk. Catch up."

"I better go," Sabine said. "My boss is getting fidgety."

After they had hung up, Cassie wondered about Sabine, the way she said things. Cynical. Or maybe sad. If she knew Sabine the way she ought to, she would be able to tell. Here she was getting all excited about a new relative, and she was incapable of getting an accurate reading on her own younger sister.

Cassie shuffled into the street in her frizzy hair, her father's shapeless coat, and squishy boots. Give her a couple of trash bags and people would start handing her money. Although she kept repeating to herself that she felt fine and didn't care about her looks, it turns out that she wasn't fine. She did care. Could she present herself at the door of Madame la Comtesse sporting a road kill on each foot? Because now it was decided: she was, without giving it any thought, finding herself heading in the direction of the seventeenth arrondissement. Cité des Fleurs, wherever that was, and whatever it was she might find there, or not find there. She had nothing better to do she had told Sabine. But mostly, she was curious. And angry. At what? At whom? She wasn't quite sure.

But first, she needed shoes. Paris did not offer many shopping options at eight in the morning. Cassie walked down rue des Martyrs, her Uggs growing wetter and heavier by the minute, searching the shop windows for a solution. Cafés, bakeries, and grocery stores were open, but everything else was closed. She stopped in front of a small vintage shop. Someone with an abundance of black curls was inside, folding T-shirts. She looked through the window. The shopkeeper was a thin woman in her fifties in a long black skirt with fingers covered in silver rings. Cassie stepped back and considered the merchandise on display in the window. It was a hot mess, part resale store, part gift and novelty, part porn video rentals. But amidst the dusty radios and food mixers, feathered whips, and old books was a single pair of red cowboy boots. The boots embodied the closest definition of shoes Cassie would not wear. For one, "secondhand shoes" struck her as a horrifying combination of words. Secondly, the boots were bright red, pointy enough to stab someone, and just so visible, so … exuberant.

Cassie continued down rue des Martyrs. As she walked, she pondered the kind of woman who would wear cowboy boots such as these. It would have to be someone with opinions. Someone who liked being seen and heard. Someone obnoxious, to be sure.

Cassie, not even clear as to why, walked back up the street and returned to stare at the boots in the window.

Yep, she thought. Here they were. On the plus side, they were not much of a risk at twenty-five euros. Odile would despise the sight of them, which added to their appeal.

She pushed open the door and entered. "Bonjour, Madame," she made sure to say. The shopkeeper jumped, startled. Her eyes were heavy with black eye makeup. Her hair was as black and wavy as Cassie's, but on her it was a fashion statement. "I must have forgotten to lock the door," the woman said. "We are not open. I'm only doing the inventory."

"Oh well, thank you then." Cassie turned around to leave.

"But since you are here, is there something you wanted to look at?"

"I need to buy a map of Paris."

The woman stepped toward a display of postcards and maps. "Here they are."

"Also, I was wondering about the…." Cassie hesitated, embarrassed. "Those red boots you have in the window."

"Les bottes de cowboy?"

"What size are they?"

The woman went to the window to retrieve the boots and handed them to Cassie. On close inspection, they looked even more rugged than they had seemed behind the window, but in a well-loved sort of way, not raggedy. Holding them, Cassie felt guilty for no good reason. "Size Forty," the shopkeeper announced. "Elles sont manifiques."

"That's my size," Cassie said, surprised. "I guess there is no harm in trying them on. They're not my style at all." When she removed her boots, her drenched socks stayed inside the Uggs. "You don't happen to sell socks, by chance?"

"We do have some, but they are spéciales," the woman said. Spéciale, in French, did not signify special at all, but plain weird.

"How spéciale?"

The woman walked to the glass counter behind which was an assortment of leather, lingerie, Eiffel Tower-shaped vibrators, and furry handcuffs. She handed her a pair of high socks in a vibrant pink covered in a small penis print. "C'est tout ce que j'ai." That's all I have.

"Penis socks?"

"Oui, Madame."

Cassie sat down and contemplated her toes which increasingly looked like miniature drowned corpses. She sighed in surrender and put on the penis socks. The penis prints stretched obscenely.

And then she slid her feet inside the boots.

Words could hardly describe the perfection with which they fit. The arch was perfect. The height was perfect. The way her feet felt, safe, warm, dry, and protected after all the abuse, was perfect. She took two steps back and looked at herself in the mirror. Not so bad. Pretty great in fact. Not at all like her, but awesome in their own genre. "I can't believe they're only twenty-five euros!" she exclaimed.

"Ha, non," the woman said. "You missed a zero. Look at the tag: They're two hundred and fifty euros."

Cassie looked at the tag, looked at the woman, then looked at her boots.

"I'll take them," she said.

She walked to the soundtrack of her cowboy boots pounding the sidewalk. Comtesse-Marceline-de-Bécasel-D'Alompe, Comtesse-Marceline-de-Bécasel-D'Alompe. What a mouthful, that name. In truth, aristocratic names triggered mixed emotions in her, something ingrained in her subconscious to which she had never given a second thought until now. Those people. They clung to their bloodline like an amulet against the evils of all things progressive. Out of principle, she resented the thought of power, or money, passed down across generations. Or did she? Could it be that she was unconsciously parroting her mother's prejudice? Growing up under her mother's dominance, Cassie had adopted much of her mother's tastes and opinions as her own, so much so that it was at times difficult to sort things out, even now. It wasn't until she was in her thirties, when she began to catch herself wondering how her mother would react to things in order to know how she should feel, that she had realized this. She had cured herself of this compulsion during her marriage by an exhausting daily practice of rebelling against Peter's authority. A calm, confident husband was the perfect person against whom to practice having a mind of one's own. With Peter, she had rebelled, and fought, and stood her ground. Not for what she wanted (that remained kind of murky) but against what he wanted, which was nearly as good.

The air was cold on her cheeks as she walked up rue des Abbesses toward the métro station. She unfolded her Paris map. Cité des Fleurs. The City of Flowers. What a lovely street name. For the first time since she arrived in Paris, Cassie felt equipped for the weather, and since she could think better when her body was in motion, she decided to continue on foot rather than take the métro. It was strange to feel so at home in Paris. It was not only how things looked and smelled and sounded, but it was also the people. In the United States, even after nearly twenty years, people felt opaque to her. Friendly, easy to categorize, yet amorphous. But here in Paris, it was as though she had an immediate, gut-level knowledge of the collective thinking, the yearning of souls, the take-no-prisoner sense of humor, the contrarian thinking, the deep and so very French appetite for anarchy, a uniquely rebellious spirit that inhabited even the most conventional individuals. She could feel the zeitgeist of the place in her bones. From rue des Abbesses, she walked down rue Joseph de Maistre along the Montmartre cemetery's wall. Maybe for a few days she could cope with her mom, her sisters, her father, and forget about her children in college, the void in between their calls, Peter, the loss of it all, starting from scratch, not wanting to start anything, not knowing where to start. The rhythmic, clipped sound of her heels on the sidewalk had a way of saying, "You exist." That was better than what Sabine had said. Sabine had said, "I'm alive." It sounded horrible, the way she said it. To be alive was to occupy space. To exist was to claim significance, to demand it. Something was wrong with Sabine, but Cassie had no idea how to bring it up without everyone in her family telling her to go to hell.

As she walked through the unknown neighborhood, she felt a sense of déjà vu. She was pretty certain that she had never been on this street, so why did the sidewalks, the sycamores, and in particular the buildings feel so familiar? What did it mean to be a countess these days, she wondered? Picturesque names – what her mother called noms à charnières, names with hinges – and useless titles, were all that was left of the French nobility. Aristocracy's power was long gone. Their great wealth had shrunk to nothing for most. Families that had passed down land, properties, and estates for five or six generations, these days often had to sell everything just to pay the inheritance tax. Fabulous properties that had been in families for several hundred years were being sold and turned into museums or hotels.

"They think they're better than us," Raymonde would say about anyone she perceived as richer, happier, or better-educated, though the underlying fear may not be how much better they were but how insignificant she felt. The neighborhood was lively, busy like a village. Boucheries, pâtisseries, cordonneries, flower shops, and cafés all teemed with activity. In front of the school, mothers held the hands of children with colorful backpacks and raincoats. Ladies with shopping baskets greeted each other and chatted in the doorways of buildings. Men in green overalls swept the sidewalks. Cassie's cowboy boots clip-clopped on the pavement, and the rhythm was beginning to sound a lot like I think I can-I think I can.

****

Cassie arrived at rue de la Jonquière and had to stop to collect herself. She stood on the sidewalk, the drizzle of rain in her face. What was going on? She had never been here before, she was certain of this, yet she still could not shake off the growing feeling of déjà vu. It was as though she knew what the next block looked like instants before seeing it. This porte cochère. The shape of this window. That gate, the sign over the butcher shop – she knew them, but how could this be? Also, something struck her suddenly. How was it that she knew all those architectural terms? She was finding herself able to recognize an arc-boutan and a travée. Why? How? She did not know any of those words in English, which means she had learned them in French as a child. And then it came to her like a poke in her heart: she had been here before! With her father.

It was years ago when she was a little girl. It was not a linear memory. It came in bits. Her hand in his. Odile was there. Him pointing at rooftops and windows. An arc-boutan, a travée. This was one of the things he did: name objects. It was not too fascinating at the time. He tended to ramble on about subjects of no interest to little girls. But as they walked, he pointed to churches, to windows, and to rooftops and told her and Odile the names of things: une rothonde, un pillastre. He was going to show them a house, she remembered. A special house. Sabine would have been an infant. She was not there. Where was their mother?

Cassie arrived in front of a metal gate with a sign that read: "Cité des Fleurs. Rue privée. Closed to the public from seven in the morning to seven at night. Chiens interdits." She walked through the main gate just as the sun managed to pierce through and the sky was revealed, blue in patches between dark, billowy clouds.

She could not believe her eyes as she advanced through the private alley. Not only had she absolutely been here before, but it was unfathomable that she would have forgotten it until now. That such a place existed in the middle of Paris was amazing enough. This was not a place you forgot. Cité des Fleurs was a long cobblestone alley about four hundred feet long and wide enough for a car, although there were no cars, not even parked ones. On each side of the alley were walls, fences topped with pointed finials painted black, blue, or green, and gates. Each gate was framed on each side by a rectangular stone pillar about ten feet high. Atop each pillar sat a large urn shaped like an inverted bell out of which tulips, narcissus, and daffodils burst like fireworks. Budding trees, cascading wisteria in purple hues, and white clematis running wild spilled from behind gates. Ivy climbed on walls, birds chirped and dashed around, and cats lay in the sun or walked around like they owned the place. The rest of Paris had felt frozen in winter, but Cité des Fleurs, perhaps because of the ray of sun, or perhaps because of the vegetation, was a pocket of spring. Behind the gates were three- and four-story houses built most likely in the late 1800s, each pretty as a jewel box, each with a small garden in front. They were what the French called hôtel particuliers, townhouses, technically, but with flair. From her vantage point in the alley, she could only see what was above the gates, the higher levels of each house. The houses all looked different, but the matching urns, out of which vegetation escaped and framed the gates, gave the street its architectural unity.

She recognized the house instantly. It was the most beautiful one on the street, painted in a pink-tinged white. She counted four stories with three large windows on each floor. The fourth story had two smaller windows nestled within the slate roof. The house had handsome proportions; the symmetry of windows gave it gravitas, but the façade had whimsical details: dainty stone carvings above the windows, a stone cornice that ran the width of the façade, intricate wrought-iron balconies. The center windows had small balconies on two of the levels. A lush, massive pine tree framed the house on one side, and the general effect was straight out of a children's fairy-tale book.

Money, Cassie thought. And lots of it by the look of things. If Marceline lived here, perhaps not all aristocrats had lost their properties to inheritance taxes.

Her castle. Was this what her mother had meant?

Buried under a thick layer of ivy she detected an aging intercom with a single button and beneath it the name Bécasel D'Alompe. She hesitated, her finger hovering above the buzzer. Her clothes gave her pause. The jeans, her father's terrible coat, and now the red cowboy boots. To press or not to press, that was the question.

She pressed.

The buzzer emitted a tiny pterodactyl noise, and Cassie's heart bounced in her chest. For a while, there was nothing. Then came a sputtering sound and a woman's voice, drowned in crackles from another world, said, "Allô, oui?"

Cassie took a deep breath. "Is this Madame de Bécasel D'Alompe?"

"What is this regarding?"

"My name is Cassandra Lombard," Cassie said in French. "I'm visiting from California. I think it's … ahem … possible that we might be … related?" She cringed. Why had she ended her sentence with a pathetic question mark? There was a long silence, but she could still hear the static. "Allô?" she said.

"Un moment, s'il vous plaît," the woman's commanded.

Cassie looked up at the house. There was no reason to feel nervous really. Except for the nagging sense that her life was about to swing wide open. It was like standing at the edge of a cliff. There was still the possibility of taking a step back. Scamper away. Hide. At one of the windows of the lower floor, a curtain parted briefly. And then another curtain moved at the window above, followed by more creaking from the intercom.

"You will now be received," the voice said. With this came a buzzing sound and a small door within the black metal gate clicked open. Sésame ouvre-toi, Cassie thought.

She flattened the frizz of her hair with the palms of her hands, readjusted her coat, and pushed open the door.

She found herself inside a large, airy, gardenlike courtyard where clipped boxwood framed a central path that led to the porch and the entrance door. To her left, a stone maiden extended her hands in a graceful beckoning. To her right, a gazebo made of six small marble columns covered with blooming clematis shaded a wrought iron patio table and chairs. She heard clipping sounds above her and lifted her head. Up on a towering thin ladder, a North African gardener, pipe in mouth, handsome and spry despite being most likely in his late eighties, was trimming a hedge, one hand holding the clipper, the other hanging on to the ladder for dear life. He nodded his head at Cassie and resumed his task.

She advanced on the narrow path and this time again saw the distinct motion of curtains in at least two of the windows. She was being observed. The thought that her curiosity was reciprocated gave her courage. The front door was flanked on each side by gas lanterns and protected by a lacy awning of glass and iron curlicues. This particular architectural element was called une Marquise, she knew, thinking how fitting it was that she had to go past a Marquise to get to the countess.

At the door, she wiped her palms on her jeans in preparation for a blue-blooded handshake. Before she could knock, a squat woman in her late forties in a buttoned-up black dress and a strict hairdo had come out of the house and onto the porch, looking at Cassie interrogatively. "How may I help you?"

Cassie propelled her hand forward and gave her a vigorous handshake. "Bonjour, Madame," she said, thinking that the woman was way too young to be her aunt. "Are you Madame…?" But in her nervousness, the name had vanished from her brain. "Madame de, de … Bbb … De, de … Aloup? Aloppe?"

"Alompe. But … which one, Madame?"

"There are several?" Cassie felt heat come to her face. "I believe she may be your … mother? Ha, yes! Marceline! I'm looking for Marceline!"

"May I tell her what this is regarding?" the woman asked. She showed no intention of letting her in.

"I'm looking for relatives of my father."

"Yes?"

"My father is hospitalized, and well, I've just heard that he might be related to Marceline – I mean, to the duchess. I mean, the countess."

"Would you please follow me dans le vestibule," the woman said.

Vestibule? The words Vulva Vestibula intruded into her mind: the entrance to the vagina. And here she was, entering the vestibule while wearing penis socks.

The vestibule was a circular entrance hall at the foot of a sweeping staircase. In the center of the room was a round mahogany table and on the table was a profuse flower arrangement overflowing with lilacs, roses, and lilies. The ceiling had been painted with elaborate and delightful trompe l'oeil of sky, clouds, cupids, and birds bashfully carrying flowing ribbons to mask the cupid's private parts. The woman pointed to a seat against a wall. "If you would please wait for a moment?"

If Cassie thought she had regressed to the eighties by losing her laptop and cell, this environment felt like going back in time a whole century. She raked the drawers of her brain for the vernacular of this world, the etiquette. Downton Abbey meets Marie Antoinette, and every other cliché bounced around in her head. She was nervous as hell. Out of place. The cupids on the ceiling, the ornate stucco molding, the beautiful wood floor, the smell of lilac; everything here was perfect. She had no clue how to sit, stand, or even hold her head in this room. She looked like a vagrant, had gotten her nobilities mixed up, had botched Marceline's name, and now had the sneaking suspicion that the woman who had opened the door was not her relative, but the maid. What now?

The woman was back in the room. "If you would please follow me," she said.

They walked on the inlaid parquet floor, Cassie trying to put as little weight as she could on the floor as her boots clip-clopped obscenely and entered a salon with ceilings that were at least twelve feet high. In the room, beautiful light poured in through the windows. Sunlight reflected on a monumental crystal chandelier in the center of the ceiling. The walls were painted a light shade of yellow with gold trimmings and covered with art, heavily framed oil paintings of bucolic settings, still lifes piled high with dead pheasants, apples, and grapes. On the floor lay dozens of immense Persian rugs. Her father too had a prized collection of Persian rugs. The more you walked on them, the more beautiful they become, he would tell visitors.

"Would you please have a seat on the bergère," the woman said pointing in the direction of a group of three chairs. Two of the chairs were matching golden fauteuils with ornate woodwork and high backs that resembled thrones, and one was a low chair upholstered in blue fabric. Cassie sat in the chair, expecting to sink in the upholstery, but finding herself perched on a hard surface with no give whatsoever. "Monsieur et Madame D'Alompe will arrive in just a minute," the woman announced before leaving.

Cassie looked around feeling dwarfed by the room. The salon was filled with Louis XVI furniture and a few Regency pieces. The desk was Regency, if not the real thing, at least a beautiful imitation. And she knew this how? From her dad. And why did her dad know those things? Wasn't this unusual knowledge in a working-class man whose schooling was cut short by the war? Above the limestone fireplace, a painting caught her eye, surprising in its modernity in such a room. It was a portrait of a woman, half figurative, half abstract, like a Modigliani that would have been reworked by Basquiat. Half of the woman's face was figurative: black mane, piercing gold eyes like those of a cat, and an ironic smile. The other side of the face looked as though it had been reworked and blurred, the mouth redrawn as if by a three-year-old. A person who would put such a painting on a mantelpiece could not be all that stuck up.

The sound of hurried footsteps preceded the arrival of a small man and small woman in their sixties. They scurried into the room and Cassie got to her feet. "Don't get up!" the woman ordered. Cassie stayed up. They advanced toward her with extended hands and took turns shaking hers as they smiled the same precise smile, with the same thin mouth, perhaps the smile they reserved for the kind of strangers in the habit of showing up unannounced at their doorstep. They introduced themselves, as Jean-Bernard de Bécasel D'Alompe and Armelle de Bécasel D'Alompe. It was immediately obvious to Cassie that the two were twins. They seemed the male and the female version of the same human being. They had taut, almost wrinkle-free skin, high cheekbones, funny little pointy noses, and arched eyebrows that gave them a permanently surprised look. They both had blondish hair, hers in a well-crafted bun at the nape of her neck, and his full on top and mounted like a toupee. They were dressed elegantly, Armelle in a pale gray cardigan, a matchstick black skirt, and a strand of pearls, Antoine in a light blue shirt and a navy sports coat with some sort of embroidered armor on the left pocket. They had the worried expressions of people propelled into a situation of emergency.

Armelle and Jean-Bernard sat on the large, golden, throne-like chairs. Down on her seat, Cassie had to look up at them. "Thank you so much for seeing me," she said. "I hope it wasn't rude to just knock at your door. Your number was unlisted."

They nodded in noncommittal unison. Jean-Bernard crossed one leg over the other, clasped his hands over one knee, and opened his mouth, but it was Armelle who spoke. "Laure said you are looking for relatives? How interesting."

"Laure?"

"Our executive assistant who opened the door."

Cassie took mental note: not the maid, but the executive assistant. She hoped she had not embarrassed herself. "My father is very ill in the hospital," she said. "I guess I am looking into his genealogy for the first time. I'm wondering if it is possible that we might be … perhaps … cousins?"

Jean-Bernard crossed his leg to the other side, clasped his hands again, opened his mouth again, and again no sound came out. "How fascinating," Armelle said, and they both exhibited the same pinched smile of polite disinterest, which seemed to indicate that the visit would be over before it had a chance to begin. Something about them was obnoxious. It was as though they were playing a game of poker and Cassie had not even been given cards.

But maybe she did have one card. "I learned only yesterday that my father has a sister," she said.

"How interesting," Armelle said again. She did not seem interested at all.

"My father told us this name we had never heard before, and then my sister found your address online."

A light of recognition came to Jean-Bernard's face but soon faded. He crossed and uncrossed his legs affectedly. Clasped and unclasped his hands.

"But of course," Armelle said.

Now Cassie was annoyed. Who were those two dinguses? And what game were they playing? "Is Marceline your mother?" she insisted. "May I meet her?"

Armelle's and Jean-Bernard's eyes darted to the portrait above the fireplace. "Our mother?" Armelle said. These people did not want to help her. And now she doubted she was related to them at all. If these two shared DNA with anything, it would be with small furry animals, perhaps hamsters or, from the way they stared at her with wide eyes and panicked expressions, prairie dogs.

Jean-Bernard crossed and uncrossed his legs again, and then clasped his hands, put them on his lap, clasped them again, then looked around the room again like in a time loop. "Mother indeed had a brother," he suddenly said in a bleaty, much too loud voice. "But he disappeared in the course of World War II!"

Armelle looked at Jean-Bernard with displeasure. "Très cher Jean-Bernard, forgive me, but you are confused. It was Mother's father who perished, in World War II." Jean-Bernard became enthralled with the tip of his shoelace, poking it through each hole of this black patent-leather shoe, one after the other, and then back from the top.

"My father is eighty-seven years old," Cassie said. "His name is Gustave Lombard. He went in for surgery, but a lung infection has developed. They're trying different intravenous antibiotics."

"And which hospital is this?" Armelle asked casually.

"Hôpital Saint-François," Cassie answered, realizing that the question revealed more interest than Armelle was willing to let on. "He was born in 1925. I wish I knew his parents' names, but I don't." Armelle and Jean-Bernard stared at her, riveted by what Cassie might say next. "He's been going in and out of consciousness."

Armelle cocked her head. "How awful," she said.

"He's been calling me Marceline." As she said the name, both Armelle and Jean-Bernard glanced at the portrait above the fireplace, and then away. It happened in fractions of seconds, but now the portrait seemed like the fourth person in the room, and it was beckoning Cassie to be more audacious. "So, tell me, does Marceline live here?" she asked. "Does she have a brother named –"

"Operation Torch!" Jean-Bernard blurted out, so loud that both Armelle and Cassie jumped. "Algiers!" he nearly shouted. "November 1942!" Jean-Bernard stopped speaking as abruptly as he had started. His eyes darted to everywhere in the room at once, and he went through a frantic cycle of leg crossings, hand clasping, and eye darting. Armelle now appeared deeply annoyed, but before she could say anything, Laure, the executive assistant, materialized and stood there, wanting to speak. Jean-Bernard turned to her, irritated. "Merci, Laure, we are fine," he said.

But Laure did not leave and was about to speak when Armelle got to her feet. "I wish we could help you," she said. "This is most unfortunate, but I'm afraid we know nothing." Mirroring his sister, Jean-Bernard too sprung up from his seat.

Cassie understood that she was expected to leave. She unfolded from her terrible chair and got up as well. She tried one more time. "Your mother, could I meet her? Maybe she knows something about my father. He was born in the eight arrondissement. On January 3rd, 1925."

Armelle put a nervous hand to the pearls around her neck. "I'm afraid that won't be possible. Her health, you see…."

Jean-Bernard echoed Armelle in tone and pained expression. "Her advancing age…."

"Let us accompany you to the door."

Cassie followed them out of the room. If they were related to her dad, this was more of the same crap. The same secrecy, the same silence, but why? What for?

They were back in the vestibule. Laure, who had followed them, coughed to get their attention and said, "I wanted to let you know that tea is served."

Armelle seemed taken aback; she pivoted on her heels and faced Laure. "That won't be necessary. Our visitor was just leaving." She took Cassie's elbow lightly but with urgency as she guided her toward the front door. "I very much hope the rest of your search will be more fruitful."

"Pardon me," Laure insisted. "But tea is served," she paused and put more emphasis on the rest of the sentence "… in Madame la Comtesse's library."

Armelle tugged at her pearls and moved her mouth into a forced smile. "The library? But of course," she said and promptly took Cassie's elbow again but this time guided her away from the door. "Would you join us for tea?"

Cassie felt something odd and exhilarating in the air. Something had just happened. What, she wasn't sure. She looked at Laure interrogatively, but the woman's face revealed nothing. "I would love to," she said.

Armelle and Jean-Bernard went in the direction of the stairwell, but as Armelle put a foot on the first step, Laure said, "I believe Madame la Comtesse intends to meet with Madame … alone."

Armelle blanched. Jean-Bernard said not a word of goodbye and stomped out of the room. There had been an upset; that much was clear. But whatever it was, Armelle's good education was well ingrained, and she regrouped quickly. "Very well then." She took Cassie's hand, shook it rather limply, and gave her a practiced smile. "It's been a pleasure, au revoir then." They were standing at the bottom of the stairs. Armelle walked off after a last sharp, military nod. Cassie now stood in the vestibule, lightheaded with giddiness. A mysterious master puppeteer was inviting her to tea, and Armelle and Jean-Bernard had been given the boot! Feeling as though she had just aced the most important interview of her life, Cassie followed Laure up the stairwell, and then through a high-ceilinged hallway lined with small oil paintings of landscapes and hunting scenes, and finally to a large door with gilded woodwork. She opened the door and let Cassie in.

The room was so unlike the rest of the house that Cassie might as well have entered an alternate universe. It was so impolite. So bohemian. The air was heavy with the smell of women's perfume and the licorice hints of pipe tobacco. It was part library, part cabinet of curiosities. On every wall were shelves upon shelves, and those were filled with books, newspapers, magazines, and bizarre, exotic artifacts: clay moldings of human parts, postcards, ostrich eggshells, Venetian masks, animal skulls, crystals sprouting out of rocks, feathers in vases. Everywhere, scattered and piled high, were cardboard boxes and trunks. Every surface and even the floor were strewn with magazines and newspaper clippings. Shelves and tabletops alike were covered with chinoiseries, porcelain vases, ashtrays, primitive sculptures, African masks, and a rather macabre assortment of taxidermy animals, from birds to bats to a large cat that could well be a lynx or a bobcat.

Next to the window, on a low, ornate Napoleon III table flanked by two Chesterfield chairs, was an Edwardian teapot, small silver forks and spoons, two delicate Limoges plates and teacups, and a three-tiered serving tray filled with an assortment of petits fours, small éclairs, and raspberry tarts no larger than small matchboxes.

Cassie was standing in the center of the library, taking it in, when a door on the opposite side from the entrance opened. A very old woman, perhaps ninety years old, marched into the room, her chin high. Her hair was perfectly white and tied in a bun, her skin thin and rosy. She was dressed to be noticed, in an extravagant, floor-length dress of red and yellow madras fabric. Around her neck was a heavy layering of two dozen strands of beads, pendants, keys, and amulets. There were bracelets on her wrists, ethnic rings on every one of her narrow, knobby fingers. Her handshake surprised Cassie: it was young and full of vigor. "Marceline de Bécasel D'Alompe," the old woman said, her golden eyes evaluating Cassie with interest. "I'm told you wanted to meet me."

Cassie recognized her immediately as the woman in the painting. Marceline was the most handsome and confident elderly women she had ever seen. Although something in her face felt familiar, one thing was for certain: she bore no physical resemblance to her father. Cassie could not help beaming as she introduced herself. Could this woman really be her father's sister? It was as though she had been invented the day before and now appeared, fully realized, a mythical creature turned to flesh and blood.

"What is your name again? Forgive me, I am tragically old and must have people repeat things to me," Marceline said.

"Cassandra Lombard."

"And what do you want from me, Mademoiselle?"

"Well, I … I'm looking for my father's sister."

Marceline studied Cassie's face with an expression of innocence layered with mirth or puzzlement. Or disapproval. Finally, cryptically she said, "But why only now?"

Cassie was not about to tell this stranger, especially if this was her aunt, that she had learned about her in a bout of morphine-induced rage filled with an expletive associated to her name. "I live in the United States," she said instead. "This is my first visit to France in five years." She added lightly, "So I thought, why not."

Marceline repeated in the same tone. "Why not?" adding, "You've met Laure haven't you? She's my everything. My brain, my eyes," she added with a wink, "and sometimes my ears."

Cassie turned to Laure. "Glad to meet you," Laure said.

Marceline nodded towards the table, and they sat down by the window. From where she sat, Cassie could see the garden through the window. The old man on the ladder was clipping a hedge in slow motion, a cold pipe between his teeth. "I hope you like Earl Grey," Marceline said. "Or perhaps you'd prefer coffee. Americans like their coffee watered down and tasting burnt. This was the kind of coffee they drank during the war. They were nostalgic for it, the taste of terrible army coffee. Quite telling, don't you think?"

"Earl Grey will be perfect."

Laure poured tea in their cups and left the room. "So you hate France I take it?" Marceline asked.

Cassie widened her eyes. "Not at all; what makes you think that?"

Marceline peered at her. "You left. You haven't been back in five years."

"I came here because my father has fallen ill. I came from California." She improvised, "And while I'm here I thought I would look for people he lost touch with."

"Lost touch, eh?" Marceline said in an acerbic tone that did not feel all that kindly. With a steady hand, she took a few petit fours and set them on her plate. Cassie drank her tea avidly. She was thirsty and badly needed to pee. In the weirdness of the moment, she had not felt it appropriate to ask the countess for a pot de chambre. "I wonder what about me makes everyone so eager to get to know me of late," Marceline mused. "Everyone wants to get back in touch, it seems. It must be an irresistible scent people my age start emitting."

"A scent?"

"A whiff of approaching death combined with money. It is quite the seductive scent."

Cassie looked at her, horrified. "I hope you don't think that's why I'm here!"

Marceline gazed at her with her yellow, cat-like eyes. "Dear, that's why everyone is here."

Cassie gasped, insulted to her core. Maybe it was the stress of the last few days, but all her restraint and good manners went out the window in a flash. "I'm not here as a strategy to claim anyone's money. I won't try to convince you of the opposite. Think what you like."

"The ploy of the long lost relative, you mean?" Marceline said sweetly as she poured more tea into Cassie's cup. "Why now, then?"

"I'll tell you why now," Cassie said, more abruptly than she wished. "Because up until yesterday I did not know that my father had a sister." Marceline who had been looking straight at her blinked a few times and looked out the window. Cassie continued, "And a week ago, I was in the United States, living my life, minding my own business while my family was planning my father's heart operation without any desire of keeping me informed. Not that this has anything to do with you, but so that you get a sense of how my family functions. Or doesn't. Neither my dad nor my mother and sisters made the smallest attempt to connect with me before taking him to the hospital for a life-threatening surgery. And no, come to think of it, I don't like France all that much."

"Oh, I see," the old woman said with a cryptic smile. "So I might not be the only long-lost relative you have in France."

The comment struck Cassie as accurate. She chose from the tray of petit fours a tiny chocolate éclair. "I'm pretty sure I suck at being part of any family," she said, popping the éclair into her mouth. "Let me ask you something. If you think I'm after your money, why even let me in?"

"Boredom?" Marceline suggested.

Cassie leaned forward, reached for her tea and looked straight into Marceline's eyes. "Don't tell me you're not just a little bit curious about me."

Marceline laughed. She seemed entertained. "Admittedly. In that case, what is it you want from me?"

"I would like to talk to you about the past."

"The past is indeed all I have going for me. There's a point when things cease to happen. All that looms on the horizon is one's mortality. At that point, it becomes all about the past. Rehashing it, wanting it to have mattered.

Could haves, should haves. You hope you made a difference. You hope it wasn't all for nothing."

"Your children will attest that your life wasn't for nothing."

Marceline raised an eyebrow. "My children?"

"They're twins, aren't they? I have twins too."

"Ah, them," Marceline said with an eyeroll.

"They weren't too keen on my meeting you."

Marceline pointed to the stuffed wild cat on a shelf above them. "This lynx has more life in him still than those two ever had." Cassie looked at Marceline in stupefaction, and Marceline laughed. "Could you think a little more quietly? I can read every one of your thoughts!" She waved an impatient hand. "They never made a life for themselves. I was told it isn't their fault. They weren't mothered properly."

"That's quite a pronouncement to make about yourself," Cassie said.

"Oh no, not me … I'm not the mother," Marceline quickly explained. "Theirs died when they were teenagers."

"They called you Mother."

"When it suits them. They certainly never called me that growing up. I did not want children, let alone hormone-laden, brutish adolescents. We've never exactly warmed up to each other. This was my second marriage. Bécasel D'Alompe was a widower." She said with no small amount of satisfaction, "I was a beauty in my youth, you know. There is little left of my looks now, of course," she added coquettishly, perhaps waiting for Cassie to compliment her. And although Cassie could very well imagine how beautiful Marceline might once have been, she did not want to pander to her, so she said nothing. Marceline registered this and seemed pleased. "A count, a widower, and wealthy to boot. You can imagine his appeal to women. But he wanted me, a fifty-year-old divorcée and older than he was by seven years." She shrugged, "I did warn him, told him that I would make a most unsuitable mother. My career demanded that I travel the world; I was never there. Armelle and Jean-Bernard had nannies – au pairs they call them these days, young women in over their heads. My becoming their stepmother did not improve things. Still, I cannot bear grown people who whine about their childhood. Once an adult, one must suck it up and start taking responsibility for oneself, wouldn't you agree?"

Cassie took that one square in the jaw. "Armelle and Jean-Bernard say that you aren't well."

Marceline cackled. "They hope I am not well. I get the use of the house until my death, and then they inherit. Meanwhile, we live under the same roof. Granted there is space, but I have been enduring their gloomy presence for close to forty years. Meanwhile, they've been so busy waiting for my death they forgot how to live their lives. Armelle is married to her last name. Some women are. She was never willing to give that up through marrying into a lesser milieu, and prospects of comparable ranks did not present themselves. As for Jean-Bernard, he's not right in the head as you may have noticed."

"What's wrong with him?"

Marceline shrugged. "A loose screw. Who knows? He never married either, and we should be glad of that." Cassie recoiled at the insensitive remark, and Marceline seemed to notice. "I say things as I see them," she said.

That would be the understatement of the century, Cassie thought. The more Marceline spoke, the less it seemed possible that she and her dad shared DNA at all. Marceline was too vivacious, too sharp, too willing to speak her mind. "Listen, I am just looking for answers to questions about my family."

"Families are more trouble than they're worth. A tremendous source of disappointment and heartache, the lot of them."

"That's what my father seems to think."

"But he suddenly remembered he has a sister?"

Cassie decided that perhaps Marceline would appreciate bluntness. "It was under strange circumstances. When he saw me yesterday, the first time in five years, he got very angry. He cursed at me. He called me names. One name in particular: yours."

Marceline had a little laugh at this and said, "Would you care for another cup of tea?"

"With pleasure."

"And you found me just like that? The next day."

"My sister and I twisted my mom's arm. She told us your last name."

"How did you find me?"

"Your address is listed. You should change that, by the way."

Marceline looked out the window, apparently pondering what Cassie had told her. Outside, the rain had begun falling again, and the strands of wisteria that framed the window swayed in the wind. The old gardener was no longer on the ladder. "Very well then," Marceline said with regret in her voice. "Why don't you ask me what you want to ask me and let this amusing game of charades end."

Cassie wasn't sure she wanted the game to end. She was afraid of Marceline's answers. This woman was far too interesting to learn that they were in no way related. "All right," she said. "Do you have a brother named Gustave Lombard?"

Marceline's expression remained unchanged. Her piercing look revealed a playful intelligence and perfectly sharp mental capacity. And something more: keen interest. Marceline was more engaged in conversing with her than her father would ever have cared to be. "I don't have a brother by that name," she said.

Cassie felt struck by disappointment. And embarrassment. She had congratulated herself for the ease with which she had found his father's sister, but she had found nothing. Instead, she had made a fool of herself with strangers. She leaned back in her chair, her bladder now threatening to burst. "I was wondering if…."

"Yes?"

"I was wondering if I could hmm … be excused."

"I beg your pardon?"

Cassie burst out laughing at her own ridiculousness and Marceline's dumbfounded expression. "I'm sorry. I can't come up with the polite way to speak of bodily functions while in an aristocratic company. I need to go to the bathroom. It's all this tea."

"Oh," Marceline said, "we aristocrats have no shortage of bathrooms or bodily functions. There is one right outside. Actually," she said, changing her mind, "why don't you go to the bathroom right that way instead?" She pointed to the far side of the room, the back door she had come from. "Over through this door. Down the corridor, and then four doors to your left."

Cassie hurried across the room and found herself in a narrow hallway and counted the doors. One. Two. Three. What a letdown. Marceline would not lie to her face, would she? And yet, the portrait: something in Marceline's countenance, the shape of her chin, her eye color.… But no, Cassie should not read everything that was missing from her life into this.

She arrived at the fourth door and turned the porcelain doorknob. She was in a sort of boudoir, a delightful room basking in warm light filtered through pink silk curtains. The light caressed the bookshelf, the daybed, the comfortable chair and ottoman. This was no bathroom; Marceline had made a mistake. Cassie turned around to leave when something incredible caught her eye on the vanity table, among the perfume bottles, the powder boxes, the ivory combs and tortoise hairbrushes. She gasped. Her pulse skyrocketed before she even knew what to make of what lay before her eyes.

Marceline, Marceline, she muttered to herself. You, naughty girl.

A few minutes later, after finding a bathroom behind the second door, Cassie was back in front of Marceline, but this time she had a triumphant smile on her lips. "You have a lovely home," she said.

"What I'd like to know is," Marceline said, "why you should be so preoccupied with your father's personal affairs. Clearly, he wishes to turn the page. Does he want you snooping into his past? Besides, for all you know he might only be attempting to shield you from it."

"I think I can handle his past."

"But what about his wishes?"

"So, you did not answer my question. Why did you accept to meet me?"

"I told you. I don't get to meet new people too often. And the people who already know me tend to find me insufferable. The sentiment is, by the way, quite mutual." She waved her hand, chasing away an objection Cassie did not express. "People find aging in others odious. I know I certainly do. It's nice to meet someone young occasionally. Someone new. So, tell me, if your father did not decide to talk about that sister of his, why get involved?"

"The truth?" Cassie asked.

Marceline smiled thinly. "Preferably."

"I don't care what my dad wants or doesn't want. I'm looking into this for me."

"And yet, some secrets are best left alone."

Cassie narrowed her eyes, "And you know the secret, don't you?"

Marceline chuckled. "Do I?"

"And you do know my father. You didn't send me to the wrong door by accident. You wanted me to find it."

Cassie and Marceline came to a standstill on either side of the tea tray, watching and measuring one another. Marceline broke the silence. "So? Am I the long-lost sister? Is he the long-lost brother?"

"You know you are."

Marceline smiled. "But can you prove it?"

"Other than the fact that you and I look alike? Same curls. Our eye color is similar. Not a common color, is it? Even the way our hairline is the same, the narrow forehead. With all due respect, since you're far prettier than I am."

Marceline nodded with renewed interest. "We do indeed seem to bear a certain resemblance with one another. My hair used to be black and fluff up much like yours."

"But that's not what gave it away."

"What gave it away, good grief?" Marceline laughed, "Are you Hercule Poirot? Is this like in those detective stories?"

"That object I saw in that pink room, on the vanity. The finial. My father owns the very same one. He said there were only two in the world, that they were a pair. One was stolen from him. You have it, right there in that room!"

Marceline sat back. She seemed to be enjoying herself tremendously. "The long-lost sister and the long-lost finial!" she said, beaming.

Cassie frowned, "Why would you not tell me the truth?"

"Point to a single lie that came out of my mouth."

"You denied knowing my father."

"You asked if I had a brother named Gustave … how did you say it? Lombard? The answer to this question is still no."

"But it is him, isn't it?"

"A woman of my rank … not that rank means anything these days, but someone of my wealth must always proceed with caution. Scams are perpetrated on the elderly. And even then, why come here after all these years if you're not here for a piece of the pie."

"The pie?"

"My fortune."

"I have no interest in your fortune," Cassie said, rolling her eyes. "That's not what I'm after. I'm interested in everything that happened before you got any of this."

"So what you're after is my memory."

"Precisely."

"I haven't lost any of my intellectual capacities you know."

"It does look that way."

"But what if my memory conflicts with what you want to hear?"

"I have no preconceived notions of what I want to hear."

"Everyone does. Aren't you worried I might tarnish the way you see your father?"

"Listen," Cassie said. "I need this."

"Why?"

"To figure things out."

"Such as?"

Cassie hesitated. "He and I don't have the closest relationship. As a child, he was wonderful to me. But as I grew up, I don't know … everything changed."

"How so?"

"When I was about twelve years old he became distant and…." She stopped, partly because she was getting choked up, partly because she felt obligated to add a disclaimer. "So that you know, as far as my family sees it, I'm inventing this." Now she felt mildly disgusted with herself. "I hate to rehash old recriminations."

"And why not?" Marceline croaked. "That's all your father ever did."

Cassie was stunned. "I … beg your pardon?"

"Twelve years old, you said?" Marceline asked pensively. "Yes. It would make perfect sense." She grabbed a silver bell and shook it. "I'm calling Laure. We're going to need a whole lot more tea."

****

They remained silent as Laure brought in a new pot of tea. Cassie could tell that the old lady had gone inward. Her haughty defensiveness was changing into a mood Cassie could not decipher. Laure poured tea for them and retreated from the room. Marceline broke her silence. "Perhaps the past is best as you remember it. The way it was told to you has shaped you in ways you might not even realize."

"I want to know the truth about my father."

"The truth? How vague."

"Vague? There only is one truth."

"Nonsense!" the old lady cackled. "There are as many truths as there are human beings experiencing them."

Cassie thought of how her family perceived her vision of the truth as lies. "My dad never spoke of his childhood, of his family, of any of his experiences. He met my mother when he was already forty years old, and it's as though he was born then. There are no pictures. No stories. You'd think he was an amnesiac."

"Trust me on this; he remembers," Marceline said. "That's precisely the problem. What does your mother know about your father's youth?"

"If she knows anything, she's tight-lipped about it."

"What if I told you that your father did not just try to make a break with the past, but that he actively proceeded to erase it?"

"What do you mean?"

"Gustave Lombardi," Marceline said, looking straight at her. "That's my brother's name."

Cassie marked a pause. "It sounds a whole lot like Gustave Lombard, doesn't it?"

"They are one and the same."

Cassie was astonished. "My father would have changed his name?"

"It would appear so."

"And you are my aunt?"

Marceline nodded gravely. "I believe I am."

Cassie beamed. "Well, hello. Lovely to meet you!"

Marceline did not waste time in pleasantries. "Do you know much about your grandparents, Cassandra?"

"Please call me Cassie."

"I will call you Cassandra. Cassie feels common. Too American. And don't you even consider calling me Marcie or anything horrid of that sort."

Cassie sensed there was no point in insisting. "Cassandra it is then," she said. "I've never met my grandparents. I saw a picture of my grandfather once, I think."

Cassie had only seen the picture once, but the man in the photograph, and the context of finding it, were perfectly preserved memories. It was summer. She had lost her first tooth. Her mother was wearing an ultra-short dress with large orange and yellow flowers that were the fashion in the seventies. Her mother looked pretty with her well-applied coral lipstick, her tanned legs and arms, her hoop earrings, and her ash-blonde hair, smooth along her back. But as always, her mother was threatening, somehow, behind the veneer. Raymonde's moods turned quickly, without warning, and she was a slapper. You'd find yourself with a burning cheek, left to ponder what you had done wrong. That morning, her mother had seemed amenable, chatty. She had brought along a Polaroid camera and taken a picture of Cassie's new gap-toothed smile. Once the Polaroid was dry, they had opened the family album where photos were few and far between, entire years left unrecorded. A picture had fallen out of it.

It was a black and white photograph of a man in his forties. He wore a straw hat, pants rolled up at the bottom. He was holding a fishing rod in one hand, and in the other hand a medium-sized fish. He was very handsome. He looked like one of those silent movie stars. But most of all he had her father's smile. He was standing on a balcony. In the background, Cassie remembered the ocean, boats in the distance, palm trees.

"Who's this man?" she had asked her mother.

"That's your father's dad, your grandfather," Raymonde had answered.

This was the first time Cassie had ever heard of a grandfather on her dad's side of the family. "Where is he now?" she had asked.

"He's long dead," Raymonde had said.

The album was closed, and so was the conversation. But Cassie thought about the man in the picture a whole lot for the next few days. However, when she opened the album to look for the picture again, it was gone. At dinner one night she said, "I can't find the photo of your dad, Papa. It's not in the album anymore."

Her father had blanched and looked at his wife.

"What?" Raymonde had said innocently.

"The picture of the man with the fish. My grandfather," Cassie had insisted. "It's not there anymore."

"I have no idea what you're talking about," her mother had said with an air of perfect honesty, so much so that after a while Cassie wondered if she had imagined the whole thing.

"He was handsome, I remember," Cassie told Marceline. "He was smiling. On a terrace. There were stone pillars. He held a fishing rod and a fish."

Marceline turned wistful. "Ah yes," she said. "I know the photograph. World War II. The photograph was taken shortly before he died."

"He wasn't wearing a uniform in the picture."

Marceline looked out the window; her face was drawn. "There are many ways to die in a war. Our father's death was the kind that will tear a family apart."

"I was under the impression that all my father's family had died in the war. His mother too."

"We lived, obviously. Although with great sadness after losing Father. I imagine it was the same for Gustave. My father's name was Albano. Albano Cohen Lombardi." Marceline's eyes moistened. She dabbed at them with a pressed monogrammed handkerchief. "In the picture you saw, was the balcony overlooking a bay?"

"Yes!" Cassie exclaimed. "A bay with boats in the background." The picture existed! Cassie's fists tightened. She should have felt vindicated. Instead, she felt angry. Why had her mother denied it all? These were the kinds of things she did. She'd do or say one thing, and then deny that she had, and in one fell swoop imply that Cassie was the one who was lying, or worse, that she was crazy. "It looked like the South of France."

"Not the South of France," Marceline said, shaking her head. She was looking tired now, and her words came out more slowly. "Algeria. Algiers to be precise. The picture was taken around October 1942, shortly before Operation Torch. I was on a mission for the OSS, part of setting up that operation."

Operation Torch. This was what Jean-Bernard had blurted out. "The OSS?" she asked. "You were a spy?"

"I guess one could call me that."

"What about my dad? Was he a spy as well?"

"That's a matter up for debate. We were children. I was nineteen years old. He was just seventeen. This was war, and we did things. I was given a mission and…. You see, there are many reasons a family's story might get erased. Sometimes, the people are no longer there to talk. Sometimes it is erased on purpose because the collective family suffering is too great. To go on, some people decide to forget."

"And in the case of your family?"

"I'm afraid both were true. You see, Gustave and I were very different. We looked different physically, and our temperaments are opposites indeed. I was the kind of person who took action, whereas he was kind of a dreamer. Also, we had different upbringings."

"Weren't you raised together?"

Marceline closed her eyes. She, who had looked indomitable ten minutes earlier, now looked her age. For an instant, she seemed to forget that Cassie was there, and silence floated between them. "Raised together?" Marceline finally echoed, opening her eyes. "Well, we were. But in all fairness to Gustave, we were not raised in the quite same way." Marceline, lost in her memories, seemed to speak to herself. "To understand Gustave, you must understand Albano," she muttered. "To understand the story of the son, you must know the story of the father. And you must understand the time and place in which each one was born. Albano, your grandfather, was the only one in his immediate family to survive one of the last great cholera pandemics of the nineteenth century. He was born in the Ottoman Empire, you see, in 1900, in Smyrna. He left Smyrna when he was twenty-two after it burned to the ground and the Ottoman Empire collapsed. Smyrna as such doesn't exist anymore. It was renamed Izmir. It's in Turkey. Albano was raised by his uncle. He was the orphan son of a prominent rabbi. He was destined from birth to become a rabbi himself."

"How interesting. So my father must have had some Jewish blood?"

"Some?" Marceline had a dry little laugh that turned into a long cough.

Laure, who must have had a sixth sense about Marceline's physical state, arrived in the room. "Madame," she said. "You don't want to exert yourself. The doctor said…."

Marceline ignored Laure, took a sip of tea, and stopped coughing. "Both our parents were Jewish," she told Cassie. "As were their parents, and their grandparents before that. Your father was as Jewish as they come."

"I don't see how that would work," Cassie said. "We are Catholic. Kind of. I mean, my father was, and my mother too. I think. But we weren't religious. My sisters and I weren't baptized. We didn't go to church or anything."

Marceline looked appalled. "Are you telling me that Gustave hid his entire Jewish heritage from his daughters?"

Cassie frowned at this. "He wasn't hiding it … I don't think. Religion was not a topic of conversation in our family. I never gave it any thought and—"

"Are you an anti-Semite?" the old lady interrupted, peering at her intently above her cup.

Cassie nearly squirted tea through her nose. "Of course not! But I know very little about Judaism one way or another."

"Clearly."

"I'm not familiar with the religion, or the tradition. It doesn't mean that I have negative feelings," Cassie said. "I studied the history of Europe like every other French student. I know about the Holocaust. Although I never understood why anyone would have issues with Judaism or the Jews. That has never made sense to me."

"Even those who take issue with Judaism have to fabricate reasons why they do. The idea that your father would not tell you about his roots surprises me, but I guess it shouldn't. I had no idea how far removed he was trying to get from us. Perhaps it is to be understood in context; I can try to explain if you have the patience."

"Go as far back in time as you need to."

Marceline set her cup down, and tapped her bony fingertips on the table, gathering her thoughts. "All right then. You should know that both your grandfather and grandmother were Sephardic Jews. They were descendants of Jews exiled from Spain in the thirteenth century."

Cassie moaned inwardly. What had she gotten herself into? Marceline continued, "To refresh your memory, this was when King Ferdinand of Aragon and Queen Isabella of Castile issued the edict that expelled all Jews from Spain in 1492. Jews were given a few months to convert to Christianity, leave, or die. You did learn that in school, didn't you?"

No, Cassie did not remember a thing about it. "It rings a bell," she answered.

"I should hope so," Marceline said. "The Ottoman Empire seemed like a reasonable destination for exile. It wasn't a shabby place either. The Ottoman Empire, at its apogee, spanned no less than three continents from Europe to Asia to parts of Africa. A single man, Sultan Bayezid II, had the fate of our family, and perhaps that of an entire segment of Jewish culture, in his hands. He was incredulous that Spain would willingly weaken its economy by evicting its wealthiest and most educated citizens, and he issued a decree extending to the Jews of Spain immediate citizenship. For good measure, he declared it punishable by death to disagree with his edict and went so far as to ridicule Ferdinand and Isabella for impoverishing their kingdom and enriching his – which the Jews most certainly did, for centuries after that. The idea of different races and religions cohabitating in good harmony is a pipe dream nowadays. So you can only imagine how things were throughout the world in the 1400s.

"Well, the Ottoman Empire of the time may have been such a dream. This was perhaps the single place in the world that would find Christians, Jews, and Muslims living and able to worship side by side, protected by a decree of the government. All religions and ethnicities were allowed to coexist in relative peace. Armenians, Turks, Kurds, Greeks, Christians, and Jews did just that, for centuries. And each group was established in free, autonomous societies called millets. Millets followed their respective religion in the places of worship they built – the Jews, the Christians, the Orthodox

Greeks, the Muslims, and so forth. Millets functioned according to their own religious and civil laws, spoke their own languages. Their children were educated in their own customs, in their own schools, all with the legal supervision and protection of the Empire in exchange for loyalty to it. Not to mention stiff taxation." Marceline stopped and said, "I don't mean to bore you, but your family's roots can be traced back to the fifteenth century."

Cassie realized that she was sitting on the edge of her armchair, her body forward. "There is nothing I want to hear about more," she assured her. But it wasn't just the story she found fascinating; it was Marceline herself. The way she spoke with conviction, her sentences unclouded by hesitation, like a person who never doubted for a moment that what she had to say deserved attention. The sort of woman Cassie had never known she wanted to be. And with this realization, Cassie felt immensely guilty of liking Marceline too much, of liking her and wanting to be liked by her, which was even worse.

"Thus arrived your grandfather's ancestors," Marceline continued. "After being evicted from Spain with their riches, talents, and education, they promptly went to work building, learning, trading, and innovating. Many Jews grew to prominent roles in finance, politics, medicine, manufacturing, and commerce all over the Ottoman Empire. This went on for centuries with everyone living in relative harmony, give or take a fair share of massacres and wars. And then it all came to a halt by the end of the 1920s."

"World War I?" Cassie asked.

"Even in 1902," Marceline continued without bothering to respond, "when my father, Albano, was born, the Ottoman Empire, after centuries of unparalleled greatness, was ailing. Well, it had had a good run. In the early 1900s, the mood of the world was tipping toward nationalism. It happens every so often; you will discover that for yourself should you live as long as I have. The budding nationalistic hysteria that would soon bring nations to wage war against one another saw itself played out within the Ottoman Empire. What had made the Empire so remarkable, its capacity to embrace immigrants regardless of their religion or nationality, was now at the very core of its demise. It was, shall we say, too mixed. Whatever aggrieved them, people found ways to blame those who weren't like them. Greeks fought Turks, Turks massacred Armenians, Arabs revolted, and everyone hated the Jews."

Smyrna was different, at least for a time. The Ottoman Empire was losing its power and girth, but Smyrna, where my father resided, remained the Pearl of the Orient. Its location on the Aegean Sea put it at the intersection of many nautical roads between Europe and the Orient. Sure, there must have been the same racial hatred there as everywhere, but the world's commercial interests kept Smyrna out of the fray, and there were fewer manifestations. When the Turks, who were on the side of the Axis, lost the Great War, World War I as it is known, the Treaty of Sèvres gave Smyrna and other chunks of the Empire to the Greeks. Another war between the Turks and the Greeks started over land control that lasted for years until

Greece was defeated in Anatolia. As the Greek army retreated, Christian and Muslim populations suffered reprisals at the hands of both the Turkish army and the defeated Greek army. Villages were destroyed, crops set on fire, women and children killed, daughters raped. This news, reported by the influx of refugees, brought the ethnic communities that had previously respected one another to a paroxysm of racial hatred. This culminated for Smyrna in September 1922 when the city was burned to the ground.

"How?" Cassie asked. "By whom?"

"No one can agree. The Turks accuse the Greeks of burning it down when they saw that they had lost control of it, and the Greeks believe the Turks did it, in reprisal against the Greek and Armenian populations. The Smyrna fire raged for days. It is said that hundreds of thousands who had taken refuge on the quayside were killed. My father left Smyrna at that point."

CHAPTER 10

Flames

Albano walked across the Smyrna pier with joy in his heart. Throughout the Empire, the war between the Greeks and the Turks still raged. Endlessly conflicting rumors as to which country was winning and which was losing never amounted to anything concrete. One could no more trust the printed news than the alarming gossips that rippled through Smyrna. But today, Albano did not feel concerned. Men could go on slaughtering each other to their heart's desire for all he cared. In only a few weeks he would become a father, and shortly after that, he, Xandra, and their child would board the boat that would take them away from the Ottoman Empire and toward their new life in Paris.

Xandra's medicinal brew had worked; until it had not. When they first understood that she was expecting, Albano and Xandra were overwhelmed with equal measures of joy and dread. They now lived a life of outcasts, and the guilt and pain of Hagop's disappearance clung to them like a shroud. For over a year, he and Xandra had been deeply happy in the cave. But with the discovery of the pregnancy came a new set of worries. It would be months before the birth, but they had to think ahead. Taking care of a newborn by themselves was daunting. At first, they had fantasized that Xandra might be accepted back into her family now that she was with child. But Yori, they had learned, had openly sworn to give her a beating or worse if she ever reappeared, and he had even boasted about killing Albano. Would Yori do it? They did not think so. They hoped that the bragging was his attempt at keeping his standing, but the more they discussed it, the less they were willing to take the chance. They resigned themselves to Xandra giving birth without the support of her mother or her community. They had then decided on the next best thing: a hospital birth at the American hospital. It would be expensive, but they could save for it if Albano added more hours of hard physical labor on the quayside and around the city.

After much discussion with Xandra, Albano decided that there was nothing to lose and everything to gain by daring to write a letter, the most important letter he would ever write, the response to which could change everything.

Dear Uncle Moshe, Albano's letter said.

I have a wife now. Her name is Xandra. Well, we are not properly married, but we have just found out that we are expecting a child. Xandra is Armenian, and because of our illicit union, her family has repudiated her. She risks her life if she as much as sets foot in the Armenian quarter, but she isn't welcome in the Jewish quarter either. We have been living on our own on Mount Pagus for the last year, with much help and generosity from Uncle Joshua, but we fear it isn't much of a future to offer our child. We have thoughts of leaving Smyrna to make a life elsewhere. What do you think of France? Do you believe it is a good place for Xandra and me? Might there be possibilities to work there for someone coming from the Ottoman Empire? Xandra and I have been learning French just in case.

Yours truly,

Albano

"How long before the letter reaches him?" Xandra asked.

"A month at most. And another one to receive his reply."

They waited patiently, barely daring to make plans out loud. Each day, Albano stopped by the post office hoping for a letter. When it came at last, Albano resisted opening it until he was back in the cave with Xandra.

It was evening, and the fire was ready, with soup cooking in the kettle. Xandra, who was rounder and more beautiful by the day, opened the letter ceremoniously and gave it to Albano to read out loud.

"My dear Albano," began Uncle Moshe's response.

In the aftermath of the bloodbath that was the Great War, France is eager for able bodies to work on their farms and factories, and desperate enough to seek out the help of foreigners. Visas are easy to obtain, especially if you are in possession of a promise of employment, which I am enclosing. Come work with me, Albano! My rug commerce has blossomed, and I have recently sought to expand into the diamond trade. I could use someone I can trust, and I trust no one as much as I trust my own blood. Come to Paris, Albano! Bring your Xandra. I will find a place for you to live. Xandra will need to do nothing further than raise your precious child. Let me know what else you might need, and I will help you.

Warmly,

Your Uncle Moshe

Incredulous, Albano lifted his eyes from the letter. Xandra looked stunned. "Does he mean this?" she asked, her expression full of wonder.

"Uncle Moshe can be a joker, but he is a man of his word."

"France," she murmured. "We can go to France and start a new life."

"Not just a new life, my love. A better life. You read what he said. He wants me to work for him!"

Xandra laughed. "My Albano, the French businessman!"

They discussed this for hours, but every conclusion they came to was the same. They had a chance of starting over in Paris, and they should grab that chance. That meant leaving Smyrna and their families behind and becoming strangers in a foreign land. But in this foreign land, they would be together without hiding, without risk to their lives. Albano wrote a second letter:

Dear Uncle Moshe,

Xandra and I will remain forever in your debt. What you are offering goes beyond our wildest hopes and dreams. We thank you from the bottom of our hearts and accept your generous invitation and offer of work. I hope I can be of help to you, although I know little about rugs, and even less about diamonds, having never even seen one.

I hear that there is anti-Semitism in Europe. Is this something I should be concerned about?

Albano

My Dear Nephew,

Paris has a thriving Jewish community that has prospered here for generations. I'm afraid the brand of Judaism practiced here might not meet with your admirably devout pursuits. Yes, people go to synagogues and light candles for the Shabbat, but I have not seen strong signs of devotion. I am afraid most of this will offend you terribly.

Uncle Moshe

Dear Uncle Moshe,

I hope it is not I who will offend you, dear Uncle. I have renounced becoming a rabbi, and both Xandra and I have vowed to renounce any religion that conspires to keep us apart.

Albano

Dearest Albano and Xandra,

Your choice does not offend me in the least. I am of the mind that it is love, not war, or religion, or power that should be humanity's chief pursuit, and thus, I trust that my personal life choices will not be of a nature to vex you either.

Uncle Moshe

Albano lifted his eyes from the letter. "What does he mean?" Xandra asked.

Albano shrugged. "I don't know."

Albano set out to write another letter in which he told Uncle Moshe he would be working hard to save up money for the boat ride. For the time being, he explained, their savings went to pay for the hospital birth, but as soon as the child was born, he would save for the trip. If all went well, he had calculated that it would take about two years before they could pay for the boat trip to Europe.

Albano set out to work even harder. There was plenty of day labor on the quayside. For the next several months, and as Xandra's belly swelled, their spirits filled with dreams and their hearts with hope.

In the cave, Xandra and Albano, lying on their straw mat and propped with feather pillows against the stone, spent hours practicing French. Every so often, Albano would place his head close to the warmth of Xandra's belly, hoping to feel the kick of the baby, a feeling that never ceased to fill him with wonderment. Already, Albano read and spoke French; now he enjoyed teaching it to Xandra, correcting her diction as she read from the newspaper, her eyebrows twisting in the effort.

They would adopt the ways of France, its language, its traditions, unquestioningly. They would apply for citizenship once there. In France, just as they did in the cave, they vowed to pray privately, and never to force their faith on each other. They also vowed never to blame each other for the choices they made together. They made plans for their child, and for future children. They would teach them about God but not impose a religion. They would teach them about their respective languages and cultures but not to fear people who were different from them. The future thrilled them. Leaving Smyrna would be hard, especially for Xandra, because it would be giving up entirely on the hope of ever connecting with her family again.

One day, after toiling all day under the hard sun loading bags of dried apricots into a boat for Aleppo, Albano went to the American Express office, which he used as a mailing address. Uncle Moshe had sent not a letter this time, but a parcel.

Albano brought it back to the cave that evening, and he and Xandra opened the small brown package excitedly. The box contained a letter, a beautiful shawl of the finest silk decorated with miniature Eiffel Towers, and a French dictionary thickly bound in black leather.

Dearest Albano and Xandra,

I certainly don't plan on waiting years for my new business partner! I took the liberty of sending you a few things. The dictionary might not thrill you, but this time, the adage that one should not judge a book by its cover will not apply. As to your boat expense, you will find within the pages of this book that one thing you said you have never encountered before.

Your Uncle Moshe

"What is he saying?" Xandra wondered, the beautiful silk shawl already wrapped around her shoulders. "Your Uncle Moshe is strange. I don't know what he means half the time."

Albano shook his head. "He's an imaginative person. He likes to tell stories." He shrugged, "This dictionary can only be helpful for our lessons," he said, turning the pages. Suddenly he stopped, widening his eyes.

"What?" Xandra asked as Albano was suddenly turning the dictionary in all directions, opening its pages, fiddling with the cover. "What are you doing, Albano?" Albano was now looking at the cover until his fingers met a slight bulging under the leather. He looked at Xandra, took his knife, and gently peeled off the glue around that area.

A small diamond fell into his lap.

They both gasped. Xandra brought her hands to her mouth. "Oh my God!"

Albano marveled. "That's the thing I said I had never seen before. I guessed what he was trying to tell us: a diamond! Uncle Moshe sent this to pay for the boat ride."

****

Thus, a month later, on a crisp early September morning of the year 1922, Albano was walking toward Smyrna's quayside dressed in his best clothes. In a secret fold of his pants pocket was the small diamond that never left his possession, the key to their safe passage out of Smyrna. Today, he would finalize his arrangement with a ship going to Marseille and pick up the stamped visas that awaited him at the French consulate. Then he would approach the many jewelers in Smyrna and see who would give him the best price for his diamond.

He had not sold the diamond right away because he found it much easier to conceal it than to hide the equivalent in currency. Albano also had a murkier reason: he found it difficult to part with such a wonderful thing. At night, he and Xandra delighted in watching it glisten in the light of the fire. During the day, when he was sure to be alone, Albano took it out of the small leather pouch Xandra had sewn for it and admired its luminescent beauty in the sun. To think that one little stone, carved just so, could hold such value and such beauty! To think that one little shiny rock could transform three lives!

It was early in the morning still, and the French consulate would not open for a little while. Albano decided he would wait for the consulate's opening by doing one of his favorite things, which was to buy a newspaper and sit on the terrace of a French bistro and order a coffee. When he was a child, Albano had admired those groomed, educated European men as they sat on the terraces before heading to work, taking their time to be served breakfast and peruse the news. They had then seemed to him the embodiment of poise and sophistication. He had known then, without believing it possible, that this was the life he wanted.

What a glorious September morning this was, he thought, as he descended toward the quays. He only wished Xandra could share this moment with him. She had not left Mount Pagus in over a year. She was even more prudent not to be seen, unmarried as she was, now that she had a large belly. In Paris, things would be different. The two of them would be able to share every moment, without hiding, without fear. In Paris, he decided, they would start every morning so: they would awaken just as the dawn broke and would walk together down the streets until they found a nice café. They would order breakfast and read the newspaper together. No one would look at them or judge them. They would be like any husband and wife, simply having their breakfast.

****

As Albano walked, the sky was bright blue, and a sea breeze ruffled the top of palm trees and caressed his skin. It was a shame to leave Smyrna now, he thought, just as the city had regained its cosmopolitan flair. The French, the British, and the Italians had returned to Smyrna. On the quayside, you could again sit on the terrace of restaurants, order a cassoulet or an eggplant parmigiana, and watch people from every corner of the earth go about their business. The Ottoman Empire had been on the losing side in 1919 and so large parts of it, including Smyrna, were now under Greek control. But the Greeks, who had taken the city without much bloodshed, ran it well. Preserving their commercial interests meant preserving everyone else's as well. For this reason, even the local Turks didn't object too loudly to the fact that their city had been taken from them.

As Albano made his way toward the pier, he averted his eyes when he passed groups of Armenians, Greek, or Turkish men. The sight of Europeans in their finest attire on their morning stroll by the water did not tell the whole story. Smyrna, open as it was to the sea and the rest of the world, was only a pocket of calm and prosperity, strangely exempt from the vicissitudes of the time. Nothing was serene in the Empire. The Greeks ran the city, but the war with the Turks still raged. Hatred was everywhere. The many years of war had turned peaceful men into soldiers and reasonable ones of all ethnicities into political extremists and religious fanatics. Every day, Albano questioned his decision to wait until their child was born to leave for Europe. Was it wise? Their situation was precarious. Everyone in the Armenian quarter was a danger to them, and they had few friends in the Jewish quarter. And then, there was Xandra who looked gloriously beautiful with her swollen belly. Her vulnerability had become a source of anguish to him. Since the early days of the war, men had reverted to their darkest instincts. Her beauty and the vulnerability of her pregnancy put her at risk. He did not tell her this, but it was something he worried about a great deal.

The moment he arrived on the quayside, Albano was startled to see not just one but several warships on the horizon. He made his way toward the row of cafés, restaurants, and brasseries, and like everyone he passed, looked out at the sea. People were agitated, exchanging speculations, wondering out loud about the presence of warships in the bay. Albano went to sit on the terrace of a French café he favored. "What is happening?" he asked the usual waiter.

"We don't know," the waiter said, setting a cup of coffee on his table. "They keep coming and coming, one warship after another. Here!" He pointed in the distance. "Another one coming! Over there!"

The arrival of a new warship sent everyone into a frenzy of extrapolations.

"Is it an attack?" someone asked.

"The Turks are here!" another shouted.

"Of course not," someone said. "This is the Greek fleet, can't you see? The Greeks aren't about to attack their own city." In the crowd, people laughed.

As more warships entered the bay, and as everyone peered at the horizon, trying to make sense of things, the flags on some of the ships became visible. A Levantine man pulled expensive binoculars out of their case and began to scrutinize the horizon. "What do you see?" people asked.

"It's not just the Greeks!" the Levantine man exclaimed. "I see a French flag. And this one is British!"

"And an Italian destroyer!" screamed another man who also had binoculars. "This makes no sense."

Soon there were about twenty European warships on the horizon as well as many Greek vessels. A post office employee came running in, red and sweaty and brandishing a printed cable.

"Kemal's army has won in Anatolia. The Greeks are defeated!"

Everyone in the café went silent. Cigarettes fell from lips. People stood up, dropped their newspapers and napkins.

Fear rocked Albano like a terrible earthquake, as though the ground had shaken beneath his feet. Everyone on the quay began to speak at once, all saying the same thing, in their language: "This was impossible. It had to be incorrect. How could the Greeks be defeated? They had the largest and strongest army. A much better army than Mustapha Kemal's."

"I heard the Greek army is bankrupt. They have no weapons, no shoes, no horses," someone said.

"The Greek newspapers have kept saying that everything was fine."

"They were only trying to raise our spirits."

"But why are there European warships in the bay?"

"Are they here to protect us against the Turks?"

The thought was both chilling and reassuring. It would make sense that the boats had been dispatched to intervene. There were too many Europeans living and working in Smyrna. The warships must have been sent here as a deterrent.

Things were happening fast. They watched, filled with dread and hope as an imposing Greek warship came close to the quay and dropped anchor.

Soon, a dozen rafts approached, each holding just a few Greek sailors. They docked, and the sailors put down their oars, prepared their rifles, and waited. For what? The sight of rifles quieted everyone. The crowd, confused, waited as well. All eyes were on the Greek sailors and their weapons. Something would happen any instant now; the crowd sensed it.

Suddenly, there was a shift in people's attention. Café chairs were pushed in unison as men rose from their tables. Gazes shifted, and hundreds of disbelieving faces turned away from the boats and toward the crowd on the quayside. People parted, revealing a lone soldier who was making his way across the quay, limping toward the water. It was a Greek soldier, bare feet, weaponless. His uniform was in shreds and bloodied. There was a thick, dirty bandage over his head. His eyes were empty, and he looked at no one. People continued to part all around him as he labored toward the water on what seemed to be his last reserves of strength. Were the rafts waiting for him? Albano wondered if he was someone important in need of an escort.

"A retreating Greek soldier!" someone said out loud, voicing what everyone understood at once.

The soldier made his way to the dock. Once there, assisted by the Greek sailors, he clambered into one of the rafts. But the raft did not move; the sailors did not take their oars. They continued to wait. A heavy silence fell on the quayside as heads turned in unison toward a second Greek soldier, in just as bad shape, now appearing through the crowd. And now another. And another, and soon there were dozens of them. All were in a terrible condition. All seemed propelled to get to the water, and all climbed inside the rafts. One soldier dropped to his knees and then to the ground before he could reach the dock. Two soldiers not much better off than he was picked him up by his armpits and dragged him toward the boats.

In minutes, the mood on the quayside had shifted. There was a sense of urgency, of mounting panic among the patrons of the restaurants, the fishermen, the restaurant waiters. Albano felt it too, the sensation of doom, like a big wash of dread that hollowed out the belly: something terrible had happened, or was about to. One moment a dozen soldiers clambered toward the boats, the next there was a hundred of them, and the reality of the pathetic state of the Greek army was revealed. The soldiers were dirty, shoeless, bandaged, and bloodied. Many had lost their weapons. On each face was painted the carnage they had suffered. But as pathetic as it was to witness the collapse of an army, no one on the quay was prepared to face what happened next. In the trail of the soldiers appeared the first of the Greek refugees. Soon there were hundreds of them: children, old men, and women, women carrying babies. Judging from their exhaustion, they must have been walking for days. They carried few belongings. They were filthy and haggard. Many immediately started to beg for water and food. There were many injured among the civilians and many burn victims dragged in stretchers or pushed in wheelbarrows. The cries and moans of pain iced the blood as much as the deadness in their eyes.

The rafts dispatched to rescue the fleeing army, now filled, began to make their way back to the Greek fleet. The incoming Greek soldiers who continued arriving down from inland in droves gathered on the dock, awaiting rescue.

"Who are these people?" someone asked.

"Did you see?" someone pointed out. "Not a single Greek refugee was allowed into the rescue boats."

"They will come back for them."

"What if they don't? How many more are there? What if they leave the refugees here? The city cannot absorb all these people."

Albano understood what everyone on the quay understood. If the Greek army was retreating, it meant that the Turks were advancing. In less than a day, Mustapha Kemal could be in Smyrna, eager to retake the city. There was no telling what would happen then. Throughout the Empire, it had been the same story. What a fool he had been to believe that Smyrna would be any different! There had been retaliation on civilian populations: the systematic destruction, the burning of villages, rapes, and murders had reached a paroxysm of madness everywhere. Why would Smyrna be exempt from all this? The state of those refugees, now advancing by the thousands, betrayed the devastation they must have suffered inland, a devastation which might soon befall the Christians of Smyrna.

"They will burn the city down!" someone cried out.

"Assuredly not," a voice said. "Mustapha Kemal would not allow the destruction of the Jewel of the Orient." There was a collective murmur of assent. The Turks would not want the city damaged. It had too much Islamic history, magnificent mosques, not to mention that Smyrna played an essential commercial role on an international scale.

"This is why the warships are here," someone said. "Every country wants to preserve its interests and its citizens. They are standing guard. Kemal will never dare create a diplomatic incident. After all, he is only at war with the Greeks, not with all of Europe." There was a collective sense of relief. People had found ways to convince themselves that they would be safe.

Albano thought differently.

He knew in an instant what he needed to do. He needed to head for the French consulate to get their stamped visas and run back up Mount Pagus to fetch Xandra. They would board the first French ship that would take them. The luxury of waiting until Xandra had safely given birth was a notion of the past. If this was true that the Turks were advancing, no Christian in the city was safe. Doubt came to his mind. Should he first pick up the visas? They were stamped at last and ready to use. Or should he not waste a moment in alerting Xandra? The Turkish army would want to take possession of the highest ground in the city, as was their symbolic way to claim it. What if they decided that Mount Pagus constituted the highest part of the city?

He needed to get Xandra first! The visas would have to wait.

Albano put money down next to his steaming coffee and abandoned the café. He rushed away from the esplanade as soldiers and refugees poured into the quay in increasing numbers. Many simply collapsed as close to the water as possible. Those who could immediately set up camp, laying claim to every nook they could find on the esplanade, against the walls of buildings, on porches and stoops, all around the fountain where he had met Hagop that first day, and under every bit of shade they could find. Women were crying out for food and water for their children as Good Samaritans came out of restaurants and cafés bringing glasses of water and bread. One thing was obvious: at the rate with which the refugees were arriving, those efforts would soon prove vastly insufficient.

****

Albano arrived in the cave two hours later. In the cave, Xandra was preparing a meal. She got up from the ground, her expansive belly weighing her down. "What is happening?" she asked the instant she saw the expression on his face, his red cheeks, and sweaty clothes.

"The Greeks have lost," Albano said. "The Turks are coming. Thousands of refugees are pouring into Smyrna in the trail of what's left of the Greek army. We need to go down to the city. Now."

He had expected Xandra to panic, but that wasn't her way. She only blanched and asked, "Why now?"

"There are European and American ships, even Japanese ones, in the bay to watch over the city. If there is looting or massacres, it will be in the mountains and inland where the rest of the world cannot see."

"Did you get the visas?"

At that moment, Albano sensed it: he had made a mistake. "I thought it best to get you first," he said.

"Why can't we stay in the cave? It has protected us this far."

"How long would we need to stay in hiding? Days? Months? How would we eat? And after that, what is to say that Kemal's Smyrna would let Christians and Muslims coexist?"

"What about Jews?"

"I think he might leave Jews alone."

"Then you can get food from your uncle, and I'll continue in the cave until the baby comes."

Albano shook his head. "I think we need to leave before the baby is born. We need to leave now. With all the sick refugees coming in I worry that you might be turned down at the hospital."

"The hospital would not turn down a pregnant woman."

Albano tried not to let his voice betray all he had seen. "I saw pregnant women and children in need of care in the streets today."

"The baby will come in the cave then," Xandra said, shaking her head stubbornly. "You will help me with the birth, and I will feed our child. We don't need the hospital."

"You have not seen what I saw," Albano implored. "I fear that a great tragedy is about to befall the city. We need to board the first French ship we can and leave. Immediately."

Xandra put her hand on her belly, protectively. She was quiet for a long while, thinking. "If you are certain this is what we must do," she said.

"I am certain of nothing," he admitted.

Xandra did not respond. In the darkness of the cave, she began gathering their belongings in silence. They packed clothes for the child, the ones she had sewn. Also food: cheese, olives, bread, and dried fruit. Albano filled their sheepskin with water. Xandra packed up their spare set of clothes and sandals. They concealed the finials in the folds of Xandra's wide skirt, in narrow pockets she had sewn especially for this purpose between layers of her petticoat.

Within thirty minutes, all was ready. From the crevice behind the boulders, they retrieved the money stashed away for the hospital birth fee.

****

They trekked slowly, hiding in bushes when they heard the galloping of a horse or the roar of an automobile. When they joined the main road, Xandra and Albano gasped. On his way to the cave, he had crossed paths with refugees by the hundreds who were going down the mountain and heading for the sea. Now, the road to the city was packed with thousands upon thousands of refugees and soldiers, perhaps a hundred thousand or more. Albano had never seen so many human beings in one place.

They joined the slowly moving crowd, felt their heat, their stench. They could not have gone any faster than the crawling pace at which this wave of sick, wounded, hungry, and thirsty humans moved. Albano stayed close to Xandra. They both carried their possessions on their back, with Albano bearing the heaviest load. Dozens of times Albano felt sick having to fend off children and mothers who were begging. How rapidly and easily a person could revert to caring only about his self-interest, even in the face of hungry children.

Already, it was dark. The slow procession of moonlit silhouettes slowed to a crawl when they finally arrived near the quayside. Xandra and Albano, pressed against many bodies, held hands and said nothing as they advanced ever so slowly, trying not to bump into those ahead of them. On the darkening horizon, one could still make out the reassuring presence of the dozen warships anchored in the harbor.

The glamorous esplanade of the morning had turned into an encampment, a lumpy mass composed of thousands of strewn bodies, parcels, goats, caged chickens, and whatever meager possessions with which the refugees had managed to escape. The smell of feces and urine was terrible, as were the moans that floated in the falling night.

On the docks, the Greek rescue boats worked relentlessly by the light of lanterns carrying soldiers to the destroyers and then rushing back to the quay for more.

Albano held Xandra's hand tightly as they walked across the esplanade in the darkness, stumbling on the limbs of sleeping children, and barely avoiding stepping in trash and excrement, until they found an open spot near an Armenian family, a mother, father, and their three small children. Xandra set blankets on the ground, and she and Albano discreetly shared a few almonds.

"As soon as it is morning," Albano whispered, "I'll go to the French consulate and retrieve the visas. I'll sell the diamond, send a cable to Uncle Moshe explaining the situation, and we will present ourselves at the first ship in the direction of France, newly purchased tickets in hand."

This optimistic plan, buoyed by Albano's falsely reassuring tone, allowed them to fall into an uneasy sleep.

****

With the call of the first caged rooster, the esplanade awakened and Albano took in the seriousness of the situation. The lighthearted atmosphere that had prevailed on the quay through both wars had made way to desperation. The entire quayside was nothing but a mass of wounded, sickly refugees, exhausted from their painful trek from inland to shore, and more of them were arriving every minute. They were Christians and, for the most part, Greek and Armenian women, children, and elderly folks. All had followed the retreating Greek army for protection. The only young men present were the crippled ones who had not been suited for war. One woman in ten appeared to be pregnant.

"Why did you come here?" Albano asked the Armenian mother and father near where they had settled.

"We followed the army to the water, and here we are," the husband answered with exhaustion. It was clear that he had no desire to converse. "We hope to escape by boat before Kemal's army enters Smyrna," he said wearily.

"But why did you leave?"

The man peered at him, dismayed by Albano's ignorance. "The Turks have destroyed our village, burned everything. They raped our women and girls. They even slaughtered children. Innocent children! From our village, we alone were able to bring our family intact. So many have lost everyone."

"This is the way of the Turks," the wife told Xandra, her face distorted with loathing and rage. "They are beasts, and they will want the blood of everyone here."

Xandra and Albano looked at each other, a current of terror passing between them. "But they won't need to kill anymore," Albano said almost pleadingly. "They have won."

"It is true what they say!" the husband said, disgusted. "You Smyrniots have suffered nothing of the wars." He spat on the ground and added angrily, "This is the way it has been. Each military victory is followed by rapes and massacres."

"But you are Armenian," Xandra said. "The Turks are at war with the Greeks."

"They are at war with anyone who is not Muslim, but they hate the Armenians the most. Jews and Muslims are in this together; they want to exterminate every single Christian in the Ottoman Empire."

Xandra seemed about to respond something in defense of the Jews, but Albano silenced her with a wary look.

"They say Kemal's army is well trained and honorable," Albano said with as much assurance as he could muster.

To this, the husband shook his head glumly. "Perhaps, but the Chettes have filled his army."

"What are those?"

"Irregulars and mercenaries. They are devoted to Kemal, but they are not soldiers. They do not follow discipline. And what of your local Turkish citizens? What will they do when Kemal arrives? They will celebrate and join in the looting, that's what they'll do. This is how it has been in every village, in every city." The man changed his tone to a whisper so that only Albano and Xandra could hear. "But if the Turkish army doesn't, the Greek army will. They know they have lost Smyrna and they will destroy everything so that Kemal won't be able to put his hands on it."

As though this conversation was spontaneously repeating itself from person to person, the population on the quay seemed gripped with collective panic. The Armenians and Greeks feared the Turkish army, but the Armenians feared the Greeks too. Everyone was terrified.

As the Greek soldiers continued being evacuated by the hundreds, everyone else was beginning to stand in lines awaiting a chance to board a ship, holding a spot for their families, clutching papers that proved their nationalities. It was clear that orders were not to evacuate. Tempers started to flare up.

"They are still not taking refugees! Soldiers first, they say," a Greek man growled upon returning from the dock.

On other docks further to the right, another kind of activity was building. Vehicles were unloading throngs of British, French, and Italian citizens who pressed themselves into lines. Levantines families were in line as well, dressed in their manner, a mix between styles of the Occident and the Orient. Their luggage was arranged in neat piles as Turkish servants fanned them and brought them refreshments from the nearby cafés. Nowhere had the divide between human circumstances been more striking:

one group hopeless, famished, filthy, and the other radiating entitlement and self-importance. But there was a single emotion the wealthy and the downtrodden shared, and that was fear. No one knew for sure what was about to unfold, but all seemed clear on the urgent need to leave Smyrna.

"Why aren't the British and French warships sending rescue boats? What are they waiting for?" someone in the crowd said.

"Word is they won't take in refugees. In their minds, this is an issue between the Greeks and the Turks, and they want to remain neutral. Each warship will only take their own citizens."

Xandra looked at Albano, panic-stricken. Albano whispered to her reassuringly. "Our situation is different. We will have French visas. We won't be refugees in their eyes."

A small boat detached itself from the Italian destroyer and docked. Italian journalists and photographers clambered out noisily and proceeded to unload their equipment, still and movie cameras. The Italian journalists made their ways to the cafés and opened their briefcases to reveal encased typewriters. They immediately took out paper and carbon and began typing. Others unfurled their equipment and started taking photographs. Albano was reminded of the story of the human zoo, and of the people who found it entertaining to visit them. Whatever was about to happen, the world would be watching indeed.

In the harbor, refugees had to make way for Levantine automobiles. The cars stopped, and servants in white livery jumped out and stacked crates, boxes, and suitcases while others loaded them onto private boats. The Levantine women shielded their skin from the sun with lace umbrellas and put lavender-scented handkerchiefs over their noses to protect their senses from the stench. "The Levantines are sending their women and children away," Xandra said. "I recognize some of my customers."

"I recognize some of them as well."

"Could we ask them for help?"

"If it comes to that," Albano said.

Xandra looked at him intently. "When will we know if it has come to that?"

"Let me retrieve the French visas as soon as the consulate opens. Then we'll know more."

"Maybe we should go to the Armenian quarter," Xandra said. "Perhaps seeing the danger, someone I know will forgive us for what we did and offer us shelter for a day."

Albano hesitated before stating the harsh truth. "Xandra, I am not certain the Armenian quarter will be safe at all once Kemal's army arrives."

They decided that Xandra would stay next to the Armenian family while Albano picked up the visas. The French government building was only five minutes away. Albano walked across the quayside trying not to listen to his thoughts. For now, at least, things were relatively calm. The many warships floated in the bay and beyond, a sight that was both alarming and reassuring.

The crowd of refugees had huddled on the quayside although the influx seemed to have slowed. But it was too many people in too close proximity. Albano sensed it; the slightest incident would trigger a chain reaction of panic. If that happened, things would deteriorate. Unrest would affect the functioning of the consulate, the banks, and the ocean liner traffic and derail his plans, plans that were very far off course already. He felt trapped. He sensed that they all were, trapped on the quayside with a single goal, a single thought: to find a boat out of Smyrna. That task, which would have been effortless just the day before, might soon become insurmountable. Why had they planned to wait for after the birth to leave? He should have known to leave as soon as the diamond arrived! Their attachment to Smyrna and to the way things were had been too strong. Xandra had asked him to stay until the birth, and he had agreed. Why had he trusted her instincts and ignored his own?

When he arrived at the French consulate, Albano's fear was confirmed. Already, there were several hundred men and women in line hoping for a visa. He joined the line and resigned himself to a long wait. At least, their visas were signed. It was only a matter of retrieving them.

He waited there, anxious about Xandra's well-being. It was safer for her out on the quayside, protected by the sheer mass of people stranded there and in full view of the European boats, than out on the streets where things felt uncertain. But the sun was fierce. At this time of the day, there would be no shade for Xandra or anyone on the quay.

There were about forty people ahead of him. People sat on the stairs and waited. The consulate opened. Everyone stood up. But when they saw that the guards only let in three people at a time, people returned to sitting on the stone steps. The long wait in the sun began. Every so often, the guards would open the door to let a few people in, and a few others would come out with relief on their faces.

Albano had been there for two hours, perhaps three, in the untenable heat of the day. Only about twenty people had entered and exited the building so far, and there were about twenty more ahead of him. He could not leave the line to see how Xandra was doing and risk losing his place. A few men had gone to urinate on the steps rather than lose their spot, and now it smelled wretched. Albano was standing in line and waiting. He felt bored and anxious, sleepy and impatient, drowsy and thirsty, but suddenly, all this was replaced by a sort of chill up his spine. He felt the chill in his body and the tingle of fear in his palms before he could even understand that something was happening. A sound, impossible to define a first, was breaking through the fabric of the day. It began as a sort of clamor; voices and shouts intermingled. Soon, it was as though the entire city were emitting a low moan.

Things happened fast. In an instant, the line Albano was in dispersed. Everyone ducked into corners, and he did as well, not knowing what was to fear or from where the threat came. An otherworldly silence fell upon the city. All sounds were sucked out of the air as though a hundred thousand people were holding their breath.

There was a tremendous vibration; he felt it. And then thunder broke. Drums and trumpets. The sound of thousands of hoofs beating the pavement. Gunshots. The terrified howls of women and children. Crowds parted only meters from where Albano stood, to reveal the phantasmagorical vision of the Turkish army entering Smyrna.

First came the cavalry mounted on majestic horses and moving in perfect military unison. The cavalrymen wore embroidered Circassian hats and gleaming curved scimitars and carried Turkish flags and banners. The cavalcade moved thunderously through the street, followed by a military band and finally a mass of soldiers on foot wearing black fezzes, long guns over their shoulders, and swords strapped around their waists.

The Muslim population of the city rushed into the street and stood at windows, erupting in jubilation, weeping with joy, and waving Turkish flags. Albano only felt dread.

At a command, the cavalry stopped, separated into two lines, and drew their swords. Albano, only meters away from all this, gasped in shock. The army's countenance was formidable. After witnessing what remained of the Greek army, there was no longer the shadow of a doubt as to who was victorious in the war.

All of Albano's expectations and rationale, everything he had thought would happen, everything he had planned, was shattered at once. All he could do was watch as the calls of trumpets and the rhythmic pounding of drums reached their climax, and Mustapha Kemal himself made his victorious entrance into Smyrna. Kemal, only feet from where Albano was, stood splendidly, very straight on his gorgeous horse. With his chiseled face and piercing eyes, he looked every bit the fearsome leader of his reputation. He did not stop, and neither did the procession. They were followed by exultant Turks, men, women, and children. All went up the streets, no doubt to reach the highest ground and thus officially claim the city.

Drenched in sweat, Albano slithered back deep into the crowd and out of sight. He walked up the deserted steps to the consulate. At the door, he knocked again and again, but no one opened. After ten minutes of this, Albano bolted in the direction of the quayside.

When he arrived, a heavy silence had seized the mass of refugees. The quayside was a zoo indeed. A terrible zoo. The refugees on the quayside had been ambushed like beasts between Kemal's army and the sea. They cowered, prayed, and cried just as the Turkish citizens of Smyrna were flocking into the streets, shooting their firearms in the air, laughing, waving flags, and shoving each other to catch a glimpse of the military procession. In the water, British, French, Italian, and American destroyers and cruisers stood guard, but the restaurants, the cafés, and the brasseries, so lively the day before, were not only closed but boarded up, the owners still in the process of hammering wood planks over windows. This struck Albano as a terrible omen. The optimism of the Smyrniots, their determination to go on living to the fullest despite the world's mayhem, their insistence that commerce could erase all differences between races ended when the restaurants and cafés that had remained defiantly open through many wars and invasions now boarded their doors. Suddenly, the boats in the bay did not reassure the way they had the day before. Albano nudged his way through the crowd in search of Xandra. The mass of people felt denser, more desperate. There were ripples of alarms, rumors, bits of sentences overheard. "The officers are in control," one Greek man said. "No one will go crazy while Kemal is here, and Kemal wants the respect of the Americans and Europeans, and they are watching from the boats." Albano prayed that was true.

Xandra was sitting on the blanket right where he had left her. Waiting for him, trusting him to fix everything. "The French consulate shut its doors when Kemal's army arrived," he had to tell her.

"What can we do?" she asked.

Albano noticed the strain on her face and wondered if she had slept at all the night before. "We can only wait for it to reopen," he said.

"Look at all these people," she whispered. "They all want to leave too."

"Their situation is very different from ours," he assured her. "They have nothing. We have money, we have visas awaiting us, and we have the diamond."

"Oh my God, Albano," Xandra exclaimed, suddenly realizing. "You have to go!"

He frowned. "Go where?"

"You have to go to Frank Street and sell the diamond. Without money, we will never get a boat, even if we get our visas."

Albano rushed in the direction of Frank Street as the sounds of Turkish celebration emanated from every corner of the city. There were rumors that looting had begun. He quickened his pace. People were in the streets, celebrating still, but the women and children were gone; only the men remained. They walked in groups, brandishing jugs of alcohol and swords, sometimes even a rifle. Albano saw a group of men coming out of a store, carrying things they had stolen. One by one, the shops and restaurants he passed closed, windows were shut, entrances to stores were boarded up. Albano began to run as fast as he could, powerlessly trying to beat the clock. But by the time he arrived on Frank Street, every jeweler had locked their front doors and closed their wooden shutters.

Crestfallen, Albano returned to the quayside and told Xandra what had happened. She only closed her eyes and did not speak. What could she have said? He spent the rest of the day going back and forth between Xandra and walking around the area to assess the situation. He walked along the quay listening to rumors, checked on the French consulate, bartered some of their food against fresh goat milk that he brought to Xandra, and back to the consulate. But the consulate never reopened that day. As the day progressed,

Albano's dread grew. European citizens on the quay were filing into boats that carried them away into the ships of their respective countries. One by one, the Levantine families sailed away in their private boats.

By dusk, all that was left on the quay were the refugees. Albano no longer trusted that his and Xandra's situation was different from theirs.

As night fell, the sounds of gunshots and celebration receded into the distance. The people on the quay grew quiet, and many allowed themselves to hope that perhaps they would be safe after all. The army was elsewhere. The looting would occupy the rowdiest elements. Thus far, there had been no violence.

Albano lay close to Xandra. She sat upright, her back against a jute bag filled with millet, and he curled up on his side, his head on her lap. Periodically, there would be the sound of guns fired into the air. Still, he fell asleep as she softly caressed his hair and as the wind carried echoes of Turkish celebration.

****

Albano was awakened by Xandra's hand on his shoulder. She was wide awake. It was nearly morning.

"Did you sleep at all?" he asked.

Xandra did not respond. She looked pale; her eyes were red. "There are rumors of looting in the Armenian quarter," she murmured.

"Who says this?"

"How do we know that my family is safe?"

Albano rubbed his eyes. "I will go and inquire."

"It's too dangerous."

"I know the back alleys. I won't take the main streets."

"I know that my father wants to kill you!"

Albano took Xandra's hands and rubbed them soothingly between his. "I will look from the street. I will make sure everyone is safe, and I will come back."

Albano drank some tea that the Armenian family had made. Then he and Xandra ate the last of their bread. He got up and trudged across the quay through the multitude of refugees. Smells were getting worse. Greek and Armenian flags, which had been everywhere just the day before were conspicuously absent from sight. Turkish flags now dangled from every window.

Albano arrived at the edge of the Armenian quarter to find not a soul on either side of a crude barricade made of piled chairs and tables. Who had set this up, he wondered worriedly? Was it the Armenians to prevent the Turks from coming in, or the Turks to stop them from getting out? Yori and the rest of the Armenian men had no doubt prepared for the eventuality of a Turkish invasion. They must have had weapons stashed away to protect themselves, Albano hoped, ammunition, escape plans and routes figured out.

From what he could see on his side of the barricade, the Armenian quarter looked deserted. Windows were boarded up, entrances to buildings bolted, streets empty. He waited for a while, pacing along the barricade, unsure what to do. He was about to move a few chairs to enter when two heavily armed Turk guards appeared before him and pushed their guns in his chest. The men did not dress like soldiers from Kemal's army.

"Are you Armenian?" they demanded to know.

"I'm Jewish," Albano mumbled.

"Do you have business in here?"

There was a muffled scream in the distance, the sounds of broken glass. "Only friends I, I meant to visit," he stuttered.

"Go back where you came from. We are under military instructions. No one can leave or enter the Armenian quarter."

As the exchange took place, both parties pretended to ignore the echoes of a woman's screams resonating in the streets.

"When will it open up again?" Albano asked, trying to appear nonchalant.

"It will open when it opens, Jew. Now go!"

Albano walked away. When he was out of sight, he leaned against a wall and tried to calm his breathing. For an hour, he went through back alleys and tried different streets, but everywhere was barricaded.

He returned to Xandra and told her what had taken place, although he mentioned none of the chilling sounds of violence and distress he had heard. Xandra swallowed her tears before they appeared. "There are rumors that they are killing people in there."

"I think that everyone is gone," he lied. "I saw no one on the streets except for Turks."

"Something is wrong, Albano. I know it. And there is looting taking place, to be sure. We can hear the gunshots from here."

"Looting, yes. But people must have run away."

"Please ask people as you wait in line for the visas," she implored.

Albano went. The line was even longer than the day before, but despite people tapping and pleading at the door, the French consulate did not open that day.

By noon, all knew what was taking place in the Armenian quarter. Smyrna's Turkish civilians, perhaps helped by Kemal's army's irregulars, and perhaps even under orders of Mustapha Kemal himself, had shut down the Armenian quarter street by street, making it impossible for anyone to see what was happening as they methodically looted stores and pillaged houses.

All through the following night came the distant echoes of the rampage taking place. Albano felt less than certain that everyone had evacuated. What if, instead of running, they had thought themselves safer inside their houses? And what if they were trapped now, with all exit routes blocked? What if behind each bolted door was a terrified family? Locked doors were no match for drunken looters. Xandra, imagining her mother, father, and little sisters cowering in terror in the cellar, cried all night long, and Albano was powerless to comfort her.

With daybreak came rumors of atrocities. The rumors spread like fire on parched land. Albano removed his caftan and the diamond it concealed and gave it to Xandra. "Keep this. It will be safer with you."

"What will you do," Xandra asked? Her eyes were red. She looked exhausted. "I will ask if anyone has any information about your family."

Once he was away from the crowd, Albano strategized. He could not pass as Turk; his accent would immediately betray him. To be mistaken for Greek or an Armenian might be life-threatening. Of all the minorities in Smyrna, Jews were, at the moment, the least threatened. So, for the first time in a long while, Albano retrieved his kippah from his pocket and placed it on his head.

When he arrived at the entrance of the Armenian quarter, the barricades seemed abandoned. He climbed over and around the mess of broken chairs and tables and slowly walked through the streets, staying close to buildings in case he needed to hide. The destruction took his breath away. The ground was a sea of broken glass, and not a single window stood. Every door was gone, reduced to splinters, every storefront turned to rubble.

Albano advanced inside the Armenian quarter, walking on the debris. The silence was heavy, painful. Where were the looters? Where were the people? Before he turned onto the main street, a smell unknown and horrendous grabbed his throat, but it came too late to prepare him for the devastation that lay before him. Dozens of bodies were strewn on the pavement. Men, women, and children; dead. Butchered. The smell of decaying flesh soon replaced every other smell. Flies circled in malefic clouds over the bodies. Drying blood ran down the length of the sloping street. Albano's legs folded under him, and he fell to his knees.

A tremendous sound of shattering glass broke the silence, and he only had seconds to get up and sprint into an open building. In the darkness, he watched as a group of men, about a dozen of them, brandishing guns, flags, swords, and bottles of alcohol, walked past without seeing him. They shouted drunkenly, laughed, stumbled on each other. Albano held his breath as they began to enter one building after another, each time exiting empty-handed. Finding nothing left to steal made them furious. They began to fire gunshots at façades and throw things at windows. Albano cowered. His kippah would hold no power against those bloodthirsty beasts. Eventually, the men stepped over the bodies as though they were logs, turned a corner down the street, and disappeared.

Albano stayed where he was, trying to gather his thoughts and breathe normally. Soon another group of men appeared, Turkish soldiers in uniform this time. They were drunk as well, disheveled, and with none of the exemplary discipline of the day before. They were dragging a young man by his arms. They stopped in the middle of the street and beat him mercilessly.

Albano, his whole body shaking, closed his eyes and waited. When the young man went quiet, the soldiers left, and the street was silent again. Albano waited a few minutes, then ran to the man. He was dead.

He returned to his hiding spot and remained there for a long time. Layered with his fear for Xandra's family, Albano felt the rise of a terrible suspicion. These horrors were not only the work of drunken men turned murderers. If soldiers were doing it, they were all doomed. It meant that military discipline had broken down. And in the absence of military rules and restraint, every soldier could transform into a well-trained and well-armed savage.

If he stayed in the Armenian quarter, he might become the next man they beat to death, but a terrible urge told him to remain here. How could he leave until he knew that Xandra's family was safe? Nauseous with fear and dread, Albano moved from carriage entrances to cellar doors, inching closer to Xandra and Hagop's family house. The magnitude of the devastation stunned him. Every Armenian household had been invaded and pillaged. Belongings were sprawled into the streets. Everything was in pieces, defaced. The pavement was a sickening hue of red-brown from all the blood now dried up. The bodies were an intolerable sight. They had not just killed, those beasts, they had mutilated, dismembered, disfigured, and then killed. Men, women, or children, even tender babies; they had not cared. Everywhere, flies swarmed. The smell was relentless, suffocating, abject.

He had hoped at first that people were hiding in cellars and attics. He had pictured mothers, their hands on their children's mouths to quiet them. Daughters still hiding under floorboards. Entire families huddled in secret rooms with men at their doors, armed to defend them. But now Albano began to pray for the opposite. He hoped that no one had attempted to hide. To run away would have been the only option for survival.

He moved through the neighborhood slowly, ducking into dark doorsteps, hiding behind doors, and plunging into dark alleys the moment he heard footsteps or drunken laugher.

****

The door to Yori's bakery was open.

Inside, all that was made of glass was shattered, every chair and table overturned. The beautiful one-hundred-year-old fresco on the wall, the one Xandra's family was so proud of, had been defaced with excrement. The air and sticky surfaces were thick with flies. The smell of warm pastries, honey, and roasting nuts still hung in the air absurdly. Albano, his heart beating wildly with fear of what he might find, walked to the main living room. Everything that could be carried had been stolen, and everything that could not was destroyed. The furniture, the rugs, the tapestries on the walls, the dishes were gone. There was nothing left of Xandra's family's cherished belongings.

He stepped over shattered objects, and his heart stopped. On the floor, sticking out from a pile of rubble, was an inert arm. He rushed to it and came to his knees. It was Ina, Xandra's mother. There was a clean, small wound in her chest that reddened her blouse. Albano brought his shaking hand to feel her pulse and recoiled at the feel of her arm cold and stiff already. He got up, staggered away, stumbled around the room. He went down the steps, bumping into everything, to the underground cellar where Yori made his bread. He found no one downstairs, only rubble and exploded bags of flour that thinly coated everything. Albano breathed with relief. If Yori wasn't there, it meant that he had run away with his four young daughters. But why had Ina stayed behind?

He clambered up out of the cellar. Standing in the room were Ina lay, he felt something fall lightly on his head; feathers and straw bits floated in the air that seemed to be coming from the sky. He looked up. They were coming from spaces between the ceiling's board. Was there a room upstairs he had not known about? Gripped with the worst presentiment, he looked around and found, behind a curtain, a narrow staircase that led to the upper floor. He willed himself to climb up the stairs. After a few steps, he stopped. There was blood at his feet and many footprints in the blood. Hearing nothing but the pounding of his own heart, he climbed slowly. Before he reached the room, he saw Yori sprawled on the floor. His eyes were open and in the center of his forehead was a small bullet hole. Albano started to run madly down the stairs; he slipped on the blood and tumbled all the way down. But once there, he knew he had to return. He went back up the stairs, stepped over Yori's body, and walked to a door. He entered the room.

There, covered in feathers coming from a punctured mattress, were Xandra's little sisters. Clara, Agda, and Octavia, and even four-year-old Tessa, lay in their blood, their dresses torn to pieces, their throats slit.

Albano ran out of the room, down the stairs, and out the door of the destroyed bakery. Outside, he collapsed on the pavement and threw up bile.

****

As soon as he could stand on his feet again, he ran away from the Armenian quarter, passing soldiers and drunken Turks. Albano ran so fast that the men only laughed and shot drunkenly in his direction.

Albano did not stop running until he found himself on Frank Street.

He stopped in the middle of Frank Street and bent forward, his hand on his knees. His lungs felt ready to explode. When he had caught his breath, he looked around. Yesterday, Frank Street had been a lively marketplace. Now it was ghost-like. The shops and cafés were boarded up, and the silence was spine-chilling. He saw not a single person dead or alive. The façades, doors, and windows were intact. The terrible violence must, therefore, have had a system; the carnage had physical boundaries. It was clear to him that the Armenian quarter had been singled out as a playground for the devil.

At that moment, he made a pact with himself. He would never tell Xandra what he had seen. He would never tell anyone. If he told no one, perhaps one day he too would disbelieve it.

****

On the quay, Albano gasped in shock. While he was gone, a new form of anarchy had taken over the quayside. The day had been hot. Trash and excrement had piled up. The odor, compounded by the number of people and the growing heat of the sun, had reached an intolerable level. Refugees were continuing to trickle down in an endless stream. Albano guessed that there must now be at least one hundred thousand refugees huddled there.

He did not find Xandra sitting next to the Armenian family where he had left her, but standing a few feet away from them, her belongings packed at her feet. "Did you see my family?" she asked, her face taut with apprehension.

He looked straight into her eyes and lied. "They must have found shelter somewhere."

She closed her eyes with relief. "Is it true that everything was looted?" she asked.

Albano nodded. "Everything."

"Even my parents' house?"

Albano looked away so that she would not read the horror in his eyes. "Yes."

"Even the bakery?"

"The bakery was ransacked. There is nothing left."

"What about the oven? Is the oven still there? Surely they cannot destroy or steal an oven made of stone?"

"It seemed fine," he said. He had paid no attention to the oven.

"Then, they can rebuild," Xandra said resolutely. "Do you think my family is somewhere on the quay?" she added. "Look how many people are here. Do you think it's possible that Hagop returned and that he led them to the cave? He's the only one who knows the way to get there. He knows the cave is the only safe place."

He marveled at Xandra's capacity for hope. In his gut, he knew that Hagop had never returned to Smyrna. He or someone would have seen him on the quayside a long time ago. Was Hagop in a camp somewhere in Anatolia? Was he sick or starving? Was he dead? Wherever he was, it was preferable to bearing witness to what Albano had just seen.

A collective call of anger resonated from the docks. Everyone looked in that direction. A British rescue boat was leaving half full and refusing to let anyone else in.

"What is happening?" he asked.

"The foreign ships are still only taking the foreign nationals, even now that Kemal has arrived," one man explained.

"This will be a disaster if they do not start to evacuate," another man said. "People have no food or water, and there is nowhere they can go."

Nearby, a woman let out a moan that turned into a howl. She was on her back with several women by her side. Some began to make a tent around her with blankets and shawls to give her privacy. "She is having her baby," Xandra said in a tiny voice. Unconsciously, she placed her hand over her own massive belly. They looked at each other somberly. "We can't stay here," she said, pointing to the terrace of Brasserie de France. "People are dying."

Albano had not consciously registered it before: from everywhere on the quay, groups of men were carrying inert bodies and lining them up against the façade of the Brasserie. "I'll go to the Levantine quarter or the European quarter," he said. "I will come back to you as soon as I find a safe place."

"No, Albano," Xandra said, shaking her head forcefully. "This time, I will come with you."

"Please stay here, with the nice family."

"The family does not want me here anymore."

"But why?"

She looked at him with sadness. "They say I am with a Jew."

"Why would it bother them?" he asked angrily. "At a time like this!"

"I am not spending another minute away from you, wondering if you are alive or dead," she said. "Wherever you are going, we will be together."

"The streets are too dangerous."

"And this is not?" she asked.

Albano noticed how pale Xandra was. The hair around her face was wet with sweat. "You look unwell," he said.

"I just need to get away from the stench."

"At least here there are the ships, boats…."

Xandra only shook her head no. Albano knew that there was no point in insisting. "Come," he said and took her hand.

He hoisted their bag onto his back, and they trudged through the multitude, heading in the direction of the Levantine quarter. Moving through the crowd was difficult as more refugees poured in, dirtier and more terrified than the ones before. In truth, Albano did not know where to go next. He held Xandra's hand and walked in a fog, the imprint of what he had seen embedded in him. The vision of horror would ice his soul, he feared, for the rest of his life.

At some point, he became conscious that he was holding Xandra's hand in public. Nothing that had mattered two days ago had importance now. "Let's spend the night in front of the French consulate and decide in the morning," he said.

"Should we try to take refuge in the Jewish quarter?" Xandra wondered.

"It is too far, and I worry that Jews too could become a target. No, we must head in the direction of the European areas. They say that Kemal wants the European leaders to think well of him. It will be the safest area to be sure." Was Albano sure? He wasn't. But as he said this, he became convinced of it.

****

There was no line in front of the French consulate. A sign on the door said that the consulate was closed. About a hundred people had opted to camp out on the marble doorsteps regardless. Albano managed to find a spot for him and Xandra on the porch right next to the entrance.

It was a hard surface, but it would be in the shade at the hottest time of the day.

Night fell. They wrapped themselves in blankets. Albano refused to eat the last of their food. "There is nothing left after that," Xandra told him. He insisted she should eat it all, and when she protested, he told her if not for her, for the child.

He thought he would never fall asleep, but miraculously, he held Xandra tight and succumbed to a dark, nightmarish slumber for a few hours.

****

He awakened in the middle of the night. Xandra was asleep and sitting upright. He delicately moved her down to her side and covered her with the blanket. People were sound asleep on the steps.

His eyes got accustomed to the dark. He walked to the door of the consulate and placed his ear against it. What would happen if he knocked now? Perhaps someone who was also awake would open the door, if for no other reason than curiosity. He knocked for an hour, politely, patiently. When one of the sleepers on the marble step moved, he stopped. He varied his rhythm, made the knocking musical so that it would be apparent that he was doing this deliberately. He made sure to keep his knocking firm but unthreatening. He had seen how things were going. Banging violently at the door was the opposite of what would lead to its opening.

After half an hour of this, and just as he was about to give up, he heard someone fiddling with the lock. He held his breath. The door opened just enough for a man's face to appear. He wore nightclothes and even a night hat. "What do you want," the man whispered in French. He was perhaps forty years old, with black eyes and a thin mustache. He did not look angry or threatening, just worried. "The consulate is closed. You have to stop knocking." He added, "You are preventing us from sleeping."

"I will let you sleep but please listen," Albano said in his best French. "I am here to pick up my visas. It would only take a few minutes, and then I will be gone."

"We're not making visas anymore."

"I am not asking you to make a visa. I am asking you to give us the visas that already exist. I received a notice of it a few days ago. I was about to pick them up when Kemal arrived."

The man said nothing but shook his head no. "I have a letter of employment in Paris," Albano insisted, unfolding the crumpled paperwork that he always kept in his trouser pocket. "We are expected there." The man continued to shake his head adamantly. "Monsieur, my wife is Armenian," Albano said, desperately. "You know what has gone on in the Armenian quarter, do you not? That small piece of paper, which is already stamped on someone's desk, is all that remains in the way of us getting out of Smyrna." And seeing the man was still listening, he added, "She is pregnant and about to give birth. All you have to do to save three lives is look for the papers and hand them to me. I don't even need to come inside."

The man thought for a long moment. "Give me your names," he finally said to Albano's disbelief. "I'll see what I can find."

Ten minutes later, the door opened again, just a few centimeters. Albano peered into the French man's eyes wordlessly as he handed him an envelope. "I stamped them," the man said. And before Albano could thank him, the door closed. No one, not even Xandra, had seen what had taken place.

Albano opened the envelope and found the stamped visas. They were saved.

****

The next morning, they stood in line at the dock where the French rescue boats continued to shuttle between the quayside and the French destroyer moored in the distance. Albano and Xandra stood up straight. Their clothes showed signs of wear. Albano hoped that they did not look as downtrodden as the Greek and Armenian refugees.

"We have visas," Albano said in his strongly accented French when it was their turn to show their papers.

"We only take in French nationals," the sailor answered.

"We have visas. Stamped visas which we got from the French consulate," Albano declared, using his firmest tone.

"The consulate is closed," the French sailor said, not believing him.

"We were given our visas; they are stamped and in good order." Albano insisted. "We have letters of employment in Paris, and we have money."

The sailor looked at him dubiously. "Where is your money?"

Albano took the money from his pocket and showed it to him. The sailor looked at the Turkish currency. It was clear that he was incapable of knowing how much what Albano held in his hands was worth. And in truth, it wasn't enough for a boat ride to France. If only he had sold the diamond when he still had a chance! "I have more," Albano whispered. "Much more. I just don't have it with me quite yet."

The French sailor looked at him with mistrust. "Coming onboard is not a matter of money," he said. "We operate under strict orders of the French government. This is a rescue mission, not a commercial venture."

"But how else can we sail to France?" Albano asked. "We have work waiting for us there," he repeated. "We are expected."

"You will need to find a private boat." The sailor looked at him and smirked, "With all your money, it should not be difficult."

"What we need to do," Albano told Xandra later on, "is find someone who will buy the diamond. Someone rich. The sailor was right; we need to find a private boat. Our best chance is with the Levantines. Perhaps we should go the European quarter and knock at the doors of Levantines we know, old customers from the bakery."

"Are there still Levantines left? A great many took boats out of the city. You saw them."

"They can't all have left," Albano said. "The women and children are away, but the men would not leave their properties and businesses unattended: their banks, their factories, their warehouses. I will knock on every door until one opens. Just as I did to get the visas."

They set out toward the Levantine quarter. Going along the water was out of the question: there were so many souls huddled in masses that it would have taken hours just to step over parcels and bodies. They decided to walk through the streets instead.

At first, they struggled to walk across the esplanade full of refugees. But as they moved away from the quayside, streets were increasingly emptier. It was as though individuals had the instinct to huddle together, holding on to each other to make a single organism, like fire ants during a flood. He and Xandra were doing the exact opposite; they were separating from the solid mass, drifting into the unknown.

The farther they walked away from the esplanade, the quieter things became. There was no one in the streets; no one was at any of the windows. Stores were shut and boarded. People had either left or were staying inside. The silence and emptiness of the street were deeply unsettling. Smyrna had turned into a ghost city. Albano knew in his gut that if people were not there, it meant that the streets were not safe, even in the European quarter. He fought the urge to run back to the esplanade. He had to reason with himself. This was only fear taking hold of him after what he had seen; none of these horrors would happen where so many Europeans lived. He wished that Xandra could walk faster, but as it was, she struggled. Her feet and ankles were swollen. Her heavy belly made every step difficult. But to rush her would alarm her.

"Where is everyone?" she asked. "Are you sure we should not go to the Jewish quarter instead?"

"No one in the Jewish quarter would be able to afford the diamond," he said. He tried to make his voice confident, rather than terrified. He wanted

Xandra to think that he was optimistic about their options, not that he had begun to fear for her life and the life of every Christian in Smyrna. The vision of Xandra's family haunted him every instant. Evil was here, pouring like black ink through the streets, up and down stairs, through every house and every bedroom. All they could do was try and run from it because if God could not stop it, there was nothing they could do. "We're almost there," he said.

"If they are not hurting the Jews, maybe we should look like Jews," Xandra suggested. Albano nodded and placed his kippah on his head. He wrapped his prayer shawl over his shoulders and let the fringes dangle. Xandra took the silk shawl with Eiffel Tower prints that Uncle Moshe had sent them and wrapped it around her hair.

They advanced carefully, along walls, hand in hand, their hearts beating too fast. Xandra abruptly stopped. "Oh, Albano, look!" she said in a strangled whisper. Albano looked. Out in the alley to their right was the body of a man. "Should we see if he needs help?" she asked.

Albano had no doubt the man was dead. "No," he said. "Let's go on."

They had not taken ten steps when a woman began to scream. The scream was unending, terrible and then, abruptly, it stopped.

Paralyzed, they waited. Xandra's face was white. "What is happening, Albano?"

"Shh!"

A deafening noise of hooves on the pavement was coming in their direction. They had only moments to take cover in one of the alleys. A group of ten men on horses rushed by.

From somewhere not too distant came another piercing scream. And then a single gunshot, followed by silence.

"We need to turn back," Albano muttered.

"But," Xandra said, "the men went in that direction."

Albano looked at Xandra as though he were seeing her for the first time. And at once he realized his terrible mistake. To remove Xandra from the quay where she could disappear in a crowd had been madness. Her beauty, her vulnerable belly, made her prey. How many mistakes had he made already, by not planning, by failing to act at the correct time? They should never have left the cave. "We can't continue walking in the street like this," he said. "We need to take cover. Wait for the night."

"If these men find us, they will rob us," Xandra said.

"I do not worry about the men pushed by greed," Albano said. "It is the men who are powered by hatred that we must watch for." He saw that she was not understanding. "They are killing Christians," he admitted.

"In the Armenian quarter?"

"Yes."

"Are you sure my family escaped?"

"They were … gone when I got there," he said without looking at her for fear that his eyes would betray him.

They began to knock at every door that was still unbroken. No one would open. Going from door to door, Albano and Xandra hid in corners when they heard throngs of men on horses. Xandra looked exhausted. She had had little to eat since they left the cave. "Do you have the strength to go on? Do you need to rest?" he asked.

"I can walk," she said. "If we reach the Levantine quarter someone will recognize us and shelter us, or at least help us with some food, whereas here there is nothing."

And suddenly, without warning, there was the sound of many footsteps. They had only time to hide in the recesses of a building's entryway. They held on to each other and held their breath.

The men were only a few meters away. Albano shrank further back into the shadow, protecting Xandra by pushing her against the wall.

A man's voice calmly said, "Stop hiding, Jew." This was said nonchalantly, as though the man who spoke did not doubt that Albano was cornered without the chance of escape.

Albano put his fingers gently over Xandra's mouth. With his eyes, he indicated what he was about to do. She tried to take hold of his hand to stop him, but he did not let her. He stepped out of the shadow and said, "I am not hiding."

There were three men. Mean-looking. One of them was on horseback, and the other two were on foot. They reeked of alcohol. Their clothes were stained with wine and blood. The man on the horse was so drunk he could barely stay up. His body kept leaning to the right. He would straighten up, then lean again.

"What are you doing, then, Jew?" the first man said. He seemed the least drunk of the three, and the most aggressive.

"I am here … like you," Albano said.

"We are taking back what belongs to us," the man said.

"So am I," Albano answered, with no idea what the man meant.

"Nothing here belongs to you, Jew. You can only have what we have rejected. Are you going through trash, Jew? Cleaning the streets, like a rat?"

Albano decided to go along with the man's thinking. "I am," he said.

"After we have gotten rid of every Christian in town, we will get rid of your lot as well."

"Give us what you have," the second man said. "Give us your money."

Albano paused for only a second before retrieving the hospital birth money from his pocket and handing it to him. The men laughed and hollered at their good fortune and pocketed the money.

"And what is that?" The man on the horse said, pointing in the direction of the shadow within the building's entryway.

"Nothing."

"Is that your woman, Jew? Come see us, woman," he ordered.

Xandra bravely stepped out of the shadow, her eyes lowered. Her stillness broke Albano's heart. She still wore Uncle Moshe's Eiffel Tower silk shawl over her hair, but she had also tied the thin cloth that had contained their food over the lower half of her face. Albano understood what she was trying to do: covered this way, she could easily pass for a Muslim woman. Albano stopped her from going forward, putting his hand on her arm. "She is with child," he said.

The third man came down from his horse. He vacillated and came close to her, looking at her befuddled. "I like pregnant women. It is like raping two for the price of one." The two other men emitted riotous laughs, which pleased him. "I like your woman, Jew," he said slurring his words. Leering, he came near her and lifted his hand to touch her face.

"Don't!" Albano shouted. He moved his body directly in front of Xandra's. The first man pounced on him, struck him across the jaw. The second man kneed him in the groin with a savage laugh. Albano folded over. They went on hitting him, with their fists, and with the handles of their guns, blow by blow. He fell to the ground, and his forehead hit the pavement hard. In one instant, all three men had seized Xandra. Albano made a superhuman effort to rise, but each time, he collapsed. The men ripped Xandra's shawl off her face, and her beauty was revealed. There was silence, awe perhaps. Immediately after, the rage in their eyes transformed into a terrifying hunger. Things happened fast. Albano watched helplessly, his face pressed against the ground, his body limp and unresponsive as his beloved received a violent push. She fell to the ground on her back. Now one of the men man was on top of her, slapping her, while the others hollered like mad beasts. Xandra made no noise. She did not moan or cry out. Albano came on all fours and tried to get up, blood pouring down his face from the cut on his forehead. "Stop!" he shouted.

The drunkest of the three men, the one who rode the horse and was the leader, was undoing his belt. "She's mine!" he told the two others. "You'll have her next." So the first man moved off her, and now the leader was on top of Xandra, tugging at her dress clumsily.

The other two men went to Albano and kicked him again and again. Through the kicks to his ribs and belly, Albano found within him a formidable power. He shouted, "She is Muslim! She could be your sister. Allah does not want you to rape your sister!"

The man on top of Xandra continued to struggle with his pants and her dress, but after a moment, he stopped moving. And a miracle happened: he lifted himself away from her and stumbled up. At first, the other two giggled and leered, but soon they stopped, careful not to humiliate their leader. Perhaps the man was too drunk to complete his act. Perhaps he saw her pregnant belly and had a change of heart. Perhaps Albano had put doubt in his mind. Perhaps he was just tired of perpetrating atrocities. Albano would never know. The man moved toward his horse. "Let's go," he said. The other two, their bloodlust not satisfied, turned to Albano and went back to kicking him in the ribs and head. But they grew tired of this too and eventually left.

When they were gone, Albano found the strength to crawl to Xandra and be conscious long enough to see that she was breathing. He managed to drag her into the shadow of the entryway before falling unconscious, next to her.

****

In his dream, he heard Xandra's plaintive voice. "Albano?" His head throbbed, but he thought he was in the cave, safe. "The baby is coming," said the voice in the dream.

"I am so happy," he answered through his haze of slumber.

"Albano…." He felt Xandra's grip on him, and the alarm in her voice awakened him this time. "The baby is coming, Albano…."

Albano opened his eyes. Xandra was sitting up, panic-stricken. Pain radiated throughout his body, in his ribs, in his groin, in his skull. How could he have slept through this? But he had not slept; he had passed out. "Are you hurt?" he asked. "How long did I sleep?"

Xandra looked at him with gaunt eyes. "Many hours. The cut on your head stopped bleeding. There is another cut on your arm. It is deep, but I was able to stop the blood."

"The baby? What did you say about the baby?"

"It is the fall, I think. At intervals, my belly is becoming hard as stone, and liquid came out of me." She looked at him gravely. "That is the sign that the baby wants to come out."

Albano rubbed the crust of blood that caked his face. "It is too early," he said.

"I have seen healthy babies born in the eighth month," she said. She took a bit of water from their gourd and used the bottom of her skirt to wash the blood from his face. "Can you see at all? Your left eye is nearly shut. Have they broken bones?"

Albano tried to sit up. Judging from the shooting pain in his torso, he was certain more than one of his ribs were broken. The wound on his forehead throbbed. The cut in his arm was deep enough to reveal the tendon and part of the bone, but he could move it. "We need a hospital for you," he told her. He looked in his pocket but found nothing there.

"The money is gone," Xandra reminded him. "The men took it, remember? Did they find the diamond?"

Albano felt the hem of his caftan. The tiny bulge was there, immensely reassuring. "They did not know to look."

"They did not find the finials," she told him.

"How could they not?"

"I had taken them out of my skirt and hid them near the wall. Now I have them again."

"The finials are not worth taking such risks."

Xandra helped him up, first to his knees, and then she helped him stand against a wall for support. She brought the gourd to his lips, and he drank. The pain was so intense throughout his body that he could not figure out what hurt most, but he could move. "Can you walk?" she asked. And suddenly, she turned pale, held her swollen belly, and moaned.

"You are in pain!" Albano exclaimed.

They hung on to each other and set out to walk alongside the buildings. They had to maneuver around piles of trash and broken furniture, bricks, glass, abandoned belongings, and, worst of all, corpses. They did not stop until Albano spotted something. He bent down and retrieved a French flag and wrapped Xandra in it. "I've seen people do this in the hope that the Turks will leave them alone."

Xandra stopped, doubled over with pain. She burst into tears. "I don't even know where we're going."

Albano took her face in his hands and kissed the tears from her eyes. Her face was hot and moist. "Anywhere that will give us asylum. The American Consulate, the American or French hospital."

"They are not opening for anyone," she wept.

"We have visas, my dearest. We have visas and our diamond, and you are pregnant. There are reasons for people to shelter us."

"But how do you know for sure?"

"Providence let us obtain visas. We were lucky enough to be given a diamond. These men let us go. You know what this means, don't you?"

"No."

"It means that God is on our side."

"Your God or mine?" she said with a small smile, drying her eyes with her sleeve.

Albano caressed her cheek. "They both are."

****

They hid when they needed to and walked when they could. They saw very few souls in the streets of the European quarter. Those who weren't here to destroy were hiding. An automobile zoomed past and abruptly stopped a few meters from them. Two men jumped out. Albano and Xandra recoiled in the shadow of a portico, but the men were not after them. They were carrying glass jars, which they thrashed against the walls of buildings. The men climbed back into the automobile, which drove a hundred more meters, and they got out again and threw more bottles through the broken windows of a building. There was the sound of broken glass. Then the automobile was gone.

"What are they doing?" Xandra asked.

"I don't know." They passed the broken bottles, and the pungent scent of kerosene filled their lungs. "Let's hurry," Albano urged.

When they arrived in the Levantine quarter, their hopes vanished. On every block the sprawling white villas and the treasures they hid lay open, disemboweled. Flower gardens were crushed, windows shattered, fountains desecrated, marble statuary tossed to the ground. Grand pianos, couches, beds: everything too heavy to be carried away had been defenestrated and laid in rubble down below. The poor servants who had pointlessly stood guard to protect the houses, likely at the command of their masters, lay among the ruins, their throats slit.

Albano and Xandra passed the residences in silence. On every street, they met the same wreckage. They encountered no one they knew, living or dead. "There is no sense in being here," Albano said. "The Levantines can't help us any more than they could help themselves. All those who could have been of assistance to us have fled. Let's go on Rose Street. There are hospices there, and maybe the Red Cross office has been spared."

"May God hear you," Xandra muttered.

"Will you be all right?"

She looked at him gravely. "I don't know how these things work, but the hardening of my belly is happening more often."

The narrow, beautiful Rose Street had been ransacked. The only people they saw were sprawled on the pavement, dead. They continued walking, with Xandra pausing every few minutes until her contraction passed. The rank smell of kerosene floated around them like a muted menace.

Albano remembered that very near the end of the Levantine quarter, near the place where he and Xandra would finish her delivery route, near their beach and their tree, was Hôpital Sainte Geneviève, a small hospital they had passed a hundred times without paying attention to it. He decided to head there. When they got near it, they heard clamoring and approached carefully. There was a group of about one hundred souls, the first gathering they had encountered since they left the quayside. They were Greek and Armenian refugees and terrified Smyrniots, most of them wounded, huddled at the foot of Hospital Sainte Geneviève's iron gate. They were calling and screaming in many languages, and shaking the gate, begging for refuge. Up in the window, Albano saw the shape of a woman dressed in white: a nun, or else a nurse.

"There are doctors in the hospital!" Albano exclaimed. "That's why those people are here."

They joined the voices, shouting and calling and shaking the gate, but no one opened. To be this close to help and get no help at all was enraging, unjust, pointless. They grabbed the wrought iron, shaking it, clinging to the last vestiges of hope, which had been shattered in so many ways in the last days, still believing that human decency was possible, that it existed still, just beyond the gate. The day was ending. To continue knocking and shaking the gate to no avail was nonsense. Albano did not think it was a good idea to join the group about to spend the night, vulnerable, out in the open.

"Let's find shelter in an abandoned house nearby," he told Xandra.

The sun was setting fast. Albano entered several buildings through open doors only to find dead bodies covered in flies. In the narrow streets, the sea wind had stopped flowing, and the air was saturated with the odor of decomposing corpses. As terrible as this was, an even more ominous feeling haunted Albano. It was unspecified. He could not name or express his fear. It was as though the consistency of the air was off somehow. Something felt wrong. And then it hit him: the wind! For the last few days, the wind had been blowing from the sea. But since sundown, it had begun blowing from inland. With the change of wind came the scent that sent chills down his spine. Xandra must have understood at the same time. "The wind has turned," she said.

"It smells like kerosene and smoke," he said.

"I think this is what these men were doing," Xandra said. "They were throwing bottles filled with kerosene through those windows."

Fire and earthquakes had destroyed Smyrna many times. Each time, it had been rebuilt faster and with lighter materials. Now built mostly out of wood, the city was more vulnerable than ever. "With the wind turning, if someone wanted to set the city on fire, it would be easy to do," Albano said somberly.

****

Albano and Xandra tried to get inside two houses near the hospital, but the smell of decomposing bodies deterred them. They tried a third house, which was located nearly across from the hospital. It had been ransacked and looted. Anything that could not be taken away had been vandalized; there was not a single chair left standing, not a curtain that had not been shredded, but there were no bodies. "This is where we'll spend the night," Albano said. He made a rudimental bed for Xandra out of the soft things he could gather, and he folded the French flag into a pillow. Despite the cramps that were coming now every few minutes, Xandra fell asleep. Albano sat on the wood floor next to her. After he was beaten and had fallen unconscious, she must have stayed awake to watch over him, and now she had no strength left. Albano caressed her hair. Her skin was hot to the touch, the hair around her face and neck soaked with sweat. In her exhaustion, she only moaned through the contractions.

He was unable to close his eyes to rest. He decided to go up to the rooftop. The house was three stories high. It had been a beautiful house, with exquisite mosaics and beautiful windows and doors. The walls were whitewashed, the floors made of expensive wood. Up on the rooftop, he stopped to take in the expansive view of the quayside, the bay, and, in the far distance, Mount Pagus. He leaned against the carved balustrade. How marvelous must the lives of the owners of this house have been. How many evenings must they have gathered here on summer nights, relishing the cooling breeze, the setting sun, and the echoes of the lively city below. How quickly and irrevocably had all their fates changed. He thought of himself and Xandra, of their future children. He pictured them at the balcony of their own house in Paris. He had imagined their future happiness so vividly that he could feel it. He had made Xandra a promise. Now was not the time to sink into despair.

Clouds hurried in the sky, and the rising moon shone brightly, revealing the outline of the many ships standing guard in the bay. From the balcony, he could see the distant mass of hundreds of thousands of refugees on the vast quayside. From where he was, he also had a good view of the hospital below and the many poor souls huddled at the gates. Inside the hospital, oil lamps were lit. Through the windows, he watched the hospital cots filled with sick and wounded people. A dozen nurses dressed in white worked tirelessly by their sides. This hospital, just out of reach, was where Xandra needed to be. What would become of them if they were not let in? Would he deliver the baby himself? What would he need? Would he need water? And where would he get food? When it came out, the baby surely would feed on Xandra's milk, which would come at some point although he did not know how to make sure it did. Xandra, too, needed to eat for strength. He had never seen her so weak, so sickly, so feverish.

A chill crept along his spine. Something was wrong with Xandra! The hot skin, the sweating, the paleness. She wasn't just giving birth; she was ill! He rushed down the stairs to her and touched her forehead, felt her pulse. Fever! He could see now, plain as day, that she was burning with it. Thoughts jumbled up through his brain. Could it be that the baby was dead inside? He knew this was possible. And when this happened, could a woman give birth to a dead child? Surely, they did. It must happen. He cursed his ignorance in women's matters. Xandra needed the proper care immediately. He spent the next hour going up and down the stairs to check on Xandra and back up to the rooftop where he stared across the street at the hospital's windows, thinking, praying, and spinning hopeless and optimistic thoughts together until he felt he was going mad.

One by one, the refugees at the gate curled into balls and went to sleep.

He was watching the hospital, mentally willing it into opening its gate for them, when something caught his attention. To the right of the hospital was a small, dark alley. Every so often the alley briefly lit up with a dim light. Peering and waiting for the next time the light would come on, he finally understood what was going on. There was a small side door to the hospital, with people secretly coming in and out of it.

He jumped to his feet, ran down to Xandra and whispered to her, "I think I found a way to get inside the hospital. I'll be right back."

Xandra only moaned.

Albano made a wide detour so that he could access the alley alongside the building and not walk past the gate where people were camped out. He found the door by touch and sat next to it in the darkness. He thought of knocking at first but decided his best chance was to wait until the door opened again, allowing him to speak to a person face to face.

After an hour, spent mad with anxiety about having left Xandra alone, he was about to rush back to her when he heard a slight click, and ever so slowly the door was pushed open. Two men came out carrying a body on a stretcher. Coming from the light and into darkness, they did not see him. What they were doing, he understood, was getting rid of their dead. The men with the stretcher walked away from the door, but before it could be shut again, Albano put his foot up and blocked it from closing. A person, having not seen Albano's foot, struggled to shut it.

"Please let me in," he whispered in English, unsure what language was likeliest to be spoken there. "My wife is about to give birth."

"Who are you?" a heavily accented voice in the dark whispered back anxiously.

"We have no water, no food. Her baby is coming any moment. Please shelter us. We will not tell anyone."

"We have many wounded," the man's voice said through his unsuccessful efforts to shut the door on Albano's foot. His accent sounded German. "We are well above capacity."

Albano instinctively realized that the man's insistence in arguing with him was a good sign. "I have seen bodies coming through," he said. "You must replace them with the living. Give us a chance. She will give birth in the street. She was struck by crazed men, and the baby is coming early, and now she burns with fever."

"Are you Armenian, or Greek?" the man asked. Albano's eyes had somewhat gotten used to the darkness, and he could see that this was an old man with furrows between his eyes and a deeply lined face. His collar and black habit revealed that he might be a priest or a vicar, or that he had a function in a Christian church.

"I am Jewish," Albano admitted.

"We cannot help Jews. We have enough of our people to tend to."

"Please, my wife is – well, she is not my wife. She is Armenian. She is Christian. I am only protecting her. Please do not let a Christian child be born in the streets with murderers running wild."

By now, the man had figured out that Albano's leg was what kept the door from closing and was kicking it as hard as he could, which was not very hard because he was an old man. "I am sorry, we're doing all that we can."

"I can pay you."

The man stopped kicking. "We have no beds."

"I have a diamond."

The eyes on the other side of the door lit up, and the old man looked at him as though for the first time. "Show me."

Albano wrestled with his caftan, tore at the lining. He opened his dirty palm and showed his diamond. For a moment, he and the man stared at the precious stone that gleamed intensely, its beauty almost ludicrous in Albano grimy hand.

"How do I know it is real?" the old man said.

"You won't know. You will have to take a chance. You have little to lose. All this gamble will cost you is to let my wife come inside."

The old man stopped wrestling with the door and seemed to be weighing this. "Come back with her," he finally said.

"Will you open?" Albano asked.

"Tap four times, and then once."

Albano ran back to Xandra and awakened her. Her clothes were drenched in sweat. "The hospital will take you!"

She looked at him with sickly eyes. "I don't know how I will walk."

Albano did not let her finish her sentence. He lifted her limp body in his arms and carried her down the stairs and into the street. His broken ribs felt as though they might pierce through his chest, but he did not care. "It smells like fire," she said dreamily.

"Let's go!"

Excruciating pain shooting through his body with every step, Albano carried Xandra down the stairs, out of the house, around the back of the hospital, and into the alley. Once there, he tapped as instructed.

The transaction took an instant. The door opened. The diamond was dropped into an open palm, and Xandra was let in. She burst into tears. "Albano! How will we pay for the boat now?"

"I will run to the quay and try to find someone we know."

"Let him inside too," Xandra begged through her tears.

"Impossible. He must wait outside," the old German man said.

"Xandra, I will run to the quay now. I will be back in a short time," Albano assured her.

"Take me with you!"

He looked into Xandra's beautiful, sickly eyes. "You and our child will be safe here. I will look for a boat, show them our visas, and secure our passage out of Smyrna. Then as soon as the baby is here, we will board the boat."

"No! Albano. Don't leave me here."

"Just think of Paris," he whispered to her, as a nurse's hand was on her arm, trying to move her away from the door. Xandra clutched her arms around his neck, sobbing. "Don't leave me!"

"You must be quiet!" The old man urged.

"Think of our dream," Albano murmured in her ear. "Remember my promise to you. You and I and our children will live in a beautiful house in Paris, remember? We will have a boy and a girl."

She tightened her grip, but a contraction engulfed her in pain, and she let go. A moment later, she was inside, and the door had shut. He heard her scream his name.

Xandra would be safe in the hospital. The gate was massive. It had resisted the looting and the madness and would continue to do so. Inside, there would be capable hands to help her give birth. Albano stood, numb with anguish at the thought of leaving any distance between them, but he had to find a boat if they were to have any chance at all of escaping. He sprinted toward the quayside, ignoring his pain.

****

He progressed slowly toward the quayside, moving from doorway to doorway and hiding when groups of men passed by brandishing swords and firearms. He was in a strange state of shock and confusion: moments of terror and despair, alternating with great pangs of numbness. Many times, he had to remember where he was and why he was there. The agonizing pain in his chest was nothing compared to the one in his arm. Xandra had wrapped it in a thin piece of cloth torn from her dress while he was unconscious. He lifted the bandage. The blood had dried up, but the flesh around the cut was red and swollen, oozing pus. He knew that all sort of terrible things could happen from such a wound. He had seen healthy men amputated after smaller skin lacerations began to fester.

He made his way to Frank Street, hoping for some semblance of normality. The day before, Frank Street had been eerily quiet but safe. Now it wasn't, or rather he was witnessing the aftermath of a terrible rampage. Bodies were strewn along the length of the street. Where there had been bustling international shops, brasseries, and restaurants, now there was only death. In the fountain-filled courtyards, beside door fronts, porches and verandas were the bodies of women, children, and men, many with bodies mutilated, ears or noses cut off, eyes gouged. The state of many of the young girls and women left no doubt as to their fate before being murdered. The smell of kerosene stung his eyes and nose. The stench of death clung to everything.

How could men do this to one another? Again and again, he had heard that these sorts of things had taken place elsewhere in the world, but those accounts had not felt real. They had felt like the fables in books. He had been incapable of imagining such hell could happen here.

Scattered ashes flew around, and a burning smell wafted through the streets. It was not the familiar scent of brush or chimney fires; it was the pungent odor of burning tar, burning oil. It was the smell of fire consuming houses.

On the quayside, it was chaos. The number of refugees seemed to have quadrupled overnight. And yet the many European, American, and even Japanese warships still stood immobile in the harbor. Could they possibly not know what was going on in the city? The presence of the foreign ships was preventing atrocities from spreading to the quayside, but for how long? If the killing and raping and robbing happened in plain view of the ships, would the

French, the British, the Americans, or the Italians persist with their preposterous neutrality? Albano felt anger consume him.

Somewhere above, on the far edge of the city, a massive black cloud was rising.

He struggled from dock to dock, visa in hand, asking everyone, looking for familiar faces. Albano was conscious that his appearance worked against him. His eyelids were nearly shut, his nose and eyes were black and blue, and there was a deep gash on his forehead and dried up blood on his face and clothes. He felt his best chance would not be with the military boats: the soldiers were under strict orders not to take civilians, so he did not waste time with them. Instead, he went toward the docks where the Levantine boats moored. Greece, Italy, Palestine, Egypt, the boat's destination did not matter. From wherever they ended up, he would contact Uncle Moshe and beg him to help them with money for their passage. Now that Albano had neither money nor diamond, only his visa, all he could do was to make empty promises of reimbursement. But very few pleasure boats remained on the quay, and among the ones still leaving, he found no one willing to wait for him and Xandra. He thought of Hagop at that moment. Only a year ago, the quayside had belonged to them. Hagop would have known people and would have had the right words to convince them. He would have laughed with them, and insulted them in ten languages, and it would have worked.

He began noticing that people on the quay were turning and looking in the direction of the city. He looked up to see where fingers were pointing. The cloud of smoke that had been hovering far back, nearly outside the city limits, was now enormous. Not only that. There were several black clouds now, coming from different parts of the city. No one understood why so many fires had sprouted at once. Someone shouted, "I smelled petroleum. They are setting Smyrna on fire!" The word spread across the quay like a noxious wave. "The Christians are setting fires to their own quarters so that the Turks can't lay hands on their new properties."

"No, it is the Turks who are setting fires. They have received orders from Mustapha Kemal's headquarters."

"All the fire hoses have been cut; the firemen can do nothing!" someone screamed.

"Why would the Turks burn a city that is now under their control?"

"They want to decimate every Christian."

"They want to burn all the bodies so the Allies will not know of their crimes."

"They waited for the right wind, the one that blows away from the Turkish and Jewish quarters. See, the fire was set in several places at once. They are methodical."

"That's the work of the Jews!"

"The Jews and Turks would not want to burn Smyrna; they need Smyrna!"

"The foreign warships need to evacuate us! If the fire continues and the wind continues blowing toward the sea, it will soon reach the quay."

In a matter of minutes, panic set in. It was pandemonium. "We are trapped between the fire and the sea!" People began throwing themselves senselessly into the water and swimming to the boats, trying to get in them, hanging on to ropes and ladders. Those who had accepted the notion that foreign ships were not taking refugees, now refused that notion and screamed and begged for rescue. People jumped from docks into the water or tried to throw themselves into boats from above. Those already onboard boats pushed down those who were struggling to get in. Sailors threatened to fire their rifles, and many did. Quite a few people began swimming towards the ships far out in the harbor.

And then came a scream. "The European quarter is up in flames!"

The revelation came to him like a sharp blow to his solar plexus. Xandra!

He pivoted and began running countercurrent to the crowd, jumping over piles of trash, tripping over bodies, falling and getting up, again and again. The fire was becoming huge at a pace he could not have imagined. He ran, despite his throbbing arm and broken ribs, as the sky rapidly, ominously darkened and as smoke rose straight above what seemed to be the area where Hospital Sainte Geneviève lay. Everyone was crazy now. A huge mass of people who must have been hiding in cellars and attics were fleeing away from the fire and towards him. He tried pushing his way through the panicked crowd, but it was impossible. He kept falling and being stepped on, but he continued, and as he did, he too had to step on fallen bodies, small children, and women crushed in the stampede. As he got closer to the European quarter's fire, there were fewer people in the streets. He should have been able to move faster, but now there was another obstacle: the smoke.

He placed his caftan over his nose. Now, between the thick smoke and the falling ashes, he was walking blindly. But worse, the temperature was rising, and he could feel the heat of the fire on his skin, as though he were stepping into an oven. Still, he advanced as burning cinders and pieces of roofs fell on him. Soon, he could not breathe, and the heat was so great that the hair on his arms was singed. He bent down as he walked, trying to stay close to the ground until he was on all fours, crawling, trying to breathe in the air at ground level. He coughed, choked. He could no longer open his eyes and resorted to feeling his way by touching the stone edges of the buildings. And suddenly there was a strange silence. Albano had just enough time to register the silence before an enormous conflagration swept him up and threw him into the air. And everything went dark.

****

Albano returned to consciousness face down in humid dirt. It was dark, and he did not know where he was. The air was saturated with smoke and ashes, and he coughed for a long while. He slowly rose to his knees, propping himself with his elbows and hands. When his eyes got accustomed to the dark, he realized that he was in a stone cellar below ground level. A dim light came from above. He could not understand what he was doing here. His head throbbed. He was covered in mud, and something viscous stuck to his neck. He felt the back of his head with his fingers. There was a new, deep, bloody gash on the back of his head, but the blood was thick and dry, so he must have been unconscious for hours.

Suddenly the terrible understanding came. "Xandra!" he hollered. He found a ladder and went up it. When he was all the way up, he understood what must have happened: either he had managed to fall into the cellar at the moment of the explosion or it had propelled him there.

Outside it was gray, opaque, and suffocating. The sky was obscured by the air saturated with smoke and ashes, and it was hard to see more than a few steps ahead. Everywhere he walked, Albano stepped into many centimeters of soft ashes, and stirred-up ashes followed him, billowing in his trail. These ashes, what were they made from? Houses? Furniture? People? How long had he been unconscious?

Out in the street, the scene of devastation he could glimpse was complete. He came to the understanding that his landing inside a cellar below ground had saved his life. The fire must have leaped through the neighborhood, caught on every building made of wood, and moved through them in mere minutes. But he had been inside a humid stone cellar, and so the fire had gone elsewhere. The air below ground must have been breathable, which was why he had not suffocated.

In the street, there were too many burned bodies to count. He alone must not have been licked by the flames! The fact that he had not been burned or asphyxiated by this torrent of fire and smoke, the fact that he was standing at all, was a miracle.

He could not recognize any of the buildings now that they were charred, and without the sun or the moon to guide him, he did not know north from south or east from west. Burning cinders, leftover parts of buildings that must have burst into flames many hours ago, still produced an infernal heat. He clambered his way through the streets, or what might have been streets. The cafés, houses, restaurants, churches, banks, gardens could not be told apart from each other: all were blackened beams, cinder, and rubble. Ashes blanketed the fallen bodies and continued coming down from the sky like soft, gray snow. From the appearance of the cinders, the fire may have swept through the place twenty-four hours ago, perhaps more. That's how long he had been unconscious.

He needed to find Xandra. Xandra was in the hospital. Hospitals were the safest places to be.

He held the cloth of his caftan over his face to filter the air he was breathing and set out, avoiding falling embers, rubble, and bodies. The desolation was immense. But he was alive. He had escaped. Xandra must have escaped, too. Why would God bother with a single miracle?

Struggling to find a recognizable marker in the desolate graveyard that had been his city, he walked and muttered the same two words over and over: "Please, God. Please, God."

****

He walked in circles until finally the smoke cloud cleared up and patches of blue sky were visible, and through it, the light improved. He guided himself better.

When he finally arrived where Hospital Sainte Geneviève should have been, he let out a howling scream. There was nothing there. Only the gate remained standing, absurdly unscathed. Behind it were the ruins of two stone walls opened to the sky. Everything else was cinders and burned debris. He stepped over smoldering wood beams, metal bed frames melted into strange shapes, the carcass of a cradle, a filing cabinet, abandoned shoes. The whole time he shouted, "Xandra! Xandra!," his heart near explosion from terror.

"They are all dead," a man behind him said.

Albano turned. The man was sitting on the ashy ground, like a dark angel floating on a grey cloud. His hair and beard were burned in patches. He wore a torn, dirty black suit rolled up above the ankles. Tears streaked his face black with soot.

Albano shouted at the man, "They are not dead. They ran away! They ran for protection."

"There was no time," the man said in a vacant voice. "The conflagration happened in an instant. There was nowhere to run to."

"But you are here. You are alive!" He turned away from the man, ignoring him, and returned to calling, "Xandra! Xandra!"

The wind opened a gap in the smoke above that let in sunlight. He saw that he was standing in what must have been the hospital's food hall, now open to the air with crumbling walls on two sides. Two men and four nurses from the Red Cross, hair, clothes, and faces black with ashes, slowly moved through the debris, the men lifting bodies onto stretchers and lining them up against one of the walls. There were dozens of bodies lined up there, charred beyond recognition. He ran to a nurse. "There was a woman here," he asked frantically in French. "She was giving birth! She was Armenian. Do you remember her? I brought her here. I think it was yesterday. Or the day before. How long ago did the fire happen?"

The Red Cross woman shook her head in ignorance. "I just arrived by boat from the shore. I don't think anyone made it out of here." She turned away, but Albano saw her glimpse at the row of dead bodies. It was as though a knife had just been planted through his belly. He tottered toward the area where the nurse had looked. Numb with terror, he walked among the corpses. None of them recognizable as people, only as human shapes. Several were twisted in terrible ways, their bodies curled into the position where they had met their fate, as though they had thrashed while on fire. Others had their arms alongside their bodies, as though their bodies had burned in their sleep. He went from body to body, forcing himself to look when all he wanted to do was run.

He saw them. It was them; he knew this immediately. Her hair, her clothes, her face, her flesh were gone. Nothing about the woman was recognizable, but he knew this was Xandra because someone had placed a minuscule dead infant wrapped in a shawl on top of her, as though in a final embrace. The infant was not burned: someone must have kept it from the fire and then placed him back on top of his mother's charred remains. Albano knew the infant was his child, and the woman was Xandra, because of the shawl in which the baby was wrapped. It was the Parisian shawl from Uncle Moshe, the one with the small Eiffel Towers.

Albano fell to his knees, buried his face in the thick ashes that covered the ground, and began to howl.

****

Later, many hours later, numb, Albano took his baby in his arms. The child weighed nothing. In the sun that now pierced ferociously through the whitening smoke, he headed toward the water and along the beach. The pain above his elbow was excruciating, but he welcomed it.

All around, emerging from the rubble, were lone, haggard, disoriented silhouettes. Survivors like himself, people who would never be able to understand why they were still alive, or why they alone must live to endure the loss of everything they knew and everyone they loved. From every direction came the screams and sobs of the survivors. But Albano remained silent.

His dead infant in his arms, he stood on the beach and looked in the distance at the esplanade of the quayside. Now the smoke had parted, and he could witness the same events that had just happened where he now stood. The fire that had consumed the European quarter had reached the quay. There, hundreds of thousands of refugees, trapped between sea and fire, awaited their terrible death. From where he stood on the beach, he could see the European boats, now frantically evacuating the people on the quayside, but it was too late. The heat was such that the sailboats that tried to get close saw their sails catch fire. For each boat in the harbor, there were a hundred people, ant-like in size from where Albano stood, treading water around it, swimming among drowned bodies.

He carried his dead child's tiny body and crossed paths with people in as much despair as he was.

He finally reached the beach. Their beach.

He walked to their tree. The tree was now a dark carcass, standing on the ash-covered sand. He stood on the beach with his infant, where the shade of the tree should have been. He set the corpse on the sand at the base of the tree and began digging. He dug with his bare hands, and when the hole was deep enough, he set his child in it and gently covered him back with the Eiffel Tower shawl, and then with sand.

He did not say a prayer.

He returned to the ruins of the hospital, wrapped Xandra's charred remains in a piece of tarp, and carried her, now weightless, to the beach. The pain in his heart was so deep that the pain in his arm was nothing compared to it. There, he dug a new hole right next to their child's grave and buried his beloved.

He did not say a prayer for Xandra either. There was no prayer left in him.

When he was done, he walked into the flat sea. Trash of all sorts floated on the water, as ashes continued to fall softly on the surface. The water felt hot. The corpses of people who had drowned trying to escape the fire floated in the water by the hundreds. He realized now that the people he had seen walking around, specter-like, those who had survived, must have been the good swimmers, those able to tread water and swim far enough from the shore not to suffocate from the toxic air or be cooked by the heat. Those people had returned to shore and entered hell.

As he swam away from shore, salt stung the open wounds on his skull and arm, and his broken ribs stabbed his lungs. He was not a good swimmer. He kept going under and swallowing tepid water. He did not swim toward the pier or the quayside. He swam forward, out to sea. The water became colder and colder the farther he swam. He turned back to see Smyrna only once. The city was engulfed in flames. His family's burial ground would be the whole city, if not the entire Ottoman Empire.

As Albano swam further and further away from the coast, the floating corpses, innumerable at first, became scarce. Further out to sea, the screams on the shore became muffled and then disappeared. He felt the cold sea caress his body, the salt, excruciating on his wounds at first, now healing them perhaps. No matter how men built and destroyed cities and killed one another, the sea was deep and eternal, and soon he would be one with it.

Albano swam towards the horizon. He would go until the Aegean Sea took him. But his body did not want to die, and it took hours before, exhausted, he finally began sinking under and swallowing water. By then Smyrna was no longer on the horizon. The only indication that it had existed at all was the mass of black smoke that tarnished the blue of the sky. He thought of the finials and how they must have melted in Xandra's skirt folds.

When Albano's body finally broke down, his eyes and nostrils filled with water, he did not feel panicked, or fearful. A last thought came to him as he went under, the most peaceful thought: the bodies burned in the fire were fixed in death in the convulsions of trying to escape the flames. But Xandra and the baby had been burned in a position of repose, she on her back, her legs straight, her arms alongside her body, and the baby set there on top of her.

This meant that they were already dead when the fire consumed the hospital.

This meant that the baby and Xandra did not die in the fire, but in childbirth.

There was nothing he could have done to save them.

He felt gratitude that they were spared the unimaginable horror of being burnt alive.

The last thing Albano did before going under one final time was to thank God for giving him Xandra.

****

Many miles away, up on the hillside above the city, sitting in the shadow of the Red Cross truck that had carried him away from the hospital, the old German priest watched the terrible smoke blanket that covered Smyrna. He sponged the sweat off his brow and got up. In the medical truck, he took out a clean compress and poured water on it. With a hunched back, he walked to the olive orchard and the makeshift beds set in the shade of the trees where the Red Cross nurses were hard at work in the implacable heat of the sun. The old priest walked to the bed where the young woman moaned. He gently applied the compress to the side of her face.

"Albano," the young woman muttered through her fever and pain.

"Quiet, my child," the old man said. "You must rest now."

CHAPTER 11

Family Spy

"Do you know what made your father decide to leave Smyrna?" Cassie asked.

Marceline shook her head in ignorance. "Why does anyone become an expatriate? I would think that for most it's a combination of things. Better opportunities elsewhere? Who knows? He must have decided that there wasn't much for him there. And the city had burned down, so there was that." She thought for a moment, looking at the rivulets of rain against the window's glass pane. "To be honest, he never spoke about it."

"So my father is not the first man in our family who preferred not to speak about the past," Cassie noted.

"Well there had been some dark stuff to be sure," Marceline said. "Somehow along the way he had lost the use of an arm."

Cassie tried to remember if she had noticed that in the picture. "He was missing an arm?" she asked.

"No, it was there. But there was nerve damage below the elbow. His lower arm and hand were nearly useless."

"It must have been difficult for him."

"After the first world war, men missing limbs and covered in scars were the rule rather than the exception. But for my father, as for most men of the time, the invisible scars must have brought the most pain."

"I can't get over the fact that my grandfather was a Turkish Jew," Cassie said. "I had no idea that I had such exotic ancestry."

"My father did not see himself as Turk. The Republic of Turkey wasn't founded until after he left the region. So he wasn't Ottoman, since the Ottoman Empire did not exist anymore, and he wasn't Turk. One thing is for certain: my father wasn't French either, and the French people would not let him forget it."

Cassie eyed the album on the table. "Do you have photos of him?"

"Not from his childhood. My father grew up extremely poor."

"I thought he was wealthy."

"Not until he arrived in Paris when he was in his early twenties and his uncle took him under his wing. Uncle Moshe's business was quite successful already, but my father became a great asset. He was intelligent and spoke many languages. At home they spoke Ladino and Hebrew, and he had grown up with so many cultures living side by side that he had learned to speak

Arabic and French and I think Armenian and some modern Greek. Languages were good for business."

"And your mother?" Cassie corrected herself, "My grandmother. She was French?"

"Her name was Lucienne. She came from an entirely different world from Father's. Their universes did not always happily intersect. Possibly the only thing they had in common was that they were both Jewish. My father did the best he could to keep up with her ways. He was a steadfast provider, a man of keen intellect, a loving father, but there was in him a reservoir of sadness, a secrecy that quite literally drove my mother mad."

"My grandmother? Mad as in crazy?" Cassie asked.

"Please do not rush ahead. I'm trying to be thorough. The main thing you must keep in mind is that your father was Jewish."

"Truthfully," Cassie said, "my father never spoke of religion. I don't think it mattered to him."

"Did not matter?" Marceline said, spitting out her words. "Of course, it mattered! My dear, Judaism, being a Jew, that was what mattered most!"

"But I –"

"Everything about your father, all his little secrets, and lies, they all spring from the fact that he is Jewish. Whether he liked it or not, his story is a tiny Marceline of the story of Jewish people."

Cassie felt that the comment was absurd and hyperbolic with nothing whatsoever to do with her reality. "I really don't think he felt that way at all and—"

Marceline raised her hand to stop her. "Darling, this is not a subjective matter. It is factual. Now please stop interrupting me." She unfolded her glasses with frail hands covered in heavy rings. There was something wonderful about being coquettish at eighty-seven, Cassie thought, when she, who in theory was on the market for a mate, could hardly be bothered to put on lipstick. "Would you like to see photographs of your dad as a child?" her aunt asked.

Did she want to see a photograph? Cassie would have given a kidney to get any information that would help her understand her father as a boy, or at any age.

Marceline opened the album and placed an index finger, covered almost entirely by an immense turquoise ring, on a black and white photograph of a baby dressed in his embroidered white gown and bonnet, his mouth wide open into a toothless scream. "I remember distinctly the day Gustave arrived," she said. "Possibly one of my earliest memories, since I was eighteen months old. I was precocious though. I am told that by that age I could speak in enough sentences to order the maids around."

Cassie scrutinized the photograph. "That's my dad? He seems from another area."

"1925 to be exact. Your father was a terribly unattractive newborn, I must say: scrawny and fussy, but I was passionate about him." She pointed to the picture of a little girl barely larger than the baby she held in her arms. "Here I am. My affection for baby Gustave was the nearest I ever got to maternal sentiments." Marceline pointed to another photograph where a baby sat upright in a massive black contraption perched up on thin wheels almost as tall as a little girl next to them. "This is me, pushing the pram," she said.

Marceline turned the album's page and pointed to a series of photographs of a fancy picnic by a lake where people in their finest attire posed for a camera. "This is us at the Bois de Boulogne. It must have been 1928 because I remember distinctly that there was a birthday cake for me and that I was turning five." In one of the photographs, a dozen women in fur-trimmed coats, beaded lace dresses, and cloche hats, sitting in folding chairs, seemed dressed for an episode of a wedding on some Victorian epoch TV series rather than a picnic by the lake. A few of the women in the group had short hair, Garçonne style. Marceline pointed to one of the women whose eyebrows appeared to have been plucked and redrawn and whose mouth was painted in that bee-stung shape that must have been the fashion. Around her neck was a long strand of pearls. Her dress, straight and loose and belted at the hip, emphasized her slenderness. Her nose and chin were a bit strong, and she was not the prettiest in the group, but she looked regal, much like Marceline did, and she had an air of confidence about her, if not superiority.

"That is Mother."

Cassie whistled softly in admiration. "Very elegant."

"Indeed," Marceline said, pointing to a toddler who sat on a blanket, wooden toys surrounding him. "This is Gustave at age three."

Cassie pointed to a stern, stiff woman by his side. "Who is this?"

"One of our British nannies at the time. I don't remember her name; they seemed to come and go interchangeably." She pointed to the photograph of a pretty little girl, pouting in a stiff white dress and curled hair tied with ribbons. "And this is me. Funny how vividly I remember that day. The adults strolling along the lake, the pretty ladies twirling their umbrellas, the mustachioed gentlemen who conversed with them. I remember that some of the men in the group were attempting to ride unicycles and kept falling, and the women laughed. Someone had set out a phonograph and was trying to make it play a tune. On the pond, they had made teams. Men and ladies clambered inside small wooden boats with much laughter. The men grabbed oars and began racing each other across the lake. The ladies, my mother included, applauded and cheered from the shore. Those were the années folles. After the sufferings and restrictions of the Great War, people wanted to behave lightheartedly. Adults dressed as they wished, drank liquor, danced the night away. Unfortunately for us, lightheartedness was not afforded to actual children who were expected to behave like miniature adults. I had been told to sit still and not dirty my dress. That is why I look so cross."

Marceline turned the page to a new photograph. A man in a suit held Gustave on his lap. Marceline had her arms around his neck. Cassie immediately recognized the man she had only once, as a child, seen in a picture. "That's him! My grandfather!"

"We called him Baba. I loved no one more."

"He looks like an actor, like a French Clark Gable or something."

"Baba was very handsome. It occurs to me now that he should have been rowing a boat and playing with the other adults. Instead, here he is in this photograph, sitting with us on that picnic blanket. I was too young to be aware that my father did not exactly fit in with this uppity Parisian crowd."

Cassie's grandfather, sitting in the dappled shade of a chestnut tree, was staring toward the lake, seemingly absorbed in some sorrowful vision. "He does look kind of sad," she said.

"Men have secret scars that they must bear alone. Whenever we asked Baba about his past, he would say that this life with us was all that mattered to him. He said he wanted to forget. This was a generation of adults who had greatly suffered from the war, and who worked, often maniacally, at distracting themselves from their suffering and loss. My father, too, might have wanted to forget, but it did not appear that he could. I would strive for his attention in the hope of bringing him back to joy. Had he not said it himself? That he was happy when he was with us?" Marceline looked at Cassie. "Did your father share any of this with you?"

Cassie shook her head. "Not a word."

"But did you not ask?"

"Here and there my sisters and I must have tried. As a child, you get rebuffed enough times, and you learn what the taboo subjects are."

"And this is how history is forgotten," Marceline said. "Forgotten and therefore repeated."

"Were you practicing Jews?"

"Sort of. We were Jewish, but we did not call ourselves that because this would have implied adhering to certain modes of behavior, and a certain devotion to the religion. We called ourselves Israelites. We were mildly observant. One of the few religious traditions Israelites upheld was to marry among themselves. For example, it had been important, when my mother was looking for a husband, that the husband be Jewish. As for the rest, it was interpreted loosely." Marceline flipped the pages of the album, "Look at this," she said. "I don't remember a single Passover, but this is us and our annual Easter egg hunt. The maids hid chocolate eggs wrapped in foil throughout the house, and Gustave and I ran up and down, basket in hand, looking for them."

"You did not celebrate Jewish holidays?"

"We regarded religious services as social events. We never thought of denying our Jewish identity; we were proud of it. But to me, being Jewish equated to little more than getting to wear my prettiest dresses and ribbons on High Holy Days. The chauffeur would drive us to the synagogue, and there was the amusing tradition of walking the last hundred yards on days when the rule was not to use cars. We celebrated Hanukah, but Mother always had a Christmas tree in a corner for reasons that were not explained to us. On Friday evenings, we were invited to Shabbat dinners at the home of the Parisian Jewish bourgeoisie, or we hosted them. We ate kosher only when we invited more observant Jews to our home, such as the occasional rabbi. Otherwise, it was not rare for pork roast to be served for Shabbat. My father refused to eat treif, but if there was boeuf bourguignon for dinner, he'd eat it, picking at the lardons and leaving them on the side of his plate while my mother rolled her eyes."

"But you said that everything that happened with my dad had to do with being Jewish."

"That is my whole point. For every Jew who wants to believe that he or she has integrated into society, there is a society intent on remembering that they are different. Post-World War I, most French Jews whose families had been French for multiple generations believed that they were French before they were Jewish. Our family and our Jewish friends' families were acutely aware that France not only protected our right to exist but was one of the very few countries in the world to impart us with equal rights. And so French Jews gave the République their unmitigated devotion. A devotion that would not be rewarded, as we all know how things turned out for the Jews during the second world war."

This gave Cassie pause. Her father was born in 1925, which meant that he was only fourteen years old when the war broke, sixteen when the Germans invaded France. As Marceline said, everyone knew how things had turned out. "How did your family make it out in one piece?"

"That is a long story, which I am about to tell you. But first, you might want to understand the setting. Within the Jewish community of the nineteen twenties, there was a strong sense of class. Mother felt secure in her knowledge that she stood proudly on the top echelon. By marrying my father, she had married below her milieu. Mother's ancestors had entertained Russian princes and Flemish countesses. She was quick to point out that she was also of Catholic descent – this might explain the Christmas tree. Some of her ancestors had gone astray, I suppose, making her, for all intents and purposes, Jewish, but she was heir to a long lineage of Christian nobility with a family tree going as far back as Saint Louis, ninth King of France and, ironically, a ferocious anti-Semite."

"I think I remember my father saying something about that," Cassie interrupted. "About some blue blood ancestry. I never paid it any attention."

Marceline looked at her mockingly. "Well, it's quite telling that he would remember this but conveniently forget the Jewish part, don't you think?"

"I don't know," Cassie said.

"Mother had class and elegance," Marceline continued, "but her father and brothers had perished in the Great War, and all that remained of their wealth was the house whose upkeep they could not afford. At twenty-five, Mother was still not married. The men, especially Jewish men who had come back from the Front in one piece, were few and far between. Concessions had to be made. Then my father arrived. He was Jewish, recently hired to work with his uncle, whose rug business was thriving. Yes, I know, the cliché of the Jewish carpet salesman. But it was noble enough commerce. Well, Mother must have had her moment of hesitation. Baba was a foreigner and a merchant without the slightest pedigree. But he was a charming and, as you saw, a very handsome man. Mother was finding herself an old maid with a family fortune dwindled to nothing and so must have been willing to overlook details of nationality, class, and upbringing. Meanwhile, marrying her would allow my father to integrate into French life in ways that would have been otherwise impossible." Marceline pointed to a photograph of her grandfather. "I wish you could see, too bad the photo is in black and white, but Baba had that golden eye color us three seem to share."

"Amber," Cassie said.

"Who wants amber eyes when they can be gold, wouldn't you agree?" Marceline said. Her haughtiness of earlier had been replaced with a certain youthfulness, as though in speaking about her childhood she were reverting to a younger version of herself. Her aunt's hair was thick and white as snow, but the beauty of her youth was still visible as the light of the day shone through the window on her face, revealing her fine features, her aquiline nose, her peach-colored skin, and the pale amber – or gold – of her eyes. "It was hard for people to place Baba's nationality," she said, "Italian, Persian, Greek. But no one could have mistaken him for French. He spoke every language with an indefinable accent, softly rolling his r's. Baba was likable. Everyone who met him, my mother included, fell under his spell. I adored my father. Gustave adored him too. And even though Mother could be dismissive at times, she was undoubtedly in love with him."

"What was your mother like?"

"She was educated, or at least as educated as the times had permitted a French woman to be. She read. She played the piano beautifully. She had a modern way of thinking about the role of women. She hated the notion that a woman was to be subservient to a man, and she may have resented men for the opportunities afforded to them. Now, of course, that changed the moment she had a daughter. When it came to my standing in the world, she was quite the traditionalist."

"How did your parents meet?"

"At a dinner party at Moshe's, my father's uncle. Like my father, Moshe came from the Ottoman Empire. He had made his fortune in Europe long before my father joined him in Paris. I often wondered what my mother was doing at Uncle Moshe's that evening. Those two did not belong to the same worlds. Uncle Moshe was boisterous, a large man with a booming voice who, when he could not be understood because of his broken French, just spoke louder. I've heard Mother refer to him as "the peacock." Mother valued restraint, decorum, and pedigree; Moshe had none of those. In any case, Moshe hosted a dinner, and Mother happened to be invited through shared friends."

"And so, they fell in love?"

"From the moment they met, my parents must have recognized in each other the answer to pressing needs. The benefits for a merger of sorts. Otherwise, they were an unlikely match. Mother was an assertive woman who did not tolerate contradiction, which might have been one of the reasons she had not found a husband earlier. She did not possess the demure qualities men of the time looked for in a woman. Mother wore the pants, so to speak. At least in the beginning. My father let her decide almost everything. He made money, increasing amounts as the years passed, but it was Mother who decided how to spend it, whom to invite to dinner, which salons to attend, where to go on holidays, and everything concerning the children's upbringing. Wearing the pants also meant she could be quick to anger and dismissive with Father. Perhaps his lack of social status became more difficult for Mother to overlook as the collective disposition of French citizens toward foreigners began to change during the ramp up to the Second World War. Or perhaps she became scared, and who would blame her? She might have perceived my father's gentle ways as weakness and felt it was up to her to display more traditionally masculine traits."

"Did they love each other?"

"Well, maybe not in the classic sense, but there was affection. Mother was possessive of Baba and jealous of every woman she perceived as prettier than she was. As for Baba, he put Lucienne on a pedestal, and he seemed aware that she was his social superior. As I mentioned, Mother's fortune had been lost, but there were nice remnants of her family's past glory. Mother's family could be traced back at least ten generations, and each generation left artifacts, jewelry, paintings, silver, and furniture to the generation that followed. Gustave and I grew up surrounded by it all. Today, little of this treasure remains. The bulk of it was stolen during the Second World War and never recovered. The few things we could salvage were pieces small enough to pack and take with us when the time came to flee the Nazis. And, of course, there was the house."

"This house? Where we are right now?"

"It has been in our family for over a hundred years and was built by my great-grandfather on Mother's side. The house has good bones, but it isn't as grand now as it was when your father and I were children. You should have seen it before the war. Our family lived in style. There was a chauffeur, a cook, maids. And an endless procession of nannies, which we called British nurses – the kind prized in society at the time – was dispatched to our care and education. The nannies lived with us. There was usually one for me and one for Gustave. If the nannies had a human nature, they made it a point of professionalism never to reveal it. It wasn't until much later, when my knowledge of English proved itself useful, that I could see any benefit to leaving small children to the care of such cold-hearted women."

"They were mean?"

"Only indifferent and strict, and expected to be that way. People did not indulge children the way they do now. In those days, they were to be seen and not heard. There was little crossover between the world of children and the world of grown-ups. We learned how to dress, behave, and speak to resemble miniature adults. Your father and I lived in fear of the British nannies. They punished us at the least perceived infraction; they took away our favorite toys and even chose if we deserved dessert or not. Our parents deferred to them for most matters concerning us."

"That's kind of hard to imagine these days."

"We did not know any different. Our parents were mostly absent when we were little. My father worked long hours. Moshe did most of the traveling and Baba stayed in the Paris office until late every day. Mother wasn't around much either. She was forever attending teas, and lunches, and the charity events of Paris's elite society. For this reason, Gustave and I found ourselves in the peculiar position of being the masters of the house, with the adult staff deferring to us. Our daily life was minutely scheduled by the nannies with lessons, restrictions, rules, and obligations. Interestingly, the British nannies had power over us, and Gustave and I had power over the maids, the cook, the chauffeur, and our tutors. It was unspoken, but we each knew our place. All Mother demanded of us was perfect behavior and dedication to our studies. She did not take an interest in us unless we accomplished something exceptional. Being groomed for the life of privilege that awaited us, that was our work. It came in the form of endless lessons and tutoring. Ballet, piano, drawing, etiquette, manners, school work. I excelled at all this. Lessons challenged my competitive nature. I've always wanted to be the best."

"Where did you go to school?"

"When we were small, we did not attend. Tutors, which we called précepteurs, came to the house for our lessons. We were sheltered but not indulged, and certainly never idle. Mother was always stressed and displeased, but our father was fabulous. Every evening he arrived from work bringing us treats, which he hid in his coat pockets. That was the bright moment of our day. At bedtime, we had a tradition of story-telling. Baba did not read to us from books, but instead, he sat on our beds and told us all kinds of magical stories from the Orient, stories of monkeys, and magic carpets caught at the tip of the Eiffel Tower, and magical grottos filled with gold crowns, and such."

Marceline took a breath, closed the photo album. "Our early childhood was carefree. But disconcerting events took place after 1929. I was too young to make sense of it. All I understood was that rich people were finding themselves in ruins overnight because something or other had crashed in a country called America. All we heard as children were bits of conversations, and our vivid imaginations took over. I imagined American skyscraper buildings, literally scraping the sky, and men in top hats and black coats soaring out of every window like crows, and into the clouds, and then crashing onto the ground. The world beyond the confines of my happy life was beginning to feel strangely precarious. Mother, who had always been fretful, became more nervous still. Gustave was a sensitive boy and absorbed it all. He began waking up at night with terrible nightmares. He was pale, too thin, and tense as a wound-up spring. He chewed on his sleeve constantly. The British nannies were blamed for this, and Mother kept hiring sterner ones."

"That seems counterintuitive."

"She was under the impression that Gustave was spoiled and self-indulgent, and that character in a child was something that required molding through brute strength."

Cassie looked at one of the photographs in which Marceline seemed to be about ten years old. Her chin was up, her body about to bounce out of the frame, her black curls barely tamed. She smiled, seemingly confident of her adorableness. Standing next to her, little Gustave looked imploringly at the camera. His body was scrawny in the suit, his collar too stiff for his neck. It was also apparent in all the photos that Gustave looked like his mother, whereas Marceline was the spitting image of her handsome father. "You were very pretty."

"Also, I looked gentile. This should have been of no consequence, but alas, as the century embraced anti-Semitism, this was no small matter. The fact was, Gustave looked Jewish, and I could pass for a non-Jew. Mother was quite thrilled about that." She paused and looked at Cassie, who must have looked confused. "You don't think your father looks Jewish?"

"I never thought of him looking like anything other than my dad. What does looking Jewish even mean? It would not occur to me to think of his physical appearance in those terms."

"Rest assured that others did," Marceline said. "The differences between Gustave and me were many and profound, but mostly I looked gentile and he did not. Also, he was a soft child, and I was admittedly a tough little thing."

Cassie felt a slight pinch in her heart. A sense of alarm. Her dad had hidden his Judaism to his own daughters. He had been raised in pre-war France. She did not like the math happening in her head. Her dad had been a selfish, neglectful dad as far as she was concerned. He had liked Odile and he had not liked her. A simple enough narrative. It had never occurred to her that he had been a child too. A child who had suffered.

Marceline looked absently around the room and out the window as she went inward, as if mentally dusting off fragments of memories, placing herself back in the same house but over half a century earlier.

"When I was seven and Gustave was five years old, and every night had turned into a sleepless mess for him, Baba insisted to Mother that Gustave needed a nurturing presence rather than a stern nanny. He wanted to hire someone gentle and motherly. Mother relented and interviewed new women. This possibly changed our lives. In fact, I remember the day of the interviews vividly. There were chairs lined up in the vestibule, and a dozen applicants, bearing reference letters, were made to sit and wait until Mother received them one by one. I was sitting in the garden by the gate and watching the women come in when I overheard our chauffeur gossip with our gardener, as they smoked on the other side of the gate. They did not see me and went on with their conversations. "Should we tell the pretty ones to turn back and not even bother?" the gardener said.

"She isn't foolish enough to hire help that might be a temptation," the driver responded.

They were talking about Mother.

"I would not worry about the boss. Surely, he has a mistress hidden away somewhere. Or perhaps more than one," said the gardener. "You'd know about it; aren't you the one driving him?"

The driver chuckled, "Haven't you seen who he works with? His uncle."

They both laughed, stepped on their cigarette butts, and went about their work. I did not know what they were talking about, but I was instinctively furious. I stomped into the house with the urge to tell Father and Mother that the staff had been gossiping behind their backs. But I was not halfway out of the garden when I had the hunch that telling on them might hurt my parents or at least mess with the order of things. Inside, I went to the library room and looked up the word mistress in a dictionary. As I suspected, the word in this context had nothing to do with a schoolmistress. I read the mystifying synonyms: kept woman; courtesan, concubine, paramour, and the even more perturbing word that gave me pause, lover.

Outside the library room, prospective nannies continued to line up, and Mother received them one by one in her study. Through the window, I saw my father walk out of the house and enter the car. The driver started the engine, and they left. A mistress? What would my father want with a mistress? Did he not love Mother?

That got me thinking. Indeed, the women on Mother's staff, the maids, the cook, the nannies, were homely, but I was convinced of Father's innocence. He did not show any interest for any of the fancy women who graced their dinner parties. He was generous with his time and attention, attentive and polite with all, but this behavior did not change when he was in the company of a beautiful woman. I felt that I needed to be more vigilant. How many more things went beyond the scope of my awareness? I decided to spy on my parents so as not to be caught off guard again. If there was something to know, I wanted to be the first one to find out about it.

Gustave was coming down the spiral staircase when he found me flat on my belly, spying on the group of aspiring nannies that sat on chairs in the vestibule down below.

"What is it?" he asked.

"Mother is hiring you a nanny," I told him. "I am spying on them."

"Why?"

"I'm a spy now."

"I'm a spy also then," Gustave said. He got down to his belly and looked down with me.

"There can only be one spy," I told him. "But you can be my acolyte."

We watched. There were twelve ladies, sitting with their backs straight, purses clutched on their laps, cheap hats planted firmly on their heads. They all dressed the same, narrow skirts, blazers, blouses all in variants of grey. Every fifteen minutes or so, the door to Mother's study opened, and one woman left and another entered. There were the thin ones and the large ones, but they otherwise looked so interchangeable to me that I wondered how Mother could tell them apart.

This went on for a while until the front bell rang. The maid opened the door to a new woman. From where we were, we could only see the bottom of the woman's long skirt, her thick, dark hose, and ugly shoes. A very unusual attire to say the least. The maid seemed to recoil at the sight of her and fumbled with her words, telling the arriving woman that the position had been filled, which was clearly a lie with all the other women still sitting in their chairs. The woman apologized in a heavily accented voice. She insisted that she had an appointment. "This won't do," the maid said sharply. "You must leave now." She began to close the door on the woman who said, "Wait! I have a letter."

This was the most captivating thing that had happened in the last hour of lying on our bellies at the top of the stairwell. Gustave and I twisted our necks to see the woman's face, but we were too high up the stairwell to see more than the bottom half of her. She handed an envelope to the maid, who took it reluctantly. From above we watched the maid open the envelope, read the note, and mumble, "In that case, if you would please take a seat."

The strange woman stepped forward and came into view below us. She did not wear the traditional outfit of nannies. She wore a shawl over her hair rather than a hat. Her profile revealed her as a beautiful young woman with dark eyes fringed with thick eyelashes, and a sensual mouth. She was pretty. And then, having sensed our presence, she turned to look up at us, and Gustave and I gasped. The entire right side of the woman's face, from her temple down the length of her cheek and covering her chin, was all a massive scar. It was as if her skin had been melted and set again. Burned. We had seen enough men return from the war with this kind of wound, but a woman, a nanny, never.

The woman looked at us and smiled, and her whole face blossomed into something kind and beautiful.

Her name was Sandra. I learned later that my mother had agreed to interview her only because of Uncle Moshe's pressure – he was after all my father's boss. It had been his signature and his recommendation on the letter she had shown the maid. Sandra was a refugee we soon learned. She had no family and, because of her disfigurement, could find no work.

The following day, she was hired.

Mother did put up a fight, but my father had the final word. I heard them argue behind closed doors. I had found an air vent on the floor of the library above the salon. If you leaned right on the vent and placed your ear tight against it, the conversations came out crystal clear. Baba made the case for the woman with the scar.

"But she is foreign," my mother said.

"Not any more foreign than the British ones," Father told her. "I think it is time we moved away from those women. They are not good for Gustave." This was news to me, as he had never criticized any of them in my presence.

"We know nothing about her," Mother said.

"Moshe vouches for her. Also, she can cook and bake the kinds of foods from my country. I am quite tired of French cuisine." That was news to me as well. I had no idea my father was displeased with anything at all.

Mother continued to argue, and Baba was calmly telling her why she would be good for the family. But at some point, Mother said that the woman was repulsive. Father became angry, he who never was angry. He raised his voice and said, "I have made a decision. The foreign woman is hired."

It was unlike him to contradict Mother, and I was shocked by this, but not as shocked as Mother was. At a loss for words, she stuttered, "But, Alban…."

"I will tell Moshe to send her at once," my father said. With this, he just left the room.

Thus, Sandra came to live with us.

At first, Gustave and I were horrified and fascinated by her scar, but within days, we did not see it anymore. The only times we were reminded of it was through the eyes of others who recoiled when they saw Sandra for the first time.

Father had been absolutely right. Sandra turned out to be the best thing that could have happened to Gustave and me. She spoke French hesitantly and never said one word more than she had to, but her quietness, her reluctance to speak up, were more than compensated by a genuinely loving heart. Although Sandra was officially Gustave's nanny, it was soon clear that my nanny was here for the teaching of manners and that Sandra was here to dispense the loving care to both of us. She had great empathy for us and cried along with us and laughed as well. Although she could barely read or write in French, she had an intelligence and pragmatism that commanded respect. She would listen to us, without judgment or advice. She would just sit and be with us. She soon became the one person I ran to when I was in trouble. When I felt ill, or worried, or mad, she was the person I counted on. With just a few words, she could turn drama into something manageable. Sandra came to love Gustave and me nearly as a mother would, caring for us deeply, and accepting us and loving us through our many flaws.

"How did she get burned," Cassie asked.

"Her burn covered the right side of her body, from her temple, cheek, and neck to her shoulder and arm and perhaps lower. We were embarrassed to ask how it had happened, and she did not volunteer the information. In all the time she lived with us, we never asked about her past. And she never offered to tell."

"Perhaps you were afraid to know?"

Marceline nodded. "Perhaps. Sandra's arrival in our lives, in 1931, coincided with Europe descending into madness. In the years that followed, she became our rock. We were lucky to have her."

"Anti-Semitism began, you mean?" Cassie asked.

Marceline was about to respond, but she was overtaken by one of her coughs. "Anti-Semitism has no beginning, and it has no end, my dear," she managed to say.

As on cue, Laure entered "Madame?" She said, pouring her a glass of water. "It's time for your rest."

Marceline looked at Casandra, dabbed at her eyes and sighed. "Being old is like being a baby all over again. They bathe you, diaper you, put you down for naps. The worst indignities."

"You have to go now?" Cassie said, disappointed. She had found out so much about her dad already, and yet there was so much more to learn.

"I am tired," Marceline admitted. "I can tell you more another time perhaps?"

"Of course, you should rest," Cassie said begrudgingly. "But I'm only here for a few short days. Would it be all right with you if I came back tomorrow?"

Marceline got up from her seat with Laure's help. "Not here," she said. "In neutral territory, away from Armelle and Jean-Bernard snooping into my business."

Cassie stood up. "Just tell me where and I'll be there."

"There's this place I like," Marceline said. "Le Valentin, Passage Jouffroy. You know where that is?"

"I'll find it," Cassie said.

"Please come at noon," Marceline said. She sighed unhappily. "That's the time between my morning nap and my afternoon nap."

"Thank you for speaking to me," Cassie said as Laure nudged her out of the room and toward the staircase. "It means a lot."

Marceline, who was at the door to her room, said, "Actually. I have not been entirely honest with you."

"How so?"

"I knew you were Gustave's daughter from the moment I looked through my window and saw you pass the gate."

Cassie was astounded. "How is that possible?"

"That coat you're wearing."

"It's my father's," Cassie said.

"To be precise, it is your grandfather's. I remember the coat being made by our tailor because I came to the fitting. This was in, let's see, I was about eight years old. It must have been 1931. It was during the Great Depression. Bad things were going on all around, soup kitchens, long lines. But we were still doing well. We could still afford tailored clothes. The treats I told you about, the ones my father used to bring us every evening," Marceline's voice almost broke. "They came out of those pockets." She looked away to hide her emotion.

Cassie stared at the coat. "My Jewish grandfather's coat? That sounds practically biblical."

"May I ask why you're wearing it?" Marceline asked. "It seems like an odd choice."

"It was in my dad's hospital room. I was freezing, so I took it. I did wonder why, of all the coats he owns, my dad had taken this one with him to the hospital."

"Your father's downfall was always sentimentalism," Marceline said.

CHAPTER 12

The Man on a Motorcycle

It was almost two in the afternoon by the time Cassie left Marceline's house. In that room smelling of pipe tobacco, perfume, and old papers, filled with books, knickknacks, and strange artifacts, with the rain falling hard against the window, Cassie had forgotten to look at her watch. Her mother and Odile were most likely at her dad's bedside, and she was late. She stood at the street corner hoping for a cab, her blood laced with caffeine, from all that Earl Grey tea. She hated Earl Grey, but she had been so impressed – intimidated was more like it – by old Marceline that she drank the brew stoically rather than admit her dislike for it. If there was a fitting metaphor for who she was, this was it.

After ten minutes, she gave up on the idea of a cab and began walking. She hurried back to the ninth arrondissement accompanied by the clapping sound of her cowboy boots on the pavement. Her mind was filled with visions of her father as a fragile little boy living in opulence in that Cité des Fleurs house, visions she needed to reconcile with the ailing old man in his hospital bed, so powerful that he could apparently hurt her while unconscious. She could not wait to tell her sisters all that she had learned. How much of it did her mother know already? Had her dad confided in her? Her mother always knew more than she let on. She walked down rue Marcadet, past cars, old buildings, neon signs, and people gazing at their cell phones amorously. Those buildings had been there when her grandfather, a young man from the Ottoman Empire, had first arrived in Paris in 1922. Albano had walked past the same buildings, along the same boulevards. Her father had strolled down these streets as a boy.

She walked along rue Joseph de Maistre. The rain had stopped. Children riding bicycles filled the playgrounds that had been empty earlier. Did her father and Marceline once play there? The wealth, the grand house, the nannies, the class-obsessed mother, the foreign father, the bratty big sister, none of it reconciled with the restrained man she knew. Her dad had a backstory now, pathos she could sink her teeth into. All Cassie had ever wanted was to break the code to her father's heart. Speaking to Marceline was like being handed the key. Or if not the key, a least a map to a key. Things revealed themselves as she walked. Why did her father own so many Persian rugs? Because rugs were the family business. Why did he know so much about furniture and architecture? Because he grew up with an eye for those things and the homeschooling to go with it. Who had stolen the second finial? Marceline had, obviously, since she had possession of it.

Marceline had abruptly ended her story in 1931. She had needed to regroup. She had been upset, that much was clear. It did not take a historian to know what came next. Her dad had grown up in a time and place when being Jewish could cost you your life. He had survived, somehow, and she was about to find out how. Marceline seemed surprised, contemptuous even, of the fact that he had chosen to hide his Judaism. He had wanted to erase the past, as Marceline had said? Or perhaps he had wanted to hide himself and his daughters from a time where history might repeat itself, as history always did.

****

When she arrived at the hospital, Odile was standing outside the dressing room waiting for her. "How come you're wearing Papa's coat?" she asked, sounding appalled by this.

"I was cold," Cassie said.

Odile looked down at Cassie's red cowboy boots. "And what in the Lord's name are those?"

"Long story," Cassie said, "an incredible story, in fact. I've had quite the exciting morning. That's why I'm late. I can't wait to tell you all about it. How is Papa today?"

"Maman's with him," Odile said. "We spoke to his doctor already." Odile appeared to hesitate. "The doctor says his condition is stable, but … well, they feel he needs a lot of rest and—"

"Let's go see him."

"I could use a break," Odile said tensely. "Let's go the cafeteria."

This was not what Cassie wanted to do, but she could not afford to pass on a rare offer to do something normal and sisterly with Odile. "Sure," she said.

In the cafeteria, a janitor was mopping the floor. The room smelled of synthetic lemon detergent. Unnerving French pop music played in the background. Cassie and Odile put coins in a machine and waited for their espressos as they were noisily expelled into plastic cups. They sat at one of the tables. Odile stirred sugar into her coffee, looking ill. "Are you all right?" Cassie asked.

"My stomach's acting out. Something I ate." Odile's stomach had always been a barometer for her moods.

"Well, I met Marceline," Cassie said excitedly.

Odile seemed very surprised. "You did?"

"I even went to her house."

"Is she really Papa's sister?"

"Unbelievably, yes. They could not be more different, though. She's eighty-nine years old, two years older than Papa. But they have opposite personalities. She is sharp as can be. And she seems … I don't know … fearless."

Odile pinched her lips. "Unlike Papa, you mean."

"No, I mean … she's a character. She's eccentric. She told me interesting things about our grandfather. Do you know that he was from Smyrna? In the Ottoman Empire?"

"No," Odile said, excited. "I didn't know that. Wait, the Ottoman Empire? Wasn't that centuries ago?"

"I know, it sounds ancient, but apparently, it only ended in the nineteen twenties. About the time the Sacré-Coeur opened its doors."

"That has to be incorrect," Odile said.

"No, really, I went there yesterday and read it on a plaque."

Odile rolled her eyes. "Well then, if you read it on a plaque."

"And believe it or not, Papa was Jewish."

Odile squinted, shook her head. "Of course not."

"He had two Jewish parents." Odile was looking at her blankly, waiting for the punchline. "Amazing, isn't it?"

"I don't see how that's possible," Odile said. "Papa is Catholic. Everyone knows that."

"Apparently not by birth."

"If you say so," Odile said, shrugging with impatience.

"And that makes us half Jewish!"

"Whoopee," Odile said flatly.

"You're not amazed?"

"I frankly don't care one way or another." The way Odile said this, it was apparent she cared a whole lot. It was apparent, in fact, that she was seething.

"Why did he not tell us?"

"Maybe he forgot."

Cassie looked at Odile in disbelief. "Seriously?"

"Who cares. If Papa didn't want to be Jewish, that was up to him."

"I'm not so sure one can decide not to be Jewish."

"It's not a race," Odile said. "It's a religion. You can convert to it."

"It's both, I think. I'm not sure how it works."

"Well, we're not Jewish."

"I don't know," Cassie said. "I might be. I'm open to it."

"Why am I not surprised?" Odile snapped. "You never met a part of your upbringing you didn't want to reject."

Cassie stiffened in her chair, "Here it comes…."

"One day you're French, and the next you're American. One day you're Catholic, and now you've turned Jewish."

"Oh please, it's not like you're some devout Catholic. When was the last time you set foot in a church?"

"The point is, you grew up in France and were raised Catholic. Is that so terrible? Is that so disgusting to you?" Odile's voice quivered, "Are we so disgusting to you?"

"What scares you so much about the idea of Papa being Jewish? Or you being a Jew for that matter."

Odile snapped, "Don't say that word!"

"That word?" Cassie's was suddenly furious. "Do you mean the JEW word? For your information it's not a disparaging term, Odile, it's what Jewish people are called." Cassie controlled her breathing the best she could. She could have said so much more. The urge to verbally crush Odile was nearly irresistible, and the urge to crush her physically was not far behind. She could easily have reached across the table and slapped her, and Odile would have slapped her back, or pulled her hair, just as they had done throughout their childhood, with the two of them transforming into a four-arms-four-legs shrieking monster right there on the cafeteria's linoleum floor. Tempting. "Marceline will tell you about Papa if you're too frigging stubborn to hear it from me," she said between clenched teeth. "I'm seeing her tomorrow. She wants to meet you. You can come along."

Odile pinched her lips. "Not interested," she said without an instant of reflection.

"But … why not?"

"My loyalty is to Papa."

Cassie was dumbstruck. "Why are we even discussing loyalty?"

"Here is a woman Papa didn't want to have anything to do with, and you're all chummy with her. I'm sorry, but no thank you."

Cassie raised her voice despite herself. "You don't get it at all! This is not betraying Papa; this is trying to understand him."

"You have your way of understanding him, and I have mine." Odile was even paler now. "Let's agree to disagree."

"Oh, bullshit, Odile!"

"Actually," Odile said, looking at the floor of the cafeteria, "there is something I need to talk to you about. Yesterday, this whole explosion, and screaming at you the way he did, that was hard on Papa."

Cassie rolled her eyes. "Not just on him."

"He's the one in a hospital bed, not you, last I checked," Odile snapped.

"True, true," Cassie said. "You think I don't know that?"

"We're so focused on fighting the lung infection right now that we tend to forget that he had heart surgery a few days ago. The last thing he needs is more strain on his heart."

"I could not agree more."

"The way he became emotional yesterday, that can't be good for his heart," Odile said softly.

"Probably not."

"Maman and I discussed this, and well … we think that it's better we do what we can to avoid any stress for him."

Cassie nodded in agreement. "We're on the same page."

Odile looked relieved. "Oh, good."

"Great," Cassie said, still nodding. She was happy that the argument had died down rather than escalate the way it invariably did. Maybe they were both mature enough to communicate without the usual drama. Maybe they could start a new chapter. Perhaps her father's illness could bring them closer. She smiled.

"Do you see what I'm trying to say?" Odile asked, suddenly worried.

"I – I'm not sure. Are you trying to say something?"

"Well," Odile said in a small voice and without looking at her, "We think you need to stay away."

"Away from what?"

"From Papa's room."

Cassie's stomach dropped. "What?"

"We decided … for the time being."

"Are you telling me I can't see Papa?"

"You said we were on the same page," Odile whimpered.

"We decided?" Cassie exclaimed. She tried to gather her jumbled thoughts through the wave of emotion: sadness, anger, a sense of betrayal and rejection. "Who's we? The doctors? You and Maman?"

Odile hesitated. "All of us, including the doctors."

"What doctors? Which doctor?"

"Doctor Dumant. We met with him this morning and—"

"Papa was on drugs. It was a freak thing! And I did nothing wrong. I just stood there, and he verbally attacked me!"

"No one said you did anything wrong," Odile said in a calm, paternalistic tone. "You don't have to take this personally."

"My own sister is asking me not to see my own father," Cassie cried out. "No, worse: my own sister is telling me not to see my own father because she believes I am harming him. And I shouldn't take it personally?"

"This is not about you."

"It is!"

"We're trying to give Papa the best possible chance at recovery."

"Unlike me, who's trying to kill him?" Cassie pushed her chair back and got to her feet. There was the anger and there was the caffeine, and she wasn't sure which of the two had taken over her brain. "Well, screw that! Nobody's going to dictate if I can see my own father. Like it or not, I'm going into that room."

"You can't!" Odile said, snapping at attention and jumping up from her chair.

"Who'll stop me?"

Cassie stormed out of the cafeteria, Odile running after her. "Cassandra, stop! Don't make a spectacle! Stop right now! Please listen to me. Stop!"

Cassie headed toward the room, but just before the door, she veered left and entered the first hallway, and then the next until Odile's calls and the sound of her shoes clip-clopping behind her stopped.

For ten minutes, Cassie walked through the hospital hallways in a fog, her chest heavy, her feet heavy, a painful lump stuck in her throat. She sat on a bench in a deserted hallway, a thousand-pound weight on her shoulders, defeated.

The image of Marceline came to her. Marceline in her multicolored dress, her posture, her pride. A spy for the OSS. How would Marceline handle this? Would she dissolve in a pool of tears? Cassie had a sense that she would not. Marceline did not strike her as the kind of woman who let other people affect the way she felt about herself.

She got up from the bench and stomped toward the intensive care unit. The reception area was crowded with patients, visitors, nurses, doctors, and staff. She made a beeline for the desk. Behind the desk, she recognized the frizzy-haired clerk she had badgered the day before. She gave the woman her name and avoided eye contact.

The frizzy clerk looked uneasy. She said, "The list of visitors has been restricted."

Cassie felt in her stomach the return of that hollow feeling. "Meaning?" she asked.

"Your name was crossed off the list of approved visitors," the clerk said, trying hard to appear detached from her victory.

Cassie was either going to burst into tears in front of all those people or attack. "That is my father in there. I flew all the way from the United States just to see him!"

"Yes, Madame, we are all well aware that you came from America." Cassie could hear the eye roll implied in the comment.

It was a small miracle that she didn't hurl herself at the woman's throat. "Yes, that's right! I am a proud citizen of the US of A!" she shouted. Around them, conversations suspended in mid-sentence, bodies froze in position. Everyone in the ICU, those who were ill and those who were well, the nurses and the aids, the visitors and the cleaning staff – everyone was watching. Cassie fought the urge to get louder. She said to the clerk in a controlled voice, "Why has the Chief of Services not seen me yet?"

"I told you, he does not see people."

"Let him decide if he will see me or not. Did you or did you not give him the message?"

"He was made aware of it."

"I sure hope so for your sake, because I'm ready to go right over your head. Tell him that if he doesn't see me, I will go over his head. All the way to the top! I will fight this with legal means. I will write letters to every journalist, every blogger, every politician and expose how this hospital treats its clients."

Doctor Dumant appeared at the desk, his stethoscope planted on either side of his neck. "What is … this?" he asked dispassionately.

The clerk fumbled with her words. "Docteur Dumant. This person is … she wants us to … she demands…."

Cassie turned to the doctor, "And you! What gives you the right to separate me from my father? This whole thing has been mishandled by your hospital from the start. You botched the surgery; you exposed him to an infection; you did not give him the correct antibiotic. You drugged him into oblivion, which made him delusional enough to go batshit crazy. And now you're stopping me from seeing him? I'm not the one harming him. You are! The instant he set foot in this hospital you proceeded to kill him by any means possible."

"What is it you … want from me," the doctor said in an exhausted voice.

"I want to speak to the Chief of Services!" She pointed at the clerk. "And this person here won't let me."

The doctor turned to the desk. "Did you forward the message, Mademoiselle Pinçon?"

"I think so," the clerk, who now had a name, said as she fumbled with papers. It was obvious from Mademoiselle Pinçon's demeanor that she was as flustered with people who were above her as she was intent on making people like Cassie feel two inches tall.

"She thinks so!" Cassie said, childish victory in her voice. "You never gave him the message, did you?"

The doctor sighed and turned to a nearby nurse, bypassing Pinçon entirely. "S'il vous plaît, Florence, could you … make sure that the Chief of … Services is aware that this lady wants to speak to him?"

"Oui, Docteur."

Without further words, Doctor Dumant walked away, looking at his clipboard. He put his hand on the door to the surgery unit, stopped, and turned toward Cassie. "By the way," he said. "So that we are … clear, I am not the one keeping you away … from the room."

"They told me you did."

"I only recommended that your … father should be kept calm. Your mother and sister … are the ones who made that decision. They took you off the list, and they … have the power to do so." With this, he left.

Odile had lied. This was essentially a restraining order against her. This was nuts. This was deranged! Cassie drifted through the hallways like a somnambulist. All kinds of hurt flooded in. All the hurt she had so carefully pushed away was pushing back, about to swallow her whole. Her heart ached, and the lump in her throat seemed made of lead. She was in enemy territory here. She was under attack. Her sister hated her. Her mother hated her. Her father hated her. He always had! She was unloved because they were hateful, hateful people!

And also, because she was unlovable.

She stepped out into the courtyard and sat on an empty bench and stayed there, not even feeling the cold, humid air.

She did not know how much time had passed before Sabine sat next to her on the bench. "I had nothing to do with this; I want you to know," Sabine said. "No one consulted me. You're not missing much; Dad's not awake. And going into that room is like stepping through the gates of hell anyway."

Cassie wiped her eyes, rubbed her cheeks, felt her blood flow return. She looked at Sabine, who was wrapped in a thin coat. Her face was drawn. "How could they kick me out?" she asked her.

"They're afraid of you," Sabine said.

"King Kong and Godzilla are afraid of me?"

"They're more scared of you than you are of them."

Cassie shook her head in incomprehension. "But why?"

Sabine hesitated, looking for an accurate answer. She spoke without passion, looking at the ground. "You challenge their way of looking at the world and themselves. You need to be wrong, or else the whole castle of cards collapses."

"I'm not trying to be right. I'm trying to be … I don't know … not exactly appreciated … I've resigned myself to the idea that that is not going to happen. Not approved of even. Forget about that. Accepted. That's the word. I just want to be accepted." She shook her head. "Right now, I'd settle for being tolerated."

"They've made you into this formidable enemy over the years. It's a story they tell themselves."

"I'm not even sure what that means."

Sabine moved her hair away from her face; she was trying to say something difficult. "When you left France, you were eighteen and I was eight. I looked up to you."

"You did?"

"You were just how I wanted to be when I grew up."

"I bet you've made some serious adjustments to your thinking since," Cassie said. Sabine did not answer. "I remember you too, of course. You were adorable." This was a lie. She had little recollection of Sabine as a child. It was the age difference. And she had been much too preoccupied with her teenage self to notice that she had an eight-year-old sister.

"After you left home I kept waiting for you to come back," Sabine said. She let her hair fall across her face as though she wanted to hide it. "And Papa and Maman hated Peter and the US. And little by little it got worse. Every time they spoke about you, it was to say that you had done or said this horrible thing. And then the letter … I guess even I started to believe that you were this … devil."

"I hope you don't mean that you've hated me for the last twenty years."

"Not hate, no. You're unpredictable. You shake things up. You're like a big wrench in the status quo. When you're here, it's impossible to go on looking at things quite in the same way. For all of us, it's damage control the minute you're involved."

"I'm Attila the Hun."

"But I think we need this," Sabine said. "Our family can use that kind of brain-shake."

"Attila the Hun, but in a fun way. You know, my kids consider me a complete bore. I consider myself a complete bore."

"You're certainly not boring."

"So, if I want their approval, all I need to do is to shut my mouth?"

"That's what I do, and I still don't get their approval." Sabine had meant this as a joke, but even her humor had an aftertaste of hopelessness.

Cassie looked at her sister and suddenly felt a terrible pang of guilt. Here she was, talking about herself when, clearly, she ought to be asking about Sabine. "Will you tell me what's going on with you for heaven's sake?"

Sabine was quiet for a minute, as though she was deciding if she should open up, or perhaps she just didn't know where to start. "Paul met someone," she said finally. "The full cliché."

From her own breakup experience, Cassie knew that platitudes only served to make oneself feel better. "I'm sorry," she said.

"I was two months pregnant."

"Did Paul know that?"

"Yes," Sabine said.

"Jeez," Cassie whistled, "what an asshole."

"I could not imagine raising children without him. Or sharing them with him and that woman. I had an abortion." She paused, looked away. "It was awful."

"I didn't know. No one called me."

"I was afraid you'd try to talk me out of it, the abortion."

"Me? I would have been supportive." Cassie reflected on this. "Actually, I'm pretty sure I would have tried to talk you out of it."

"One day, I'm happy, expecting twins –"

"Twins?" Cassie exclaimed.

"And the next, I'm –" Sabine shook her head. "I couldn't do this alone, be a mother, I mean. If it had been just one baby, maybe … but Paul had just broken my heart. I was sinking. It was all too much." She took a deep breath, shook away whatever emotion rose in her. "I thought if I didn't do it then, I would never do it. And so, I did. It's done. It's over. The babies are gone."

"Sabine … I don't know what to say. I wish I had been there for you."

"Since that, everything feels … flat."

"How could it not? Have you seen someone about that? They have great medications nowadays."

"No."

"And therapy. What about therapy? Peter always said I needed therapy."

"For what?"

"Anger. Blaming. For not knowing myself. Not knowing what I want."

"You're describing everyone in our family."

"You don't seem to have anger, the way we do."

"I just redirect it."

"Where?"

Sabine pointed at herself, "Here."

In the hospital garden, a young father was walking behind his daughter. The little girl was learning how to walk. She was dressed in a navy coat, white wool stockings, and tiny Mary Jane shoes on her feet, like a child out of another century. Each time she almost toppled, the father lurched forward, but then he let her fall so that she could get a feel for it. Cassie smiled at the little girl and at the dad who smiled back. She realized that Sabine was looking right past them, not even seeing them.

"You're still young," she told her sister, knowing full well this was beside the point, but what can you say to someone who is grieving. "You have your whole life ahead of you. And you are beautiful."

"Thank you. I wish I could enjoy it. My youth, my life; I don't think I've ever felt carefree or young."

"Is there anything I can do to help?"

"This helps. The killer in this family is the feeling that you can't talk, that everything emotional is off limits. Speaking up is like stepping on land mines."

"Yep. Since I got here, they've been blowing up all over the place."

"And yet you're still standing."

"I am," Cassie said in surprise. "I am still standing."

****

They said goodbye, and Cassie left the hospital. She felt wiped out. All she wanted now was food in her belly followed by a long bath in that fantastic tub and then bed.

She entered La Jument Bleue at 7:10 p.m. Like clockwork, Indiana Jones was putting the lock on his motorcycle. Cassie hurried her step and rushed to the table they both coveted. Two could play this petty game. She zoomed inside and got to the table first. She folded her coat over the chair to claim it and was about to sit down when she sensed that Indiana was right behind her. She pivoted on her feet, ready to flash him a gloating smile. But she was faced with his expression of puzzlement and felt suddenly disarmed. "You wanted this table?" she asked.

"I did," he admitted. He was standing awkwardly, his helmet in one hand.

"Is that why you've been looking at me angrily?" she said. "Because I have your favorite table?"

Indiana blinked. "Not angrily," he said. "It's just that we all have our little habits."

Cassie sighed. She did not have another battle in her. "You can have your table." She grabbed her coat and moved it to the chair facing the only other empty table, which happened to be the table next to his.

"Merci," he said. "I like to be next to the window, to watch my bike. You have no idea how fast you can find yourself without a tire or a wheel." He removed his leather satchel, his jacket, his wool scarf and sat down.

Cassie settled in her chair. She was glad she had not been ridiculous about the table. It was a refreshing feeling to be the bigger person. "No explanation necessary," she said.

"When you park on the street, you can end up missing a rearview mirror; it's an antique. The parts are so hard to find. That's why I like to keep an eye."

"Hmm … hmm," she said.

They were now sitting next to one another at their respective tables, almost shoulder to shoulder, their backs to the mirrored wall, which was beyond awkward. "I've had lunch here every day for the last year," Indiana said.

"You like it that much?" she asked. They were talking, something she did not want to do, but because they sat side by side, they did not look at each other.

"Force of habit," he said. "As of late, I've been having dinner here as well."

He was trying to make conversation, she realized. He was being nice. Why had she assumed this would turn into a fight? When had fighting become her default mode? With her mother and father, with Peter, and now with the entire staff of a Parisian hospital that she wasn't so convinced deserved it. What was wrong with her? She was at her worst with Odile. Was there ever a time when she and her sister had not been at war? Odile was no better. She was always on the attack too. They reacted to each other, fed off each other's lunacy. But the thing was, it was the same pattern with her twins, always at each other's throat. Why? Could everybody else be to blame, and more important, could she be blameless when the only common denominator between all these fighting people was herself?

Indiana frowned and said. "You look mad. Are you're angry with me? Would you like the table back?"

She was surprised to see the intent look on his face as he waited for her answer. "Of course not," she said. His eyes were the palest of blue and his face nicely rugged, the face of a man who spends a lot of time outdoors. "I am angry," she admitted. "Furious, in fact. But not at you, and not about the table." And seeing that he seemed upset, she added, "I promise."

The waiter came to inform them that the dessert on special was profiteroles au chocolat. He set their tables and left. "The patronne usually reserves the table for me," Indiana said. "She did for years, and now I think

I've fallen out of grace. At any rate, either you're doing something right, or I'm doing something wrong."

"We can't be still talking about the table?" Cassie said. "You did nothing wrong with the patronne. It's just that by the time you arrive in the morning, I've usually been sitting here for a while."

"Writing on placemats," he said.

"Well … I guess, yes," she answered, flustered that he had noticed. "I assume she doesn't have the heart to kick me out."

He feigned terror. "Are we speaking of the same patronne?"

She laughed. "I don't just write on placemats, you know. I order food, too."

"Steak au poivre and frites?"

She felt herself blush. "You're quite observant."

"With ketchup?"

"The way you said ketchup sounds like a reproach."

"That's not what people usually eat with a steak with pepper and cream sauce."

"What do they eat with it?"

"Well, pepper and cream sauce."

She tapped her hand to her skull. "So that's why they put it there!"

"The sauce is there to enhance flavor, you see," he said. "So that people won't have to resort to ketchup."

"It has nothing to do with flavor. I use ketchup strictly for comfort."

Indiana mimicked head to toe chills at the prospect. He then dug into his well-worn leather satchel. "I have something for you," he said.

"For me?" Cassie said, astonished.

"I hope you won't mind." He handed her a thin, flat package wrapped in brown paper. "I took the liberty of assuming that you could use this."

She stared at the package, then at him. "Do you always carry gifts around to give to perfect strangers?"

"Not until today."

She hesitated, but because he looked so earnest, she took the package from his hands. She stared at it. "This is weird," she said, not knowing exactly how to feel or why she even went along with this. She opened the package. In it was a single five-by-eight Moleskine notebook with a bright pink cover.

"Better than writing on placemats, no?" he said. "Do you like the color? I can trade it for any other color. It took me a while to decide. Women like pink. Some of them do, at least."

"Thank you," Cassie said. She felt helplessly moved by the gesture. When was the last time someone cared one bit what color she liked? Perhaps no one ever had. It was her first time being the object of random kindness, and it was coming at a vulnerable moment. She was usually the one anticipating the wants and needs of others, and to care for them was enough to fill her with love. But in the last years, those she loved had become self-sufficient, or they had moved on, and there was no one left to care for. Cassie steadied herself not to betray her emotion. "Did you plan on giving me this so that I would relinquish your table?"

"It was going to be either a bribe or a gift, and since you so generously gave me the table, it's definitely a gift. You should use a laptop, you know. Although I didn't feel that giving you a laptop would be appropriate at this juncture in our relationship."

She burst out laughing. "You and I are in a relationship?"

"We do share custody of a table."

Cassie shook her head, still laughing. "This is the most thoughtful gift I've received in a long time," she admitted.

"Oh, great, I'm glad."

This had been one seriously bizarre day. This morning she was learning about her ancestors from an aunt she didn't know existed. This afternoon she was being treated like a leper by her family. And here she was now, engaged in a shoulder-to-shoulder conversation with a handsome stranger over the ownership of a bistro table. "I thank you for your kindness," she told him. "The table is now yours without any grudge from me whatsoever. And for the record, I do own a laptop."

"Then it must be an invisible laptop," he said. "I'm Hervé," he added, extending his hand.

"Cassandra," she said shaking his hand. "Cassie."

"Ha!"

"Ha?"

"Cassandra," he said. "Daughter of King Priam and Queen Hecuba of Troy."

"Not that one, sorry to disappoint."

"She was given the gift of prophecy by the gods, but Apollo cursed her for not returning his love."

"What kind of curse?"

"He made it so that no one would believe her prophecies."

Cassie smiled, charmed against her will. "Well, that serves her right. What fool turns down Apollo?"

"You are new in the neighborhood?"

Cassie was not going to get into the big mess of the last few days with a stranger. "Sort of new," she said. "Returning."

"You come to La Jument Bleue every day," Hervé said. "But I had never seen you before three days ago."

"It's convenient for me," she said evasively. "What about you. You seem to live here."

"I work nearby, and since my home life has…." He searched for the appropriate word. "Well, deteriorated, I'm here a lot. It's close to work, and the food is good."

"Divorce?" she said, fishing for information.

"We were never married," he said. "What about you? I hear you're staying at Hôtel Petite Seine?" To her surprised expression, he eyed the old manager who was sitting at the bar. "I have my spies."

"So much for customer privacy."

"That's all he would tell me. So? How come you're staying there?" he asked. "A deteriorated home life too?"

Cassie thought about it. No, she didn't want to open up to this stranger. Not when stupid tears threatened to burst out of her at the slightest provocation. "It's kind of silly, carrying on a conversation while eating at separate tables," she noted.

"I was just thinking the same thing," Hervé said, and with this, he picked up his plate, knife, and fork and set them on her table, got up, and sat across from her. "Here we go," he said, reaching for his glass and setting it in front of his plate. "Have you tried the house wine?" he asked, peering at her with lagoon-colored eyes. "It's not bad at all."

Cassie's face burned. This she had not expected. To hide her surprise, she made a joke of it. "But what about the table?" she whispered, darting a worried look at the table Hervé had abandoned. "What about its feelings?"

Hervé spoke to the table as though it were a child, "If you remain very still we will come to you for dessert."

"You work in this neighborhood, huh? What kind of work do you do?" she asked, masking her growing self-consciousness by taking a large gulp of her water.

He shrugged. "I'm an administrator."

"That's vague."

"A bureaucrat," he said with a slight grimace. "I was forced to take this lousy administrative job. I'm wretched at it, and I hate every moment of it."

"You were forced?" she asked. She was flustered and was having trouble looking him in the eyes.

Hervé shrugged again, apparently one of his favorite things to do, and he looked pretty cute doing it. "I made a mistake," he said. "Well, it was not a mistake. Let's say I played with fire, I was burned – caught, I mean, and my boss sent me to purgatory for a few years. In actuality, it feels more like a pact with the devil. But I should not complain. They pay me well enough, and it allows me to pursue other interests."

"Such as Greek mythology?"

"For example, yes. I have many hobbies. What about you?"

"My latest hobby involves getting into arguments with anyone who comes within ten feet of me."

"I'll consider myself warned."

"As for work…." She thought about it. "I too made a pact with the devil. Although I'm pretty good at what I do."

"What do you do?"

"I'm a writer. Perhaps more of a ghostwriter of sorts."

"Ah, now it all makes sense!"

"What?"

"It explains the ghost laptop."

She laughed. "My laptop and my cell phone both just broke down. Mercury must be in retrograde."

"Oh no, it isn't," Hervé assured her. "Quite the contrary. Venus is in Mars. This is a time for action, and for love."

"I take it that astrology is another hobby of yours? Maybe you'll be able to tell me what's going to happen to me next."

"You're Cassandra," he said. "You're the one with the gift of prophecy."

"You know my gift is useless since I'm cursed. No one believes me anyway."

He raised a finger. "I predict," he said in a cavernous, prophetic-sounding voice, "that for dessert you'll have profiteroles au chocolat."

"You're cheating. That's not prophecy; it's mind reading."

"All right," Hervé said, and returning to his prophetic voice, added, "I predict that tomorrow you will not eat steak with ketchup."

"Now that's interesting. How do you know that?"

"Because you and I are going to eat in a place where they do not serve either."

"Are we?" Cassie felt herself blush to her roots. Was he asking her out? He was asking her out!

"I will pick you up right here tomorrow," he said. "And I will take you to a fantastic fish restaurant I know."

Evidently, she needed to say no. But what reason would she give? Looking out the window, she contemplated the deluge outside and Hervé's motorcycle that glistened in the rain. "I'm not climbing on that thing if that's what you have in mind."

"You might need to wear something insulating."

She pointed to her clothes. "Jeans and this coat are all I have."

"I'll bring a jacket and helmet. And a scarf." As he said this, and just as the waiter came in to take their orders, the patronne called from behind the counter.

"Hervé, phone call for you."

"Ha," he told Cassie. "If you'll excuse me." He got up from the table and walked to the counter.

"I am tired of being your secretary," the patronne grumbled as she handed him the receiver across the bar. "Get yourself a cell phone. Comme un homme normal," she said. Like a normal person.

He got up, listened to the person on the line. After a few minutes, he returned to the table. "I'm sorry, I can't stay. I must dash. An emergency at work." He hurried, putting on his jacket. "So, we're all set? 7:10 pm tomorrow? At your hotel?" he said, hoisting the satchel over his shoulder.

"I don't even know why, but I'm going to say … yes."

"Excellent. See you then."

He left money on the table for her dinner and left her sitting at La Jument Bleue, stunned and speechless.

****

After dinner, in her hotel, Cassie removed her boots and coat and sat in bed. She thought of Hervé and smiled. Did she really just accept a date with a handsome stranger? She giggled to herself, feeling like a teenage girl. Here she was in Paris with no computer and no phone. The last time this had happened, she was eighteen years old. She had been about to meet Peter, but unaware of it, about to leave everything behind and move to the United States, a country where she did not even speak the language. What had she been like at eighteen? She had been angry with her family, confused, rebellious. She had only known herself through the eyes of others: her secretive, passive-aggressive mother, her resentful sister, her indifferent, if not hostile, father. She had wanted an adventure. She had wanted another life. She had wanted a romance, something sweeping and wild. She had even dared wish she could shine one day, learn to be herself, whatever that meant.

Cassie closed her eyes. Marceline. That's the kind of woman she had wanted to become. But her life had taken a different turn, a twenty-year bifurcation away from the person she had hoped to be.

She went to stand by the window. Outside, the city sparkled, beautiful even in the rain. In Paris, there was a strange alchemy in the air. The moment you got there, forgotten yearnings emerged. Maybe the last twenty years had just been a detour. Maybe she could still become the person she wanted to be and live the life she had dreamed of. Maybe it wasn't too late.

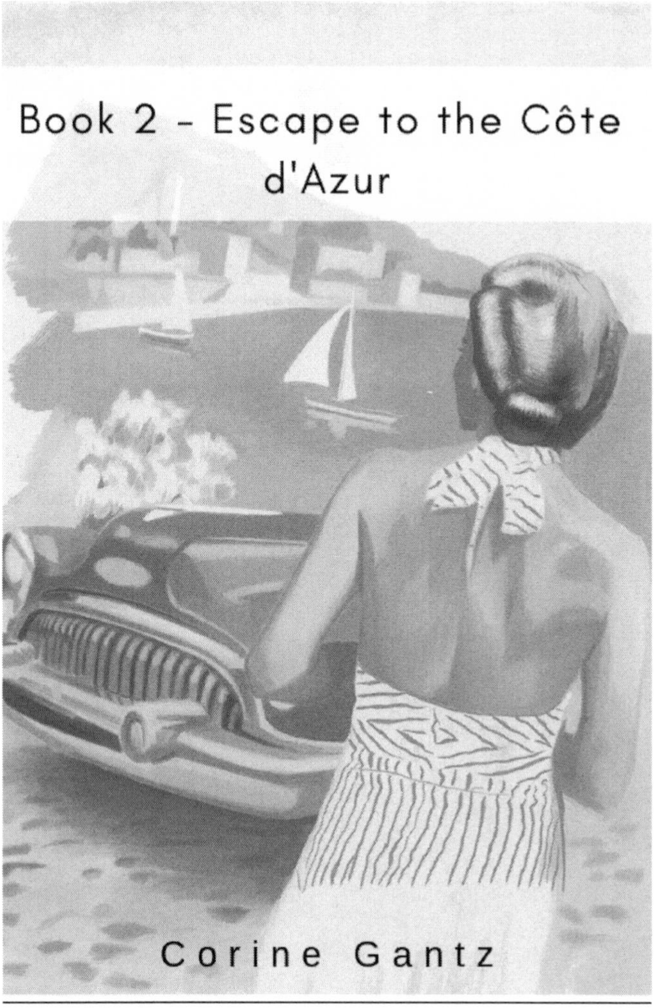
Book 2 - Escape to the Côte d'Azur
Corine Gantz

To refugees past, present, and future.

CHAPTER 1

Ketchup All Over the Place

The early morning light, soft and wintry, entered through the glass pane of Cassie's hotel room window. She lay on her back, the covers up to her chin, wishing she were safely at home in Los Angeles where she belonged and not in Paris where everyone hated her.

Upon arriving four days ago, she had tried to charge her cell phone and laptop by plugging them into a medieval converter, causing them to implode. Now that she was reduced to using public phones like in the eighties, throwing her back into the precise era where she had chosen to get the hell away from her family in the first place, there was the real possibility that she too was about to implode.

She could run away, rush back home on the next flight, but what was there to return to, really? An empty house? A garden in shambles? Motherhood had been her purpose, but Jeanne and Alex were away at their respective colleges, clearly not needing her at all. And was Los Angeles really home? After twenty years, she felt American, but no one let her forget her French accent. She was a foreigner. An immigrant. In Los Angeles, there was work, but her ex's lack of compunction about letting her write his screenplays while he reaped Hollywood's accolades was starting to look a lot like indentured servitude. And the daily witnessing of his matrimonial bliss with Jessica – and by the way Cassie still had not brought Jessica's little gifts to her parents. The perfect little packages were still on the mantle – was beginning to look a lot like masochism.

Peter exploited her. That much she was clear on. But the reason he did, was that she let him. And she let him because five years post-divorce she was still terrified of a life without him.

Damn the mess of her life. Damn the loneliness. There were so many changes she should make, but all of them required bravery and more losses perhaps. The unknown.

Cassie was staring at the ceiling when a faint ray of sun entered the room and hit the crystals that dangled on the chandelier. Blue prisms appeared on the crown molding and swept across the aging wallpaper, briefly transforming the walls of her small hotel room into a kind of fairytale scene. And then, as fast as the enchantment of the light had come, it was gone. She got out of bed and peeked out the window. On the small balcony, the metal table and chairs glistened with dew. Beyond that, shy sunrays bounced off

Paris rooftops, and the silhouette of the Eiffel Tower emerged against a pink sky. Beautiful.

She felt a flutter of excitement. Today she had another meeting with Marceline, her father's estranged sister whose existence had been a complete secret until two days ago. Her spry eighty-seven-year-old aunt had already revealed more about her dad than she had known her entire life. And maybe Cassie did have one friend in Paris: Sabine, her younger sister, who did not appear to carry hostility towards her. So, that was something. And there was Hervé, the man with the motorcycle she had met at the Jument Bleue who wanted to have dinner with her, tonight!

She should *never* have said yes to dinner, for so many reasons. Not the least of which was her failure to mention that she lived in the United States and that she was only in Paris for a few more days. She wasn't a monster full of deceit; it's just that it had not come into the conversation. Not that she owed this perfect stranger information about her life. But still, she had flirted, and maybe he had flirted too. Unless he had not; she couldn't be sure. He could as easily be a friendly man (or gay perhaps, or friendly and gay), making amends after their squabble over coveting the same table.

The reasonable thing to do was to cancel dinner, but how? Hervé had not given her his number, and anyway she didn't have a phone. She looked at the clock: seven a.m. He had mentioned that he had breakfast at the Jument Bleue every day before work, so maybe she could catch him there and nip things in the bud nice and clean. It was time she acted like her steady, serious, dependable self. The self that seemed to have gone missing from the moment she had landed in Paris a few days ago. All she needed to do right now was to imagine her twins' reaction to the idea of her having dinner with a stranger to realize how ludicrous it was.

She jumped into her jeans, put on the second-hand red cowboy boots bought the day before, wrapped herself in her grandfather's ill-fitting coat, and ran down the stairs.

At the desk, the elderly proprietor, his bushy white hair and eyebrows uncombed, was trying to button the top collar of his shirt with trembling fingers. "Bonjour, Monsieur!" she called out as she zoomed past him.

"Doucement, doucement," he sighed. "The youth, always rushing."

"I'm forty years old," she called out as she pushed open the door.

"You're a child," the old man responded.

Outside, it was another glorious spring day in Paris: cold, blustery, and wet. She put her purse over her head and, hopping around puddles, hurried toward the Jument Bleue.

The café was loud and filled to capacity with people having their last espresso of the morning (and in some instances their first glass of Beaujolais) before work. Remembering the Open Sesame of all French interactions – something she would have done well to remember the day before when dealing with the creeps at the hospital, Cassie spotted the owner. She called out over the roar of the espresso machine, "Bonjour, Madame. Comment ça va ce matin?"

The patronne, who seemed even more bosomy, pink-cheeked, and small-waisted than the day before, which was remarkable for a woman well into her sixties, looked at Cassie crosswise. But her expression softened somewhat when she recognized her. "Almost no complaints," she said, adding, "a café au lait?" After only two days, Cassie was being treated like one of the regulars, a small reward that made her feel good in a pitiable sort of way.

She took her café au lait and waited with a mix of dread and impatience until 7:30, but Hervé did not appear. "That man," she asked the patronne finally, "the one who comes here all the time, was he here this morning?"

The patronne shrugged. "A hundred men come here every day, Madame."

"The handsome one," Cassie said. "With the motorcycle."

"Ah, oui. You missed him. He left five minutes before you got here."

"Do you know how I could reach him?"

"You can always telephone him," the patronne said.

"Do you have his number?" Cassie asked too eagerly.

The patronne laughed out loud. "Well, like you, the one he gives away is the one to the Jument. It looks like you people have put yourself in a bind."

Back in her hotel room, Cassie mulled over her options. Her meeting with Marceline was not until noon, and hospital visiting hours started after that. After seeing Marceline, she was determined to see her dad, even if that entailed forcing her way into the hospital, wringing her mother's and sister's Hermès-clad necks, and stepping right over their still-warm corpses. She hated, HATED them! It would be a relief, it would be a joy, it would be a gift from heaven never to interact with them again! Ever.

She took a shower standing in the massive bathtub, her thoughts running amok. She had not come all the way to France to be denied access to her own father. She too had feelings, in case they had forgotten. She too was a human being! It was not her fault that her dad had hallucinated when he saw her and thought that she was Marceline. It was not her fault that he hated his sister deeply enough to hide her very existence from his three daughters.

Lost in the comfort of warm water over her body, Cassie rehearsed in her mind all the mean things she might tell her mother and Odile. She then toyed for a few more minutes with morbid images involving strangulation until she changed her mind and decided that her overriding urge was to apologize to them, implore, beg, and crawl on her hands and knees, whatever it took, until they saw how lovable and humble and harmless she was. Sabine did not seem to see her as this formidable opponent. If Sabine did not see her as the enemy, maybe there was hope to get through to Odile and her mother.

She got out of the bathroom and dried her hair with a towel. With the humidity, all hope of looking appropriately polished would need to be abandoned at once. Her hair would look like a cross between lichen and a crow's nest, and that was that. She still had about three hours before going to Marceline's. Maybe in the meantime, she could go to her mom's apartment with the excuse of bringing Jessica's gifts. She would pretend to come with a peace offering and then give her and Odile hell about what they had done. Unless they apologized to her. Or felt guilty. Or something. If they put her name back on the list, she would consider being magnanimous.

****

She stepped out of the hotel and into the street. The rain had stopped. Her parent's apartment was at the corner of Boulevard Barbès and rue Ordener, about a twenty-minute walk from her hotel. She was wondering how in the world she was going to cancel that dinner with Hervé when she walked past the gate of the hospital where her dad was being treated. She stopped to face the building, which looked more like an annex of the Louvre than a hospital, with its stone archways and planted center courtyard. A flurry of people freely came in and out, which was bitterly ironic considering that she was not allowed in and that her father was unable to get out. No good whatsoever would come from going inside she realized. Not only was she banned from her dad's room, but she had alienated the doctors, nurses, and staff with whom she had come into contact. Every interaction at the hospital, whether with the staff, her mother, her sister, or, worse yet, her very ill father, had been an epic disaster. But before she quite realized what she was doing, or why, she was walking through the gate and heading for the intensive care unit.

She knew the way by heart now, loathing every inch of it. She walked through the colonnaded marble walkways alongside the series of tall, arched windows that looked out into the central garden, passing through the peculiar mix of state-of-the-art medical facilities and nineteenth-century architecture. She peeked through the glass of the double doors to the intensive care unit. The waiting room was empty. Only a few nurses and doctors in white coats passed by, busy looking at files or on their cellphones. There was no one behind the reception desk.

She stood by the door, thinking. Two doors down the hallway was her dad, so close and yet so out of reach. She felt a pang of angst. What if she returned to the United States before he awakened? Would their last interaction be one where he screamed at her, mistaking her for someone else? No, she could not bear the thought of this. She had not come to France hoping for a reconciliation, but now she desperately wanted one. Especially now that, thanks to Marceline, she sensed the suffering of his childhood. In the back of her mind, there had always been time to make up with her father. She thought it would eventually happen when she stopped being angry at him. How ridiculous. He was eighty-five years old. If they did not speak now, if he did not see her and feel her love at long last, if there was not some kind of healing between them now, when would they get the chance?

If she were to go through the door, past the now empty reception desk, she could be by his side in a dozen steps.

She slowly pushed open the door and slithered inside the waiting room. She was alone! She walked toward her dad's room as furtively as she could manage, stepping on the tip of her red cowboy boots in slow motion, cutting through the regulations and interdictions like a knife going through butter. Her hand was on the door to her dad's room when she heard a woman's voice. "You know that's not happening!"

She felt nauseated. It was the odious Mademoiselle Pinçon, the intensive-care unit clerk and obstructionist-in-chief. The woman had her arms crossed on her chest, an expression of outrage on her greenish face. Today she wore her hair pineapple-style, in a fuzzy bun on top of her head.

"What's not happening?" Cassie asked disingenuously.

"You know very well that you're not allowed in that room," Pinçon said.

"I know that," Cassie snapped. "Why do you think I'm showing up here outside of visiting hours?"

Pinçon did not buy this for a second. "Then why are you here?"

"To make an appointment with your Chief of Services. What was his name again?"

"I told you we do not give out names, and I told you that he does not see people."

"And I told you to give him a message that I wanted to meet him regardless. Did you?"

"He's well aware of the entire situation."

"Then let him know that I want to see him and let him decide for himself like a big boy!"

"Madame, there is no reason to raise your voice!"

"You raised yours!"

"You need to leave," Pinçon said. "You aren't welcome here."

Cassie had the urge to grab Pinçon by the bun and shake. "You better tell him about me, or I will go right over your head."

"And what if he won't see you? What will you do then?" Pinçon asked with a smirk.

"Then I'll go right over *his* head. You tell him that. Also tell him that I will fight this with legal means if I have to. But before that, I'll write letters to every journalist, every blogger, every sick person in Paris and expose how this hospital treats its clients."

They were facing each other, both of them breathing hard, both of them overflowing with righteous indignation. In Cassie's peripheral vision, she noticed nurses, interns, a security guard, all looking at her. She turned around toward the exit door and said, "I'll be back today. And by then you better have an appointment time for me."

Outside, she took a huge gulp of fresh morning air to steady her lungs, then hurried away. She needed for Odile and her mother to put her back on the visitor's list and to do that today. Fuming, she hurried up rue Thimonnier. It took her a while to notice the motorcyclist who was driving alongside her, slowing the cars behind him on the narrow, one-way street. There was a honking sound, and she looked in his direction.

"Hervé?"

"Bonjour!" he shouted over the noise of the engine. He still had his helmet on, and she could only see his eyes, which were smiling and so very blue.

She walked faster with the hope that he would not notice how flustered she was. "Ah, hem. Hello," she said.

"What?" he shouted.

"Hello," she shouted back. Behind them, cars began to honk. She trotted faster.

"Do you need a ride somewhere?" he shouted.

"No, I hmm. No. As a matter of fact, I was looking for you this morning," she said, but loud honking of the cars behind Hervé covered her voice.

"What?"

She looked over her shoulder at the cars and angry drivers. "I was looking for you this morning!" she shouted.

"What?" he said.

"I went to the Jument this morning to tell you that I'm busy tonight so I can't—"

"I'm picking you up at the hotel then," he shouted.

"I can't," she shouted back. "I need to cancel."

"D'accord. Around seven p.m."

"No, but—"

"Ok, perfect, see you tonight!" With this, he lowered his visor and drove off.

She stood on the pavement as his motorcycle sped away and turned the corner. "What? No …," she mumbled.

She walked toward her parent's apartment replaying the interaction with Pinçon and the one with Hervé, wondering how they both got mangled so fast and so beyond repair. When she arrived at rue Ordener, the outdoor market was in full swing. The rain was dripping along the sides of awnings, and people in raincoats struggled to fit their umbrellas in the narrow aisles. Merchants called out their prices as people took money from wallets and put groceries in baskets.

Cassie cut through the aisles, the flower shop, the cheese shop, the butcher, the vegetable stands, all so familiar to her, and arrived at the foot of her parent's building, a graceless structure built in the sixties. She buzzed several times without an answer. A woman let herself in and, recognizing Cassie perhaps from years ago, let her enter. In the elevator, Cassie stared at her feet. The woman's straw bag was full of groceries from the market below. There was a baguette in her bag, and from the smell of it, cheese too. But the smell of bread and cheese did not mask the scent of the elevator, so familiar from her childhood. Polish, metal, and perfumes all combined to form a specific alchemy of scents that was like that of no other elevator, in no other street, in no other city. It was the smell of her teenage years, of being bored to tears, of dreaming of escape, of sunlight, of vast expanses of sky.

She knocked on the door to her parent's apartment, but no one answered. Her mother was probably at the market. Cassie felt with her fingers for the key her mother left in a small crack hidden in the wood casing above the door jam and let herself in.

Even in the dark, the smells in the apartment, of her mother's cooking, of that lemony detergent with which she washed everything, the faint scent of mothballs emanating from the coat closet, and her father's lavender aftershave swept her back to childhood, to adolescence, but also back to an underdeveloped, meeker, and more frightened version of herself.

She turned on the light. The entry and living room looked as she remembered it. She inspected the apartment, walking from room to room. The bedroom she once shared with Odile was full of stuffed animals and toys, probably for Odile's children when they came over. Sabine's bedroom had become a laundry hub. There was a drying rack next to the heater, an ironing board in the center of the room, a pile of neatly folded towels on the bed. The rest of the apartment appeared frozen in time. It was dense with her parent's furniture, all in excellent taste, mostly copies but a few authentic eighteenth-century pieces. Her father's rug collection covered the wood floor: Afghan, Turkish, Persian, each precisely in the spot where it had always been. The art on the wall was unimaginative: prints of famous masterpieces, posters of museum exhibitions. Everything was in its place; everything was safe. The throw pillows matched the curtains and what could be in pairs, was: a pair of ceramic owls, a pair of leather armchairs, a pair of candelabra on the mantelpiece. In a corner, the glass cabinet where they displayed their special things. The result was an air of properness, of permanence, of whatever one might call the opposite of free spirit, the opposite of possibilities.

There were so many memories in this apartment or not quite memories – her family was not big on that concept – more like feelings. Not pleasant ones. The feeling of claustrophobia, of starving for daylight. It was the location of the apartment, on the second floor in a narrow street with windows facing north. How many hours had she spent looking out the window staring at the rain, staring at the windows across the street for something interesting to see, never seeing anything? How many hours had she spent at the kitchen table, doodling and procrastinating when she should have been studying? How many hours sitting on that couch, in front of the TV, watching reruns of *Dallas* and *Starsky et Hutch* in a state of apathy so complete and so deep that even going to the bathroom to pee took effort? How many hours, days, years, waiting for her life to begin at last?

In the kitchen, there were the same table and four chairs, same pans lined up on the wall in order of sizes, but now everything had more of a worn look. The stove sported a few permanent stains. The cabinets' paint was chipped in places. The walls had taken on a yellowish hue.

She realized she was hungry. Knowing her mother's clock-like schedule, she was certain Raymonde would soon return with a baguette. But on second thought, Cassie decided that she would look bad for waiting for her mother to feed her like a child. Despite being renowned in the family as a disastrous cook, a label she shook off while in the United States, where every other person was a self-proclaimed disastrous cook, in France that title stuck to her like infamy. But she was perfectly capable of making herself a couple of fried eggs. She opened the refrigerator. There were eggs and, thank goodness, ketchup.

She took a pan from the cupboard, turned on the heat on the stove, added a dollop of butter to the pan, cracked the eggs into it, added salt and pepper. She took the ketchup out of the refrigerator and smiled in spite of herself because it reminded her of how Hervé had teased her about her passion for the condiment. There was only a little bit left at the bottom of the bottle. She shook it, but nothing came to the top. She hoped she would not be thinking about Hervé every time she used ketchup from here on out. She was too old to flirt like that. But it had felt so nice to have a man talk to her. A handsome man. A handsome man who rode a motorcycle like in dumb romance novels.

She contemplated the bottle, shook it more energetically. Still, nothing came to the top. She tapped it against the kitchen table and suddenly, for no reason at all, the top snapped off, and a thick red spray squirted out, volcano-style, onto the table, all over the floor, and even on the kitchen wall. "Merde!" she said. There were no paper towels or dish towels in sight. She stepped over the ketchup spill and zoomed out of the kitchen toward Sabine's room and grabbed a small embroidered towel from the pile of laundry.

She walked through the living room on the way back to the kitchen and stood for a minute in front of the glass cabinet that contained her parents' few precious things: the set of six Baccarat champagne glasses, the silver ice bucket, the Limoges porcelain dishes that were only taken out at Christmas. Christmas: what a joke, what a travesty. Why had her father hidden from his daughters that he was Jewish? What did it matter if he was? These were not the 1930s for heaven sake! No wonder Christmases at her house had always been depressing. It had all been a big lie.

Her father's finial was here, on the shelf, identical to the one his sister Marceline possessed. The finial wasn't much to look at for something he made such a fuss about. In fact, the matching finial in Marceline's Cité des Fleurs house, where everything was so bohemian and bigger than life, had glowed like a precious object imbued with mystery and meaning. But here, in her parents' cramped, puny life, the finial looked insignificant. It was about the size and shape of a toilet paper roll, only made out of some kind of intricately carved metal, hollow in the middle and shaped sort of like a crown with tiny bells dangling here and there.

She opened the cabinet and took the finial out, turning it in her hands. She felt its weight, its fragility, between her fingers. This was not the first time she was looking at it up closely. When she was a child, she had sneaked it out of the cabinet many times when her parents were out of the house, mostly because it was forbidden to open that cabinet. So how could she resist? She was perhaps fifteen or sixteen when she had first paid attention to the inscription inside, engraved in tiny letters: 29 Boulevard Haussmann, Paris. A few days later, she had taken the métro there with romantic notions to uncover powerful family secrets. She had expected to find an antique store at that address, or an art dealer, where some wise old men knew … something. But it was only a Société Générale Bank. She remembered going inside and being struck by the beautiful art deco glass dome, the polished wood counters, the intricate mosaic across the floor. She learned that the bank had been built in the early 1900s and that it was one of the oldest banks in Paris, but she had not known whom to ask about a finial, so she had returned home.

Cassie turned the finial over, looking inside and under it. What part of her had reminded her father of Marceline so strongly, she wondered, that his rage at his sister had spewed out of him like out of a flamethrower the moment he saw her at the hospital? Was it the way she looked? She and Marceline had similar eye color. And Marceline too had black hair in her youth. Was it the way she spoke? The way she moved? And for how long had her father perceived those similarities?

Was it only that day at the hospital, in a morphine haze, or had it been going on for much longer?

And what was that red stuff at her feet on her father's best Kilim rug?

Her heart sank. Was this Ketchup?

She must have accidentally stepped in it in the kitchen, and now it was everywhere! She looked around and could practically retrace her steps. She had tracked ketchup all over the house. On every frigging Persian rug!

At that moment, her mother and sister entered the apartment. What they saw upon entering was the cabinet wide open, ketchup everywhere, and Cassie red-handed with the finial in her hands.

Odile gasped. "Cassandra?"

"Were you taking my finial?" Raymonde asked.

"I – no, of course not. I was just looking at it."

"How did you get in?" Odile said as she snatched the finial out of Cassie's hand and placed it back on the shelf.

Cassie let her do this without resistance. "The key above the door jam," she murmured.

Raymonde rushed to inspect the stain below Cassie's feet. "Oh, mon Dieu! Is this blood?"

"Just … ketchup."

"Just?" Raymonde bellowed.

"Relax," Cassie said. "I'll wipe it off."

"Not with my best towels you won't," Raymonde said, pulling the embroidered hand towel from Cassie's clutched fingers.

"You can't just barge in here without warning," Odile said.

"I don't see why not. It's my childhood home too. I have as much right to be here as you do," Cassie said, her face hot with embarrassment.

"Why would you want to take the finial and spill ketchup everywhere?" Raymonde said.

"I was not taking it, I—"

"Why did you come here?"

Cassie improvised. "To bring you presents."

"What presents?"

Cassie looked at her hands in the hope that they might magically appear there. "I guess I forgot them at the hotel." Raymonde looked at her with increased suspicion.

"Regardless, you could have called us first," Odile pointed out.

"My cell phone is fried, remember?"

"Which by the way makes no sense at all," Odile said.

"Stop treating me like I'm irresponsible!"

Raymonde sniffed the air, frowning. "What is that smell?" she asked no one in particular.

Odile sniffed, looking around. "Something's burning," she stated.

Cassie's eyes widened. "The eggs!"

All three sprang toward the kitchen and opened the door to a thick black cloud that emanated from a flaming pan. In an instant, Raymonde had put water in the pan and Odile had opened the window and was fanning away the smoke. Cassie stood there feeling horrible.

"I can't believe this. Incroyable!" Odile said.

"I was starving."

"You have a genius for chaos."

"Oh, give me a frigging break, Odile. Like you've never had a pan catch on fire."

"Actually, I don't believe I have."

"Of course, Mademoiselle perfect!"

When the smoke was gone, and they had spent thirty minutes on all fours carefully dabbing at the ketchup stains with damp cloths and baking soda, they sat at the kitchen table. Raymonde put jam, butter, and a baguette in front of Cassie and Odile. She then told them about their dad. She had already spoken to the doctor on the phone this morning. Gustave's status had neither improved nor worsened in the night. The topic of the ignominy of having taken Cassie off the visitors' list was carefully avoided by all.

"I didn't have a phone," Cassie explained, chewing her baguette while Odile and Raymonde sat across from her, observing her like she was a strange animal. "So, I thought I'd stop by. Maman, I met Marceline. I went to her house yesterday."

"The Cité des Fleurs house?" Raymonde asked.

"Have you been there?"

"Your father mentioned it."

"I think I had been there before," Cassie said. "It looked very familiar to me, at least the street, the outside. Do you remember it Odile? I'm pretty sure Papa took us there when we were little."

"I don't," Odile said.

"I don't think I ever went inside, though. I would have remembered. It's pretty grand. Papa grew up there before the war. Marceline lives there now with two adult children from one of her marriages. They take care of her in some ways, but she doesn't seem the kind who likes to be told what to do."

"Was she surprised to meet you? Was she happy?" Odile asked.

"I can't say that she welcomed me with open arms. She did not want to talk at first. Eventually, she warmed to the idea of speaking to me. She told me how they grew up. Marceline is two years older than Papa. Papa's father was from Turkey, believe it or not. He arrived in Paris in the early twenties. His name was Albano. He had a successful rug business for a while."

"Is that why Papa is so into rugs?"

"Must be. Papa's mother was named Lucienne. She was uppity. And they were wealthy."

Odile's face registered doubt. "It's hard to picture Papa with a silver spoon in his mouth."

"Well, believe it," Cassie said. "And there is that other thing." Cassie looked at her sister. When she had broached the subject the day before, it hadn't gone well. "Like the fact that Papa is Jewish," she said tentatively.

Raymonde looked at Cassie, and then at Odile. But Odile was keeping a poker face.

"Apparently, he wanted to hide this," Cassie said. "So much so that he changed his last name,"

Odile tilted her head back in disbelief. "What?"

"Our grandfather's name was Albano Cohen Lombardi. It seems that Papa dropped the "i" at the end, not to mention the Cohen part."

Odile looked genuinely aghast. "Of course not! You're making things up."

"Marceline told me so."

Odile raised her voice. "Well, then *she's* making things up."

Cassie immediately matched Odile's tone. "Someone is making things up, for sure. Me or Marceline. Or Papa. Or Maman. Or you. Someone in this family is lying."

"Maman, is that true?" Odile asked. "Did Papa change his name?" Odile sounded more upset by the thought that their father might have changed his name than by the notion that he had been in the closet regarding religion. Or maybe she had digested that part since learning about it the day before.

"I wouldn't know," Raymonde said. But she was not making eye contact with either of them, which was suspicious.

"If it was true, he would have told me," Odile said with waning assurance.

He had clearly kept Odile in the dark as well, but the reminder that her father and her sister had a privileged relationship hurt Cassie nonetheless. "Would he have? How much do you know about his past? He's not exactly a chatterbox." Raymonde was now going around the kitchen filling the sink with water and putting dirty dishes in it. She was making sure they could not see her expression. "You knew he was Jewish, right Maman?" Cassie said.

Raymonde did not look up from her dishes as Cassie and Odile watched the back of her head. "I did not know about the name change," their mother said at last with a sigh. "But I knew that … part."

"That he was Jewish," Odile insisted. "He told you?"

"It didn't matter," Raymonde said.

"But he told you that he was Jewish? He said it?" Odile was not about to let Raymonde off the hook. If their father had been present, Odile would not have cross-examined their mother. None of this would have been discussed. But the balance of power was altered by his absence.

"Not exactly," Raymonde mumbled. "He was, hmm … I just … knew."

"You guessed it?" Odile insisted.

"There are … ways to know," Raymonde said mysteriously.

"Papa's circumcised!" Odile exclaimed.

"Don't be crass," Raymonde said.

"Talk about the elephant in the room," Cassie said.

"The *circumcised* elephant," Odile added, and they both giggled.

"Oh, you two are so annoying!" Raymonde said. "When I tell you it did not matter, it did not matter!"

Odile rolled her eyes. "Maman, you can't actually believe this. It was a secret, obviously, some crazy mind trip between the two of you. He was obviously trying to hide it, and you pretended not to know?"

"Did you know he grew up rich?" Cassie asked.

"Kind of," Raymonde said. "Well, yes. That, he told me. But he never wanted a penny from them."

"I'm definitely super curious about that," Odile admitted.

"You want to hear what Marceline told me?" Cassie asked.

"Sure."

"And you Maman? Do you want to know?"

"No sense in stirring up the past," Raymonde said but in a limp way.

"I can just tell Odile another time when you're not here," Cassie said cunningly. "If you prefer that."

Raymonde shrugged. "At this point, it doesn't matter," she said, which was her way of admitting that she burned with curiosity.

As they sat around the small kitchen table, with the not-so-faint smell of burnt eggs and spilled ketchup floating in the air, Cassie repeated to Raymonde and Odile the story that Marceline had told her.

CHAPTER 2

Années Folles

Through her window, Marceline watched Cassandra leave her home that first day. She watched her walk on the gravel path and go through the gate dressed in Albano's coat, and she wondered if she would be coming back.

She sat back in her armchair and rang the bell for Laure to bring her electric blanket. One by one, she removed the bangles on her wrists, the rings, the all-too-heavy loop earrings she had quickly donned when her new-found niece had stunned her with the surprise of a visit. She rubbed her sore earlobes. Gustave's daughter, here in the house, staring at her and speaking with her from across their tea!

All those years, Gustave had shunned her. Four decades of sibling estrangement. All this time, Marceline had been certain that Gustave had dragged her through the mud, that he had told his three daughters all kinds of lies about her. She had inoculated herself from that. But to think he had simply erased her, pretended that she did not exist at all. She did not know what to think of that. It was painful and cruel. Everything that ever happened between them was.

Gustave was incapable of seeing things her way. Incapable of listening even. Albano's death had not been her fault. Or it was Gustave's fault just as much as hers. He knew this, evidently. But it did not fit the narrative where she was the enemy, and he was the victim. That's what she would tell Cassandra when she returned tomorrow. If she returned.

She liked the niece. The young woman – well, not young exactly, but young compared to herself – was dressed every which way. And those red boots were peculiar. But the family resemblance was clear. Lucky for her, Gustave's daughter did not look like him at all. She had gotten the good genes, Albano's genes.

Marceline undid her bun so that her head could rest comfortably against the back of the chair. In the story she would tell Cassandra, where would she start?? What was relevant? But relevant to what? To her relationship to Gustave? To anyone's relationship to Gustave?

Would things have been different between them had they not been children of the war. Gustave was only the end product of the time he grew up in. And so was she.

As a child, Marceline had had the sense of being special. She had been too young to understand that was simply growing up privileged. In the early years of the 1930s, Europe's mounting financial and political troubles had not affected her family. They had a beautiful home and plenty of money. Albano marveled at everything his children did, no matter how lackluster. Her piano playing, for example. Did he realize she was no Beethoven? Truth be told, she did not particularly enjoy artistic pursuits. She perceived it a great injustice to be subjected to tedious ballet, drawing, and penmanship lessons that her brother Gustave did not have to endure because he was a boy. She was athletic. She wanted to ride horses, ski, play table tennis and badminton. She liked to win. Unfortunately, since they were schooled at home and hardly ever in contact with other children, the only person available to compete against was Gustave.

Her mother liked to tell Marceline and Gustave that they had royal blood. Where did she get this idea? Who knows? Lucienne was besotted by the aristocracy. She liked to entertain and had friends, many of them Jewish, some of them not, in government, in the military, at the préfecture. They were magistrates, deputies, politicians, physicians, attorneys, and remnant members of the French aristocracy. The latter you could recognize by the way her mother fretted over them. Lucienne was caught between two worlds: the world of the bourgeoisie and the world of the nobility. She had failed to acquire one of those elusive hyphened names or titles by marriage, but no matter. No sooner had Marceline been born than she began projecting that dream onto her.

They owned many nice things. The finials were kept in a locked glass cabinet. To Marceline and Gustave, they looked like tiny metal crowns. She had once asked her mother what they were. Her mother said that they were Torah ornaments. "Uncle Moshe brought them back from a trip. They belong to your father's ancestry as a Kohen."

"What is a Kohen?" Gustave asked.

"The singular form of Kohanim. They are from an ancient Jewish priesthood line," her mother answered. "They used to fit on top of an ancient Sefer Torah, which was hidden and brought back from Spain hundreds of years ago."

"Where is the Torah now?"

"A Torah is made of fragile materials and are too bulky to conceal, so there are a number of things that might have happened to it over the years. We don't know. The finials are small and made of metal, and so they are easy to hide and are all that remains."

"Why are there two finials?"

"Each one fits atop the cylinders the Torah is rolled on. They are a pair. They mustn't ever be separated. Gustave will inherit them."

"Why him and not me?" Marceline had asked.

"Gustave is a boy and son of Kohanim, so he is Kohen as well," her mother said.

"Because I have royal ancestors?" Gustave asked.

"You're a Kohanim from your father's side of the family, not from mine. There is an ancient Jewish priesthood line coming through your father, but the royal line comes through me."

Gustave turned to Marceline and exclaimed, "I have royal blood!"

"So do I," Marceline said.

Lucienne laughed that same dismissive laugh she used when Uncle Moshe was mentioned, or when her husband mispronounced a word. "I suppose you both have royal blood," she said. "But Gustave might have gotten the bulk of the Jewish blood."

Perhaps, in retrospect, this could have been a compliment. Only at that time, it had felt like a pronouncement that reverberated within their beings. Marceline had recently understood that a person could be disliked simply for being Jewish. She was old enough to understand that there was such a thing as anti-Jewish sentiment, and here was her mother crowning her brother as the designated Jew of the household. They understood this has something to do with what everyone repeated all the time: that Gustave looked Jewish whereas Marceline didn't.

When Marceline was ten and Gustave eight years old, it was decided that home schooling was no longer sufficient. They were to attend the local private school in the Quartier des Épinettes. Marceline had immediately thrived there, finding in school an outlet for her spirit of competition, as well as something new and thrilling: social intrigue.

Gustave was not so fortunate. He had always been a solitary boy who spent hours alone drawing, carving ships out of balsa wood, or playing with miniature train tracks. He was always bent over lead soldiers, a tiny paintbrush between his fingers. At school, Gustave's quietness was misconstrued as aloofness. He did not know how to make friends. Each morning, he pleaded with their mother to stay home. He said that the other boys hated him. Lucienne dismissed this. Why would anyone hate Gustave, she asked? What was there to hate about a seven-year-old boy? She refused to see that Gustave had been thrown into an environment against which he had no defense. He was exposed to the vitriol of other children not only at a fragile time in his development but at the wrong time in history.

Marceline never believed that there was much wrong with Gustave. Under other circumstances, other boys might have left him alone. But this was a time when the core principles of entire countries were rotting out, when a bizarre, uncontrollable perception shift was sweeping through Europe like a noxious wave. Their mother's generation had not suffered from overt anti-Semitism in France. But in a single generation, everything can be forgotten. Now that the economies of entire countries were sinking, being Jewish, and looking Jewish, started to mean something different. It was to *be* different. Gustave, her sweet and sensitive brother, became the perfect lightening rod for all that is hateful and detestable in other children's natures. He was shy, introverted, and Jewish, attributes that could make a little boy the object of children's cruelty, and this in the context of social hatred that soon permeated everything.

As anti-Semitism grew, Gustave's Jewishness, so to speak, turned into a liability, not only for himself but, Marceline soon started to believe, for the entire family.

When Marceline was born, in 1923, few could have predicted that the political and financial decisions made on an international scale after the Great War, such as the conditions imposed on Germany, for example, or the financial permissiveness that led to the American stock market crash, had already activated the gears of the World War II machine.

The twenties had been the années folles, the roaring twenties, and for a while at least everyone had been determined to be happy and optimistic. The virus of hatred had remained dormant. But give a virus the right environment, allow it to propagate, and it starts spreading. The financial crisis in America had triggered a ripple effect of economic turmoil throughout Europe. In the whispered conversations of the staff, in the headlines of newspapers that she was too young to understand, on the grim faces of teachers, in the long lines of destitute families in front of the soup kitchens that sprouted across Paris, Marceline detected an alarming sense of anomaly.

She remembered one particular dinner in 1934. At eleven years old, she was still told nothing of world politics. Children's questions were brushed off, but this much she knew: France, which had taken pride in weathering the world's economic upheaval, was now on the brink of financial catastrophe. Hundreds of thousands of people were out on the streets without work or shelter as France grew hungry and restless. Adult conversations are the last thing the youth wants to be subjected to, but Marceline was starved for clues as to the workings of the world around her, so she paid attention. That one dinner, in particular, put words to the anxiety she felt.

It was a Shabbat dinner and the guests were gentiles as well as Jews, husbands and wives, all well known to them – although now she could not remember their names – all part of the upper echelon of French society. Shabbat wasn't a religious thing to her family, but rather an excuse to entertain, and the gentile friends lent themselves to the traditions with good humor and gastronomical enthusiasm. She remembered she wore a dress made of burgundy velvet with a white lace collar. She remembered that Gustave was sitting next to her and that his pockets were filled with marbles and that he was playing with them under the table on his lap, which he was not supposed to do. She remembered that Uncle Moshe was there that night. She loved her uncle, he was so funny and playful, but his presence always irritated her mother.

The prayers were said over the bread and the wine. The candles were lit. Marceline did not remember the meal, what was served or discussed. Everyone seemed in a jolly mood. That was until dessert, when the atmosphere changed. Perhaps it was the arrival of Sandra into the room. Sandra had a great talent for baking. There was a cook, but when they entertained, Sandra was asked to make dessert, and then for reasons important to her father, Sandra herself would bring the sweets she had prepared. Marceline thought that her father meant to give Sandra the sense that she was valued, but Sandra, who was a self-effacing woman, only seemed to do it to please him. Lucienne, for her part, felt it a ridiculous and unnecessary charade as Sandra reluctantly became the center of attention, receiving lavish praises for her talent.

That night, Sandra shyly entered the dining room with her tray. The arrival of this foreign-looking woman with a ghastly scar on her face seemed to make some people uncomfortable. Port and brandy helping, voices began to change pitch. It was barely perceptible at first but politeness, along with sobriety, was going out the window.

People began to discuss that little man in Germany. One guest said that he could not help but admire the German man's certainty when France's own politicians were corrupt and ineffectual. "His rise to political power is impressive, you must admit," the guest said.

"If not chilling," someone replied. "In the last two months, he abolished the title of president and declared himself Fuehrer and Reich Chancellor, and eliminated the rivals in his party."

"A purge, you mean," Uncle Moshe pointed out. "A series of murders. And you see what he is doing now, he is rearming Germany, in direct violation of the Treaty of Versailles."

Marceline wondered if Uncle Moshe would mention Hitler's purported ill-treatment of German Jews, but this was not a topic of polite conversation around non-Jewish guests. At home, she heard Uncle Moshe, Baba, and her mother speak about Hitler, but the gentiles did not seem terribly concerned about what happened to the Jews in another country, at a time when France was suffering such economic woes that all it could do was focus on domestic issues.

"Hitler must do what needs to be done," a Jewish guest, a walrus of a man, tall and thick with a white mustache, said. "Our own politicians would be well advised to do the same." He looked at Sandra. "The influx of racially dubious foreigners is out of control." Marceline looked at Sandra, who did not look up. Instead, she set the tray on the table, wiped her hands on her apron, and left the room. Uncle Moshe and Baba looked at each other. Her mother was absorbed in conversation with the woman who sat next to her. "After the war, France essentially no longer had a labor force, and so it made sense to recruit workers," the Walrus continued. "Immigrants were desired, needed, without a doubt. But now, between the political unrest in all those barbaric countries, and the financial crisis, everyone wants to be a political refugee. France is weakened by the arrival in droves of undesirables of every creed and conviction."

In conversations, her father was not one to impose his opinion, so Marceline was surprised when he said, "Refugee does not mean unworthy," he said. "Most are hard-working and capable."

A young man who was not Jewish, and whose polished manners and tall stature Marceline admired, addressed her father conciliatorily. "We needed people like you, Alban," he said. "And look how well you have adapted. You've earned your stripes. You have been here for years. But times are entirely different now. Refugees are draining France. Surely you must agree that immigrants are taking the scarce work there is."

The Walrus stabbed the air with his fork "Precisely! We take on more immigrants than any other country in the world. Even America is second to us. It is madness. Uncontrollable madness."

"Immigrants are also consumers who pay taxes," Baba said. "Are they not contributing as much to the French economy as they are benefiting from it?"

"The depression, Dear Alban, is caused by overproduction, not underconsumption," the young man said. "This is self-evident economics. The last thing France needs is more workers. The more foreigners this country absorbs, the worse the situation."

"However," Baba said, insisting in a way that was uncharacteristic of him, "I believe that there are few more loyal subjects. Who would be more likely to take arms to defend France, should it be threatened by war, than a grateful refugee with nowhere else to go?"

Her father had mentioned war, and now everyone looked upset.

"Would we ever trust them?" interjected one of the guests, a pompous-looking man with reddish skin. "Who is to say that they wouldn't infiltrate our armies with spies and stab us in the back?"

Another guest, a thin, nervous man with a goatee interrupted, "Besides, with France weakened by the present low birth rate, our government thought it beneficial to encourage mixed marriages, but we are all recognizing the mistake that was. We thus not only weakened France, but we weakened French blood and the French race."

Uncle Moshe, usually loud, had taken to gathering crumbs on the tablecloth with the blade of his knife and said nothing. "The French race?" her father wondered out loud.

"When immigrants came from Belgium or Switzerland, it was one thing, but now they come from Italy, Spain, and Portugal. Or worse," the goatee man said. "You must admit that those darker complexions stand out." Marceline's stomach knotted.

The Walrus yelped, "They will never integrate, nor would we want them to! French families don't wish for that kind of mixed-race offspring."

Her eyes met her father's for only an instant, long enough for her to witness the hurt in his eyes. This was not only about Sandra. Her father and Uncle Moshe were foreigners from a country now called Turkey, a country of Muslims, of dark-skinned people.

And the mixed-race offspring were no other than she and Gustave.

At the other end of the table, her mother pretended to hear nothing and breezily instructed a maid to fetch coffee. Gustave was pinching bread dough between his fingers and shaping it into little mice with almond slivers as ears and cherry stems as tails.

Moshe's voice resounded, sharp and clear. "Aren't you concerned that the desire to reject foreigners might extend to people like us?" he asked.

"People like *us*?" the Walrus said with the tone of someone who cannot think of a scenario where a person such as Uncle Moshe and a respectable man like himself could be put into the same basket.

"Jews," Moshe said.

The collective unease grew thick. And Marceline suddenly understood a truth: the Jewish men wanted to convince themselves that they were more similar to the gentiles in the room than to those undesirable foreigners, and Moshe was suggesting that as Jews, they would *all* turn into undesirables.

"Religion has nothing to do with this," the Walrus scoffed. "With all due respect Moshe, we Israelites have integrated into the very fabric of France, generation after generation, each more educated and assimilated than the next. We are doctors and lawyers. We are generals. We are at every echelon of politics. We have never known any language other than the French language. Sir, the Israelites of France are French, have always been and always will be."

The gentile man with the goatee came to the Walrus's rescue. "There is simply no point of making comparisons between foreigners who arrive by the thousands, cause a hemorrhage of values, and tarnish our culture and the French citizens of Israelite conviction," he said.

The Walrus grunted his approval. "To protect the best among us and reject the worst is a natural sentiment."

"Not all instincts that are natural should be encouraged," her father pointed out.

"Plainly said, Dear Alban, we feel justified in wanting France back to the French, and foreigners out," the young Jewish man said.

"Isn't this xenophobia?" her father calmly asked.

"Alban!" Mother exclaimed.

"Not at all," the young man said. "It's economics."

"It's common sense!" the Walrus said.

One of the Jewish wives giggled and said, "If you wish to call it xenophobia, so be it. We have France at heart, and I won't make apologies for it. I think those foreigners have no place here and should be chased away."

"I think like Moshe that from xenophobia to anti-Semitism is not such a wide gap to bridge," her father said.

The thin young man said venomously, "Fear not Alban. What are you so worried about? That we will send you back to your country?"

Terror seized Marceline's heart. Could her father be sent away for being a foreigner?

"I don't have a country to return to," Baba said. "The one I left no longer exists." He paused and added, "But before leaving, I was a witness to how hatred can be used to dismantle governments and break up countries. I saw what hate does once it takes hold in the hearts of men."

Her mother dismissed Baba with a fluttering of her long, thin fingers. "Alban, don't be such a wet blanket. If they ever try to revoke your citizenship, there are at least five men at this table who will vouch for you."

Marceline looked at those red, hostile faces around the table, and one thing was clear to her: should her family ever need these men's help, they would never give it.

****

Gustave came home from school with his first black eye a few weeks later. He had been shoved to the ground and called a dirty Jew.

Sandra was inconsolable. Lucienne only seemed exasperated.

Bullying, which did not even have a name then, was perceived as a failing of the victim. His parents were told that Gustave needed to stand up to the other boys. He needed to learn to get along with others. While at school, Marceline pushed for things to be done her way and would negotiate and cajole and charm everyone into giving her what she wanted. Gustave did not seem to require anything. Gustave did not seem to need friends. He did not need attention, nor did he need to run around and create mischief. Had he been mischievous, all parties would have been greatly reassured. But here he was, quiet, sensitive, or that word never pronounced but on the tip of everyone's tongue: weak. Her father must have blamed himself for not preparing Gustave better. So he immediately enrolled him in boxing classes where poor Gustave was even more miserable.

Following the black eye incident, the mood in the house mirrored that of the rest of the country. The year was 1935. People were losing their jobs in droves. Banks went bankrupt. Factories closed overnight without so much as a sign on their doors. Social panic ensued. Political rhetoric became nonsensical. Desperate people clawed at every scapegoat they could blame for their predicament and, throughout Europe, the mood about foreigners in general, and Jews in particular, morphed into something sinister.

Over the next few years, as Hitler's power grew and the world made its inexorable progression toward the hell that was to become World War II, her father, the Turk, the immigrant, became an undesirable acquaintance, even amongst Jews. If in 1934 there were more dinner parties and salons than could be attended, by 1936, those couples her parents had considered friends all but disappeared. The non-Jews did not want to mingle with a Jewish family, and the Jews did not want to associate with foreigners such as her father and Uncle Moshe. This should come as no surprise to someone familiar with the mechanisms of war. As people try to save their skin, they push to find someone who can be taken in their place. Marceline had witnessed this behavior over the course of her life. She had even recognized it in herself. Righteous people are a rare breed. Heroism usually confines itself to those dearest to us. We will do anything for those we love to survive, even if that comes at the detriment of others.

Xenophobia began to stretch its ugly tentacles within their small family circle. It crept in in subtle ways. Her mother, for whom Baba's lack of belonging to her social class had always been difficult to swallow, began speaking to him with disdain. The core of her wrath was focused on Uncle Moshe, whom she described as a salesman without refinement or manner. But that was not the worst. The pernicious way of thinking toward foreigners crept into Marceline's consciousness. She too wished Uncle Moshe did not look so conspicuously foreign. Now even she could not help but perceive her father differently. He did not speak perfect French, and his accent now shamed her. She began seeing him through the eyes of an entire nation and, with horror, saw what they saw: an immigrant from the wrong side of the world.

She found excuses for him not to take her to school. She stopped inviting friends over. She impatiently corrected his diction. When he spoke in another language to Uncle Moshe, to Sandra, or to a supplier over the telephone, it made her angry. If her father noticed this, he did not mention it.

Her father could not have been more prescient. Within the year, it was no longer about immigrants. Virulent anti-Semitism became acceptable discourse in the press, in the inflamed rhetoric of the intelligentsia, in the work of revered authors such as Robert Brasillach or Louis-Ferdinand Céline. Journalists, thinkers, and politicians began competing for the most extreme anti-Semitic discourse. Anti-Semitism ripened into a noxious fruit. And once racism and anti-Semitism were encouraged in the public discourse, it moved into the streets.

They were powerless as they watched things snowball. The things said about the Jews were absurd, irrational. How could Jews be formidably powerful and, at the very same time, disgustingly weak? They were bloodthirsty warmongers and, at the same time, cowards. Jews were said to steal work away from the proletariat, and in the same breath, accused of controlling and owning everything.

Marceline would awaken in the morning with a ball of anguish in the pit of her stomach, and she would go to bed with it. What she feared exactly was not named, but she needed to look no further than neighboring Germany to populate her nightmares.

Soon, Lucienne was shunned from salons of which she had been the very pulse. She was voted out of her horticultural society chairmanship. A literary salon she had founded and hosted moved elsewhere. A charity for war daughters she presided over stopped receiving funds and withered away. But her mother's torments were mild next to Gustave's. There was not a week when Gustave wasn't called names or beaten. At lunchtime, kids threw things into his food. His books were stolen, his homework destroyed. He would return home from school with his back covered with ink blotches, his study folders torn to bits. Marceline didn't know what she was angrier at: the vicious kids, the system that allowed for these kinds of things to happen, or her brother for being the butt of it all.

In the midst of all this, she turned fourteen. The year was 1937. Her piano playing had improved, thanks to daily lessons and hours of practice, and for her birthday her father bought an Imperial Bösendorfer in utter disproportion to her aptitudes. She remembered feeling guilty about this, as though it made her a fraud. Already, there were signs that she was being treated differently than Gustave whether she deserved to be or not. It was not only happening at home. She looked gentile, but even if people knew she wasn't, she seemed immune to anti-Semitism at school. Boys passed her notes professing their love. If some of the girls hated her for being Jewish, or for any other reason, she had a certain dominance over the group, and none of the kids dared attack her.

One day, her father told her, "You are a beautiful girl and will become a beautiful woman Marceline, but do not let it be the most important thing about you."

"I don't," she protested. "I am learning the piano. I spend hours on it."

"You must also strive to become a mensch."

She thought he was speaking of protecting her brother. "What can I do about Gustave?" she said. "I don't know the boys who mistreat him. Besides, there's a wall eight feet tall that stands between the boys' and girls' buildings."

"I mean that you must look past the social position and physical appearances of others," her father said. She wondered if he could read the content of her soul, how she secretly felt about foreigners, the shameful embarrassment she had begun to experience at being the daughter of one. "When people appear strong, you must see their fragility," he said. "If they seem fragile, look for their strength. Learn to see past the flaws, even when they seem beyond repair, and know that their suffering is just as valid as your own."

Now she knew he was talking about Gustave. Her father was worried not about how he was treated by other boys at school, but how he was treated at home by her.

That evening, she wrote in her journal that from now on she would strive to be nicer and more tolerant, that she would stand up for her brother at school and fight off anyone who did or said bad things to him. She wrote this perhaps in the hope it would be read. What she did not write in her journal was that she knew popularity to be fickle. She wished she could go to her brother's rescue. But the last thing she wanted was for his Judaism to draw attention to her own.

One day, in the winter of 1938, Gustave returned from school with a bloodied uniform and a broken nose. By the time he arrived home, his nose has swollen to twice its size, and already the space around his eyes had turned purple. They congregated in the bathroom where Gustave sat on the edge of the bathtub holding ice on his face while Sandra helped him out of his blood-stained shirt. He was twelve and growing taller and thinner. Now he even had hair on his armpits. When the undershirt was removed, they all saw the large bruises on his pale body.

"What are those?" her father exclaimed.

Gustave, holding the pack of ice to his nose, glared at them. "No one has ever bothered to know where my bruises came from until now," he said under his breath.

Her father was taken aback, "I … well. Is it not from the sports you do?"

Sandra dabbed at the dried-up blood with a wet cloth. Her mother, who had been watching with her arms crossed said, "We shall speak to the schoolmaster!"

"You never fight back?" her father asked anxiously. "You are taking boxing. You know how to punch. Isn't that helping?"

"Punch who?" Gustave raged. "They come from behind, several at once; they call me a kike, kick me, push me to the ground."

Her mother sighed, exasperated. "And look at your nose! There are doctors we could hire to repair this, make it look less … prominent perhaps?"

"If the only thing those savages will understand is violence, then you must hit back," her father said. "You can't just stand there and wait to be punched."

"I've never seen *you* hit anyone!" Gustave snapped. "How easy do you think it is? I wonder what you would do."

Marceline chimed in, "Well, personally, I would hit back."

Gustave threw the ice pack to the ground and shouted, "You're all pretending like I did something, or didn't do something. You're pretending not to see that it's about one thing: it's about the way I look."

They said nothing, but they all knew what Gustave was referring to. There were drawings in the newspapers and on billboards sprouting up all over Paris. They knew the satires, in plays, at the movies, and on the news. Everywhere, the hideous caricature of the loathsome Jew with the hooked nose, the large ears, the pale face, the bags under the eyes. Jews were made to look like sickly vultures. It was all just so confusing and terrifying. Marceline did not recognize this invented beast in herself, but it was impossible not to hate that creature, a creature that could embody humanity's worse qualities, both morally and physically. Was her brother recognizing himself in that terrible fiction?

Her mother said, "Alban, I think it is time we proceeded with what we discussed."

The notion had been floating around for a while. Her mother had gotten herself convinced that Gustave should attend a pensionnat. She loved the idea of boarding schools in general. They were expensive, a sign of good breeding, the clear mark of a superior education. But lately, her reasons were murkier.

Albano turned to her. "Lucienne. I have told you before. We are not doing this."

"I don't want to go to boarding school!" Gustave said with fury. "I don't and I won't!"

"It would be a Jewish boarding school," her mother continued sweetly. "How could you be attacked there? New children, new teachers; with a new attitude, you could make a fresh start. Make friends." She turned to her husband. "His education is suffering, Alban. You know that he needs that fresh start."

"No, Lucienne," her father said.

"But, Alban…."

"The world is going mad again," her father said before leaving the room.

At dinner, Gustave, dressed in a robe like a convalescent, chewed without appetite. Her father was silent and seemed to be churning grave thoughts in his head. They ate wordlessly, oppressed by a sense of foreboding. Her mother broke the silence. "I attended a pensionnat," she said with artificial cheer. "There are clubs and functions, and there are games in the evenings, and on the weekends, you get to go on outings and lovely field trips with your classmates."

"You just want to send me away so that you don't have to deal with me," Gustave said below his breath.

"Lucienne, Dear, let's us have a nice dinner," her father said.

Her mother was not deterred. "It will benefit you. They will keep you safe there."

"How could they?" Gustave nearly shouted.

Her mother gazed around the dining room as though the validation of her thinking might be written somewhere on the walls. "There is more thorough oversight in boarding school," she said in that decisive tone that left no room for questioning. "The children sleep there, so the educators are responsible. They can't very well let the boys hurt one another, or the parents would take them out."

Gustave shrugged, disgusted. "I would be hated there too. Only for more hours of the day. And the nights. And on lovely field trips."

"There is camaraderie," her mother insisted. "Bonds are forged. It isn't like school, I assure you. Not at all."

Tears of rage welled up in Gustave's eyes. He turned to their father. "I don't want to go, Baba. Tell Mother to stop! Please."

"We do not need to be discussing this right now," her father said firmly to everyone at the table.

"I'll make it work at my school," Gustave said imploringly. "I will start getting along."

Her mother had one of her dry laughs. "I'm not certain any of this is within your control, darling."

"Please, Baba, don't send me away!"

That evening Marceline went to Gustave's room. These days he closed his door to her, accusing her of touching his things. To be fair, she did like to touch his things quite a bit. The balsa airplanes dangling from fish lines, the miniature sailboats on shelves, the toy soldiers in formation: it was all so irresistible. And it was fun to move things around or even hide things. That evening Sandra was in Gustave's room, organizing his desk but mostly, Marceline suspected, so that he would not feel alone. She knew that Gustave would be on his best behavior around Sandra. She had a way of looking at you, pained and at the same time believing in you, and neither Marceline nor Gustave wanted to disappoint her.

Marceline sat on his bed where Gustave lay, furious. The area around his eyes was awfully swollen and blue by now.

"Why are you here?" he said. "You are not allowed in my room."

Sandra looked at her with insistence, so Marceline understood that she needed to apologize to Gustave. "You're right," she told him. "I would not know what to do either if people hit me."

Gustave sat up in bed, raging. "Mother says that Paris is the problem, or that the school is the problem, or that the other boys are the problem, or that being Jewish is the problem. But what she means, in fact, is that *I* am the problem. Me."

"You're not the problem," Marceline said, watching the swelling in Gustave's eye nearly shut it closed.

"I am a problem for Mother! That's the truth."

"She has shown me brochures of girls' boarding schools for years. She wants me to go too. You know Mother; she gets fixated."

"Of course, she doesn't want *you* to go to boarding school!" Gustave nearly spat out the words. "She's having too much fun making you her lapdog, and taking you places to show you off."

"I am no one's lapdog, you pest!"

"You see how bored she is now? You're her only activity."

Marceline could have argued that this wasn't the case, but truth be told, it was. "Baba won't let her send you anywhere," she said. "They will go to school tomorrow and ask them to suspend the boys who are attacking you. In fact, they will make sure those boys are kicked out."

"That won't happen," Gustave said as Sandra arranged the pillow behind his head.

Her parents did go to the school, accompanied by Gustave. But the meeting with the school's headmaster did not turn out as hoped. The complaint was that Gustave was a source of conflict and distraction. To her parents' surprise, it was recommended that, for Gustave's safety and the sake of the good functioning of the classroom, he should leave. This was in no way the headmaster kicking a Jewish kid out of school, he unctuously protested. It was a mere suggestion. But he also inferred that they were done defending him. Her mother and father understood the subtext. Gustave, if they chose for him to attend, would do so at his own risk.

Upon their return from their conference with the headmaster, her parents walked straight to the small salon and shut the door behind them. Marceline rushed up the stairs to the library above. She closed the door behind her, lay down on the wooden floor, put her ear to the air vent, and listened.

"I cannot believe Gustave should be the one removed!" her mother said, her voice trembling with outrage.

"Paris is taking a turn for the worse," her father said.

"Can there be no recourse?" her mother asked. "Is there no higher authority? Surely there must be someone we know at the district level, or else at the ministry of education. Perhaps I should speak to Monsieur Hébert. Do you remember him? He is the Minister of Commerce's brother-in-law. He is Jewish."

"Perhaps Gustave should be taught at home for a while," her father said.

"You said it yourself, Alban; you want him to become a man. How will this be accomplished by keeping him sheltered between these four walls? Already, he runs to Sandra at the slightest setback. And he is too old for a nanny anyway. How long do you plan on keeping that woman around?"

"With everything going on, all the negative things being said about Jews, maybe he should indeed be sheltered."

"Would that be to his best interest in the long run? I know you don't want me to speak about this but…."

"What?"

"The Jewish pensionnat, the one I told you about in Rânes. Gustave would not stand out there, but neither would he be overindulged. He would continue his studies in a proper fashion."

My father's answer lacked conviction. "It is the middle of the school year," he said.

"I have enquired," my mother said. "They have room. They will take him."

Marceline was shocked. Her mother had essentially made the arrangements. All she needed now was for her husband to say yes.

"I fear that…." her father began, struggling to find his words. "You know how shy he is … but on the other hand…."

Her mother must have seen in her husband's hesitation that he was waiting for her to persuade him. "You want him to gain strength, but you won't allow him the opportunity," she said shrilly. "If you believe him too weak to cope with life, how will he think anything different? It is by practicing facing his fears that he will master them. You were an orphan. You raised yourself. You had no choice but to become a man."

"But I am different. I am more resilient. Each person is made differently and—"

"Whether they are or aren't is immaterial," her mother interrupted in that clipped, dismissive tone she took with her husband of late. "He might need to learn to be resilient. You are the one who constantly speaks of war. Would you let Gustave face impending war without strengthening him first?"

The mention of war sent the familiar shiver of fear down Marceline's spine. Suddenly, her mother's idea made sense to her. Gustave needed to breathe in some fresh air, grow muscles, make friends. She held her breath, hoping that her father would agree. She realized now that she *needed* Gustave to be sent away from Paris, away from her, so that she could stop worrying about him and the bad feeling in the pit of her stomach could ease.

"Perhaps boarding school would be best," Baba said at last. There was defeat in his voice. "But how shall we tell him?"

"Display strength and resolve, Alban. Lead by example." Marceline did not like her mother's tone, the contempt in it. But she made sense. Baba needed to act firm and tell Gustave about their decision.

"Maybe you are right," her father said.

Gustave was called in to meet alone with their father. Marceline resumed her position, with her ear on the air vent. Her father, who had shown compassion toward Gustave when it was just he and her mother, now forced himself to speak quite coldly to him. He explained that it was for Gustave's best interest so that he could become a man. He would not return to school. He would be attending Jewish boarding school in Rânes as soon as his wounds healed.

At first, Gustave wept and begged. After a while, he stopped protesting. Marceline imagined him sitting there, trying to swallow his hurt. She imagined him feeling abandoned. For the first time in her life, and this would not be the last, she realized her good fortune to have been born a girl. Being a girl, she got to be as strong as she wanted, but without the pressures men faced. For women, strength came as a bonus. Her generation was the first for which university study was possible. Her mother had been denied that advantage in her days. The bar for women was set low when it came to education, or strength, or intelligence. Women did not have to display them the way men must. Strength was a gift women could use at will but was best concealed. Or else you became like her mother, hard, and no one liked you.

Gustave left for boarding school after the winter break of 1938. Marceline felt lighter at first and wondered if her parents did as well. But in the following weeks, meal after meal, Gustave's absence was like a reproach. Her parents repeated to one another that sending Gustave away had been the correct thing to do, the best thing for him. They said that he would make friends among Jewish boys and that anti-Semitism had been the obstacle. Now he would be protected from the violence of bullies. But she doubted they believed this.

They wrote letters, and Gustave wrote back. Three times between January and June, they visited him. If there were problems, Gustave kept them to himself. His teachers and the boarding school headmaster assured them that he was doing well. But his taut face, his clipped responses to questions, and the tension Marceline sensed in him told a different story. It wasn't until he came back home for the summer that they found out how terribly unhappy he was. They monitor the mail, Gustave told them. One of his letters, where he had spoken of mistreatment by his Latin teacher and some of his schoolmates, had never arrived and probably had been intercepted. A subsequent letter where he complained of loneliness had been read out loud to his class – a much-used technique of intimidation through humiliation. After that, he had stopped writing anything of substance.

That summer, Marceline's attempts at conversations with Gustave led nowhere. Dinner times were tense and fraught with peril. Any little thing she said could set him off. He was angry with all of them. He hated boarding school and begged them not to send him back come September. But there were demonstrations against Jews in Paris and in the streets of France's largest cities. Jews were warned to avoid synagogues. Her parents decided that putting Gustave back in a regular school was not an option. The pensionnat was the correct place to prepare him for the university.

How could they have imagined that within a few years Jewish boys would no longer be allowed to receive higher education?

And so, Gustave was made to return to Rânes. Once there, Gustave stopped writing. His silence weighed heavily on the family. When they sent this fragile, sensitive, lonely boy away, her parents had said they wanted him to turn into a man. What they neglected to consider was the kind of man the experience would turn him into.

While Gustave was in boarding school, the continent unraveled at a pace and with an intensity that baffled them all. Each day came news more worrisome than the next from across Europe. The vitriolic discourse of politicians, journalists, and writers had corroded the general opinion. Even in moderate circles, virulent anti-Semitism and had become commonplace. French Jews, they said, had a personal vendetta against Hitler because of his treatment of Jews in Germany and were manipulating at every echelon of power to push France toward a war against the Fuehrer. Hitler was an expansionist no doubt, but if he wanted Czechoslovakia and Austria, let him have them. What did this have to do with France? And if Hitler had a beef against Jews, who in Europe didn't? The horrors of the Great War were too fresh, the losses too deep. No one wanted to rock the boat with someone as apparently unreasonable and belligerent as Adolf Hitler. It was easier to create a narrative with a villain of manageable power, a villain that, unlike the Reich, could be thwarted. Who better than France's small population of Jews to be that villain?

Everywhere, in the papers, in the schools, on billboards on the streets, Jews were described as moral delinquents, as threats to French racial purity, as warmongers, as enemies of the State. Solutions were suggested, from instating professional quotas, to creating a ministry of race, to purges.

Marceline turned fifteen.

In November, they heard the news of Kristallnacht. The Jews of Germany wound up accused of destroying their own property and were ordered to reimburse the government to the tune of a million Reichsmarks. Following this, German Jews were prohibited from all commercial activities.

Meanwhile, in Paris, the mistrust toward foreigners was ratified by law through a government decree whereby foreigners needed to acquire a special permit to work and could be detained if suspected of being dangerous to the security of the country. Naturalized citizens, such as Albano, could see themselves stripped of their French citizenship and be imprisoned if suspected of behavior harmful to France.

Which one of those events tipped the balance for her father? Following the decree, her parents held a tense discussion behind closed doors. Marceline had rushed to the vent the minute they had shut the door of the small salon behind them, the sign that something important was about to be discussed.

"Moshe and I believe that the time has come to make a change to our business," Albano told Lucienne. "The economy being what it is, rugs aren't selling."

As much as her mother enjoyed their lavish lifestyle, she considered business talk distasteful. Money, to her way of looking at it, was to be spent but not earned or at the very least, not openly pursued. "What is it you should sell, then?" she asked with detachment. "No one has money. Nothing is selling."

"We plan to shift to diamonds," Albano said.

"Alban, Dear, if people cannot afford rugs, how will they afford diamonds?" Lucienne scoffed.

"We don't want to sell diamonds, Lucienne. We want to buy them."

"In heaven's name, why?"

"Moshe and I think that it is time to liquidate."

"Liquidate?" she echoed in an empty voice.

"Sell. Sell everything we own," Albano said. "And buy diamonds with the proceeds. Money can be devalued; banks can go under; assets can be frozen, but diamonds endure."

Marceline naively took what her father was saying at face value. This was a new business venture: rugs to diamonds. But her mother read between the lines. "France will weather the depression," she said aggressively. "And if you think the diamond business is any better than the rug business, so be it, but you're married to a French native. No matter the crisis you will not be affected politically."

"I do not worry about being from Turkey. I worry because we're Jewish."

"Nonsense."

"You see what is happening in Germany," her father said.

"This is precisely the primitive mentality you and Moshe never could shake off. France is a republic. We have laws. We have a government. We have rules. French people are not savages. No one here takes anyone's business away."

"If there is war—"

My mother wanted to stop him from saying what she feared. She raised her voice. "There won't be!"

Undeterred, Albano continued. "And if France loses the war—"

"We won't!" she shouted.

"I am preparing our family for this eventuality," Albano calmly said.

Lucienne fell silent. Marceline would have preferred to hear her scream and yell at her father, telling him that he was an alarmist, that there was nothing to fear, that they were safe. She did not. Marceline imagined her mother, sitting on the sofa, her head in her hands, as she had seen her do so many times in the last few months. "Why not gold?" Lucienne asked in an empty voice. "Everyone is buying gold."

"Too heavy to easily transport," Albano said.

"Why would we want to *transport* diamonds? I don't follow you."

"I know you have little interest in business affairs, Lucienne," Albano said soothingly. Marceline could picture him standing next to her, gently rubbing her shoulder, something he did to each of them when they were upset. "But should the time come to leave the country, we must be prepared."

"You won't leave us, will you?" her mother said, her voice close to panic.

"Of course not," Albano said. "We will all leave."

A shockwave of emotions rolled through Marceline's body. Were things that bad?

"All of us?" my mother whimpered. "But how? To go where?"

Where was her mother's certainty? Why was she not reassuring her husband? Why was she not reminding him that they were rich and powerful, that they had friends in high places, that they were immune to the Depression and would be immune to Hitler as well? Marceline felt the crumbling of her safe world. The denial she clung to flew away like straw in the wind.

In the room below, and through the airshaft, there was a long silence. "I think we should sell the house."

"Never!" Lucienne said.

"If that is your wish," Albano said. "I understand. It has been in your family for generations. But know that if we are to leave, there is no telling what will come of it."

"How do you mean?"

"It might be pillaged, burned, who knows."

"Pillaged?" Lucienne laughed angrily, and her anger was a relief to Marceline. "Where do you think we are, Alban? This is not your village in the mountains! Besides, the best way for our things to be stolen is to leave them unattended. I am not leaving this house. You hear me? You can go wherever you wish if you are scared. I shall stay!"

"When it is time to leave, you will leave," Albano said. There was no hesitation. No anger in his voice. No room for arguing.

Surprisingly, this seemed to appease Lucienne. She remained silent for a long minute and then asked, "Where will we go?"

"Away from Paris, see how things are away from the capital."

"And then what?"

"Moshe and I are discussing the options."

"Why is it always Moshe having a say in how we conduct our affairs? Moshe, a man who leads a life of utter depravity and who never even learned to speak decent French!"

"Make a list of what you are willing to sell."

"I shall not sell a thing! If we must go, we'll go. We'll just close down the house for as long as this charade continues."

"If that is your wish, Lucienne. Let me know how I can help you prepare. Meanwhile, Moshe and I will liquidate the business. Also, Moshe is planning a trip to Switzerland. We will put valuables in a Swiss bank: money, gold, diamonds, the finials, and any family heirlooms you would like protected."

"That won't be necessary. My family's heirlooms will wait right here for our return," her mother said.

****

For the next five months, Europe continued to brew, but life for Marceline and her family didn't change. There wasn't any noticeable activity in the house. Nothing was openly being bought or sold, save for a few paintings, and her father continued to go to work every day, until one morning in early April 1939 when her parents summoned her.

"We are going on a journey," her father said while her mother sat beside him, rigid. "You will go to school today, and this will be your last day. Do not tell any of your friends that you will not be returning."

Marceline feigned astonishment. Her heart was pounding. "My exams are next week. Where are we going?"

"We cannot tell you this, ma chérie. Not quite yet."

"But why?"

"Think of it as a holiday," her mother said, but there was no joy on her face.

Marceline was told to pack her schoolbooks, pictures, anything of sentimental value to her. There was a flurry of activity around the house: the furniture was covered with sheets, paintings were taken down and moved to the cellar, crates and suitcases, brought up from the basement, were dusted and filled with belongings. When this was done, the entire staff – save for one as Marceline was soon to learn – was let go and given a month's severance pay. It had all been so sudden, everyone looked as though in a state of shock.

We are going south, her mother told her. And then she admitted, "Your father has convinced himself that Paris is too dangerous for Jews."

"So, Hitler hates Jews. What of it?" Marceline said, echoing the reassuring words that Jews throughout France said to convince themselves and each other. "He doesn't get to decide what happens here."

"Every one of our friends has attempted to explain to your father that there is nothing to fear for Jews," her mother said. "Especially those who have assets and connections in high places. A few months and we'll be back, I'm sure. Your father seems ready to leave at the drop of a hat every time he senses danger, real or imagined. I decided that, rather than fight him, I would go along and let him take us wherever."

"What about my lessons?" Marceline asked, not because she cared but because she needed more information.

"We will find teachers."

"What about my piano?"

"Your piano will be here upon our return, like everything else. Meanwhile, I will make arrangements for one to be rented in the South of France."

"That's where we are going?"

Lucienne rolled her eyes. "Just keep this to yourself, will you?"

"Oh, Mother, please, can it be a baby grand? You know I am ready for one."

Her mother smiled. "We'll see," she said, which usually meant yes.

The South of France? A baby grand? Secrecy? This did not sound so bad. Marceline hoped that maybe there would be interesting boys there. The boys she knew in Paris were tame, and she was bored with them. "What about Gustave?" she asked.

"Gustave will remain in Rânes," her mother said. "The point is to be away from Paris, and that is already the case for him."

The day of the departure, Marceline came down to the breakfast table, where the atmosphere was strained. The maid went from cup to cup, pouring coffee or tea. Marceline could tell from the stiff way her mother brought her cup to her mouth that she was seething. As soon as the maid left the breakfast room, her mother could no longer contain herself. "Why *her*, of all people? How can you make such a decision and just impose it on me, Alban? She would not be my first, second, or even third choice!"

Albano didn't look up from his newspaper. "This is one less person you will have to interview when we get there," he said.

Marceline looked from her father to her mother, trying to understand. What were they talking about?

Lucienne was red in the face. "I just don't see why it is your business to make this decision. I am the one who handles the staff."

Her father said, "She would not find work if we left her behind."

Marceline immediately understood that they were speaking of Sandra, whom her father had wanted to keep even after Gustave had gone away to boarding school. That had been a contentious point between them, her mother wanting to part with Sandra and her father insisting that she stay.

"She is not even Jewish!" her mother exclaimed.

Albano was staring at his newspaper, avoiding to look at his wife. "She will be helpful," he said.

In an instant, Lucienne blew up. "How will a disfigured foreigner be helpful just as we are thrown into a new house in a new city? The help I need is someone whom people can look at without fright."

"Enough," her father said between his teeth.

"You seem blind to the fact that people find her physically repulsive!"

"Enough!" he shouted.

They both looked at him, her mother trembling with rage and Marceline stunned. She was used to her mother's anger, but in her fifteen years had never witnessed her father's. Albano threw his napkin on the table and said, "Get ready to leave," and he exited the room.

All morning, what remained of the staff covered the furniture with sheets and closed the window shutters. It was a cold, blustery day, and from her bedroom window, Marceline watched them load up the two cars in the pouring rain. She gave her bedroom one last look. The bed was stripped of bedding. All the smaller objects had been packed, put into storage, or shipped to the new place. Would she see her bedroom again? She repeated to herself that she would be all right, that a good star had been watching over her and would continue to do so. She wasn't so certain about Gustave. Her brother would now live days away from them by automobile or train.

She slowly put on her coat and gloves, taking in her bed, stripped of bedding and the top of her dresser, now bare. The thought that she might be permanently leaving happiness behind gripped her and she felt ill. What if there were no good star? What if she was, along with all of France, on a descent toward something dark and unnamable?

The staff looked resentful as she stepped outside. Some of them would not make eye contact. She could see how they might feel deserted. There was no work in Paris, and here was her family, off to an extended holiday, or so they perceived. The staff did not see them as a family doing what it could in an uncertain political situation, but as rich Jews.

The Alfa Romeo 2500 and the Renault Juvaquatre were parked in front of the house. Both automobiles were filled to the brim with crates and luggage, with more crates attached to the roofs. Her father took the wheel of the Alfa Romeo. It was not their usual driver in the other car, but one of Uncle Moshe's trusted men.

Sandra came out of the house holding her small cardboard suitcase. She was dressed entirely in black with a peasant skirt and a shawl around her face that made her look much older than she was. Marceline put her arm on Sandra's shoulder to reassure her as she climbed in beside Moshe's man in the Renault.

Lucienne strutted out of the house in her best coat. She refused to look at any of them and walked to the Alfa Romeo. There she waited for Albano to get out of the automobile, come around it and open the door for her to climb in the passenger seat.

Before Marceline climbed in the back of the car, she looked back at Sandra who warmly smiled at her through the window, and suddenly Marceline wasn't sure who was supposed to be reassuring whom.

They drove off, the Renault following their Alfa Romeo. Outside, it was pouring still. In the streets of Paris, Marceline watched men and women, their clothes slick with rain, waiting in long lines outside bakeries. Her mother turned to her and said, "We will drive to Lyon and spend the night there. The following day we will drive to the South of France."

Baba, at the wheel, cleared his throat. "Actually, Lucienne, there is going to be a detour."

"What detour?" Lucienne said in an astonished voice.

"First we will go to Rânes and pick up Gustave."

"But it's on the opposite end of the country!" she exclaimed.

"I know," Albano said.

"It's a fine Jewish establishment. It's in the country. You said it yourself; he will be safe there!"

Her father interrupted her. "I changed my mind."

"And what about me not being given a say?" her mother said shrilly.

"We are not leaving Gustave behind, Lucienne. End of discussion."

Marceline relaxed in her seat. There was something endlessly reassuring about her father's new way of taking charge. Her mother had made all the decisions in the past, and although she continued to say things in that way that tolerated no contradiction, lately she had appeared confused and afraid, and Marceline wasn't sure that her mother had any idea what to do at all.

They arrived, unannounced in the early afternoon, in front of Gustave's boarding school. Gustave was called from his class while she, Baba, and Lucienne waited for him in the schoolmaster's office.

When Gustave entered the room, he blinked at them, not understanding. He looked frail in his uniform. Had he lost weight? She had not seen him in a few months. He had acne now, and he was very pale "What's wrong?" he asked.

"Your parents are here to take you," the headmaster said.

Gustave's eyes widened. "Take me where?"

Her father beamed. "We'll tell you when we're in the car."

"For how long?" Gustave said, his voice shaking.

"You're not coming back here," Albano simply said.

Gustave's eyes filled with tears, and it was too much for all of them. What had they been doing, keeping him away like an outcast? Weren't they all outcasts at this point? There was no sense of pretending to the contrary. Gustave threw himself into his father's arms. "Thank you, Baba," he cried, and they all sobbed, even their mother.

Marceline closed her eyes. This many years later she still could taste the relief, the fear, even the love they all had for each other then. She would not get into all this with Cassandra. How much did the young woman know about her father, when she had not even known that he was Jewish. The abyss of information might prove itself too immense to bridge. However, Cassandra had appeared eager to know the truth. But would she really return, or would she avoid her the way Gustave had?

Marceline wanted Cassandra to return. For the past forty years, she had wanted to tell her side of her story, but everyone who would have cared to listen was either dead or wished to forget.

****

In the kitchen, there was still a whiff of burnt eggs mixed with toast and coffee. Cassie looked at Odile and Raymonde for their reaction to Marceline's story, and they looked at her, waiting for more. "And then what happened?" Odile said.

Cassie shrugged. "That's all Marceline told me. She was tired."

"She's getting up there in years," Raymonde said. "She's must be close to ninety years old."

"She's *really* old," Odile said, emphasizing the word really.

"She's perfectly with it, if that's what you're wondering."

"Something runs in that family. The mother went crazy in old age," Raymonde said.

It was clear to Cassie that they were both looking for ways to invalidate anything Marceline might have said. "How is it possible that Papa never spoke about any of this?" she asked. "He was a Jewish boy, in France, at the most dangerous time in history. And he somehow escaped the Nazis. I mean, wouldn't that be something he would want to tell us about?"

"He wanted to forget," Raymonde said.

"I think he made the best of it," Odile said.

Cassie was walking on thin ice with her questions, but she insisted. "How could it not leave an imprint on him? You know, post-traumatic stress of some kind?"

What they all knew was implied in her comment, was the possibility that Gustave, her father, had a problem, or at least had grown up in a fertile terrain for some psychological scarring.

Raymonde found something to stare at on the floorboards, and Odile ignored Cassie's question and asked, "So how did they survive the Nazis and all?"

"I don't know," Cassie said, omitting to mention that she was meeting Marceline for lunch and that she had every intention to find out.

"Thank goodness," Raymonde chirped. "These kinds of terrible things will never happen again."

"They're still happening, Maman," Odile said coldly. "Only in other countries, to other people, out of sight from you."

Raymonde pouted, upset. "Civilized people have decency now; they have morals."

Odile shrugged. "Until the next economic downturn when the decent, civilized peoples will latch on to the first-power hungry wacko who tells them it's okay to hate."

"That's a gloomy vision of humankind," Cassie said.

"I'm a realist," Odile said. She turned to Raymonde. "Do you know where Papa went? Where he was during the war?"

Raymonde protested, "I was born after the war."

The non sequitur was so classic Raymonde that Cassie and Odile looked at each other as if to say "can you believe it?". Odile was the one who said, "Obviously, you don't have to have lived through it. Papa might have *told* you about it."

"All this is news to me," Raymonde admitted. She shook her head. "He never said a thing about any of this. Not a word."

"What do the two of you speak about?" Odile said, exasperated. "You've been married for over forty years!"

"We talk plenty, I'll have you know," Raymonde said. And with that, she crossed her arms. After a moment of thinking, she said, "He did mention being royalty or something like that. And then there were the finials. They were Jewish he said. The one his sister stole and the one here that Cassandra was about to take."

"I just wanted to look at it!" Cassie exclaimed.

"The finials came from his ancestor," Raymonde said. "Via his father."

"The Jewish Turk?" Odile said.

"He wasn't quite a Turk," Cassie corrected. "He was born in an area that since became Turkey but—"

Odile ignored this and continued grilling Raymonde. "Did Papa ever mention his parents to you?"

"Never his mother, but Gustave was very close to his father. He died long before your dad and I met."

"What did Papa say about him?" Cassie asked.

"Albano? Your father loved his dad. I know that he was a good man, very warm. Other than that, I don't think there was much to say about him," Raymonde said.

CHAPTER 3

Unreasonable Union

Albano had no memory of his rescue, no awareness of the large vessel that floated beside him as he was drowning or of its men who sifted through the sea water, looking for survivors. He had no sense of being scooped up and hoisted into the boat, no recollection of the care that was given to him as he lay barely conscious for days.

As providence would have it, the vessel was a well-equipped British hospital boat. It deposited him and a thousand other wounded refugees in Marseille, where Albano was hospitalized for weeks before he gained awareness of his surroundings. He found himself recovering from an infection on his arm that had nearly cost him his life. He was in a vast room crammed with beds, anonymous among hundreds of men who wailed and moaned day and night. His nights were haunted by terrible nightmares, and when he woke up, it was to discover again and again that reality was far worse. For weeks, Albano could not leave his bed. He needed assistance with the simplest tasks and ignored the hospital workers' attempts at communicating with him in Arabic, Greek, or Armenian, until one morning when he surprised them by asking in French if they would send a cable to his uncle in Paris.

Two days later, Uncle Moshe, who had left Paris immediately upon hearing the news that Albano was alive, was by his side in Marseille.

The doctors explained to Uncle Moshe that Albano refused to leave his bed, hardly spoke, and barely ate. His body was healing. They had been able to save his arm despite the infection, although they feared that permanent nerve damage had occurred. They weren't as optimistic about the state of his mind. Albano's disinterest in food stalled his recovery. Like many of the people rescued from the Smyrna fire, there was little left of him but skin, bones, and a crushed spirit.

Uncle Moshe ordered a wheelchair and had the workers lift Albano onto it. He tucked him in a blanket and wheeled him out of the room and into the sunlight of the manicured hospital grounds.

Outside, Albano saw clouds, thin, swaying palm trees, bougainvillea, and pink laurels and thought that he was back in Smyrna. Uncle Moshe told him that Smyrna was no longer. The city as they knew it had been annihilated by the fire.

Albano wished never to speak of what he had seen, but he owed Uncle Moshe an explanation. Moshe sat on a stone bench under a tree and listened. Albano, with an excruciating economy of words, told him about selling newspapers with Hagop, about how he and Xandra had fallen in love, and about how it had cost them Hagop's friendship. He told him how Hagop was taken by the police when he had left the cave where Albano was hiding him. He told Uncle Moshe about the baby so close to birth when Kemal's army overtook the city. He told Uncle Moshe about trying to find a boat with all the other refugees flooding the quayside. He told him about the carnage in the Armenian quarter, the destruction, the atrocities, the massacre of Xandra's family, how the men set the houses on fire. He told him how he and Xandra were attacked as they tried to escape with the small diamond they possessed, how Albano had given the diamond to a priest in exchange for letting Xandra give birth in the Christian hospital. How he had tried, unsuccessfully, to gain safe passage out of the country. How he had made his way through the burning city and eventually to a hospital reduced to cinders and burnt corpses.

"I killed them both by leaving them there," he said. "I should never have left Xandra's side. I buried Xandra, and I buried our child. Then I went into the water, not to live, but to die." There was a long pause with neither of them speaking. Finally, Albano said, "I never want to speak of this again."

Uncle Moshe listened and wept for Albano who could no longer weep. "Albano," Uncle Moshe said, "you are my family. There is little left of it, and whoever is left would rather pretend that I don't exist. I will care for you if you'll let me. But first answer this question: What do you want your life to be?"

"I don't know life without Xandra. I don't want a life without her."

"Come with me to Paris. You could work with me. Unless you want to resume rabbinical studies. That is possible too."

"I want nothing to do with God."

"You can start life anew in Paris, maybe raise a family one day."

"I can never love again, and I can never again give love."

Uncle Moshe did not contradict him. He stayed in Marseille for two weeks and, through friends, was able to secure Albano a refugee's visa.

When the visa arrived, Uncle Moshe booked two first-class train tickets from Marseille to Paris.

On the train, Albano looked in incomprehension around the cabin. He had never been in such close contact with luxury. The mahogany wood paneling, the polished brass, and copper metalwork, the velvet-covered seating, all so precious and alien to him. At lunchtime, Albano sat facing silver cutlery and porcelain plates, as obsequious waiters poured wine into their crystal glasses and placed menus in their hands and crisp, pressed napkins on their laps. Finally, he asked, "Uncle Moshe, are you rich?"

Uncle Moshe smiled. "Yes, my dear nephew. It appears that I am."

Albano watched how comfortable Uncle Moshe was in these luxurious surroundings and wondered how rapidly one could learn to behave with the confidence brought on by wealth. "I hope you are not wasting your time with me," he told Uncle Moshe. "I'm moving in a fog of memories. I do not take pleasure in things. My memories torment me every instant I'm awake. The happy times and the darkest of times are all I can think of. I worry that I will disappoint you. I have failed so many."

"How have you failed anyone?"

"I brought ruin to those I loved most. Every decision I made was the wrong one. Now I cannot even show you proper gratitude for rescuing me."

"Perhaps it is you who are rescuing me."

"How so?"

"You give me something worthwhile to do. You will be my project."

"I am not even sure I want to survive."

"You will survive nonetheless. I will see to it. Better than survive, you shall thrive. I have my mind set to make a French gentleman out of you."

Albano shook his head at the concept. "How could I ever become a French gentleman?"

"It will be in the way you dress and speak. The company you keep. The way you spend your money."

"I have none."

Uncle Moshe, thrilled like a child who brings his mother a gift, exclaimed, "This also is about to change now that you will work with me!"

Albano recognized in Uncle Moshe's eyes the joy and excitement that came from dreaming up a future for someone else. It was the same joy and excitement he had felt for Xandra at the prospect of giving her a new life in France. But now this very life was offered to him, and it was pointless. He was inclined to tell Uncle Moshe this, but here was this kind man, treating him like a son, and he didn't have it in his heart to disappoint him. "Is it a difficult business to learn?" he asked.

"You who have memorized the Talmud should not have too much difficulty."

****

Uncle Moshe lived in a rooftop apartment on one of Paris's most prestigious streets, Avenue George V. Inside the apartment, Albano walked through the rooms in a state of utter disbelief. It was like a castle, immense, with spacious rooms and tall ceilings and bright with many windows with balconies overlooking Paris. It was on the top floor of a four-story building, with steps to the rooftop, which had a garden on it. There were five bedrooms and as many bathrooms. Uncle Moshe's décor had the feel of Levantine villas. He liked gold-leafed furniture, mosaics, and inlays, statues of Adonis, red velvet, heavy draperies. In his apartment, there were crystal bowls filled with sweets, lavish flower arrangements, tasseled toss pillows, gilded mirrors, and deep sofas. The art inside the apartment was often scandalous in nature, with many nude sculptures and paintings, most of them men. The herringbone wood floors that ran through the apartment were thick with rare rugs. Uncle Moshe, he soon found out, liked to shop for art, furnishings, and clothes. At home, he wrapped himself in embroidered silk robes belted over his ever-expanding belly. Each morning he groomed himself carefully and dressed in only the finest clothes, shoes, hats, coats, and watches. It was all so extraordinary. All this time, Albano had dreamt of wealth, and yet his dreams, compared to the reality of Moshe's life, had been small and unimaginative.

Uncle Moshe was always in motion and could bear neither stillness nor silence. This was perhaps why his apartment was filled day and night with an endless stream of guests and visitors. Some visitors came and went, and others stayed for weeks or even months at a time. They had little incentive to leave. Uncle Moshe was generous to a fault. His guests were spared no luxury. They were brought breakfast in bed by the maid, and Moshe's cook catered to their eating whims. When they left, at last, it was not because he asked them to, but usually because of an argument or some drama with other guests. Uncle Moshe never passed on an opportunity to throw a party. Beautiful, perfumed men and independent women with their short dresses, cropped hair, and long cigarette holders came there to dance, drink, smoke, play poker, and do many other things that kept a staff of four occupied around the clock. Uncle Moshe was always the first one up and the last one in bed. At work and at play, he was indefatigable.

For a month, Albano did not leave the apartment. Many days he slept the whole day through. There was nothing he could do about it: lethargy overtook him with the first morning light. Consequently, he could not sleep at night. He learned which of the floor's waxed wooden boards creaked so that he could pace without awakening the neighbors below or the guests. For hours he stood at his bedroom window, staring into the night at the falling rain. He observed, disinterested, the loss of the use of his left hand. What was a loss of a limb to a man whose heart had been ripped from his chest? He now was a cripple, like so many men in Paris who were lucky enough to have returned from the Great War. In Paris, it seemed that the majority of men were scarred, missing an eye, an arm, or a leg. Albano ate without appetite. Food no longer had any taste. The alcohol he drank made him forget nothing. Books remained unread on his lap. He found no joy in music. When Uncle Moshe entertained, which was frequently, Albano retreated to his room.

That first month, Uncle Moshe showed no other expectation of his nephew than to remain clean, gain back some weight, and rest. He offered for him to come along on rides through the city, and on occasion, Albano obliged. Uncle Moshe's automobile was a sparkling blue de Dion Bouton Torpedo, a gleaming jewel with a removable top. Dressed in fancy coats with fur collars, they meandered through Paris in the magnificent vehicle driven by a chauffeur. Paris reminded Albano of Smyrna in many ways because his city's architecture had mirrored that of the great capitals of Europe. All of it was familiar, but at the same time, it was alien. The beautiful buildings were there, and the fancy shops, and the restaurants and cafés, but there was no ocean, no camels, no dust; nothing smelled familiar, everything was flat, and rain and cold prevailed even though this was now April. Uncle Moshe was thrilled to show him Paris, but Albano's attention remained focused on the hood ornament, a delicate young woman who appeared to be jumping up, or dancing, her hair in the wind. He imagined it to be Xandra's spirit, preceding him, guiding him happily through the city, as the car glided past the Trocadero area, with its sweeping views of the Seine River and the Eiffel Tower, the Arc de Triomphe, rue de Rivoli, the Louvre Museum. During the day, Albano could imagine Xandra, her smile, her hair, her laugh. He played with imagining that she was alive and marveling at all the extraordinary Parisian sights. But his nights were populated with frantic nightmares in which he was carrying her through a burning Smyrna.

Albano found the strength to read the newspaper clippings Uncle Moshe had kept. In Smyrna, the Armenian, Greek, and Levantine quarters were gone, as was most of the population, who had either perished or found a way to flee. The Turkish quarter had suffered minor damages and, amazingly, the same was true of the Jewish quarter. This is where they should have gone rather than trying to get to the quay with all the refugees, he thought. If I only had listened to Xandra.

He and Uncle Moshe received letters from Uncle Joshua. The family was struggling in the aftermath of the destruction, but they did not plan to leave Smyrna. To go where? Now that the Ottoman Empire had been dissolved, there were no more millets or protection for anyone. Uncle Joshua did not want to attempt taking the family to France. He wanted to stay in the community where he was born and raise his children and future grandchildren there. Uncle Moshe sent them monetary help, but it was nearly useless in a city turned to ashes where little commerce took place, where food was scarce, and water wells polluted. In the end, there was strangely little to gather from the newspapers. It was beyond reason that such a human catastrophe, hundreds of thousands of deaths, the destruction of an entire city would come down to headlines, small articles, footnotes, and everything seen through the lens of the country's political and commercial interests. The alleged neutrality of the ships in the harbor, the failure to act, the indifference, how the captains of those ships obeyed orders rather than consider the human tragedy before them were scarcely mentioned.

"History will sort this out," Uncle Moshe assured him. "One day the destruction of Smyrna will be remembered as one of the most brutal acts of humanity. All through the world, children of future generations will learn of it in schools. You'll see."

When Albano was back to a healthy weight, from the twenty kilos he had lost, Uncle Moshe took him to his tailor. There Albano stood, passive, as they fitted him for a new wardrobe while Moshe fretted over every detail. The shoes, the hats, the jackets, coats, and suits all were custom made for him. "Uncle, I do not need all those beautiful things," Albano protested.

"If you're going to live in France, it can either be in luxury or indigence," Uncle Moshe answered. "For a foreigner from our part of the world, there is practically no in-between. Your attire must convey your importance, or else your race and accent will remind them of your insignificance in their eyes."

Besides enlisting the help of a private tutor to perfect his French and reduce his accent, Uncle Moshe personally handled Albano's lessons in etiquette. He showed him the peculiar ways Europeans ate. He showed him how to hold his fork with his left hand, the knife in the right, only cutting the small bit of food that was about to go into his mouth. He taught him that there were a special fork and knife for fish and how to tell those apart from the regular ones. He taught him how to unfold a napkin onto his lap (Uncle Moshe had a way to do it that was full of flourish), how to order wine, how to call for a taxi, how to bend to kiss a lady's hand to varying degrees depending on one's motives. He taught him how to comb his hair parted, how to use pomade. He insisted that Albano wear a monocle he had no use for to appear older, and taught him how to take a handkerchief or a gold watch out of his buttoned-down vest pocket to great effect. Even how to clear his throat knowingly and how to suppress burps. As Uncle Moshe mimicked the behaviors of French gentlemen, Albano was reminded of Hagop's antics. Hagop, who was surely dead now, another life wasted, another heartache too hard to bear. Whatever Hagop had done that last day at the cave before the police took him, hitting Xandra, running away with all the money, the cruel words, were of no importance. He only blamed himself. Hagop had been the victim of society's ills. None of it had been his fault.

Uncle Moshe told him one day at the office where Albano devoted fourteen hours a day learning the rug trade, "You learn fast and you are good with numbers, but it is your good looks that will be the greatest asset to our business. You will make an impression on the ladies and their rich, carpet-buying husbands." In this way Hagop and Uncle Moshe were the same. They had both convinced themselves that Albano had magical powers of persuasion because of the way he looked. When Albano glimpsed himself in the mirror in one of Uncle Moshe's gilded bathrooms, he saw nothing other than sad eyes with an unusual golden hue, and lips that no longer knew how to smile.

Once Albano was suitably attired and better versed in the ways of French society, Uncle Moshe began taking him around town to restaurants, to plays, to the opera, and to the many places where all of Paris danced, drank, seduced, and dined. It was 1923, and Paris was one large celebration. What were the Parisian thinking, Albano wondered? Did they know of a place once called the Ottoman Empire? Did they know anything about his land and its arid summers, its bay with the myriad boats, the caravans of camels? Had they learned of the fire that destroyed Smyrna? Did they care? Parisians did not seem to care about much, other than entertaining themselves.

But it was not fair to resent Paris's apparent insouciance. Although it had emerged victorious, France was devastated by the war. The many crippled men on the streets served as a constant reminder of this. France seemed pulled between two forces: on the one hand the physical and emotional scars of war, and on the other, the youth willing its future into existence with forced joyfulness. Frantic; yes, this was the word that came to him. Paris was frantic. He was arriving in a country in the crux of great change. There was a mad dash toward modernity. Women were becoming emancipated. A cultural and artistic evolution was taking place in the arts, in writing, in plays, in clothes, and political ideas. The notion of what was acceptable behavior was in a state of constant reinvention. Women cropped their hair like boys and dressed garçonne style. They wore fluid, revealing dresses cut at the knee and no corset. They favored bell-shaped hats, long strands of beads; they showed their arms and legs, and in the dancing spots at night, occasionally bared their breasts. The city was looking for absurdist's ways to play. There were carnivals, disguises, parties where men dressed as women, and women as men. And then there was the obsession with racing. There wasn't a week without a new race, sillier than the one before. There were races for café waiters, dressed in their garbs and carrying trays. There were newspaper deliverymen races, chimney sweepers races, boat races on the Seine, even races where legless men raced each other in their wheelchairs, and races of drunken men who had to drink a glass of alcohol every 100 meters. Since the end of the Great War, there was in Paris an almost desperate quest for laughter and enjoyment of life, and Albano was incapable of either.

"Where are the Jews?" Albano had asked Uncle Moshe early on as they rode through Paris. "I do not see any of them in the streets."

"They dress just like French people. Over time they have integrated into French society. They've abandoned many of the customs and ways of our culture. Their children have attended Parisian universities for generations. They are doctors, lawyers, writers, artists, politicians. In fact, they do not feel a kinship with us. They see us as too Jewish. Too ethnic. They see themselves as French, and they see us as foreigners. France might tout itself as the most cosmopolitan place on the planet, but immigrants are still immigrants."

France was what he and Xandra had hoped for: a place where a Sephardic Jew and a Christian Armenian could love each other free of judgment and threat from their respective ethnic groups.

Again and again, the same thought haunted Albano. Why had he decided to stay in Smyrna until *after* the baby was born? They should have left as soon as they had received Uncle Moshe's diamond. Had he done this, they would be together today. A family. It was impossible not to be bitter as he moved around Paris, watching people in wonderment, baffled at the affluence and freedom all around. Why be given the key to this heaven only to be robbed of Xandra, the one person he cared to share it with?

Albano threw himself into his new work. Uncle Moshe's rue des Rosiers store was so successful that it could barely hold enough inventory. Now his uncle entertained the notion of opening an upscale store on rue d'Uzès, one that Albano would run.

Each day they had lunch together at one of the restaurants near the shop. One beautiful June day they walked to a brasserie. The owner hurried toward them, beaming. "Ah, mon cher Monsieur! What a pleasure to see you again. You are bringing a new friend today?"

"This young man is my nephew," Uncle Moshe told her. The woman nodded knowingly.

"Have you ever eaten a choucroute?" Moshe asked.

"What is it?"

"Every part of the pig served on a plate of fermented cabbage."

Uncle Moshe ordered the choucroute. Albano nibbled at the cooked cabbage, careful to avoid everything else on the plate while Moshe dug in with his usual gusto. They discussed work. Uncle Moshe spoke of the bank loans he was securing and the contacts he was making in the diamond trade. He said, "Perhaps we should diversify."

"Diversify?"

"Go into the diamond trade."

"Why do so when the business is doing so well?"

"Rugs are cumbersome," Moshe said.

"Is that a problem?" Albano asked.

"It is not a problem today, but it could become one."

Albano looked at Uncle Moshe, not understanding.

"It's not smart to keep all your eggs in one basket," Uncle Moshe said. "What if there is another war? And don't tell me that we just had the war to end all wars; that's just a fallacy. Wars are only a jumping board to the next war. You saw how it was in the Empire and every empire before that."

"How would we get into the diamond trade?" Albano asked.

"First, we need to learn. Your eye is good and discerning, I have said this before. There is a man I know who could train you. He can teach you how to look through a particular kind of lens and recognize a diamond's quality and flaws even before it's been cut."

Albano said he would learn. But what he was thinking and did not tell Uncle Moshe, was that every glimmer of every diamond would remind him of Xandra and of the day when he put the diamond in the hand of a priest, and all hope was lost.

They finished lunch and ordered dessert. Around them, gentlemen with curled mustaches, starched collars, and waxed hair sat at tables next to their plump wives. Cups filled with chocolate mousse were set in front of them.

Uncle Moshe patted his belly with satisfaction. "France is a good country for us. We must count our blessings that we are here."

"I guess this is a blessing," Albano said, unable to mask his bitterness.

"Don't you think that those who died in Smyrna would have wished a different fate?"

Albano looked away. He already condemned himself for every decision he had made in the last year, and even for failing to die that day in the water. But lately, he also felt shame at his indulging in this deep sadness, at his incapacity to move on. "You are right. They would wish for my fate. I am standing, and of sound mind, and healthy, and I can work, and the work interests me more than any other work I would imagine doing. And the money flows in beyond my wildest imagination. Yet I sink in melancholy."

"That is because work and money won't give meaning to your life," Uncle Moshe said, taking a spoon full of desert into his mouth. "I guess it might be enough for some men, but not for someone with your disposition."

"What is my disposition?"

"You're a man of heart, my dear nephew. You need more than material gains and earthly pleasure. Power does not interest you. What you need is a purpose."

Albano shook his head. "Then I'm at a loss."

Uncle Moshe set down his spoon and stopped eating his chocolate mousse. "I have meant to speak to you about this. I thought about it a great deal. You know how, as part of the rebuilding, France's desperate need for children makes sense. Not only economically, demographically, but also emotionally. France needs to regain strength, hope, and a future."

"True."

"Those happened to be the very things you need."

"I suppose."

"Well, Dear Albano, then you will agree that, like France, the solution is to bring children into your life."

Albano watched his uncle, dumbfounded and amused. "Where am I to find children that will have me?"

"You told me a few months ago that you would never love again. Do you still think this to be true?"

A shadow passed before Albano's eyes. "I am in love still. Only to a person who is no longer."

"You are a loving man and you need a family for which to care and provide."

Albano smiled in spite of himself. "And so, I shall find a family to love? How would you suggest I do that?"

"There are ladies in Paris that will have you, as you must know."

"But I shall not love them."

"But you could care for them! In all the ways women need to be cared for. And they would bear children that you would dearly love."

Albano dismissed the notion with his hand. "But Xandra—"

"This would not be betraying her!" Uncle Moshe interrupted. "Do you think your beloved would have wanted you to spend the rest of your days childless, womanless, and alone?"

Albano was astounded. "You are asking me to marry a French woman I do not love?"

"I am asking you nothing. I'm merely telling you about options you might not have thought about. You could find a nice person and like her enough. Someone with whom you could grow in fondness over time."

"I'm a foreigner, a refugee. Someone who struggles with the language. A crippled man whose heart belongs to a dead woman. No sane French woman would have me even if I wanted her, which I do not."

"You are also a healthy young man, a rare commodity in France these days, and one with a growing business and bank account at that. You are intelligent, hard-working, capable, kind, and caring."

"Please," Albano said, embarrassed. But Uncle Moshe would not be stopped.

"And you are very handsome. Women will line up to marry you." Albano was shaking his head, closing his eyes, rejecting all that Uncle Moshe was saying. Moshe paused and then said, "Think of it as a business arrangement then. One that favors both parties." He added after a longer pause, "Another aspect of marriage not to be dismissed is that it will be your ticket to French naturalization."

"You don't have a wife," Albano pointed out accusatorily.

Uncle Moshe rolled his eyes. "I cannot subject a poor woman to a life of lies."

"But you think *I* should?"

"If you can go to bed with a woman, and provide for her, and treat her kindly, give her children, that's love enough. Together, you can build a life."

Albano dismissed Uncle Moshe's idea that day. But as he walked through Paris over the next several months, watching the trees go bare and then green again, the gaping void in his heart and soul did not fill. Albano had been in France for five months, and he was concluding that his pain might never go away. He began to wonder if Uncle Moshe might be right. What if he could find a French woman? They would have children. Through marriage, he would get respectability and French citizenship. Together, they would create a home life. Uncle Moshe's plan was not just a good solution. If Albano did not want to turn mad with grief and despair, it was the only solution.

****

In March, he met the woman who would become his wife. He met her at a party Uncle Moshe had thrown at his house. Moshe had brought in a small jazz band, fresh from America. There were a trumpet and two saxophones making a ruckus. The butler could barely keep up with the pace of the flowing wine. Young Parisian men and women, already drunk, for the most part, were dancing, drinking champagne wine, eating caviar canapés, and laughing. Albano made the effort to attend, rather than stay in his room. He stood in a corner, watching the French women. Their appetite for life scared him. How would he be able to give any of them happiness? He was about to retreat to his room when he noticed a serious young woman who stood slightly removed from the scene. The other guests were dancing feverishly, but she just leaned against a door, her arms crossed over her slight chest, and observed the dancers with an air of reproach on her face. She was dressed in the new fashion, her blonde hair cut below her ears. She was not a beautiful woman. Her nose and eyebrows were a bit pronounced, her eyes small and dark, her silhouette angular. But her body lent itself perfectly to the favored tomboy look, which she wore with more elegance than the other, prettier women in the room. As he watched her, he noticed that she had looked at him too. Albano did not for a second think that she was the kind of woman he would want to marry, or who would want to marry him, but he felt that he could speak to her, perhaps because she looked grave, pensive, and maybe upset, emotions he could relate to. He cut through the dancers and came near her. "Do you not enjoy jazz?" he asked.

"Of course, I do." She frowned before adding, "Actually, no, I do not."

"Myself, I don't understand it," Albano said. "Where I come from, melodies are quite different, as are the instruments. My ears must first be trained to recognize all this noise and cadence as music."

"Oh, by all means, tell your ears that there is nothing wrong with them." She was not looking at him as she spoke.

"What music do you enjoy?"

"I'm classically trained, and I intend to remain this way."

"Classical? Aren't you a flapper? An emancipated woman?"

She turned to him for the first time, as though surprised he was still speaking to her. "Not in the sense that I want to dance and drink my life away, only in the sense that I reject the subjugation of corsets."

"I hear that much has changed for French women."

"Is that so? We cannot vote and aren't represented in government. If we want to work, we need the authorization of our husbands or fathers. While our men were at war, we ran the country. We proved that we are so much more than a vehicle for corsets. Most of us do not intend to remain in men's shadows."

Albano had never considered any of this and found himself without an opinion on the subject. "What instrument do you play?" he asked.

"The piano, of course." Albano could see she was happy he was speaking to her, but that she was not trusting, not relaxing. "I have started to give lessons," she said, shrugging.

"I admire women who work."

"Alas, I do not do this by choice. I am unmarried, and I have my mother to support." She seemed bored with speaking about herself. "Where do you come from?" she asked.

"A country they are now trying to rename Turkey."

"Ah! Mustapha Kemal. I hear he is quite the progressive himself."

"That remains to be seen."

"A Muslim country ...," she said. The sentence was unfinished, the question not formulated but he understood.

"I am Jewish," he answered.

"As am I," she said, visibly pleased. "And what are you doing in Paris, Monsieur?"

He bent slightly to take her gloved hand, and brought it to his lips without quite touching it, the way Moshe had taught him. "My name is Albano. I live here now that my country was destroyed."

"Are you a refugee?"

"I am a businessman."

"And what is your business?"

"The oriental rug trade, with my uncle," he said, pointing to Uncle Moshe who stood in the company of two young women. All three were laughing at something or someone.

"Ah ... our dear Moshe," she said. "Quite the character." She peered at him. "He and you are related you say?"

"He and my father were brothers."

"Were?"

"My father passed."

"As has mine," she said.

"The war?"

"It wiped the nation clean of three generations of men. My mother has lost every man she held dear, her father, her husband, and her two sons."

"And so, you have lost them too."

"And so, I have," she said with a sadness devoid of self-pity. "My name is Lucienne," she said, handing him her hand. Having already kissed her hand earlier, he shook it this time, which made her laugh. "Forgive me. I am still learning your customs and your beautiful language."

They walked to the adjoining salon, which was empty, and where the sounds of jazz were muffled, and sat on the sofa. "And what do you intend to do in Paris besides selling rugs?" she asked.

Albano thought of this. "I intend to marry and have a family."

She remained pensive. "I intended to marry as well ... but the war has ruined Mother and me, and without a fortune, I seem to hold little appeal."

"You are a distinguished lady, an accomplished pianist, a forward-thinking, intelligent woman. You will find a husband."

She smiled at him. It was clear that she was enjoying his company but was trying hard not to seem too interested. "Oh, but it is too late for me you see. I'm already an old maid."

This was not an expression he was familiar with. "An old maid?" he repeated.

"A woman passed the age when she can find a husband."

"But you are so young!"

"I'm twenty-four. That's the age when the world decides that if no one thought you had anything to offer before, it won't start happening now."

"I am twenty-one years old myself. Am I too late to marry as well?"

"Don't be absurd. Only women's value depreciates with age." She observed him with keen interest. "You look older. I would have said thirty."

"Oh no!" he said playfully. "Do I look that old?"

She laughed. Her serious, almost severe expression vanished. "I'm sorry, I meant it as a compliment. You seem wiser than your years."

Albano was quiet. He thought of Uncle Moshe's advice. Treat her kindly; that's love enough. "I have a question for you. Or rather, a request," he said.

"What is it?"

"Would you accept to have dinner with me?"

This flustered her. "You hardly know me!"

"I am attempting to remedy that."

To mask her pleasure, she took a cigarette out of a thin silver box and brought it to her lips and let him light it for her. "I accept your invitation," she said, taking an elegant small puff out of her cigarette.

****

Lucienne's family, he learned, was of Tsarfati ancestry, but the last few generations had been born and raised in Paris. Several had distinguished themselves for their social, political, and economic achievements. But over the years, the bloodline had not quite replenished, and she and her mother had become its sole remaining members. After the death of Lucienne's grandfather, father, and brothers in the Great War, all that remained of their fortune was a modest military pension and the family house, a three-storied hôtel particulier in the Cité des Fleurs in the seventeenth arrondissement of Paris. Lucienne and her mother were proud women, but they were pragmatic. The house's upkeep and taxes made it impossible to keep, and soon they would have to find an apartment and sell generations of cherished belongings to make ends meet.

Lucienne had qualities that Albano respected. She was socially confident. She was serious. She was intelligent and had a clear sense of her beliefs and what she wanted in life.

The courtship wasn't a long one. By marrying Albano, Lucienne would save her house and aspire to a comfortable lifestyle. She and her elderly mother would be cared for. She would have to overlook the fact that Albano was foreign-born and of humble roots, but he was Jewish, which mattered to her and her mother very much. Albano, in return, would receive citizenship.

And despite Uncle Moshe's opinion that Lucienne was too cold, Albano convinced himself that by choosing a woman for whom he felt neither love nor lust, he would not be betraying Xandra.

They were married at the Synagogue des Tournelles. They were both eager to have children. Marceline was born precisely nine months later, in December 1923. Two years later, in December 1925, they welcomed their boy Gustave.

The children came into the world at a time of tremendous vitality. These were the années folles indeed. The population of France seemed engaged in a frantic effort to forget the austerity and horrors of the war. The mood, forced perhaps, was to lightness, to dancing and drinking, to excesses and indulgences, to modernization and consumption. The economy thrived, as did Albano and Moshe's business.

Uncle Moshe had been correct. Albano immediately fell in love with his children, a deep, all-encompassing love that allowed him to live again. Marceline was a vivacious and self-assured little girl who had inherited his physical features, and unruly black curls, and that strange eye color, neither gold nor green. From her mother, Marceline inherited a strong will and commanding personality.

Gustave was Marceline's opposite. He had dark brown eyes, pale skin, and his mother's aquiline nose. He was a tender soul, fragile and shy, and was easily made nervous by noises and people. Emotions flooded out of him at the slightest upset. Marceline was fearless from an early age and stood her ground unflinchingly before children and adults. Her one soft spot was her little brother, whom she treated as her personal possession. She bossed him around, dressed him like a doll, and rewarded him according to her whim, and Gustave accepted her authority absolutely. Marceline enjoyed her brother's company when he was compliant, but his tears exasperated her.

Albano was concerned about Gustave's gentleness, his vulnerability. Should a boy learn toughness from his sister? Should he not learn it from his father? Albano noted how much more entertaining Marceline was in Lucienne's salons. There, from the earliest age, his daughter's wit and aplomb delighted everyone. In contrast, Gustave would not look people in the eye, and he tended to scamper away the minute he was addressed by a stranger. It was impossible not to compare the two children. Thoughtful, shy Gustave reminded Albano of himself. And lively Marceline, absurdly, reminded him of Hagop.

Lucienne liked to remain active. She found meaning in literary and artistic salons and philanthropy work. She did not tend to the minutiae of the children. This was the function of the nannies, British nannies always since they were, according to Lucienne, the only appropriate choice for French children of high society.

For Lucienne, a good standing in society and the right kind of manners were of utmost importance. This was the way she had grown up and the way she intended to raise her children. Albano, for whom everything in France was a discovery, was blind to many of the subtleties that Lucienne, a well-bred French woman from elite Jewish society, was well attuned to. She could detect in an instant people's good or inferior breeding from the way they moved, spoke, or dressed or from the company they kept. Those she admired most, those at the very top of her personal hierarchy, were the people issued by birth from European aristocracy. Family standing, to Lucienne, meant everything. And although she enjoyed their lifestyle, money – the kind which was not inherited but which she dubbed "nouveau riche" money – was something to be vaguely ashamed of. Albano, for example, learned that in France, all Jews were not equal in the eyes of the French Jewry. He was a Sephardi, and she was Ashkenazi, and for reasons he still could not understand, and according to his wife, the former was inferior to the latter.

Albano did not fit Lucienne's ideal of status and education, and he often sensed that his having been raised in a poor village in another country was embarrassing to her.

For his part, Albano would have preferred if Lucienne showed more tenderness toward the children. But she believed this was not her role, and perhaps she was right.

All in all, they got along well. They did not argue and spoke to each other with civility.

Lucienne's mother lived with them. Grand-mère was a wonderful woman who adored her grandchildren, and since she doted on them from the moment they woke up to the moment they went to bed, the children were never deprived of the warmth of her kind and loving heart.

At the heart of Albano's life were the children. They ate early with the nannies, but at every dinner, Albano sat with them at dessert time. At bedtime, he went into the room they shared and told them stories. Often during the day, he would meet them at the park and play with them or take them to the zoo. Every chance he got, he held them tight and told them how much he adored them. Still, each day, as he watched Marceline and Gustave get tucked into bed, he thought of the baby he and Xandra had lost, and he thought of Xandra and of the life that had not been.

As the years passed, Albano watched Marceline and Gustave become little French children. He observed them inside the nursery, surrounded by stuffed toys bigger than they were, dollhouses, and wooden horses. Marceline's black mane was tamed into polished curls. Gustave was dressed like a miniature gentleman. They knew how to hold their elbows tight against the side of their bodies as they cut their meat with children-size silverware. They said, "Bonjour, Madame," and "Oui, Monsieur," and "s'il vous plaît," and "merci." They did not know a word of Ladino, Arabic, Armenian, or Greek. They would eventually learn Latin and English with tutors, Lucienne said, and when they were old enough, they would attend Hebrew lessons.

When the time came, Lucienne planned to send them to boarding school for the best possible education.

As Albano watched his children, dressed in perfect little outfits, practice their piano, or write letters with an ink pen, or color within the lines, he marveled at the difference between their childhoods and his. If Marceline and Gustave had no idea what other children in the world must endure, it was a good thing. His children would forever be safe. They would never lack for anything. Their lives would be perfect.

All too often, Albano found himself dreaming awake about Xandra. Year after year, the daydream continued. Marceline was born, and then Gustave. He and Lucienne celebrated their second anniversary, their third, their fifth, their sixth. Still, it was Xandra he dreamed about. He rose early every morning and went on long walks by himself, but he was not truly alone. He imagined himself with Xandra, walking with her. He dreamed that he showed Xandra the gardens of Paris, the Arc de Triomphe, the banks of the Seine, the Trocadero, the Grand Palais, the bridges. In those dreams, he had conversations with the ghost of Xandra that he could never have had with Lucienne.

He and Lucienne stayed out of each other's affairs and scarcely argued. Alban, as she preferred to call him, aspired to be the most accommodating of husbands. He wanted, above all, to make Lucienne content. He was in charge of their finances, about which she never asked questions, and she handled the details of the house and the children, where to go on holidays, whom to hire and fire, what to wear, whom to see. Over the years, under Lucienne's capable direction and impeccable taste, the house was repaired and modernized with new plumbing, comfortable bathrooms, central heating, and a telephone. They soon owned two automobiles. A full-time chauffeur was hired as well as a cook. Lucienne held salons and dinners and surrounded herself with members of Paris's high bourgeoisie and even the occasional aristocrat. Albano was a bit overwhelmed by the role he was supposed to hold in society, but he was open to meeting new people, and his time living under Moshe's roof had taught him to observe without judgment.

Lucienne became increasingly hard to please, but Albano knew he was to blame for this. He had stopped visiting her bed when she became pregnant with Gustave and had not found it in himself to rejoin her. They now each had their own bedroom in the house. He had moved into his own room on the pretext of insomnia. At first, at bedtime, he would come to sit on her bed and say a few words to her so that she would not feel abandoned. But soon, he could not even make himself do that.

Lucienne grew angry and dismissive. "Don't feel that you need to come here," she said one night after she had worn a new silk nightgown, perhaps in the hope of inciting him, but had only received a kiss on her forehead. "It's obvious that you're only going through the motions."

"I came to bid you good night."

"You clearly loathe to touch me."

"Lucienne!"

"I know you have mistresses."

"I do not."

"You want me to believe that a twenty-eight-year-old man can do without intimate relations?"

He tried his best to reassure her, but this did not calm her jealousy. He felt great guilt at the suffering he had inflicted upon Lucienne by marrying her. She suffered from his lack of social standing, which diminished hers. And now she suffered from his lack of physical engagement. Albano felt alone a lot of the time. But all in all, those were beautiful years watching the children grow up. Still, every day, there was the loss of Xandra, like a feeling of a void in his heart.

****

In the next few years, as Paris continued to lose itself into the general intoxication of the années folles, as Lucienne continued to host dinners and salons, and as his and Moshe's business grew, Albano began to keep a tense, watchful eye on the political situation throughout Europe. He did not like the excitement about National Socialism and its racist theories in Germany, and in Italy, Mussolini's fascism worried him. But when he brought those worries to Moshe, his uncle told him he was only looking for reasons to explain why he was so unhappy, and that he had warned him against marrying Lucienne whom he found cold and snobbish.

In 1929, the world began to unravel. It started with a personal loss. On the night of the New York Stock Market Crash, Grand-mère collapsed of a heart attack. Marceline was six then and Gustave only four. Marceline, being older, was able to grieve and adjust, but Gustave was inconsolable. For months, he had nightmares, and during the day he cried at the smallest frustration.

Albano was pained by Gustave's vulnerability but did not know how to help him. Lucienne felt that Gustave needed more discipline. Lucienne hired and fired more British nannies, capable women trained to be uncompromising. This only made Gustave more anxious. Albano wondered what might become of a boy who seemed to be afraid of his shadow. Life was treacherous as it was, even when faced head-on.

Albano tried not to resent Lucienne for her impatience with Gustave. She was, after all, doing the best she could, frantically going through a new caregiver every few weeks. Why could Gustave not be more like his sister, Lucienne wondered out loud? At six years old, Marceline was a paragon of strength and determination, unsentimental to the point of ruthlessness. Even Lucienne was less unyielding.

This disagreement over how to help Gustave went on for months and created a wedge between Albano and Lucienne. But the hiring and firing of nannies was a new source of tension between them. If the women were pretty, or young, Lucienne would make a scene, accuse Albano of all sorts of evils, and fire them. It wasn't rare for Gustave to awaken with one nanny, and be put to sleep that same night by a different one he'd never seen before.

Immediately following the American Stock Market Crash, Uncle Moshe left for Tripoli, Lebanon, Athens, and Naples to secure arrangements with his suppliers. He would also visit Uncle Joshua and his family in the Jewish quarter in the city now called Izmir.

Uncle Moshe's trip was extended an additional month. Upon his return, he called Albano on the telephone and asked that they meet at the Tuileries Garden the next day. They needed to talk, he said.

As they walked together down the central alley, along the neat hedges of clipped boxwood and chestnut trees, Uncle Moshe was uncharacteristically quiet. "Was your voyage a good one?" Albano asked. "You didn't tell me why you extended it. Is anything the matter?"

"I wanted to speak to you about something. You will want to sit, Albano. What I have to say to you will be difficult."

Albano became worried. "Are you ill, Uncle?"

They sat on one of the stone benches around the garden's large round basin. Little boys sailed their wooden boats, and little girls played with hoops and jump ropes. Mothers and children's nurses sat on chairs, catching the spring sun's timid rays.

"The reason I extended my trip is that I ended up spending much more time in Izmir. The change of name is a good thing. There is little left of the city we loved."

"Please do not speak to me of Smyrna."

"Albano, I must," Uncle Moshe said somberly. "As you know I saw Uncle Joshua."

"Is he not well?"

"The whole family is well and much appreciative of our help. These are trying times for the non-Muslims who stayed, but they are making do. When I saw Uncle Joshua, I could tell there was something he was trying to conceal from me. He was not looking me in the eyes, and I know my brother. He was upset, and when I asked him what was wrong, he would not tell me at first. I pressed him to tell me what was on his mind, and he eventually did." Uncle Moshe hesitated, staring at his round fingers, searching for words. "Uncle Joshua spoke of a visit he had received two years prior. A visit about which he had kept silent."

"What kind of visit?"

"A person came to his door. A woman."

"What kind of woman?"

"A veiled woman. At first, Uncle Joshua found it strange that an unknown Muslim woman would come all the way to the Jewish quarter and ask to speak to him. The woman said she was not Turkish but Armenian."

"Armenian?" Albano became excited. "Had she known Xandra perhaps?"

"Albano, the woman asked about you."

"About me?"

"She wanted to know if you were alive. Uncle Joshua told her that you had escaped the fire and almost died of drowning, but that you had been rescued and moved to France, and that now you were married and had children."

Albano racked his memory for any Armenian woman he might know from the past. Xandra's mother and sisters had perished. There were women he saw at the bakery, but none that knew him by name. "Who was this woman?" he asked.

"She didn't want to say. She thanked your uncle and walked away. Uncle Joshua did not speak of this to anyone. But he … when he saw me, he felt guilty I guess."

"Guilty of what?"

"He felt you deserved to know, or at least he wanted to place the burden of telling you, or of not telling you, on my shoulders."

Albano was getting impatient. What was Uncle Moshe trying to say? "What burden?"

"Uncle Joshua believed that this woman was, in fact, the same woman he said you left your family and religion for. He believed the woman was Xandra."

Albano shrugged. "Of course not."

"Whoever she was, Joshua felt guilty about keeping that impression to himself. He also said she had asked for your address in France and that he would not give it to her."

"Why not?"

"You had started a new life, and he did not want to be the one to ruin it."

Albano got up from the bench and began pacing. "A childhood friend of Xandra and Hagop perhaps? Who could she be? Uncle Joshua was a fool not to give her my address. This woman obviously wanted to speak to me and had every right to."

"In Uncle Joshua's mind, it would have been uncalled for if this woman was indeed who he convinced himself she was."

"But she was not."

Uncle Moshe hesitated. "There was the complication of her appearance. If this woman was indeed Xandra, she was not the way you remember her."

"Uncle Moshe," Albano said with force. "The woman was not Xandra. Xandra perished in the fire. I buried her."

"Even with a headdress, your Uncle Joshua saw that she was burned," Moshe muttered. "Terribly disfigured by the fire." Uncle Moshe, still sitting on the stone bench, was pale and distraught. He did not look at Albano but still stared down into his lap.

"What are you trying to tell me, Uncle Moshe?"

"You want to know why I spent a month in Smyrna when I was supposed to leave after a week?" Moshe said.

"Why did you?"

Uncle Moshe took in a large breath. He got up from the bench, took Albano by the shoulder, and faced him. "I stayed to look for the woman."

Albano was dumbfounded. "Why would you do that?"

"I needed to know. What if Uncle Joshua had been right? What if the woman was indeed Xandra?"

Albano was angered by this, annoyed by Uncle Moshe's hands on his shoulders. He answered as patiently as he could, "I buried her with my own—"

"I found her," Uncle Moshe interrupted, his eyes filling with tears. "Your Xandra is alive, Albano!"

The two men faced each other. Uncle Moshe strengthened his grip on Albano's shoulders. Neither moved. Albano looked at Uncle Moshe imploringly. There was so much more in Uncle Moshe's expression than the meaning of his words. Moshe seemed both devastated and thrilled. Albano tried to speak, "I … I don't understand."

"Uncle Joshua was right, Albano. Xandra is alive."

Albano was very pale suddenly. He shook his head vigorously and, freeing himself from Moshe's grip, walked away saying, "It cannot be. It cannot be. I took her in my arms, she and the baby. I carried them to the sand, under the tree, I dug their grave!"

"Your child did perish," Uncle Moshe said gravely. "But the woman you buried was not Xandra. Xandra gave birth to a stillborn child as the fire raged. She was saved! She was evacuated before the hospital burned down. She was carried to safety and was between life and death for weeks. She suffered severe burns, but she lived."

Albano's legs folded under him. He sank onto the park bench. He was panting, nauseated. None of this made sense, but suddenly he had the terrible urge to believe. He did not, could not, believe, but he wanted to. He could not bear to think Uncle Moshe was wrong. He muttered, "How can you know that this is the right person?"

"There isn't the shadow of a doubt. I met her. She and I spoke at length. The cave, Hagop, her parents, the pregnancy, the diamond, the visas, the arrival of Kemal, the fire. She knows everything about you, every small thing. And she looks just like the picture you once sent me."

Albano curled over himself. "I can't have abandoned her!" he muttered. "It's not true! I can't have abandoned her and married another woman. I could not have left her to die alone in childbirth and run away. I have children! With someone else … I forgot her; I tried to forget her. If she were alive, I could never forgive myself. I … she.…" He looked up at Uncle Moshe. "But still … It would be the most wonderful gift from God."

Uncle Moshe beamed. "She is alive."

Albano got up from the bench, frantic, speaking loudly. "I am taking a boat. I am leaving today!"

"That won't be necessary."

"I must go to Izmir at once. If this is Xandra—"

"She is here, Albano," Uncle Moshe said.

"Here?"

"Here in Paris. I brought her back with me."

Albano's mouth opened and closed. Words didn't come out. "Xandra is in Paris?" he finally said. His knees buckled again, and he stumbled to the boxwood hedge, bent over, and threw up.

Uncle Moshe patted him on the back. "I debated whether to respect her wish. Although she finally agreed to come to Paris, she made me promise not to tell you a thing."

"But why?" Albano yelled.

"She thought you would be better off not knowing."

Albano was crying now, tears rolling down his face. "How could I be better off?"

"She respects that you are married. She asks for nothing."

And this alone, her demonstration of selflessness, convinced Albano. "That is my Xandra! She is alive!" He was laughing now through his tears.

"Albano, you must know," Uncle Moshe said gravely, "she suffered. She is not the way you remember her. It's been a great many years of grief and physical pain for her."

"Seven years! Seven years later! How will she ever believe I didn't mean to abandon her? How will she ever forgive me?"

"She understands and forgives you."

"That is what she is like!" Albano said, with immense pride. There was on his face enormous hope and excitement. "Where is she?"

"In my apartment."

"Your apartment?" Albano exclaimed.

"She knows that I am here with you now. She hopes for your visit."

"Today?"

"Whenever you are ready. She knows this will be a shock to you, all this. She has known you were alive for a long time. She says to tell you that she understands if you need time or if you prefer not to come at all."

"Let's go right now!"

Uncle Moshe's apartment was only a short drive away. In the back seat of Moshe's automobile, Albano's entire body trembled violently, and he was incapable of a coherent thought. He asked a million questions, but Uncle Moshe said it was better if Xandra explained everything herself. When the driver stopped in front of Moshe's apartment, Albano sprang out into the street, into the building, and up the stairs while Moshe waited for the elevator. Moshe found Albano at the door of the apartment. "I don't know if I can do this. I'm … I'm so afraid this isn't her."

They entered the salon, which for once was empty. Uncle Moshe had managed to make the houseguests disappear. "I will get her," Uncle Moshe said. "Be courageous. What you are about to see and hear will be difficult."

A few minutes later, there was a rap at the door. Albano rushed to the door, then hesitated, his hand on the doorknob. Finally, he opened it.

Xandra faced him, her grave, beautiful eyes staring unflinchingly. Her long, silky black hair was draped over one side of her face. Albano stood there, his arms alongside his body, his heart pounding, his pulse racing. She did not run to him, and his impulse to run to her was stopped. She was dressed in black. Despite the hair hiding most of her face, he could see the extent of the ravages: the skin pink, crumpled, as though melted. All the right side of her face from her temple and below her eye and all the way down to her neck had suffered a terrible burn. Her hand on that side of her body was burned as well, and he suspected a great deal of her body must also be. She watched him watch her, her eyes overflowing. "Albano," she murmured.

Albano rushed to her, but his legs gave out from under him. He sank to his knees and embraced her at the waist, his arms wrapped around her, burying his face in her skirt. "My Xandra," was all he managed to say. He stayed there a long time, weeping. Then he got up and took her in his arms. She was sobbing too. "My Xandra," he sobbed, "I left you for dead."

She took him by the hand, and they huddled on the couch by the window, crying. Albano took her hands and kissed them a hundred times. When they had cried all the tears in their bodies and could finally speak, Albano, now buoyed by joy, could not stop laughing and smiling, and so Xandra could not help but smile too.

"Are you a dream? You are a dream. Swear to me you aren't a dream!"

"I am real, Albano. You have not changed. You look like a true gentleman."

"You are just the same!" he exclaimed. He moved away slightly so that he could take in her whole appearance. "No. You are better!"

"I am disfigured."

"I believed you dead. I was certain I had buried you. Do you think that I am worried about a scar? Do you think it even matters?" With extreme gentleness, Albano moved the long strands of her hair away from her face and observed the scar carefully. The burn started at the temple, down the eyelid over her right eye, her right cheek, and down her neck.

"All the right side, down to my waist," she said, answering his silent question. "Also, part of my calf and my right foot."

"How you must have suffered," he said, caressing her burned cheek.

"The skin on my foot is the most painful because I have to wear shoes," she said lightly. "One cannot go barefoot in Paris! Moshe failed to tell me this."

"You have found me when I could not find you. I am so sorry. So, so sorry." Albano's words came out rushed and jumbled. "I was hit. Something exploded. I lost consciousness. I returned to the hospital, but it had already burned to the ground. A single wall still stood. There were bodies. Corpses lined against the wall. There was this small, burnt infant … next to a burned body of a woman, and the scarf, it too was burned for the most part, but I recognized it. And I thought … I believed…."

Xandra lowered her eyes. She thought for a long time, putting the pieces of the puzzle together in her mind. "I must tell you what happened. But do not blame yourself, dear, dear Albano. It is all my fault. I can see now how my actions … How you would not have known … You see, already the building had caught on fire as I delivered our child. People were running everywhere. They were trying to evacuate and here I was, pushing our baby out. I pushed. But our son … It must have been the fall when those men attacked us. He never breathed, the poor angel. I saw him. He was beautiful."

"A boy!"

"He looked just like you. I did not know what to do. I wrapped his tiny body in the scarf. I had nothing else. There was no time. The room was hot and filled with dense smoke. A whole side of the building was already in flames. I had to go. They were helping me, but I could not bring the baby. They would not let me. And I could not leave him alone." She wiped her tears, and then Albano's.

"There was a woman, a kind woman, who had died just a few hours before. She was lying there. I did not want our baby to be alone in the fire, so I placed his small body wrapped in the scarf over hers, and I moved her arms over him so that they would have each other's company. I did this. I don't know why I did it. Then a beam fell, my hair caught on fire, and my dress. People helped me put it out, and then they carried me into a truck, and we were gone."

She shook her head, understanding at last. "I never thought you would come back and see that woman with our baby and think that she was me. I never imagined that both bodies would burn to the point of being unrecognizable. And yet the scarf was not burnt? I thought for all those years, about the reasons why you did not come back, but never once did I think of that."

"I came back and found them. I buried our baby, and this woman, thinking she was you. And then I swam out to sea. I wanted to die. I tried to die."

"Moshe told me this. It was five years after the fire before I had the strength to try to find out what had happened to you. As long as no one told me you were dead, I found reasons to hope. Finally, I had the courage to face the truth. I went to the Jewish quarter. I asked to see your family. People were suspicious. Your aunt chased me away. I left, but I was surprised when a man came after me on the road. He said he was your Uncle Joshua. He told me that you had survived the fire, that you had been rescued from drowning by a British hospital ship. He said that you now lived in Paris.

"This made me so happy. But, at the same time, heartbroken. I could not understand why you had not looked for me, why you had gone to France without me. He asked my name, but I did not want to tell him, I did not know yet if you should think me alive or dead. Your Uncle Joshua had the same thought, I imagine. He felt he was protecting both of us, asking me to move on, by revealing that you had married a Jewish woman in Paris, that you had a beautiful house, and a boy and a girl."

"How was telling you this protecting you?" Albano said. He was furious with Uncle Joshua for attempting to play God and control his future.

"He wanted you to continue your life without the burden of caring about me. Here I was, disfigured. Do not be angry with him Albano. He thought he was giving both of us a chance at happiness, and—"

"I will never forgive him."

"You must," she said, bringing her hands to his cheek as she always had done to soothe him.

"How could you for an instant believe I would just abandon you and our baby? You know I would have searched everywhere."

"Maybe you had looked for me and not found me and believed me dead, or you had learned of our dead child, or you had found out about my wounds. I could hardly expect—"

"Xandra, you know me better than this."

"At first, I was despondent. But over time, I was glad that your dream had come true and that you had found happiness."

"It was never my dream; it was *our* dream!" Albano exclaimed. He added bitterly, "There was no happiness to be found in this dream unless we shared it."

"But you were alive, and that was enough for me," she said. "I accepted this fate. I found comfort in knowing that you had children and that you were well. I could have continued like this for the rest of my life. I felt that imposing myself into your life now would have been cruel. It was your Uncle Moshe who convinced me otherwise." She smiled at the recollection. "One morning, two years after I spoke to your Uncle Joshua, this huge, fancily dressed Jewish man appears in the bakery where I worked, asking to speak to me. I recognized him right away from your description. I was wearing a headdress because I was working in a Muslim shop. The headdress was a good thing. I liked it. I was ceaselessly thankful for it so that I did not have to suffer other's disgust with my appearance. And by protecting my face from the sun, the pain slowly subsided. But when Moshe came, he asked my name and asked to see my face, and he recognized me as the woman he had seen in the one photograph we sent him many years ago. Right away, he asked me to come back to Paris with him."

Albano gently traced the contour of her face with the tip of a finger. "How you must have suffered."

"A part of me welcomed the physical pain. It gave shape to the terrible grief I felt at losing you and our son. Also, I had learned that my whole family had perished. It was hard to find a reason to live. Only my faith stopped me from killing myself. And in time, my faith helped me live. Moshe promised me a better life in Paris, even if I never saw you again. I felt it was what I should do. I agreed to come to France. You see, my life in Izmir was hard. I was bedridden for too long, and I missed the possibility to run away. By the time I was ready, the borders were closed to refugees. The surrounding countries had absorbed too many already. I had no money, no home. I was the poorest of the poor, a crippled woman in a destroyed city." Albano stopped her words by kissing her lips softly. She let him do this, but she continued her story. "The man you gave our diamond to, do you remember him?"

"The priest?"

"Fire was upon us; cinders rained from the sky; we could not breathe. He put a blanket over me to choke out the fire in my hair. After that, he made sure I was carried to safety. We never discussed the diamond, but I believed it save my life. By accepting the diamond, he felt entrusted with my care. There was a time when I should have thanked him, but I cursed him for saving me instead. For forcing me to live."

"What became of him?"

"There was an influenza epidemic. He died. But before that, he found work for me. There was a bakery, a Turkish bakery. They took me in. They were not bad people. They were not good people. I was not mistreated. I took care of the children and worked in the bakery, but I was a pariah in the community. I was not paid. I worked in exchange for food and shelter.

"I explained all this to Moshe, and he said that I was entitled to pay and dignity. He told me that I could find such dignity in France if I followed him. I told him that I had accepted my fate. He told me to then accept my new fate since it had now changed, and my new fate was to live in Paris." Xandra laughed. "What could I respond? He said he would find me work, paid work. That I did not deserve a life of servitude in a dangerous country that had decimated my people. It took him weeks to convince me, but he wouldn't give up and said he would not leave Izmir without me."

"But why hesitate?"

"I was afraid to see you. As long as I did not act, I could still dream. Once you knew about me, then I would have to face the truth."

"What truth?"

She looked at the polished wood floor. "That there is no room for me in your life."

Albano opened his mouth to respond, but she put a finger on his lips. She said, "Moshe stayed and waited. And then I accepted. But I did not want him to tell you about me. Not yet. I was willing to accept the kindness of this stranger. I wasn't yet convinced, though, that I wanted you to know about me. I didn't think that was the right thing to do."

"But, of course, Uncle Moshe told me anyway."

She smiled. "I get the sense that Moshe does whatever he wants."

"He has his own sense of what is right and wrong. He is a man of integrity to his convictions."

"Also, I needed to return these to you," she said. She leaned toward a bag at her feet, took a package out and unwrapped it.

It was the Torah finials. Albano stared at them, speechless. "I thought they were stolen."

"They were with me," she said. Still in a pocket of my skirt.

"But, Xandra, if you had those you could have sold them. I am sure they would have brought you a good sum."

"They are sacred. They belong to your son."

Albano contemplated the Torah ornaments unhappily. They were back in his life at the same time as Xandra. Why should two small artifacts be treated with such deference? Why had he not sold them ages ago? And what did this mean to him? Was it a sign from God that He wanted him to pursue his duty as a Kohen? But the scripture clearly opposed it. He had lost the use of a hand, which made him unsuited for the task according to the sacred text. He had also taken part in a burial and could therefore not be a Jewish priest. But he could see how pleased Xandra was, and to what lengths she had gone to protect the finials, and so he pretended to be overjoyed. And in a way, he was, but only because they were a testimony of her love for him.

"Have you found happiness here?" Xandra asked.

"Now that you're here, sitting beside me, I am happy."

Xandra's eyes filled with tears. "But it's too late now. Much too late."

"Why?"

"The way I look…."

Albano smiled. "I still see the most gorgeous woman in the world, only the most gorgeous woman in the world has a burn on her face."

Tears fell down her cheeks as she said, "And there is your life, your beautiful life here."

"Everything in my life changed the instant I learned you are alive."

Everything had to be told, every torture, every pain, and even – and that was more difficult at times for Albano knowing everything Xandra had endured – all the blessings. Albano had to tell Xandra about Lucienne. Why he had chosen her as a wife, the arrangement of convenience that was their marriage. He tried to explain what his wife was like, even though he was not sure he understood it himself. He described her as a person full of rules and strong ideas, who, much like the Levantines, thought that people must be divided into groups and that to be born in a certain family made you a better person. He told Xandra what it was like to have wealth, to produce wealth, and how it never brought the peace and happiness they both had imagined.

He told her about Gustave, his sweet boy who was five years old now, so wonderfully innocent and fragile, and about Marceline, his spirited seven-year-old daughter. He told her what it had been like to make sense of this life, what it was like to go on living when so many had not. He told her of his guilt about Lucienne, how he no longer would share her bed, and her ensuing suspicion and jealousy.

"How could I tell her that I married her *because* I did not love her? How could I tell her that I didn't desire her then or now, but that I wanted children? How could I tell her that I was in love with a dead woman?" He told Xandra how without Uncle Moshe he would have sunk into despair and madness, and how this family had given him a reason to live. "Yet despite all the richness and joys in my life, despite my love for our children, my thoughts always came back to you, and also to Hagop." He added, "And your family … I felt as though I had let everyone perish and it was unjust that I should be alive."

Xandra listened. And then she asked her question, "That day in Smyrna when I was on the quayside, and you went to the Armenian quarter. Do you remember?" Albano nodded. He knew what Xandra was going to ask. "You said that my parents and my sister had escaped." Albano lowered his eyes. "But you saw them didn't you," she pressed. "You saw that day what had been done to them? You saw them, and then you came back, and you felt you needed to lie to me because you didn't want me to suffer?"

Albano took her hands. "Oh, Xandra, how could I have told you otherwise?"

"I learned of what happened to them from another survivor," she said.

"Our baby, me, and now your entire family. How could you bear such pain, my poor love?"

They wept, holding hands, lost in the brutal memories. Around them was Uncle Moshe's luxurious sitting room, with high ceilings and chandeliers, and silk drapes, and beautiful furniture, all so much more lavish and beautiful than inside the Levantines' houses they used to peek into when they delivered pastries. They were sitting beside the heat of the fireplace. Outside the window, Paris glistened with rain. The trees that lined the street swayed to the force of the wind. But for the moment, they were back in Smyrna, in those fateful days of 1922.

"What about Hagop? Did you learn anything?" Albano asked.

"For years it was chaos and lawlessness. It was impossible to get information. But over the years some people returned, very few of them. They told us who they had seen die, and who they believed might still be alive, who was executed on the spot, who was walked to Syria or sent to forced labor camps. But no one could tell me about Hagop. No one saw him. No one remembered him. I wrote to the Red Cross and the Syrian refugee camps, but no answer came back. And there is not a day when my spirit is not tormented by thoughts of my brother. When I think of the brutal death of my sisters and parents, I can grieve and pray for their souls to rest in peace.

But Hagop's mystery is something else. Some days I feel sure he is alive, as though our souls are still connected."

"If he were alive, he would have found a way to return to Smyrna and see about his family."

"What if he is crippled, or blinded, or cannot speak? There are many reasons a man would be unable to call for help." She added, "I had the same thought about you, Dear Albano. I could not help but feel that you were alive. And since I was right about you, maybe there is a chance that I am right about Hagop as well."

"You are proof that miracles exist. I will write to every consulate, every embassy, every government, every church, every office of the Red Cross."

"He could be anywhere. In Syria or Greece, or back in Turkey."

"If he is alive, I will find him. If he is not, I will try to get that confirmed so that we can move on and grieve him properly."

"Do you think that he would still hate us?"

"Not after everything. Not after all these years. If Hagop is found, he will forgive us."

"Oh, Albano. That would be so wonderful."

They spoke for hours and cried until there was not a tear left in them. In the streets of Paris, the rain had subsided, and now they sat by the fire as night fell. Wrapped in each other's arms, they fell asleep with the most profound joy in their hearts.

Albano returned to the Cité des Fleurs house in the early hours. Lucienne wanted to know where he had spent the night, and he told her he had been at his office. She wanted to know why he looked so pale, why his eyes were red, but Albano was not ready to express what had just happened. One day Lucienne would be told, but for the moment he wanted to keep his beautiful secret.

It took Xandra and Albano days to tell each other what had taken place in the eight years since the Smyrna fire. For Albano, Xandra had returned, and it was like she had never left his side. That first week, they spent all of their time together inside Moshe's apartment. He wanted to take her outside and be the one to show her Paris, but that would have to wait. Albano could not take the chance of anyone he knew seeing him with a woman other than Lucienne. He needed to speak to Lucienne first, tell her the truth, but he did not doubt that the truth would destroy her. Each time he thought of this, he felt more incapable of hurting her. Lucienne had done nothing wrong. She did not deserve such cruelty.

After a month, Albano still had not found the right words to tell Lucienne. What could he in good conscience tell her? That the love of his life had returned? That no matter how deep his responsibility and love for his family, his bond to Xandra was deeper? How could he explain to Lucienne that the steel vice that had entrapped his heart for eight painful years, preventing him from experiencing happiness, had vanished the instant he had laid eyes on his beloved? That even the birth of Marceline and Gustave had not felt as miraculous as holding Xandra in his arms again?

Xandra was the antidote to all that had been ailing him. And God, even God, had returned to his life. By bringing Xandra back to him, He had revealed Himself in all of His mystery and glory.

To Xandra, he said, "What can I tell Lucienne? She is innocent. She is a good, decent person. She loves me despite my indifference. I have tried to love her, Xandra. I have tried. She is not unlovable. She is stern and haughty, and difficult at times, but how could she not have become that way when I never let her blossom into the loving marriage she deserved? She gave me two children. Already, she suffers so much that I am in a separate bedroom. And now, to think that I am betraying her this way?"

Xandra said, "In the eyes of God, and in the eyes of the law, she is your wife. I have no claim to you."

"You have every claim!"

"I was first. But she is your wife."

"You are more of a wife to me than she ever could be."

"We have a past. And yes, we love each other. But the covenants of marriage are sacred. I respect your marriage. I would never want to do anything to alienate you from her."

"I will divorce her. People do."

Xandra looked at him. "Not in my religion, Albano."

Albano frowned. "No divorce?"

"I am a Christian woman."

Albano contemplated this. "What are we going to do?"

"I don't know," she said, shaking her head.

"I want you to be the first person I see when I awaken in the morning. I want you to be the last person I see when I close my eyes at night. And when comes that final time I close my eyes, I want you to be the person whose hand I hold."

"I will not be the one who will break up a family. Perhaps we can be friends. The closest of friends."

"I want you in my bed too," he said.

She lowered her eyes and turned pale. "I cannot, Albano. This cannot happen."

Albano looked at her in shock. "But we love each other! I want to hold you in that way."

"We must be strong. God has not spared us to watch us be sinful."

"But we have kissed already? Won't I be able to kiss you?"

"I … I don't know," she said. "I don't know what is right. I need to go to church and ask God."

"We have already missed so many years of happiness!"

"We can be happy. I am happy now. I am so happy that my heart sings."

"I will find a solution so that we can be together every day," he told her. "I don't know what the solution will be. But I will find one."

The crazy idea that Xandra should take care of Gustave and Marceline as their nanny revealed itself to Albano as the perfect solution. She would live with them and take care of the children now that Grand-mère was gone. It all made perfect sense. Lucienne was looking for a nanny able to handle Gustave's broken heart. Albano insisted that Xandra, who he said was a refugee rescued from their home country, be considered. Albano interceded in her favor, telling Lucienne that it was time that a more nurturing woman be hired. When Lucienne protested, he said that Gustave had enough of the circus of uninterested nannies. This time, Albano would choose the nanny, and he was choosing a nurturing woman from his country, someone gentle and loving the way Grand-mère had been. Lucienne, who was always suspicious of other women, was not suspicious this time, only annoyed that she did not have the last word. Because of the way Xandra looked, she did not see her as a threat and ultimately hired her.

Gustave and Marceline quickly bonded with Xandra, who fell in love with them at once. She had much experience taking care of her siblings and, later on, the children of the Muslim family whom she worked for in Izmir after the fire. She was given the nanny's room next to the large nursery the children shared so that she could tend to their needs at night. She bathed them, got them dressed, and put them to sleep. She took her meals with them. She brought them to the park, accompanied them on all their outings. She supervised when tutors and teachers gave them lessons. She played with them, drew with them, helped Marceline make clothes for her dolls, assisted Gustave in creating stories for his stuffed animals. The staff was wary of her at first because of the scars on her face and because she spoke French hesitantly. But they saw that she was helpful and that no task was below her. She was a hard worker, a person who rose early to attend church, someone level-headed who avoided gossip and drama.

Lucienne alone did not warm up to Xandra. She had little affection for her employees in general but displayed a particular impatience for Xandra. The rumor among the employees was that her hiring had been done without Lucienne's consent. Or perhaps she resented that the children had taken to Xandra so rapidly. Also, Lucienne liked to maintain a certain standard of esthetics and propriety. A broken window could be fixed, a drab plant repotted, fading wallpapers replaced. In her house, everything was the very best. But Xandra's appearance was something she could do nothing about. One day she told Albano, "I am sure with our recommendation she would get all the work she wishes."

"What do you mean?"

"There are families in Paris who do not share our standards. She would do well there. But here…."

Albano had shrugged, irritated. "What standards have we?"

"I don't want people to think ... I understand the poor woman did not choose to look this way, but must we be the one family to take her in?"

"She is good for our children. Who cares what people think?"

"Haven't you heard what people are starting to say about Jewish families? The last thing we want to do is fuel gossip. I would prefer to stay completely above the fray."

"And so, you think that a nanny with an unscarred face will ingratiate you with the anti-Semites?"

"I simply want the children to fit in."

"And I want the children to be well cared for."

"I shall never understand your attachment to this woman," Lucienne snapped. "And besides, I am the one who makes these decisions around the house. Since when do you even care who I hire and fire?"

"She is staying," Albano had said, and he left the room.

One night, Albano was enduring one of Lucienne's dinners, with many guests, when the maid arrived with a tray of Oriental desserts. Now that Xandra lived with them, Lucienne's dinners had become famous in Paris for the exotic pastries she served. The compliments guests paid to Xandra's pastries were the only redeeming moments of those insufferable dinners where each guest was more pompous and self-important than the next. Albano loved to listen and later repeat the compliments to Xandra. And so, instead of tuning out the conversation Lucienne was having with a woman in the yellow dress and hat, he listened.

"How extraordinarily delicious!" the woman told Lucienne. "And so unusual. Is this marzipan? Are those pistachios? You must give me the address of your baker."

"We have an unusual situation," Lucienne answered. "My children's nanny happens to be a wonderful baker."

"Oh goodness, don't ever let her slip away. Or else your guests will abandon you one by one."

"My guests will keep coming then," Lucienne said good-naturedly. "She cannot leave us; she has no place else to go. She's a foreign refugee and entirely depends on us for survival."

"How horrid," the woman said. "You must feel trapped, poor darling. Those foreigners have ways of insinuating themselves into every corner of our existence."

Lucienne laughed too loudly. "Well, I did marry one of them, so I should know."

The woman smiled. "Your husband had the common decency of being rich, which puts him into a very different realm."

"Indeed."

"Only make sure that her foreign ways don't rub off on your children."

"I know what you mean. She's a mystery to me. I don't know what she thinks or if she thinks at all. It's quite an irritation."

"Those refugees are masterful at self-preservation," the woman said.

"The children are getting older. I would let her go, but these are hard times, and my husband doesn't have the heart."

"A decent nanny who bakes? She would find employment in no time."

Lucienne lowered her voice. "I'm not certain in her case. She has a tragic appearance. Burned. From head to toe."

"Ghastly!" the woman said as she popped the rest of a pastry into her mouth.

Albano felt disgusted; he was done listening. He tucked his fists into his pockets and went up to the children's bedroom.

Marceline and Gustave were already fast asleep, with warm blankets pulled up to their chins. They were as cozy and warm as birds in a nest. Xandra had dozed off in the armchair, a nearby candle softly lighting her face. Albano's chest expanded with love for the three of them. What Lucienne said or thought did not matter. Still, though, he would speak to her.

After the guests had departed, Albano tapped at Lucienne's bedroom door. She was sitting at her vanity, removing her jewels. When he entered, he could tell that his arrival into her room flustered her. She began combing her hair. They had not been intimate in years, and this created a terrible chasm between them that was never discussed. If she missed it, she did not say. If she wanted it, she did not ask. Facing her now, he regretted giving her the wrong impression. It felt cruel. But now that he was in her room, he would say what he had meant to say, but he would do it without showing the anger he felt. "I heard you speak of Sandra to that woman."

Lucienne stiffened. She stopped brushing her hair and got up to stand by the window. "And so?" she asked.

"You were denigrating refugees, denigrating Sandra, who is a hard-working, excellent person. Whereas that woman you were speaking with is an arrogant snob."

"An arrogant snob who happens to be the Minister of Agriculture's second cousin."

"Beware of letting the prevalent xenophobia taint your thinking."

"It does not."

"It is an insidious thing, Lucienne. And I want none of it in our house." Lucienne did not answer. "Have a good night," he whispered as he left her room. Again, she did not respond.

Albano saw Xandra during the day, but they had to be careful not to express closeness in public. Albano would meet Xandra and the children at the park or the zoo. There, they would sit on benches side by side as the children played, always cautious not to sit too close or to appear intimate. Sometimes Albano would drive them himself, and they would bring a picnic lunch and eat it at the park, just the four of them, like a regular family. At the children's bedtime, Xandra would sit in the armchair by the fireplace as Albano told stories. Sundays were Xandra's day off. In the morning, she would go to church. In the afternoon, she and Albano met for as many hours as they could manage without raising suspicion. They could not be seen together without the presence of the children, so the only way they could be alone was to meet at Moshe's house. Moshe kept a room just for them and had special meals prepared and deposited in front of their door. Albano and Xandra would spend those Sunday afternoons speaking, eating, listening to music, playing card games, laughing, and kissing. But they would not make love. That had been Xandra's condition. "I will take care of your children, and I will live inside your house, and we have our Sunday afternoons, but I will not be the mistress of a married man," she had told him early on.

"That is because you won't let me leave Lucienne and marry you," he would say.

"You know how I feel about this," she would answer stubbornly.

Again and again, they had the same argument about love and God. She would tell him, "Divorce is a great sin. God saw what we were doing in the cave when we were not married, and He punished us. He did not let our boy live, and He wounded both of us almost mortally. And then He separated us. But then, He had mercy on us and gave us a chance. We are living this chance right now."

Albano did not know how he felt about God, but he felt certain that if God had a hand in the minutiae of humans' daily dealings, He would spare innocents and punish evil. Judging from the state of humanity, it seemed to be the opposite that took place. "I want us to love each other like a proper couple," he would say.

"I do not need that to know that I love you."

"But I do need it. I don't … but I do…."

She moved her hands toward herself. "Why would you even want this disfigured body."

His eyes lit up when he said, "It is today as it has always been: beautiful."

"We can still kiss."

"Oh, Xandra, what is it you want from me? Please allow me to leave Lucienne so that I can marry you."

"Isn't it enough cruelty that I have stolen her husband's heart? Must she see her family torn to pieces as well?"

"My heart was never hers to steal away, and you know that."

"Yet what crime has she committed that she would deserve to be abandoned?"

"If you do not want me to leave her, at least let us be lovers."

"I cannot be an adulterer," Xandra would say. "When I face my God, and you face yours, it will be with a clear conscience."

"But I want you. I want you just the same as I have always wanted you."

"I want you in that way too. But we both must resist. That is our trial, Albano; please do not put me in the position to deny you."

Albano felt that in this way his relationship to Xandra mirrored his relationship to Lucienne, whom he no longer was intimate with. Thus, he had two wives but no wife at all. Abstinence was his lot. But he was a twenty-eight-year-old man with desires, who got to hold and kiss his beloved but little else. "All I have are the memories of the cave. Maddening memories," he told her.

She would blush. "I have those memories too."

****

One Sunday afternoon, in 1932, when Marceline was nine years old and Gustave seven, Xandra told Albano, "Something ugly happened this week. At the Bois de Vincennes, in the area where they have the wooden horses and the swing sets and slides. There was a group of ten-year-old boys. They came to Gustave and called him names."

"What kinds of names?" Albano asked.

"The kind of bad names they give to the Jews. I did not know what they meant. Marceline explained this to me afterward."

"Were those boys from Gustave's school?"

"They were strangers."

"Marceline and Gustave dress like any other French children. How would those boys know they are Jewish?"

"They looked at Gustave, and they knew."

Albano marveled at this. "In Smyrna, each group dressed differently, so it was easy for people to know. Here they can simply tell?"

"Marceline was angry," Xandra said. "They were targeting her little brother, and you know how fiery she is. She was not about to let that happen. She's had practice defending me when people say things about my face. She rises to her feet and huffs and puffs like a little dragon. And at the park, she faced the boys, and I don't even know what she told them, she was speaking so fast; she just stood tall and told them off. The boys snickered, but they left."

"How about Gustave?"

"He cried at first, but then he was angry at himself for crying. And then he was angry at Marceline for helping him. It humiliated him that a girl would appear stronger than he is."

"He needs to learn from his sister and become more aggressive," Albano said. "That's what Lucienne thinks. She feels that Gustave needs training to be less timid. She also thinks that Marceline would do well to be a little less forceful."

"I don't think Gustave needs to be compared to his sister any more than one should compare a bear to a fish. The bear is perfect at being a bear, and the fish is perfect as it is, being a fish."

Albano shook his head. "But the fish cannot survive on land."

"The fish is not supposed to. If you let Gustave be himself, he will find his own way. That little boy feels deeply. Many things of the world are an aggression to him. He has the talent of being quiet and pensive when others seek distraction and amusement."

"What you see as Gustave's qualities, Lucienne considers weaknesses. Do you think he could become the rabbi I never could be? He is a Kohen after all."

"Or he may become a poet, or a writer, or an artist," Xandra mused.

"He is only seven years old. I supposed he has plenty of time to become more assertive."

"The world is not composed of just one type of man, Albano. There is room for Gustave to be just the way he is."

"Yes, but look at how people have come to think about Jews everywhere across Europe, even in France. And now I learn that even children are acting this out, as you just witnessed. The world is out of balance, and I'm afraid that at the moment it has little use for poets."

"The world precisely needs people like Gustave to return to its balance. He is a wonderful boy. In every way, wonderful."

"But his sister is—"

"Marceline has leadership and emotional strength."

"Marceline needs to learn to become more girlish, just as Gustave must learn to be boyish. She has to learn to tame her dominance. She can be callous, much like her mother."

Xandra smiled teasingly. "Do you want her to have female qualities only?"

"Well, yes." He looked at Xandra and could tell it was not the correct answer. "Why not? Is that not what women aspire to?"

"Perhaps she is a woman destined to greater things."

"Her mother certainly seems to believe so."

"I think Marceline will do greater things than even Lucienne imagines," Xandra said.

Albano returned home on foot from Moshe's apartment. He enjoyed long solitary walks through Paris, which allowed him time to think. He walked briskly from Avenue George V, walked across the eighth arrondissement toward the seventeenth arrondissement and the Cité des Fleurs house, cutting through the Parc Monceau. In the park, the sycamores had lost most of their leaves. Already, the air was crisp. Albano braced himself for another frigid European winter. He had not wanted to alarm Xandra, but the climate against the Jews, throughout Europe, worried him. Now, Parisian children parroted their parent's prejudices all the way to the playground, and Marceline and Gustave were beginning to experience racial hatred. This was the very thing he had sought to protect his children from.

Hagop was once again on his mind. Two years of effort, of letters to consulates and embassies in every country throughout what used to be the Ottoman Empire, had brought no news of Hagop. With each negative response, his hope of finding Hagop alive shrank further. Albano found much to regret about the way he had treated Hagop and much to blame himself for. Had he been straightforward about his love for Xandra when they were young boys, instead of waiting until they were men, had he found the courage to tell Hagop the truth early on, Albano was now convinced that the course of all their lives would have been different. Hagop had learned about Albano and Xandra's love in a time of religious persecutions and political upheaval when the Ottoman Empire's Armenian population was imperiled. Because of this, the thought of Xandra with someone who wasn't Armenian had been intolerable to him. But Hagop, he could see this now, had only meant to control his environment as best he could by hanging on to traditions.

Yet, Albano reasoned, had Hagop given himself some time to cool off, had he not reacted and thus thrown himself into the hands of his enemies, things would have been different. Once again, Albano imagined himself running after Hagop that day on Mount Pagus, and talking him into returning to the cave. Other times, he imagined clubbing Hagop over the head and dragging him unconscious into the cave to keep him protected, against his will if need be. Albano replayed various scenarios in his mind: he and Xandra staying in the cave; Xandra giving birth there instead of in that hospital; both of them leaving for Paris months earlier. If they had done any of those things, the baby might be alive today. He would be ten years old by now. In one scenario, they would not have needed to go to France. He and Xandra would have stayed in the Jewish quarter with Uncle Joshua and his family. In another scenario, they would all have wound up in Paris, and Hagop would be working with him and Moshe. He would never have met Lucienne. He would live in a nice house in Paris with Xandra and their children, although this scenario, which implied that Marceline and Gustave could not have been born, wasn't one he liked to entertain.

Hagop's impulsive nature had been his undoing. He had let his pride rule over his actions. Albano had known all along that Hagop could be reckless, but he had never tried to change him. He had accepted his friend the way he was, even the parts that were flawed. He shouldn't have. He should have reasoned with him, tried to shape him. But he had been afraid to contradict Hagop, afraid to take a stand and say unpleasant things. Now he saw the way Gustave and Marceline were. There was an opportunity to observe them, identify their weaknesses, and mend them while they were still young. He did not need to make the same mistake again of loving without helping, which was not loving at all. Yes, it was easier to accept the other person for whom he or she was. But wasn't to accept people as they were a more selfish act, perhaps a cowardly act? The difficult thing to do, the responsible thing to do, was to help give those you loved the strength to go past their limitations.

And so, Albano began to think that perhaps Lucienne was right, and Xandra was wrong. Gustave might be a fish who would need to be taught how to behave like a bear.

CHAPTER 4

Life in CGI

Cassie left Odile and Raymonde and walked down the street toward the métro station. Had this been progress? Maybe. At least they had listened to her. She had not exactly been the picture of poise and dignity, and she might have reinforced their opinion that she was an unpredictable nut by tracking ketchup throughout the apartment and nearly setting the kitchen on fire.

In the end, she had chickened out of confronting them. She should have demanded that they let her see her dad instead of treating her like she carried the bubonic plague. This was what she did: fight useless battles about insignificant details while what mattered to her festered inside.

In the métro, Parisians were indifferent, half asleep. Most were absorbed by whatever gadget they were holding: smartphones, e-readers, electronic games, and what-have-yous. If hers had not disintegrated, she'd be doing the same thing. She buried her hands into the depth of her father's coat pockets to stop them from craving the immediate gratification of scrolling, swiping, and poking. She was left with no choice but to look around and be with her thoughts, and many of them she did not like.

And she had chickened out of canceling the date with that man too; let's face it.

Maybe she wanted the date?

She got out of the subway at Havre Caumartin and entered the first café she saw. She went to the back and walked down uneven stairs through a narrow, dark corridor looking for the bathroom. She opened the door to the "toilettes" and recoiled in horror: a squat toilet! Nope. Thank you. She turned around to leave but saw the public telephone, and just above it an advertising display for their movie assaulted her. *Women in Black, Part Two*: the title in gold letters this time. It was as though the telephone were beckoning her to call Peter. She swiped her credit card and dialed his cell. From the café above came the sounds of French pop music and the clanking of dishes. A door opened, and a waiter walked past her. She caught a glimpse of the kitchen: a sink, piles of plates and glasses, and a man in a grimy sleeveless shirt, a cigarette at his lips, setting a cast-iron pan on a stove. The phone rang. A rank bathroom odor mingled with the smell of French fries.

"It's me," she said when Peter picked up.

"Cassie!" he exclaimed. "Do you know how frustrating it is not to be able to reach you?"

Cassie felt transported elsewhere. To California, to her house, that haven of calm, the view of the mountain from the porch, hummingbird feeders. "How is everything at home?" she asked.

"Home?" Peter echoed, revealing how absurd her question was. Wherever he was, it was not her home.

"The twins, I mean, how are they? College? Any news?"

"No news is good news," Peter said jovially.

"No news from my children isn't good news to me."

"You're tense for early morning."

"It's not early morning here."

"Did you have your coffee?"

"It's just that…." She hesitated. How could she describe what was happening without starting to blubber like an idiot? She inhaled for strength. "My mom and Odile are not letting me see my dad."

"What?" Peter said with the exact amount of indignation she had hoped from him.

"They took my name off the visitors' list."

"What the hell, Cassie?"

"There was this thing yesterday, this … hullabaloo. My dad got overwrought or something. When I came to his room, he got into this … rage. And they are blaming me."

"What did you do?"

"I did nothing of course!"

"I meant what did you do when they said you could not see your dad?" Peter said diplomatically.

"I cried, what else?"

"You're going to take this lying down?"

"You know how I get with them. I get confused."

"Let me unconfuse you. It's always the same shit show with them. You're the black sheep. They always side with Odile."

"If my dad gets dangerously agitated around me, maybe they have a point."

"Trust me; they don't."

This was the type of thing Peter always told her. It was his role to remind her to trust her gut, that she was entitled to feeling offended and outraged, that she must fight for her rights. Except when it came to him. Was Peter correct about any of this? Could he be trusted? He could be self-serving. Maybe it suited him that she remain alienated from her family.

And Peter lied, too. Things he said were layered with omissions and half-truths. She had seen him lie to others, and she had caught him in lies with her. Sometimes she had the energy to ask him to clarify, but most of the time it was easier to let things fly. It was easier not to listen to her intuitions, to that little voice that warned of danger. "So, I went to my parent's apartment to talk to them," she said. "Confront them, you know but I…."

She stopped talking. Peter was not listening. He was in a conversation with someone.

"Oh," he said after a moment. "Jessica is telling me to ask you if your parents liked their presents."

Where were they? On the beach? At their house? Were they shopping at Trader Joe's? Had they just had sex? "Tell Jessica Rabbit that this is not about her right now," she said.

She overheard Peter call out to Jessica. "They loved the presents, Honey!"

"Tell Jessica Rabbit that I forgot to give it to them. But I will soon. If I don't kill them first."

Peter called out to Jessica. "Cassie's family says thank you. They say that they hope to meet you one day."

"Lying is truly effortless to you," Cassie marveled.

"It's all smoke and mirrors, darling. Just trying to keep peace and harmony going."

"Okay. So, now I'm in Paris, and I don't know what to do with myself," she said. "Although I'm having lunch with that new aunt I told you about." She did not think it necessary to bring up dates with good-looking French men on motorcycles.

"It would not be such a bad idea to come back early. I'm sensing tension with the studio. Some pressure to rewrite some scenes," Peter said.

"We have plenty of time."

"Ahem … for the one that's coming out now."

"What? That ship has sailed. They're advertising it here like you would not believe. It's all over the subway, posters, at bus stops, in magazines. I'm staring at one of them right now."

"The studio is thinking of a few added lines, in voice-over."

"To say what?"

"There is a sentiment that perhaps our heroine is all leather and kung fu, but you know how it's the man who saves the day? Well, apparently it might be misconstrued."

"As what?"

"As chauvinistic."

"Not inaccurate. How are they going to pull that off without reshoots?"

"She could speak as we see her from the back, or maybe they could shoot a close-up of her face where she says … stuff."

"What kind of stuff?"

"They're thinking a sentence or two, something empowering, something feminist. Give the movie more of a girl power sort of thing. Maybe you can think about it, throw around some ideas."

"Why me?"

"You're a woman."

"And that would make me an expert at bullshitting other women?"

"You know the trigger points, what pisses off women, where they take offense."

"I think this conversation just demonstrated that you're the expert at it."

Peter laughed uneasily. "Work your magic, Baby."

"More of that good old smoke and mirrors?" she asked.

"On the plus side, they solved the diversity problem," he said.

"It that still an issue? They should have thought about that at casting."

"No, they're cool with it. They found a way to fix it."

"How?"

"With CGI."

Cassie closed her eyes and groaned, "Don't tell me they're just going to color in the – I'll have to pretend I didn't hear this."

"I'm thinking I should look into changing your ticket."

"Change it to what?"

"To come back earlier. I mean why stay if they're going to treat you this way?"

"You were the one who talked me into coming here in the first place!"

"You were right, love: France is enemy territory for you."

Before she knew why exactly, she saw red. "This realization conveniently coincides with you needing me for work."

"Why do you have to be antagonistic all the time?" Peter exclaimed.

As was the case so often when she was in conversation with Peter, Cassie's mental sharpness blunted, her sense of right and wrong blurred. She could see her own point, the one she was pressing so hard to make, at least in the beginning. And she could see his, but all too often it was the validity of her own point that she began to doubt. She *was* being antagonistic. Perhaps not all the time but a majority of the time. She was being reactive, but reactive to what? She wasn't sure. With Peter, two and two did not always make four. For example, he had professed his love and devotion to her throughout their marriage, so why had she not felt loved? Why did she feel that his devotion to her always took the back seat to his devotion to himself? For example, the affair. He had denied it at first. Or her feelings that he was taking advantage of her professionally. His first line of defense was to say that she *imagined* things, that she was making things up, when he knew that this was precisely what her family said about her, when he knew this was her weak point. And in the face of that, she became confused and harassed and helpless at knowing her mind or trusting the content of her own heart. If Peter could be so casual about her writing credit, then his moral compass was flexible, and everything he said should be looked at through the lens of truth flexibility.

"Maybe that's because you and I have unfinished business," she finally said.

"Such as?"

"Such as you *know* what." She let this hang, and there was a difficult silence.

"Are we still talking about the affair?" he said, in a tone that blended sadness and outrage.

Cassie hesitated. "I'm talking about that and the stuff after that."

"What stuff? There is no stuff!"

"Stuff is everywhere, Peter. It's a euphemism for bullshit!"

On the line, there was the sound of a sharp inhale, and then silence. "I have to go," Peter said at last. "I promised Aidan and Liam to take them to Travel Town, you know, that train thing in Griffith Park? They're breathing down my neck."

It did not sound like Peter's boys were nearby, breathing down his neck or otherwise. "Go where you have to go" she sighed. "Do what you have to do."

"I'll look into changing the return ticket then?" he asked.

"I guess."

She hung up and faced the movie poster. Even the tone-deaf studio saw what she was unable to articulate: her fictional alter ego was no more capable of taking the lead than she was.

She turned away from the poster and tried to calm herself. Maybe she should start small. Try and channel her inner superhero and brave that terrifying bathroom.

She stepped tentatively inside and locked the door. Facing yet another advertising display for *Women in Black, Part Two*, she contorted, pulled down her jeans, bunched up her coat to waist level, held it and her bag tight against her, squatted and tried not to pee on her boots, or touch anything, or breathe.

She left the café. Outside, it was, no surprise, raining. She wrestled her way through hordes of harried shoppers on their way to and from Galeries Lafayette and Le Printemps.

Across from Galeries Lafayette was, interesting coincidence, the beautiful Art Déco Société Générale Bank, the very bank where she had come as a teenager, the address of which was engraved inside her father's finial.

She trudged up Boulevard Haussmann, bumping into people. In this sea of humanity, she noticed everyone and could filter out nothing: not the smells, not the sounds, not the way people looked and dressed. In her frizzy hair, shapeless coat, and cowboy boots, she looked like a garden troll as she walked past Parisian women in trendy winter coats and fabulous shoes. The men were elegant too. Where were the garish baseball caps, the black socks in white sneakers, the T-shirts tucked over beer bellies? Parisian men wore slacks ending at just the right length, polished shoes, and groomed beards. Even the children were nerve-rackingly elegant.

She still had thirty minutes before meeting Marceline. She stood in front of the Galeries Lafayette. Enter or not? A flock of Japanese tourists engulfed her, and before she knew it, she was inside, jolted by the scents of hundreds of designer perfumes.

She walked through the aisles, brushed her fingers against cashmere, leather, silk, cotton, and wool wondering where even to start. The light came through the art nouveau stained glass of the famous Byzantine cupola thirty feet above and shone on the balconies, which looked like suspended gilded alcoves. She was inside the church of fashion. Proper worshippers were able to distinguish what made one sweater, one pair of pants, one shade of lipstick more desirable than another. But no swiftly tied new scarf would make a dent in her disastrous outfit. Cassie would have to start from scratch. She would have to start from the inside out, in fact, since she was at the moment wearing the last of her clean underwear and bras. She laughed to herself, picturing the disaster of a man, say, to name a person at random, handsome Hervé, setting his eyes on the horror of her subpar underwear. She pushed the thought away. She was not letting him go near that. Not at her age, not on the first date. IF this was a date.

In the lingerie department, she hovered around nightgowns, silk negligees, ruffled organza boy shorts, black guêpières, and stopped in front of a lacy bra in a scandalous shade of purple. If she were to, hypothetically, wear such a bra with all that lace, and those half cups, and that wild purple, it might put the wrong thoughts into Hervé's head … or worse, her own!

She charged out of Galeries Lafayette and landed outside in the humid air. Her comfy, 100% cotton high-waist briefs would be an insurance policy against even *wanting* this unsuspecting man to get anywhere near her.

Outside, the rain was pouring down. Cassie's umbrella, bought for ten euros in the street, overturned in seconds in a gust of wind. How was Marceline going to get here, she wondered? She had visions of the ancient lady fighting off the weather, helplessly clambering through the métro. Boulevard Montmartre was a hair-raising nightmare complete with bumper-to-bumper traffic, exhaust fumes, and maniacal honking. Inside their cars, drivers gesticulated, yelled, and hammered their horns as though they were missile launchers.

She waited for Marceline on the sidewalk in front of the exit of the Grévin Wax Museum, where they had agreed to meet. She was stretching her neck for signs of Marceline when the driver of a long, black Mercedes, sleek with rain, swiftly and in a blazing demonstration of hubris, drove right off the pavement, over the curb, and from there proceeded to use the sidewalk as his private driveway. Furious pedestrians yelled and cursed at the car. The Mercedes continued on the sidewalk with the perfect indifference of a black whale through a school of mackerels. When the car got to Cassie's level, it slowed to stop right in front of her. Out of it sprang a hefty man in a black raincoat – a chauffeur, or possibly a bodyguard, judging from his stature – who clicked open a bright red umbrella the size of a parasol, walked around the car, opened the back door, and reached in to assist his passenger out of her seat. To Cassie's astonishment, the passenger was Marceline.

Pedestrians, upset that they had to struggle to walk around the stopped car, hurled insults at the driver and Marceline, but both appeared thoroughly unconcerned. Marceline gingerly put one foot and then the other on the slick pavement and with the driver's help got out of the car. She was the picture of Parisian elegance in black heels, black, lacy pantyhose, orange silk scarf, and long black coat decorated at the top with a large gold brooch. Marceline hooked her arm around her driver's elbow and together, at a snail's pace, they moved toward Cassie who came forward to help. Marceline stopped her with a raised hand. "I'm not crippled! Maurice will get me inside the passage, and then you can take over." To the driver, she said, "Maurice, be here at 1:30 p.m. sharp, will you."

"Oui, Madame la Comtesse," Maurice said.

Inside the passage, Marceline let go of Maurice's arm and stumbled two steps in Cassie's direction, flailing her arms. "Damn Manolos," she said. Cassie took hold of her arm. "No, not like that! I hang on to you, not you to me." She hooked her right arm around Cassie's left, and they walked forward on the marble floor.

"Careful. The floor might be slick."

"This is not my first rainy day, très chère," Marceline grumbled.

Both breathed in relief once they were on dry ground.

Next to the cacophonic street, the Passage Jouffroy was soothingly quiet. Visitors strolled, speaking in hush tones. Grey geometrical mosaics covered the floor, and a diffused, cheerful light flooded the gallery from above through a skylight dome of glass and iron, like a lace glass ceiling. On both sides of the covered alley, there were antique shops, rare books sellers, lithography, old stamps and postcard shops, cafés, and restaurants, all with façades and details restored from an era some 100 years earlier.

"This place is fantastic," Cassie exclaimed.

"You've never been here? It's a Parisian institution. There were over a hundred glass-covered shopping arcades such as this one across the ninth and second arrondissements in the first part of the nineteenth century. Haussmann tore most of them to the ground when he rebuilt Paris. Galerie Vivienne and Passage Jouffroy are two of the nicest that remain." She eyed Cassie. "You're still wearing my father's coat,"

"I forgot to bring a coat to France."

"Nonsense."

"I'd been promised a heat wave."

"Ha!" Marceline croaked. "Here it is. Le Valentin, the tea salon I like."

Le Valentin was an old-fashioned tearoom which opened onto the Passage Jouffroy. The shop windows, framed by green scalloped velvet curtains with dozens of tassels, displayed Easter candies under glass cloches to make it look like terrariums. Pastel marshmallow bunnies, sugar baby chicks, and colorful eggs covered in metallic paper rested on fake grass. There was an assortment of decorated chocolate eggs, jars of confiture, and cake stands of various height displaying pies and pastries.

They entered. "Bonjour, Madame la Comtesse," said the woman behind the counter. Inside, it smelled of liquorice, caramel, and hot chocolate, and maybe a bit like staleness and wax. On the marble shelves and the countertop were glass jars filled with candies from another time, pale guimauve ribbons, and glossy fruits confits. A waitress in a white apron rushed in to help them out of their coats and whispered a greeting in Madame La Comtesse's ear. "They know me here," Marceline said with undisguised satisfaction as she sat down. Over a chic black cardigan, she wore around the neck her bohemian assortment of beaded necklaces, trinkets, old keys, and tassels. "Bring me a Petit Coeur, a Forêt Noire, and a cup of chocolat chaud, ma petite," she told the waitress without even so much as glancing at the menu.

"You're not having lunch?" Cassie asked.

"This is lunch."

"All sweets?"

"Are you worried this might shorten my life expectancy?"

Cassie smiled. "And no guilt?"

"Guilt is a senseless waste of energy. Do what you're going to do, or don't do it. The rest is an exercise in self-mortification."

Cassie laughed. "Maybe we should all follow your diet."

"Try the millefeuille au chocolat and you'll be a centenarian."

Cassie studied her menu. "A chocolat chaud and a millefeuille," she told the waitress. "Doctor's orders."

The smell of chocolate reduced to a thick elixir permeated the air as the waitress filled each of their cups out of a tall ceramic pot.

CHAPTER 5

Côte d'Azur

Marceline took a sip out of her cup and watched Cassandra with curiosity. She had never entertained the idea of having children and, because of Gustave, she had been denied the privilege of knowing her three nieces. So it was a strange feeling to sit across from one of them – a woman she was related to by blood. Marceline could not help but look for, and think she could recognize, something of herself in Cassandra: the tenacity perhaps; the curiosity; a certain form of intrepidness, of contrarianism. "Your father had a difficult time in school before the war," she told her niece. "Children have a way of acting out the pathos around them, and in the year that preceded World War II, Gustave embodied, for lack of a better description, the consummate scapegoat. Something had to be done about it. My parents had no choice but to send him away."

"No choice? There had to be other choices," Cassandra said. "He could have been home-schooled, for example."

Marceline felt irritated by this, by this woman who knew nothing of the details of Marceline's life at the time intent on doing exactly what Gustave had done, which was to point the finger. She had better keep in mind that she was not speaking to a younger, more naïve version of herself and that Cassandra was a different person, one who would not necessarily agree with her, one whom she would need to convince. "You have to see it through the lens of the time. Now boys can be whichever way they want to be. Back then, it was believed that Gustave needed to be fortified, hardened, toughened, or whatnot. He had to be made into the acceptable kind of boy that is ruthless and dominant."

"My dad is as communicative as a doorknob, at least with me, but dominant, no. So, in that sense, sending him away did not work one bit."

Marceline nodded in agreement. "The absurdity, looking back on it, was that society wanted to make Gustave into a leader and me into an artist when, in fact, I was the one with leadership qualities and Gustave was the artist. The fact of the matter is, people can never change the essence of who they are."

"Do you think your mother deserves the blame for sending him away?" Cassandra asked.

"I can't say it was all her doing. If our father was against her plan, he was meek in standing up to her. But our father must have been at a loss. He wanted to do what was right for Gustave, and he listened to those who considered themselves experts. But in the end, I think Gustave resented me the most."

"Why you?"

"He would do nothing but compare my fate to his from that point on. It was a tremendous injustice, seen from his perspective, that I was able to stay with my parents while he was sent away. Gustave got into his mind that our parents favored me. But even if he were right, how must I be blamed for it?"

"Even if it was done with good intentions, it seems a harsh thing to do to a child," Cassie said.

"You must understand that within the context of those years, and the fear and uncertainty that we inhaled with every breath we took, my parents were torn as to what to do." Marceline put her cup down. "Although in hindsight, we might have convinced ourselves that having him in a Jewish boarding school away from Paris was the best thing for him when, in fact, it might have been the best thing for us."

"What do you mean?"

Marceline sighed. It cost her to admit the truth. "Gustave was drawing attention to us – to the fact that we were Jewish. Society was going mad, and perhaps we were going mad too, unable to adjust, unable to understand and accept the new reality of how the Jews were being perceived. We wanted to deny it."

"I can't begin to understand how society would shift just like that."

"Not exactly 'just like that,' but it all happened fast. There was the Great Depression. Well, we did not know what to call it then. No one could imagine an end to it. People were losing everything: work, food, a sense of safety. When people feel out of control, they grasp for causes and solutions to their problems. What they readily find are the wrong causes and the wrong solutions. Powerlessness makes one likelier to embrace the single-minded doctrine of those with the most venom, those who embody the anger people feel within. When given a chance, it is always fear and suspicion that take hold. Hatred is more visceral, easier to access than decency or self-restraint. They began putting Jews into one of two categories: either they were, like our family, among the rich and influential, just when the French population felt increasingly powerless, or they were immigrants and refugees, allegedly stealing whatever little work was available. It was all propaganda-driven. Believe me when I tell you that behaving like a sheep is not just for the impoverished or the uneducated. Propaganda has just as much power over the clever and the rich. Society needed a scapegoat, and who better served that purpose than the Jews?"

"Actually, I don't know why Jews would be so easily pigeonholed into that role," Cassandra said.

Marceline shrugged. "I would guess that it is faster to reignite the collective memory of hatred than to start with a brand-new group of people. At any rate, the whiff of war was too hard to ignore for my father. Everyone else might be in denial, but he wasn't. We children did not quite understand what was happening. All I knew was that one day, I was told to pack my things, and the next, we were sweeping Gustave away from the pensionnat and fleeing Paris." She closed her eyes, let the memories flood in, and began to tell Cassandra about the months before the war.

****

At the Rânes boarding house, Gustave went to his room and gathered his belongings. To the question of where the bill should be sent, my father responded by handing the headmaster a thick envelope filled with francs. No, there would not be a forwarding address, my father told him.

We left Rânes within the hour. My father was at the wheel of the Alpha Romeo. My mother, in her best Chanel suit, sat primly in the front seat. Gustave and I were in back. Following us closely behind was the Renault, driven by Moshe's man, with Sandra and all our luggage.

There was in the air a new strangeness, a trepidation at the unknown. There was dread also. The sense that we were running from a nameless threat. There was at the same time a new closeness with my family, a closeness that is not emotional, but visceral, born from the suspicion that, from this moment forward, we would have nothing and no one but each other.

In Le Mans, we stopped at a charming hotel. For dinner, I remember that we ate the local specialty: buckwheat crêpes and apple cider. We ate in an atmosphere of forced gaiety. Were we trying to fool ourselves, or the people at the hotel, by acting as though things were normal, that we were a regular family on holiday? This gaiety was not our norm. We were just playing a part.

Early in the morning, we left the hotel and drove across France as torrential rain poured. The roads were slick and treacherous. My father's shoulders tensed up under his coat, and his knuckles stiffened on the wheel, and yet I felt relieved. There was comfort in having all those I held dear under one moveable roof, speeding away from Paris, away from our anguishes. War could come and go, I told myself. My father's injury made him unfit for combat, and as for Gustave, he was too young to be drafted. Other men would be sent to die in the trenches. Men I did not care about. If it amused Hitler, he could well knock down our house. We would not be there when he came.

The rain had been omnipresent ever since we left Paris. But as we headed south, past France's mid-point, the curtain of clouds lifted, the downpour stopped, and the landscape turned bright-green. I realized something, which the weather and ominous headlines had made me forget: it was springtime. We drove through large stretches of empty roads, past vast expanses of rolling hills, and beneath clear blue sky, our spirits lifting higher with each turn of the wheel.

Gustave read the map and gave Baba directions. I was in charge of selecting restaurants off the Michelin Guide. In Beaune, we ate Oeufs en Meurettes, a dish of poached eggs and red Bourgogne wine sauce. This time, our father insisted that Sandra and the driver have lunch with us. It was a lovely sentiment that made for a terribly awkward meal.

Past Dijon, the temperature rose noticeably. We rolled down the windows and the scents of wild thyme and sage wafted into the Alpha Romeo. Past Valence, the earth's coloring soon changed to a vibrant red. Oleander bushes as tall as trees lined the side of the road.

On the third day of our journey, we came upon the cobalt blue expanse of the Mediterranean Sea.

"La mer!" Gustave and I exclaimed.

My father, without warning, stopped the car on the side of the road. He got out, and Gustave and I hopped out after him. My father took a few steps toward the cliff that overlooked the sea. He stood there, in his waistcoat and shirtsleeves, his face turned toward the warm sun, his arms slightly open as though they were antennas that allowed him to take in all of that warmth and blue.

"What is it, Baba?" we asked.

"The sea, the smell, even the dirt…. It reminds me of my country." He contemplated the sea that shimmered on the horizon. "Can you hear the wind?" he beamed. "Even the wind sounds the same."

The other car pulled up and parked behind ours. Sandra rolled down her window, and Baba leaned in to speak to her. They said a few words, and both smiled.

Now that he had seen the sea, anxiety seeped out of my father with each kilometer that moved us farther away from Paris. In the car, he became talkative. Now the gaiety was real. My father's joy was communicative. We played charades and twenty questions. Even my mother participated. A nearly tangible weight lifted off me. It was as though we had left blustery Paris sick with worries and had magically stepped into summer and out of the shadow of war.

We drove along the Massif de l'Estérel. Below us, vertiginous cliffs plunged into the foam of the Mediterranean. Cypresses stood like giant swords around ancient stone houses, and the songs of the first cicadas throbbed in our ears. Gustave and I put our faces out of the automobile's windows to smell the unfamiliar fragrances carried by the warm wind that ruffled our hair. Our coats and socks were off by now. Gustave was down to his white sleeveless undershirt, and Mother did not object.

At last, we arrived. We drove past a gate with a sign made of ceramic tile that read "La Bastide." The cars went up a circuitous driveway lined with knobby olive trees until a magnificent house perched on a hill came into view. It was a sprawling villa with a terracotta tile roof, warm ochre stonewalls, and wooden shutters painted blue. A bougainvillea wrapped itself lazily around the side of the house and part of the roof. Cascading ivy and petunias spilled out of dozens of pots. The tires crushed the pebbled driveway, and my father stopped the automobile in front of the house. We got out and took in the scenery. La Bastide had sweeping views of the Bay of Cannes and the Mediterranean. The horizon filled with nothing but blue. The air buzzed with insects, and the pungent smell of rosemary mingled with the perfume of lavender's early blooms.

One by one, the staff selected by the rental agency hurried outside to greet us. With dramatic flair, they stood by the entrance porch as though we were royalty. Be assured that Mother liked that very much. But then an insect zoomed past her face, and she began swatting the air spastically with a copy of her *Vogue* magazine.

Inside, Gustave and I ran from room to room. Light flooded into the house as the staff opened the shutters that had been kept closed to keep the rooms cool. Apparently, in this land of wonders, the sunshine we Parisians were starved for was in such overabundance that they thought nothing of keeping the shutters closed in the middle of the day.

Inside, the décor was sparse but warm. Rather than the moldings seen in Parisian buildings, there were exposed dark beams and white-washed walls typical of the region. Red, hexagonal clay tomettes tiled the floor throughout the house. In the bedrooms, the blankets on the four-poster beds, the curtains, and even the wallpaper were covered with Provençal fabric. "This place swarms with Provençal motives," my mother declared. "There seems to be no running away from it, whether you like it or not." In the dining room, a thick, dark, varnished table with sturdy, graceless legs and matching chairs could have easily seated twenty. There were hutches, and cavernous fireplaces, and nooks and crannies everywhere. "Positively medieval," Mother dropped with a sigh. "I guess it will have to do." But I could tell she was satisfied.

My father smiled a Cheshire cat's grin and gestured toward the living room. He opened the door ceremoniously, revealing not the baby grand I expected but a beautiful Steinway grand piano.

"Baba! Thank you!" I said, jumping at his neck to hug him as my mother and Sandra smiled. Only then did I notice Gustave. My brother stood by the door, looking dour, perhaps stricken. Our eyes met, and he quickly looked at the floor.

A conscience can manifest itself at bizarre times. That day I felt it. At that moment, I felt ashamed of my advantages. I was so catered to, so adored and doted on, that it nearly sickened me. And now, having fetched Gustave as we did, I was reminded of the condemned man's expression on his face each time he had to return to his boarding school after holidays. The brutal coldness of it all now seized me. How had we, for nearly two years, rationalized sending Gustave away? How had this been admissible? I walked to the Steinway and, conscious of Gustave's eyes on me, I brushed my fingers on the keyboard, but I did not play.

We were introduced to the groundskeeper, Monsieur Malou, a Provençal man with a face as gnarly as the pit of a peach. Despite his old age, he had labored on the grounds until they became a veritable Garden of Eden. There were water features with tiny goldfish, lawns that were not mowed with military precision as they were in Paris but allowed to mingle with wildflowers. There was a brook, flowerbeds bursting with lilacs and clematises, an orchard lush with apple, peach, plum, and cherry trees, many of them in bloom. Mr. Malou, in his musical Provençal accent, named the trees and spoke of them with affection. This apricot tree was the sweetest. This peach tree had fruit with yellow flesh. This cherry tree had been a disappointment for the last few seasons, but there was hope for a comeback. On the arid slope below La Bastide stood a small vineyard where buds exploded in tender leaves. We were shown the vegetable garden. Gustave and I had our first experience pulling carrots, onions, and radishes out of the ground, which felt nothing short of miraculous. "We are canning as much as we can," Monsieur Malou told my parents with a knowing look. He added, "We are prepared." I wondered if Gustave understood that he was hinting at the prospect of war.

As we walked back toward the house, my father lifted his nose in the air and took in a big whiff. "Can you smell it?" he said, beaming, "Can you smell the sea?"

"I can't," Gustave said. "Water doesn't have a smell."

"Oh, I can smell it from here," my father said. "I can hear it too! And it is calling our names."

"When can we go to the sea?" Gustave asked.

"We can go now," my father said.

"We haven't got our swimming trunks unpacked," I ventured, hoping this would not stop us from going.

"We'll only take a look," Baba said.

We arrived in front of the house. Sandra was by the automobiles, helping with the unloading and instructing the house staff where to put things.

"We'll go tomorrow," my mother said. "Today we shall get settled."

On a normal day, in a normal world, this would have been the end of it. But to my surprise, my father only shrugged and headed toward the car. "Why delay?" he said. "Let's just go now."

Did my mother's unmitigated ruling of the Paris house have no jurisdiction in the South of France? We looked from my mother to my father. Gustave and I had a quick decision to make, lest we miss the window of opportunity. How we reacted might well set a precedent for the rest of our time here. The decision was whether to go by my mother's boring rules or be free with Baba. It took me but two seconds to run after him. Gustave was perplexed for another few seconds, and then he also piled into the car. My father then turned to my mother. "Come on along, Lucienne, Dear," he said playfully. It will be lovely. I heard the call of the sea, and when the sea calls, we must not be impolite.

"I have had enough driving," my mother said, tight-lipped. "Besides, someone needs to give instructions for the unpacking."

"Please Maman, come," I said. "Don't you want to see the Mediterranean?"

"I shall see it plenty since we must abandon a perfectly good life to bury ourselves here," my mother said.

"As you wish, Dear," Baba said. And then he did a terribly imprudent thing, one that would have lasting repercussions. He turned to Sandra and asked, "Would you like to join us?"

Sandra should have declined and stayed behind to help my mother. That was, in theory, her function here, the reason we were taking her along. But she did not look at my mother. She did not hesitate. She only entered the car. I was surprised by this small act of subversion, quite an uncharacteristic one I might add. But it was enough for my mother to begin resenting her presence even more. My feeling is, she should have sided with my mother. But then again, Sandra was a simple woman who did not perhaps understand the ramifications of her actions.

In the automobile, Baba and Gustave sat in front, Sandra and I in back. We drove down the hill with all the windows open, the warm wind billowing our clothes and ruffling our hair. The colors here were the most vivid. The earth was brick-red, the distant sea emerald green, the sky blue, and everywhere yellow mimosa trees released their powdery scent. The late April sun in the South of France bore no resemblance to the meek Parisian light. It was hot on the skin and quite fierce. It made you want to be reckless.

We arrived in the town of Cannes and drove down the Boulevard de la Croisette. The Croisette was a sight to behold. On one side were luxury boutiques, cafés, restaurants and their terraces, and glamorous hotels painted bright white. We drove past Dior, and Cartier, and countless expensive boutiques. We had to put our faces out the automobile's window to take in the immensity of the Hotel Carlton, a towering palace seven stories high, with twin domes at each corner and a white façade layered with hundreds of small balconies overlooking the sea. To our eyes accustomed to the gray austerity of Haussmannian architecture, Le Martinez hôtel and Le Majestic hôtel took on the air of sugary confections.

The Croisette was all so bright and cheery. At the foot of each hotel, the restaurants' terraces were filled with diners sipping their aperitifs. Servers in black vests and bowties scurried about the terraces carrying tall glasses of pastis and bowls of local olives. Orange and lemon trees in large planters framed the terraces with barrages of fragrant blooms. On the curve, drivers in livery stood by gleaming Rolls Royces and Bentleys, chamois skin in hand.

The sea and the promenade were on the other side with a center divider planted with colorful flowers and palm trees standing between the two. My father turned to Sandra and spoke in a foreign language, which might have been Armenian or Arabic. When my mother was present, Baba only spoke to Sandra in French, but when it was just us around, he used languages she spoke more fluently. He pointed to the palm trees. "Those are trees from our country," he told us. I would soon find that everything in Cannes reminded him of Smyrna: the sea, the beaches, the vegetation, the warmth, the smells, and the gentle, almost inaudible lap of a calm sea on sand beaches.

We could see the sea from the car, but a low parapet hid the sand beach from sight. Baba parked the automobile, and we stepped out onto the promenade. I wished I had come properly dressed. The place was nothing short of a fashion show. Men wore pale summer suits and tipped their hats to the passing ladies. The women protected their complexion from the sun with lacy umbrellas and had the effortless elegance of those for whom mink, cashmere, and pearls were the ordinary. Had Mother not been so stubborn, she would have been perfectly in her element in this setting, she who would never be seen outside without white gloves, even in the scorching heat of summer. In Cannes, everything smelled of money and high class as though this pocket of the world were immune from the blight of the impending war and endless financial depression by which the rest of France and Europe were so alarmingly affected.

We leaned over the parapet to discover the beach below and its many rows of parasols and cushioned chaises, like small beds fit for an Egyptian queen. The Carlton's beach was all yellow and white stripes, the Martinez's, blue and white stripes. In the sand, ladies reclined on chaise lounges. Children in swimming trunks frolicked in and out of the water, carrying metal buckets and shovels. In the distance, the sea, punctuated by sailboats of all sizes, lay like a shimmering sheet beneath the cloudless sky.

I gazed at the sea, at my father's relaxed smile, at his arm draped over my brother's shoulders, at Sandra, whose face looked luminous as she lifted it toward the sun. My anxious thoughts washed away. For that moment, all was right.

No matter what we had promised my mother, all four of us in concert went down the stone steps and made a beeline for the beach. Sandra immediately removed her shoes, bent down, and took a handful of sand that she sifted between her fingers. I removed my shoes too and stuffed my socks in Sandra's bag. The sand was warm and voluptuous under my bare toes. My father stooped, and he too touched the sand. Squatting, he gazed wistfully at the sea. I saw that Sandra's eyes were drowned in tears. My father gave her an indecipherable look. Were those tears of joy or sadness? I did not let myself imagine it could be anything other than the return of happiness to our lives.

Gustave rolled up his pant legs, removed his undershirt, and hopped wildly into the water. "It's glacial!" he screamed.

"It is only April," Baba said. "It will warm up."

We had promised my mother only to look at the water, but no matter;, it was irresistible. I did not care about my clothes and went straight to the sea. I was baptized by Gustave's spray of icy water. "Oh you!" I roared. "I will...." I took water in my cupped hands and hurled it at Gustave, who received it square in the face, surprising us both. He and I began a mad splashing. And now Father joined in. We laughed and screamed and splashed some more while Sandra watched us, hiding her giggles with her hand.

At that moment I felt reconnected with something rare as gold but as necessary as oxygen, something irrepressible: joy. I had been holding my breath for years and not even known it.

My mother, it dawned on me, never would have permitted such freedom. She surely would have forbidden me to remove my shoes and socks in public. And thanks to her absence, Father could be joyful and carefree as well.

My mother's disapproval was always there, whether it was silent or voiced. For sixteen years, my mother had carefully orchestrated my life, my outings, my social circle, and my activities, always with eyes on the future. She had groomed me for a specific life, and because her certainty was absolute, and because I had excelled at meeting her expectations, I had no concept of rebelling. My mother and I, the way I saw it, had a common objective. But at that moment on the beach, it struck me for the first time that I never thought independently from my mother. Her thoughts, her plans, her decisions, her judgment of me and others had a hold on me. Was I even capable of an original thought? Her lapdog, Gustave had called me.

Gustave and I continued frolicking on the beach. When I had enough, I stepped out of the water, drenched, guffawing, my hair wet in my face. I walked into the warm sand. Sandra removed her shawl and offered it to me so that I could dry off. But before I got to her, I saw something that stopped me in my path. Drenched, cold, and disheveled as I was, I stood there and stared, my mouth ajar. The public beach was only separated from Le Carlton hôtel's private beach by a three-foot-tall white fence. There, to my left, under the shade of a Carlton hotel parasol, reclining on a padded lounge chair, was a striking woman in a scandalous, strapless, two-piece white swimsuit. She may have been a French starlet. In my memory, she looked a lot like Betty Grable, the American actress. Her hair was luminescent platinum and coiffed in firm, glossy curls. Her lips were painted incandescent red. Most incredible was how tanned her long legs were. The moment froze into one perfect image: the woman extending her hand toward the iced beverage a server brought on a tray. A cigarette materialized between her fingers. The waiter bent down to light it. She had an enigmatic smile. She brought the cigarette to her red lips, and glamour perfection was achieved.

And to think I had believed myself of this world! I was an awkward little girl in white socks and silly curls without an ounce of glamour to her. In an instant, I knew the kind of woman I wanted to become, and this was it!

I had thus far blindly followed my mother's plan for me. I had understood the goal and worked towards it. But so far, it had been all my mother's goal. What did it have to do with me?

I stormed off the beach, suddenly furious. I ignored Sandra and her shawl and went toward the stairs, hating my hair, my childish dress, my appalling lack of sophistication.

I remember that time of laughing and splashing on the beach as one of the last events of my childhood. I would reappear at the top of the stairs, an adolescent.

We arrived at La Bastide in time for supper. Dinner had been prepared and set on the long Provençal table, but my mother was still pouting and refused to come out of her room. Baba, Gustave, and I ate in awkward silence. Afterward, my father went to my mother's bedroom to smooth things out. The number of hours my father patiently spent trying to make my mother feel better to no avail can probably be counted in years of his life. I'm not sure why he bothered. Some people just seem to want to feel terrible. They want to be cross, and they want to remain that way. My mother, I now realized, was one of those people.

After dinner, Gustave and I stepped into the garden. It was night, and the air pulsated with the songs of crickets. We walked out in the balmy air that smelled of citrus blooms. The huge moon reflected on our skin, giving us an eerie glow.

"Do you think there will be war soon?" I asked Gustave.

"Baba seems to think so," he said.

"But don't you think Mother would know more? She is more French than Baba. Maybe she understands things better?"

"Of course she doesn't," Gustave said, "Mother is hateful and knows nothing."

I was shocked by this outburst. "Mother is not that bad," I said.

Gustave stared ahead, his jaw set. "Yes, she is."

We walked in the moonlight in silence. If Gustave hated Mother now, was it because she had sent him away? I wondered if he held me responsible too.

Perhaps that night was my chance to ask him, but my thoughts were not properly formed in my head yet. Had I acknowledged the injustice, had I asked for his forgiveness, perhaps the course of our relationship would have been different. But words did not come to me. Instead, I spoke of myself. I told him about the woman on the beach, and how horrific my clothes were, and how I was going to become a world-famous concert pianist one day, or an aviator like Amelia Earhart, or the next Vivien Leigh. Gustave listened, as was his habit, nodding, as though he never doubted I would achieve greatness.

A few days later we were having breakfast and making plans for the day when Baba closed his newspaper and slammed it on the table. "Something should have been done about Hitler years ago. And now France and Britain scramble to side with Poland. Can't they see we need to make a pact with the Soviet Union before Germany does?"

My mother had taken to dismissing my father's political opinions, perhaps to reassure us. "The French government knows what it is doing, Alban. France must sign the pact with Poland. That is precisely how we stop Hitler."

My father shook his head somberly. "Hitler will invade Poland. If we sign this pact, we'll have no other choice but to enter the war."

"So, let that hideous little man invade Poland, and let us intervene. What will Hitler do then? It's not like he will attack France if this is what you're worried about."

"If he does invade, France does not have the army to fight him," my father said.

My heart thumped painfully in my chest. Gustave and I looked at each other. My mother blinked in incomprehension. "How so?" she said.

"Our equipment is outdated and insufficient; our generals are set in their ways. Our military won't be able to cope. Not when Hitler has been building his army for years, and certainly not without the Russians by our side."

"So, we could lose the war?" I asked, my throat dry.

My mother shrieked, "You are frightening the children! Besides, you are wrong on all counts. We will hardly need to fight Hitler. He's not stupid enough to risk public humiliation trying to break the Maginot Line."

My father shrugged, "I'm afraid that the Maginot Line is just a line in the sand, Lucienne. If determined armies can invade across oceans, I don't think Hitler will be so easily deterred."

Horrified, we looked at my father. Discrediting the Maginot Line, the impenetrable military fortification along the German and Italian borders, the first line of defense against the enemy, the genius design of our most decorated intelligence: this was tantamount to blasphemy. "The Maginot is unbreakable," Gustave said. "That's what they say in *Le Monde*."

"Oh, but your father needs no Maginot Line," my mother said, putting as much derision in her tone as she could. "He's got himself a fortress up here. Haven't you, Dear?" My father poked at his eggs uncomfortably as my mother went on. "And should the enemies attack, we shall defend ourselves by pelleting them with peach pits, which we'll have plenty to spare come summertime." She laughed and, seeing that no one else did, added, "Alban, when will this silliness end? My friends are mocking us for leaving Paris, and I don't know what to tell them. Frankly, I am beginning to feel embarrassed."

Shortly after that, in May, France and Britain rejected the Soviet Union's proposal for a pact of mutual military assistance, and they agreed to give Poland military help against Hitler. In other words, the opposite of what my father had hoped for. My mother stopped asking to return to Paris, and I willed myself not to think about unpleasant things.

To my disappointment, and in contradiction of the original plan, Gustave and I were not enrolled in school. Instead, tutors came to the house. In what felt like an endless holiday, Gustave and I tended to our studies without much élan, swam in the pool, and ate Provençal food. Madame Malou was a superb cook and treated us to snails with parsley and garlic butter, or boeuf en daube with carrots from the garden, soupe de poisson, and pissaladières. Under her tutelage, Sandra learned to prepare calissons d'aix and lavender-infused ice cream. We competed daily in angry tennis matches that sent Gustave into paroxysms of fury when he did not win, which was almost always. I played the piano and perfected my English with a British boy, red and pimply but with whom I mostly perfected my kissing skills. I was antsy for more excitement and would have loved to meet more people, but my father said that our presence in the South of France needed to be inconspicuous.

"It is only a measure of precaution," my father said during one of our early dinners at La Bastide.

"Baba, our Jewish friends in Paris aren't worried, so why should we be?" Gustave asked, repeating our mother's sentiments.

"It doesn't matter what the greatest number of people think," my father said. "What matters is what we think and what we decide to do."

"But how is one to decide?" I asked.

"The signs are there for those who pay attention," my father answered.

My mother had a little laugh. "Don't you know that your father receives special intelligence from Président Lebrun? Or is it the generals of the Wehrmacht, letting you know their plans before they know it themselves?"

My father stared down at his plate. "I am sorry Lucienne if I am causing you grief."

The next few weeks revealed an upset of the balance of power at home. My mother might have sounded confident, but it seemed to have been an act to reassure Gustave and me. Also, in this new house, and isolated from her friends, she was out of her element and no longer all that mighty. At night, her sleep was fretful, which she blamed on the croaking of hundreds of frogs that emerged out of the pond and onto the lawn at sundown. In the morning, there would often be a few dead ones floating in the pool.

Our mother's poor sleep resulted in cranky moods and lethargy. During the day, she wandered aimlessly around the house, deeming the sun too hot for her disposition. Perhaps there were other reasons for her fading spirit. Maybe she was more afraid of an impending war than she let on. Maybe she knew of Father's plans, still secret to Gustave and me. The thing was, my parents argued now. If they had done it before, it had been discreet, and I had not quite noticed. Before Cannes, there were distractions: Father's work, Mother's charities. Before Cannes, there had been decorum. My future, mapped out by my mother, had seemed a series of straightforward steps. Follow those steps, schooling, manners, a certain attitude, connections, friendships, salons and dinners, the right kind of marriage, and life would follow the desired trajectory. But now my mother was grasping for the way things ought to be while we wandered off course, into uncharted waters. The plan was no longer simple. There were imponderables. There was xenophobia, and there was anti-Semitism, and soon there might be war, terrifying things she could not face, and so she fought Baba instead. Everything seemed to be a reason for her to take offense.

One of the points of contention between my parents was Sandra, whom my mother resented having around.

"Why are you not utilizing Sandra?" I heard my father ask my mother one day.

My mother straightened, "Oh, so she talks behind my back now?"

"She wants to work, and you've given her nothing to do."

"I don't know, Alban," my mother said with lassitude. "This house is fully staffed. Am I to invent things for her to do? Should I have another child so that she can be useful? The children no longer need her, and neither do I."

I felt bad for Sandra, but I was not clear that Sandra felt bad for herself. Her resilience was quite impressive. If my mother yelled at her, which she did quite often, or if she disparaged her, or told her to get 'out of her sight,' Sandra simply lowered her eyes or left the room quietly without appearing upset. Sandra was never one to resist, or take a stand, or even advocate for herself. Instead, she saw what was needed to be done and dove right in without fanfare.

Having known Sandra only in the context of the city life, I had a narrow definition of what she could do. But, apparently, Sandra had no such limitation for herself. She observed the groundskeeper and without being instructed, found things to do in the garden. She weeded and picked vegetables, learned to tend the beehives, picked fruit from trees and bushes, and volunteered for any errands within walking distance. She took it upon herself to drape every bed with fine netting to protect our sleep from mosquitoes. She even did nice things for Mother without being asked. Every evening, she set out to hunt for frogs by flashlight. She collected the little horrors in a large bucket and walked a kilometer to pour them into a nearby pond. No one believed it would make a dent, but it did. Soon there were very few frogs haunting our sleep or polluting our pool.

One day, I saw that Sandra was holding something in her lap. It was yarn, and she was knitting socks by the dozen.

"Do you know how to sew?" I asked her.

"Yes," she said.

I looked at her with renewed interest. "If I were to show you a picture in a magazine, would you know how to make something, such as a dress or a blouse?"

She thought about it. "Yes," she said.

"Mother won't buy the sort of clothes that are fashionable." I went to get the *Marie Claire* magazine on the coffee table and opened the page to a skirt I coveted. "Could you make this if I can find the fabric?"

Sandra gave me a cockeyed look and asked in her disjointed French, "Your mother doesn't want to buy, but you want me to make for you?"

I sat next to her and put my arm around her. "Oh, pretty please, Sandra, could it be our secret?"

"If your mother sees new clothes, she will ask."

"She won't, I promise. I'll never wear any of it when she's around. It's just for me to enjoy. It's just clothes. What harm is there in that? And besides, I don't care if Mother is angry with me."

Sandra frowned, but her lips turned up slightly. "She will be mad at me more than you."

I shrugged, "So, who cares."

Sandra pondered this for a moment. "Get the fabric," she said.

****

I was not the only one whose temperament was expressing itself in new ways. Gustave, too, was changing. Was it the strain of the last few years, his experience at boarding school, or the alchemy of puberty that morphed my sweet, timid, cautious brother into a fourteen-year-old bundle of fury and resentment? The only emotion he willingly expressed with me was brewing anger. Gone was his willingness to resume the role of docile playmate. He seemed to prefer being alone to being in my company. He hardly acknowledged Mother, or me, and when he did, it was through eye rolls, dismissive shrugs, snapping remarks, and slamming of doors. When he did not disappear into his room, he roamed inside the house and out in the garden like a ghostly presence, appearing without being heard, and startling me on purpose. The one person who seemed to find grace in his eyes was our father, to the exclusion of everyone else.

As for our father, he took to going out at night without telling us where or why. He had a telephone installed at the house and made calls behind closed doors. He and Mother argued incessantly, but in whispers. Mostly I could hear my mother's hissing and Father's unflappable reassurance. "Lucienne, I assure you. Lucienne, I promise. Lucienne, please calm your nerves." I began to suspect something. I had never forgotten the words of the servants. My mother was jealous of other women. Could my father have a lover here in Cannes? Could that be the reason he had made us all come here? When those thoughts entered my mind, instead of feeling bad for Mother, I secretly rooted for my father.

The thing was, Baba wasn't going to the office anymore. And so, what was he doing exactly?

"Have you retired, Baba?" I asked him one day.

He laughed. "I am only thirty-eight; I am not an old man yet."

"But you don't go to an office."

"I still do business with Uncle Moshe."

"Where is he?"

"He is abroad," my father said. And that was all the information he would volunteer.

It was good to have Baba to ourselves, at least in theory. It presented some problems, though. For one, he was bored. How else to explain all the time he now spent with Gustave? In Cannes, my brother resumed his carving of little wooden boats for days on end. He'd fine-tune a sail, or a tail, or whatnot and present it to my father to be admired. They had long discussions on the merits of automobiles. They'd visit auto shows. They'd make daylong excursions to neighboring towns to get this locomotive or that miniature forest. They'd construct floating things and test them in the pool. They'd bend over train sets, forgetting the world around them, forgetting I was even in the room.

And me? Well, I was only a girl. Although he was genuinely proud of me, my father understood not one bit about my mastery of the piano, my tennis prowess, or the fact that I could recite Shakespeare with an affected upper-crust British accent. He adored me; this much was clear, but his awkwardness around me grew nevertheless. My new womanly figure was a hindrance to our physical closeness, my breasts a source of embarrassment to us both.

My father now kept me at the respectful distance reserved for people who make you nervous and around whom you're not sure how to behave. Gustave could be wrestled with underwater. Gustave could kick around a soccer ball with him. Together, they could discuss boating and the merits of various train engines. Gustave knew his keel from his rudder, a steam dome from a sand dome. For a while, I tried to be one of the boys, but the appeal of miniature boats was lost on me.

Up until now, my parents had seemed to delight in being my captive audience. But now I was too old to be indulged in such ways. I played the piano, but no one seemed to have much enthusiasm for my nightly recitals. My father was distracted and often would leave the room to take a telephone call. My mother appeared lost in her unhappy thoughts. As for Gustave, in a display of open animosity, he refused to sit and hear my music at all.

So, as Gustave and my father sat side by side in fascination, watching obnoxious little trains make endless figure eights on a plank of wood, I was reduced to the only option left to me, 'turning into a young woman.' My mother and I had different definitions of this. Hers was something out of an 1800s etiquette book. My definition involved boys.

I'm not precisely sure when the resentment between Gustave and me turned to open aggression, but I know when our cold war started. One day in mid-July, Gustave – or I assumed it was he – told Mother that the British boy and I had been kissing. I found out I had been betrayed when my mother, red-faced, her eyes gleaming, burst into my room and slapped me across the face. "Needless to say, you are not to study with this boy anymore."

I held my hand to my burning face. "What did I do?" I shouted.

"You have conducted yourself improperly. Don't you act surprised young lady; you are not fooling me!"

"Who told you? It's Gustave, isn't it? That little brat!"

"Gustave, unlike you, knows the difference between right and wrong."

"If that were the case, he would not tattle."

"How I found out is beside the point, Marceline. Your privileges are revoked starting right this instant."

"What privileges?" I screamed. And with dramatic flair, I added, "What could make my situation here worse than it is already is, with no friends and nothing to do?"

My mother was very upset, and perhaps it was about more than my misbehavior. "The fact that we are here has nothing to do with me," she said. "It is your father who has chosen to isolate us from our social circle, not I. I am as punished as you are."

As it was, Mother seemed more interested in preserving the status quo. My punishment turned out to be a delicate affair because neither of us wanted my father to know what I had done. My father came from a conservative background. I did not want to disappoint him, and I think my mother had an investment in my appearing beyond reproach. Consequently, my punishment was a secret one and tantamount to no punishment at all. For two weeks, I was forbidden to eat ice cream and sweets, and I was not allowed to leave the house.

I bided my time. I read, I swam, I lay by the pool till I turned golden brown. In the privacy of my room and my mirror, I practiced being glamorous, like the woman I had admired on the beach. I stole Mother's cigarettes and smoked them in the orchard when no one was looking. Tutors continued to teach us. As to the matter of learning the English language, my British kissing partner was fired and replaced with an American woman. Gustave and I loved the new accent, which sounded wild and free to us, so we began to pay attention to our lessons. It turned out that by getting that British boy fired, Gustave was instrumental in our properly learning English, a skill that would eventually alter the course of my life. When the need for a translator arose many years later, I was ready for the job.

To be honest, I wasn't certain that Gustave had ratted me out about the British boy. My mother could have found out through Sandra, or Madame Malou, Monsieur Malou, or anyone else on the staff. Still, I stopped trusting my brother with my secrets. When he walked by me or peeped over my shoulder as I wrote, or if he materialized on the same dirt path when I took walks around the property, I accused him of snooping and of being a pest.

One afternoon, my parents were out, and he caught me in the act of practicing in my bedroom mirror the bewitching hand movements of Hedy Lamar in the movie *Algiers*. My lips were red with lipstick, there was an ivory cigarette holder in my hand, and I wore my mother's too-big-for-me Jean Patou black lamé sheath. Gustave opened the door, sneered, and left. I was humiliated. Later on, I cornered him. "You're not allowed in my room anymore," I said.

"You're acting like a fool."

"And stop tattling."

"I don't," he said.

I did not know what to make of this response. "You're the one acting like a fool," I said. "Maybe you should grow up, instead of playing little boy's games."

"Oh, not like you, playing dress-up like a six-year-old?"

"The childish toys you and Baba play with.... You're fourteen years old, Gustave."

"How is it childish, if Baba likes them too?"

"You and Baba are both being childish."

"You're jealous."

"What would I have to be jealous about?" I scoffed. But perhaps he was right.

The other problem with my father not disappearing to the office every day was that with him around, it was harder to ignore the war. One thing about war is that you can pretend it is happening elsewhere and to other people only for so long. It requires vigilance and concentration to remain in the dark. With Baba at home, I could not avoid overhearing troublesome conversations between him and Monsieur Malou. I could not avoid the newspapers left on couches and coffee tables. I could not always turn off the radio when the program I had been listening suddenly made way for a chilling newsbreak. It was on the radio that we all first learned in August that the Soviet Union and Germany had signed a non-aggression treaty. My father's prophetic worst-case scenario had become reality. What this meant, I was too terrified to imagine. Two strong armies, two aggressive nations, now had an alliance. Where did this leave France?

Following these events, my father's secrecy increased. But he did not seem scared. Rather, he seemed determined. His calm was the only thing that allowed me to sleep at night. If he wasn't worried, he whom Mother called a doomsayer, this meant that things would be all right.

That same month, my father did something extravagant, considering that he lately had been lecturing us on the virtues of thrift. One hot afternoon, promising us a surprise, he took the whole family to the pier, where he parked the automobile. We walked on the dock, admiring the beautiful boats that bobbed over the dark, steely water. I was convinced he had hired one for the afternoon. But when we faced a thirty-foot, pristine fishing boat, named Jolie Fille, my father planted on each of our heads a captain's hat and announced, "I have bought us a fishing boat."

Gustave and I jumped up and down and threw ourselves at our father's neck. "Baba, can we use it now? Do you know how to pilot it?" we asked.

"I have hired a skipper for the month, but soon we shall learn to navigate it ourselves."

"Can we rename it?" I asked.

"What do you want to rename it?" Gustave sneered, "Jolie Marceline?"

The fishing boat was lovely. It had two small, well-decorated bedrooms, each with two sets of bunk beds. It had sleek, varnished wood paneling, handsome naval motifs, a darling kitchen with all elements fitting just so, and a padded chaise lounge out on deck. Mother alone did not appear surprised by the sudden purchase. She narrowed her eyes at the boat, measuring it, as though she were contemplating fate itself.

My father, who had not expressed the slightest interest for boating in the past, now seemed obsessed with learning to pilot his 'toy,' as our mother called it. He practiced taking it in and out of the harbor. He learned to read a compass and maritime maps. Gustave was enthralled by it all. He wanted to be on the boat every day, all day long, if that was an option. Throughout August, he and Baba fished, plunging into the Mediterranean from the boat wearing underwater masks and brandishing thin harpoons. They'd emerge from the water with all manner of loathsome sea creatures, fish, gnarly gray seashells, and small convulsing octopuses that Gustave loved to see wrapped around his wrists. I tried to accompany them at first but soon learned that I was not the type who enjoys staring at the water for hours on end. My brother was in heaven to share yet one more thing with Baba.

On September 1, 1939, the Wehrmacht invaded Poland. Immediately, the French government mobilized its troops. We were listening to the radio when we found out. Everything had pointed in that direction, and yet we had all refused to believe Hitler would be so brazen. For the next few days, we stood by the radio, listening for news.

On September 3rd, France and Great Britain declared war on Germany. Fear swept through me like a million darts attacking my chest, my heart, my belly. War. War with a country whose modern, fanatical army terrified us. My father lowered his head, as in prayer, and Mother just clapped her hands over her heart. Neither found anything reassuring to say.

Over the course of the week, everything my father had said and done up to this point began to make sense. Friends had called him an alarmist and a pessimist when he was in the process of liquidating his assets. They had waited to see what would happen. They had listened to each other's reassurance, and few of them were prepared. Most of our Jewish friends had not planned on the fact that with France entering the war, there would suddenly be no buyers for houses and no takers for businesses. Banks stopped lending. People stopped buying. And no one could liquidate anything.

We sat around the dining room table. There was something my father wanted to discuss. It was a sweltering day without a hint of a breeze, inside the dining room and out.

"With the proceeds from the sale of our business, Uncle Moshe and I bought diamonds," he explained. "Those await us in a Swiss bank."

"Why a Swiss bank?" we asked.

"If France is defeated, French banks won't be safe," he said.

"Do you think that's possible, Baba?" Gustave asked.

My father did not answer. "It is possible that traveling to Switzerland might become impossible, so the bulk of our money will be inaccessible to us."

"Oh, goodness, Alban, what if the war lasts for years?" Mother said.

"I have French and foreign money, several diamonds, and some gold. Those need to last until the end of the war."

"What a disaster!" my mother exclaimed.

"Financially, we are better off than most, Lucienne." He lowered his eyes, reluctant to say more. "On the other hand, children, you are old enough to know that being Jewish puts us at risk." Mother gave him an incendiary look to silence him. My father hesitated but forced himself to speak. "We need to look no further than what is happening in Germany to know what an eventual defeat could mean for Jewish families: frozen assets, confiscation of property, requisitioning, interdictions to practice certain professions, limitations of rights, numerus clausus."

"What is that, Baba?"

"A cap on the number of Jewish students accepted in each school."

There was a lump in my throat. My parents, even Mother, had tried so hard to protect us from the truth, and now Baba was articulating the fear we all felt. There were rumors coming from Germany, at once incomprehensible and terrifying, that Jewish families were being made to leave their homes and forced to congregate in giant prisons.

"What will we do, Baba?" Gustave asked.

"Our most immediate risk is to be dispossessed. This is why I took these financial precautions. As for the rest, I do have plans, but it's too soon to share them with you children." I thought of our friends in Paris. Most of them had dismissed my father as crazy and had no exit strategy. Now I felt grateful for his strength, for the fact that he had a plan at all. "For the time being, remember that a thinking mind is better than a reactive mind," he added.

"Also," Mother said pragmatically, "know that nothing in the newspaper can be trusted from now on. It will be nothing but propaganda; you can be assured of it. That's how it was during the Great War."

****

The French put their faith in the counsel of the old generals who had triumphed in the Great War twenty years prior. What else could we do? To think otherwise would have led to despair. But those old generals, glorious and experienced as they were, could not imagine modern warfare any more than we could. We understood war as it had been in the past: that young men would get foot rot in trenches, that there would be air raids with nights spent in cellars, that there would be pride, patriotism, and, eventually, victory. We were ignorant of modern warfare and unprepared for it. We could not imagine submarines and tanks, the atoms bombs. The few who felt that France was unprepared and anticipated defeat, my father included, still couldn't predict a war without trenches, a war fought for ideology. No one predicted genocide. But all this would come later. For now, there was only clinging to our patriotism and our belief in the powers that be.

For the next eight months, we waited.

There was little military action on French territory, no bombing, no attacks. The people of France did not quite know what to make of it. People began to wonder if perhaps they had worried unnecessarily. Perhaps, they thought, Germany was intimidated by our power and deterred by the Maginot Line. Over those eight months, the French population settled into the new normalcy of the Drôle de Guerre. In this 'phony war,' most everyone in France began to relax. When they ran out of funds, or out of fear, those who had left the larger cities returned. In the end, the place where people want to be is home. It doesn't matter where home is: it is the notion of home, of one's personal things on shelves, of being sheltered under a familiar roof that gives people the illusion of safety. But my father did not relax. He showed no sign of wanting to return to Paris.

In the South of France, temperatures dropped over the winter months. We had not thought of bringing our winter clothes. There were restrictions already, on fuel, on fabric, and Baba mandated that we be more prudent with money. This did not sit so well with me, as it coincided with a time in my life when I wanted to be pretty and meet boys. The inactivity and the waiting were hard on the nerves for everyone. I walked alone around country roads I knew by heart and spent hours reading by the chimney fire, feeling afraid and cold. Anxiety was the only emotion. The only pastime was waiting.

Maybe because we had no control over the world around us, my mother and I engaged in a constant tug of war. She seemed to want to pull me back into childhood, while I pulled to come out of it. She wanted me in smock dresses, Mary Jane shoes, and white socks. I dreamed of nylon stockings and A-shaped skirts. I read *Marie Claire* and *Vogue* magazines, gorged on espionage novels, and the minute my parents were out of the house I'd make a beeline for Mother's makeup, heels, and cigarettes. I discovered in myself a great appetite for disobedience.

Soon enough, Mother's patience with the South of France grew thin. She begged Baba to leave Cannes, and I agreed with her wholeheartedly. Why could we not return home to Paris? Nothing was happening, and it drove us mad.

One late October day at dinner, my father tried to appear casual as he explained that he would be doing business in Nice for a week or so. There was excitement on his face, but that was all he would say. But when the week turned into a month of him going to Nice every day, and often spending the night there, I heard my mother accuse him of seeing another woman. My father insisted that he was only tending to business. "What kind of business has you coming home in the middle of the night reeking of cigarettes and wine?" she asked.

"I neither smoke nor drink as you well know, Lucienne."

"Then why then do I smell it on your clothes?"

"Do you smell women's perfume?" my father asked. "No, you do not. That is because I am not around women."

"Then tell me what it is you do! And please tell me you are doing nothing illegal."

"Of course not."

"Then what is it?"

"An old friend from my country is in town. I am helping him to get acclimated to France. He does not speak the language well."

"Are you helping him with money too?"

My father hesitated. "A little," he said.

"Why am I not surprised?" my mother shrieked. "And is this man the reason I must do without a driver? I scrimp so that you can spend our money on a stranger?"

"He is not a stranger to me," my father said.

"Why the secrecy then? Why not introduce him to me, take him to dinner with the family."

My father hesitated. "In time. For now, he has gone through a lot. He needs to rest."

"Is he troubled?" my mother asked.

"He is a very smart man, and I have faith in him." With this, my father left the room so fast that I barely had time to dart away from the door before he saw me spying.

As the months dragged on, I found myself wanting something to happen: war, violence, bombing, a Nazi invasion, anything to take me out of my torpor. And it wasn't just me being a silly girl. No one could bear the standoff, the terrible latent anguish. Action, of any kind, appeared less intolerable than this state of suspended animation. Perhaps, at a global level, as a nation, we had an intuition of the truth. And the truth was that this period of military standoff wasn't due to Germany's apathy, or German fear, but to the fact that the Germans were preparing how best to devastate us.

Soon it was March. We had been in Cannes for nearly a year, and it had been seven months of non-war when spring began to warm the hills. Spring in the South of France did not creep in slowly the way it did in Paris. It arrived in full fanfare, all the fruit trees bursting with blooms, the sun hot, the very nature of the air festive. For my father, the week of helping his friend had turned into two months, and his excitement must have waned because he now looked pained and preoccupied.

"Why can't we meet your friend," Gustave asked him one day.

"He is a troubled man, my son. He has suffered much and is haunted by too many demons. I am helping him the best I can, but some people are harder to help than others."

"What happened to him?" I asked.

"He is Armenian. Terrible things happened to the Armenian people where I come from."

"Armenian, like Sandra?" I thought of her burn scar and shivered.

"Yes," my father said, a shadow of sadness passing over his face.

"Why would bad things happen to Armenians? What did they do? Who wanted to hurt them?"

"Fanatics did."

"Was it about religion?"

"It was about fanaticism, which needs no other excuse or explanation."

"I don't understand," Gustave said.

"That is because you are a logical person. You want reasons for hatred to exist. You want to justify it in your mind. You want to know if it is about land, or race, or nationality, or politics, or past events, or even religion when, in fact, for the fanatics, butchering and torturing are their own purpose."

"How do people become fanatics?"

"Many are born that way. Just take away the rules that stop them, and it is like unleashing a wild beast."

"Is your friend hurt?" Gustave asked.

"Not physically," my father said. "But his wounds are deep."

"Can he get better?"

My father shook his head with profound sadness. "Once, I loved him like a brother, but he has been changed by his sufferings. Now there is too much violence in him."

"Has he turned into a fanatic?"

My father watched us. I could see in his expression that perhaps he understood something for the first time. "He might have," he said.

After our conversation, I found myself wishing that my father had a secret woman, someone who could comfort him. It pained me to think that he carried so much weight with no help at all from my mother.

In early April, a wealthy Parisian family moved into a nearby house, a quarter of a mile or so from ours. My parents never met the family, but I found myself crossing paths with their only son. He was twenty-two years old and quite attractive. His name was Patrice, and he kept appearing on his bicycle as I walked around the countryside. He had stark, pale-blond hair, smooth as a helmet, which he wore long and combed to one side so that it covered one eye. He dressed in the Zazou style: floppy pants, too long and rolled at the hem, and a plaid sports coat. My father had warned me of the shallowness that can come with good looks, but that wisdom had fallen on deaf ears. I began to stroll the countryside in my best outfits, hoping that sooner or later he would have to stop to speak to me, which did not take long.

"I'm terrifically bored here," he said, his slightly cruel mouth pursed in vague disgust. "But the paterfamilias wants to be here for a while until things settle."

"Aren't you old enough to enlist?"

"Father pulled strings," he said. "A heart murmur purchased at considerable cost from an accommodating physician."

We admitted that neither of us could wait to return to Paris.

"Are you at the university?" I asked.

He flipped his hair back and smiled. "I have done enough schooling for what I intend to do with my life."

"Which is?"

"To enjoy it."

He wasn't Jewish. I did not need to ask to be certain of it. Everything about him screamed Catholic privilege. His parents had wanted to keep a bigger distance between themselves and the German border and had the financial means to do so. Patrice did not ask me if I was Jewish. The question did not occur to him because asking me about myself did not occur to him.

In Paris, he told me, he spent his days recovering from his nights at underground jazz clubs where Negroes played swell tunes, and there was all this dancing, and the place was full of Americans who liked to have a swell time. He was partial to swell American beer. So, yes, he was vain. But in my sixteen-year-old eyes, he was just, well … swell. I knew about sex in some vague, theoretical way. I was innocent enough to think that boys' interests in me mirrored my interest in them: it was all very chaste, a game of seduction that culminated with love professed through written notes and the occasional heated kiss.

We continued to meet 'by accident' that week, and although his conversation was dull, we mostly were looking for hidden corners to kiss. One day he suggested a nighttime rendezvous. It was my idea that we meet in our property's vineyard at midnight. That night, I crept out of my room, after Mother and Baba had gone to bed, and set out. I had put makeup on, and perfume, and my best skirt. He arrived on his bicycle. He had brought wine and a wool blanket, which we laid on the dirt just below the grapevines. It was chilly and the moon cast long shadows in the strange darkness. Silly cow that I was, I thought it was romantic. I did not know much about the risks. I did not know that men could turn to beasts. Oh, it was sweet enough at first. One kiss led to the next, and soon he was overheated and rough. I told him to stop. I told him to back off and that he was hurting me. He did not stop.

By the time I understood what was happening, I yelled and raged for him to stop; I tried to shout, but he pressed his hand on my mouth. I bit his palm as hard as I could and tasted blood. I felt a roughness between my legs, and then an acute pain that felt as though it were breaking me in half. I turned my face, freed my mouth, and bit again. I spat in his face. But already he was pulling away.

He came off me, and I curled upon myself, reached around, struggled to gather my torn panties. An immediate sense of shame overpowered every other emotion. Whatever had just happened to me, I already sensed that no one should ever find out about it.

He was up on his feet above me, pulling his pants up.

At that moment, a silhouette emerged from between the rows of trees. It was Gustave. Had he heard us? Had he seen us? My brother was younger than I, but his time in boarding school must have informed him that something was awry. He was only a few feet away. I was still on the ground. Gustave said nothing, threw a rock at Patrice, and, in the dark, missed him. Patrice faced him menacingly. Gustave turned on his heels and began to run toward the house. Patrice started after him but his pants were still unbuttoned, and it was dark, and the ground was uneven. Patrice made three steps; his arms flailed, and he fell flat on his stomach with a thump. He let out a muffled shout and sat up, cursing. I was up on my feet now, my shame replaced by immense fury. I grabbed a large rock at my feet. Not feeling its weight, I raised it above my head and threw it hard at Patrice's face. It made a terrible sound. He screamed in pain and was knocked unconscious. I saw blackness spread on his face in the moonlight. Blood. His nose was smashed flat against his face. Had I killed him? I didn't know. I was drunk with rage, and at that moment, I truly hoped that I had.

I hobbled back home, unable to fully comprehend what had just happened to my body. In silence, I searched the sleeping house for Gustave, my blood laced with adrenaline, the sound of my pulse pounding in my head. All I knew was that Gustave was going to tell on me, and he needed to be stopped. Mother would send me to a convent in the mountains or a home for lost girls. But mostly I thought about my father. He would never again see me as his princess. Whatever I had just become through this terrible act, I was not sure, but I knew it to be something vile and shameful.

When I found Gustave in the dark hallway, Sandra was behind him. What particular kindness or calculation prevented Gustave from telling Mother and alerting Sandra instead? Did he believe, as I did, the offense unforgivable? He disappeared into his room as Sandra wordlessly took my arm and guided me to the bathroom at the farthest end of the house where my parents could not hear us.

In the bathroom, Sandra turned on the light, a look of anguish on her face. "A boy touched you?" she whispered as soon as I entered. "Did he hurt you?"

"Leave me alone!" I whispered back, furious.

"Did he hurt you?" she pressed, caressing my cheek. "Are you hurt anywhere?"

"What kinds of filthy lies did Gustave tell you?" I said. Sandra looked into my eyes and caressed my hair. Something in my chest burst open. I began to sob, and for a while, I could not stop. "Something happened," I told her at last. "The boy. He did something to me." I looked down at my body. "Down there."

She looked at me with profound sadness. "You will wash," she said. "And then you will drink something I will make for you. And then you will sleep and forget what this boy did."

"I don't even know what happened," I wept. "We were kissing and … we were only kissing…."

She searched deep down into my soul with her melancholy eyes. "You promise me. You forget this boy. All that he did to you."

Sandra helped me wash. She brought me a glass of an awful black concoction, some remedy from the old country, or what have you. She said nothing other than, "This will stop babies from coming." No lectures, admonition, or judgment, bless her heart.

The following day was April 9, 1940. I had slept fretfully, waking up a dozen times, each time to be reminded of what had happened. And in the morning, I had a new anguish: what if Patrice was dead? What would become of me if they found out I had killed him? Would I be made to confess to what he had done to me? I came down to the breakfast table, where my father and mother were reading the paper. "Are you quite all right, my lovely," my father asked. "Sandra said you were ill last night?"

"Food poisoning, I think," I muttered.

Mother lifted her eyes from the newspaper. "I hope it wasn't that dessert she made. We all had it." "She" and "her" were how my mother referred to Sandra. Ever since we arrived in Cannes, Mother was determined not to call her by her name.

Gustave pretended I was not in the room. He had his ear close to the radio as he adjusted the antenna and turned knobs to hear more clearly the news bulletins on Radio Sud-Ouest.

"How horrific," Mother said, reading from the local pages. "Madame Malou said that there was a brutal attack in the neighborhood last night. A young man was savagely assaulted less than a mile from our house." Gustave and I didn't look at each other as our mother went on. Gustave resumed his position, ear glued to the radio, fiddling with the knobs. "Two men attacked him, she said. They hit him with rocks, and bit him."

My father raised an eyebrow. "Beat him?" he asked.

"Bit him," Mother said, gnashing her teeth to demonstrate.

My father laughed. "Are you sure his vicious attacker wasn't a squirrel?"

"Children, stay near the house until they catch these men. Speaking of men," my mother continued, "what about that purported friend of yours, the one draining our resources?"

"Don't concern yourself with this," my father said. His good mood was gone.

"I know you see yourself as the defender of the orphan and the oppressed. First her, and now him. I'm only surprised you haven't moved him in to live with us as well."

"Let's not discuss this now," my father said.

"As if there isn't enough unknown in our life as it is," my mother said. "And of all places, why must we go there?"

I perked up, curious. "Go where?" I asked.

"Not now, Lucienne, please," my father said.

"Shhh, everybody" Gustave said. "They're saying something on the radio."

"You cannot insist on dictating what I can and cannot tell my friends," Mother told Father.

"Tell them what?" I asked.

"Shh!" Gustave commanded.

My mother switched gears, pointing to Gustave. "And besides, you are neglecting your son."

My father gazed up from his newspaper in disbelief. Although it was true that my father's visits to his friend resulted in him all but stopping his outings with Gustave, my mother's concern was entirely self-serving.

This is when we all saw Gustave rise from his position near the radio and look at us, all the color drained from his face.

"What is it?" Mother asked.

"The Germans attacked Denmark and Norway."

"The th … what? Gustave, darling, this is impossible," Mother said. "These countries are neutral."

"Denmark has already surrendered," Gustave said in a hollow voice. "within six hours of the attack."

The telephone began to ring, and we knew this was true.

To me, that morning remained engraved in my memory as the turning point for the rest of our lives. I will never know if my father had lied about having a friend he was helping in Nice. Perhaps it was all a cover for everything else he and Moshe were doing at that time and which I only found out about after the war.

From that point on, things went fast. Throughout April we anxiously followed the naval combats between the British and the Germans, our hopes soaring and plunging with news of the fighting. We attended a Passover service in the Grande Synagogue de Nice. I think we went to get a sense of what people in the community were saying. They seemed mostly concerned about friends and relatives in other parts of Europe. They felt safe in France. I heard that years later, in 1943, local French people had rounded up Jewish families in that very synagogue before they deported them.

In early May, the Germans attacked the Netherlands, Belgium, and Luxembourg.

A few days later, my father announced that we would be spending the night on our boat. We had done this before, so it was not particularly unusual. The house was being fumigated, and Mother and Sandra were coming as well, he informed us. That should have triggered suspicion as it was unlike my mother to spend the night on a boat when the Hotel Miramar was only a stone's throw away. Also, I had seen no sign of bugs.

After dinner, we drove down to the dock. Sandra brought a large basket of food, which also was unusual. Why not eat at a restaurant near the pier or anywhere on the Croisette? On the drive, Mother and Baba were tense, but again, I did not think much of it, as used to their fights as I was.

The boat was safely moored in the Bay of Cannes, among hundreds of others. We climbed into our respective bunks for the night. Gustave and I bunked in one cabin with Sandra. Our parents were in the other cabin.

I fell asleep quickly. I had a scary dream. Gustave's toy tanks were coming up our driveway in procession, but as they got closer, they turned out to be massive Nazi tanks, so loud that the ground shook, and the house began to crumble. I woke up in a fright, my heart pounding. The noise was real. The boat's engine was on. In fact, we were moving. Why would that be? This was the middle of the night? Why would we be leaving the dock? I leaned down. Gustave was sound asleep in the bunk below, but Sandra wasn't in the cabin. I slipped a warm sweater over my nightgown and walked up on deck. I looked for city lights, but it was pitch black. We were nowhere near the pier. I don't know how long we had been at sea. I turned around and saw Mother and Sandra. They were fully dressed. They were holding lanterns and had life jackets on. Their faces were strained. "What's the matter?" I said. "Why are we at sea?"

My mother handed me a lantern. "Wake your brother and the two of you get dressed."

That's when I saw our luggage neatly stacked on the deck. All the suitcases and hat boxes we had brought with us from Paris had miraculously materialized on the boat. How had Sandra packed all this without my seeing anything? My heart began beating faster. "What are we doing? Why would the boat—"

"Not right now, Marceline. Do as I say."

"But, Mother—"

"Go!"

I ran down the metal steps and shone the lantern in Gustave's eyes. "Wake up, Gustave; you're missing everything," I said.

"Are we sinking?" he asked through his yawn.

"Probably."

We dressed in a hurry and came up on deck. Sandra, inscrutable, fitted us with life jackets. We saw that my father was absorbed in piloting the boat, going from his compass to his map. He did not even look at us.

"Mother, are we really sinking?" Gustave asked.

"We're not sinking," I said, exhilarated. "We're going somewhere!"

My mother opened her mouth to speak. Words had trouble getting out. "Your father believes it's best to leave France. Immediately."

Leave I could understand, but leave France? "Where are we going?"

"I, um, we shall tell you later. Now please, be quiet. This is stressful enough without a barrage of questions."

I gave Sandra an interrogative look, but her face registered nothing I could read.

"Maybe we're going to Italy," I whispered to Gustave. "Or Spain."

"The boat doesn't carry enough fuel to go that far," he said. "Corsica or Sardinia maybe."

Gustave and I sat on the deck in our life jackets and waited. The night was moonless, and the sea flat as oil. Above us, the number of stars was dizzying, and I had a vertiginous sense of how insignificant we were. After about an hour, Baba abruptly stopped the engine. We were plunged into an immense silence. "Turn off the lanterns," my father ordered. We did. With the remaining one, he began signaling in a rhythmic pattern. Soon across the sea appeared a light that shone intermittently. "They're here," he said. Mother and Sandra sighed in relief.

Ten minutes later, we heard the approaching flapping sound of oars scooping water. Baba shone his light on two wooden dinghies, which were heading toward us. In them, two strange-looking men in turbans and loose white shirts rowed silently. The dinghies touched our boat. My father threw down ropes, then the ladder.

"All three of you go on the larger dinghy," my father said. "First you, Gustave, then Marceline, and then Lucienne."

"Goodness gracious, those things are flimsy! How are you expecting me to do this, Alban?" my mother said. She sounded terrified.

"Come down the steps and climb on board."

"I'll go first," Gustave said.

Gustave easily descended the short ladder and climbed aboard the dinghy. I came down the thin ladder. The dinghy moved quite a bit as I came on board. The man in the turban offered me his hand, and I tightened my grip on his as I made my way to the back. When came my mother's turn, she looked down at the ladder and recoiled. After a while, she did manage to put her legs overboard and her feet on the ladder, but then she froze. She lifted her foot off the ladder, dipped it one inch down, and promptly put it back on the ladder as though she had just been bitten by an invisible creature. The man with the turban tried to help her but seemed hesitant to grab hold of her.

"Mother, come down already," I called from below.

"It's easy. It's only a few steps down," Gustave said.

"Alban!" she whimpered. "Alban, I'm afraid I shall not be able to do this!"

"You can do it," my father said. "Just put one foot below the other, and the man will set it in the right place on the ladder; just don't look down."

"I don't want this stranger's hand on my foot. What if he pulls me?"

But the man seemed just as unwilling to touch her foot as she was to give it to him. She managed to go down two steps, but the boat swayed, and she went right back up the ladder.

"Mother!" I urged her. "Just come on down. It took me seconds."

"I shall not make it," she said, near hysterics.

The men in their turbans sat in each boat, their faces masks of forbearance. I looked up at Gustave and saw that he was trying not to laugh.

Baba realized he needed to change tactics. He came down the ladder, and from below guided her down by gently moving her feet on each step. "Come on down, Lucienne. That's good. One more, just bring your other foot down. No, Lucienne, not up, no, no, down, that's right, good ... almost there, that's it."

"I'll fall," she wailed.

"If you fall, I'll catch you."

Hearing those words, our mother inexplicably let go of the ladder, flailed her arms, and fell backward, down onto Father. Both of them collapsed to the bottom of the dinghy, Baba mashed under, and Mother sitting confusedly on top of him. Looking down from our boat, Sandra covered her mouth to hide her smile. Despite the tension of the moment, Gustave and I began laughing, and we were powerless to stop.

Baba extricated himself from under Mother and came back up the ladder and onto the boat. The rest proceeded without further trouble. My father went back up. The suitcases were lowered into the dinghy, and then he and Sandra came down and sat together in the second dinghy.

"Are we leaving our boat in the middle of the sea?" Gustave asked. "Isn't it too deep to anchor? Won't it drift?"

"Shh," my father said.

The turbaned men secured our luggage and began rowing effortlessly on the flat sea. There was no wind and only the sounds of oars touching the water. We moved, guided by the dim light of a structure in the distance. Next to me, my mother trembled violently.

To find oneself on a small floating device in the middle of the sea, imagining the depth below, was terrifying. We were alone with infinite blackness above and infinite blackness below. When the dinghy holding my father and Sandra moved ahead of ours and we could no longer see them, Mother sobbed helplessly.

Minutes later, we were beside the metal hull of a large vessel. It was a large commercial fishing boat, rusty and slick with grime. We had to climb a ladder at least fifteen feet up. Thankfully, Mother was able to go up better than she had fared going down.

The boat stank of fish and unwashed men. My mother, usually the picture of strength, now looked as vulnerable as a small girl. Sandra put her arm around Gustave. I tried to ignore the looks of the dark men on board. A man came out and spoke to my father in an unknown, guttural language. To my amazement, my father answered in the same language, a language I had never heard him speak before. The two spoke in low tones for a few minutes. My father was handed a pistol. Without so much as looking at it, he casually slipped the weapon into his belt.

Two of the men returned to one of the dinghies and headed out toward our boat, which could not have been more than a few hundred yards away, but that we could not see in the deep night. "What are they doing?" Gustave whispered. There was light on our boat, and then a brighter light. He understood before I did. "Holy mackerel," he said.

In a matter of minutes, our boat was in flames. As soon as the two men returned, the fishing boat started its engine and cut through the water away from our boat. The blaze, close at first, diminished into the distance until it disappeared from our sight.

It's not that I wasn't afraid. I was. But along with the fear came a new form of exhilaration. I knew then that it was my first time feeling truly alive. By alive, I mean that there was no thinking, and worrying, and being self-conscious. There was no past, and there was no future. There was only action, instinct, my racing pulse. While Mother, Sandra, and Gustave were understandably petrified with fright, I felt ready to jump up and grab one of those pistols and shoot at any pirate or anyone who would be mad enough to stand in our way.

We spent the next three days hidden on board the fishing boat. There we learned of our parents' plan as the mysterious boat took us away and we sat, all five us in a cramped cabin, on terrible mats set on metal bunks. "We're heading for North Africa," my father explained. "We are going to be living in Algeria. Everything there is arranged for our arrival."

"But why did we leave in the middle of the night?" Gustave asked.

"Because there is nothing to lose by being prudent. If the Germans do invade France—"

"Which is unlikely," my mother interrupted, but I could tell she was only trying to convince herself.

"And in case they start to detain foreign Jews, as this has happened elsewhere, I feel it is better not to leave a trail. And so, we will have false papers in Algeria, a new identity. New names."

"Is that why you bought the boat and learned to pilot it all those months ago, Baba," Gustave asked. "Did you already know we would do this?"

My father nodded, "Yes."

Inside the fishing boat's cabin, things creaked and clanged from every direction. The rocking of the sea compelled us to hold on to the cots and walls. The news that we would live under a false identity in a strange country swept through me like a shockwave of confusion, dread, and something resembling excitement. You have to understand that up until that moment war had been theoretical and vague to me. There had been words in newspapers and on the radio, gleaned fragments of conversations. We had no capacity to measure it against anything known to us. To Gustave, war was strategy. War was play. To me, it was an unpleasant state of affairs I carefully avoided thinking about. And for neither of us did there seem to be direct implications for our family. Sure, we had left Paris to humor my father, but this was something else entirely. We were fleeing. We were in danger. "This is an industrial fishing boat," my father said. "It is monitored by the authorities. It has to do its work and bring its catch to port, so as not to raise suspicion. These men will fish, and we will wait until they are done, at which point they will take us to Algiers. We'll arrive early in the morning so that there won't be too many people in the streets."

"Where will we live?" I asked.

"In an apartment Uncle Moshe found for us," my father said.

An apartment in Algiers. The word apartment sounded like an adventure in itself. I had no frame of reference. My father could have just as well suggested a yurt in the plains of China.

"What about the new name? What are we supposed to call each other?" Gustave asked.

"The thing is, children," my father said, "we want to make it harder for authorities to find us, should the authorities be … German. And so we won't let anyone know where we are going. We will stop all communication with anyone we know in Paris or the South of France."

"No letters to friends?" I asked, astonished. "No calling people on the telephone? Won't they wonder where we went?"

"It needs to remain an absolute secret for the time being."

"What if they think us dead?"

"That is a risk your father is more than willing to take," Mother said bitterly. "Since he hates all my friends."

"I do not hate them, but neither do I trust them," my father said.

"But, Baba," Gustave pointed out, "Algeria is still part of France. If you're worried about the Germans winning the war, would they not rule Algeria, too?"

"Indeed, Gustave, but although Algeria is French territory, the Germans are quite a bit farther away. It buys us time and distance."

"Why did you and Moshe choose Algeria, Baba?" I asked.

"Because it is open to the entire continent of Africa. And we know people there."

"What kind of people?"

"Friends of Moshe," my father said. "From this point forward, you must remember only to trust Jews. And even then, not all Jews. Moshe will give us our identity papers when we arrive. We will keep our first name but will use a different last name."

"But even if Germany wins the war, things will return to normal at some point, won't they, Baba?" Gustave asked. "We won the Great War, and we did not make the Germans abandon their language and start speaking French."

My father looked at him gravely. "The world has gone mad, my son, and it is getting worse. Even reasonable people are speaking nonsense. You've seen anti-Semitism, how it took hold in France. The more insane the hatred and the accusations, the more willing people are to embrace them. I saw this happen in my country as well. I have seen with my own eyes madness taking hold in the hearts of men. I am not worried about the kind of war fought between soldiers. Those are the wars of history books, which speak in numbers and offensives, as though war is fought by masses that move as one without feelings. In actuality, war is about the suffering of individuals. You are my family, and I will do everything to protect you. In this war, there will only be us. We will be the only people who matter."

"But we can't very well run away indefinitely," my mother said weepily.

"If what we must do to get away from the Nazis is to circle the globe one hundred times, that is what I plan to do," Baba responded.

I felt as though I were seeing my father for the first time. My soft-spoken father was, in fact, a man who plotted and planned, a man able to orchestrate secret missions to save his family. He was in his element on this strange boat, among these scary men, speaking their mysterious language. And Mother, the dragon that she usually was, was listening to him, expecting him to have answers. My purportedly meek father was decisive and assertive, while the pompous loudmouths who had disparaged him in Paris scrambled. It was the most exciting event of my life, and my father was at the center of it.

We stayed at sea for two whole days while the men caught fish. None of us could get much sleep on those metal bunks covered with dirty burlap mattresses. Sandra's basket of food did not last, and we were fed inedible things. The latrine was impossible to stomach. My father discouraged us from going up on deck unless it was nighttime. By the second day, we reeked of fish and were desperate for a bath and a decent bed. Making things worse for them, Mother, Sandra, and Gustave were seasick. By the second day, they had a hollowed and exhausted look in their eyes. Sandra and Gustave were stoic about it, but my mother was at her wit's end.

I was the opposite. Although I did not sleep or eat much either, I felt vibrant with energy.

In the early morning of the third day, we crept up on deck to glimpse the strange new land ahead of us. The dawn was barely breaking over a white city that appeared to climb the flank of a mountain. As our fishing boat neared the bay, it was daybreak, and the sun peeked slightly over the mountain, its rays reflecting against the minarets of many mosques. At the top of the hill, overlooking the Bay of Algiers, was what I later learned was the beautiful Basilique Notre-Dame d'Afrique, which to my Parisian eyes resembled the Sacré Coeur. Below the city, the vast bay was breathtaking. My father turned to Sandra and said a few words to her in Armenian. Sandra nodded, her eyes flooded with tears.

"What is it, Baba?"

"This looks like the Bay of Smyrna. Before the fire. That was our land."

"Where Sandra got her burn, and your arm was hurt?" Gustave said.

"Yes," my father said darkly. "It is said that over three hundred thousand people perished in the flames."

"You and Sandra were the lucky ones then?"

My father nodded. "Indeed, we were."

****

Marceline took a sip of her hot chocolate. It had turned cold. She called the waitress and asked her for a fresh pot. "For the better and for the worse, Africa changed my life," Marceline told Cassandra. Inexplicably, her eyes clouded with tears, and she lowered her gaze, hoping her niece had not noticed. This was such an infuriating aspect of old age: one could forget essential things, but emotions one spent a lifetime keeping at bay could helplessly resurface without warning.

"Perhaps this is a good time to stop," she said. "Maurice will be here momentarily, and I'm feeling a bit wan." This was not the truth. She did not feel tired or weak but profoundly overwhelmed. Now she would have to tell Cassandra about Algiers. About Fernand. About Khaled. About all the events that had precipitated the terrible things that had driven her and Gustave apart.

"How did you recover from the assault?" Cassandra asked.

"The assault?"

"That boy," Cassandra said. "The one in the orchard."

Marceline waved away the question. "There is no point in raging and lamenting about it. What would dwelling on it accomplish?"

"I don't know how people recover from those sorts of things."

"One just does."

"It's that simple?"

The waitress arrived with the fresh pot of hot chocolate and poured the thick liquid into their cups. The rich, velvety aroma rose to their nostrils. Marceline waited for the waitress to leave and asked Cassandra. "Why does it sound as though you are not angry at the rapist, but at me, the victim, for not appearing to suffer enough?"

"Oh no, absolutely not but—"

"Women get on because they have to. Name a woman who was not violated in one form or another."

"I wasn't," Cassie said.

"Perhaps you think that you did something right? That you deserved not to be? Or perhaps you believe that you've earned the right to a peaceful, predictable life? Well, that isn't the case, my dear. You had the good fortune not to cross paths with a predator; that is all."

"I was only saying that you've earned the right to feel sorry for yourself."

"All that does is rob people of their strength." She looked at Cassandra, who appeared distraught. She looked at the doorway. "Maurice is here," she said. "I guess this means nap time for me."

Cassie did not hide her disappointment. "You need to leave? I really was hoping to learn what happened to your family."

"This is *your* family, in fact," Marceline pointed out. "Your ancestors. Your bloodline." Marceline looked at Cassandra. "I have an idea," she said. "Maybe it's time for me to write that memoir, you know. So many good stories, and my fair share of horrible ones."

"Oh, you should definitely do it," Cassie said enthusiastically.

"Perhaps I am too old," Marceline said, shaking her head with apparent discouragement.

"There is really nothing to it. Set an hour every day," Cassandra assured her. "Step by step and day by day. Writing is more about being consistent than anything else."

Marceline marveled briefly at her niece's innocence. "Alas, my eyes and fingers are weak," she said. "Books used to be my greatest joy. Now I must hold a magnifying glass to the page, which is tiresome. My fingers betray me when it comes to turning pages, let alone hold a pen."

"I can see how that would be difficult," Cassie said.

"So, you'll do it then?" Marceline said.

"Do what?"

"Write it down."

"What?"

Marceline rolled her eyes with impatience. "Well, my memoir, evidently."

"But I don't … I … I mean I'm only in Paris for another week…."

"And so?"

"I don't think you realize, but it would be a momentous undertaking."

"Bah! I tell you the gist of it, you jot it down and find the right words later when you're back in America. How hard can it be? Be consistent is all. You're a writer. Isn't that what writers do?" She sensed that Cassandra was about to try and explain the months, if not years, of work this would entail. But for some reason, Cassie decided not to. Instead, she sighed heavily and shrugged. "Don't you own one of those nifty portable typing machines people have?" Marceline asked.

"A laptop?"

"That's it."

"Mine's in repair."

"So, that's a yes! Wonderful."

"But I …," Cassandra protested feebly.

Maurice was beside them now, helping Marceline out of her chair. How infuriating it was to require help for the slightest things. She pointed to the notepad. "You stay and write down what we just talked about while it's still fresh in your mind. I don't want you forgetting things. You really ought to have recorded our conversation. That would have been the professional thing to do."

"But I – you only asked me today," Cassandra objected. Marceline concealed her smile. What an excellent idea. A memoir. Why had she not thought of it earlier? And now she had the perfect person to do it. "It's settled then. Meet me at the Fontaine Médicis at eight in the morning. Do you know where it is?"

"Inside the Jardin du Luxembourg."

"Correct. You will be punctual, I hope?"

"To a fault."

Marceline gripped Maurice's arm and left Cassie, the tearoom, and the bill without looking back.

CHAPTER 6

A Menagerie

Cassie settled back into her chair. On either side of her, French women, young and old, sipped tea. Marceline had expressed real tenderness toward Gustave. They had both grown up under the menace of war and the looming shadow of the Holocaust, but it seemed like Marceline had enough empathy to paint a clear picture of her dad's unique hardship. Sent away to boarding school because he was conspicuously Jewish, he must have felt rejected by his family and loathed by all of Europe. Cassie could detect in Marceline's account of those years the seeds of resentment, but nothing that could explain a mutual hatred followed by a complete rupture. Something must have occurred. Something ugly.

She ordered a coke and wrote furiously everything she could remember about what Marceline had told her. Three hours later, she put her pen down. Le Valentin was almost empty except for a table with four elderly ladies who giggled like schoolgirls. One of them said something that, if she heard it correctly, included the word penis, and they guffawed.

It was too late for visiting hours now, which conveniently postponed the fight that awaited her at the hospital. She'd have to call Sabine for news.

She left Le Valentin and walked around the covered passage. There were antique booksellers, merchants of old posters and records. How could such a place make money long enough to justify its existence, Cassie wondered? In the United States, a prime retail location such as this one would have been filled with Jamba Juices and nail salons. She stopped in front of a collectible postcards shop, and after a moment, she entered. The place had the mildewed scent of old papers. A man with a Cossack mustache and black sweater vest was sitting behind a counter, looking down at a series of old documents with a magnifying glass. Behind him were rows of wooden shelves, carefully numbered. He lifted his face, in all appearance, none too pleased to have to deal with a customer.

"Do you have anything from the South of France?" she asked.

After a brooding, awkward moment the man barked. "Time period?" She had again forgotten to say bonjour.

"Late 1930s. Before World War II," she said, and hurried to add, "s'il vous plaît, Monsieur."

Grumbling but somewhat pacified, the man got up and pushed a stool up to the shelving. He climbed, reached above him on one of the shelves, and pulled out a box which he placed on the counter in front of her. "Merci!" she trumpeted.

She foraged through the box. The Riviera that Marceline had described came to life between Cassie's fingers, on yellowing postcards heavily stamped: Hôtel Le Negresco, Hôtel Carlton, men and women at the terraces of cafés, smiling for the photographer, palm trees and long antique cars, and little children knee-deep in seawater. She dug through the box, which was well organized by cities and dates: Cannes, Juan Les Pins, Saint-Jean-Cap-Ferrat. This was such a finite number of postcards; thirty of them in the stack she was going through, maybe forty. Was that all that was left of that era? In the future, there would be an infinity of images, now that everyone was a photographer, so many in fact as to render them meaningless. Or perhaps it was the opposite. The pictures we took nowadays were on hard drives that could self-destruct in an instant, as her experience with her cell phone and laptop had proved. But no, she reasoned, digital photos could be recovered. Most were safely stored in The Cloud. The Cloud, whatever that meant. But what if The Cloud was as tenuous as its namesake? An illusion. A delusion, more likely. A single fiber-optic glitch, a satellite hack, and all might vanish in an instant: recordings of and by an entire era of humanity, gone poof! into thin air. Come to think of it, digital photos had even less physical substance than thin air. What were they even made of? Neutrons, atoms, Higgs Bosons particles? She stared at a postcard of three women on a beach in hats and bathing suits, showing some skin and looking playfully at the camera. "How much for that one?" she asked.

"Twenty-five euros."

"Twenty-five euros? For an old postcard?"

"Twenty-five euros for a one-of-a-kind remnant of history, Madame," the shopkeeper answered glacially.

She bought the postcard and left the shop. She walked past more shops selling antique postcards, stamps, posters, and books. She realized that she was thinking about her father. Her father as a small boy. Her father as a young man. Her understanding of him was shifting so rapidly that even her memories seemed altered by what she had learned: her feeling of closeness to him in childhood as well as her sense that he had drifted away from her emotionally as she got older. Her subsequent disappointment and eventual resentment could not be reassessed fast enough. Already, she was losing her old notions of him and would never recover them, which was maybe a positive thing. But in a way, the more she found out about her dad, the more elusive he became. She starved for the real him, but the closer she got to the story, the more secretive she realized he had been, the less she felt she knew him. She longed for her father, for his truth, his voice, his emotion, for a window into the depth and hurt she suspected in him but that he never expressed. What trauma, what pain turned a child into a man so closed-up and protected, so unwilling to tell his story? What made a man turn away from his own sister, his own mother and father? This morning, at her parent's apartment, when she had suggested his past experiences might not have been digested, what she had meant to intimate was the possibility that pathos had affected his relationships. Specifically, his relationship to her. What made a man turn away from his own daughter?

Growing up, she had stuck out like a sore thumb, always. She had been talkative, opinionated, even as she tried to be perfect to gain his approval. Was her craving for his attention a particular turn-off? Her father had called her a know-it-all, a motormouth. He had told her she should not be so bossy, pushy. He had called her *harsh*. Over time, she had learned to smother her exuberant self into something more acceptable, something more lovable. Keeping that bubbly part of her alive had ultimately not felt worth the risk. Adapt, accommodate, or die.

Marceline was *harsh* too. She was bossy to a nearly military level. She was intimidating even in old age. Cassie did everything she could to appear unintimidating. She wanted to be perceived as nice, as accommodating. And if she wasn't feeling so nice or accommodating, she tried to hide it as though it was something shameful. Her anger eventually came out the other end, and she would end up blowing up at the wrong time and making a mess of things.

She headed back to the hotel to face the inevitable. The date or non-date, with Hervé. She would explain to him that she lived in another country. She'd make that clear from the moment he picked her up.

Her stomach churned with anxiety on her way to the métro station as she hurried past the Galeries Lafayette. What would Marceline do, she wondered? Young, fearless Marceline of 1942 seemed no more a slave to convention than old Marceline was. Young Marceline would welcome the adventure in every sense of the word. Young Marceline would say not a single peep about living in another country, and she would most definitely have bought that purple bra.

****

Cassie stepped down from Hervé's motorcycle, steadied her legs, and removed her helmet.

"Your hair is fluffy," Hervé observed.

"Pure music to a woman's ears," she said, loosening the wool scarf he had lent her.

He peered at her. "Are you all right? You're a little green."

"This was my first time on a motorcycle."

"Vraiment? Did you like it?"

"Is hanging on while shutting your eyes the same thing as liking it?"

"I see," he said. "You must be one of those adrenaline junkies."

"Believe me, I have already reached my adrenaline quota for the week."

They had parked in a public garage. On their way up the street, Cassie groaned under her breath as they walked past walls covered with dozens of *Women in Black, Part Two* posters glued side by side. They walked a few more steps and emerged into the street. Outside, it was cold and humid and so quiet that it felt as though she were screaming her thoughts. I'm on a date! With a handsome man! I'm going to lose my lunch!

And there it was again, at the bus stop, a six-feet-tall incarnation, the title in giant red letters this time: *Women in Black, Part Two.* Hervé shook his head at the posters. "What *is* this crap?" he said.

"Beats me," she said.

They crossed the street, and now they were above the quays, facing the Seine. The sun was setting, giving an orange glow to the surrounding buildings. Hervé led her down the stairs and onto the quays. As they walked on the uneven cobblestone, the river's water was just a few feet below, grey and reflecting the orange hues of the sky. "Our reservation is in ten minutes," he said, taking her elbow gallantly. "So, tell me, what is the matter with you?" She looked at him interrogatively. He clarified: "the adrenaline?"

"Where to start. My week was traumatic," she said. "I moved into a crappy hotel thinking I had made a reservation at a much better one."

"It happens."

"To me, mostly. But it's for the best. I was supposed to stay at Hôtel de la Seine, but the people there were awful."

"Ah yes, a friend of mine works there, at the reception desk."

"The mean blonde who comes to the Jument?"

"She's only mean to people she doesn't know."

"Would that not be everyone finding themselves before a reception desk?"

"You have a point."

"People like her are the reason foreigners find French people rude, you know."

He seemed genuinely surprised by this. "Foreigners think French people are rude?"

"Americans do." Cassie had already walked into her own trap. She added, "Supposedly…."

"Americans should know," Hervé said. "They happen to be the world's authority on what is rude and what isn't."

"The hotel where I ended up turned out to be lovely. Once you've climbed the two hundred stairs, you're rewarded with the prettiest view of the Eiffel Tower."

"I'd love to see it."

Under his leather jacket, he wore a sweater that matched his eye color, lagoon blue. "Any time you want," she said glibly.

"Tonight?"

"Of course," she said and regretted that immediately.

"And so, the adrenaline?"

It was not that she intended to *mislead* him about where she lived, but she had this nebulous sense that if he had a shred of interest in her, she wanted to find out. At that moment, she did not feel like pushing him away with something as annoying as the truth. It was an overwhelming impulse not to rock the boat. So, she said nothing about her dad being hospitalized and told him instead how her father had only just admitted that he had a sister, how she had met her, and how she was only now discovering her father's past. "It turns out my grandfather was a Jew from Turkey who came to France after the first war and made quite a bit of money selling rugs. The crazy thing is, my father never told us anything about him, or about growing up wealthy, let alone Jewish. This is all brand new to me."

"When was your father born?"

"1925."

Hervé made a quick mental calculation. "Let see. He must have been fourteen when World War Two started. How did his family survive the Holocaust?"

Cassie felt a chill, a sense of dread. Why had this never gone through her mind? "They went to the South of France?" she said, involuntarily making her sentence sound like a question.

"How would that protect them? Jews were no safer in the free zone, especially after 1942 when Germany changed its mind and rolled their tanks right over it. At that point, the Jews of the South of France were rounded up and sent to death camps, just as terribly as anywhere else throughout most of Europe."

"Apparently, they were able to go to North Africa. I'll know more tomorrow. She's agreed to meet every day until I have the full story."

"It must be a pretty long story."

"She goes into details. And we have to cut it into chunks. She's very old."

"And you don't want to ask your dad, rather than get the information second-hand from his sister?"

Well, there *was* the coma thing. "He refuses to speak about it," she said, which was not a lie. "He went about his life without telling us a thing."

"What is he like?"

"Worked dutifully all his adult life, but not a day past retirement. He raised three daughters, kept the same wife."

"Is that all there is to say about him?"

"He's not a chatterbox, but he's a decent man. He doesn't have a big ego. He is quiet. He is nice enough to people." As she said this, she realized that this was actually true. And so, what sick point was there in her looking for anything else, especially now, if he had indeed survived the Holocaust? So what if he was not the warmest to her? A part of him was damaged or unresolved, that was all. How many people turned into a mess after far less than that? "I would think that he was intent on rebuilding and forgetting," she said. "He didn't dwell."

They arrived at the restaurant, which was at the level of the river. They were given a table that overlooked the Seine and Paris in the setting sun. They looked at the river in silence. There was music in the background, a woman's voice singing "Le Tourbillon de la Vie." The waiter came in, and they ordered each a glass of wine.

"So, what about you?" she asked.

"What about me?"

"For one, I have to ask how come you spend so much time at the Jument."

"I work close by, and I go there to cool off when I can't stand my job, which is increasingly often."

"You said the other day that your life was complicated?"

"I have recently ended a two-year relationship, yes."

"With a woman?" she asked.

He shrugged questioningly. "As opposed to what? A possum?" He looked at her. She quickly looked away. He scowled. "You don't think I'm gay, do you?"

She swallowed. "Do *I* think you're gay?"

"You obviously think I am," he said.

"Not at all. Absolutely not!"

He frowned. "Is that why you accepted to go out with me tonight?"

"Why would I accept to go out with you if I thought you were gay?" she said breezily. "Because it would feel *safer* or something?"

"Well. Good," he said, looking upset.

"You don't give out a gay vibe whatsoever."

"I knew I shouldn't have worn this stupid cologne."

"I assure you—"

"Okay, fine, fine."

"So, tell me about your work," she said, desperate to change the subject.

"I am not my job," he said glumly. "It does not define me, my dreams, or even my daily thoughts."

"Have I offended you twice in thirty seconds?"

"I'm a physician. Was. I made a few choices that cost me my license for five years."

"Such as?"

"Nothing I would not do again in a heartbeat. It's all very noble you see. I was on a mission for Doctors Without Borders and, well, I saw a need, a need for vaccines. But there was red tape. So, I took it upon myself to smuggle them into the country."

"Yikes."

"Another year and my license will be returned to me."

"What will you do then?"

"Probably get in trouble again."

"You're lucky they didn't put you in jail."

"Oh, but they did worse: they put me in charge. That was a pact with the devil if I ever heard of one. Now I work in administration. All I do is administrate. I don't like the people I work for, the people I work with, or the people I work around."

"Why not quit?"

"That is the irony. My marriage was ruined because my ex-wife resented the fact that I traveled too much. She begged me for years to take a position that would keep me in Paris. Apparently, she wanted an actual marriage, a man able to be a parent to our kids. I would have none of it. I needed to feel free, if you know what I mean. I do give her credit: she put up with my beautiful idealism for quite a long time. But in the end, she left. Met someone. The kids were still young enough that my taking a desk job ultimately was better for them. Interesting to note that I'm now the embodiment of the perfect man, with the type of desk job she always wanted me to have. But, you see, back then I could not be fenced in."

"And now?"

"Now I'm fenced in."

"It doesn't seem worth it, spending all those hours doing something you loathe."

"I've become quite philosophical about it. How about you, your writing work, do you like it?"

"I made my own pact with the devil. I work with my ex. We've been divorced for years. But yes, I like my work."

"You're both ghostwriters?"

She laughed. "Hard to explain, but let's say he's the writer and I'm the ghost. Well, I'm his 'editor' according to the divorce settlement. I guess it would be more accurate to say that I like *his* work. I'm good at it."

"Do the two of you get along?"

"We used to bicker like a couple, and now we bicker like a brother and sister."

"What kind of writing do you do?"

How could she tell him about the screenplays without telling him she was American, living in California? "Oh well, things here and there. That kind of stuff…." Just as she said this, a huge billboard of the movie floated by on a specially chartered péniche. When the studio decided to put its back into a promotional event, it was shameless. Nothing was off limits, not even the Seine River, not the sky, not the moon. "But work does not define who we are, does it?" she said, eager to bring this conversation to a close. "By the way, the Jument's patronne said you don't have a cell phone? Is that true?"

"You tried to call me? To cancel, I bet."

Was she going to insult him again? "Not at all," she said, bringing her list of lies to a stratospheric height. "So, why no cell phone?"

"Do you remember ever needing one before those were invented?"

"No, but—"

"Me neither. I have not felt the need to join in the madness since."

"How Zen of you. I've been feeling crazy in the head ever since mine broke."

"Of course, you do. Our society has an addiction to convenience. After a few days of pain and withdrawal, you might find that you get on better without one."

"I doubt that. No one can reach me; I can't reach anybody."

"Perfect. Technology shackles you, and now you are set free. Allow some time for re-insertion into sanity. But notice how freeing it is not to have to give everyone a minute-by-minute account of your whereabouts. Also, you no longer have to interrupt your train of thought constantly and substitute your thinking with theirs."

"Although it's nice to stay connected, don't you think?"

"What connection? Only sound bites. Noise. Faux relationships. Heavily curated faux experiences that slowly turn our species into subhumans."

"I guess I better not ask you how you feel about social media."

"Just the fact that those two words were put together without irony whatsoever should raise some red flag."

"All right. But cell phones aren't that bad. Of all the evils of society, cell phones don't top the list."

"Quite the opposite; evil is precisely what cell phones are. Evil in a sleek metal suit that fits into the palm of your hand. Nobody is where they are, you see. People might be with you in one spot, but they are also carrying on all kinds of emotional and intellectual relationships in another spot."

"Hmm ...," she said, unconvinced.

"Look, you're having an experience, you're at dinner with a very polite gentleman, and suddenly you get that buzz in your pocket, and it's your ghost husband telling you to pick up some ectoplasm on your way home. Now your mind and attention have been hijacked into being subjected to the caller's experience. And there is no running away."

"You can run away. Just don't answer. We have free will."

"Was there free will when we rushed to purchase the phones, like sheep? And there is no such thing as not answering, by the way. Everyone always answers. They're addicted to that. And as soon as we pick up that call, or answer that text, or check out that notification, we forget where we are. We forget with whom we are. We shift our focus to where we aren't and who we aren't with. Reality disappears. The moment is missed. That ringing is like a jolt, a reminder that we do not belong to ourselves. The devil's way of keeping us on a tight leash."

"Okay ...," she said, trying not to smile at how passionate he was about the whole thing.

"For example," he insisted, "had your cell worked, would we have met?"

"I don't see why not."

"You would have been head down, developing sciatica and carpal tunnel typing on one of those tiny keyboards. Or someone would have called you:

that ghost ex-husband of yours. You might have rushed across town to help him perhaps. Only once there, you would have found him on his phone carrying on a conversation with yet another person."

"You might have a point."

"Also, would you have stayed at the Jument, waiting for a call."

"How did you know I was receiving phone calls at the Jument?"

"I asked."

"What did you ask exactly? And who answered?"

"I asked the patronne why an unknown woman was being given my table, and why she seemed to be there at all hours. The patronne responded that you were waiting for calls because you didn't have a cell phone either. She saw it as a sign that the two of us were meant for each other."

Cassie laughed. "Doesn't she think that relationships should be based on more solid ground?"

"They rarely are." He looked at her, and she felt herself blush. A few days ago, she was slashing through bougainvilleas like an unhinged jungle woman, and tonight she sat at a beautiful Parisian restaurant at sunset across from a charming man. "Why don't you get a new telephone if you love them so much?" he asked.

"Mine is in repair," she lied.

She ordered a sole meunière, and he asked for a lotte au fenouil. He chose the wine, a Meursault, and they watched in silence as boats glided along the Seine, illuminating the façade of buildings. Down on the quay, lovers walked hand in hand. She found it hard to look at him as she tried to calm her thoughts.

"Why don't you tell me your story," Hervé said.

"I have a story?"

"You arrive out of nowhere. You move into a hotel. No computer, no telephone, not even paper to write on. Like you've been picked clean. What happened?"

He wasn't being nosy she could tell. He was giving her the opportunity to unburden herself. She felt a slight tightening of the throat. Picked clean. Yes, that was exactly how she felt. She took in a breath and dared say it: "I'll give you the short version. My son and daughter have left the nest. My ex is remarried, with little kids and a baby on the way. The fuller all of their lives get, the emptier mine feels. Meanwhile, I'm in this horrible fight with my parents and at least one of my sisters over some old gripes." Of course, there was all that she was leaving out. Not lying exactly, but omitting.

"What's your ex like?" Hervé asked.

"Warm and friendly, at least on the surface. Likable, but self-serving. Selfish for the most part."

"What animal would he be?"

She halted her fork in mid-air. "What do you mean?"

"You know, like you: you would be a cat."

"Me? A cat?"

He looked at her intently. "Your eyes are yellow like a cat."

"I prefer gold if you don't mind."

"And you have a funny way to eat, with little bites, where you bring your fork up to your mouth and lap it up really fast."

Cassie looked at her plate, her fork. "I did not know that about myself." She thought about Peter as an animal. "He would be a fox, quick and calculating. I always wonder what he wants from me. If there is an agenda. I get bogged down by his small offenses and can't always see the forest for the tree. Same with my father. I feel that there is a bigger picture. Something I must have missed."

"What kind of animal?" Hervé asked.

"Uh?"

"Your dad."

She thought about it. How inscrutable her dad was. "I guess, an owl would do."

"And your mother and sister?"

Cassie made a rodent face. "A wallowing wombat and a honey badger."

He laughed. "You're getting good at this. See, now I can picture them perfectly. And me? What animal?" he asked.

"I don't know you well enough to tell."

He changed the subject. "What does your family reproach you?"

"I dig, I ask questions. They consider it a betrayal that I am getting to know my aunt. They punch. I counterpunch. I'm reactive. They're intense. They push me away; I set their house on fire." Hervé raised an interrogative eyebrow. "A mishap in the kitchen," she explained. "You'd be amazed at the inordinate number of things and relationships I've bungled in the last few days."

"Is that why you moved into a hotel? A bungled relationship?"

She was circling around her lies. But if she told him the truth, why she was here, for how long, would he lose interest? She did not want him to lose interest. "What about you?" she asked. "What about that complicated home life of yours?"

Hervé shook his head. "I love women, don't get me wrong...." His voice trailed off.

Cassie laughed. "You know that is a terrible pickup line."

He smiled. "Maybe I'm getting older. I don't need the validation the way I used to. And the chase, well that's exhausting. Often it's more trouble than it's worth."

She had no idea where he was going with this. All this candidness unnerved her. "I'm curious. What usually happens when you have to explain to a woman that you can't give away your cell number because you don't own one?"

"Usually, she thinks I'm lying."

"And then you give a lengthy explanation about the devil and his leash."

"And she runs the other way."

"She thinks you're trying to get rid of her."

"And she would be correct about that."

Cassie stepped back mentally. She was sitting in an incredibly romantic restaurant in an incredibly romantic city across from a very seductive man. She had many conflicting emotions to reconcile, and she was in no shape to reconcile anything. The key now was to calm the hell down, appear cool and collected, whatever that looked like. She changed the subject. "Your notebook has come in handy. My newfound aunt asked me to take notes as she is telling me our family's history. I wrote for two hours this morning, with a pen, mind you. It was exhausting. I'm so used to typing."

"Exactly! We've come to rely on technology so much that we're devolving."

"I prefer to devolve."

"You can't even write using your hands without risking physical exhaustion. That should tell you something."

"You certainly have unique ideas about things."

"More of a life's philosophy," Hervé said. "And you must be thinking, a man with a life's philosophy most likely makes little room for someone else's." He smiled an apologetic smile. "But I am consistently amending it."

Chill, she told herself. This is just a dinner. "So, what are the latest amendments?"

"I've been dabbling in simplicity," he said. "You know, slowing down, using less. Needing less."

"No electronics?"

"It goes beyond that. But I'm still figuring it out. Take coffee for example. People buy complicated machines to brew coffee. But would you not agree that it's better to put expensive coffee in a ten-euro coffee maker than cheap coffee in a thousand-euro machine?"

"I … guess."

"And pasta. People buy pasta already made; this is madness. All you need to make pasta is flour and water and eggs."

"And time."

He lifted his finger. "And time!" he declared. "That is the true currency. People with money are those who miss out the most. They delegate all that is fun for someone else to do. They pay someone to walk their dogs, to take care of their children, to drive their cars, to wash their hair."

"Wash their hair? Come on…."

"How many hair salons do you count on a single street?"

She laughed. "Touché."

They were interrupted by the arrival of their plates. Outside, the city's monuments were lit up. "The rich pay people to cook their food," Hervé continued, unfolding his napkin and setting it on his lap. "I'm surprised they have not found people to eat their food for them."

"That's a fantastic business idea."

"Or at least to chew it for them."

"That already exists," she assured him. "It's called purée."

"Speaking of which!" Hervé foraged in his pockets and retrieved a tiny bottle of ketchup. "This is for you."

She turned the bottle between her fingers, touched that he had thought of it, touched that he had gone out of his way for her. "They're not going to kick me out of this restaurant for drenching their fancy food in ketchup?"

"You'll have to do it when the waiter's back is turned. As a matter of fact, even eggs are optional."

"Eggs?"

"In pasta-making. Would you like to make fresh pasta together one day?"

"*You* can make pasta, and I can watch you do it," she said.

As night fell over the river, they spoke about their children, about what it was like to be parents, about marriage and divorce, about their exes, about books and music. Hervé was interested in everything and jumped from science to psychology to art. Not in a pedantic way, but with child-like enthusiasm and curiosity. By the time dessert came, Cassie was picking the crunchy caramel off his île flottante, and he had his fork in her chocolate cake. "I hope you don't think I'm selfish," he said out of nowhere.

"Selfish?"

"The whole table debacle – I must apologize about that – And having a life philosophy. The fact that I don't want people to interrupt my precious thinking with phone calls. I worry it all makes me appear self-centered."

"You don't fit the profile of the selfish person."

"What profile is that?"

"The little bottle of ketchup, the notebook, the scarf you brought because I might get cold on the ride here. You anticipated my need."

"There must be a different definition of selfish then because I clearly recollect being called that by quite a few women."

As the dinner progressed, she forgot to be self-conscious. There was a masculine earthiness to him, something genuine, and gruff. No mind games. He was at the same time eager to please, and terrible at altering himself to be liked. He was intelligent, educated, and attentive but had an uncomplicated straightforwardness that was unexpected, unsettling even. Peter was a charmer, someone who would manipulate you into what he wanted, and you could not even be mad at him once you realized you had been manipulated. Hervé was charming not because he tried to be, but almost in spite of himself.

On the way back, the thunderous roar of Hervé's motorcycle vibrated up her spine. She opened her eyes this time, because now – and the delicious Meursault was partly to thank for this – she was in the moment and did not want to miss an instant of it. Hervé rode steadily this time, mindful of her comfort. Paris was all glittering lights and sumptuous architecture as they rode along the Quay des Tuileries, passing the Musée de l'Orangerie, the Louvre, and the Pont Neuf, veering left at l'Île de la Cité and then up Boulevard de Sébastopol. Each turn of the wheels drained her mind of thoughts. She did not feel the cold and drizzle. It was as though she were sitting on a carousel of colors and lights. She pressed herself against Hervé's back, wrapped her arms around him, and let Paris unfold around them.

At the foot of her hotel, she hopped off the motorcycle, composed the grin on her face into something dignified, removed the helmet he had brought for her, unwrapped his scarf from around her neck, and handed it to him. "Keep the scarf," he said as he turned off the engine, removed his helmet, and hopped off his motorcycle. "For next time."

Next time? "If you were an animal, I think you'd be a bear," she said.

"A bear?"

"A bear likes his little habits. He likes his alone time, in his cave, making egg-less pasta and good coffee in lousy pots."

He thought about it and nodded. "I do like honey. Although I've had terrible luck catching salmon upstream with my bare claws."

"I'm not judging you. I'm increasingly turning into a bear myself."

"Thank goodness you don't smell like one," he said, stepping closer and leaning toward her cheek sniffing in a bear-like fashion. "You smell very good." He sniffed some more, along her cheek and then silently, as she froze in wonderment, her neck.

"It's the coat," she said, flustered. "I think there must have been lavender sachets in the pockets or something."

He shook his head. "It's not lavender."

"What is it?"

"Bear men lack the vocabulary to describe."

She too had noticed his scent, an amalgam of unknown things: cologne, leather, pipe tobacco, diesel fuel, and a mysterious something else. Something that made her want to burrow her face in his neck. "Well, thank you so much for dinner," she said. But to her dismay, Hervé was busy moving the motorcycle to the sidewalk. What is he doing? He rolled the heavy machine closer to the bus stop where a light box was shining with a poster of *Women in Back, Part Two*, like her good fairy's bitchy way of reminding her that this moment was an aberration and not her actual life. Hervé nodded in the direction of the film poster. "This merde is everywhere," he noted.

He crouched to lock the motorcycle. "You … are you parking your bike?" she asked. There was perhaps a hint of panic in her voice.

He lifted his head above the seat and raised an eyebrow. "You invited me to see the view, remember?"

"But that was when you were gay!"

He laughed, a contagious, unbridled laugh. "Is the Eiffel Tower canceled over such a trivial detail?"

"I can't even offer you a drink," she said. "The only liquid I have up there is a bottle of Scope." *Oops*, she thought. She had put her foot in it, in her manic attempts at deflecting her panic with humor. French people didn't know what Scope was. It was an American product: an invented American need. What else was scattered around the room that would give away that teeny-tiny white lie large enough to fit fifty states? She needed to tell him that he could not, absolutely not, come up to her room. View of the Eiffel Tower or not.

And that was when she realized that there was no way in hell she was going up without him. She wanted him to come up to her room more than she remembered wanting anything else in her life. "I'm warning you," she said, in a voice she did not even recognize as her own, "my room's way up, and no elevator."

He followed her inside the hotel. The old hotelier wasn't there. She began up the stairs with Hervé following. Halfway up the first set of stairs, realizing that she'd rather not have him stare at her butt for five sets of stairs she stopped and said, "Would you mind climbing ahead of me?"

"Are there ghouls hiding in the recesses of the stairwell?" Hervé asked.

When they arrived at her door, he doubled over to catch his breath and looked at her. "Either I'm totally out of shape, or you're a triathlon athlete."

"I just do a lot of laundry," she said. "It keeps me fit." Maybe she had not lost her breath, but her heart pounded loud enough to be heard from another arrondissement. They entered the room, and she turned on the light. Hervé looked around. "That's rare, a hotel that has not been remodeled to look generic." He pointed to Jessica's four little packages, which were still on the bed. "Isn't it early for Christmas?"

"Ha, those," she said. "They're gifts for my parents and sisters. They're not from me. They're from my ex-husband's new wife. I don't know why she is giving them anything, come to think of it."

Hervé picked up one of the packages, held it between two fingers, and made a disgusted grimace. "They're horrible."

"What are you saying? They're adorable. You don't like bows and glitter."

"I mistrust a gift that is too well wrapped. Good presents come in ugly packages."

"You do have theories about everything."

"This wrapping forces you to fuss much more about the gifts than the gifts deserve. The person guilty of this wrapping job is a phony. And where does she get off sucking up to your family at a time you're struggling with them?"

"You might be reading too much into this."

"Well, I don't know how you can stand to look at them."

Cassie stared at the four glittery boxes. "I *can't* stand to look at them," she admitted. "They're reminders of all my failures."

"Well, I think that was precisely her objective," Hervé said.

She looked at him. "I'm not even sure why you're here," she mumbled.

"I'm here for the view. And to try a glass of that Scope you told me about. It's that liquor from Norway made with gooseberries, right?"

"Scope? I, hmm … I don't think you'd enjoy it."

She opened the French window, and they stepped outside on the balcony. The Eiffel Tower sparkled and shimmered. They looked in silence, leaning over the balustrade. If the air was cold, she wasn't feeling it.

"Beautiful, isn't it?" she asked in a small voice.

"Mesmerizing," he said. She felt his eyes on her. She did not dare to turn to look at him. By now her heartbeat was thunderous, and her entire body was on high alert. He came closer to her, leaned, and ever so slowly went to kiss her. For one second, she wondered what in the world was happening, the next, she was melting into his kiss, and he had his arms around her.

Now they were not on the balcony, somehow, but on her bed. Jessica's presents had been kicked off to the floor; her coat was off, and so was his jacket, and he was brushing his lips up and down her neck, moving down her clavicle and sending shivers of expectation through her body. "I am not …," she muttered. "I did not think—"

He kissed her lips. "I have condoms," he said.

"No, I mean, I can't … I don't—"

"Do you want me to leave?" he whispered, still kissing her. "I'll leave. I'm a gentleman."

"You did climb so many sets of stairs …," she said, breathless.

"If you ask me to leave, I'll go. No need for stairs. I'll throw myself out the window." Saying this, he kissed her again, and her body turned to mush.

He made love to her in the most luscious ways. She was hungry for this. Hungry for him. She had a hunger in her she did not know possible.

Later, they rested side by side, naked in bed, her head on his chest, her brain incapable of a single thought. How easy this all was. How simple. A one-night stand. Just like a grown-up. How wonderful.

"You really were only going to show me the view," he said.

"I told you I was."

"Now I believe you."

"Why?"

"Your panties."

"What about them?"

"My granny would not wear those. A woman who did not mean it about the view would have worn pretty lingerie. That's how I know."

She opened her mouth, and then closed it, speechless. Then she said, "I am speechless."

"It proves my point that the best gifts don't come in the best packages."

"Hmm … I'm not sure if this is a compliment or…."

He lifted himself on his elbow and looked at her. He caressed her body with a finger. "It's very much a compliment."

"Well, I'm pretty certain you did not come up just to see the view."

"How did you guess? My underwear was mute as to my intentions."

"But not your jeans pockets, which were filled to the brim with condoms."

"I have no idea how they got there," he said, kissing her stomach. Then he lifted her like a rag doll and moved her on top of him.

CHAPTER 7

The Refugee

There had been so much Lucienne needed her to organize at the Cannes house that it was an entire month before Xandra was allowed a day off. War was brewing, of that Moshe and Albano were convinced. They had liquidated their assets, sold the business, opened bank accounts in Switzerland. Moshe had left Paris and gone directly to Algiers. Albano thought that the South of France would be less traumatic on Lucienne.

So now, without Moshe's apartment to meet at on Sundays, he and Xandra needed to find other ways to see each other in private.

Albano told Lucienne that he had business to tend to in Nice and that he'd drop off Sandra in town. Instead, he and Xandra were now driving in the direction of Théoule-sur-Mer, and then to Fréjus, where he had a plan for them to spend the day.

It was the last Sunday of May 1939. The tourist season was near, but for now, the roads and villages still had the quietness of wintertime. The cold winds had all but subsided. With each passing day, the sun shone longer and warmer, and the smells and feel of the air resembled Smyrna's climate a little bit more. Across the Côte d'Azur, roses bloomed in every garden, birds chirped, and cicadas began their vibrating songs. The inexorable descent into another worldwide war, the uncertainty, the fear, the folly of men had no effect whatever on nature. As he drove, Albano watched Xandra from the corner of his eye. She was sitting very straight and nervous, so he took her hand. She smiled. In the South of France, they knew no one. All they needed to do was to drive a few miles from the house to experience freedom. And so, today they would authorize themselves some happiness. They drove following the coast along the jagged volcanic cliffs that plunged into the foam of the sea, past the coves and beaches, and the twisted pines shaped by the mistral, the tree roots that clung powerfully to the red earth. They drove past small restaurants by the sea, and medieval towns, and harbors filled with boats. In Agay, they parked the automobile in the street and, for the very first time since they had met as children, Xandra and Albano were able to sit on the terrace of a restaurant, together in plain sight.

It was as though by leaving Paris they had flown away from judgment and even from their own limitations. He was thirty-seven years old, and so was Xandra, but they were giddy like children at the novelty of sitting across from each other at a restaurant table, their forearms resting on the red-and-white checkered tablecloth, their fingers entwined. After lunch, they walked down to the cove and stepped on the empty beach. They found a nook under the shade of pine trees and set a blanket on the sand. They lay down on the blanket and looked up at the white clouds in the azure sky. Before them was the Mediterranean Sea. Behind them, as if standing guard to protect them, was the bright red Massif de L'Estérel. They spoke about Marceline and Gustave as if they were the children they had had together, expressing pride and concern the way loving parents would. When Albano and Lucienne spoke of the children, it was usually about logistics, the need for money to tend to this or that, or informing each other about a new tutor or some event that needed attending. Xandra told him of little things, a funny comment that one of the children had said, a good grade, or even something sad she had noticed. Xandra sat in the sand and Albano lay on his back, his head on her lap. She was passing her fingers through his hair when he announced, "Marceline is growing up!"

"And you only see this now, my love? She is sixteen years old and has been a young lady for quite some time."

"Men look at her," Albano said worriedly. "Why do men have any business looking at my daughter? It will be good for her to be away from Paris. With all the distractions of the city, the silly functions her mother organizes for her."

"You know how Marceline thrives on being active and meeting people. It is isolated up at La Bastide. She can't walk into the streets the way she could in Paris."

Albano shrugged. "And so, she must learn to do without."

"A young woman her age wants romance."

"And should not get it! I see no need to anticipate such a thing."

"You might have to. So that you can prepare."

"If there is something she is unhappy about, she will tell us. Marceline is a practical person. In fact, I wish Gustave were as easy to understand."

"Are you concerned about him?"

"If only he told me how he felt," Albano said, "I could give him guidance. But since he doesn't, the advice I give him feels awkward or unwelcome."

"Continue to speak to him. Do not mistake his quietness for a desire to be left alone," Xandra said.

"I have been preoccupied the last few years, with our business, and with preparing to come here, and looking for Hagop, and seeing you on Sundays, and with all the things Moshe and I plan to do if the war comes."

"You have more time now. Maybe you should spend it with Gustave."

"I might have lost his trust by sending him to boarding school. I listened to his mother again and again, about the boxing, and boarding school, when I should have listened to you. Gustave has suffered. I do not want him feeling fearful and untrusting toward the world, no matter how treacherous it has become."

"But he has also watched you be a loving father and a capable man, and he will, in turn, know how to become a wonderful man. He is a good boy, a big-hearted boy who wants to please you and impress you."

Albano sat up. "This is what I shall do! I shall make time for him. I shall strive to become a better father."

"Only make sure Marceline isn't left out."

"I do not worry about Marceline. When she needs attention, she knows how to ask for it."

"And what about Lucienne?" Xandra asked quietly. "Should we not worry about her?"

Albano tensed up. "This is such a beautiful day. Must we spoil it?" He seldom wanted to discuss Lucienne, as though she were a permanent houseguest, a relative whose presence one must endure.

Xandra looked at her fingers and pursed her lips. "We must discuss her at some point."

Albano sighed. There was no subject he could avoid if Xandra had her heart set on bringing it up. "All right then, what of her?"

"Her entire life has changed, Albano. The politics in Paris, the alienation from her social circle, and leaving her home to come here against her wishes—"

Albano interrupted. "It is hard for me to feel empathy for her when she has so little for you."

"She suffers that you do not tend to her happiness."

"When Paris is under attack, she will come to her senses and see that all I ever intended was to save her."

"She senses our closeness."

"I doubt she does. She lives in a world of her own."

"When you brought me here, you proved to her what she suspected: that you cared about my well-being. And at the same time, she feels that you do not care for hers."

"And so, what choice do I have?" Albano said, agitated. "With all that is happening and the threat of war, divorcing her is out of the question, even if you finally allowed it. I could never leave the mother of my children to fend for herself now. It's too late; I missed my chance. I should have asked her for a divorce the very day you returned. Perhaps she would have understood then. And she was still young. She could have remarried. But now, after nine years of your living with us, it would be just terrible." Albano closed his eyes and shook his head. "I don't want to think of all the mistakes I've made."

"We made a choice that kept your family intact," Xandra said. "We did the right thing."

"And so, given the circumstances, I am taking care of her the best I can. I treat her kindly. I give her all she desires."

"Except for your love, Albano. None of this is Lucienne's fault," Xandra said, and the fact that she used Lucienne's name turned her into a full human being, with feelings and wounds. "The French turning on the Jews is not her fault. Neither is our story or the feelings you cannot have for her. She is hurt and does not deserve to be. Lucienne is not well. The way she holds her body, her new way of stooping, or sitting in a chair and not speaking, and the way she looks at the horizon without really seeing. She is troubled and sad, and the children are impatient with her."

"How can you be so kind, so empathetic, when Lucienne has done nothing to deserve it?" He took her hand and kissed it. "What am I to do to make you happy? Tell me, and I will do it."

"If you cannot see her as your wife, then perhaps you should see her as one of the children. She is a little girl again. She is sad and needs your care."

Albano sat up and kissed Xandra on the mouth in broad daylight, and they both laughed at the novelty of this. "And so, it is that you and I are raising yet another child together," he said.

****

The letter addressed to Albano bore the stamp of the Red Cross refugee camp in Aleppo Syria. It had been sent to the house in Paris and then forwarded to La Bastide. Xandra was the one who took the mail from the postman and turned it back and forth between her fingers. The letter had been mailed from Syria a full month ago. She hid it in her pocket and waited all day for Albano to return. He opened it and read it.

Dear Mr. Cohen Lombardi,

We think we have found the person you have been looking for. As the old refugee camps are dismantled, we're able to conduct a more thorough survey of each camp's population. The chief humanitarian preoccupation of the League of Nations' workers in the field has been the children. Adults can often be more elusive to identify, especially when there are no known relatives, or they do not come forward. Our research indicates that an individual responding to the name of Hagop Katsukyan might still be living in proximity to the camp. It is unclear if the individual is of sound mind, but he appears relatively healthy. Records show that he arrived at the camp around the dates you mentioned. He appears to be about the correct age, although he says he does not remember how old he is. We have attached a photograph. Please advise if this person might be the relative in question. In the hope of hearing from you soon to resolve the matter.

Salutations,

Mlle. Durant, Secretary of Mr. Pontou
Office of the Red Cross
Aleppo, Syria

The photograph was of a frail, stooping, bearded man wrapped in something that resembled a frayed blanket. He was barefoot in galoshes, and his ankles appeared swollen and covered in scabs. How could this old man be Hagop? No. It was impossible. But there was something so familiar in the man's stance. Those eyes, defiantly staring at the camera. The mouth. The striking resemblance to Xandra. Albano was so shaken that he nearly dropped the picture. Hagop! Was it really him? Albano realized he had been holding his breath, and a warm feeling enveloped him. He had to be sure. He could not let Xandra hope. But she was waiting on the other side of the door, and he would have to tell her the truth.

When he handed her the photograph, she stared at the man and made the sign of the cross. "It is him," she said gravely. "My brother is alive!"

The next few months were a whirlwind during which worries of an impending war with Germany were eclipsed by the efforts put in place to rescue Hagop. Albano hired a man who spoke Armenian to find Hagop in Aleppo with instructions to locate him inside the refugee camp, facilitate his departure out of Syria, and secure his safe passage to France. The man, Monsieur Perrin, a broad Alsatian in his sixties, was a retired official from the League of Nations who came highly recommended and would not be intimidated by the task at hand.

Upon finding Hagop, Monsieur Perrin had described him in his letter as reluctant to communicate, covered in vermin and scabs, dressed in rags, and grossly underfed. Such were the conditions of the encampment where so many other Armenian refugees languished. With Albano's instructions via telegraph, the man had taken Hagop to a doctor to be deloused and given medication for his various ailments. He was also put up in a decent hotel room and was bathed, fed, and clothed. According to Monsieur Perrin, Hagop hardly spoke but was amenable. He had accepted to be taken out of the country and showed deep gratitude at the things presently offered to him. He had suffered trauma to be sure and appeared confused and disoriented at times, but he was responding well to being cared for. His appetite was excellent, and already he had regained a few kilos.

More telegraphs were exchanged. Monsieur Perrin helped procure the necessary papers. It took months to obtain consent from the French government, but, finally, Albano had procured an authorization for a temporary visa. Eager to avoid a perilous journey across Europe where conflicts were making the crossing of borders uncertain, Monsieur Perrin suggested that he would bring Hagop to France on a specially chartered boat. The ship would sail across the Mediterranean, leaving the Syrian coast to reach Cyprus, with stops in Malta and Corsica, and at last, arrive in Nice.

In September 1939, six months after Albano and his family had left Paris, France declared war on Germany. Borders began closing one by one. In November, Hagop was on a boat making its way to the southern coast of France.

On the day of Hagop's arrival, Albano paced the length of Nice's harbor with tremendous excitement, but also something else. As he peered at the horizon for the chartered boat, an emotion he had pushed aside until that moment surfaced. Facilitating Hagop's exit out of Syria had been of all-consuming complexity, but now, walking up and down the harbor, a conversation with Xandra, one he had dismissed at the time, nagged at him. When they first learned that Hagop was alive, Albano had instantly made up his mind to bring him to France. "Hagop's struggle will end," he had told her. "It will be a wonderful thing to bring him here. His life will be changed."

But Xandra had said, "I wonder how it might affect us."

"What do you mean?"

"I wonder what kind of man he is now."

"What kind of man would he be?"

"He was taken in 1919, never to be heard from or seen. Twenty years have passed."

"And what do you suggest we do?" Albano had teased her, "leave him to rot in a refugee camp when I have the financial means and the wherewithal to rescue him?"

"What will you tell him about us?"

"There is nothing to tell him. We are doing nothing wrong. We have only to make sure he does not tell Lucienne that you and I knew each other before we came to France."

"But will he listen?"

"Of course, he will. We are rescuing him. He will be in our debt."

At first, Albano had planned on Hagop's living with them at La Bastide, at least until he was healthy and could find work and begin his own life. But Xandra had warned him against it. "Before you let him meet the children, you must be certain that he is who he says he is, and that he is of sound mind and a positive mindset toward us."

To soothe Xandra, Albano had rented a room with a view at Le Negresco hôtel and arranged every detail: fresh flowers, plenty of towels, iced champagne, and food to be brought the minute Hagop arrived. Xandra would not be there. As much as she wanted to see her brother, she said she preferred to wait a few days. The closer to Hagop's arrival, the more anxious she had been. Albano's happiness could barely be contained. He remembered so vividly the day when Moshe had rescued him in Marseille when he was sick of body and soul. When all hope was lost, Moshe had been his guardian angel. Through patience, support, and good humor, he had offered him a key to a new life and given him a future. Now, and the thought thrilled him, Albano was about to do the same for Hagop!

They predicted a harsh winter throughout Europe. But the Mediterranean climate, the sea, the pier, the palm trees would, he hoped, make Hagop feel more at home.

Standing in the chilly November wind, which could be cutting even in the South of France, Albano watched French soldiers walk by. It was possible to think himself back in 1914 on Smyrna's quayside when he and Hagop had watched soldiers from every nation, mobilized for war, gather on the dock to return to their respective countries. The French soldiers were dressed in khaki color instead of indigo as they had in the last war. But in other ways, the French uniform appeared recycled from the Great War: the suspenders, the belts, the laced boots designed for trench warfare, the golf pants, the haversacks, the standard Adrian helmet, even the Lebel rifles looked as though they were taken out of mildewed storage bins. The German army, in comparison, seemed to be marching in from the future with modern weapons, well-cut uniforms, and a steely discipline that was frightening to witness.

For now, his family would not see any of this. Albano's infirmity made him unfit for combat. As for Gustave, he was only fourteen, young enough that he might avoid combat altogether if the war was short-lived. Albano forced himself not to think of it. There was no point in worrying about things he had no control over. What he needed to focus on were the things he could control. He and Moshe were making plans, not only for themselves but with larger context in mind. Their plan was broader than their temporary safety. Germany had to be stopped, or else there would soon be no safe place in Europe for Jews. He and Moshe were operating from the standpoint of a worst-case scenario. A military defeat. If this happened, there would be an underground popular movement. The time to plan and put things in place was now while they were free to roam and communicate, when borders were still porous, when railroads and telephone lines were up and running, when the news was still mostly uncensored. And this was what they were doing, through a network of connections. They were creating a matrix of communication. There were codes, routes, fields for drop-offs, banks to channel monies, houses for hiding and gathering. For the last few years, he had felt the frustration of not succeeding in warning others to prepare. It was as though his personal experience was useless to others. What he had seen happen in Smyrna could take place anywhere. He recognized the signs. He recognized the discourse. This war would not be like the Great War because it wasn't about politics, this time around, but ideology. In this war, the Germans would not be obedient soldiers, but fanaticized ones. Yesterday, the Armenians. Tomorrow, the Jews.

The French Jews were extremely worried, yet he and Moshe had not convinced anyone they knew in Paris to act. Lucienne especially dismissed it all. But he was the husband and father, and so she followed him with the children, and in the end, that was all that mattered. What he had not quite admitted to Lucienne was that, to him, the principal appeal of the South of France wasn't the pretty house, or the climate, or the distance from the capital. It was its location, a boat ride away from another continent. Moshe was the principal architect of their plan. He had crisscrossed the world enough times to have a broader view of the geography and politics of various nations. He had left France without a forwarding address, hidden his and

Albano's assets in Swiss accounts, and was at the moment making connections throughout France's colonies in North Africa, in Morocco, Tunisia, and Algeria.

Albano looked out over the water. He had made sure to dress simply. He had left his gold watch and leather shoes at home and was wearing an old suit. He did not want to make his old friend feel embarrassed by his appearance after he had spent weeks at sea in less than luxurious conditions. He did not know Hagop's particular sufferings, but he was familiar with the state of shock brought on by a rapid change in circumstances. After a long time of dejection, the human mind grew so callused that it could not easily switch back to happiness. Depression was common, as was anxiety. He was prepared to find Hagop changed.

"What if he is still angry with us?" Xandra had wondered.

"We were young and impulsive. Twenty years is a lifetime. Years change a man."

"But not always for the better," Xandra worried. "There was always a brash side to him."

Albano recognized the name of the boat that made its way toward the dock. This was it! His heart pounded as men threw ropes and the boat moored.

As if by enchantment, the cold wind stopped. The façades of the hotels shone in the soft light of late fall. In a moment, he would see his friend, lost for twenty years. Life was full of miracles.

He recognized Monsieur Perrin who was walking down the ramp toward him. But the man who walked next to him was an old, toothless man with an ashen face and a hesitant gait, a man much too old to possibly be Hagop.

Albano stood in place, dejected. Had he helped a stranger who would now be at his charge? And that would mean that Hagop was still lost. What would he tell Xandra?

Now the old man was next to him and murmuring in Armenian, "Albano. My brother."

Albano, shocked to recognize the voice looked into the old man's eyes. What he saw in them nearly brought him to his knees. "Hagop! It is you!" Albano's voice broke into a sob of relief and sadness at witnessing his friend's terrible state. They fell in each other's arms. At first, they could only cry and hold each other. Hagop was emaciated; he who had been taller than Albano by a head, now was so hunchbacked that he was noticeably shorter. His teeth were rotten, most of his front teeth missing, his movements difficult, as though every one of his bones suffered from rust. "I am so happy you are here," was all Albano could say.

He could scarcely pay attention as Monsieur Perrin gave him all the paperwork for Hagop's entrance into the country, his visa and his application for immigration as a political refugee. Albano gave him an envelope with the rest of the fee he owed. As Monsieur Perrin spoke, Albano and Hagop just looked at each other, Albano grinning and crying, Hagop red-eyed, confused. When Monsieur Perrin was gone, Albano said, "You are so thin."

"And you are so young," Hagop said. "And as good-looking as when you were a boy." He tried to smile, but it looked more like a grimace of pain.

"How was your voyage?"

"It was terrible," Hagop said. His voice was low, monotone. "My temperament did not agree with the sea. All the weight I had gained is lost again."

"I will not be done with you until you are plump as a baby," Albano said, putting his arm around Hagop.

"No hell was worse than the one you just put me through, bringing me here on a boat," Hagop said. "Why could you not have me come here by train instead?"

Albano was taken aback by the acerbity in Hagop's voice. "The frontiers are closing," he answered. "The railroads are insecure. There were fewer chances of being stopped at sea. I was not sure your papers would withstand the scrutiny of frontier agents, especially now that France is at war."

"You speak Armenian well, my brother. Where did you learn? You did not speak so well years back."

Albano smiled. He could not wait to tell him all about Xandra, but they were still standing in the harbor, and Hagop needed to rest, eat. They had so much to tell one another, but all would be shared in due time. "I had a good teacher," he only said.

Upon entering the lobby of Le Negresco hotel, where doormen stood in their blue and red coats and black hats, Hagop removed his cap and crumpled it between his hands, lowering his head. Albano thought back to the time when he too was first introduced to wealth. He had felt insignificant but also mystified and awed. This time of war and uncertainty called for frugality; already he had tried to broach the subject with Lucienne, and it had not gone well. But for the next few days with Hagop, he wanted to be extravagant.

Inside the hotel room, Hagop looked around and clucked his tongue in appreciation. Albano was thrilled like a child. "This is one of the best rooms in this hotel, and it is one of the best hotels in Nice. Look at the bathroom! You must be eager to take a bath. Are you hungry? You can order food, and they will bring it right up." Hagop did not seem eager to take a bath, although he smelled quite bad. He said he would eat.

Albano took the telephone and ordered breakfast. He was aware of Hagop's eyes on him as he spoke French. After seventeen years in France, he had become accustomed to giving orders with the confidence that comes from having money and thought nothing of it. But it must look strange, even extraordinary to his friend.

A waiter came to the room to set a table on the balcony, which overlooked the Bay of Nice. Breakfast was brought up. Hagop dove upon the food, eating without decorum, throwing himself at the croissants, the jam, the eggs, the orange juice. Albano watched him eat and worried. Something in the way Hagop ate ran deeper than hunger. It resembled despair. As he ate, Albano asked him questions, but Hagop was too focused on the food to respond, and Albano did not insist.

As he waited for Hagop to finish, he forced himself to take in the startling deterioration of Hagop's physical body. If his friend's life had been dire enough to impact his body so dramatically, what might have happened to his soul? He would have to prepare Xandra for this. In many ways, Hagop's appearance was more shocking to him than Xandra's disfigurement had been. It was not only that the body was different. He kept looking for signs of the Hagop he knew, the easy laugh, the cunning, the gusto, the life force, but the man who grabbed food and thrust it into his mouth, swallowing it without being able to chew, appeared to be someone new entirely. Albano closed his eyes to fight the onslaught of emotions. I will heal you, he thought. I will glue you back together, all the broken pieces, just like Moshe did for me.

At last, Hagop leaned back into his chair away from the table. There were crumbs and bits of eggs around his mouth. He belched loudly. Now there was a spark of contentment in his eyes as he asked, "How did you come upon such good fortune, Albano? Your letter said you are married and you have a boy and a girl, and now you work for your uncle. Does he live here too, that fat one?"

"He's in North Africa at the moment."

"Where?"

"Algiers."

"Still, how did this happen?" Hagop asked. "How did you come to escape the Smyrna blaze without a scratch on you?"

Albano presented his arm. "There are a few scratches. Four fingers of my hand are paralyzed, but I got used to it, and I make do." He regretted saying this immediately. It was obscene to compare his hand to what Hagop must have endured. He wondered how Hagop knew that he had escaped the blaze rather than left Smyrna long before the fire, or for that matter, years later.

But Hagop continued with his questions. "And how did you get so wealthy that I am now brought to France at your expense?"

Albano felt that these answers demanded lengthy responses, but first, he asked a question about a mystery he wanted to understand. "After Monsieur Perrin found you in Aleppo, I sent you many letters," he said. "I know you received them, and the man read them to you. But you did not write back. You agreed to come here, but the only news I received was through him."

"I see I have offended you," Hagop answered in a plaintive voice. "Do not be angry at your poor old friend."

"I am not offended or mad," Albano said. "I am only curious."

"Oh, please forgive me. Look at me, and look at you. You look like a prince, and I'm like a bum twice your age. I am not educated the way you are. I was never so good with reading, and writing even less. And my eyesight is impaired." He thought about it and added, "Also, it was hard for me. How could I hear about your good luck when my life has been so miserable?"

Albano remembered Moshe's words from years ago, and told Hagop with a smile, "My good fortune is now your good fortune, dear friend."

"And will my good fortune extend to a few more of those pastries, or is this all I am allowed to eat?"

Albano ordered more food and said, "Speak to me Hagop. Tell me how you survived."

"My parents and sisters were killed when Kemal's army arrived," Hagop said. "Do you know this?"

Albano nodded. There would be time to tell him the details and reveal that Xandra was alive. He had a sense that first, he needed to know more about Hagop, about what the years might have done to him. "I want to tell you about all this, but please first tell me what happened to you?" he insisted.

Hagop shrugged impatiently. "You think you want to hear. But perhaps it is better if you don't."

"I want to know."

"There were maybe thirty of us arrested that day, the day I left with the money after we had that fight in the cave. Do you remember?"

"I shall never forget that terrible day," Albano said somberly.

"You remember that man who had come once to the Armenian quarter when we were children? The survivor? You and I listened to his tale."

"I remember him."

"Remember how we could not believe him at the time?" Hagop stared at Albano who nodded. "Everything he said was true. Those stories we were fed of displacements, of wanting the Armenians to be moved elsewhere. Those were lies. They didn't want us moved out of the country. What they wanted to do with us is wipe us from the surface of the Earth."

Albano sat down at the table and listened to Hagop's story.

"The first groups of men they took out of the Armenian quarter they took further up the mountains to be shot dead," Hagop said. "By the time they arrested me, their tactics had changed. They had been disorderly about burying the bodies. Too many cadavers of Armenians found rotting on the outskirts of town. The government wanted things done more discretely. Important people from around the world had eyes and ears in Smyrna. This is why the Armenians of Smyrna were not experiencing the same fate as villagers throughout the Empire. But eventually, they began to take the men of the Armenian quarter, inventing lies to do it. They started with men they thought were community leaders. You see, they are the ones who organize others. You start with the leaders, those who make decisions, and suddenly no one knows what to do."

"This is why they took your father?"

"This is the reason they took me! They knew I was the son of Silas, the baker. They recognized in me things I myself was not yet aware of: my natural leadership and my gift." He tapped his finger to the side of his head to illustrate. "My superior intelligence. They took me, beat me, and they stole all my money."

"The satchels?" Albano asked. The satchels were filled with the money they had both earned from years of selling newspapers in the streets of Smyrna. For Hagop to refer to it as his money was simply inaccurate. That day in the cave he had been furious at Xandra and Albano because he had discovered their love. He had beaten Xandra, and he and Albano had gotten into a fistfight. Hagop had then left the cave, taking with him all the money, his share and the half that belonged to Albano. But this was water under the bridge.

Hagop's eyes flashed with anger at the memory. "They did this quietly. They were waiting right outside the Armenian quarter. Everything they did in Smyrna, they did in secret."

"They?"

"The police."

"It was easier to take us out of town one by one, and then do with us as they pleased. And what pleased them was to make us die slowly of thirst and hunger, of despair, of exhaustion, of physical and mental torture." Hagop felt in his pocket and retrieved a pouch of tobacco. For a moment he was engrossed in the task of rolling a cigarette. His fingers trembled as he did. The result was uneven. He put the misshapen cigarette between his lips and lit it. His middle finger and index were yellow from tobacco, almost orange.

"They took me and others into the Syrian Desert," he said, inhaling. "At first, they had many gendarmes surrounding us, later on, less so. Still, I should have attempted to escape when I still had the strength, in those first few days, before the dehydration rendered me as weak as a little girl. Whatever food the villagers had brought with them ran out quickly. It did not take long before the first of us died from thirst. The first to die were the children too old to be nursed, the old folks, the pregnant women. Then, everybody else."

Hagop stopped and looked at Albano, as though he was observing the effect his account had on him. Albano had nothing to say. What could he say to this? Hagop went on. "Each time we stopped for the night some of us did not wake up. Our caravan moved forward. At that time, you could almost believe they were trying to take us someplace. But then, when we were far enough from the city, the gendarmes got the help of blood-thirsty mad men full of hatred. They were armed, and they began to rape and beat all those defenseless people." Hagop crushed the cigarette into an ashtray. His chin trembled. "Those who rebelled they just attacked with bayonets. There was nothing we could do. By then we were very weak, all of us were. Any rebellion meant instant death. So, we huddled and hoped we wouldn't be next, at least those of us who still had the will to live."

There was a rap at the room's door, and a hotel server entered with a basket full of chocolate croissants and brioches. The crumbs on the white tablecloth were removed, the pot of coffee refreshed. Hagop eyed the basket the entire time. When the server was gone Hagop began to take the pastries out of the basket, but he was no longer hungry, and so he took one bite of this one, one bite of the next, putting the pastries down on the table until he had taken a few bites of each. His fingers and face were covered in crumbs.

"This continued for what seemed like weeks," he said. "So many died, and yet there were always more villagers joining our caravan, and so there were always more people to kill. The gendarmes grew tired of this. It was taking too long. We weren't dying as cooperatively as they wished. They too were thirsty, and hungry, and tired, and wanted to go home. And yet there were so many of us still. I think that they had instructions that not one of us would make it to Syria alive, and they were trying to complete the task. They needed ways to kill us faster. Now they became frantic about it. They made us remove all our clothes so we would have no protection from the burning sun and icy nights. They made us walk on the ledges of mountains. When there were cliffs, they pushed the children down to their deaths, knowing that many of the women would jump after them, which they did."

"By God! Hagop. I—"

"Certain women, they would get rid of their children and keep them alive to do what they wished with them until they were tired of them or the women turned insane." Hagop shook his head in disgust. "When there were rivers, they would throw us in the water to drown and then shoot at us if we seemed able to reach the bank. If you lagged behind, you were beaten to death. If you could not go on, you were left to die."

Albano was sickened and astounded. Not only did Hagop's story echo that of the man who had spoken to the Armenian men back in Smyrna, but the way he described those horrors in a tone detached to the point of numbness sounded almost identical. "How did you survive?" he asked.

"I don't know how long we walked, perhaps weeks, perhaps months. I made sure I was never in sight, never noticed, always in the center of the crowd. I made myself invisible. I had no one I loved to watch die either. That made a difference. Despair killed people faster than any other method they used. Also, I had a strong body and the endurance of youth."

"You had strength of spirit."

Hagop dismissed the notion with an impatient motion of his hand. "I was like cattle. Unthinking. I just moved. Put one foot in front of the other, waiting to die I suppose, only I did not. In the end, it was not those who deserved to live who did. Not the loving mothers, not the children, not the old people, not the pretty faces who incited their lust, but those of us who were like sturdy goats, people that nothing can quite kill, not starvation, not thirst, not humiliation." Hagop had a small laugh. "You will see, Albano. One day you will want to kill me, but hard as you might try, you won't be able to, that's how tough I am."

Albano shook his head at the absurd notion. "You must be tough indeed to survive such atrocities."

"Humans survive. Cattle just exist. By the time we arrived at the refugee camp, there was no one left that was not destroyed by despair in one way or another. Including me."

Albano thought of his despair when he had hoped to drown off the coast of Smyrna. "How did you recover your will to live?"

Hagop shrugged angrily. "What makes you think I have? What keeps me standing is this body, which refuses to entirely fall apart. And also rage." He peered at Albano, as though measuring his words' impact on his friend's face. "Yes. Often I can make it through a day on rage alone."

"Your rage is understandable," Albano said.

"As this was happening, and in the years of hunger and agony that followed, all I thought about was how others in the world ate and drank and lived in abundance, people who rejoiced and had children and wives, with lives that were nothing but bliss. Yes, that injustice fueled me with enough rage to power me like coal does a steam engine. Why did I suffer so? I asked myself again and again, while others have all the luck. The opportunists, the sweet-talkers, the greedy and conniving, they did not only survive; they profited. They thrived."

Albano swallowed. He hoped it wasn't blame he heard in Hagop's words. Of all the horrors in Hagop's account, the idea of survival with rage as the sole motivator seemed to Albano the epitome of hopelessness. "And so, after this, you did not want to return home? You stayed in Syria."

"What home? My country was gone, and it had betrayed me. My family was gone. I had no reason to return. But life in the refugee camp was grim. There was no work. Little food. Everyone was ill. Everyone had to contend with their losses."

"You did not marry?"

"I've had women," Hagop said. "None of them fit to marry. Not a single one left still a virgin and most of them crazy by then. And outside the refugee camp, the Syrian women wanted nothing to do with Armenian men."

Albano wondered how virginity had relevance when one sought someone to give and receive comfort, someone to share a burden. "What was it like inside the camp?" he asked.

"Searching trash for something to eat? What was that like?" Hagop hissed. He then smiled thinly. "I guess now that you have spared no expense to rescue me you want your money's worth. You want to hear all the details of my misery. You want to know every one of the indignities I suffered." This was said in jest, but Albano did not think it funny. "Well, my brother," Hagop continued, "let me tell you about a life where you are eaten by scabies so much so that there isn't an inch of skin that doesn't render you mad. I was sick a lot. Typhus, even cholera, both of which I miraculously survived. I tell you I am like a scorpion. I can live in a crack in a wall for years without sustenance. My eyesight was damaged by the desert sun and poor nutrition. My hearing is bad. I had broken bones that did not reset properly, and so my limbs are crooked and gnarled like tree branches. The few teeth I have left are of no use. My body is nothing but pain."

"I will take you to the best doctors."

Hagop emitted a roaring laughter. "Listen to yourself: the best doctors, the best hotel, the best boat, a man hired just to pay my bills, procure my papers, and whisk me out of a place where all others have been left to die. You are a powerful man, Albano."

Albano laughed too, but uneasily. In the compliment was the kind of teasing that was Hagop's alone. He remembered how he used to both love and fear the cleverness of the spunky little boy Hagop used to be. He had been a boy full of mirth, ready to challenge everything that was serious and turn it into a joke. Hagop had been a grabber of opportunities, a jester, and also someone who told truths that were sometimes unpleasant to hear. "I am so happy to have found you at last," he said.

Hagop beamed his near toothless smile and said, "Not as happy as I!" He tore some bread and put it into his mouth. Instead of swallowing, he let it stay in his mouth as he spoke defiantly, almost angrily. "Here is something you don't know perhaps," he said. "Xandra is alive."

Albano was taken aback by Hagop's tone as much as by the news itself. "I … when did you learn this?"

Hagop shrugged. "She left a message at the Armenian Prelacy in Aleppo maybe ten years ago." Albano tried to reconcile this. Xandra told him she had looked for Hagop for years. There had been much more than one letter. "Do you know she was burnt in the fire?" Hagop said, with no more emotion than if he was speaking about a stranger. "Disfigured. Now she's a slave of sorts to a Muslim family in Izmir. She thought you might still be alive; she said so in a letter. She said she looked for you. She went to the Jewish quarter where they treated her like a dog. They wanted to keep your secret, those smart Jews. Yes, Albano, fate has treated you more kindly than the rest of us. I can see how with your new life you would have little use for her."

I found her! Albano wanted to say. But he stopped himself because of the callousness of Hagop's words. Also because of the way Hagop had already returned to eating, putting his fingers in the butter and jam dishes and wiping those clean with a great smacking of his lips. His long-lost sister, the last remaining member of his family who he knew to be injured and practically enslaved, was already gone from his mind. "And so, you did not look for her?" he asked uneasily.

Hagop laughed, and now his laugh sounded different to Albano. Not full of mirth, but bitter. "What I needed was a rich, powerful man such as yourself. Not a woman more downtrodden than I was."

Albano got up from the breakfast table and came to stand by the window. A cold breeze from the sea cooled his face. Xandra, at this moment, was at La Bastide, waiting expectantly for his return. How would he explain that in the years she had relentlessly searched for her brother, Hagop had known she was alive and had not cared? Hagop was avidly pouring leftover coffee into his glass and topping it off with all the milk and sugar that was left. The task absorbed him fully, reminding Albano of the way little children and very old people engrossed themselves in a treat. It was possible that years of suffering in solitude had made Hagop unable to think past his own survival. He would need to prepare Xandra for Hagop as much as he would need to prepare Hagop for Xandra.

He left Hagop at the hotel at the end of the day and told him he would return in the morning. He showed him how to use the telephone to order food and drove back to La Bastide.

Back at the house, Albano waited past midnight for Lucienne and the children to be asleep and met Xandra in the orchard. He told her about Hagop's distressed appearance, his tale of capture, his agony through the desert, and the hopeless stagnation in the refugee camp.

"Many have left the camp and started anew. Why didn't he?" Xandra asked. "The camp was a terrible place no doubt, but he wasn't imprisoned."

"It is as though he was put in a hole and forgotten there. He will need time to come out of the hole, like a man who was deprived of daylight and is made to face the sun. All he can do at the moment is eat," he said. And be angry, he thought.

"What did you tell him about us?"

Albano scratched his face, uneasy. "I had planned to tell him so many things, Xandra, but Hagop did not act curious, or even interested in any part of my life. It is too soon. By the look of things, it will take time for him to expand himself any further than the next meal."

Xandra asked in a small voice. "You didn't tell him about us?"

"He was overjoyed to learn that you were alive," he lied. "But … I did not get a chance to tell him that you were here in Cannes, let alone living with me."

"Where did you tell him I was?"

"He did not ask," Albano said. This admission spoke volume. They were both quiet for a few minutes. "It might take time before you can be reunited. When he sees you are here, questions will surface. You were right that I should not bring him to La Bastide. It is too soon. You and I struggled with the moral ramifications of the choice we made. It is a choice that few people besides Moshe can understand."

Xandra lowered her eyes in sadness. "I will wait to see my brother since you think it is best," she said.

"I should have thought of all this before. In my eagerness to bring him here, I did not think of all this."

"Had you anticipated it, you would have wanted to rescue him all the more," she said. "He is alive, and he is here. That is all that matters."

Albano had encouraged Hagop to enjoy a long, hot bath, have a good night's sleep, and order as much food and wine to the room as he liked. But when he knocked on the hotel room's door the next morning, there was no answer. Thinking that Hagop must have gone on a walk, Albano let himself in with his hotel key. Overnight, the pristine room had turned to a pigsty. Hagop was not inside the bed but on the floor, snoring loudly. He had moved most of the bedding and pillows around him like a sort of nest, which was surrounded by toppled glasses, ice buckets, plates of leftover food, and empty wine bottles. By the smell of things, he still had not bathed. More worrisome were the broken chair and a cracked mirror, the shattered wine bottle on the floor, and the red splatter on the wall, as though, at some point in the night, Hagop had been in the throes of a fit of rage. But now he slept like a puppy that looked contented and unrepentant amongst the ruins he had created. Albano went around the room and picked up trash. He placed the empty dishes and bottles on a tray outside the door and tidied up the room the best he could. When Hagop woke up an hour later, his first words were, "When will we be on our way?"

"On our way to where?" Albano asked.

"Do you live far away? Will we take a train or an automobile?" Hagop yawned and stretched. "I hope not a boat. Do you remember how we used to admire the Levantine's wealth, their palaces and the way they dressed, and their many servants? Now you are just like them. Better than them!" He laughed like a child on Christmas morning. "Your fortune has changed and now mine has too!" Hagop reached around him. Lifting covers and pillows and finding nothing he asked, "Can you call for more wine?"

"It is only eight in the morning," Albano said. He hesitated. "What happened here last night? Were you all right?"

"Does your palace have a cellar full of wine bottles?"

"I will disappoint you, I'm afraid, dear friend. I do not have a palace, or anything resembling the ways of the Levantines. Tell me, do you always drink this much?"

"I am only celebrating my freedom. So? When are we going?"

If Albano had any notion of introducing Hagop into his life, those thoughts vanished the moment he had entered the chaos of the hotel room. He did not know what to tell Hagop, and so he improvised. "I thought that for the time being you would be comfortable living here, while you gain strength."

"Why would I be made to stay in a hotel rather than one of the many rooms of your palace?"

"I don't have a palace."

Hagop continued; he was chatty, in a great mood. "Do you have servants, and cars, and many rooms, and a cook?"

"I, eh, yes, but … I want to take you to see a doctor, heal some of that vermin, and get some health back into you, and then when I have fattened you up a bit, I shall buy you clothes that befit you."

Hagop found a bottle under his pillow and drank from it. "God is good to me at last. I have found my savior!" Albano could not decide if Hagop was speaking of him or the wine.

"How about we run you a nice bath," Albano suggested. Hagop finally took his bath, but Albano had to undress him and coax him for an hour into stepping into the water. Hagop mistrusted the whole thing, only accepting a small amount of water at the very bottom of the tub, as though drowning was a very real possibility. He pushed away soap and washcloths angrily as if they were instruments of torture. Perhaps this was natural. Hagop's body had the frailty of a near skeleton. He was wobbly on his feet. His skin was nothing but sores and scabs. His filth was such that all the grime could not come off. Albano hoped to do a better job on subsequent baths, but for today it was a victory.

After Hagop's second night in Nice, Albano arrived to find him still drunk. To his relief, nothing in the room was broken. The repairs of the night before were sure to cost him considerably. Hagop asked to see Albano's palace again, and so Albano took a deep breath and said, "If you do not like this hotel I can find you a place of your own."

Hagop asked coldly, "Is it that you don't want me to live in the same house as your wife and children?"

The question was direct. It was the first time that Hagop mentioned Albano's family, and Albano caught himself trying to remember just how much he had told him in the letter. Had he said that his house was in Cannes and not in Nice? Had he told him his address? "It's just that, my family is in transition," he said. "My wife … well, she has not acclimated to the Côte d'Azur yet. She feels I have uprooted her from Paris, and now to impose a permanent houseguest would not be the right time." But Hagop was drinking the last of his wine and not paying attention.

That day, Hagop continued to order wine and to drink until he was sick. Albano did not have the heart to slow him down, but he worried. If Hagop had gotten used to drinking to numb his pain, the road to good health and a good life would be far harder to climb.

The rest of the week, Hagop continued to be interested in nothing outside his own physical comfort. He wanted cigarettes. He wanted food. He wanted a whore or two brought in. Albano conceded him all his requests but remained vague about possible prostitutes. Hagop still did not ask Albano about his family aside from brief, incoherent questions about "the palace." That entire week, he made little progress aside from learning to sleep in the bed. Each day, he woke up drunk, and that's how he went to sleep. Neither of them mentioned Xandra again.

This went on for an entire very expensive month, and the progress was slow. Each day, Albano would leave La Bastide early in the morning, and he would return late at night. In all his time with Hagop, he had not been able to coax him into taking another bath, but Hagop began to wash on his own, one body part at a time, over the sink, which felt to Albano like progress. For unknown reasons, he refused to leave the hotel room. He did not act fearful of the exterior world, only disinterested. He accepted for a doctor to come to the room to look at him and the doctor, a self-important man who acted disgusted during the entire visit, prescribed ointments and potions as well as an experimental drug that showed great promise in treating syphilis.

By the end of the month, there were at last signs of progress: the vermin was gone and his skin looked better. A barber came to the room to cut his hair and trim his beard. He and Albano had their first meal in the hotel restaurant rather than inside the room. During that meal, Albano was deeply uncomfortable. Hagop did not know French table manners. He burped, ate with his mouth open, wiped his lips with his sleeves. He spoke so loudly and drank so much that people asked not to be seated next to them. Soon, there was a circle of empty tables around theirs. Albano decided it was best for everyone not to repeat the experience until he could teach Hagop the ways of the French.

The second month, Hagop appeared to drink less, and Albano felt encouraged. They ventured on short outings around the hotel. They visited an excellent dentist, and Hagop was fitted for a denture, which would take some time to build. Together, they shopped for clothing. Albano said he would take Hagop to a proper tailor once he had regained some of his bulk. It was more difficult to find shoes that fit his distorted feet, and so Albano bought him several pairs of espadrilles. As he did all this, Hagop was passive. He silently observed things, and it was difficult to know if he was pleased, dissatisfied, or emotionally absent. All through that time, he acted like a demanding child that tolerated no lapse of attention and found it perfectly natural that Albano spent his days doing nothing else than care for him, order things for him, translate the newspaper for him, play endless card games with him, shop with him, take walks with him, and then return to his family at night.

To Albano's relief, Hagop no longer asked to move into his palace. He was capricious, mercurial, at times ebullient and playful like a child, and at other times, for long stretches of the day, sometimes for the entire day, he became sullen and antagonistic. By the end of the second month, Albano felt no closer to introducing him to his family. Every evening he would tell Xandra what Hagop had said and done, and they agreed that his behavior was too unpredictable. Early on, Albano had admitted to Xandra that Hagop had known all along that she was alive in Smyrna, burned and destitute, but that he had been indifferent to her fate. He had received her letters, had known that she was looking for him. He had not cared. This was as sad as it was peculiar. They decided that Hagop could not be told that she lived in Cannes. Hagop was in no shape to be reasonable.

In early January 1940, the phony war was still going on, without much combat. Whatever this war was supposed to look like, it didn't feel like one. There was in the air a sense of suspended animation, part anticipation, part dread. In Cannes, the temperature dropped, the sky was gray, and the sea turned nervous and black. They felt the sting of the first food and oil restrictions. Albano rented, in Nice, a small but handsomely furnished apartment with plenty of light. "The apartment is close enough from the center of town that you can be independent. You can walk to shops and restaurants and to the market. See, in this kitchen, you can make your meals," Albano said as Hagop followed him wordlessly from room to room. "There is running water, hot and cold, in both the kitchen and the bathroom. See, there is a radio for music."

Hagop looked around morosely. "How will I buy all this food and wine you promised?" he asked. "I have nothing." Albano handed Hagop several hundred-francs notes. Hagop pocketed the money and continued to brood.

"I'm afraid he is angry with me," Albano told Xandra that evening. "He is hurt that I don't introduce him to my family, and he has every right to be. He is bored; he is depressed; he drinks a frightening amount. He wants to live like a hermit. He hasn't a taste for much."

"Up until now, he had to keep moving to survive," Xandra suggested, "and now that he has a roof over his head, he is left to think, and thinking is painful."

"You and I know what it's like to live in a kind of fog when the only times of clarity bring unendurable mental pain. To be idle is a dangerous thing. The mind is left to roam and lick every corner and interstice of one's pain. And I understand all this. Only he always seems on the verge of saying something irreparably hostile. Hagop has moments of energy between stretches of lethargy when his anger flares up. But rage is the lone emotion that seems to make him feel good."

"You never took to the bottle or to anger," Xandra noted.

"It is a strange thing, Xandra. He is the Hagop we love, and at the same time he is not."

"You loved him more than I did. He is my brother, but he was never my friend."

"Maybe my expectations were selfish. I wanted to have him returned to us intact. But that would have been impossible; I realize this now."

"What will you do?"

"I'm sure he will get back on his feet soon."

"Perhaps the solution is to introduce your family to him by bringing them to him rather than the other way around. You could meet at a restaurant. He doesn't need to come to La Bastide. That way, he will not feel rejected, and neither will he see me."

"You might be right. Also, I want him to begin to change his mind about me and stop seeing me as a rich "Jewish Prince" as he calls me now."

"My brother never seemed the kind of person whose mind could be changed," Xandra said.

Over the following months, and through February, March, and April, those plans were abandoned as Hagop's behavior did not improve. After he moved into the apartment, which lacked the luxurious amenities of Le Negresco, letting him win at cards was the only means to briefly lift his spirit. He still would not take care of himself the way Albano had hoped. In fact, it was worse now that there was no maid to straighten the place or room service to feed him. He often didn't bathe or shave. The apartment was a disaster of dirty dishes, clothes, and cigarette butts in every empty dish. The only food Hagop consumed was bread from the bakery that stood at the street corner, and ever-increasing quantities of wine. Daily, for a month, Hagop asked to move back to the hotel and pouted when Albano explained that it was too expensive, that there were the war and restrictions, and they were all living on his savings. Although Hagop complained of boredom, he did nothing to entertain himself. He waited all day for Albano to arrive so that they could walk by the sea, go on an automobile ride, or shop for groceries. Despite Albano's encouragement, he refused to visit the Apostolic Church, where he was sure to meet members of the Armenian community, people that spoke his language. Hagop always came up with new excuses. "People look at me with disgust," he would say.

"It will take time, but if you try, you will succeed."

"I am not like you with languages. I never learned to speak French more than the few words it took to sell newspapers in Smyrna."

Albano hired a tutor to come daily, but the tutor complained that on most days Hagop refused to open his door. "Do you not want to learn the language?" Albano asked him.

"France was never the country where I wanted to live," Hagop moaned. "This is your idea of where I should be, and what can I do but comply?"

"I am only making suggestions so that you can live better in France. Is there a country where you would rather be? I thought you might like Nice. It's a beautiful city."

"It's too cold."

"Spring is coming. I will buy you warmer clothes until you get accustomed."

Hagop burst into laughter. "Buy me warmer clothes! Listen to yourself speak as though I am a woman for whom you want to buy fur."

"July and June will get warmer."

"I am alone here. I know no one, and no one speaks my language. At least in Aleppo, I had friends."

"Friends who would have murdered you in your sleep for a loaf of bread," Albano pointed out. "Why have you not tried to meet other Armenians, as I urged you to do?"

Hagop spoke bitterly. "You come, you go, in your fancy automobile. I don't even know where you live. A friend would not cast me aside. He would welcome me into his life. Not keep me hidden away like a leper."

"You aren't quite your old self yet. I thought that a few more weeks—"

"What is the harm in me meeting your family?"

"When you meet them, would you not want to be at your very best? And besides, would you not want those new teeth that will come soon?"

"So, do I scare you? Do you think I would scare them?"

"Nothing of the sort."

Hagop looked at him with drunken malevolence. "Come on, Albano. You must be just a little scared of me."

Even though it did not feel right to leave Hagop by himself, Albano made a conscious effort to spend less time with him and more time with his family. He had been neglecting them for months, and they were too isolated. He thought that it would do Lucienne good to meet other people, so they joined the synagogue in Nice. The pretext was that Gustave was fourteen, the age when he ought to be bar mitzvahed. But in reality, Albano thought that it would be good for the whole family to have a reason to get dressed up and get out of La Bastide. For some weeks, they took the automobile down to Nice to attend the Shabbat services on Fridays and stayed afterward to share the wine and bread and mingle a bit. But it did not seem to cheer Lucienne much.

One Friday night, as they walked down the stone steps after service, stopping to offer a few francs to the ever-growing sea of downtrodden men and women that awaited their help, Lucienne removed her hat, and Albano saw what he had not noticed before: her hair was turning gray. Lucienne was forty-one years old, so that was not so strange in itself. What bothered him was that she did not use hair coloring the way she always would have before. And she smoked too much. What did this all mean? Lucienne, usually so proud, was letting herself go.

To ask about this might offend her, so it would be best to say nothing and ask Xandra what she thought of it. On the steps, he paused long enough to observe his children. Marceline, in sharp contrast with her mother, was resplendent. Boys looked at her, and so did men. She was only sixteen years old, but the way she stood and moved, he realized now, and the kind of clothes she wore, made her appear to be a woman. The years, the worries, leaving Paris, all the time he spent with Hagop had blinded him to the fact that his family was changing. Gustave too was in between states. He sometimes looked like a child, sometimes like a man, but at still other times, he appeared to be a wounded creature that needed rescuing. The thought of

Gustave getting older gripped Albano with anguish. The war had better come and go before Gustave was of age.

Lucienne, in the end, said that she did not like the synagogue. She felt that the Jews of Nice kept to themselves and that they did not like Parisians, which might or might not be the truth because, as Albano saw it, Lucienne was the one with the tight lips and the absent gaze.

No one mentioned the bar mitzvah after that.

It was a joyful thing, the following week, to watch Hagop be fitted for his new denture and to see him emerge out of the dentist chair an entirely different man. He smiled in front of the mirror again and again, trying on his hat, straightening his necktie, trying out this new face of his. It was as though his new smile brought forth the transformation that had been slowly happening to the rest of his body, and now it all came together splendidly. He had put on a good twenty pounds. His face was fuller, he looked healthier, and in the clothes Albano had him fitted for, Hagop looked almost distinguished.

The two of them went for a walk in Nice. Hagop stopped in front of every mirror and every glass-paned window to admire himself. He had learned how to behave in restaurants. They ate at Acchiardo in old Nice, and Hagop tipped his hat to women, and the women smiled. Albano was sure they had turned a corner. He was so encouraged that he nearly told him about Xandra. But as lunch went on and Hagop ordered a second bottle of wine for himself, Albano decided to say nothing.

The next few weeks were difficult at home. The war, phony or not, was putting everyone on edge, Lucienne especially. She endlessly confronted Albano for spending time away from La Bastide and the family. She had convinced herself that he was having an affair with a woman in town. He decided that the best approach would be the truth. He explained to Lucienne that he had been helping a friend who was a refugee from Syria.

Also, Lucienne's ways clashed with the financial constraints of war. She gave Xandra hell whenever she wasn't able to procure an item she wanted. She accused Albano of avarice when he asked her to be more circumspect with money. She did not go a day without demanding to return to Paris. And so, Albano decided to spread out his visits to Hagop. Between Hagop and Lucienne, Albano did not know which one was more difficult to handle. Both of them made demands and were angry with him, but at least with Lucienne, the complaints were something he could address. Lucienne ranted, but Hagop sulked. Both of them continuously asked for money and nice things despite his protest that money could soon be devalued or that his funds could run out entirely. Neither took the threat of a German invasion seriously, Lucienne because of the long hours she spent on the telephone with Parisian friends who told her that Albano was acting foolishly and urged her to return to Paris, and Hagop because he felt this war had nothing to do with him since he was neither German, French, or Jewish.

Albano was disappointed in Hagop and disappointed in himself. He felt every day less willing to bring him in contact with Lucienne and the children, less ready to tell him about Xandra. His own naiveté had brought on an inextricable situation. Hagop was devoured by demons Albano could not begin to understand and emotional wounds he was powerless to heal.

Xandra asked of him too. She told him to pay closer attention to Marceline.

"I am torn between Hagop and Lucienne. There is not a moment of peace. And besides, Marceline and Gustave behave less like children than the adults."

"Still, they are children. Marceline needs fatherly guidance."

"Why? Is there something I should worry about?"

"She is defiant with Lucienne, and Lucienne doesn't know what to do. And Gustave is confused. You were spending all kinds of time with him, but now that Hagop is here, you aren't available the way you were before."

"What I want most of all is be alone with *you.* I want to take *you* away for the day as we did months ago. Do you remember that beautiful time we had in Agay? Please meet me at the orchard tonight. The evenings are warmers. It will be a moonless night, perfect for romance."

Xandra hesitated. "The children go there at night."

"It's not as though you let me do anything they could witness," Albano said. Realizing he sounded bitter, he said, "I only want to talk to you in peace." He smiled and admitted, "And kiss you some." He thought about it. "Why would Marceline or Gustave go to the orchard at night?"

Xandra lowered her gaze. "They are teenagers, and I cannot control them."

"And I cannot control Hagop. But he is showing a few positive signs. Do you know that he is finding interest in bird watching? He wanted me to buy him binoculars the other day when we walked into town, and now he never leaves without a small notebook in which he records his findings."

"That is unlike my brother," Xandra said.

"Soon I am hopeful Hagop will re-enter the world of the living. He will accept employment, find a woman to marry, and hopefully put aside his rancor."

"May God hear you," Xandra said.

Because of all the time he spent with Hagop, Albano's affairs were being dangerously neglected. There was the matter of his work with Moshe. There was Lucienne, who was becoming more strident and upset. There was poor Gustave, who found himself without the closeness of the relationship they had when they arrived in Cannes, and Marceline, who in the blink of an eye had metamorphosed from a precocious girl into a headstrong young woman. On top of all this, he could find no time to replenish himself with his Sundays with Xandra. Also, if he was honest with himself, being around Hagop was a drain to his spirit. "It is time you find things to do for yourself," he found the courage to tell him one day in late April. "I need to tend to other things. You need to look for work, look for friends. Maybe meet a woman and fall in love. The truth is, I spend too much time with you and not enough time doing everything else."

They were inside his apartment playing cards. Hagop, who had been in a fine mood, whistling between his teeth and joking around, walked away from the table. He went to the window and lit a cigarette, sulking in silence. Finally, he said, "The money you give me is not enough."

Albano, who still sat at the card table, took out his wallet. "How much would you like?"

Hagop took a deep inhale of his cigarette and let the ashes fall to the rug. "When I was in Aleppo, I was a poor man. A man without even a house to call his own, a man dressed in shreds, a man full of lice and vermin. I was the lowest of the low. And yet I had more dignity than I have now, waiting for your visits, your money, and your whim."

Albano put his cards down and breathed through the hurt he felt. He had given Hagop every waking minute he had, neglecting his family, neglecting Xandra the most. "Let me find you work," he said. "That is the only way you will get your life back."

"Why, brother, can I not meet your children and wife?" Hagop said resentfully. "Is it that you find me unfit to breathe the same air as them?"

Albano had nothing to respond to this. Again and again, Hagop was returning to this complaint, and no matter what Albano tried to do for him, Hagop turned it around, mistaking everything for a slight. He wanted to tell Hagop that he needed to take responsibility for his life. Instead, he said, "We will find good work that suits you, and so you'll earn your own living."

"What is it that you'll have me do?"

Albano had tried to broach the subject of work many times, but this was the first time Hagop seemed receptive. Now he told him his plan excitedly. "You should learn the way I learned, from the bottom up. I worked in Moshe's warehouse at first, learning all about manufacturing and shipping, and then I took accounting classes and went into the finances, the marketing. And you must take French lessons. Once your French is good, you can enter management and sales." What Albano had in mind for Hagop was something different, something to do with resistance work, if and when he was sure that Hagop could be trusted. There was no rug business anymore. There was an office in Algiers; there were employees, invoices, and orders but no inventory. It was a front.

Hagop pursed his lips. "That is not the way family works in my world. You do not start your own relative at the very bottom of the ladder but at the top."

Albano thought of all the shelling of nuts Hagop's father had put him through. "This is the same way Moshe taught me," he said.

"I can see how that pachyderm would delight in watching a pretty boy sweat and carry heavy loads. But you know I am an intellectual. I am as smart as ten French men. It would be better for them to learn to respect me from the start by having me manage them."

"If it was my own company, things might be different. I would have more leeway. But I have sold my business to come here."

"How sweet it must be to be retired at such a young age."

"I am involved in a different kind of work," Albano said. "It's something to do with the war, but I do not make any money."

"What is it you do that makes no money?" Hagop said with contempt.

Albano was surprised that it had taken so long for Hagop to wonder about this, and even more surprised he had never prepared for an answer. He had no time to ask himself how much was safe to reveal, especially when Hagop took so poorly to vagueness and secrecy. "Many of us believe France unprepared to face Hitler," Albano said. "In the eventuality of a German invasion, and in case the enemy takes control of France, we are putting in place channels so that underground groups will be able to receive funds."

Hagop placed a new cigarette between his lips and lit it. He came back to sit at the card table, blew smoke in Albano's face and said, "You look tired my friend."

Albano looked up at Hagop and admitted, "I am tired, indeed."

"It takes energy to maintain all those secrets." Hagop smiled and took an inhale of his cigarettes and added, "and all those lies."

There was an expression on Hagop's face Albano didn't like. The same expression he'd had years ago before confronting him about Xandra when he had found the embroidered handkerchief she had made for him as a memento of her love for him. "What lies?" Albano asked, sounding unconvincing even to himself.

Hagop looked at him with satisfaction. "Your dirty secrets. Oh, do not bother with the charade; I know them all."

"My secrets?"

"I have secrets of my own," Hagop said.

"You do?"

"I have lied to you, I confess. Please do not hate me, my dear friend. I told you I didn't go to the Apostolic Church, but it was a lie. I have been there many times."

"You have?" Albano said happily.

"You were correct in one regard: the Armenian community is a close-knit one." He looked at Albano intently and smiled his Hagop smile. "People were eager to tell me who they knew from Smyrna who has ended up here." Albano felt a chill sweep through his body as Hagop went on. "Lo and behold, they told me of a woman who had survived the Smyrna fire, disfigured the poor soul, and who now lives here, in the next town, as a maid to a Jewish family. You can imagine my surprise when I learned her name was Xandra." He paused for dramatic effect and said, "And you can imagine how even more surprised I was when I learned that the family she worked for was *yours*."

Albano looked at his feet, shook his head. He was sweating. Had Hagop screamed at him he would have preferred it. "This was not the way I wanted you to learn this," he said. "I was trying to find the right time to—"

"Is this why you never wanted me to see your house? Because you did not want me to see that she was there?"

"It is complicated," Albano said. His face was hot, his hands unsteady. "I must explain everything from the beginning for you to understand how this came about. I had started a family in Paris. I believed Xandra dead! And then—"

Hagop interrupted, "You are married to a French woman, that much is true. And so, my sister, she is *what* to you, exactly?"

"Moshe was the one who discovered her and brought her to France. She had nothing, and so I offered her to…." He hesitated, all the words that came out of his mouth, all his reasoning, all his justifications, now sounding trite and wrong. "Live with us," he added.

"So, I am forgotten in an apartment, and Xandra gets to live with you and your wife." He looked at Albano and smiled meanly. "A harem of sorts?"

"She is the caretaker of my children who love her very much, and she loves them back."

"Your wife knows that she was your whore, back in Smyrna?"

"It has nothing to do with—"

"Is she, still?"

"Hagop, how can you say such things after all this time? I have always had deep feelings for Xandra. She and I have a deep … bond … as well as … a friendship."

"Does your wife know about your little arrangement?"

"I did not want to tell her that Xandra and I knew each other in the past," Albano admitted.

"What would be the harm in telling her if you are doing nothing wrong?"

"It was simpler not to say … It didn't matter … and we … I did not want my wife to be upset. And so, my wife thinks of Xandra as our children's nanny. Which she is. And that is all."

Hagop pondered this for a moment. "But you do fuck her, don't you?"

"I do not. We—"

"If you did not, you would have no reason to hide the past from your wife. Or your present from me."

"It's not like this. Not at all!"

Hagop burst into laughter. "And so, you expect me to believe that you fuck that ugly wife of yours, but not my sister?"

A new chill swept through Albano's body. He had trouble finding his voice. "How … how do you know what Lucienne looks like?"

"Do you think that I would hear the news that my sister is here and not go look for myself? I saw your ugly wife. And I saw those children of yours." He laughed triumphantly. "The binoculars you bought me? Those birds I was speaking of? It was them! That daughter you have? Now, that is a beautiful girl." He added, shaking his head, "But the wife?" He shook his head and clicked his tongue disapprovingly.

Albano felt a pulsing energy shoot through his arms and fists. "When was this?"

"Where do good Jews go on the Shabbath? Not to be closer to God, but to be seen and admired by other Jews. There isn't a grand enough synagogue in Cannes, is there? The good one is right here in Nice. All I needed to do is wait by the temple. I recognized your car. I saw you with them. You didn't see me. That is my genius, you see? I can make myself invisible. All those good Jews walk right past a hobo sitting on the steps of their temple." He took an inhale of his cigarette, waved his hand agreeably. "Oh, do not feel bad, it is the same with Christians and Muslims. If you want to hide in plain sight, dress in the way that ensures that no one will want to look your way." To demonstrate, he took the denture out of his mouth, hunched his back, made a terrible face, and laughed.

Albano put his elbows on the table and took his face in his hands, looking contrite but thinking fast. "I feel terrible Hagop. I did not know how to tell you any of this."

Hagop plopped his teeth back in his mouth and sucked them back into place. The act would have been comical had he not added, "Here is what I want to know: why bring me to France if it was to make me feel like a pariah?"

"I wanted to help you. I still do."

"Another thing I don't understand is how your wife lets you have a mistress right under your roof. Is it because the mistress is even uglier than the wife? Your wife could never believe you'd want to fuck her."

"Please stop using those vile words. Xandra and I don't have that—"

"Why concern yourself with vile words just as you are committing the vile deed, dear friend? I am told that Xandra is so ugly now no one can look at her. But you're trying to keep us apart, aren't you?"

Albano finally erupted. "How could I not? I had every intention to welcome you into our lives. Every intention! But you knew Xandra was alive all these years, and you didn't even bother to answer her letters. I am trying to help you, Hagop, you know I am, and yet you keep refusing to be helped. And you are refusing to help yourself!"

Hagop was nonplussed by Albano's anger. "Do you know what this looks like?" he asked sweetly. "Not to me, but to a stranger that might enter this conversation? It looks like my sister, whom you left to die in Smyrna, my sister who is so deformed that she will never find a husband, has become your slave."

"She is no one's slave!"

"She is, unless she can leave if she wishes."

"Of course, she can."

"Even with the way her face is? And war happening on every continent? Is she left with any choice other than to be at your mercy? It would seem to a stranger's eye that she is, in fact, your prisoner."

"I pay her a wage. I only took her from Paris and to the South of France to protect her!"

"The Russian nobles paid their serfs too; only they had the right of life and death over them. What would happen to an Armenian girl, the most hated and persecuted race in the world, if she was left on her own without protection from a rich Jew?"

"I wish you could understand. Xandra wants to be here."

"But you legally have no right over her."

"None whatsoever."

"So, she is mine," Hagop said.

Albano was astounded. "Yours?"

Hagop pursed his lips. "She is my blood. When I leave France, she will come with me."

Albano crossed his arms to control the shaking of his body. "This is not how the world works. Not this part of the world."

Hagop chuckled. "Which is why I must take her to a part of the world where it does." He slapped Albano on the shoulder, "You are so pale. You know I am having fun at your expense, don't you?" Albano looked at Hagop, relieved at first, but then he saw that the angry light in Hagop's eyes was intact. "Is it why you won't show me your family, dear brother? Why you cannot let me see the nice little Jewish family full of lies and deceit you have crafted for yourself? You are afraid I will tell your wife the truth."

Albano felt a profound sadness fall over him. "What is it you want from me?"

"I will tell you one thing that could be of comfort to me. I, exhausted as I am, must do everything myself. I must shop and cook for myself like a woman, and clean after myself when I am so tired. I am a beast of labor, no better off here than in the refugee camp."

"Do you want me to hire you a servant?"

"Never, Albano. No charity, please. You are already doing so much for me I am starting to feel insulted." Hagop sat down in an armchair, crossed his legs and tilted his back against the padding of the chair, observing him. "No," Hagop continued. "I will only take what is mine. My sister. She can tend to me." And with this, he smiled his new bright white smile, and his eyes shone with cold calculation.

Albano's mind raced. Hagop did not seem like a victim of anything, at this moment. He did not seem miserable. He was dominant, very much in control; perhaps he had been in control the entire time. Had it all been an act? The man Albano faced was not the Hagop of his youth, but neither was he the helpless immigrant, the traumatized victim of genocide he had appeared to be ever since he arrived in Nice. Had the absence of a response to his letters, had Hagop's every move since the boat brought him to Nice been nothing but manipulation and brewing resentment? No, it could not have been. You must be a little scared of me, Hagop had said weeks ago. And Albano had denied it. But now he realized that he had been wary of Hagop all along.

Albano felt the overwhelming urge to leave now, dart to the house, take the family and Xandra and drive off toward a different city. Where, he didn't know. Away from Hagop was all that mattered. It would be days until Hagop discovered where they lived if he didn't know already. No, no. He was overreacting. Hagop was his friend. A friend in need who had just learned news he disapproved of and was justifiably angry. Albano made sure to speak in a steady voice. He needed to gain time. "Xandra is busy with my children who cannot be without her."

Hagop flew his fingers impatiently. "Then at night. After they have gone to sleep she can come to my place, mend and clean my things, make me supper."

"I will ask her," Albano lied.

"What ask her?" Hagop said. "She doesn't get a choice. You *tell* her."

And so, that night Albano went to Xandra and told her the terrible thing that was happening. "And so, his anger is placed on you, wanting you, as though you're his property."

In Xandra's expression, Albano could read that she was not surprised. A part of her had expected this kind of thing from Hagop all along. "He is a traditional man from my culture. From his standpoint, this is a natural thing," she said.

"Do you really think it is about being served? No, it is about claiming you as property. It is about challenging me. I am worried, Xandra. Those things Hagop says … one minute he is laughing, the other he praises me, the next he threatens. I see it now. From the first moment, he resented me. For being rich, for having avoided the terrible things he endured. Now your brother sees that while he was in deep misery, I went on to do precisely what he had forbidden me to do, which was to be with you."

"But we are not together in that way."

"He doesn't believe it or doesn't care."

"What brother is he to me who would rather know me dead or trapped in poverty and servitude than happy with you?"

"I am deceiving Lucienne and the children, and now Hagop. Also, I am not giving you the life you deserve. I am asking you to make all the concessions."

"We are both making concessions."

"What if Hagop is right? My life is nothing but lies."

"The deceptions are the only way to keep all those you love close by and protected, and that includes Hagop."

"I thought that finding him would be one of the greatest joys of my life. I thought that at last, I would be complete. Instead, I am afraid it will be my family's demise."

"You think he is about to tell Lucienne?"

"I don't know what he wants to do. I cannot understand his motives or his designs."

"Do you think he will blackmail you?"

"I'm not sure," Albano said, although he had to admit to himself that he was already being blackmailed.

Xandra breathed in and looked resolute. "I can go to his apartment and work for him if this will appease him."

Albano shook his head forcefully. "Never. I will not let you near him. Tomorrow I will tell him I can hire someone to serve him or nothing at all."

"And then what do you think will happen?"

"I am afraid he will want to punish us for being together."

"Do you think he wants to physically harm us?" Xandra asked.

"Of course not,"

"He has done that before."

"He was young then."

"He has it in him," Xandra said.

"He will not harm anyone," Albano said with as much conviction as he could put into his voice. "But he might tell my family about us, and this I cannot have. I will make a telephone call to Moshe in Algeria."

"You will ask for his counsel?"

"His counsel, and once again for his help."

The following day, Albano came to Hagop's prepared, but to his great surprise, Hagop refused to let him enter the apartment. He was waiting for him at the foot of the building and coldly asked for Albano's set of keys back. Albano handed them to him, not understanding. "Let's go to the park," Hagop said.

For someone claiming not to know the city, Hagop now seemed perfectly at ease in the streets. Also, he walked straight now. The limping, that hesitant gate, was gone. Albano had the sinking understanding that Hagop had been pretending to be worse than he was.

The park was deserted but for three French sailors on leave. It was early May. Trees were in bloom, as were the tulips planted in well-groomed beds at the foot of the trees. He and Hagop sat on a stone bench facing a water feature where a dozen sparrows cleaned their feathers, sending sprays of water around them. The ground of crushed stone was covered in the pink petals of ornamental cherries. Hagop scooped a handful of pebbles and flung them at the birds with surprising accuracy. "You ask what I do in my days since you have refused me the dignity of employment?" he said. "I have been very busy. I take my bus to Cannes in the morning, and I wait. Many days I am able to catch a glimpse of those rare birds that are so fascinating to me with my pretty spyglass you bought me yourself." Hagop let the sentence float, his silence heavy with meaning. Albano knew exactly what it meant, and what it meant iced his blood. He said nothing so Hagop went on. "That nice, polite boy of yours. And that daughter, such a gorgeous girl. I do not think much of the ugly wife."

What to say now? What to ask? Albano sensed that he had entered a dreadful game of chess with an opponent far more advanced than he. "Why do you spy on my family?" he finally asked.

"For me to survive this long required a superior mind, a crafty mind," Hagop said. "You and I are the same in that way, cunning and clever. The question remains, who is the cleverer one between us. You brought me here and thought I would become one of your admirers. Someone whose life and thoughts you can control. But I am not that crippled man I appeared to be. I am in fact powerful."

"I don't want you around them," Albano said icily.

Hagop guffawed. "Oh, now it comes: the truth!"

"You need to take control of your thoughts. Until you do, I cannot let you into my life."

"Let me into your life? Why would I want to be in your life of lies? I despise everything about it. You brought me to France for your own vanity. You thought I would become indebted to you, forever speechless with admiration, forever humbled by my own shortcomings, forever blessing the ground on which you walk."

"You're speaking nonsense."

"You underestimated me. Just as you did when you thought you could trap me in the cave so that you could steal my money."

"Can't you remember?" Albano exclaimed, outraged. "You were robbed! This, after leaving Xandra and me in the cave with nothing!"

"You trampled the values I held dearest by desecrating my own sister—"

"Only I hadn't touched her."

"Leaving me no choice that day but to either kill you both or exile myself. I had twenty years to think of this, Albano. I loved you like a brother, and so I could not kill you that day at the cave. Instead, I chose to leave, and my life was a nightmare thereafter. And to this day I have nothing. Whereas you have everything, and all this because I sacrificed myself for you."

"Had you stayed put in the cave as I begged you to do, you would not have been taken by the police!" Albano exclaimed, furious. "Your demise was your own doing."

"And your vanity will be your undoing! You wanted me to witness your superiority; only you cannot control me. You should never have brought me to France, Albano. I will never stop short of gaining justice."

"What are you saying?"

"I have not yet decided what would please me. One word from me and your children and wife will find out who you really are and who their dear nanny is. Do I want to destroy your family? Or do I demand that you sign over to me all your money? It would only be fair. Or should I not be so merciful and repay myself for my sister's honor."

"I don't know what you mean?"

Hagop casually said, "You have a virgin."

Albano jumped to his feet and faced Hagop. "You are insane! If you touch a single strand of hair on my daughter's head, I will kill you indeed. I will!"

"Then do not fail, Albano," Hagop said with icy calm. "As each time you have damaged me, I have come back stronger. As you told me that day on Mount Pagus, one of us will die. And so, we shall see who it is."

Albano was seized with panic. He steadied himself. He thought of nothing to say, and so he turned away and left.

As he moved toward the exit of the park, past the row of ornamental cherry trees, he heard more pebbles being thrown into the water and birds scattering away. Once he turned back to look at Hagop, but the bench was empty.

On the drive back home, Albano stopped on the side of the road. He squeezed the wheel with his fists until they turned white. What would he do now? The madman Hagop had become had left nothing of the Hagop he loved. No matter what Albano and Xandra had dreamed up, that man, that friendship, no longer existed. The rage and contempt Hagop had expressed that day at the cave had taken root over the years, nurtured in the fertile terrain of his psyche by the terrible persecutions he had suffered and witnessed. In his few months in France, Hagop had gained in strength, but not the kind of strength Albano had imagined. His strength, bred of agony, had transformed into a sinister force. A force that could not be reasoned with. A dangerous force. Now Hagop was threatening his family, threatening to harm his daughter. How could this be?

Xandra would not be surprised. She alone had been able to see Hagop for who he was. She had witnessed his temper and harshness before. Even as she had prayed for the safety of her brother, she had been wary of him. Albano had been blinded by a ridiculous idea of how things could be that had no basis in facts. And now, to think that this crazy man knew his family's whereabouts, that he possibly even knew his address!

He thought of the conversation he and Moshe had had just a few days before. Moshe believed that Hitler would not relent. He was certain that this phony war was only giving Hitler time to prepare. The time to leave France was immediately Moshe had said.

Albano got to La Bastide transported by a new form of urgency. He stopped the car in front of the door, stormed into the house, walked past Lucienne and went straight to the kitchen to speak to Xandra. In Armenian he told her everything Hagop had said as Lucienne stood in the kitchen, her arms limp along her body, a look of complete confusion on her face.

"What will we do?" Xandra answered in Armenian, trying not to show her own panic or to look at Lucienne.

"This is what Moshe and I prepared for. We are ready. A few telephone calls are all it will take."

"When?"

"In the next few days."

"How?"

"We'll take our boat at night. We will meet another boat Moshe arranged once we're at sea. Once in North Africa, we will get new identities. No one here or elsewhere will know where we have gone."

"What about Hagop?"

"I will pay for his rent for two years in advance. I'll open a bank account in his name with enough money to live reasonably. I will leave that information for him, which he will receive once we are gone."

"This will enrage him," Xandra said.

"There is no better solution."

Albano then turned to Lucienne who was still standing near the kitchen door. "We are leaving," he said.

"What? Where? Why?"

"The plan you and I discussed, our departure for Africa. We're putting it in motion."

"What I want to know is –?" Lucienne began to say.

Albano interrupted her. "If the Nazis invade, the frontiers will close. Then they'll be no one to protect the Jews of France and no way to escape."

"What I don't understand is—"

Albano raised his palm to stop her from speaking. "Lucienne, I know that you think I am overreacting, and I know that you fear that I might be wrong. But whether I am or not, the result is the same. We are leaving France."

Lucienne said in a small voice, "What I don't understand is … why did you rush to tell Sandra all this? Why tell *her* before telling *me*?"

Albano could not respond. After all these years of keeping his secret, in his anguish and his hast, he had been careless. Lucienne was looking at him interrogatively, and then a cloud passed over her face, a terrible realization. She stood very still, trembling and pale. But what could he tell Lucienne at this point? The menace came from everywhere, and they needed to run away, to go as far as possible. He did not expect Lucienne to understand. But in time, she would come to appreciate that he had wanted to save her life even if she was, as he could read on her face, suddenly finding out that he loved someone else, and that the person he loved might well be Sandra.

CHAPTER 8

The Naked Man

Three in the morning. Cassie kept her head firmly grounded on her pillow, her arms alongside her, afraid to move a muscle. Her skin tingled. Her palms tingled. She just needed to wait this out. Breathe.

Beside her, Hervé was sleeping peacefully, his bare back rising gently with each breath. What would this man whose name she did not know twenty hours ago think of her if she woke him up at three in the morning because she was having an anxiety attack?

Breathe.

The pain in her chest grew sharp. Her erratic little inhalations did not fill her lungs. The pain was not real, she told herself. It was an illusion. She had enough of those episodes under her belt to know that she was *probably* not dying. No actual physical danger came from feeling heartbroken.

How many of her memories were real? And even if they were, the offenses were subtle. Nothing that would allow her to point a decisive finger. And like the pain in her chest, nothing real had happened, no sexual abuse, no physical violence, not even shouting, threats, or insults, nothing that could justify her existing in a semi-permanent state of heartache. Her childhood was not exactly Oliver Twist material. Her father didn't drink. He didn't take drugs. He provided. Cassie had only suffered from benign neglect, small meannesses, cruelties that could be just as easily dismissed, even by herself, as a figment of her imagination. The pain came in weird waves, like this, and after what had transpired in the last two days, she should have expected a relapse, especially at night, when she felt most helpless. With her dad, there had been nothing overt. Nothing she could quite point to that would be considered a proof. No, he didn't drink. No, he didn't take drugs. Yes, he provided. But he did not love her.

The worse part of it was not the objective part: being treated with indifference, the micro injustices. The bad part was the sense of unreality. As Cassie massaged the memories in her mind, those gripes, as she called them, those recriminations, she could not, to this day, trust her suspicions. She could not even trust her memories. She was an unreliable narrator of her own life story. Was she one of those people who functioned in the world by believing themselves victimized? That's what her mother and sisters thought, which was sufficient to invalidate her experience. As for her dad, what did *he* believe? Was her dad aware that he had played with her mind? *If* he had played with her mind. But if he had, and now that she had met Marceline, could she dare think that he had done so on purpose? Was it, possibly, a form of retaliation twice removed?

Peter had played a role in all of this. His brief affair soon after the twins were born was something he had denied at first, he had said that it was *all in her imagination.* She was paranoid and insecure, he said, knowing full well that she did not always know how she felt, that she had a hard time trusting her intuition. After owning up to it – but only *after* she found the emails – Peter had called the affair a wake-up call, a chance for their relationship to evolve. In their sessions with the couples' therapist, he had been sincerely remorseful but also had expressed his loneliness in the marriage. Cassie was not always emotionally or sexually available. And she was angry. The general therapeutic consensus seemed to be that if Cassie chose to stay, she needed to forgive Peter. To stay but forever hold a grudge would be to punish him, but also herself. She forgave. With two babies, what other choice did she have? And besides, she loved him.

It was in one of their sessions that the therapist asked about Cassie's childhood, and, after listening gravely, coined the phrase "benign neglect." The benign neglect Cassie suffered as a child, the therapist explained, had possibly engendered a certain sense of anger and insecurity on her part. That neediness in her, that sense of longing, the suspicion that she was not all that lovable were always dangerously near the surface and could be the product of unrequited love for her father. And what might be happening, the therapist had explained, was that she could be emotionally unavailable at times, just like her father had been. Could Peter be blamed for feeling lonely with a distracted and distrusting person such as herself?

Cassie's pulse slowed. The sense of terror subsided. She inhaled fully at last. The anxiety attack ran its course in about twenty minutes, as it usually did.

Hervé's back, lit by the soft glow of the moonlight, was strong and smooth. When she returned to Los Angeles, she would have to add an item to her bucket list, a new, surprising item, one she did not know she wanted. One Night Stand: Check. But wasn't it the gentlemanly thing to do *not* to spend the night? It was unfortunate enough to be in the throes of an anxiety attack in a hotel room far from home. This one was happening while in bed with a stranger with nowhere to hide.

Hervé's light snoring stopped. He stirred. Cassie froze up. He turned on his side toward her and wrapped an arm around her waist. This was so unexpected, the weight of this warm man's arm on her, someone holding her for the first time in years, that she could have burst into tears with relief. His voice came in the dark, whispering. "You're up?"

"No, no," she said.

"Can I stay the night?" he asked sleepily.

"Now you ask?"

"I would love to make love to you again, but I don't have the ardor of my youth."

"Oh, no. By all means. Please go back to sleep."

"What are you thinking about?"

"I'm not thinking."

"I can hear you think from here."

"Just old gripes; please go back to sleep."

"About me being here?"

"Not about you. Nothing you want to hear about at three in the morning. Go back to sleep."

Hervé propped himself on one elbow. She saw him rub his eyes in the semi-darkness. "I want to hear."

She took in a breath. "My dad. He is kind of an asshole to me. That's all."

"Tell me about it," Hervé whispered.

"It's all petty stuff."

"Then be petty."

"I've had this feeling forever that my father favored my sister. Not even favored. Loved her, while he actively disliked me." Cassie stopped herself.

"Tell me," he said. He put his arm tighter around her waist and squeezed her arm gently.

Cassie sighed. "When I was a kid, he used to do and say small, mean things."

"What kind of mean things?"

"Small ones. When no one was watching. I have no witness, no proof, and my sisters and my mother think I'm paranoid."

"What kind of mean things?" Hervé insisted.

"No hitting, no verbal abuse. Nothing like that. All right, this is going to sound stupid. There were traps. Or things that felt like traps. Just little things, from him looking away when I spoke to not laughing when I was trying to be funny to showing no interest in my schoolwork, my friends, my boyfriends, and even my kids later on. Although none of that would have been a big deal had he not been so charmed by everything my sister said and did."

"Did you confront him about it?"

"Not at all. Part of me was sure I deserved it."

As she spoke, Hervé rubbed her arm, warmly, reassuringly. All Cassie had to go on were her feelings, of hurt, of pain, of jealousy toward Odile, of injustice. But every time she tried to explain what had happened to someone, it fell flat. It made her sound vindictive. By insisting, she dug herself into a bigger hole and still proved nothing.

"You think he was gaslighting you?" Hervé asked.

"A father gaslighting his daughter?"

"Why not? It's a form of control like any other."

"But what would have been his motives? Why me? If he were a controlling, mean guy, would he not be that way with my sisters too? So, in all logic, the problem was with me. Either I was unlikable, unlovable, and annoying, or I imagined things. The whole craziness of this affected my choices, how I looked at people, how I looked at myself, how I behaved."

"You seem fine now," he said, still caressing her arm comfortingly.

"It was a pretty deep hole to climb out of," she said.

"Why are you thinking about all this now, at three in the morning?"

"All these thoughts are coming back to the surface because of his sister. It's that aunt I told you about. You see, now there is a whole new piece to the puzzle. He hated his sister, and I now think it's possible that I reminded him of her."

"Now there is a motive for the crime."

Crime, yes. There was something hard lodged deep inside Cassie's heart that released its poison slowly, and her dad had put it there. "That's what I need to get to the bottom of," she said. "My life has never quite felt like my own. It feels like a collection of broken parts. And I carry the burden of making them all fit together. And suddenly, it's like I can see an outline for the whole. I don't know what it is yet, but I don't think it's just me being crazy in the head. Not anymore."

Cassie sighed deeply. The anxiety attack had passed, and she felt flooded with relief and also hope. Her relationship to her father might have been broken long before she got there. Her marriage to Peter had never been salvageable, and her current relationship to him might not be worth hanging on to. Her connection to her sisters could only be repaired if they wanted it to be. Her computer and phone were broken, and she was doing just fine without them. Her house, which barely held together, did not anchor her; it jailed her. And it was filled with discarded items no one wanted or needed but that she nonetheless felt obligated to keep. But being here, meeting Marceline, meeting Hervé, she felt herself on the cusp of something new, the discovery that she did not need to hold on to those things, that they were not her responsibility to fix.

Hervé had sensed the relaxation of her body. He was caressing her differently now, gently up and down her body, lightly, following the contours of her breasts, her waist, her hip, her thigh. "The ardor of my youth seems to have suddenly returned," he announced. With this, he began to kiss her.

****

Cassie awakened to the coos of a pair of pigeons on the balcony. Hervé was again sound asleep next to her. Had she dreamt their discussion in the middle of the night? Had she dreamt the sex? She slipped out of bed and into the bathroom, careful not to make a sound. She stared at herself in the mirror. Yowzer! She mouthed to her reflection. Yowzer, yowzer, yowzer. The mirror was too small to reflect anything below her shoulders, so the inner critic could only lament the bed hair, the smudged eye makeup, and what might very well be a love bite on her neck. Down below, where the mirror did not spread its accusatory reach, she was definitely naked. And there was one gorgeous male specimen sound asleep in her bed. Yow-Zer! How did she, of all people, let her guard down long enough for a man to charm her into going to bed with him?

She looked at the bathtub. She always wondered how in the movies people had sex, hopped into the previous day's clothes, and walked right out, or worse, had more sex without so much as the contact of a toothbrush on a stale tongue. This was no movie, she thought, spreading toothpaste on her toothbrush. She brushed her teeth energetically and removed her eye makeup thinking as fast as her comatose brain would let her. If she ran a bath, she would wake him up, accelerating the inevitable, the humiliating morning after when the man can't wait to leave, the woman feels guilty, and both parties avoid eye contact. She decided that she needed a bath and she needed it now. Perhaps, hearing the water, he would gather his things and run away. A bath was the perfect solution to all her problems, simultaneously cleaning her and allowing him a quick, wordless escape.

The old pipes whined and moaned as the water hit the tub with a thunderous splash. She dropped some shampoo into the water and the tub filled with foam. She got in and submerged her head completely and floated there with only her nose and feet out of the water. Bursts of panicky thoughts mixed in with flashes of recollection about her nighttime behavior. What in the world had she just done? This was thrilling in the way tightrope walking is thrilling. She, the poster girl for middle-age righteousness and modesty, had just had casual sex with a stranger on their first date. How could she have done that? Of course, she could. Anyone with a pulse would have, wouldn't they? The real question now was how she had managed all these years without a man's touch. It was all so wonderful. Better than wonderful. Her craving frightened her. It had been like going from a restricted calorie diet to binging on a giant plate of brownies. Forbidden. Desperate. Delicious. Wrong. But why should this be wrong? Her conscience was clear. She was a grown, unattached woman. And yet, she knew this was dangerous in ways that she hadn't begun to contemplate.

She pushed her head out of the water and found a naked Hervé standing in front of the mirror, looking critically at his tongue. "You don't have a second toothbrush, do you?" Hervé said.

"A second toothbrush? I don't even have enough panties to last me a week," she said, pointing at the half dozen bras and underwear in various stage of dryness hanging over the cast iron radiator.

He shrugged, squinted at the toothpaste, unscrewed its top, pressed a bit of paste on his finger, and proceeded to use his finger as a brush. "Why yo too-pash an ininch?" He asked, his mouth filled with foam.

"What?"

He bent over the sink, rinsed his mouth, and stood up again, looking as natural naked as if he were Adam himself. "Your toothpaste," he said, presenting her with the tube. "Why is it in English?"

She stared at the toothpaste in shock. "Hmm … yes … yes, indeed. I guess I never noticed."

He looked at her face, which rested above a mountain of foam. "I hope you're naked in there."

"Ahem … yes—"

She had not finished responding before Hervé stepped over the tub and lowered himself into the water and sank in to his shoulders opposite her. "But…."

"What?" he asked.

"There is a naked man in my bathtub."

"And a naked woman," he said, tilting his head back and groaning with pleasure. "Nice tub."

"Can I ask you a question?"

"Usually not before coffee, but all right."

"Why did you go to bed with me?"

"You're surprised?"

"I am."

"Why would you be surprised?"

Cassie shrugged.

He blew on the mound of bubbles between them, making a hole in it. "I don't know why. I wanted to. Do I need to know? Is it important to know why? I mean, why did *you*?"

"Because you're charming and you asked nicely," she said.

"All right," he said. "I went to bed with you because you're desirable. And also, because you're interesting."

"Interesting?"

"Very much so. You do all kinds of interesting things."

"That's your reason?"

"And you're strange."

"Oh, that can't be good."

"No, no … it's good. It's excellent. Sex is not everything, you know. Well, it is everything, but not if the next morning you can't stand the person you wake up next to. I like to wake up next to a person who's interesting."

"And strange."

"Strange is the icing on the cake."

They dressed and went down to the Jument for breakfast. They sat at their table, giggling like school children because the patronne had peered at them with suspicion. After their First Date (considering how unlikely all this was, Cassie giddily capitalized the event in her head), and their First Sex, and their Second Sex, all in under twelve hours, followed by their First Bath, they were sitting down together for their First Breakfast. Why Hervé had not darted out of the room after First Sex was no longer a question she asked herself. Why ask why about anything in this new bizarro world? In the recesses of her memory, she was a woman with grown children, an antagonistic family here in Paris, and a pressing life that awaited her in Los Angeles. But for the moment, all was right with the universe. "Our matchmaker is looking particularly disagreeable this morning," she told Hervé.

Hervé got up from his chair and moved to sit right next to her. He put his arm around her waist. "That's better."

"People are going to see …," she whispered.

"Oh, they have not seen anything yet," he assured her, lowering his arm and caressing the small of her back under her sweatshirt.

"You don't know this about me," she said, "but I'm a bit of a prude."

"Against all evidence to the contrary," he said, moving his hand away when the waiter approached. "What would you like to order?"

"Everything!" she said.

Hervé ordered two cafés au lait, two glasses of orange juice, buttered baguette, and confiture. They ate ravenously, whispering to each other, and laughed about everything. There could have been a hundred people around them, or none at all; she felt swallowed into this moment, this man, his eyes, his two-day-old beard, every pore of her body still reverberating from his touch.

"This is the best breakfast I ever ate," she said.

"Let's go back up to your room."

"Don't you have to go to work?"

"I'll call in sick."

"You will?"

"My absence won't make a bit of difference. You can't imagine the number of non-emergencies thrown at me in a single day. Grown people having tantrums like two-year-olds. I've had people break things, hurl insults at me over situations I can do nothing about. The other day, there was this angry old woman who barged into my office with her small purse and her thick glasses, clutching a bottle of mineral water. I see her, and I think, what can a frail old woman do? Well, she poured the contents of her water bottle on my keyboard! Just like that, the entire bottle, in front of my nose. There was nothing I could do."

Cassandra laughed. "That is something I can picture myself doing."

"What do you say? I'll call the office and let someone else handle things however they want. We could go out and play all day."

"Your coworkers won't resent having to pick up the slack?"

"They'll have my back today, and another time I'll return the favor."

"That's nice."

"They're idiots, the lot of them, but we show a united front against the people who come and go. Bureaucracy is first and foremost about self-interest." He pondered this. "It is quite awful when you think about it."

"This job might not be good for the soul."

"I'd say this is a correct assessment." He put his hands behind her neck and caressed it. "So? What do you think?"

They kissed, and at that moment she felt her life happen in real time, rather than in slow motion or rushed. How rare it was to be caught in a delicious moment and be aware of how delicious it was. "I can't. I'm supposed to meet my aunt at eight a.m. What time is it?"

Hervé looked at his watch: "half past seven."

She widened her eyes. "I'm supposed to be in the Jardin du Luxembourg in thirty minutes!"

"You'll be late."

"She is almost ninety years old, and she's going to be standing there waiting for me in the middle of a park!"

"Be careful she is not holding a water bottle."

"I have to leave right this minute."

"I'll take you there. It's on my way."

"You work in this neighborhood. How could the Jardin du Luxembourg be on your way?"

"It is now. Let's hurry. If I take the périphérique and go down the Champs Elysées, as long as there isn't a grêve or a manif, we'll get there in time." He set cash on the table and, taking her hand, helped her out of her chair. Once she was standing, he enveloped her in his arms. "How about tonight?"

"Tonight?"

"Why do you seem so surprised?"

"Aren't we supposed to play it cool? Isn't that what people do? You know, keep the other person wanting and worrying?"

"Maybe in lousy movies."

"All right," she said. "Tonight."

Outside, the sky was clear and blue, and the temperature surprised them both. "Ha, is it possible that spring has returned?" Hervé said. "Wasn't that incredible? Summer, then back to winter overnight, and now spring?"

They drove through the city. The streets were packed with cars and buses. As Hervé swerved his motorcycle gracefully in and out of lanes, the cars honking in blocked traffic were of no concern to them. Cassie, her body glued against Hervé's, sunk into the moment, the speed, the city, the warmth of him. If this was all so dangerous, why did she feel so safe?

Thirty minutes later, they arrived at Place Edmond Rostand. "I'll park and walk with you to the fountain," he said.

"No, too much of a hassle. You go to work. How's my helmet hair today?"

"Creative," he said, looking at her appreciatively from his sitting position on the Bonneville. He extended a gloved hand and attempted to smooth out her hair. "There is an interesting spring to it."

"I have to run!"

"Seven at your hotel?" he asked taking her hand and bringing her toward him and kissing her.

"Okay. What time is it now?"

"Eight a.m."

"I'm toast!" She ran toward the park's entrance and sprinted toward the fountain as Hervé's motorcycle roared away. No time to contemplate what had happened to her in the last twelve hours; already she could spot Marceline standing by the fountain. She looked regal in a long, green wool cape, a black fringed shawl around her shoulders, a masculine black hat perched on her head, and small-heeled buttoned boots firmly planted in the dirt path. Maurice was standing by, five feet away, ready to pounce should she waver.

CHAPTER 9

Algiers

Marceline stood by the Medici Fountain. The day was going to be beautiful. She loved how the public parks of Paris seemed untouched by time, and she was pleased not to see too many tourists for a change. Without tourists dressed in their garish shirts and flip-flops, she could imagine this was 1930 before World War II, and she and Gustave were children in a game of hide and seek on a Sunday afternoon. And her beloved father was about to spring from behind a bush surprising them both.

She thought of that spring of 1958 when she had waited here, her heart racing, for Khaled to come, knowing that he was risking his life to do so. It was a messy time in history and in her life. The Algerian War was raging. The Fourth Republic was on the cusp of falling. De Gaulle was about to return to power. Fernand was with the OAS then, and she worked for the French secret services. There was a price put on Khaled's head, and he could only have been in Paris to carry out FLN activities. And yet they had both risked everything for a few minutes together by this very fountain.

She was interrupted in her thoughts by Cassandra, who was running toward her.

"I'm sorry! I ran … but still … I'm late," Cassandra said, panting. She was rosy-cheeked, her hair was a mess, and there was an expression of glee on her face.

"You look different," Marceline announced.

"A friend gave me a ride on his motorcycle. I must look awful."

"To the contrary. You look…." Marceline studied her before declaring, "Happy."

Cassandra blushed. "Do I?"

They began by walking around the Medici Fountain. The canopy of plane trees, filled with nascent buds, reflected in the water. Around the rectangular basin, stone vases connected by a rough iron fence were filled with tulips about to bloom. "How pretty," Cassandra said.

Something had changed, Marceline could tell. Her niece looked alive in a way she had not the day before. A man, Marceline decided. She knew that look. Above the basin, an enormous bronze cyclops watched over a white marble couple in a languorous embrace. "This is Polyphemus," Marceline said. "In the act of discovering Galatea, the nymph he madly loves, in the arms of Acis."

"That can't be good."

"Not for Acis," Marceline mused. "Polyphemus ends up crushing his skull to death with a boulder of sorts,"

"No one likes being cuckolded. Or betrayed," Cassandra said.

"How is my brother this morning? The correct thing to do would be to visit him in the hospital, but you understand that my presence would only inflame things."

"There wasn't much of a change last I heard," Cassandra answered in a tone of confusion.

"What are you not telling me?"

Her niece rubbed her forehead, as though she was massaging a difficult thought. "It's difficult to admit, but my mother and sister are not letting me into his room."

"I'm perhaps the best person you could admit this to."

"I guess we're in the same boat."

"Pariahs," Marceline agreed.

She gripped Cassandra's arm. "I hope you don't mind if I hang on to you. I'm in no mood for a broken hip."

"Absolutely."

As they walked around the Jardin du Luxembourg under the warming sun, Marceline told Cassie about Algeria.

On May 13, 1940, our family docked at Algiers's fishing mole as dozens of boats of all sizes unloaded their catch. It was early morning, but already the air was soft and warm. In our rumpled clothes and teetering on our sea legs, we got off the boat and stepped between piles of glistening sardines and mackerels.

Like the men from our boats, the fishermen and workers on the dock had tanned skins, dark eyes, and black hair. Some wore loose-fitting pants and no shirt. Other wore long tunics. Many wore turbans or felt caps. There were women, although in smaller numbers. They wore billowy white fabric garments that covered them from head to ankle. Many had a handkerchief-size piece of fabric covering the lower portion of their face. Some older women wore the same outfit but in black. My heart raced as I walked. It was all so exotic. The smells, the quality of the air, the city above, vast and white and foreign.

I looked back to speak to Sandra, who, to my surprise, had covered her head with a shawl that she held tight under her chin with one clasped hand. But it was my mother who suddenly seemed absurdly out of place in her precious skirt and blazer and her little veiled hat.

For a few minutes, the four of us waited on the dock while my father spoke to men a few feet away.

Next to us, a group of crouching men repaired a mountain of fishnets, their bodies sinuous and muscular. Others moved crates and buckets filled with fish, shrimp, and black urchins, or laid larger fish on tables or directly on straw mats on the ground. The market was being set up in muffled silence, but I had the sense that the quietness had been brought on by our arrival. The men made a point not to look at us directly, but it felt as though they were tracking our every move. Only a group of elderly, toothless men sitting on crates and smoking their pipes, examined us frankly until one cleared his throat and spat noisily on the ground, as though pronouncing judgment. Mother turned pale and uncertain on her feet.

Baba was still speaking to one of the groups of men crouched over the nets. We heard him speak in that guttural language that we now knew was Arabic. Finally, four of the younger men he had spoken to wiped their hands and walked to the boat to fetch our luggage. Mother, Sandra, and I huddled together, while Gustave crossed his arms and stood aside. It was though in this world we knew nothing about, we instinctively knew to adopt the expected behavior of our genders.

One of our porters, a boy about my age, tall and wiry with a striking face and smooth, beautiful skin, returned from the boat carrying our largest suitcase with one arm. In his other hand dangled my dainty, turquoise hatbox, incongruously precious in his rough hand.

"Thank you," I said and held out a gloved hand to take it from him. He ignored my outstretched hand and just peered into my eyes dauntlessly for a brief, disconcerting moment, challenging me. I removed my hand, and he walked passed me, carrying the cases.

We followed our porters and our luggage, walking away from the water and across the deserted wharf. The light of dawn was soft, and we could have been at any of the piers in the South of France. But there was a different taste and texture to the air, something rough and tempestuous. I had the sensation that rules were different here, and that perhaps there were no rules at all.

Ahead of us and up above was a long row of European-style buildings anchored by a series of massive arches. In the sky, seabirds screeched and flew in circles by the hundreds. Two automobiles were parked a short distance away. From one of them emerged a familiar silhouette.

"Uncle Moshe!" Gustave shouted. He and I ran and jumped into our uncle's arms. If Uncle Moshe was here, it meant that things would be alright!

Moshe, dressed as dashing as always despite his formidable girth, kissed us and laughed out loud. He and Baba hugged tearfully, and my mother and he exchanged their customary glacial hellos.

Moshe appeared as much at ease with himself in this Algerian port as he was in Parisian salons. He did not fit in one bit, yet it was everyone else that seemed awkward in comparison. With Uncle Moshe, others could be as stiff or disapproving as they wished to be; it did not seem to trouble him in the least.

The four young fishermen loaded up both automobiles, and Moshe gave them money, a generous amount judging from their pleased expression.

Each automobile had a driver, both menacing-looking men with fedoras planted deep on their heads. This time again, Sandra climbed into the automobile that contained our things, and we piled into the other.

As we drove up a ramp along the row of stone arches, Moshe asked. "Did you hear?" My father, who sat in the passenger seat, looked at him questioningly. Moshe shook his head, "I have bad news. The Germans have made it past Sedan. They are advancing toward Paris."

The next few seconds felt like a plunge into a new dimension. Moshe's words crept inside us, stealing beats from our hearts, turning our palms into pools of sweat. We held our breath in stunned silence. Outside, a white mosque stood, serene. Palm trees swayed in the morning light. My mother broke the silence. "But what about the Maginot Line? Surely they could not have broken through the Maginot Line in three days!"

"They went around it," Moshe said.

In the back seat, my mother placed her face in her hands. "Oh mon Dieu!" she murmured. My father turned, patted her shoulder, and looked at us with great sadness. My mother remained with her face in her hands for a long time. The one thing we had held on to, the one thing we had put all our hopes in, now had disintegrated as though it had no more substance than fog. The Nazis, unlike us, had been able to see the Maginot Line for precisely what it was: an illusion.

"No one believes Paris is safe," Moshe said. "People are expecting bombings. A mass exodus is underway. People from Belgium, Luxembourg, Holland, and France are moving away from the north. There are people on every road; they're in freight trains, automobiles, bicycles, pushing wheelbarrows, even on foot. It is mayhem. Many are running out of provisions and gas already. Millions of people are fleeing.

"What about the people we know in Paris," Baba asked. "Have you news of any of them?"

"Everyone is trying to go South."

"Oh, but this is terrible!" my mother exclaimed. "Our friends are probably trying to reach us, hoping to get shelter in the Cannes house, expecting to find us there!"

"They probably are," Baba said. "The house will be open to them. I gave instructions to Monsieur Malou to let in any of our friends who want to stay there."

"See, Alban?" my mother said, "Our friends are trying to get to the Côte d'Azur. That is where everyone wants to be, and you just made us come here, to this lawless place."

My father looked at her with discouragement. "Lucienne, Dear, if Germany has gone past the Maginot Line with such ease, how long do you think it will be before they invade the rest of France?"

My mother clutched her purse and opened her mouth, but she made no sound. So I asked, "You think it's possible, Baba?"

Moshe is the one who answered. "I want to tell you it isn't. But the truth is, this Maginot Line debacle makes it clear that our generals aren't prepared."

"But we have a great army, and our soldiers are brave!" Gustave said.

"It doesn't matter how brave our soldiers are if the generals aren't using their heads," Moshe answered.

Moshe explained that the Nazis had taken Czechoslovakia, Poland, Norway, and Denmark in just days. What made France any different? What would prevent us from being swallowed in a single gulp? My mind was full of the terrible news of the German offensive, and I took in the scenery with confusion as we drove through the streets. The city was starting its day as our automobile drove past rows of tall apartment buildings. On this block we could believe ourselves back in Cannes or Nice: there were tree-lined streets, Haussmann-style apartment buildings, bakeries and butcher shops, hairdressers and tailors, cinemas, shoe stores, cafés, palm trees, and laundry drying on windowsills. And then on the next block, the sights were unmistakably foreign. There were men in loose, white breeches and turbans that led camels and donkeys and their heavy loads. Veiled women carried woven baskets on their heads. Children no more than six years old did the work of men, sweeping sidewalks and throwing buckets of soapy water on the pavement in front of the entrance of buildings. The air smelled of unknown spices, and many of the trees might as well have been from a different planet. But in the middle of all this exoticism, there were familiar sights: French housewives carrying groceries and baguettes and men in suits and hats hurrying through the streets, briefcases in hand. Everywhere we could see the kepis of French policemen on patrol.

We reeked of fish and sweat, and I desperately wanted a bath, but to anticipate the next minute, hour, day, or lifetime was pointless. The Maginot Line was no more. Countries were capitulating in a matter of hours. The German army was advancing toward Paris. We were in Africa.

Moshe pointed out the window to the strange terraced construction on the flank of the hill: hundreds of low buildings with white façades and tiny windows, all perched on top of each other. "The old city," he said. "The Kasbah. It is the reason Algiers is called La Blanche, the White One. For the most part, Muslims live there. It's a veritable maze of streets. All walks of life coexist inside the Kasbah. There are respectable people, but also prostitutes, pickpockets, deserters, and fugitives of the law. If you find yourself lost there, keep going down, and it ultimately leads to the sea."

"You will never set foot there, of course," my mother said in a horrified tone.

"Baba, how did you know?" I asked.

"How did I know what?"

"How did you know to leave France?"

"I did not know, sweet one. I only feared."

I sank into my seat, letting the vibrations of the automobile rock me. Gustave, Mother, Father and Sandra everyone important to me, was right here, safe for the moment in this vast new country. The French generals might not have been using their heads, but my father was. My faith in him was all that I had, and I clung ferociously to that.

As we drove, my father explained that we would be living under the name printed on the false identity papers Moshe had handed each of us in the car. Our last name was now the Dupont, one of France's most common names.

"I'm not sure who this name is supposed to fool, with your accent," my mother told my father.

"It's a good idea to be named like a hundred other families in Algiers alone," he answered.

We were to have a common name and live amongst common people in a nondescript apartment. We were to blend in rather than be noteworthy. It was the opposite of the way Mother had always told us we ought to be. She had always demanded that we distinguish ourselves, that our name be known, our standing noted.

We arrived on rue Mogador in front of a mastodon of an apartment building. It was imposing enough but by no means fancy. Past the front door and the lobby, there was an elevator, a dark spiral staircase, and the faint smell of bleach, soup, and trash. I smiled to myself thinking that to our mother this was the smell of 'everyone else.' The smell of common lives, of common people. A row of chipped mailboxes displayed French last names: Miramont, Pellerin, Perrier. And there was ours, ludicrous on that mailbox: Dupont. We had never lived in an apartment building before, so it was all very exciting to Gustave and me. What a new concept it was for people to live atop one another, without a garden, without a driveway, without many separate rooms for each function. I had always wondered about the strangeness of sharing an elevator or climbing stairs with strangers.

My mother and Baba squeezed inside the tiny elevator that could only accommodate two. "Let's go next," Gustave told Sandra when the elevator came back down. Sandra shook her head stubbornly, "It's like a coffin," she said, made the sign of the cross, and headed up the stairs.

"She'll come around," Moshe said. "It's a long way up."

Moshe squeezed into the elevator with us and showed us how to fold the metal gate and then the door. "We're on the fourth floor!" Gustave said with excitement as he pushed the button. He looked at me, cockeyed. "It smells like cod in here something awful." He sniffed me, "Oh, wait, it comes from you."

"This will be the best bath of our lives," I said as the elevator made its slow, creaking ascent in the center of the spiral staircase.

My parents were already inside the apartment. Mother was standing in the center of the foyer as though afraid to take another step. The high ceilings, tall windows, and a fresh coat of paint did not mask the obvious fact that this had nothing to do with the luxury she considered her birthright.

"What is this?" my mother asked, pointing to the living room furniture with an accusing finger. The décor of the main room reminded me of illustrations in an *A Thousand and One Nights* picture book. The Persian rugs were not only spread on the floor but hanging on walls as well. The dining table was at knee level and surrounded by low benches covered in embroidered cushions.

"That is nice," my father said, smiling. "It is the Algerian way."

"Alban, please have a proper table and chairs brought in."

"No, let's keep it this way," I said. "Dining will be like having a picnic."

"Marceline, no one has inquired about your opinion quite yet," my mother said. "Moshe! It's you, isn't it?" She said, turning to him. "You did this on purpose."

"Me? Never!" Moshe said in protest, looking falsely contrite.

My mother's discomfiture was such that I began to laugh. "Enough, Marceline," she said. "Your lack of empathy astounds me!"

I pointed to Gustave whose shoulders were shaking. "He's laughing too!"

Our mother was livid, and our contained laughter was making things worse. "It's not because we are in Africa that we shall turn to savages!" she said.

Gustave and I exploded into laughter.

She was angry and tired and under a lot of strain. Perhaps it would have been better for me to say nothing, but I, too, was under stress. I unconsciously knew that this new phase of our lives would require being open to new ways of being. I sensed this as clearly as I doubted my mother's capacity to adapt.

The apartment had three bedrooms, a single bathroom, and a kitchen. Sandra would be living in a maid's room under the rooftop.

My mother gasped at the kitchen, "Is food supposed to be prepared only steps away from the bedrooms?"

"We must make do," my father said apologetically.

"I just don't think that's possible, Alban. Do you realize that the smell of food cooking will be wafting through the entire place?"

There was no piano in the apartment, and no one suggested that we should rent one. My father explained that in the spirit of blending in, and until we were sure whom to trust, we would not be hiring any staff.

"Who will cook and clean?" my mother asked in a clipped tone.

"Sandra can," my father said.

"How perfect," my mother said icily.

"Perhaps we'll all learn how," Father said.

"How can you do this to me?" my mother said, her voice quivering.

I thought her drama entirely inappropriate when we were lucky to be safe and hundreds of miles away of the closest German soldier. "Mother," I said with impatience. "Baba is doing the best he can."

My mother spun toward me. "Young lady, I shall not tolerate your disrespect another minute!"

"Why be so narrow-minded?" I mumbled under my breath.

My mother took two steps toward me and without warning slapped me hard across the face.

I stood in shock. She had never slapped me before. My cheek stung. But I was not about to give her the satisfaction of showing it. I stared at her defiantly. Moshe, Gustave, and my father, embarrassed by the whole thing, avoided looking at me. My cheek hurt and my pride was wounded, but my anger demanded that I show none of it. My revenge would start by my acting indestructible.

"Bring your eyes down and apologize right this instant!" she shouted.

I just turned on my heels and walked away from her. Moshe jumped in and changed the subject to explaining how the kitchen worked.

Seething with anger but determined to appear unbothered, I accompanied Gustave and Sandra on an exploration of the apartment.

There were so many amazing new things that I soon forgot my anger. We were greatly entertained by a system whereby the trash went down from a small opening in the wall of the kitchen and fell into the apartment building's underbelly, four floors below, never to be seen again. We walked out on the narrow balcony from where we could see the hundreds of other balconies of buildings across the street. Gustave and I stood aghast, realizing that we could easily peer into the living rooms and bedrooms of the neighbors who lived right across from us and, with a lack of modesty that to us bordered on obscene, did not bother to draw their curtains. Beyond the rooftops was the Bay of Algiers. To our right, minarets stood against the azure sky. Invisible in the distance, an entire sea away, was France, and on the other side, past the mountain range, the mysterious rest of the African continent.

I took in the hectic street below, the balconies of countless apartments, the mingling sounds of French songs over the radio and of the melody of unknown instruments. The smell of the Mediterranean air, which had a different texture here, weaved itself together with the arid winds from the Sahara Desert that began right behind the city at the Atlas Mountains. In instants, I had fallen in love with Algeria.

The following day, my father took us for a stroll around the European quarter where most of the French and local Jews lived. "The French influence started in the 1880s when Algeria became a French overseas territory, through no choice of its own," he said.

The French, he explained, had built the city on the flank of the mountains in an architecture reminiscent of Paris, in a succession of terraces around the Kasbah, the old Algerian fortress. Two civilizations mingled in a patchwork of architectural styles. There were tree-lined streets and rows of Haussmann-style buildings. There were wrought iron lampposts at every street corner. Automobiles crisscrossed the city. An elaborate system of climbing and turning trolleys served as public transportation. We walked past stores of the kind we were used to, from the simplest boulangerie to the fanciest department store. But the soul of the city came from the Neo-Moorish architecture of the older buildings, the horseshoe arches, the rounded windows, the columns, the ornate mosaic motifs, the fountains, the shaded arcades over the sidewalk to shield pedestrians from the hot African sun.

The vegetation in Algiers went mostly unchecked, sprawling, wild. Foliage we considered houseplants in Paris climbed trees like monkeys. The palm trees we had discovered in the South of France here were indigenous. There were churches and temples, but it was the domes and minarets of a hundred mosques that dominated, shining like jewels in the skyline. Algiers smelled of the sea, of tagines cooking in stone ovens. It smelled of camel dung, and trash, and rose flower essence. As we took in the city, the smells, sights, and sounds moved through my senses like a shockwave. It was as though I had been asleep my entire life and were awakening at long last.

"There are three distinct cultures in Algiers," my father explained. "There are the North African Muslims, the North African Jews, and the French colonizers. Algeria is run by the descendants of Europeans who settled here about one hundred years ago after winning their war, and by the North African Jews because they were given French citizenship soon after, and so their children were able to have a French education and do well."

"What about the Muslims?" Gustave asked. "Weren't they given French citizenship and education?"

"No," my father said.

"Why not?"

"This is the kind of injustice that happens after wars," he said.

Father, Mother, Gustave, and I walked in the shade of trees along rue d'Isly. The cinema house still showed *Le Jour Se Lève* with Jean Gabin and Arletti, a movie that had come out in Paris months ago. We entered the librairie-papeterie. Gustave bought a comic book, but those, too, were a month behind. The many boulangeries were filled with the familiar aroma of brioche and baking baguettes, and we relished that small normalcy. We walked inside a beautiful building built in the Neo-Moorish style, the famed Galeries de France, where we would be able to buy everything nice we liked, from Mother's Guerlain face powder to the Schiaparelli scarves I coveted.

We had lunch on the terrace of a brasserie, and, sitting on the outdoor chairs, we could have believed ourselves back on the Riviera: same obsequious service, same spotless silverware and starched white tablecloth, same escargots à l'ail and choucroute garnie on our plates, same customers in dark suits with thin mustaches, same wives in blooming hats and tailleurs, with the same spoiled poodles below the table licking foie gras off their fingers. Mother relaxed. For a moment it seemed possible she might acclimate. But as soon as we stepped out of the restaurant, the smell alone reminded us of how far from France we were. It was the smell of kebabs and spicy merguez sausages grilling on impromptu cast iron grills set up by a street vendor right on the sidewalk outside the restaurant. To my mother's dismay, the Algerian way of life, its foods, its colors, its scents, could not be contained as it spilled out of the restaurants and markets onto proper-looking European streets. "They are cooking out on the street? Just like that?" my mother exclaimed. 'They' would become her code name for everything Algerian and anything that frightened her, which was one and the same.

We walked toward the sea. On the waterfront, the local French people, who were known as colons, were easy to distinguish from the fresh arrivals from France such as ourselves. The men wore suits, and the women dressed in Paris fashion. Yet there was a certain languor and self-assurance to them that could only come from several generations of feeling both entitled and superior to the indigenous people. The attitude of the colonizer, I presumed. My father said that although they were French, many had never seen France, nor had their parents.

I wasn't sure how to tell the Jews from the non-Jews because they all dressed in the European style, but the Muslims looked, moved, and dressed in their own ways. Some of the Muslim men dressed in European pants and shirts and even suits, but most dressed like the fishermen we had seen at the dock. They had fezzes, caps, or turbans on their heads, loose pants gathered at the ankles under long tunics called djellaba. Some wore woolen capes wrapped around their bodies. The Muslim men spoke in Arabic interspersed with French as they sat at the terraces of cafés, or had their beards trimmed in outdoor barber shops, or played cards on flimsy tables. There were men guiding donkeys loaded with belongings, men pulling camels, men carrying goats. We saw an autobus go by with a dozen men perched atop its roof. We saw a group of Bedouin from the desert sitting on the sidewalk, smoking and conversing with animation. The Muslim men had a disconcerting way of never looking at us. We walked among them, and they acted as though we were invisible. The Muslim women moved through the streets in small groups. Most women, but not all, covered their hair and faces according to Islamic law, and all you could see of them were their ankles and sandaled feet, the tip of their hennaed fingers, and the eyes, lined with black Khol, they averted when we looked at them. I was flustered to see that the women of European descent got to dress like French women, speak like French women, behave like French women, and not cover their heads. I wondered how offensive this might be to the Muslim population. But no one else seemed to be asking themselves that question.

"This town is a veritable Tower of Babel," my mother said. "Are you sure it is safe for us to walk like this?"

"The French police are everywhere," Gustave said. "I see more kepis than turbans."

"Just as in Paris, or any other city, there are areas of town to avoid," my father said, taking Mother reassuringly by the elbow. "Remain in the European areas and you'll be perfectly safe."

"Still, They are everywhere," she said. "We don't know what They are like."

I too wanted to know what the Algerian Muslims were like and how and where they lived. How different were they from us? How did the women feel about their veils? What did they discuss when they were amongst themselves? What did they care about? In Algiers, we would be living side by side, yet our worlds seemed hermetically shut off from one another.

Not all Muslims ignored us. To many who sold goods or begged, we represented their livelihood. We walked down one block, and a man in djellaba with a shaved head waved for us to get closer to the small table he had set out on the sidewalk, which was covered in a bright heap of mandarins and lemons. A boy in rags pursued us to offer, for a few francs, fried sardines rolled in newspapers. Further down the street, an old woman shoved in front of us a mound of sweets that resembled the kind that Sandra made. Because we were raised on the stuff, Gustave and I had a particular taste for fried dough drenched in honey. The woman pointed to her pastry and said in broken French, "Fruits déguisés, Cornes de Gazelles."

"Mother, can we buy some?" we asked.

"Out of the question! It isn't hygienic."

My mother never did allow us to eat street food. So we learned, along with many other infractions to her rules, to do it behind her back. Life was about to change for Gustave and for me. We were about to get a taste of something new: freedom, the kind achieved through sneaking, and lying, and doing things the moment our preoccupied parents had their backs turned.

We did not have far to go; down the steps from the apartment were new tastes and sensations just at our fingertips. I was seventeen and Gustave was fifteen, and the lure of a culture that charmed us, that intimidated us, and that we wanted to understand was too compelling to resist.

We ended our first stroll through Algiers by shopping at Le Bon Marché, the French department store. My father bought Gustave a miniature replica of a super heavy FCM F1 tank and for Mother a bottle of Soir de Paris. "And you my Princess, what will make you happy?" he asked.

I jumped at my chance. "Baba, I'm positively dying for a bottle of Chanel Number Five. Oh, pretty please, say yes!"

"She's far too young for that," my mother said.

"Isn't this a woman's perfume?" my father asked.

I put my arms around his neck. "That is what I will be in just a few months, Baba. I'll be eighteen, like it or not."

"Well, I do not like it at all," he said, kissing me on top of my head.

I went through that bottle so fast. I would have bathed in it had I been able to. I might have been more parsimonious had I known that it was the last bottle of perfume I would get my hands on for the next five years.

That first week, my mother made an effort. Baba went to work with Moshe, and so she tried to be brave and take Gustave and me to the department store. Afterward, we sat in front of grenadine syrup and madeleines on the terrace of the Le Bon Marché's restaurant. My mother struck up a conversation with a French woman in pearls. Her daughter, a bosomy girl about my age in white gloves, white ankle socks, and a smock dress, pouted and seemed set on not making eye contact. The girl's name was Béatrice. The family was Jewish. She did not tell this to us, but we could sense it, and she probably could tell we were Jewish as well. They were from Le Vésinet, a suburb of Paris. The father worked at the préfecture, and they had lived in Algiers for a year. The conversation, pregnant with euphemisms, started.

"Are you here on holiday?" the woman asked.

My mother scoffed. "Some holiday this would be, if you know what I mean!"

The woman laughed, displaying an impressive row of buck teeth. "François and I were biding our time until we'd be able to return," the woman said. "But with the situation, he wonders if we would not be better off staying here for a while."

"Indeed, perhaps it is best to stay put until things quiet down in France," my mother said, acknowledging in our presence for the first time that she approved of our coming here.

"Who would want to be here, if not compelled to be? I suppose you have to be born here. But if you ask me, the local French are much more like the Muslims than they care to admit."

"They are very local indeed," my mother said.

"What brings you here? I hope it doesn't have to do with the unfortunate affairs in Europe?"

"Oh, not at all," my mother lied. "Only my husband's business venture."

"François says that the German forces should never have attacked us."

"Why could they not content themselves with Denmark and Belgium?" my mother said.

"It is a delusion of grandeur for Monsieur Hitler to think that he can face our generals," the woman added with genuine conviction. "This war shall be over before it has begun."

My mother brightened, "Is this a fact?"

"My husband's colleagues at the Préfecture assure us of it."

"What a relief!" my mother exclaimed.

"And so what is your husband's business?"

"He's in the fine rug trade."

"Why we must exchange addresses! The girls are the same age. They absolutely must become friends."

Béatrice gave me a bored look.

We bid them goodbye and agreed to meet a few days later. Mother said that we did not yet have a telephone number. The lie showed that no matter what she said about not being worried, she regardless took the secrecy part seriously.

When we left the restaurant, my mother had a spring in her step. We chatted as we walked on one street and then the next. We discovered that Algiers went from the sea and climbed the hillside following the curves of the canyon and that the various levels of the city connected through an intricate assortment of ramps, stairs, terraces and gardens, most of them built on an incline. We went up and down stairs that connected parallel streets we did not recognize. We went up and down, and down and up, right and left, argued, attempted to retrace our steps, and before long, we were lost.

The realization came to us as a shock when we came face to face with a crouching camel next to which sat a turbaned man. My mother clung to her purse. "Oh my," she said with a shrill. "Gustave, do you know the way back?"

Gustave shook his head. "I don't know this city any more than you do."

"But aren't you good at maps and such?"

"I can read a map," he said impatiently. "Only as you can see, I don't have one at the moment, or else we would not be lost."

"Lost? Oh, but we must, must find our way home! Oh goodness!"

We turned into a small street bustling with brown men in djellaba. Where were we? My mother kept muttering "Oh goodness!" in a panicked voice. We walked into a street that was dark, odorous, and littered with trash. We turned around, and at the end of it seemed to sprout three narrower streets. "Which one have we come from?" my mother wailed.

We tried the largest of the three and found ourselves at the foot of stairwells which led to an animated public square were, bursting out from every door, street merchants sold grilled meat, baskets, rugs, piles of dates and dried apricots, fabric, live chickens, baby goats, and small dead animals. Women draped in veils sat on mats made of woven dried fibers with flat baskets filled with pastries in front of them. Feral-looking children, dogs, and cats ran amok. There were taverns outside of which Berber men smoked pipes and drank unknown beverages.

I gazed upward. We were at the foot of a series of lime-washed structures built on the side of a hill, with meandering stairs, haphazardly placed windows, and flat roofs.

"It's the Kasbah!" Gustave exclaimed.

"Oh my God," my mother whimpered. "They will murder us!"

The place was dense with Muslim men and women, but they ignored us completely and went about their lives in the jumble of cafés, workshops, and fruit stands. "No one will murder us," I told her. "Look, they're just regular folks." Despite my reassuring words, I remembered what Moshe and my father had said: this was not a place for French children or French mothers. And it was certainly not a good place in which to get lost.

My mother must have had a similar thought. She froze in place, white, trembling. She grabbed me with clammy hands. "I … can't go on. I can't … can't move," she said, supplicant, her eyes glazed with panic. She went limp. Gustave and I supported her and led her to steps away from the crowd. She sat heavily on the stone stairs. My mother sitting on the bare ground of a city, was an almost incomprehensible sight.

"Are you ill?" I asked. "Let's ask for help."

"Not *Them*!" Mother shrieked. She added below her breath. "We need to find someone like *us*."

"We ought to find a policeman or someone," Gustave said. "But where?"

Indeed, wherever we were now, there was not a kepi in sight.

"You stay here with Mother," I told Gustave. "I'll go find a policeman." My mother did not object to this. She, who usually took charge of the minutest details of my life, was looking at me imploringly. "Neither of you move away from here," I ordered. "Or I'll never be able to find you again."

"What if you get lost too?" Gustave said.

"I'll try my best not to."

"Goodness," my mother whimpered.

I decided that the best course of action was to head up. At least the stairs weren't crowded, and perhaps from above, I would be able to see where the streets below led and thus regain a sense of direction. The instruction from Moshe had been to go down toward the sea, but it did not make sense to me. We might find dangerous streets on the way down. I left Gustave and Mother and started up the nearest staircase.

If anyone paid attention to me, I did not bother thinking about it.

I did not have to venture far inside the Kasbah to be stunned at the world before my eyes. I passed buildings with deep arches and wooden doors that opened to private courtyards. An entire civilization existed here, just meters away from the European area, one with its rules, its rhythms, its timelessness. Had I gone back in time a hundred years, I felt certain that very little would look different. Away from the bustle of the lower streets, people lived and breathed, children played in the dirt, mothers called them, grabbed them, and pulled them inside the many doors. Men disappeared behind doors. Through a window, there was the sound of two men speaking to each other. A little girl stepped in front of me and laughed. An old man sat on a rug against a wall and watched me as he drew on his pipe. Somewhere, someone pinched the cord of a sort of guitar, and a strange melody rose, echoing through the alley. I had the sense that people could be born, marry, have children, and die without leaving these walls. If you never wanted to be found, this is where you could hide. If you wanted to slit a throat and disappear into a crowd, this would be the place to go. There would be no one to rescue you if you were an outsider and they wanted you dead. The stairs I had gone up led to more stairs and more dark alleys. The names of streets were marked in both French and Arabic. As I climbed, I had taken a mental note of guideposts and street names, but soon they all began to sound and look the same. I had wandered inside the Kasbah for less than ten minutes, and already I was losing confidence that I would be able to find my way back, when at last I saw a respectable-looking Frenchman dressed in a suit and fedora descending the steps. The man looked perfectly at ease and unworried. I threw myself at him and asked for his help. I described the place where I had left Gustave and my mother. In less than two minutes, we found them.

He followed me back to Mother, who was huddled against Gustave. Both looked wretched, Mother because she was still in the midst of her episode, and Gustave because he had been forced to endure her.

The French man offered to guide us back to the apartment, and we accepted eagerly. My mother eventually got up and walked. Her face returned to its normal hue, but she did not say a word. Upon our return home, Mother forgot any good manners, and it was left up to me to thank our rescuer. The man just tilted his hat at us and left without giving his name. Mother ran up the stairs of the apartment building and locked herself in her room. An hour later, we could still hear her sobbing behind her door, and she did not acknowledge our knocks.

"What's the matter with Mum?" Gustave asked me.

"I haven't the slightest clue," I told him.

Our indomitable mother had just suffered the first of many attack of nerves, as it was called at the time, the dynamics of which no one in the family, and no one at the time, understood.

It was May 1940 when our family arrived in Algiers. It was in Algeria that I transformed from a spoiled adolescent girl to an idealistic young woman with a delusion of invulnerability. It was in Algeria that Gustave went from a timid boy to having something to prove, at the risk of endangering us all. It was in Algeria that the Allied forces had their first breakthrough in 1942, with a direct impact on the outcome of the Second World War. The Jews of Algeria were instrumental in making the Allied landing in Algeria possible, and our family was at the heart of that day and the days that lead up to it.

It was also in Algeria that Gustave and I turned on each other. And it was in Algeria that our family collapsed, with our beloved father attempting one last time to do what he had done since we were born, his single objective, the reason for his existence: to keep Gustave and me safe.

****

We were arriving in Algeria at a time of unprecedented turmoil. Everyone's fate was up in the air. In the days after our arrival, the news from France went from bad to worse. On June 10th, a *Le Figaro* newspaper headline declared, "The German rush continues to face admirable resistance by our troops." On June 11th, it said: "The enemy has reached the lower Seine River but is being contained by our attacks."

And then nothing. It was as though, overnight, *Le Figaro* had stopped publication.

Paris fell on June 14th. On June 16th, a new government was shaped, led by the beloved Maréchal Pétain, who, to most everyone's dismay, promptly signed an armistice.

The week following Pétain's armistice, all of Algiers had their ears glued to the radio, hoping to decipher the facts through the rhetoric. Many tuned into the BBC in the hope of hearing more from General de Gaulle and his talk of worldwide war and his vow of armed resistance. Rumors spread faster than facts, and then, with the propaganda machine taking hold, there soon was no longer such a thing as a fact. In Algiers, we were spared the pain of seeing Nazi boots under the Arc de Triomphe, but we felt guilty for not sharing in the suffering. Didn't our luck, or cleverness, not imply a certain selfishness? We imagined our friends and neighbors reeling; we pictured the exodus out of Paris, our fellow Parisians powerlessness before the occupiers. The fact that we were far from all this gave us a secret sense of guilt, a shame that, perhaps, was the reason we all wanted to appear heroic in our own ways.

How to describe Algiers of the 1940s? How to separate this place and time in the context of the maelstrom the world had become? We were on French soil, following French rules, enforced by French police within the boundaries of the zone libre, the armistice's agreed-upon French territory unoccupied by the Germans. But the free zone was controlled by the Vichy government, which in turn was controlled by Hitler. And so, this was France under German control, and we were the vanquished. But to Gustave and me, there was a sense of disconnect between the way we were supposed to feel and the reality of our new life. In Algiers, the sky was spotless, the sea and air were warm, the vegetation luxuriant, the people alive and vibrant. Restaurants and cafés brimmed with people; the streets were bustling. By early June, just a month after our arrival, the air became hot. The local architecture was designed to harvest cool air and permit it to flow through houses. The city was a web of arcades, porticos, and courtyards. A briefly opened door would allow for a glimpse of the quiet private gardens that existed in the middle of the city. In those indoor courtyards and breezeways, mosaic fountains trickled water and gave the impression of an oasis. There, people napped, met, talked, had dinner, and lived their lives.

We wished Monsieur Baron Haussmann had been made aware of techniques known by generations of North African builders. In our apartment, the air was as stifling as a woolen blanket. Soon we saw how other people organized around the hot and cool hours of the day. French families that had settled in Algiers for generations, ruling the city and making every effort to shape it, had learned a thing or two over the last hundred years. Whether they admitted it or not, when it pleased them, they hardly resisted the Arabic influences of a culture developed over thousands of years. Concessions had been made. Even those who lived in buildings like ours ended up spending their evening hours on their apartments' terraces and balconies.

We began closing the windows during the hot hours and reopening them at sundown the way the locals did. In Paris, you would have no idea how people lived behind closed doors. Here, people lived their lives in the open for all to see. In the evenings, balconies came to life one by one and entire families flocked outside looking for a breeze, relinquishing inhibition and privacy in exchange for a breath of fresh air. There they watered their potted geraniums, played with their children, kissed, argued, dried their laundry, ate, and drank their aperitifs in plain sight. As the war progressed, people would often end up keeping livestock on their balconies: chickens for eggs, sometimes even a goat for milk. The balconies soon became vegetable gardens were people planted tomatoes, zucchini, eggplants, peppers, and herbs.

It wasn't long before our family started spending evenings around the small table on the balcony, tentatively at first, and then with relish. The first few weeks, my mother wanted to have nothing to do with it. She didn't want to appear common. But as spring made way for summer and the torpor gained on all of us, the clouds of her cigarette smoke joined the smells of the food that rose from a hundred apartment kitchens below. From up on the fourth floor, we watched the lives of our neighbors unfold, and they watched us. Sandra, who feared heights, refused to put a toe on the balcony and would hand us plates of food with her eyes shut.

Almost as soon as we arrived, my father got involved in activities that took him away from the apartment. He and Uncle Moshe opened an office in town, although it was unclear what kind of business they did. I had the sense there was a lot he and Uncle Moshe were not telling us, and an even stronger sense that it was better not to ask. Baba was an ardent anti-Vichyist from the start. To him, the armistice was a disgrace, a betrayal, and he believed that nothing good could come out of an alliance with the Nazis. He was the first to openly and prophetically declare Pétain a puppet. It took the rest of France and Algeria several more weeks, if not months to come to a similar conclusion.

I had to adjust to a new understanding of my father. In France, he had been a mild-mannered businessman, a hapless foreigner who appeared dominated by his wife. In Algiers, he was a man comfortable living under a false identity, who thought nothing of secretly moving his family to another country overnight, a man who conversed in French, Hebrew, Arabic, and Greek, a man who told people what to do. Now Mother, Gustave, and I were the foreigners. We were the ones who did not know the customs, the language, or the conventions. And now it was Mother, not he, who embarrassed me.

Mother did not appear to overcome her anguish of the day when we had gotten lost. She scarcely wanted to go out of the apartment. As summer went on, she closed all the shutters, allegedly to keep the heat at bay, but it might have been her way of tuning out the war. The balcony became her sanctuary. As soon as the sun began to set, she positioned herself on a chair, smoking cigarettes, her body leaning against the balustrade to better scan the street below for Baba's return. She seemed in a constant state of alert. What we all came to call her 'nerves' dictated her life. She ventured into the city only if my father accompanied her, and even then, she was jumpy, angry, and suspicious of all. She developed a panicky distrust for food and would not eat anything unless it had been prepared by Sandra, which was ironic since Mother insisted that Sandra was, in fact, crafty, lazy, and not mindful enough of how things needed to be properly washed and cooked. Once we managed to convince her to have dinner at a local restaurant that served Algerian specialties. My mother scanned the place. "Is this place hygienic?" she asked worriedly.

"This place is perfectly fine," Gustave reassured her.

She laid a napkin on her chair to protect her clothes before sitting, as the Algerian waiter looked at her with puzzlement.

I rolled my eyes. "I wonder what good you think that will do, which is none at all."

"Mind your mother, Marceline," my father said.

"She is acting rude," I said. "It's embarrassing."

"Quit speaking about me as though I am not right here," my mother said.

"Well, are you?"

"Marceline, don't be cruel," my father commanded.

"I think you're looking for reasons to complain about this country. Why can't you adapt as we do?"

"Marceline!" my father said.

"Why can't you make an effort! Your obsession with decorum, the name-dropping, all that might have been the basis of your existence, but now that has become outdated and senseless."

Mother's lips quivered. She stood up. "Take me home, will you Alban?"

We left the restaurant. I was furious at my mother for her inflexibility, and at my father for catering to her whims. It did not occur to me that she might be struggling with a psychological ailment, or that she needed empathy and care.

Soon after that, she got worse. She behaved like a hermit and spent most of her days complaining about her stomach, her teeth, her sleep, the lack of comfort, the heat. Without a staff to manage, a house to run, functions to attend, or friends to visit, she began to lack the will to get up or get dressed. She stopped reading newspapers because she found them too depressing and said she did not have the concentration to read books. She slept a lot or sat on the balcony and smoked.

Sandra was left with the responsibility of the apartment, the cooking, all the errands, and, now that my mother displayed a new, astounding disinterest for our education, the supervision of our lessons and homework. It is not that my mother asked her to do any of this, but Sandra just took it on. We thought we had saved Sandra by bringing her along, but the truth was, I'm not sure how we would have coped without her. Unlike my mother, she quickly adjusted to the ways of a Muslim country. Like Father, she was in her element here. She was Armenian and Christian but seemed more at ease with the humble folks of Algiers than she had ever been in Paris. She spoke Arabic well. Here, she was free to wear a shawl over her hair, which better masked her scar. In Paris, wearing a headscarf made her stand out as too foreign. She said she felt more comfortable that way. People stared at her less. The heat did not affect her. She was confident walking in the streets of Algiers, and was a natural at haggling and navigating the markets. She never got over her fear of the elevator and climbed and descended four flights of stairs several times a day carrying heavy food baskets or, if such was my mother's whim, just to fetch a pack of Gitanes or a special type of tea to settle her stomach or her nerves. My mother, for all her resentment toward Sandra, was the one who depended on her the most. As my mother fell apart, Sandra continued to do anything and everything for us children: the kinds of things usually done by mothers, I suppose.

****

From that time onward, the apartment, dark and overheated, without a whiff of air except at night, began to feel like a mausoleum. I could not bear it. And how could I when everything outside was so new and exciting? North Africa was as messy and uncharted as Paris was proper and familiar. To Gustave and me, the limitations imposed by our upbringing could hardly compete with the vastness of the Sahel, and of the Sahara Desert, immense and dangerous, that began just behind the city. I was a young woman who craved freedom. War was raging in Europe, killing men, bringing nothing but uncertainty into our lives, and redefining the role of women. And here, the sky was blue, the sea emerald-green, and a vast, mysterious city lay at my feet.

As a French demoiselle, I was penned within the boundaries of the European quarter. Sandra was my chaperone everywhere I went, even if that meant picking up a baguette one block away from our apartment. Sandra, unfortunately, took her role seriously. No matter my pleading, she refused to take me to lively areas such as Bab-El-Oued or let me enter one of the mosques or get a closer look at the market at the foot of the Kasbah. I could go on Boulevard Foch, rue Michelet, rue d'Isly. I shopped at the various pâtisseries and bookstores, spent hours trying every dress and every shoe at Le Bon Marché and the Galeries de France. I went to the library and the nearby parks, feigned interest in the local museums, pretended to be pious at temple. All of that with Sandra as my shadow. Meanwhile, Gustave, because he was a boy, roamed freely. Gustave would set out on his bicycle to explore the city in ways I could only dream of. The infuriating double standard accentuated the growing tension between Gustave and me. With Baba in the midst of a vanishing act and Mother acting so strangely, we were left to our own devices, and everything was cause for discord between us.

I soon paired up by default with Béatrice, the daughter of the woman we had met early on. Béatrice pleased Mother because her father was a prominent local bureaucrat who worked at the préfecture and because the family was Jewish, which inspired blind trust in my parents. It turned out that Béatrice pleased me too. She was neither attractive nor unattractive, neither smart nor stupid, and she accepted my dominance completely. She lacked imagination but was game for everything and would follow me, no questions asked, into whatever mischief popped into my mind. However, what pleased me most about her was that her passivity masked a cunning nature. She was entirely devoid of scruples when it came to parental disobedience.

At first, Béatrice and I spent most of our time at each other's homes, leafing through magazines and dreaming of actors we liked. But soon, we were bored. Bored with our little girl clothes, bored with our braids and ponytails, bored with the war, bored with the utter absence of boys in our lives, bored by our parents' sudden obsession with saving money. Rationing had been ordered from the moment France declared war. At first, it was a symbolic gesture to give us a sense of participation in the war effort. It was seen as uncouth to be wasteful, and sacrifices were expected of everyone.

"Nowadays, countries wage war, sending young men to be killed while life at home can remain precisely the same. But back in 1940, the war involved our entire nation. Before we could personally feel the dire privations and wounds of war, and before Germany began bleeding France of its riches, everyone did his and her bit. We acted patriotic, dressed and behaved in a way that was appropriate to the time, and were made acutely aware of the sacrifices of our men."

Well, Béatrice and I, or rather our bratty, seventeen-year-old incarnations, did not quite have rationing on the mind. We were consumed by the desire to get our hands on silk stockings or, better yet, some of those American nylons everyone talked about. But already they were impossible to find, even on the black market. Béatrice and I learned to do each other's hair to be more fashionable in smooth curls and victory rolls, and those immediately added five years to our features. We wore what we called, 'hosiery in a bottle.' Elizabeth Arden had issued a lotion to color the legs. We then enrolled Sandra's help to paint a thin line of henna to the back of our legs, which gave the illusion of nylons' back seam. With the exception of taking elevators or stepping on a balcony, there was nothing that Sandra could not do. When asked to attempt something she had never done before, Sandra had a funny way of mulling it over quietly in her head. Then she would tilt her head and say, "All right." The tricky bit was to hide our painted legs from our parents, but we managed by avoiding angles where they could see them.

Béatrice and I soon ran out of things to do or say. I was supposed to reveal nothing of our family's identity, and Béatrice had nothing to say of interest, or else she had secrets of her own. I grew restless. "We need to meet boys," I told her one day.

"But how?"

"Where are the boys? In cafés, in the streets, I guess. But our mothers will never let us talk to them."

"Well, there is the one place," Béatrice said.

"What place?"

She smiled a wry smile, "A place that crawls with all sorts of boys."

Béatrice had lived here for a year and knew the city well enough. She asked her mother to convince mine to let us go with Sandra to the University of Algiers, allegedly for its extensive library and gardens filled with rare plants. Mother agreed, and we set off. We picked up books at the library and strolled in the gardens. We sat on a bench in the dappled shade of a giant Strelitzia, refreshed by the mist of a water feature, and opened our books. Sandra sat at a short distance from us and took her mending out of her basket. Béatrice and I read and read, but it was hot even in the shade of the fountain. I lasted about an hour without a single boy in sight before saying, "Let's go back."

"Not quite yet," Béatrice whispered, eyeing Sandra. There was the loud ringing of the university bell. Béatrice perked up. She sat straighter and lifted her chest, and within minutes the appeal of the university revealed itself. Boys. Hundreds of boys, our ages and older, began filling the garden. Needless to say, we had to return to get new books the next day. And the day after that.

As we sat on the bench near the fountain, open books on our lap, we set out to reconnoiter so as to discern who was who. Many of the boys moved in groups, carrying textbooks. Some, a few, were here to study or eat their lunch. Most were clearly no more interested in the garden's botanical wonders than we were. A few of the boys began to walk in increasingly closer ellipses around us.

One group of boys appeared to be more audacious than the others. They always seemed to be loitering in the gardens at the same time we were there. We knew that they were law students because they carried textbooks and made sure to sit on a bench not so far from ours and loudly debate law principles. We knew that they were Jewish because of the Star of David pendants they wore around their necks. The best-looking of the three, a confident boy with pomaded hair and expensive clothes, looked at me with insistence and was not shy about his interest.

One day, in a rare show of initiative, Béatrice took it upon herself to wear her Star of David around her neck too, a rallying cry of sorts. It was ironic to think that the symbol we wore with pride would within a short time be used to brand us as society's lepers.

We did not quite know what we wanted with those boys, but the blood in our veins ran hot, and so did theirs. We observed them, and they inspected us, but the activity was discreet because of Sandra, who sat there, pretending not to notice our shenanigans. As long as she was there, they would not dare approach us.

After a few days of this dance, it became clear that we needed to ditch Sandra. This would be a grave offense, and both of us would have a lot of answering to do, but Béatrice embraced the idea right away.

The following day, we put our plan into action. In the afternoon, Sandra and I picked up Béatrice at her apartment and headed for the university, as we had done daily for a week. But once we were deep into the streets, I turned to Sandra. "We want to be on our own now," I told her.

Sandra blinked, not understanding. "On your own?"

"Without a chaperone," I said.

She shook her head violently. "Your parents—"

"Will never know about this," I insisted.

"I cannot let you," she implored, still shaking her head. But we both knew that Sandra's resolve was no match for my willpower.

"Listen, I am doing this either way," I said. "I'm only telling you so that you won't worry."

"Is it to see those boys?" Sandra asked miserably.

"You can sit here and relax for a couple of hours, or run your errands. We won't do anything bad. Don't worry," I whispered to her, "no funny business. I'm never drinking that horrible concoction again."

"Funny business?" she repeated, confusion painted all over her face.

"We'll just walk around, talk to people our age. You know, be free for an hour or so."

"Marceline, it is war time. No one is free to do as they wish."

"It's the opposite; we're all free, Sandra. Including you." I kissed her, knowing it always softened her to mush. "Two hours. I promise! We'll meet you right here." With that, Béatrice and I scampered off and left her standing at the corner of rue Michelet and rue Richelieu. We ran into the crowd and hopped on a trolley as we had done many times with Sandra. We arrived at the University of Algiers's gardens just as the bell rang and walked the stairs casually, conspicuously without a chaperone, and pretended to take an interest in the bamboo forest. The boys pounced. Where did they even come from? Did they wait in the garden day after day hoping for us to stop by? They followed us for a while. We played coy for a respectable amount of time, and then the boys introduced themselves.

"Aren't you supposed to be in class?" Béatrice asked. "The bell just rang again."

"Mens sana in corpore sano," said one of the boys, his standing as an intellectual of the group made evident by the small round glasses I later found out he did not need. "It's not healthy to exclusively fill up your brain. One needs to enjoy the fresh air as well."

"I am Fernand," said the handsomest of the group. Fernand oozed shrewd charm and sported a Clark Gable mustache. Parted hair combed with shiny, scented pomade accentuated the resemblance. "This is André," he said, pointing to the intellectual. "And this is Émile," he said, introducing the biggest of the three, a boy tall and wide, an impressive specimen of a man. They were about our age. All three boys had black eyes and hair and skin tanned to a golden brown. They were an exotic kind of Jewish, more Sephardic than Ashkenazi. They were also, in my impression at the time, more self-assured, more virile-looking, more audacious than the boys, Jewish or gentile, one could find in Paris or the South of France.

"Our classes are in the building that looks down on the garden," big Émile said, pointing to one of the windows of the university above us. "When we see you, we come down."

I immediately liked his honesty. "What are you studying?" I asked.

"The law," André said, examining a leaf he held between his fingers rather than makinge eye contact. "First year."

"We've been friends since childhood," Émile explained.

"And you all want to be lawyers?" Béatrice giggled.

"one for all, and all for one. We do everything together," Émile said.

Fernand looked at me and smiled. "Not quite everything," he said.

"Where is the woman who is usually with you?" André asked.

"Oh, her? We lost her," Béatrice said, unconcerned.

I didn't think it too smart to let strangers know we might be vulnerable. "She's nearby," I lied.

"What happened to her face?" André asked.

Béatrice made a nauseated grimace. "I know, isn't it awful? I can't bear to look at her."

"She was burned in a fire," I said. The boys nodded gravely. Their respect told me something about the type of people they were.

They were Algerian-born Jews. As such they were different from the French colonizers, different from the local Muslims, and different from the Jews I knew in Paris. They were the descendants of Jews who had lived in North Africa for many generations but were given French citizenship with the Crémieux Decree of 1870. They were part of Algeria's human landscape, and this citizenship had been issued to a population caught between two worlds, with two sets of resentments and prejudices.

"To the Arabs, we're the French colonizer," Fernand explained. "Even though our families were in Algeria long before it was colonized by the French. Our families have been here for centuries."

"But to the French," Émile said, "we're Arabs."

"But we're a stupider type of Arab in that case," André said. "The kind that insist on being Jewish and doesn't even have the sense of being Muslim in a Muslim country."

As my father had explained to us, the Crémieux Decree had come with a priceless advantage not bestowed upon the local Muslim population: a free French education. The boys' grandparents had been the first generation to benefit from the law and thus were able to raise their income and social level. The boys' parents had integrated and slowly shaped Algerian society. In a generation, these Jewish families spoke only French, enrolled in universities, and became doctors, lawyers, politicians, and businessmen. Fernand, André, and Émile were born into a life of privilege. All were sure to inherit their family's businesses. And so, they moved with assurance and carefree exuberance and none of the restraint of self-conscious Parisian boys. Their life of amusements and privilege had afforded them a freedom they took for granted. They were passionate, political, and determined to live life to the fullest. I could not have known at the time that this group of boys would change my life.

"Are you allowed to leave the university gardens?" Émile asked.

I smiled. "We're not allowed to be here in the first place."

"Where are you supposed to be?"

"Shopping for hats on rue Michelet."

Fernand locked eyes with me., "Would you like to taste the best ice cream in town?"

"Where?"

"In Bab-El-Oued."

"I'm not sure we're allowed to go to that quartier," Béatrice said with widening eyes.

We knew the implication of following boys we did not know without our parents' knowledge. It might not seem like such a feat nowadays, but at the time, this decision put us at a crossroad. Refuse, and we would continue our dull existence with our reputations intact. Accept, and at last we would get to taste life, but it might be with our reputations forever soiled. It did not matter what we did with those boys. Being seen with them would put us squarely in the category of girls of ill repute.

I had already made up my mind. Béatrice only needed a slight push on my part. "Aren't we already well outside the rules?" I suggested to her.

"A bit of ice cream has never led anyone to jail," big Émile offered, flirting with Béatrice.

"I could be tempted," said Béatrice, who had never met a boy she didn't like.

Together, we took the trolley back across town to Place du Gouvernement. We arrived at a café with striped red-and-white awnings and rattan chairs set out on a terrace cooled by the mottled shade of sycamores. Above the door, a sign read "Café Djurdjura." Fernand helped me to my chair, and Émile helped Béatrice, thus implicitly laying claim to each of us. The five of us gathered around a small table. Around us, older men drank anisette. André crossed one leg over the other, his body away from the table, and took out a Nietzsche book, which he read ostensibly while not missing a bit of conversation. His father was part owner of Galeries de France. He was serious, conscientious about facts, and had an unsettling way of looking away as he spoke, so it was unclear what he thought of you and if he even wanted you there. Émile's father worked at the préfecture and could 'pull strings,' or so the story was. Émile's shirts were never large enough for his frame, and when he laughed, which was all the time, it seemed his clothes might burst.

He was without anger but often got into fistfights, perhaps because hoodlums considered his mere appearance a challenge.

And Fernand. Women were quite into him. He was cool and self-assured, and his overuse of cologne and reputation as a womanizer made him easy to discount. But he was the leader of the group. It was he who, much like an army officer, could recruit, motivate, and organize his troops and later did.

Émile and Fernand lavished us with attention. I sat straight, folded my legs to one side, and lifted my bust as I had practiced so many times in front of the mirror. "This terrace reminds me of the South of France," I said.

"We've never been to France," Émile said. "I've always wanted to see Paris."

"I hear we're not missing anything. Paris is filled with stuck-ups." André said, not looking up from his copy of *Beyond Good and Evil.*

"At the moment it's crawling with Nazis," I said.

"The weather is dreadful in Paris. Gray, gray, and more wretched gray," Béatrice said. "You would positively loathe it."

As we chatted, the waiter, an Algerian boy about our age, moved through the tables. He was tall and thin and wore his white shirt, black pants, and black bow tie with surprising elegance. His body was chiseled, hard. His hair was cut very short, practically shaved, a style that was in contrast with the well-coiffed hair, glossy with pomade, of our new friends. For a brief moment, something about the Algerian waiter felt familiar. Had I seen him before? But the next moment, the illusion dissolved.

The waiter arrived at our table. "What is it you want?" he said abruptly.

Fernand looked at him angrily. "I hardly think that's a proper way to take an order," he said.

"You don't want anything?" the boy asked. Was it sarcasm in his tone? I could not be sure. He spoke French with a slight accent.

He and Fernand looked at each other in a way that made it clear that the two had a history. Was this boy the reason Fernand had brought us to this place? Perhaps to display us?

"Let it go, Fernand," Émile said. "He's not worth it." He turned to the waiter. "We'll share a coupe géante."

The boy looked above our head, as he asked, "Flavors?"

Émile declared with panache, "For these beautiful ladies, only the very best. Chocolate, mint, Grand Marnier, vanilla, raspberry, rose water, and coffee. And double whipped cream."

"Oh, please," Béatrice pleaded, her eyelashes fluttering, "what is it about Algiers that you have to add rose water to eve-ry-thing; tea, pastries, perfume? If I have to ingest anything that tastes of rose water again, I will positively die!"

"But what a beautifully-scented death this would be," André said.

"No rose water!" Émile clamored. "Please replace that scoop with … more chocolate!"

"Bring us six spoons," Fernand ordered.

The waiter walked away, feline, his forearm muscles taught under his caramel-color skin. "Do you know this boy?" Béatrice asked.

"He's not one of us," Fernand said.

"What do you mean?"

"Muslim." André only said, as though no further explanation was needed.

"His people don't respect women," Émile explained to me.

"Whereas you do?" I asked. I might have sounded terser than intended, so I compensated with a smile.

"Not only that," Fernand said lyrically. "Women are our muses, our inspiration, our raison d'être."

The boy returned a few minutes later and set at the center of our table a bowl the size of half a soccer ball overflowing with colorful ice cream scoops, and topped with whipped cream and toasted almond slivers. He set a single spoon on a napkin next to the ice cream bowl. His fingers were rough and covered with scratches. I glimpsed up at him. His eyes pierced through mine.

"I asked for six spoons; can't you count? And bring us all water!" Fernand said.

The boy left our table wordlessly and came back to set five additional spoons and napkins on the table. He then put on the table a single glass of iced water and produced six straws, which he plopped one by one into the glass. Before Fernand could register the affront, the boy had turned away, feline and unhurried.

"I'll kick his teeth in for this disrespect," Fernand said under his breath.

Unlike Fernand, André and Émile seemed to find the whole episode very amusing. "Compare his day to yours," Émile said conciliatorily. "Fisherman by night, lowly waiter by day, the closest he'll ever get to beautiful Parisiennes is to serve them ice cream."

Fernand changed the subject and turned to me. "Do tell. What is life like in Paris?"

"Curfew at nine in the evening. Limited rations. Clocks set to Berlin time," I answered.

Fernand played along, "I meant to ask, what are people wearing? What kind of music are the clubs playing?"

"I guess we'll need to wait until after the war to find out," André said.

"Are you ladies students?" Émile asked.

"Or are you looking for husbands?" André added.

Émile grabbed André's Nietzsche and whacked him on the head with it. "Ruffian!"

Béatrice threw her head back and laughed.

"Some fancy law students you all are," I said.

Everything for the boys, as Béatrice and I would come to call them, was an opportunity to have fun. They loved to joust verbally and to challenge each other. They loved to play games and tell stories. As soon as the ice cream was consumed, they started a contest where Béatrice and I had to throw olives into their mouths to see how many they could catch. They wanted to make us laugh. We wanted to laugh, so we did. I was well aware of the reproachful eyes of European women who sat at nearby tables. We were trollops, as far as they were concerned. It bothered me, but it did not bother me enough. Sitting on the terrace of Café Djurdjura on this hot June day, I felt more optimistic. In the company of these boys who competed in wit and goofiness, away from my mother and the apartment, it seemed possible to breathe at last.

As the five of us chatted, I made a conscious effort not to look at the Muslim boy who stood at the door that separated the café and its terrace, his arms crossed over his apron, his eyes half closed like those of a cat. From that distance, I had the sensation that he was watching me but I could not be sure.

Fernand, Émile, and André gallantly walked us back to rue Michelet. We found Sandra standing in the exact spot where we had parted over three hours before. Her hands were clasped over her basket, which was still empty. When she spotted me, her whole body relaxed, but she did not look at me or speak to me. The boys, determined to make an impression, introduced themselves with utmost politeness. Sandra only narrowed her eyes at them.

When they were gone, and we had walked Béatrice back to her apartment, Sandra turned to me and said, "You cannot do this again."

"Sandra," I implored, "you need to understand: Mother is acting crazy. There is war. We don't know what the future will bring. I only want to live before it's too late." I had meant to sound dramatic, but suddenly it rang true.

She shook her head. "What if something had happened to you? What would I tell Albano?"

"You and Baba are on a first-name basis now?" I said to tease her. She blushed, embarrassed. "Tell Mother and Baba that you're not up to the task of watching me," I said. "And in the end, you'd get into more trouble than I would."

Was it a manipulating thing to say? Without a doubt. The poor thing must have known that her presence in Algiers was on a precarious footing with Mother being so upset that she was here at all. But I knew what I wanted, and I could not let Sandra get in my way.

The following days, we repeated the same scheme, and soon it became routine. Sandra went along with it, letting us ditch her and meeting us hours later. I came to wonder if she did not tacitly agree that I should be able to experience a bit of freedom. As always, she never told a soul. If Sandra was good at one thing, it was at keeping a secret.

The war, which had begun as surreal words printed in newspapers or heard on the radio, soon started to color everything and became palpable. Paris, our symbol for all of France, had been subjugated, trampled, and humiliated in defeat. When the Vichy government was first created, we put our faith in it. But in July 1940, less than a month after the Germans invaded Paris, Pétain's government abruptly revised naturalizations obtained after 1927. In doing so, it denaturalized my father, stripping him of his French nationality overnight and without the possibility of appeal.

"No one will come all the way to North Africa to take away my citizenship," my father told us at dinnertime. "That is because no one knows where any of us are. As long as we keep who we are a secret, we will be safe."

My mother clenched her fork. Her face was panic-stricken. "But if you are to take back your original nationality, what will it be? You left the Ottoman Empire before it became Turkey. Does that make you a Turkish citizen?"

My father thought about it with his usual equanimity. "I think, yes. And Turkey is neutral."

"For now!" she exclaimed. "But what if it chooses a side? What if it takes the side of the Axis? Then you could become an enemy alien!"

"Lucienne, I am a French-Algerian citizen, born and raised here as far as anyone is concerned, and so are you, and so are the children. That is all you need to remember. We are Alban, Lucienne, Marceline, and Gustave Dupont, and we are French."

"But who gave you these papers? Moshe? How can you be sure they will continue to work? Can you even trust that man?"

"The identity is fake, but the papers are real, not counterfeit. Moshe has friends, Jewish friends, in high places here in Algiers."

"Oh, Alban!" she wailed. "How can you put us in this situation?"

Gustave, who had been looking at our mother with disgust, exploded. "Baba is saving us! Can't you understand *anything*?" He stood up from the table and left the room, slamming the door.

Mother dissolved into tears "Everyone hates me!"

Now it was my turn to be disgusted. I too took refuge in my room, leaving it up to my father to console her.

We settled into this new life, with the Vichy regime and Nazi Germany as a background. We had to continue our education while keeping a low profile, so it was determined that we would study at home. Our mothers having decided this was the most economical way to educate us, Béatrice, Gustave, and I took tedious lessons from uninspired tutors. The lessons were a special kind of torture for Gustave, who was flustered by Béatrice's presence. She paid him no more attention than if he had been one of the stray dogs that roamed the streets of Algiers. After our lessons, Sandra would feed us lunch, and Béatrice and I would disappear into my bedroom, do our hair, and pool our clothes and accessories, coming up with endless combinations. Once we were dressed and our hair was nicely coiffed, we went into town with Sandra, ostensibly tagging along as she did her errands, but ditching her as soon as we got to the trolley station.

We did not have to worry about Baba finding out since he spent his day with Uncle Moshe in his Algiers office. My mother was usually asleep in her room or taken ill with one of her migraines. But Gustave was suspicious. One day, we did not dart out of the apartment fast enough. He was at the door to the elevator. "Why are you getting all dolled up?" he asked.

Sandra hurried down the stairwell to keep above the fray.

"Mind your own business," Béatrice told him.

Gustave was too shy to address Béatrice. He turned to me. "Does Mother know that you paint your faces like this?"

The question was tricky. Makeup was not acceptable for girls our age, so before our parents saw it, we removed it as carefully as we had applied it. The only option was to take the offensive. "Would you be more comfortable if Béatrice and I stayed home?" I asked Gustave. "Would you prefer us to be like the Muslim women, veiled, and unseen?"

"That's not the point!"

"If you want to make a fuss about a little rouge, you can," I said.

"Are you going to tell?" Béatrice asked him.

"There's nothing to tell," I said. "Unless you want to upset Mother even more. Or you can burden Baba with it, who is so tense as it is. Do as you wish."

Gustave considered this. "You better not do anything bad," he said. "And you better not cause Sandra to get in trouble."

"Attaboy," Béatrice said, tapping him on the head. Gustave's face turned crimson.

Day after day, Béatrice and I left Sandra behind, hopped on a trolley, and for a few hours met up with Fernand, André, and Émile at favorite cafés around Algiers where we had "la kremia", the local display of appetizers, and drank Perrier-grenadines and smoked untold quantities of Gauloises. By August, Béatrice and Émile were going steady. They kissed, hidden in public parks in the bushes behind shade trees, while we kept watch. Fernand courted me, and I found him attractive, but my experience in the south of France had made me wary of sweet-talking, confident young men. He and I played a game of cat and mouse that pleased me. I was getting the attention without committing to something I was not ready for.

Despite the war and the strange mood at home, my life was starting at long last. Béatrice and I wanted to ignore our worries. We wanted to spend time with boys and feel young and free. Our new friends were not parent-approved. With them, we did not feel shackled by propriety or decorum. For the first time, I experienced what it was like to be in the company of young men that did not involve strategizing or analyzing lineage. I loved the boys' directness, their passion, and as the year progressed and Hitler's path of destruction broadened, their outrage and desire to act. The boys knew the city; they were smart, educated, quick to laughter, carefree by birth. When the time came, they would also prove themselves to be courageous men.

Café Djurdjura became our favorite place to meet, although we soon had to forget the ice cream. One by one, the flavors were discontinued until there wasn't even milk or refrigeration.

****

The Muslim waiter's name was Khaled. He worked at Café Djurdjura most afternoons. He spoke French with a soft North African accent. From what I garnered through observation, Khaled worked two jobs. Like most of the native Muslims of Algiers, he was probably extremely poor. The cuts on his hands, those gashes and blisters that never healed, were from working at the fishing mole. Unlike the other waiters or my blabbermouth friends, he hardly said a word and made no effort to be sociable. If Khaled was capable of smiling, I never saw it. His somberness made us all seem shallow, or him very deep. He and Fernand had disliked each other at first sight, each representing one side of Algiers that resented the other, but Fernand's creative ways to mock and humiliate him were no match for Khaled's silent contempt.

Some days, I thought I felt Khaled's gaze on me, but I did not want to look up for fear that my friends would notice. His presence unnerved me. I thought about him too much and my continuously thinking about him unnerved me. His attitude angered me: his arrogance, his lack of apparent interest for me, his contempt for our group, the pride he displayed by not touching our tips were just all so infuriating. It was months before I could admit to myself that he was the reason why I was drawn to Café Djurdjura. That in the morning, I dressed thinking about him. That when I did my hair or put on lipstick, it was he who was on my mind. I was clear on two points: that I should not let my feelings be known and that I should not have them in the first place. I trusted no one with my growing fascination with Khaled. Not the boys, not Béatrice, not even myself.

The summer went on like this, my pretending not to pay Khaled any attention, and his ignoring us. Every day, our group, with affected lightheartedness that masked our fear, sat around the same small café table on the terrace of Café Djurdjura, as we waited to hear about the fate of France.

In late August, we were sipping watered-down orangeade when André arrived, brandishing *L'Écho d'Alger*. "The Marchandeau Law was abrogated," he said, flopping down on a chair. A terrible silence fell on us as we digested the news. We all knew the Marchandeau Law. It was a new law, barely a year old, that had declared anti-Semitic propaganda in the press illegal. The importance of this law had been deemed a vital necessity by the Troisième République, and now they wanted it gone? The abrogation of the law was an open invitation to hatred. "Soon there will be no one and nothing protecting Jews," I said, voicing what we all thought.

"The Maréchal's hands are tied," Émile offered. "His focus is on getting our prisoners of war back from Germany, and to make sure our cities aren't bombed. This doesn't have to mean anything."

"The Maréchal Pétain can do no wrong in Émile's eyes," André said.

"After all, if it weren't for him there still would be a French army," Émile argued. "He's the reason we are not on our way to a battlefield."

None of us answered. We wanted to believe in Pétain. We wanted to ignore our nagging doubts.

The temperature had not yet dropped by late September. The only signs that summer was gone were the shortening days and the softer sun. With September came the chilling news of a first official census of Jews in the occupied zone.

"Pétain's regime wants free reign to implement the racial policies it has been drooling after," Fernand said.

"A census doesn't have to signify they mean us harm," Béatrice said.

Fernand, André, Émile, and I did not even bother to respond.

Vallat and other notorious anti-Semites were given prominent roles in Vichy, and thus began the government-sponsored anti-Jew witch hunt. Every day, it seemed, the newspaper reported on measures reducing the rights of Jews and making their living situation more precarious. In early October, things got worse. A French official "Statute on Jews" was announced that mirrored Nazi policies in Germany. It was just as my father had predicted. It closed French Jews to a number of professions. One signature on a decree and French Jews could no longer be teachers, lawyers, or journalists.

Overnight, André, Fernand, and Émile were seeing their education become worthless, their future canceled.

We met at Café Djurdjura the day following that news. When Béatrice and I arrived, we found the boys slumped despondently on their chairs in front of a full ashtray. They had spent the night talking about the situation and drinking. Seeing them in such a pitiful state, unshaven, unwashed – even Fernand, who took so much pride in his appearance – morphed my worry and empathy into a feeling of anger I could not explain. It was not anger at the injustice, but anger at them.

Béatrice began to cry the minute we sat down. "My father said he might be fired from the préfecture. What are we going to do?"

"Will they let us pass the bar exam?" André repeated to himself, stunned.

"Will they even let us graduate?" Émile said.

I thought of my father, of our fake papers, of the money he had put away. Were we the only family who did not worry about employment or money? I noticed that the boys no longer wore their Stars of David pendants. I wondered if this was a conscious act.

"Can't the rest of France see how terribly unjust this is and rebel?" Béatrice said.

Fernand shrugged. "The French aren't going to rebel because they're all too glad this is happening to us."

"Everyone has their problems. Uncertainty, lost work, the long lines, the rationing, and the price of butter if there is butter at all," Émile said.

André rebelled. "How can you wax poetic about the suffering of gentiles at a moment like this?"

Fernand asked of no one in particular, "We can't join the army, we can't study and we can't find work; what is left for us to do?"

"There is no disgrace in working with your hands," I said. "You can become a fisherman or a merchant."

"Sweetheart, don't be rude," Fernand said with a thin smile.

"Whatever you decide to do, don't spend too much time feeling sorry for yourselves," I said.

They collectively stared at me with an expression of dismay. André, who had been holding his chin in his hands as he sipped his drink morosely from a straw, said, "Don't you realize what is going on?"

"They are trying to break our spirit," I said. "Don't tell me they've already succeeded."

My comment seemed to jolt the boys out of their melancholy and into anger at me. But their anger was reassuring. Anger meant action. "Easy for you to give us advice, Marceline," André said. "The situation changes nothing for women."

"How so?" I asked.

"Women can continue to care for their men, feed their families, make babies: what they've always done." Fernand said.

"Sweetheart, don't *you* be rude now," I said.

"In Russia, I hear they let women get equal pay as they do equal work," Fernand said. "Women are actually given guns to fight, and they can be soldiers. They even have female airline pilots."

"You better keep your mouth shut about your Bolshevik sentiments," André told him. "It will land you in jail faster than you can say Rasputin."

"I'm only stating a fact," Fernand said. "I'm not saying I am for equal pay or the vote for women or anything like that."

"America has given women the right to vote," I said. "Britain has too. Even Germany has since 1918. They're not the worse for wear."

"Oh, so women, that's who elected Hitler?" André said.

Émile, all too happy to move away from the topic of Communism asked, "Do you think that the women's right to vote would magically make them equal to men?"

"Being equal to men would be a demotion," I said. "Women are already superior. Especially to André."

Béatrice giggled nervously. André raised his palms, "What did I say?"

"The only injustices you perceive are those happening to you," I said, quite loudly. "We speak of the rights of men, and the rights of Jews, and the rights of Arabs. But in each group, there is a subgroup with no rights at all. No one ever speaks of the rights of women." Khaled, who was setting plates of appetizers on a nearby table looked up at me.

Fernand took my hand and patted it. "What's eating you, baby doll?" he asked.

Something was eating at me indeed, but I was not going to share that information with them. It was about another law that struck my family directly. My friends did not know my father or the fact that he was a foreigner. The new law concerning the ressortissants étrangers de race juive authorized the internment of foreign Jews on the sole basis of them being foreigners. That morning, we had learned through Moshe, who had eyes and ears in Paris, that there was a protectoral order tracking my father. He and Moshe were wanted for anti-French activities, namely the timely liquidation of their holdings, the closing of a profitable business, and the disappearance of capital. The police had looked for ways to expropriate us and confiscate our assets and had found them missing. The police had come to the Paris house and had learned that we had left for the South of France a year before. Another police team had knocked at our door in Cannes and had been told that we had taken all our belongings and vanished overnight. The Cannes commissariat de police confirmed that burned pieces of our boat had been found off the coast of Corsica when we had attempted to leave the country and that we were presumed dead. From there, they had not been able to trail us. If it hadn't been for our fake identity, the French police in Algiers would have easily found us. The strange exit out of Cannes, leaving the boat behind in the middle of the Mediterranean, all the precautions my father had taken, and that frankly had seemed overly dramatic then, were saving us.

And now Baba and Moshe were fugitives, and by extension, so were we.

In the weeks that followed, Jewish businesses in both occupied and unoccupied France were put under Aryan leadership or, to put it plainly, were stolen. All bank accounts changed hands. Jewish assets were frozen and controlled by the Vichy-run administration. One day, my father gathered Mother, Gustave and me in the salon. His face was grave, but he was calm. "This is how we are affected," he began. "Our assets are safe in Swiss accounts, but we will not be able to access that money. We will have to make what we have here last."

"What do we have?" Gustave asked.

"We have diamonds."

"How many? How much?" I asked.

"Enough. We are going to sell some. Not all of it, in case money gets devalued. I am hoping we can make it last a couple of years if we are thrifty."

My mother straightened and said with earnest bravery, "If things have come to that, I shall sell the Cité des Fleurs house."

"Are we going to sell our house, Baba?" Gustave said.

My father shook his head. "Lucienne, children, I am afraid I need to tell you the truth about our house. I've known of this since June, but I did not have the heart to say anything."

My mother blanched., "For goodness' sake, Alban, what is it?"

"The house has been appropriated by the Nazis as a habitation for their upper echelon operatives."

"I don't understand?" my mother cried out.

"Nazis have been living in our house," Gustave said with a degree of spite she did not deserve. "Sleeping in your bed. Eating out of your china, with your silverware. Sitting on your toilets."

"Gustave, please," my father said.

"For three months?" my mother murmured. "They've been in our house for three months?" She paused and stared into space.

"I am so sorry, Dear," my father said.

Without warning, she shot up from her chair and screamed at my father. "How could you let them? How could you give our house to the Nazis?"

The accusation was entirely absurd. "Lucienne, that is not how this happened," my father said in a soothing voice.

My mother was wailing now, "First, this woman! And now, my house!" She ran to her room and slammed the door yelling, "You take everything from me!"

We stood in the dining room in awkward silence.

"This time, she's really flipped her wig," Gustave said.

"What woman is Maman talking about?" I asked.

"She's overly exhausted," my father said.

"From what?" Gustave said. "She does nothing but sleep."

"We must all help your mother. This is a very hard time for her."

"It's a hard time for everyone!" Gustave shouted. He turned to me, yelling, "Except for Marceline."

"Stop concerning yourself with me!" I yelled back.

My mother had always given us the notion that she was the dominant force in our home. It was clear to us now that her intransigence, her domineering ways had masked her fragility. Taken out of her country, downgraded from her status, stripped of her money, the pillars on which she had rested all of her life crumbled. She fell into the deep state of despondency that had been threatening to engulf her. Now she refused to leave the apartment. Some days, she never dressed or got out of bed. She barely ate; her face was gaunt. She hardly paid attention to any of us and refused to come to the table at mealtimes. Sandra had to bring her trays with the few foods she would tolerate, bizarre things such as jasmine tea, hearts of palm, and canned sardines and toast. Whatever energy my mother still had, she used it to berate Sandra. Sandra, whom she relied on for everything; Sandra, who did the best she could to make what little money we had last longer. Sandra understood bartering and haggling very well indeed. She could make a lot out of very little and worked relentlessly while Mother cried and spent her time in the suffocating heat of the apartment, all curtains drawn.

The biggest blow for Fernand, Émile, and André, and for all the Algerian Jews, came a few days later. With a single signature on a document abrogating the Crémieux Decree, the Jews of Algeria were stripped of their French nationality. This was unbelievable news. Overnight, by virtue of being Jews born in North Africa, my friends and their families were no longer French.

"How could this be?" Émile repeated, dozens of times a day. "How could this be?"

"This is the excuse they've been waiting for!" André said. "They can say that Hitler made them do it and not bother themselves with public opinion."

"Do you not think that the Maréchal has to do something to appease the Germans?" Émile said limply.

André's face turned red. "Shut your mouth with your Maréchal, or I will punch you square in the jaw."

"I don't blame Émile for clutching to the hope that the Maréchal has the answers since no one else does," Fernand said. "The Vichy propaganda is efficient. They have you believe that he is Jesus reincarnate."

"And this Jesus hates the Jews," Béatrice said.

"This is Maréchal Pétain, Verdun Hero, Savior of France," André said. That's why he can't possibly blame his military for our defeat. He wants to convince us that France's defeat is a moral one. How else can we justify our terrible debacle? He wants people to believe that the Nazi occupation is only a symptom of the problem, and that the problem is us.'"

"Us the Jews?" Béatrice asked.

"Us the French, and the alleged slow rotting of society," André answered.

"Admit it," Émile said, "ever since the Great War, people have wanted to do nothing but have a ball, dance, and drink themselves into a stupor. Maybe a return to sound values would not be such a bad thing. Maybe it's true that the German's over took us in a matter of weeks because we were lazy and complacent."

"And let me guess," Fernand sneered, "And the only way France can regain pride in itself is through some sort of purification process, a strengthening of patriotism through wholesome outdoor physical activity and renewed patriarchy?

"And do not forget an invigorated form of bigotry," André said.

"Family values and outdoor life have never done people any harm," Émile suggested.

"Here we go," André exclaimed. "The glorification of physical strength in a frantic effort to cure ourselves of imaginary complacency!"

Whether in response to the frustration of being forbidden to fight, or because testosterone combined with the deep urge to act made men restless, or whether it was in admiration of those Germans' strong military bodies, every man in the city suddenly wanted to exercise, do manual labor, work in the fields, strengthen their bodies.

"It is all propaganda, Émile," Fernand said between his teeth, quietly enough so that people at the next table could not hear. "Our nation is ripe for it. Like drowning people latching to remnants of a sinking ship, we're looking for reasons for our terrible failure. We saw how Germany reinvented itself after the Great War. Whether we admit it or not, Goebbels' speeches and the Nazis' propaganda about race and strength are having an insidious effect on us. We hate the Nazis, and we hate Hitler, but how can we not admire the way Germany rose from the ashes? And here is Pétain suggesting that the French need some of that beautiful discipline, outdoor work, calisthenics! We're ashamed; we're blindsided; we're *conquered* for god's sake! We're not lazy or complacent: we're defeated! And we're defeated because Pétain capitulated on our behalf like the coward that he is. Pétain is making us think it is unpatriotic to point fingers at our incompetent army. *His* army. He wants us to blame ourselves. He wants our self-loathing."

"Pétain is exploiting our shame," André added, "and then points the finger at the obvious scapegoats, in line with the German propaganda; Communists, Freemasons, homosexuals, foreigners, and Jews. When in fact it is Pétain and his minions who are at the beck and call of the Fuehrer, not the Jews, or whatever foreigners they can find to hate. The first thing to purify is this damn government filled with an incompetent bunch of old fuddy-duddies." André was getting too loud. At the tables around us, people stared. From the other side of the terrace, Khaled made eye contact with me and slowly shook his head.

I put my hand on André's sleeve. "André, shhh…"

"Is the notion that our beloved leader has betrayed us too painful to contemplate?" André raged, not even noticing my hand. "The Nazis aren't even the greatest enemy of France. No," he shouted, "The greatest enemy of France is the Vichy Government!"

"My friend here has had too much sun and anisette," Fernand said with a bright smile to everyone on the terrace.

Khaled approached our table, he picked up empty glasses, and gazing above our heads said, "If you want to spend the rest of the war in jail, this is the way to do it." He picked up the rest of the glasses and walked away without another word.

We looked at each other in bewilderment. "I am amazed," Émile bellowed," "he does speak!"

Fernand was livid. "It is not his place to. He's not supposed to eavesdrop on us, or for that matter, to have an opinion."

"Although he is right. I am drunk," André said.

"You're missing the point," Fernand snapped. "He should not be allowed to speak to us at all."

"Can't you learn anything?" I said angrily.

Fernand frowned. "What is there to learn, sweetheart?"

"Your superiority is only in your imagination, Fernand. It is that attitude of the colonizer I presume. Can you not see that we are all one law away from having no standing in society at all?"

"What a nasty thing to say, young lady," Fernand said, smiling to soften the mood.

"It applies to me as well," I said. "Arabs, Parisians, Algerians, Jews, we're all in the same boat now."

The following week, Khaled began to work on the other side of the café's terrace. I suspected that Fernand had something to do with Khaled being given an area away from us, but to ask him would be to give the issue too much attention. Fernand knew the owner, who was Jewish. Perhaps he needed to feel that he still had some measure of influence over his environment. Now it was easier to watch Khaled come and go from a distance as he moved through the tables. On the one hand, I could observe him inconspicuously. But on the other hand, I had felt his presence and, his overhearing our conversation as a sort of closeness between us, if not a friendship. It bothered me that he could no longer hear us. Or at least not hear me.

As fall progressed, the weather changed. Temperatures dropped, café terraces closed. We met the boys inside cafés rather than on terraces, and so we had to keep our conversations even quieter. We weren't the only ones. An atmosphere of mistrust, more acute with every week that passed, was sweeping through the city. We learned to look around us for indiscreet ears. There were words and names we avoided.

Week by week, Jewish teachers in France and North Africa were fired from schools, Jewish bankers replaced, Jewish businessmen dispossessed, if not thrown into jail, without an explanation. André, whose father was part owner of Galeries de France, saw his assets confiscated. Émile's father and grandfather, who had worked at the préfecture all their adult lives, found themselves without any means of supporting their family. André, Fernand, Émile, and their families, in the space of a few months, had lost their nationality and their livelihood. Béatrice's family's fared even worse. Her father was fired, and they had no idea what to do. They considered returning to occupied Paris. German occupation or not, at least they had family there. It was my father who convinced Béatrice's father to stay put for the time being and even lent him money to do so.

Apathy seemed to fall upon Fernand, Émile, and André. They lost all desire to open a class book. What for, when most professions would be denied to them? There was little to do but sit for hours at Café Djurdjura and pore over the Vichy-controlled *L'Écho d'Alger* and *Gazette d'Alger* for hints of truth and sparks of hope for the Jews of France. But reading the newspapers was painful. Now sanctioned by the press, anti-Semitism was rampant. Every day in the news and plastered on billboards, Jews were depicted as dangerous, treacherous, and physically repulsive. I couldn't bear going to the movie theater where the official news channel, France Actualité, blasted carefully crafted propaganda disguised as news bulletins regarding our religion, which was now considered a race. Posters depicted us with noses like slices of Brie cheese, evil smirks, and clawed fingers. It would have been laughable if it had not made us physically ill to see how the madness was appealing to everyone and how powerless we were to stop it.

Meanwhile, the Vichy regime's deceptions were not yet so obvious that they might cause the French population to rebel. The French were lulled into torpor by the cult of Pétain's personality, which seemed to be turning into a bona fide religion. The Maréchal's portrait was everywhere. As the Germans began to plunder all of France's riches, and French people could no longer feed themselves or keep their homes warm, any thought one might harbor against Pétain was deemed unpatriotic, or worse, actively anti-French. What André had felt free to express just a month before was now akin to treason.

Outside, in the shade of entrances of buildings, little girls played hopscotch and jumped ropes. Little boys ran through the city, played marbles, and chased after cats and pigeons, but mostly they played war with increasing violence.

Winter 1941 was a trying one. To make ends meet, Jewish doctors became pedicurists, Jewish lawyers drove taxis, Jewish teachers shined shoes, and Jewish bankers sold in the streets the lemons and oranges from their gardens. For all my friends, money became scarce, and so did food. The boys grew thin; we all did. No one was getting appropriate nourishment for our growing bodies. But pangs of hunger were nothing compared to the terrible knot of anxiety ever present in our bellies.

In January, I turned eighteen.

When they are too old to play in the streets and forbidden to work or enlist, what is left for energetic young men to do? Disgusted, angry, terrified, stripped of a future, denied higher education and work, but relatively free to come and go, the Jewish men of Algiers young and old began to congregate. In no time, our favorite cafés served as outposts and rallying places. But Vichy spies were everywhere. We had to be discreet. Other French colonies in Africa, the Ivory Coast, Tchad, Cameroun, and the Congo had rallied to the call of General de Gaulle and France Libre. Why not Algeria? We received the news of colonies joining France Libre like cool water on a parched throat. Hope was a beautiful thing, and it was the only thing we had. There were rumors that the United States would soon end its neutrality. Most of it was little more than wishful thinking and jumbled signals on the radio. We did not know whom to turn to. We could trust no one. In Algeria, even more than the rest of France, there was deep distrust for the British ever since

Churchill's decision to sink our ships right here in Mers-El- Kébir when he anticipated that the French fleet posted there would fall under German's control. This had resulted in the death of over a thousand French sailors.

"And what of America, who does nothing?" Émile said. "Will they ever enter the war? Show some courage?"

"They're not doing nothing," André sneered. "They're providing the Brits with weapons to use against us."

"That's propaganda," Fernand said. "Whoever our allies are, when they reach out to us we need to be ready."

"Ready how, without weapons or an army? And how would they reach out to us?" I asked.

"Think about it," Fernand said. "The police in Algiers are in Pétain's pocket. Who are the only people the Allied forces can absolutely count on being against the Germans? Who would have absolutely nothing to gain and everything to lose with France remaining under German control?"

"The Jews!" Béatrice said.

"That's right, sweetie."

I had my doubts about the Jews of North Africa being able to make a dent in this war but I understood the boys' need for hope. Still, I began to worry when it became apparent that the boys too seemed contaminated by the exercise mania bug that must have been in the air. Could it be that my friends were being lured by Vichy's lies? Every day, young, old, crippled or not, the Jewish men of Algiers made their way to the Gymnase Géo Gras, one of Algiers' gymnasiums, to partake in vigorous calisthenics. Fernand, André, and Émile stopped bothering to go to school and, joining other mustachioed men in tight clothes and pomaded hair, spent most of their time at the gym.

One afternoon, the boys arrived after one of their workouts and flopped down on their café chairs.

"Must you really work so hard?" Béatrice asked.

"Order of the Maréchal," Fernand said with a wink.

Béatrice turned to me. "Really?"

"Your brother was at the gymnasium's door today," André said.

"My brother?" I asked, surprised.

"That skinny fellow, Gustave."

"How do you even know who my brother is?"

"It is a small town," Émile said.

"He's been showing up on his bicycle every day, trying to get in."

"So, he wants to exercise like all of you fools?" I shrugged. "Let him in."

"He's too young," André said. "You should tell him to stay home."

"What harm is there in him exercising?"

"He's a nuisance, asking questions," Fernand said. "You have to tell him not to come anymore."

"I have no control over my brother," I said. "And by the way, if you know who Gustave is, does this mean he knows who you are?"

"Is that a problem?"

"I don't need him knowing my business," I said.

"He can't be trusted?"

"I don't know," I said. "He can be slippery."

"I'll tell him not to go to Géo Gras," Béatrice said giggling. "I think he's stuck on me."

"Stay out of this, Béatrice," I said. "I'll deal with my own brother."

In truth, I did not know what Gustave was doing with his days. Did he have friends? Was he still smitten with Béatrice, or had he found some girl his age to care about? He seemed to be home quite a lot, stuck between Mother and Sandra, perhaps ensuring the former didn't kill the latter. When I came home, he usually was in his room reading his comics, drawing, or melting his ear to the radio. He continued to be obsessed with war: armaments, tanks, navy equipment, deployment, and maneuvers. He read everything he could on the subject. Drawings of tanks and weapons and helmets and flags were all over the apartment. He was an excellent artist; too bad his talent was being used for something so pointless. At dinner, he incessantly mentioned that if it were possible for Jews, he would enlist as soon as he was old enough. But I think it was only to drive Father mad. This gymnasium thing would be good for him. He could use a physical outlet. "I see no reason why you boys have a problem with him," I told Fernand, Émile, and André. "Why do you even care?"

But the boys did not answer my question.

I came home that same afternoon, dreading the sight of my mother's uncombed hair, Father's tense jaw, the suffocating family silence. Lately, we had to change our lifestyle, and this didn't help. No more visits from private tutors, no more French restaurants or shopping excursions to the Galeries de France. Everyone in town was struggling one way or another, so it was something you resigned yourself to. And so, my mother lost her last few reasons to get dressed in the morning.

After leaving the boys, I met up with Sandra on rue d'Isly, and we walked back to the apartment together. "I finished this today," she said, opening her basket as we walked to show me what was inside. With rationing, it was hard to find the clothes I wanted. Sandra, after many pleas on my part, had hand sewn a girdle and porte-jarretelles – my first – with fabric she had bought on the black market.

I threw my arms around her. "You're a life-saver," I said.

She grumbled. "Tell your mother nothing."

"My lips are sealed," I said.

Before we got to the apartment, I asked Sandra, "What is Gustave up to these days?"

She shrugged, "This and that."

"But where does he go?"

"Here and there."

I laughed. "I know when you are trying not to answer my questions. It looks exactly like that right now." I took her arm and leaned against her. "Of course, you must know where Gustave is. He's your little favorite. I bet you know just where he is and what he does minute by minute. He is working with Moshe and Baba, isn't he? People say they saw him in town. By the way, what kind of business is this they're doing? Baba won't tell."

We arrived at the door of the apartment building, and Sandra pushed it open. "Everyone wants to do their own things," she said evasively.

"Yes," I said soothingly. "And what are those things exactly?"

"I do not ask."

"Oh, but you know."

She pinched her lips. "I don't tell what you do, and I don't tell what they do," she said, and she started up the stairs to our apartment.

"Oh, come on Sandra, come up the elevator! You're killing yourself."

"I like stairs."

"No one likes stairs."

"Everyone is stubborn," Sandra said. "I am stubborn, too."

"That you are," I said, shutting the metal gate of the lift behind me.

Later, in my room, I tried on the girdle Sandra had sewn. I liked how it shrank my waist and accentuated my hourglass figure. It was the fashion, and I always loved fashion. I also wanted the attention of men. In our group of friends, Fernand stuck out as the desirable one. He was an attractive fellow to be sure. Always well dressed and suave as well as educated and intelligent. He had a confidence and authority that I found very appealing. But I was clear on one thing as I looked at myself in the mirror: Fernand was not the man I was dressing for. All I could think about was Kahled, and this needed to stop.

The instant I got out of my bedroom, my mother pounced on me. She pinched my side and lifted my skirt in an uncharacteristic fit of crudeness and rage. "What is this!" she shouted.

"Don't you touch me," I said, staring her down.

My mother pushed me out of the way and stormed into the kitchen where Sandra was peeling onions for dinner. "I know what you're up to!" she screamed at Sandra. Gustave peeked his head out of his bedroom, and we followed our mother into the kitchen just in time to see her grab two onions from the countertop, and throw them at Sandra. Mother missed, and the onions rolled to the floor. "You're turning Marceline and Béatrice into whores!" she hollered. Sandra stared at us, at my mother, then at the onions on the floor. I stepped in, took my mother's arm and tried to move her out of the kitchen. "Don't be ridiculous, Mother. You're being mean for no reason."

"She stole everything from me!" My mother screamed. What she was talking about, I had no idea. Sandra bent down to pick up the onions with shaking hands.

"You're not making any sense!" I said. "You're mad at me, not at Sandra."

Before I could stop her, my mother had grabbed another onion from the countertop and thrown it at Sandra. Her arms were too weak to inflict much damage, but her rage was painful to witness. "You ruined everything!" she shouted at her.

Sandra backed against the kitchen's wall, put her face in her hands and began to cry silently. "Don't listen to Mother," I told her. "She has lost her mind."

My mother turned to me and hissed, "You think I'm crazy, but I know! I know what she does, and I know what you do!"

"That's it, Mother. I shall not listen to your mad rambles for another moment. I'm leaving!"

This shook my mother out of her fog, "Leaving? Where will you go?"

"Out. I'm going out."

"You can't go into the streets by yourself!"

"Well, I'm going to do it anyhow."

"Who will you see?" she shrieked.

"You answer that question yourself, since you think you know everything."

"You have to have a chaperon!"

"I do not."

"I'll tell your father!" my mother wailed.

"Tell him. Why should I care?"

"You can't! You – you can't – go with men. If you do, you'll be – *spoiled*."

"Spoiled for what?"

"You will never marry well," my mother said pitifully.

"Again, this?" I scoffed. I went through the front door and slammed it behind me, and ran down the stairwell.

Once in the street, quite officially without a chaperone for the first time, and feeling very feminine in my girdle and high heels, I inhaled deeply and felt free. But as I walked in the street, all the streets seemed to lead to Café Djurdjura, and all my thoughts returned to Khaled.

When I returned to the apartment an hour later, Mother was eerily calm. My father was not home yet. I braced myself for his return. My mother was about to drag me through the mud, but I was resolute to tell him all the insults she had hurled at Sandra. To my astonishment, when my father came back, my mother did not tell him a thing. It was as though nothing had happened. From that day forward, my mother, perhaps realizing that by not telling Baba about my disobeying her that day, she had been complicit in my misconduct, chose to look the other way. All her fortitude and principles were washed away in this strange land. She withdrew even more. A kinder soul would have stayed by her side and taken care of her needs, but I hated her for not pulling herself together, and I would not spend a minute more than necessary inside the apartment. What little communication we had at home, what little openness was left between my mother and me, disappeared. And when these kinds of things take hold, it is difficult to find a way back.

Perhaps what was happening at home was an expression of the strain of the time, the secretiveness, the mistrust, the anger, the anguish. At home, no one dared mention our fears, the war, politics, or the Vichy government and what could be done about it. With my friends, that was all we talked about. At home, we considered my mother's nerves too fragile, and so we avoided the subjects. But even when my mother was asleep, my father did not discuss it. All he seemed to care to do was go to the office and carry on with business as usual with Uncle Moshe.

A few weeks later, in one of our rare dinners as a family, I tried to awaken my family out of its torpor. "What we need is a system to combat anti-Semitism at its roots," I said. "We've let it creep up on us. We thought it would pass, and look at us now."

"It's too late for that, Dearest," my father said. "In another century, perhaps."

"How come we Jews don't fight? We let people make up stories about us. We let them trample on whatever rights we have left. We need to rise, collectively."

"Now is not the time to rise," my father said. "Now is the time to survive."

This infuriated me. "All this beautiful pragmatism is precisely what brought us to where we stand now. Make no waves, behave, and wait it out until it goes away. Only it doesn't."

"Hitler is unstoppable for now," my father said, "The willingness of men to follow him is bottomless. But he will make mistakes. His army will exhaust itself."

"What will you do in the meanwhile? Nothing?" I said in a tone that was more condescending than I intended.

My father sighed. "We are not doing nothing," he said. "We came here."

"But if Hitler gets closer, what will you do? Will you put us in another car, on another boat? And to go where?"

"Jews have been persecuted for thousands of years. That is the way the world is. And then, wars are lost and won, governments change, countries are reshaped, new policies are made."

"And so?"

"If we are patient, if we don't get killed, if we think ahead and know when to flee and where to go, then we can endure. Then when people forget their hatred, or direct it at some other group, we can be free again. For a generation or two."

"What kind of life is that? A life of injustices and persecution?"

"We can survive injustices."

"What's to say that this current wave of hatred is not going to last another hundred years?"

"For Jews to be free again, first they have to stay alive. That is all I'm asking of you children. Be prudent. Be smart. Be discreet."

"To cower is not enough of a life for some of us," I said haughtily.

My father scowled. "And yet you and Gustave are going to stay put and hope everyone forgets about us," he said.

And then, out of nowhere, my mother pointed a finger at me, "This one," she screeched. "This one is a wild one! She goes with men!"

We stood, stunned by her outburst. My father's face reddened and he turned to me. "Do you, Marceline?"

I shrugged, "Absolutely not."

"Ha! my mother said." Mother spat.

Father turned to Gustave. "Does she?"

Gustave made an unconvincing gesture to signify his ignorance, his eyes locked on his plate.

My father turned to me with sorrow on his face, "Marceline," he said. "Please tell me this is not true."

"You would rather believe Mother, who's completely irrational, or Gustave who would do anything for attention?" I asked.

My mother did not like the bit about her being irrational. "She's at the café all day long," she shrieked. "With the riff raff of this town."

I turned to her "Who told you this?" And then said, "so, I go to cafés with friends. So what?"

Mother, again, pointed an accusatory finger at me. "She is promiscuous!"

"Are you being promiscuous Marceline?" my father said in an icy tone.

"I am not. But so what if I were?" I said.

My father refused to look at me, and this was more painful than shouts and screams. He turned to Gustave, "I want you to keep an eye on your sister," he said.

"What?" I yelled. "I don't need my baby brother as a shadow!"

"I'm sixteen!" Gustave said.

"Oh, but let's not forget, he is *a boy*! Boys have all the rights, all the freedom, and all the fun. And now I must have a little boy spy following my every move?"

"I don't know how else to safeguard you," my father said in an exhausted tone. Was he disappointed in me, or was he tired? "If you do not have the good sense to care about your honor, at least you should care about your safety. I do not need to remind you how dangerous a time this is."

"Your daughter is out of control, Alban!" my mother raged, "and you're going to let her do as she pleases?"

"You're the one who's out of control, Mother!" I screamed, throwing my napkin on my untouched plate. "Get out of your bed and pick yourself up. Do something. Stop thinking you're the only one who suffers. Besides," I told my father, "Gustave has too much time on his hands. He's the one you better watch. I heard he keeps pestering the Géo Gras crowd, asking questions."

To my surprise, my father got up from his chair, livid, and raised his voice. "If anything happens to either of you it will be as though you have killed your mother and me. Ask yourself if this is what you want!" He stormed out of the room.

I turned to Gustave and said between clenched teeth: "You better not follow me, or I'll have my friends beat you up!"

The last thing I heard as I left the room was my mother mumbling to herself, "She must marry well!"

****

Despite all that was happening, in the world and at home, and as day after day as war raged throughout Europe, all I could think about was Khaled. Was this how I coped? Was that how I created a window of happiness for myself? I dreamt of him at night, and during endless, empty days spent at Café Djurdjura watched him move through the terrace's tables, nimble, tanned, the posture of a dancer, more grace in his little finger than in any parts of my mother's silly counts and bankers combined. My sense of power lay in my ability to appear as aloof as he was. At times, I was sure he looked at me. Other times, I doubted it. The emotional distance I put between others and myself was my strength, or so I believed. I was cool-headed. I was smart. When it came to Khaled, however, I was an imbecile. I spoke too loudly or made a show of throwing my head back in laughter at something profoundly unfunny that Béatrice had said. Every one of my movements when I was in Khaled's presence, every word, every smile, was an act. After leaving the café, I felt embarrassed by my behavior and resolved to be better the next day, only to behave like a foolish girl all over again. I only hoped I was not too transparent. I only hoped I did not seem pathetic or, worse, attracted to him.

The answer came, and Fernand was the one who gave it to me. We were all sitting out on the terrace of café Djurdjura. Fernand met my eyes just as I looked up at Khaled. He waited for Khaled to be out of earshot and whispered in my ear. "I can see the games you two are playing."

"What game is that," I said innocently.

"The seduction game. I watch you, you know. I see how you dress. How you make yourself pretty. You're a beautiful girl, Marceline. You can do much better than him." I was embarrassed and eager to deny everything, but to deny too much would be an admission of guilt. "Are you jealous?" I said.

"Should I be?" he asked.

"If you think I'm being seductive, why assume you know who I am hoping to seduce?"

"Well," Fernand said, "I don't think it's for André or Émile."

"I don't think it's them either," I said, staring at him flirtatiously.

Reassured, Fernand sat back in his chair and smiled. I had always sensed that Fernand was attracted to me, but the same could be said of Émile and André. This brief interaction changed the dynamics between us: from that moment on, Fernand saw me as willing to return his advances. Days went on. Fernand now flirted with me openly. He was always touching my waist, giving me his seat, petting my hand. Khaled had noticed; of this I was certain. I let Fernand flirt with me openly. I even flirted back. I was sick of waiting, sick of not knowing, sick of wanting. I hoped that it would change something, that it would force Khaled to come out of hiding.

It did.

One afternoon, Béatrice and I got up from the table and, as we had so many times, headed for Café Djurdjura's bathroom. It was a hot day. For the last hour, I had flirted with Fernand and watched from the corner of my eyes as Khaled impassively went from table to table. My pulse throbbed. I felt under pressure, like the countdown of a doomsday clock.

Outside, the nearby church bell marked three in the afternoon.

Béatrice and I walked away from the terrace and went inside the café, past Khaled, past the tables and chairs, past the side looks of French men who drank red wine at the counter, and down the windowless corridor that led to the bathroom.

Béatrice went in first, leaving me alone in the corridor, which was lit by a single small fixture. I leaned against the wall and waited in an exacerbated state of alertness. It was as though I knew that something was about to happen. Suddenly, the light went off, and the corridor was flooded in darkness. I waited, breathless. I felt a move toward me in the dark. In a few steps, Khaled was facing me. I shivered. He placed his hands on either side of me, palms pressed on the wall against which I leaned, encircling me with his arms without touching me. He was taller than me by a head. I lifted my face. His lips were inches from mine. My entire body vibrated. I smelled him. I felt his body's warmth. He said nothing. I felt that I heard his heartbeat and his breathing. Or were those mine?

A moment later there was the sound of the bathroom lock opening, and Béatrice was in the corridor. "Marceline, what are you doing in the dark?" she asked. An invisible hand turned on the light again. In the narrow hallway, it was just Béatrice and I. Khaled was gone.

****

Marceline smiled to herself. Cassandra was smiling too. "Young love," Marceline sighed.

"Did Khaled become your boyfriend?" Cassandra asked. "Please tell me that he did."

Marceline realized that they had walked all around the park and now they stood by the Medici Fountain, were Acis and Galatea, locked in their embrace, awaited doom. Rain was falling again, barely a drizzle but enough that Cassandra's black hair was covered in minuscule glimmering drops, like a spider web blanketed in dew. "I believe I see my car by the gate," Marceline said. "Isn't that Maurice over there?"

"Yep. Double-parked, as usual."

"I guess this is as good a point to stop as any."

"Not without telling me about Khaled first!" Cassandra exclaimed.

"Is that a command?" Marceline asked wryly.

"Oh, no. I did not mean it that way. I'm sorry. I can be pushy," Cassandra said. "I've been told that before."

Marceline found it endlessly irritating the tendency women had to put themselves down for attributes that were considered qualities in men. "So, be pushy," she told Cassandra. "Don't apologize for it. Persistence is a strength, my dear. Not something to feel wishy-washy about."

Cassie shook her head. "My dad did not like that about me, I don't think," she admitted.

"Well, I guess not if you mean to get into Gustave's good graces. But as far as the rest of the world is concerned, passion, grit, and perseverance are perfectly wonderful traits."

They reached the Luxembourg Garden's gate. Maurice retrieved a large umbrella out of the trunk and helped Marceline into the car. "Meet me tomorrow at my house," she told Cassandra. "Eight o'clock in the morning. And this time, don't keep me waiting."

In the car, Marceline settled in her seat and looked out the window through the droplets. Decade after decade, people dressed differently, the cars changed, but Paris remained the same. She watched Cassandra cross Place Edmond Rostand and head inside the brasserie at the corner, then come out again and sit at the terrace. Marceline never again would have that kind of freedom, the ability to rely on her body to come and go as she pleased. That old carcass of hers had had a good run; she was in no position to complain. She had been blessed with exceptional health and vigor. How old was she when men stopped looking at her? Her sixties perhaps? Her niece was not even forty yet: young and free. But she did not seem the type of woman who could grab that freedom and enjoy it.

People had a way of creating barriers for themselves: politeness, convention, guilt, the opinions of others. It was a blessing not to care about those sorts of things at all. Although Marceline wasn't a stranger to guilt, she chose not to let it cripple her. Women like herself got things done and were chastised for it. It did not matter that she had spent her life – risked her life – in the service of France. She had not played nice, and she had more enemies than friends. Gustave was not her only enemy, only her earliest one.

The rain seemed to subside. Maurice turned off the windshield wipers and things went silent inside the car save for the groan of the engine. Marceline sank deeper into the leather of the seats as they raced through Paris. What a bother how certain events of one's life were mired in so many shades of gray. As she had recounted that family fight to Cassandra,

Marceline had been clear on her own innocence. But now, after telling her story, she wasn't so sure it held ground. Was she truly blameless? She understood now, and with utter clarity, that she should never have threatened to have her friends beat up Gustave, her father should never have asked Gustave to surveil her, and Gustave should never have taken that challenge to heart. But all that had happened, and the seeds were planted. And there had been no going back from that point.

CHAPTER 10

Lingerie

The drizzle had stopped, and sunshine peeked through the scattered clouds. On the terrace, the tables and chairs, protected by the wide awning, were dry, so Cassie decided to have her lunch outside. A waiter came, first looking surprised to find her alone there. She ordered the plat du jour, poached eggs in wine sauce with extra ketchup. Her senses felt strangely heightened. The air felt crisper, as though cleansed, the colors brighter. She felt sexy for no reason at all. Was anyone noticing? The Paris of today felt very different from the Paris of the day before. Even as Marceline was speaking, Cassie had kept replaying in her mind how Hervé had taken charge of things, how he had touched her. None of it felt real or possible: not her response to his touch, not his touch, not the fact that he had wanted to touch her at all.

Her lunch arrived. The eggs were perfectly poached, the sauce so heavenly that she took the brave step of forgoing ketchup. She ate ravenously. When she was done, she ordered an espresso and took out Hervé's notebook.

She wrote quickly, in bullet points, trying to be as thorough as possible. At every turn of her story, Marceline came out as the star character, with her dad in a supporting role. She seemed to be making every effort to be honest, but Marceline could not help but see the world as filled with orbiting people, and with herself at the center, radiating her influence. Cassie wondered if her dad had had a hard time asserting his masculinity with such a commanding, confident sister. Maybe that's why he had chosen a wife eager to accommodate him and make excuses for everything he did.

She had trouble reconciling the father she knew with the man Marceline described. First, he had been a little Jewish boy navigating the lead up to World War II, and now he was a teenager. She felt her previous ideas of him slip away. Who was her father? What did he want in life? How did he feel about things? About her? She still had no idea why Marceline deserved his hatred. In fact, had he not tried to rescue his sister from her attacker in the South of France? Had he not kept her secrets? In Algeria, he had wanted to prevent her from getting into trouble. He must have cared for her. And in her own way, Marceline cared for him. There were signs of sibling rivalry, but nothing that would explain his eventual hatred. Cassie lifted her pen. What was Marceline trying to convey? She seemed intent on building a case. Marceline had spent plenty of time explaining what it was like to live at a time when the information fed to you was propaganda, and you did not know what was true and what was not. Cassie wondered if she should question Marceline's story. After all, she still had not heard her father's.

Two hours, one lip-smacking île flottante, and two more espressos later, Cassie closed her notebook. Once again, she had been coaxed into writing for someone else. It must be life's karma to toil over what other people were too lazy or unfocused to do. What story was she going to write? Marceline's story, or her father's? After hearing the events from Marceline's standpoint, it would be more difficult to write a story that honored her father. And if she didn't do him justice, would her family hate her for it? Was she willing to take that risk? She stared at her hands. There was an indentation on her right index finger from the pressure of the pen. Already, her body was becoming accustomed to a life without electronic devices. Her hands did not feel like they belonged to the person she was four days ago. For some reason, they felt like more capable hands. Notions of a book fluttered in her mind. Marceline's memoir was not what she had in mind. She wanted to write a novel. Change the names and call it fiction. Fill in the blanks with her imagination.

****

After lunch, Cassie set out following the outer edge of the Luxembourg Garden, turning right on rue de Tournon until it became rue de Seine. Rather than take the métro, she decided to head to the hospital on foot and try not to think of what would happen once she got there.

Tonight, she would see Hervé.

See. Hervé? Since when was she "seeing" anyone?

The next portion of the street brimmed with shops, bakeries, and art galleries, and she wanted to enter every one of them. She could not help but see her surroundings through Hervé-tinted glasses. Even this butcher shop was quaint. And this patisserie. And how interesting people looked, how beautiful Paris was, and how vast and varied the city was from street to street!

She scanned the shop windows, realizing that she had been unconsciously looking for a lingerie store. How had she allowed for the garments closest to her skin to be so pitiable? What did it say about her? She had told herself she wasn't shallow enough to care, but wasn't it more likely a lack of self-worth?

She entered Monoprix and wandered through the clothing aisle until she stood in front of the bras and panties. She needed nothing as fancy as the designer lingerie at the Galeries Lafayette, but what about a little something lacy and cute? And why just cotton? Who made that rule? In the dressing room, she looked at her legs in the full-length mirror. Not bad at all. All those stairs at home had done her good. Her butt wasn't horrible for a woman her age. Her curves seemed positioned in right places. Whatever imperfections, Hervé had not seemed to mind. She tried half a dozen bras and matching panties and quickly narrowed down her choice to two sets, one light pink, one dark gray.

She left Monoprix and walked ever so slowly toward the hospital, stopping in front of shop windows, delaying the inevitable: the idiotic bureaucrats at the hospital, Odile and her tears, her mother with all her secrets. Odile's tears were the trump card. The fact that her sister had no control over her lachrymal glands did not prove that her suffering was superior to everyone else's. As for Mademoiselle Pinçon, that horrible woman, she needed to come up with a way to bypass her. Cassie was outnumbered, and it made her do and say nutty things. Walking into the hospital was stepping into the unknown, which was not the staff, or her mother, or Odile, or even her father – she knew what to expect of them. No, the unknown was herself. There had been more than a few instances in her life when she saw red, and all modicum of self-control had gone out the window. Cases in point: the letter of gripes she should never have sent her parents and telling Peter she wanted a divorce when a good cry should have sufficed. She felt, at this juncture, dangerously ripe for an outburst of crazy.

She passed a craft shop window with boxes to build miniature airplanes and boats. Alex, like her father, loved building things. He was in the robotics club in high school and even won a prize for it. Engineering seemed to be his thing. Had they known each other, Alex and her dad could have bonded perhaps. Had her dad loved her children, she could have forgiven him everything. Her dad's incapacity to love her children was her fault because she had left the country – at least that was the narrative. But she had always felt as though his rejection of her country of adoption, of her children, of her marriage, and of herself was her dad's way to punish her for a crime she was unaware of having committed but of which she bore the weight.

She realized now that as Marceline was telling her about Gustave, it was Alex that Cassie pictured. The similarities between her son's and her father's personalities jumped at her for the first time. Both were sensitive, introverted, and shy, more comfortable working and functioning in solitude, and yet lonely. But whereas Alex was loved for being who he was, her father at the same age had been victimized. It was awful to think of the kind of damage this could do to a boy. Her father had never let anyone know his suffering, but in doing so, he had prevented everyone from truly knowing him. Cassie thought of her dad as a boy. She thought of Alex and of all the boys who grew up feeling that they fell short of society's expectations.

She took the Pont du Carrousel across the river. The Louvre was on one bank; on the other was the Musée d'Orsay. Above, blue sky and shapely white clouds. In the distance was the metallic Pont des Arts and the stone arches of the Pont Royal. And couples. Couples who walked hand in hand below on the quays made her long for something.

Love. How could she not want it now?

She put her elbows on the balustrade and looked down. Below, on the stone ledge of the Seine's bank, a young man and woman were nestled in each other's arms. When the man leaned forward to kiss her, and his lover tilted her neck back and lifted her arm around his neck, the two replicated the statue of Galatea and Acis.

Without being sure why, Cassie began to cry.

****

At the intensive care reception desk, there was a new woman with a warm smile that Cassie had never seen before. She looked like a decent person with proper human feelings and emotions, not like that nightmarish Mademoiselle Pinçon. Maybe if Cassie played it cool-headed and normal, in other words, if she acted the opposite of how she felt, this new woman might not ask for an ID and thus not discover that Cassie was banned from the room.

There were four people in line ahead of her, and quickly several more came after her. As she waited in line, Cassie rehearsed in her mind how she was going to put this new clerk in her pocket by killing her with kindness. But when her turn came, Pinçon was back at the desk, looking at her angrily from above her computer screen.

"I'm here for my appointment," Cassie said, improvising.

"What appointment?" Pinçon asked without as much as lifting her gaze.

"With the Chief of Services," Cassie snapped. "Docteur Juin told you to make it happen. We've gone over this how many times now?"

"Ah, yes," Pinçon said, pretending to remember suddenly. She looked down at her screen and said resentfully, "He will see you next Thursday at eight in the morning."

"Ha! I told you he would see me! Wait, what day is it today? Did you say next Thursday? But that's a week from now! I'll be back in California by then."

Pinçon shrugged, indifferent. "That's what's available."

"I'm sure he can squeeze me in for five minutes."

"I'm not a miracle worker, Madame."

"Look, he obviously accepted to see me, so what is it to you if it happens now or later?"

"He is extremely busy."

"Me too, and yet here I am, wasting my precious time with you."

"Madame, it is not necessary to be rude," Pinçon said with just the right amount of superiority.

"I flew across a continent to see my father."

"If you want a different time, I can give you the email address of the Chief of Services' secretary's assistant."

Cassie felt hot. "His assistant?"

"His secretary's assistant. The secretary's communication has to pass through her assistant first."

"But why?"

"That's the proper channel."

"Fine, okay. Could I see her now, rather than email, to expedite things?"

"Oh, that will be impossible."

"Why is that?"

"The Chief of Services' secretary's assistant is on maternity leave until January."

Cassie's face must have turned crimson. "You know what your problem is?" she began to say, with no plan on how to finish her sentence.

"Non, Madame, what is my problem?" Pinçon asked defiantly.

"You're part of a giant bureaucratic maze. Did you see the movie *Brazil*?" Behind her in line, people began to groan.

"Do you want that email address or not?" Pinçon asked.

Cassie did not even know what she was saying. She was trying to say something, make a point, but her sentences came out jumbled, nonsensical. "Red tape, glued everywhere. Employees on maternity leave clocking their nine to five and protecting each other's back."

"Madame, there are many people in line behind you."

"The result is, nobody cares! You're like mini-Hitlers, with your Fascist ways, and...." Cassie paused, searching for a powerful ending to her rant. "And an utmost disregard for human lives!" Audible snickers came out from the people in line behind her.

"Madame, that is absurd," Pinçon said. "The hospital saves dozens of lives every day."

"Give me the name of the Chief of Services!" Cassie said, much too loudly.

"Madame, as I have explained again and again to you, we do not give out names of employees."

"Oh, stop 'Madaming' me!" Cassie yelled. "It's my dad in there! My dad! I'm going to see him whether you like it or not." With this, she turned away from the desk. The people in line parted and watched with keen interest as she marched toward the patients' rooms.

Pinçon was up on her feet, calling after her. "Madame, please be reasonable."

"I've been reasonable my entire life!" Cassie shouted. She heard the shuffling of feet behind her, and she pressed forward. Now she had her hand on the knob to her father's room, expecting to be yanked out by the scruff of her neck, or tasered, but they were not stopping her.

Just as she opened the door to her dad's room, her mother came out of it.

Raymonde looked at Cassie and then at the two interns on her heel. Everyone stood around awkwardly. "Oh. Bonjour, Maman," Cassie said sweetly. "I was just coming to see you. Are Odile and Sabine in there?"

"Just me," Raymonde said distrustfully. She stood by the door, her arms crossed, a stubborn expression in her eyes. "Odile's boy has an ear infection," she said, eyeing the interns. "Sabine ... I don't know where she is, as usual."

"What did the doctor say?"

"He's not stopped by yet."

It was one thing to fight strangers; pushing her way past her mother was another. Cassie's fury and righteous indignation drained out of her to be replaced by the realization that she was, in fact, terrified to enter her dad's room, to risk being rejected by him once more. She sighed and asked her mom, "You want to have coffee?"

"I guess," Raymonde said.

Cassie took her arm and said, "Let's get out of here." The interns, embarrassed for her, took a step back, then another. No one was making eye contact. On the way out of the hospital, she avoided looking at Pinçon, the interns, the people in line, and those sitting in the waiting room.

They crossed the street and entered Bistro Saint-François. Inside, they found a table by the window with a view of the hospital. The café was filled with hospital personnel and a handful of people whose shell-shocked expression told her they too were here to visit a loved one. There was a huddled family of redheads, a solitary man looking fixedly out the window, a red-eyed Muslim woman and her small daughter, and a young Asian man in an elegant suit. Raymonde pointed to Cassie's Monoprix bags.

"You've been shopping?" she asked. It sounded like a reproach, as though she was accusing Cassie of frivolity.

"I ran out of things to wear."

"There are laundromats you know," her mother said.

Yes, and you could also offer for me to use your washing machine, Cassie thought. Instead, she said, "Are you hungry?"

"I don't eat at all hours." By this Raymonde meant that Americans ate "at all hours," whereas in France there were proper and improper times to eat. This was an infuriating theme: France good; America bad. But she had better act calm and composed if she was going to talk her mother into letting her back into her father's room.

"I'm glad we could have some time just the two of us," Cassie said conciliatorily, "and I'm sorry I messed up your rug." Raymonde grunted an unintelligible answer. "How is Papa feeling today?"

"His vitals are the same."

"Still sleeping?"

"Still sleeping."

"Don't they plan on waking him up? Doesn't he need to eat?"

Raymonde tensed up. "They are feeding him through tubes and whatnot."

"What about you? Are you sleeping all right?"

"A few hours here and there."

"I've meant to ask you about Sabine. She seems exhausted." The exact term she was trying to convey was "clinically depressed."

Raymonde sighed, relieved perhaps that they were talking about something safe. "We don't get to see too much of her. Apparently, she has better things to do than to come over and visit her parents."

"Not even for Sunday lunches?" Sunday lunch. That fraught, tension-filled family institution Cassie had been glad to elude for the last twenty years, although moving to another continent hardly exonerated her.

"She's never had us over either. Not even when she was with Paul. You know she still doesn't cook? Odile says that Sabine has yet to become an adult," Raymonde added, looking sideways to avoid Cassie's stare. "But you know me: I'm neutral."

"I'm not even sure what being an adult means," Cassie mumbled.

"I guess that's the women of this generation. They want a career so badly that they compete with men. Well, men don't like competitive women."

"They don't?"

"They want a woman who can take care of them. How can you be in a relationship if you won't cook for your man?"

"I managed."

Raymonde made a small, undecipherable grimace, which Cassie instantly interpreted as scorn. Her warming feeling toward her mother dropped down a few degrees. Raymonde's way of being judgmental was undisguised and made worse by the fact that she saw her bluntness as honesty, although in her relationship with her daughters, honesty was expected to be a one-way street. "What's the point of Sabine coming here if she's going to make this long face. The last thing we need is her negativity."

"Maybe she's struggling."

"It's better for her that Paul left her when he did. Better that than a divorce. That's what Odile says."

"Tell Odile that staying married is not a sign that your relationship is not a complete failure." She bit her lip. Too late. Her mother would give Odile a report of this before the day ended. "I'm a bit concerned about Sabine."

"You can't be all that concerned. Sabine said the two of you hardly speak."

This hurt Cassie. More of that wholesome honesty. "I think she is trying to manage her emotions on her own," she said defensively. "I didn't know anything about this. I would have been there for her."

"If she had needed you, she would have told you about it I think."

"She looks awful. Something is wrong with her," Cassie insisted.

"Sabine isn't the one in a coma, last I checked," Raymonde said. "She had two hands and two feet. She should be more helpful in this time of crisis, not just waltz in here when she has five minutes."

Maybe that's what becoming an adult meant. That moment when your parents cease to see you as vulnerable and in need of their care and start thinking you should take care of them. "You don't realize that your father has been a lot of work. And that's even before he got the surgery. And with

Gustave, forget sleeping! He has to get up to pee four or five times a night. And the snoring. And to go up and down the métro with him is out of the question. And I can't very well leave him alone, so I'm sequestered at home. And I do all the shopping and cooking and cleaning and laundry. But you know me, I don't like to complain." The waiter arrived and set two espressos on the table. Raymonde downed hers like a shot of tequila before adding angrily, "You'd think Odile was the one taking care of him from seeing her here every day. But let me tell you, she is not. I am."

Cassie rolled her eyes. "I'm sure Papa is head over heels in appreciation of her regardless."

"Well, you know how her smile 'lights up the place,'" Raymonde said. Those were Gustave's words. Her mother's sarcasm wasn't lost on Cassie, who had often wondered how come her own smile never managed to light up anything. "She comes over once or twice a week," Raymonde continued. "So, of course, she has all this energy and patience. She does her two bits and then she's out the door looking like Mother Theresa. She doesn't know what it's like to take care, and take care, and take care some more. The minutiae of it and the exhaustion."

Cassie felt the urge to defend Odile. "She has young children. She must have a pretty clear idea of what exhaustion feels like."

Raymonde shrugged. "You know how Odile is. She likes everyone to walk like they're her little soldiers. She always says that you gave your twins too much freedom. She said that's what all their troubles sprang from."

"They're over it now. They made it into college," Cassie said defensively. She considered it an amazing feat to be the parent of modern-day teenagers. They were guinea pigs in a global human experiment with parents acting as the blind leading the blind in the age of sexting and cyberbullying. Modern-day kids did not only have to keep up with the Joneses, the way past generations did; they had to keep up with the superrich, the infamous, and the shameless. Alex and Jeanne had gone through this, plus a divorce, and miraculously come out in one piece. "I don't think that I have ruined their lives quite yet."

"To each their own," Raymonde said.

Did she really expect positive reinforcement from her mother? The temptation to provoke became irresistible. "I saw Marceline again," she said.

Raymonde was visibly shaken. "You did? When?"

"Right after I left your place this morning."

"But why?" Raymonde whimpered.

"For one, I had nothing better to do since you're not letting me see Papa."

"It's one thing to see her once, but it's another to have a relationship with her. Your father's not going to like that," Raymonde said. Her eyes darted around the café for a solution. "If he asks you, don't tell him that you saw her."

"Why not?"

"He's going to think I told you about her."

"Which you did."

"He's the one who mentioned her!" Raymonde said, indignant. "When he was unconscious."

"But you're the one who gave me her last name. I could not have found her without it."

"You and Odile were pressuring me!" She had raised her voice. They eyed each other like boxers in the ring.

So, this was what her mother feared? She was afraid that her husband would be mad at her? "What I still can't figure out," Cassie said, "is why Papa hid his last name from us? Was it so that we could not find Marceline, or so that we would not learn about his childhood?"

"In those days, it wasn't uncommon for people to drop a syllable or two from their names," Raymonde said, sounding unconvinced. "To sound more French."

"Or less Jewish?"

Raymonde shook her head in defeat. "Your father is *really* not going to like that."

"It doesn't surprise you that you know so little about his life before he met you?"

Raymonde was agitated, defensive. "When he married me, he wanted to start from scratch. He did not want his new family to be polluted by … old stories."

"Was his Judaism part of the pollution?"

"I told you! It wasn't important to him!"

"But important enough to hide."

"He wasn't trying to hide anything," Raymonde snapped. "Why do you always have to make accusations? Your father made his choices, and it has nothing to do with you."

"Hiding his heritage from his daughters? It seems to have plenty to do with us."

"Your sisters would not care. They would respect his decision."

"But what was his decision? And why?"

"What is it to you?"

"For one, I'm curious about the idea that I'm half Jewish."

"You could not be Jewish if you tried. I'm not, and if your mother is not, you're not either. End of story."

Apparently, her mother had done her homework. "Is that why he married you, Maman? So that his daughters could never be suspected of being Jewish?"

"That's an awful accusation!"

"Is it?"

"Here you are, digging in the dirt and trying to drag us all into it?"

"If by digging you mean being this family's archeologist, I'll take it as a compliment. Unless being Jewish *is* the dirt you're talking about?"

"Stop it, Cassandra. Cut it out!"

"Is Papa hiding his Judaism from us or from himself? Is he ashamed of it?"

"Shame has nothing to do with any of this." Raymonde's expression had changed. She looked about to become hurtful. "Why do you keep disparaging your father, especially now."

If Cassie did not want to get demolished, she needed to back the hell off. She braced herself and pushed ahead instead. "If there is no shame, then why do you react like I'm accusing him of war crimes?"

"Why do you take so much enjoyment in hurting people?"

"Oh jeez, Maman!"

"And you make up stories. You always do that."

"What is there in his past that you are both trying so hard to hide from us?"

"There is nothing. Absolutely nothing!"

"How about a living aunt? Don't tell me you're not hiding stuff. She's more than eager to tell me the story if I can't hear it from you."

Raymonde's face turned crimson. "You know what your problem is? You're a pathological liar! You always were! Something is very wrong with your brain!" She sprang up. "I'm going to see Gustave."

This was a lost cause, but Cassie tried anyway. "How about letting me see him too?"

"Why? So that you can accuse him of being an anti-Semite?"

"You're twisting things around."

"No, you are!" Raymonde shot back. She was standing by the table, red and vibrating with fury. "You come in, spread your venom, spill your accusations, create a whole big mess of things with your lies. And you steal!" With this, she left the café. She would have slammed the door, had there been a door to slam.

Cassie sat, shaking. This was their M.O. Their kryptonite against her. They called her a liar when in fact it was they who were doing the lying. And it worked. Usually, she shut up. Or left the country. She wanted to leave the country now. She sat back in the pleather of the bench seat and controlled her breathing. This was what they did. This was what her parents' forty-year marriage could be summed up to: the wife covering for the husband, closing her eyes, taking his side blindly, no matter what. Even to the detriment of her daughters.

Cassie stayed in the café to regroup. Her tantrum at the hospital and this fight were not making things easier. She watched the rain fall in the street. At times, gusts of wind were so strong that all umbrellas overturned at once. When would the rain stop? How could people live like this, trapped in shitty weather, in drudge, in car exhaust, in lies, self-loathing, and loneliness? She ordered a chamomile tea to counteract the effect of an espresso with her mother. She wrote in her new journal details of Marceline's story she wanted to be sure to remember. About thirty minutes later she raised her head.

Outside, Sabine was crossing the street and was heading toward the café. Her face was pale, drawn; the collar of her coat turned up. She entered and made her way toward Cassie and plopped down across from her. "Maman said you might still be here," she said. "She was livid. Her anger at you seems to be on a whole other level."

"What a shocker."

"You don't care?"

"I care, and at the same time, I don't. She's trying to shut me up. The usual intimidation."

Sabine nodded in understanding. "We just saw the doctor," she said. "They think they'll have to start giving Papa dialysis. He's severely anemic. They'll give him a blood transfusion too."

"What about the infection?"

"They're trying something stronger."

"Shit."

"You think I look terrible?" Sabine asked with a forced smile.

"I do? What? No!"

"That's what Maman just told me."

"She what? No! I did not mean it that way. You look beautiful. I guess I was just asking about you. You're right. I should have asked you directly."

"Asked me what?"

"It's just that you seem sad. I was wondering if I could help."

"She made it sound like I was somehow failing in your eyes."

"I care about you. I'm not judging you. I don't know how Maman does it: pitting us against each other, creating this environment of suspicion."

"Maman said that you think I need to grow up."

"What? No! That's complete bullshit! *Odile* was the one who said that," Cassie yelped. "It wasn't me!"

"Oh, great," Sabine said.

"See, she did it again! Now I'm throwing Odile under the bus. I'm sorry. No one thinks you need to grow up." Cassie shook her head in admiration. "How does Maman do it? She's a genius at this, like a criminal mastermind."

"As long as we hate each other we might not turn against her," Sabine said.

"You think it's deliberate?"

"I don't think she has any idea she's doing it. It's more like a hyper-developed instinct of self-preservation."

"I'm beginning to think that she resents Odile the most."

"Why?"

"Because Odile's perfect. At least we're the official fuckups."

Sabine laughed softly. "Well, I certainly am."

Cassie looked at her beautiful, sad-looking sister. "Tell me, how are you doing?"

Sabine sat deep in her seat, brought her hands to her coat's collar like she was trying to disappear into it. "I would have given birth this week," she said. "The due date was supposed to be right now. I would have two babies. Two car seats, you know, double stroller, that kind of thing."

"I'm so sorry."

"You know what's weird?" Sabine said. "I never knew them, but I miss them. Or maybe I only miss the life I had imagined. I made that choice. It was my choice to end the pregnancy. I tell myself that it's for the best, that I could not have given them a good life. I tell myself I'll have other babies; life goes on. But it doesn't feel as though life is going on. It feels like life kind of stopped."

"Do you have friends who can support you?"

"I'm avoiding everyone. I can't keep up the effort of being witty or pleasant."

They were quiet for a long time. The waiter came and Sabine ordered a hot chocolate and Cassie a second espresso. There were new people inside. People came and went, never for long, here to have a cup of coffee, or a bite to eat, before resuming their workday, facing their problems: the café as a respite from the mini-traumas of life, the minutiae, the stress, the loneliness.

"Maybe you could take a break, go elsewhere," Cassie said. "Travel. Pretend to be someone else; I don't know. That or maybe have the space to think. Time to just digest this, instead of having to go on keeping on while you're feeling like this."

Sabine shook her head. "I don't think running away is the solution."

"It worked for me. At least temporarily."

Sabine looked at her watch. "I have to go back to work. Do you want to have dinner together?"

"Okay … I want to but I can't. Keep this to yourself, but I have sort of a date."

Sabine sat back in her seat and smiled. "A sort of a date or a date-date?"

"This man. I met him yesterday."

"Met him?"

"And what a meeting this was," Cassie said significantly, emphasizing the word meeting.

Sabine laughed. "How is that possible? You've only been here for two days!"

"He wants to see me tonight again. That's the incredible part. And, well, I need to run back to the hotel to make myself pretty with this." Cassie dug into her Monoprix bag and dangled below the table a demi-cup bra and matching panties, pearl grey with baby pink lace trims. "See? This is me pretending to be someone else."

"Put it on right now so that I can judge the full effect," Sabine said. "I cannot believe that you already have a lover!"

"Believe me, neither can I."

****

At seven-thirty in the evening, Cassie heard Hervé's Bonneville roar in the street below. She looked down from the balcony, and he looked up and waved to her. She rushed down the stairs to meet him. He was still sitting on the motorcycle. "What are we doing?" she asked.

"It should be a dry evening. Do you know where you'd like to eat?"

"Anywhere there is food. I'm starving."

"What? I could not hear," he said. "Come closer."

She stepped closer to him. "I was telling you—"

He interrupted her by extending his arm to bring her next to him. They kissed a fantastic kiss. "I could wait to eat," she said, already breathless.

"Is the Eiffel Tower still up there?" he asked lifting his chin toward her balcony.

"There is no way to know for sure. Unless we check."

He parked the motorcycle and fastened it quicker than she had ever seen him do it. Within minutes they were up in her room, and he was undressing her.

****

Two hours later they were on the motorcycle, zooming through Paris. Her body against Hervé's, she felt like mush as they drove past the Opera, down Boulevard des Capucines and rue Cambon, and around Place de la Concorde, then on rue de Rivoli and along the Parc des Tuileries toward Bastille. Paris was a swirl of lights.

He took her to dinner in a small wine bar, cozy and dark. They sat across a tiny table, their legs entangled. Dusty rows of bottles and a couple of locals were their only witnesses. Over oysters and Bordeaux, she told him about her time with Marceline at the Jardin du Luxembourg. She described the interaction with her mother, how the cross-examination had culminated in spitefulness on both sides. He listened to her, interrupting only for clarifications. She could not help but compare him to Peter. Peter never asked her how her day was; he told her how his went.

"So, this is how my father made it in one piece through World War II," she said. "He was in North Africa the whole time under a new identity. I am still waiting to find out why he chose to discard the Jewish part of his name, married a non-Jew, and broke off all relations with his mother, father, and sister."

"His mother and father made it out alive too?"

"Sadly, my grandfather died there."

"Of old age?"

"Probably. No, wait. He was born in 1902 and died in 1942. So, he must have been forty when he died."

"He died in 1942. In Algiers?"

"Yes."

"How?"

"I don't know yet."

"Wasn't there some military coup there? Ah, yes. That's it. The Allied forces liberated Algeria, Tunisia, and Morocco in 1942. It was a whole landing operation. The Germans never saw it coming. In retaliation they broke the agreement with Vichy and invaded the rest of France."

"How do you know this?"

"Bah, I read stuff."

"You're a good listener, you know."

"The quality of my listening skills depends entirely on the order of the evening. Had we had dinner first, I might have been distracted."

"I would not have lasted through dinner," she admitted.

He took her hand and kissed the inside of her wrist. "You and I are very compatible."

"I have noticed that."

"I like where this is going."

She cocked her head. "Where *is* this going?"

"I'm hoping for more of the same," he said. "Seeing you. I like you a lot."

She laughed. "Can we maintain this pace? When would we ever sleep?" Her mother's words rang in her ears. You're a liar. You've always been a liar. In her account of what had happened during the day, Cassie had been careful to leave out the humiliating time at the hospital. When Hervé asked her if she was planning on confronting her father, she had remained evasive. When he asked her what her kids were studying, she had left out the fact that they attended schools in New York and Miami. What had started as a harmless white lie by omission was beginning to look a lot like an elaborate scheme of deception. If there was a moment to come forward with the truth, it was now. "I … I want to tell you that I'm not … as available as…."

He pulled his hand away and frowned at her. "Is this the moment when you tell me that you are involved with someone else? Because let me tell you right now, I am not the kind of guy who has an affair behind someone's back." The interruption of the contact of his hand felt jarring, awful, an abrupt withholding of tenderness.

"No," she said, wounded. "I'm not involved with anyone." Hervé took her hand back, and she could breathe again.

"What are you afraid of then?"

She only had another five days in Paris according to her return ticket. That's what she was afraid of. If she told him this, the moment would be ruined. "Maybe it's just that this is all so very unlike me. I'm the mother of teenagers. This seems like something they should be doing. Not me."

"Aha, I see. A case of too much fun? Where does that come from?"

The truth. Any delay in telling the truth would make things worse and turn her into a deceitful person if she wasn't already one. And the truth was that there was no room for Hervé in her life. It was materially and logistically impossible, and he needed to know this. "It's just that, the way my life is at the moment, you and me.... It ... complicates things."

"Cassandra," he interrupted, "I'm attracted to you. You appear to be attracted to me. It doesn't need to be a complicated thing."

"It's just that I don't think I will be in Paris ... forever."

"Neither will I! Who's speaking of forever? There are a lot of places I'd rather be. Any place without desks, preferably somewhere without internet reception. A place where people know what matters. Somewhere closer to the essence of things. Anywhere would be better than Paris."

"The countryside?"

"I was thinking more in the vein of Southeast Asia, the Middle East. That's where I'm headed first chance I get."

She felt a hurt she had no right to feel. Here she was, afraid to push Hervé away by revealing that she lived in the United States when his future so clearly did not include her. "I hear India is incredible," she said.

But Hervé was telling her that there was one thing she could have right now, and that was lust. And golly, did lust sound good. And she was single. And he was single. And they were both adults. She'd be an idiot to mess this up, this little bit of magic that had just come into her life unannounced. Her sense of self had always been an unsolvable puzzle, with every layer of experience adding to the confusion. Was she French or American? Was she Christian or was she Jewish? Was she brave or afraid? Was she strong or weak? Was she talented or destined to remain in someone's shadow? Was she lovable or not? Should she not be able to know who she was by now?

But maybe because of her family's secrets and lies, pieces of the truth had been lost. And without them, the puzzle of who she was could never be solved. And as in a puzzle, everything was interconnected. Each piece recovered brought meaning to the next one: her father hiding his Judaism; Odile as the favorite daughter; her mother's silence; Sabine's hopelessness. What did this all mean when put together? And strange things were bubbling up to the surface. Intuitions about her marriage she had been reluctant to examine: Peter's rearranging of the truth; the increasingly suspect Jessica narrative. Disparate things now appeared as part of a cohesive whole. There had been rules and regulations in her life. There had been a system, a rigid one, put in place by herself for her own safety. But walls were crumbling. Control was escaping her. Revelations about how she should understand the world and herself were on the tip of her consciousness. And now there was Hervé, like a major upset in the order of things. She felt like a color-blind person allowed to see the blue of the sky and the green of forests for the very first time. She sensed tectonic shifts about to take place.

Cassie looked at Hervé and smiled. She had only a few more days in Paris, and she would need to fit another lifetime into those few days, carpe diem for all it was worth, because this was her shot at experiencing, for the first time, really, what it felt like to be a teenager. She raised her wine glass.

"To an uncomplicated thing, then." Hervé reached across the table, took her hand, and kissed it, and she felt as though she was falling.

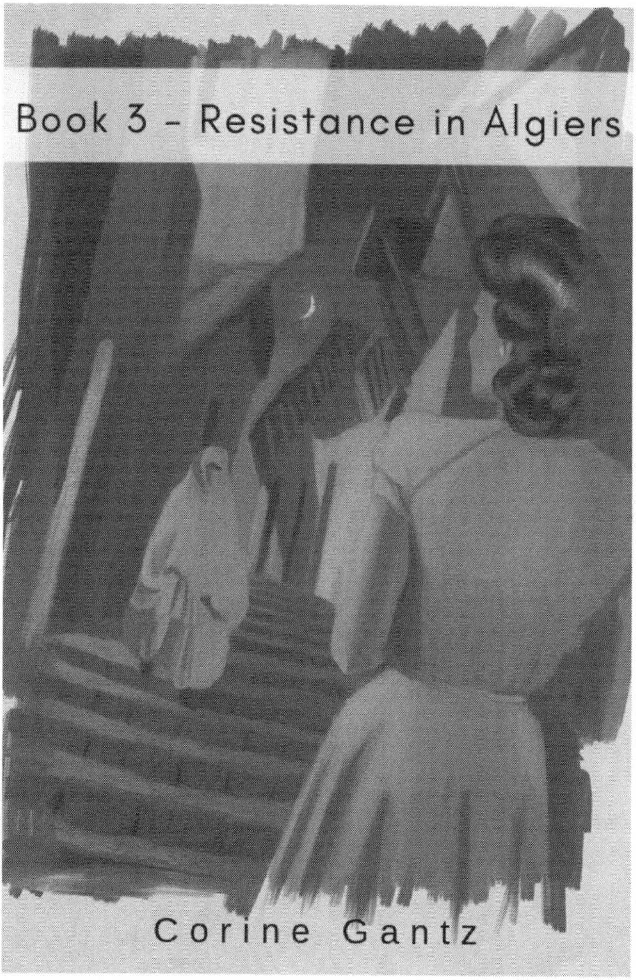
Book 3 - Resistance in Algiers
Corine Gantz

To everyday heroes.

CHAPTER 1

Springtime in Paris

Hot water pounded Cassie's shoulders; water rivulets slid down her neck, her breasts, her thighs as she stood inside above her Parisian hotel bathroom's claw-foot tub. Steam turned the glass of the small window above the tub opaque, and Paris's skyline blurred, mirroring her thoughts. How easy, and natural and lovely it had been with Hervé. Dinner the night before. Conversations about small things. The laughter. The kisses. His skin. His hands on her. How could it be that five years after her divorce, long past the time when she thought she cared about physical things at all, her body suddenly remembered that it felt things, that it wanted things?

And yet, when she had awakened thirty minutes ago, Hervé had already left. A couple of dinners and two nights of lovemaking did not exactly constitute a relationship, and yet it stung. It was for the best. The romance, if that's what this was, was headed for the cliff anyway. Her omissions – okay, her lies – insignificant at first, had grown the size of an entire continent. She had not told Hervé that she lived in the United States and had not lived in France for a good twenty years or that she was in Paris for only a few more days. She had deliberately moved the conversation away from the truth in big and small ways. She had told Hervé that she had children in college, but not that her twins were Americans, in American colleges. She told him that she was a writer and worked with her ex, but not that the career took place in Los Angeles. It had been easier to let Hervé think that she had landed in this ninth arrondissement hotel room because of an imaginary breakup. She had told him that she lived in the United States and would only remain in Paris for a few more days to visit her father who currently drifted in and out of consciousness in the hospital a few blocks away from her hotel.

At first, she had only meant to withhold information from a stranger. After finding herself in bed with said stranger, and finding herself liking him very much, she had not revealed details that might reflect negatively on her, details such as the country where she lived, or the fact that her mother and sister were barring her from her dad's hospital room because they saw her as unpredictable and perhaps even potentially damaging to his recovery. True, her dad had gone into a rage when Cassie entered the room, but it was only because of the drugs; it was because he was confusing her with Marceline, the sister from which he was estranged and whose existence he had kept hidden for over forty years. Cassie blamed the morphine for his outbursts, but apparently, the hospital, her mother, and her sister Odile blamed her. The fact that Cassie lived in another country where she was still in love with her ex-husband, and that she was presently at war with her father, her sister, and her mother, not to mention the entire French hospital, would have been topics on the heavy side for a first date. She did not judge it necessary to elaborate on how much of a nut she was. Anyway, the curated version of her life had not stopped Hervé from running away while she was asleep, so her lies did not matter at all.

Cassie got out of the shower and wiped the fog from the mirror. The day ahead promised to be fraught with drama. Her mother would intimidate her out of asking questions about the past. Her sister Odile would tell her that cozying up to Marceline had been a betrayal of their dad. She planned to escalate her fight with the bureaucrats at the hospital because she now saw it her mission, on behalf of every French patient they had or would callously ignore, to point out how robotic and heartless they were. Perhaps that was the real reason she was in Paris: to be reminded of the infuriating reasons she had left France and her family in the first place.

Cassie put on her last pair of clean jeans, layered two T-shirts, and pulled on the red cowboy boots. Jessica's little gifts to her family were still on the mantelpiece, reminding her precisely of what awaited back home: work with Peter, not to mention his matrimonial bliss rubbed in her face day in and day out. She had no right to resent Jessica. Jessica had won Peter over fair and square long after Cassie could claim any ownership of the man.

She looked at the little packages. Hervé had hated those gifts the minute he set eyes on them, and now she saw them in a new light. He had belittled the frilly wrappings and even pointed out that her ex-husband's new wife had no business giving presents to her parents. Hervé. His skin. His smell. The way he had kissed her. After five years without a man's touch, she was desperate. Had she been too eager? She'd definitely been eager.

In time, perhaps, there would be other lovers. Hervé's materializing into her life, however briefly, was a reminder of what was possible. Maybe her time in Paris was opening her world in unexpected ways. Sabine, her younger sister, was in need of her friendship. And there was Marceline, with whom she started to feel an unexplainable kinship. She had not told Odile or her mother that she planned to see Marceline again today. Estranged or not, betrayal of their father or not, Marceline was the only member of the family willing to speak of the past.

She left her hotel room and went down the many sets of stairs. The hospital was not open to visitors in the morning, but maybe she'd be able to speak to someone more open-minded, someone more human, who would let her enter her dad's room. The horrible people she had dealt with thus far hid their incompetence and natural cruelty behind nameless superiors and nonsensical clerical rules, and she had hit a wall. At this point, her only plan was to continue to hit that wall again and again until she cracked it open.

At the reception desk, the old hotelier, his white hair straight up on his head like Albert Einstein in a fright, stood behind the desk, his eyes closed, so immobile that he looked as if he might be asleep standing up. But as she walked by the desk, he opened his eyes and handed her a dozen scribbled pieces of papers. "That American man," he said sourly. "He called all night. Every hour." He grimaced with contempt. "Always gave me the same number. He thinks I'm an imbecile."

Cassie narrowed her eyes at the handful of notes. It was Peter's number, written over and over on various scraps of paper. She could well imagine Peter, who did not speak French, as he shouted the numbers at an elderly Frenchman determined not to speak English. "I'm sorry," she said. "He can be single-minded."

The old man grunted. "Is he your boss?"

"My ex-husband, calling from California. He refuses to accept the concept of time zones."

The old man shook his head and made a whistling sound of empathy between his teeth. "The new one," he said, evidently referring to Hervé, whom he had seen going up and down the stairs with her. "At least he knows the difference between night and day." With this, he handed her a separate note. The handwriting was atrocious; the letters looked like a succession of tiny waves, but she managed to decipher it. "*Je ne voulais pas te réveiller. Je viens te chercher vers 20 heures. Ce soir je fais la cuisine. Hervé.*" Cassie looked up from the note and beamed at the old hotelier. She had not been dumped! Hervé had only meant not to wake her up. He was picking her up around eight p.m. and was cooking dinner! In the span of two days, she had gone from divorced and bitter to having a French lover who cooked for her! "I need to make a phone call," she told the old man.

"Well, it still works for now. We're about to get rid of it. Who doesn't have cell phones these days," the old man said, pointing to the dark corner of the reception hall where stood the bizarre phone booth, the one inexplicably upholstered in mushy red velvet, like the inside of a cake or the lining of a coffin.

She entered the phone booth and slid the glass door closed, remembering that Hervé had mentioned something about making pasta from scratch. Apparently, it was a thing, some sort of French mating ritual new to her. Still giddy, she made a collect call to Peter's number in California.

"Cassie, at last!" Peter exclaimed. "For heaven's sake, what were you doing for the last eight hours?"

"Sleeping," she sighed. "Peter, it was night here."

"And there are no phones in the rooms?"

"Still nope."

"And yet they wouldn't wake you up to tell you I was trying to reach you?"

"Apparently not."

"This is ridiculous, Cassie. You need to get yourself a new cell phone, immediately."

"I don't know; I'm kind of liking it."

"Liking what?"

"Being unplugged. There's something to say about it."

"Well, you better re-plug and fast because we've got a crisis on our hands." Peter was using the urgent tone that usually preceded his turning frantic. "*Women in Black, Part Two* is getting *creamed* by the critics!"

Cassie thought of the movie, how important it had all seemed only a few days ago, and now how trivial, something not worth wasting a minute of mental energy on. "Bad reviews don't mean the movie won't do well," she said.

"Across the board, *The New York Times*, *Variety*, *Huff Post.* They say it's formulaic."

"Of course, it's formulaic," she said. "We gave the studio a paint-by-number of what they wanted."

"Same difference. You know how studio executives are. They want guarantees."

"Tell them the usual garbage: reviewers are failed intellectuals who like to hear the sound of their own rants. Although you and I know they are correct in their assessment."

"What? I don't know that!" Peter said, indignant. "How do I know that? It's a perfectly good film in its genre."

"Correct. The genre is the problem."

"Regardless, the studio's freaking out. They're pumping another fifteen million into promotion."

"Really? You can't take a step in Paris without being bombarded with their ads. Besides, I don't see how any of this is our problem at this point."

"Well, here is how it's our problem: they're freaking out about the one we're writing now,"

"They want to pull out of the prequel? *An Inter Galactic Dramedy.*"

"They would if they could, but lucky for us there are too many big names attached."

"So, what do they want from us?"

"Take a wild guess."

"They want a rewrite?"

"And we better give it to them, and fast, or else the franchise is in peril."

She chuckled despite herself. "Thank God for that."

"Can you cut the cynicism? What's gotten into you? They want to pump up a few things, the humor, the sex, the violence. Oh, and they hate the subplot."

"I hate the subplot too."

"*Now* you tell me?"

Cassie stated something that was suddenly obvious to her, like a cosmic revelation. "I hate the entire film."

"Which *you* wrote with me every day and never said a word!"

"True."

"They think it's not broad enough."

"It's so broad you could stretch it from here to Jupiter."

"What is it you want, Cassie?" Peter said, exasperated. "This is our livelihood. You want to spit in the soup? Bite the hand that feeds or whatnot? I don't know what to tell you. They want a rewrite, and we're going to give them a rewrite. That's what we do. That's why we're the best."

"It's like being the best at clubbing yourself over the head with a rock."

"It's entertainment! Five days in Paris and you've turned into an intellectual snob?"

"Would it be so terrible if our short time on this planet could contribute to improving it, not making it sink to lower depths."

"Oh, please spare me the existentialism."

"I'll remind you that my dad is unconscious in the hospital. It's par for the course."

Peter was silent for a moment, recalibrating. When he spoke again, it was with an almost cheerful voice. "Listen, I know about your dad and all, very tough. You must be going through hell."

"Actually—"

"I hate to do this to you, love, but you need to get your cute butt back to L.A. I'll call the airline to see if there is a penalty for returning early. How about I upgrade you, huh? My treat. There might be a flight leaving today. Or tomorrow?"

"And leave my dad?"

"You can go back to France as soon as we knock this new draft out. You know what? I have an idea. How about I get a service to buy you a new laptop and deliver it to your hotel in the next few hours. I bet that can be done. France is not the Third World."

"The Developing World," she corrected.

"I can email you the studio's notes, and you can start working on the rewrite on the plane. It's what, a twelve-hour flight? You could make a serious dent in twelve hours."

"What about my dad?"

Peter's voice was humble, pleading. "Well, since they won't let you see him anyway…."

Cassie took a breath. Around her was red velvet, both safe and suffocating at the same time. "Peter, Listen—"

"And like I said; you could turn around in a few days and get back to Paris if need be."

She exhaled, looked at her watch. She had just enough time to get to Marceline's house. "I can't get into this right now. Let me call you back in a few hours, alright?"

"I'll get you a laptop," Peter said cheerfully.

****

Outside felt like springtime. The Parisians had a bounce in their step; an optimistically summery wardrobe had replaced umbrellas and raincoats. Cassie entered the boulangerie at the foot of the hotel and bought a pain au chocolat and an Orangina. She walked to the métro at Barbès-Rochechouart. Just like the day before, the station's walls were covered with posters for *Woman in Black*, and there were three men at work gluing more. The studio had wasted no time in printing new posters, but they must have run out of space because they were being smacked right on top of the old ones. That's what fifteen million bought you these days. She laughed out loud and was surprised by the sound of her own laughter.

In the packed métro, a hand on the vertical metal pole, swaying along with every turn, Cassie ate her pain au chocolat feeling not at all like the grown-up she was, but like an eighteen-year-old with a crush. Hervé was cooking pasta. For her! Could someone please pinch her? She had heard of that fantasy, the man who could cook. And she was about to experience it.

Last night, Hervé had talked more about what he wanted to do with his life: something to do with water purification systems in remote parts of Africa. An evening of pasta making was the extent of Hervé's commitment to her. Her return ticket was four days away, and she planned to use those days well. She would have to explain to Peter that saving him, and by extension Hollywood, would have to wait a few days.

Cassie stood facing the Cité des Fleurs house. The first time she had seen the house, it had felt like a foggy dream. But now, moments of her childhood were unlocking as though they had been hidden away in drawers of her mind and were opening up one by one. The smell of wet stones, the chirping of birds, the grey trunks of sycamores, the distant noise of car traffic. Odile in a yellow woolen hat. Her father, towering above them in his winter coat. Her hand in his. All three of them him looking up at the house.

"Why are we here, Papa?" Odile had asked.

"I lived there once," Father said. "In this house."

"When you were little?"

"When I was a boy."

"Did you have a family?" Odile had asked. She must have been six or seven years old. That means that Cassie was four at most.

"Everyone has a family," their dad had said.

"Where are they now?"

"They're dead," he said.

"Can we go inside the house, Papa?" Cassie had asked.

"Oh, no; there are people living in it."

"What people?"

"Just people," he had said.

He had taken them to the Cité des Fleurs twice, maybe three times. They had stood there, the three of them, never walking through the gate, never entering it, never as much as ringing the bell. What strange compulsion brought her father back to the Cité des Fleurs house? Why show it to his daughters but never tell them what it all meant? Why not describe to them the bullying he had endured as a child. Why not mention the years in boarding school or what it was like to be a Jewish boy during the rise of French anti-Semitism? Why not explain how his family had to flee the Nazis, first to the South of France, and then to North Africa where they lived under a false identity? Why did he not tell them that he had a sister? And why say that his family had died, which was clearly a lie?

Cassie hesitated before pressing the buzzer. She was coming here against her mother's and Odile's wishes and, she was pretty confident of this, against her father's as well. Her dad had made a choice to separate from his family and later to hide his sister's existence. He had chosen to alter his last name and to hide his Judaism. And here she was, unearthing it all.

The bell made a screechy, otherworldly noise when she pressed her finger on it. From somewhere in the house, the wide metal gate was unlocked and clicked open. She pushed on the gate. In the garden, the old North African gardener with the handsome face raked the gravel of the path, a cold pipe at his mouth. "Your garden is enchanting," she said as she walked past him.

He touched his cap and tilted his head. "Merci, merci."

"I have a crazy garden in Los Angeles," she told him. "But it takes discipline to groom a garden, and that's not my forte. I can't even discipline my hair."

"C'est une belle journée," he answered with a smile. She was not sure if he had understood her and her lame humor at all.

"Yes, a gorgeous day," she agreed. She walked up to the stoop. The front door opened and Armelle, Marceline's stepdaughter, placed herself firmly in the doorway. "Mother has been quite exhausted," she said nervously fingering her pearls. "I'm afraid you might have to reconvene another time."

"Reconvene? But I'm returning to the U.S. in a few days."

Armelle perked up. "Oh, are you?"

"What is wrong with Marceline?"

Armelle's eyes avoided hers. "Oh, nothing much," she said. "She needs more rest is all."

Cassie was about to insist when she heard Marceline's voice from upstairs. "Armelle, for heaven's sake, stop your nonsense, will you."

Armelle sighed and moved out of the way. She reluctantly invited Cassie to come in. "She's in her study," she said.

Cassie walked past Armelle and up the stairs. She tapped at Marceline's door. "Come on in," Marceline called out. "No need to knock. I'm not the Queen of England."

The study smelled of old books, heavy women's perfume, Earl Grey tea, and pipe tobacco. Laure, Marceline's assistant, was up on a stool and moving what appeared to be a family of stuffed owls from the bookshelf. Magazine and books covered every surface. Laure next began to sort through old papers. Marceline wore an orange silk kimono pantsuit. Her hair was wrapped in an orange shawl, and her neck and arms were heavy with bracelets and necklaces covered in charms, beads, old keys, and trinkets. She looked the picture of health and vitality. "Are you feeling ill?" Cassie asked.

"I'm perfectly well, Dear."

"Why did Armelle make a fuss then?"

"Ha," Marceline clucked. "Long story."

"She's quite protective of you."

"Not protective of me, that's for sure."

"Of who then?"

"Of herself."

Cassie shook her head. "I don't get it."

Marceline pointed at the two leather armchairs by the window, and they sat down. "Laure, would you bring us hot chocolate? Is it too early for hot chocolate? Or rather, bring us mint tea, the way they make it in Algiers. To put us in the mood." She shifted her gaze to Cassie. "How is Gustave feeling this morning?"

Cassie had a defeated sigh. "I will try to see him this afternoon."

"Try?"

"To tell you the truth, well … I'm in a fight with my mother and my sister. They're making a problem. They're acting as though I might harm him in some way since that first day when he was so agitated, and well … they've barred me from his room."

Marceline did not appear surprised. "Agitated, when he thought you were me?"

"What is it about me that reminds him of you, I wonder."

"Well, it's pretty obvious. It's your spark!"

Cassie raised her eyebrows. "I have a spark?"

"Call it what you will. That fire, that curiosity, that defiance, that life force."

"Me? No. I'm terrified of the slightest risk."

"And yet you are here, aren't you?"

What Marceline called a spark, might have been a reference to Cassie's temper. It was a part of her that she strived, and mostly failed, to restrain. It was the part that acted on impulse, that got into fights, the part that kicked out a perfectly good husband and then regretted it, the part that rebelled against injustices, real or perceived. But that was also the part of her with the fire to create, the drive to claim a small part of the world for herself. "I want to know what happened between you and my father," Cassie declared.

Marceline sighed heavily. "Death happened."

"Who died?"

"Things began to take a turn in the spring of 1941," Marceline said. "It's a long story, Cassandra. I haven't told too many people about it. A portion was classified top secret, but who cares now. I have a foot in the grave. Are you going to write all this down?"

"Sure."

"Then take out your pen and paper; what are you waiting for?"

Cassie obediently opened her tote bag, set her pad on the table, uncapped her pen, and listened.

CHAPTER 2

Resistance in Algiers

I was only eighteen, and I did not know my heart. I confused sexual attention for love, and I confused the pangs of unrequited love for hatred. Fernand and I had become lovers. This happened after an afternoon when I had stumbled upon him with an attractive girl at his arm. The two of them were looking through the window of a department store. She was giggling, and I could tell that she was smitten with him. A few paces behind them, small purses in hand, their respective mothers followed. Fernand saw me and quickly looked away, pretending not to know me. The reaction mystified me. I cross-examined him the following day, and he admitted that the girl was his fiancée, and had been for months.

"Why have you never said a word about her?" I asked him. We were sitting at the terrace of a restaurant. Only a year before, the Algiers restaurant scene had been vibrant. Now everything was drab. Menus were shrinking, and prices were going up. We could barely afford to eat out at all and usually shared a few items between us, stuffing ourselves with bread lathered with margarine until even those items began to disappear from shops and restaurants. We were waiting for Béatrice, André, and Émile and were alone until our friends arrived.

"What is there to say?" Fernand answered. "It's a boring story. We are engaged. She's seventeen. We have to wait until she turns nineteen to marry. She's a good Jewish girl. No hanky-panky. Our mothers are always chaperoning. You know how it goes."

"How can you be certain she will still want to marry you two years from now?"

"In all practicality, we've been engaged since we were kids. Our families have known each other for generations. The union has been heavily plotted."

"An arranged marriage?"

"Not arranged," Fernand said with a wry smile. "Merely facilitated."

"Do you love her?"

"She is beautiful and sweet. Her folks are important in Algiers. The families approve. What's not to love?"

"In the street the other day, you pretended not to know me. Who are you embarrassed about? Was it her or me?"

He looked at me with those velvety eyes, both commanding and ironic. "I'm embarrassed by neither of you. Only discreet. So as to hurt no one's feelings."

"Do you think I care? Do you think my feelings would be so easily bruised? You and I are friends, nothing more."

He smiled wryly. "Now it is *my* feelings that are being hurt."

"You are capable of feelings?"

He looked at me in an unmistakably sexual way. "You know all too well how I feel about you, Marceline. I am tortured with thoughts of you day and night. It's a miracle that I manage any sleep at all. You have that effect on men, don't you know?"

"Well, you should be ashamed of yourself," I said, flattered. "You are engaged. Try warm milk at bedtime; you'll sleep just fine. Leave me out of your nights."

"Tell me you are incapable of guilty thoughts yourself. Or rather, don't tell me. I won't believe you."

I played with the straw in my glass. I was capable of guilty thoughts indeed. I too tossed and turned at night, and it had quite a bit to do with lust. Ever since that day in the café's corridor, my baffling, thrilling encounter with Khaled replayed in my mind on a loop. Had he meant to kiss me? Had he wanted to speak to me? Had he intended to frighten me? He had appeared in the dark hallway, wordlessly bent toward me, and I had felt engulfed by all the things he had perhaps meant to convey without words or touch: tenderness, threat, desire, amusement, domination. What drove me mad was that the strange courtship had ended as enigmatically as it had begun. Since that day, nothing. Dozens of times since, I had stubbornly returned to Café Djurdjura, and he had not so much as looked in my direction. I was left not knowing his feelings at all and mine even less. I felt eager, and I felt powerless. I was furious, and at the same time drunk with a sort of secret happiness about the thrill, the hope, the romance of it all. It was an unexplained craving, a feeling of desperation, a sense that it had been a cruel game and that I had lost. Was this how things would end between Khaled and me? Over and done before they had even begun? Often anger would take over. How dare he corner me like that? Who did he think he was? He was nobody. He was my social inferior. He was part of a culture and a religion alien to me.

"There are several sorts of people in one's life," Fernand said. "She is the girl I'll marry, the future mother of my children. But I'll admit I didn't want this to push you away."

"Is that so?"

Fernand put his hand over mine and began to gently caress it with the tip of his fingers. "Perhaps I thought you would like me less."

Fernand was handsome. He and I had played a game of seduction for years, but I had no desire to pretend to love him, and I made sure never to cross a line. He and I had not so much as kissed. But his being engaged, his attachment to someone else, changed things. Perhaps he was just what I needed to get my mind off Khaled. I did not remove my hand. "Maybe it's the opposite," I said. "Perhaps I like you more now."

"Now that you know I'm engaged?"

"To become the mother of someone's children is not every woman's dream, Fernand."

And so, we secretly met in cheap hotel rooms. Although I was just two years older than his fiancée, I felt like I was a mature woman. I liked the thought of having a lover with no emotional attachment, no commitment. I liked that he wanted to keep me a secret because I too wanted to be discreet. We met a couple of times a week. Fernand was an attentive sexual partner, and there was a lot of excitement in the secrecy of those meetings. But in a strange way, I felt closer to Khaled after only a few moments with him in that hallway than I felt to Fernand, skin against skin in bed.

It was during one my secret rendezvous with Fernand that I learned about what was really taking place at Géo Gras.

It had been one of those warm spring afternoons. Sprawled under the white sheets of Hotel de Paris, my head rested on Fernand's chest as the blades of the ceiling fan struggled to move the air, already hot for the season. There wasn't much to do in Algiers in the spring of 1941. There was no school to attend, no work to get paid for, no money, and little available to buy or eat. Fernand and I met in secret from our friends twice a week in the middle of the afternoon.

"My family is onto me," I told Fernand as he absentmindedly caressed my naked body with the tips of his fingers. "I'm pretty certain that my brother is spying on me and reporting to my father."

But Fernand had his own frustration. "They say we're not French," he growled. "They're the ones selling France out to Hitler. They fill their pockets stealing Jewish businesses and emptying our bank accounts. Their hateful little minds have no concept of patriotism. How they love to hate the Jews so that they can plunder us!" Fernand sat up in bed, suddenly incensed by his own words. "I will show them what true patriotism looks like," he said. "To my death, if I must."

I shrugged, "Jews have demonstrated their patriotism time and again. Your dying for France will not prove a thing."

"Regardless," he said, "I'd rather die of a bullet, shot proving my allegiance to France, than from typhus in an internment camp."

"Well, I intend on living," I said, sitting up in bed next to him. "We will accomplish far less by being dead wouldn't you think?" Rays of the sun came through the spaces between the window's shutters. It was already late. I had to dress, arrange my hair, and meet up with Sandra before she needed to get to the apartment to fix dinner so that we could both walk home together. "I want to shape my own fate, not bob along the way I have been," I said. Those were just words. I had shaped nothing and knew it.

"Then you better do something soon before you run out of opportunities," Fernand said. "Look at the Jews of Europe. Their chance has passed. They are trapped. But here in Algeria, you can still act." He added, "If you have the nerve."

Did I have the nerve, when for months now I had done nothing concerning the nature of my obsession? I had failed to speak to Khaled, failed to get his attention, failed to get him out of my mind. But I also knew that no good would come out of pursuing Khaled, or him pursuing me. I knew better than to go down that rabbit hole. "I would join the Resistance in a heartbeat," I told Fernand, not even knowing what that meant. This was not the first time I had mentioned the Resistance, perhaps to push him to act.

Fernand looked at me fiercely. "What's stopping you?"

I shrugged. I took the sheet from the bed, wrapped myself in it, and went to sit in front of the vanity. "How would they know to find me? I don't have any idea how to find them? It's not as though I can place an advertisement in the newspaper."

Fernand propped himself up on one elbow and watched me comb my hair. After a long while, he asked, "And what would you do for the Resistance?"

"Whatever it takes," I answered, not meaning it.

Fernand got up from the bed and came to stand behind me. He put his hands on my shoulders. In the mirror, I watched his face turn serious. "You would not have to place an advertisement in the newspaper," he murmured in my ear.

"You know people?"

The fan's blades turned in slow motion as he whispered, "We are part of a Resistance cell. André, Émile, and I."

"You are?" The questioning in my voice betrayed that I was more dubious than stunned.

He smiled. "What is so hard to believe? That we would be, or that we would be without you suspecting a thing?"

"There is resisting, and there is The Resistance," I said. "It's one thing to have good intentions, and another to be properly connected."

If Fernand had planned to keep things a secret, my lack of conviction goaded him to say more. "Do you have any idea of what is really going on at Géo Gras?" he asked.

"You do calisthenics I thought."

"Do you truly think that we care one way or another how healthy we are? Obedience, honor, discipline, willpower, travail, famille, patrie, all that nonsense. Did you actually believe that we bought into that? No, that has only been our excuse to meet."

It was then that Fernand told me all about the activities at Gymnase Géo Gras. The gymnasium was a cover, a meeting place for the Resistance. While Béatrice and I thought that our friends were parading around in shorts, climbing ropes, lifting iron bars, and fine-tuning their musculature as the world fell to pieces; they were doing Resistance work! They gathered intelligence on Vichy hotspots, kept records on boating activities throughout the region, mapped out the coast and mountains, recruited, established codes, and chains of communication and command, and made plans on how to overtake strategic points in the city.

In many ways, the Jews of Algiers were ideally suited for such clandestine organizing. They were a tight-knit group accustomed to a hostile environment. Their trust in each other had developed from parents to children over generations. The arrests, the humiliations, and the privations that had hit the community in the previous two years had only served to reinforce the strength of their bond.

"In theory, we're preparing to defend ourselves should the situation against the Jews deteriorate. But lately, there has been word that something bigger is on the brink."

"How much bigger?"

"Huge," he said. A thrilled silence lingered after his word.

"Are you armed?" I asked.

"You know how the gunsmith had his shop shut down and his stock confiscated by order of the préfecture? That was after we hid away hundreds of firearms in the basement of the gymnasium. Nothing that compares to the Germans MP43, but enough to put a bullet through a Nazi's head. Enough to capture, or kidnap. Enough for the Allied forces to know they can count on us in the eventuality of an invasion of North Africa."

I was enthralled. "You think that's a possibility?"

"Yes ... Especially in light of recent events," Fernand said. "We've received contact. Someone was sent to Algeria by the French Resistance to organize us. They're trusting us! The Jews are the only people they know for certain will never be on the side of Pétain or the Nazis. You see," he said, "the Allies see us as the last true patriots!"

I felt thrilled, buoyed for the first time in months by hope and excitement. "I want to be part of this," I said.

"It's dangerous business. And besides, many men think a woman is a liability."

"We raise less suspicion."

"Being part of this means risking your life. Your father would not allow you to get involved."

"My father would never know about this."

"Chances are that he would be one of the first to know."

I shrugged, "How so?"

Fernand gave me a quizzical look. "Your father is one of the cell leaders."

I laughed. "Of course, he's not. What are you talking about? My father is the most cautious man you'll ever meet, and the most risk-averse."

"Him and that big man, Moshe."

"*Uncle* Moshe?" I asked in disbelief.

"They've been channeling money from England and the United States. They have air routes and drop-off points throughout France and North Africa. Their cell is the one that helps finance all the others. Without your father, there would be no funds."

I felt goosebumps all over my body. Baba, my father! With all his talk of being safe, I had never paid attention to his secretive behavior. Now it all made sense. But as proud of him as I felt, I also wished he wasn't involved. I might have romantic notions of risking my life for freedom, but I didn't want my father to risk his. "It there any way I could help without my dad or my uncle finding out?"

"There is a way," Fernand said. "You could help, and it would just be between us two. Underground in the underground sort of thing. In fact, it might be best. The less you know, the safer you are. This is how the cells have to work anyway. Things have to be compartmentalized. That way, if one of us gets caught, only his cell goes down. He can't give out anyone else's names or confess what they do."

"Do you have something in mind for me?"

"Translation," he said without hesitation. "You're fluent in English."

I looked at him askance. "You had always meant to ask me this, didn't you? You've been planning to ask me, and you knew I'd say yes."

"We need you, sweetie. We translate loads of stuff coming our way, but we aren't always sure of the subtleties."

I had no idea that my next sentence would place me at the center of a mission that could soon change the course of the war. "I can do this," I told him, with all the fervor I felt. "I want to do this."

I left the hotel, careful to leave before Fernand did, so as not to be seen near him. As I stepped into the bright light of mid-afternoon, my head buzzed with what I had learned. But just as I walked out of the hotel, I came face to face with Gustave on his bicycle!

"What are you doing in there?" Gustave demanded to know.

"Have you been following me?"

He straddled his bike. Gustave had turned into a hybrid between a boy and a man. He was tall now and muscular from the incessant push-ups and lifting weights in his room, yet he still had no hair on him, and his eyes were still those of a child. He crossed his arms. "Are you being a tramp?" he asked.

I stepped toward him and grabbed him by the arm. "I'll skin you alive, you little rat!"

He shook his arm from my grip, furious. "Are you telling them not to let me in?"

"What are you talking about?"

"You're telling the Géo Gras men not to include me, aren't you?"

Gustave must have caught wind of what was taking place at Géo Gras, tried to offer his services, and been shooed away. If that was the case, it was most likely because our father had ordered it. "I had nothing to do with that," I said, which was the truth.

Gustave twisted his mouth angrily. "You're lying, as usual."

"You better stay away from trouble," I said. "You've heard what Baba said."

"And you heard what he told *you*," he sneered. "You're not obeying either."

"What are you trying to prove, Gustave? That you're a brave man? A big hero? You'd be nothing but a liability to them. One look at you and they can tell you don't have what it takes."

Gustave looked hurt, then furious. "You're nothing but a whore." He spat out the words and darted away on his bike.

I worried that Gustave would run straight to my father to tell on me. But mostly I wanted to punish him for what he had said. Why could men go to bed with whomever they wanted, but a woman doing so was a whore? At the same time, my rage was partially due to shame. I knew that I was being promiscuous not out of love but out of idleness.

Could I have fallen in love with Fernand if not for Khaled? Would I have been infatuated with Khaled had it not been forbidden? The thing was, sex with Fernand did not feel right. I felt blemished by it. Nonsensically, I felt as though I was betraying Khaled.

My Resistance activity thus began. Newspapers from Britain and the United States were contraband items on which the members of the Resistance depended for intelligence. It was terribly dangerous to be caught in possession of one. No one at Géo Gras was fluent enough in English to know for certain that they understood the contents. Fernand soon put me to the task. For hours at a time, by the light of a candle, while the rest of the family slept, I translated all manner of English newspaper articles, brochures, and annotations on maps. At last, those dreadful British nannies had proved themselves not entirely useless.

From May 1941 to January 1942, when we celebrated my nineteenth birthday without enough flour or eggs for a cake, I translated. My fingertips were raw from flipping through the pages of my dictionary with a fervor I had seldom applied to my schoolwork. I was good at this and got better with practice. My English improved exponentially. I was too busy, and nervous, to wonder what had come of Gustave's own Resistance dreams. To me, he was a child. I could not imagine that others saw this pencil-thin seventeen-year-old as a man.

For a young Jewish woman in 1941, it was unfathomable to hope that the world would recover from its spiraling descent into hell. Hitler's maniacal plans and politics went unopposed. His army was unstoppable. But it wasn't just Hitler. Hating the Jews appeared to be the one point on which the entire world agreed. There might have been righteous and well-meaning people not intent on wiping Jews off the face of the earth, but they were few and mostly focused on their own survival. So very little was being done to stop the hatred against us. We felt it down to the marrow of our bones: soon, Jews would have no place to hide, no country to run to. The information we received from friends and relatives cemented our understanding that we had become the entire world's prey. How would we ever overcome this, even if Hitler lost the war, which at this point seemed impossible? Hatred was closing in on Jews, squeezing us out of existence.

I needed Fernand because his anger was so much more reassuring than our collective apathy and discouragement. Fernand believed that the Jewish people's fate wasn't written yet. He admonished us not to count on the return of human decency or to hope that the government would set up protective policies. These, to him, were paralyzing delusions. He believed that we would prevail because our fight had only begun. It wasn't prayer or hiding that we needed but guns and grenades.

Another person I depend on for hope was my father. As nurturing to me as air or water was the way Baba found reasons to rejoice. In June 1941, when Hitler invaded the Soviet Union, and the Russian army seemed unable to stop him, my father promised us that Hitler would not be able to sustain a war on two fronts. When Japan attacked Pearl Harbor on December 7th, 1941 and the United States officially entered the war, my father tried to convince us that the combined will and brain power of Roosevelt and Churchill would save us. Now that I knew that my father was a prominent person in the Resistance, I hung on to his words and hoped he knew something we didn't.

And so, in the absence of tangible signs that things would improve, what carried me through these dark times was my father's optimism, Fernand's exhortations, my modest efforts with the Resistance, and, perhaps more essential to me, the mystery of Khaled.

As months passed and he still made no eye contact with me, I had to admit to myself that I had fallen under his spell. When I got up in the morning, he was my first thought. The way I dressed, the way I did my hair: it was all for him. I had only one interest in my day, and that was to see him, even from afar. I had no name for this, for my feelings, but in them, I recognized hope. Hope was a fragile thing, it was all we had in that terrible war, and so I protected mine like a weakly beating heart.

Throughout the rest of the winter, I dutifully translated the papers Fernand gave me. Information never changed hands between us. We communicated via a system he had devised. Every day I went to the market and stopped at the flower stand owned by a Jewish woman who was part of the Resistance. We would then exchange matching straw bags. Hers contained the day's documents to translate. Mine contained my translation from the day before. While I have no doubt that the work Fernand gave me was important, it was also a test to observe my grit and dedication. I did not know this at the time, but this assignment was a way for him to calibrate me, and in many ways train me, for the future mission he had in mind.

This pickup and drop-off of papers went on for months without drama until one day when I arrived home after an afternoon with Béatrice. From the moment I entered the apartment, it was clear that something was wrong. Mother, Father, and Gustave were sitting in the living room, waiting for me in ominous silence. Mother looked vindicated. Gustave stood sheepishly. My father immediately brandished one of my translations and a copy of *The New York Tribune*. "What are these?" he said.

"Where did you find that?" I said, knowing just where he had found them. Gustave, whose nose was everywhere, must have dug them out from inside my bedroom fireplace where they were hidden. I turned to my brother and shouted, "You little rat!"

"Who is your contact?" my father asked without bothering to pretend he did not understand what I was up to.

"Give that back to me," I said. "People are expecting this translation. It's my duty to give it to them."

For a man who worked for the Resistance, my father did not exactly give my demand much respect. "What duty?" he said, rolling his eyes. "Your duty is to mind your mother and me."

"I know who she spends her time with," Gustave volunteered.

"Snitch!" I said.

"Your brother speaks only out of concern for your safety," my mother said.

"He's all too happy to get me in trouble."

"You got yourself into trouble without his help," my father pointed out. "And besides, Gustave understands something you fail to comprehend, Marceline. His loyalty to this family has to be greater than his loyalty to you. That's because a family is greater than the sum of its parts."

"What does that even mean?" I said, exasperated.

"It means that if one of us is wounded, or imprisoned, or killed, the others would never … ever recover." My father choked on his words and paused to gather himself. "What if the police had searched the apartment and found this? An American newspaper and a recent one at that! Do you realize how damning that would be?"

"Then what?" I shrugged. "What would they do?"

"They would interrogate you," my father said. "They would want the names of your contacts."

"I would never speak."

"They would torture you until you did," Gustave said.

"Unlike you, I am not afraid of torture," I said haughtily.

"How can you be so daft?" Gustave said.

My father lifted a palm to quiet us. "The thing is, Marceline, we would *all* get interrogated. They would not have to investigate for long before realizing we're here under a false name. From there they would see that I am a wanted man in France. And they would send me to an internment camp."

This chastisement was unfair coming from my father. He clearly had no idea that I knew of his involvement with the Géo Gras group. As the head of a cell, he put himself, and us, at risk every single day. Either Fernand was wrong, or my father was a fantastic actor. Either way, arguing with him was counterproductive. So I changed my tone, knowing it would serve me better to act contrite and repentant. I begged Father to at least let me give the translated documents to my contacts and tell them I could no longer help. He agreed to this but confiscated the dictionary, which I hardly needed anymore.

It never occurred to me, at any point, to obey my father. Had I not always gotten what I wanted? I resolved to be more discreet, and I convinced myself that no matter how angry my father seemed, he was secretly proud of me.

In early spring of 1942, things started to move fast.

The boys were already at Café Djurdjura when Béatrice and I arrived one afternoon. Fernand appeared to be in a jovial mood. "They are getting rid of him at long last," he said.

"Who?" I asked.

"That worthless Arab," Fernand said watching me intently. He squinted in the direction of Khaled, who stood by the entrance of the terrace, in his waiter's uniform, the usual white shirt, black pants, and long apron, his arms crossed in front of his chest, his expression inscrutable. We all turned to look at him, and he stared straight back at us, or, it felt, straight at me. Then he turned on his heels and disappeared inside the café.

"I heard that he quit," Béatrice said.

"Trust me, sweetheart," Fernand said, "these people are in no position to voluntarily leave a paying job."

"Why was he fired?" I asked, as casually as I could.

"The owner's Jewish," Émile said. "The government is putting a Frenchman from Lyon in his place. The new chap is hiring his own people, all pearly white French. Everyone here is laid off; the Jews and the Arabs."

"And we all know who will be the next undesirables: the Jewish clientele, present company included," André said.

I was stunned. Where would I see Khaled now? I had planned on the cat-and-mouse game playing out in my mind to last forever. "Let's not come to this wretched place anymore," I said. "Boycott the anti-Semites before they boycott us."

Fernand had a sarcastic smile. "How convenient, darling, now that the Djurdjura will have lost all its charm."

"What charm?" Béatrice asked. But the boys looked elsewhere and did not answer.

I buried my nose in my glass of iced lemonade, furious at Fernand, at myself, at Khaled. Had I been that transparent? And if so, did it mean Khaled knew? I was humiliated. Fernand hated Khaled. If he knew my feelings, he must have taken a perverse pleasure in watching me hide them.

As my friends bantered about other things, my mind raced. Khaled was leaving Café Djurdjura. He would forever disappear into this wide city, of which so many parts were forbidden to me.

Would I see him again?

A sense of powerlessness washed over me as the reasoning that I had so far managed to keep at bay suddenly imposed itself: I was being ridiculous. Khaled's silent, brooding good looks had been the perfect blank canvas onto which to project my fantasy, the romantic pull of impossible love. The thing was, nothing could ever take place between us. Had he been interested in me I would have no choice but to reject him. Between our two cultures and classes were nothing but animosity and suspicion. Our worlds only intersected in one place, Café Djurdjura. The café had been the gateway between our two very different lives, and now that door was closed shut. There were powerful rules, unwritten rules and some written ones, that forbade us to be in any form of contact. Muslims boys had to abide by a set of laws and constraints as restrictive as those imposed on French Jewish girls.

Khaled and I never could, and never *would*, become anything.

A lump in my throat swelled up. The notion that I might never see him again was intolerable.

The following day, a wiry boy from Montpellier had replaced Khaled. That week, all the Arab waiters, even those who had worked at the café for twenty years, were replaced one by one with friends of the new owner. That same week, the name of the café was changed to Bistro Belle France, but by then we had stopped going.

I had been feasting on glimpses of Khaled. Now that he was gone, there was nothing to sustain me. That was when I realized how much I had needed his presence, even on the periphery of my life. I had a consuming need for him. I felt depressed and angry at the same time. The thing was, powerlessness was not an emotion I handled well. I needed to do *something*. What, I did not know. I had the sense that, given the slightest push, I might do something irreversible.

All week, I walked through the streets of Algiers in a fog. At the sight of a thin, muscular silhouette, a shaved head, or a white shirt, my heart would race senselessly. Soon I had no choice but to admit the truth to myself: this walking through the street wasn't aimless; I was actively searching the crowds for him. I began to walk in and out of cafés and restaurants like a crazy woman, bumping into patrons. I was in and out of plazas and markets. I looked everywhere short of venturing out alone in areas of Algiers where men could be killed and women raped.

Then I remembered what the boys had said. When he was not working at the café, Khaled was a fisherman.

It took some convincing to get Béatrice to accompany me the next morning. "The fishing port? But why," she whined. "I hate the smell. What's the point? It's a bore."

"Oh, but it's so picturesque: the little boats, the market! I hear it's a lot of fun."

Béatrice looked unconvinced. "Let's go with the boys," she said.

"Must you do everything with them?" I said, exasperated. "Well, I shall go alone then."

Béatrice relented. She was grumpy when I picked her up at seven in the morning. "Why so early?" she asked. She contemplated my outfit. I wore my mother's best navy blouse paired with my new cream trousers. They were tightly belted at the waist, form-fitting at the hips, loose fitting around the leg and came floating down around the ankle. "You're wearing trousers?" she said without trying to mask her envy.

"Sandra sewed me a pair from a pattern," I said. This was the new fashion, a more masculine silhouette, although there was a gap between what we coveted in magazines and what was available in Algiers shops. I wanted to look like Ingrid Bergman that morning. I wanted to be irresistible.

Béatrice still pouted as we made our way down to the pier, straw baskets in hand. The market smelled of fresh fish and the sea. People were hungry and standing in lines all over the city for milk, eggs, and bread, but there was still plenty of fish if you had money. All around us were crates of sardines, anchovies, sea bass, red mullets, and groupers. There were cuttlefish, octopus, shrimp, and black sea snails by the bucket displayed over beds of crushed ice and algae. The shoppers were men, Arab women covered from head to toe, cooks of wealthy families, dozens of maids, and French housewives. The restaurant buyers and personal chefs of Algiers's elite loaded crates into automobiles while the rest of the populace, from French housewives to Arab mothers to maids to young kids holding fists full of coins, were left to haggle for inferior cuts.

I walked around the market, Béatrice in tow, scanning the crowd and ignoring the merchandise on display as I made my way closer to the boats.

A group of a dozen Arab men crouched around a long net punctuated with small red buoys. And there was Khaled among them! His focus was on his task, his hands agile as he passed a large needle in an out through the rough netting. I placed myself in front of Béatrice so that she would not see him.

"Oh, goodness gracious, this is awful!" I whispered to her with as much alarm in my voice as I could fabricate.

"What? What?" she asked in the same tone. "What's the matter?"

"I'm into a heap of trouble," I said, signifying to her with eye rolls that my period had just come unannounced: a complete lie. "If I take another step, I will stain everything."

"What do you want me to do?" she asked dully.

"I can't move. Find me a shawl or something to wrap around my waist."

"I don't have anything!"

"Then run home and get one! Quick!"

She looked at me with suspicion. "You want to stay here alone?"

"It's perfectly safe. Look, there are plenty of women here. And the police are here too. I'll stay right in this corner, and I won't move."

Béatrice dropped her straw bag and darted away. When she was out of sight, I advanced out of the shadows and stood about ten feet away from Khaled. Finally, he lifted his face and saw me. He expressed no surprise. He stood up, wiped his hands on a towel, walked away from the net and the crouching men and came towards me. When we were face to face, he watched me with keen interest, waiting for me to speak.

"You work here?" I said, stating the obvious.

"I remember you," he said softly, in his Arabic-accented French.

"From the Djurdjura. Yes." I smiled, fearing I was blushing. "I'm one of your best customers."

He shook his head. "I mean that I remember you from right here."

"The pier? I've never been here before."

He smiled. "You have. With your family."

I was astonished. "You saw us? That was nearly two years ago."

He cocked his head mockingly. "That day I was working. You don't remember? You had a white dress."

"I did?"

"I carried some of your luggage."

I searched his face, haunted by the faint memory. "Is that why you've been looking at me?"

He smiled with his eyes only. "I've been looking at you because you are beautiful." He said this without pretense or flirtation.

My chest swelled up like a balloon. "You know I really can't be here," I said. "I can't be here, and I can't speak to you."

"No, you cannot," he agreed. He seemed amused.

"And you can't talk to me either," I said. "Some people would have your skin for this."

His eyes were smiling. "Including that boyfriend of yours?" he asked.

I looked away. It did not matter how secretive Fernand and I were; everyone assumed we were together. "He is not my boyfriend," I said. Was that a lie? We spent time in bed together. And I sounded so terribly eager. Coming here in the first place reeked of desperation.

He seemed distant for a moment, looking past me. Then he said. "You see that area under the pier, to the right of us?" he said this without looking in the direction he was indicating. I looked to my right. Below the pier, dozens of dark wooden pillars created a shaded area that extended from the sand into the sea. A few men, their feet in the water, stood in the shade of the pier with their fishing rods, the lines taut in the water. "I go there every day to fish after work."

"You work at a fish market and you fish?" I said inanely.

"The fish I catch don't cost money."

"I see," I said, not seeing anything for the summersaults my heart was making inside my chest.

"Come here after six tonight," he murmured. "Meet me underneath the pier."

"I will," I whispered.

"I better return to work," he said.

"Yes, yes of course."

He turned away with a graceful economy of movement and went back to his crouching position working on the net. I watched the back of his neck, the tanned skin, and wanted to touch it. Our exchange had lasted all but two minutes, and already Béatrice was running toward me. "I got it!" she said. "I just remembered I had a shawl in my bag; we can wrap it around your waist—"

"False alarm," I said.

She pouted at my lack of appreciation and then looked at me askance. "Why do you look so happy? Are you playing some trick on me?"

"I just love fish!" I answered, taking her by the arm and guiding her away from the area with the fishing nets. I looked away so she wouldn't see that I was beaming.

At five that same evening, I told Mother I was going down to buy her cigarettes and hurried down toward the pier. Mother was taking her sleeping medication earlier and earlier, and by the time I left, she was already groggy. I had under an hour before my father returned from the office where he and Uncle Moshe worked. If I arrived home after him, he would demand to know where I had been.

It was tricky for a young woman to walk alone in Algiers's streets as curfew approached. Already overzealous French policemen did not need an excuse to stop people to inspect their papers, especially if they were young and pretty. I walked from store to store, pretending to be window-shopping. The police seemed more interested in Algerian men they could harass than in me, and so I went on undisturbed. When a policeman watched me too insistently, I entered a building as though I lived there. I came out again minutes later and continued down the street. Once there were no more shops, I wrapped a shawl around my head and shoulders and hurried down to the pier without being stopped. When I reached the beach, I removed my shoes and walked on the sand toward the fishing pier, more nervous as I got closer. In the distance, I could see a half dozen men, some on top of the pier and some on the beach. As I got closer, I recognized Khaled. His pants were rolled up, his feet were in the water, and his shirt was open and billowing in the warm evening sea breeze. He held his fishing rod with one hand and stood perfectly still, the lean muscles of his arm flexed. He glanced in my direction, and then straight ahead at the water, showing no expression. I stood silently about ten feet behind him with the intuition that if he was acting as though I wasn't there, that meant he expected me not to come any closer.

Someone looking at us from any vantage point would have seen two strangers standing on the narrow beach: a man fishing and a woman watching the sunset. Above the beach, a tandem of policemen on their rounds saluted me from afar. I waited, the wind ruffling my hair. The air and the light were soft. A hundred seagulls swirled in the sky above a tiny wooden boat painted white and blue. I did not feel impatient but expectant. I had the sense that the next moment would change my life.

After a few minutes, once the policemen were out of sight, Khaled lifted his rod and reeled in the line. A foot-long fish dangled from the hook, flailing and twitching, his silvery scales catching the light of the fading sun. Khaled unhooked the fish, dropped it in a bucket, and wiped his hands on his pants. He took his time bringing a cigarette out of a pack and to his lips. Only then did he walk toward me. But he did not come close. He stopped to my left and lit his cigarette. Still ten feet away from each other, we now both faced the sea. The sun approached the horizon, and our skins took on a golden hue. The water lapped the beach. Khaled's shirt billowed, and I caught sight of his smooth chest, his tanned skin. I watched him from the corner of my eyes, making sure not to turn my head toward him too conspicuously.

"I'm happy you came," Khaled said to the sea.

"I'm sorry that they fired you from Djurdjura. We're boycotting it, so that you know."

"Do not feel bad," he said. "It was time for me to leave."

"You were not happy there?"

"How could I have been?" he said.

"We will never be able to speak like two regular people, will we?" I murmured.

"Have you ever visited the Jardin d'Essai?" he asked.

"Yes. It's beautiful."

"Could you come there alone?"

"I think so."

"I will be there tomorrow. In the Allée des Dragonniers. At eleven in the morning."

"Is that a place where we can speak more … freely than here?" I asked.

Khaled's profile moved imperceptibly toward me, and his lips curled into a thin smile. "Up to a point," he said.

"I'll be there," I said.

"One of us has to leave now," he said, taking a puff of his cigarette and bending down to grab the rod he had planted in the sand. "People are watching." He was right. Up above, standing over the parapet, a European couple there to enjoy the sunset was looking at us.

"I'll leave," I said, and I walked past him, continuing my stroll on the sand as though he and I were strangers, which in many ways we were.

I had been near him for only a minute, and yet those few instants felt so rich with meaning, so palpably exciting. I went home but could barely sleep that night.

The next day, I told Sandra that I was off to visit the Jardin d'Essai with Béatrice and my friends and hopped on the first trolley that took me in the direction of the garden.

The most mundane thing could become the pretext to check your papers and even detain you. Hoping to pass as older, since the police tended to show extra zeal toward unaccompanied girls, I wore Mother's fitted jacket, belted at the waist and widely padded at the shoulders, and my favorite A-line skirt. I had done my hair in the new style: hair parted in the center, small victory rolls on each side, the rest loose above the shoulders. If on the outside I appeared polished and collected, on the inside I was all in knots.

In the botanical garden, I made my way past the ten-foot tall strelitzia and the oleanders in bloom, up the cascading set of stairs, and past the circular lake surrounded by a lawn and flanked on each side by tall, willowy palm trees. From the central pathway, the view of the sea was majestic. It was windier than usual, and the wind carried the crisp smell of the sea. I followed the dirt alleys and made my way past more lawns and fountains, past the ficus alley until I faced the sign that read "Allée des Dragonniers." I thought I had stepped on a strange planet. This alley was a wide dirt path planted on each side with primeval-looking plants, half-trees, half-cactuses, with strange limbs that formed a canopy dense enough to block the sunlight almost completely. The thickness of the vegetation muffled all sounds besides that of my footsteps. There were no birds. The scent of the place was unknown to me, musky and sweet. I was alone in the alley save for an old man sporting an oversized turban who sat on a bench, his unlit pipe in his mouth, his eyes half-closed. I walked slowly, trying to calm the wild activity in my chest when a male voice said. "They call these dragon trees." I turned. Khaled was standing in front of me, tall, thin, beautiful. His eyes were on me, inquisitive. To my surprise, he was dressed in a garden guide's uniform. "The Latin name for them is Dracaena. I would love to tell you more about the Jardin d'Essai if you'll allow me," he said. I only nodded, unable to speak. It was the first time I saw Khaled truly smile, and it was like a beam of sunlight, an urgent happiness he was not trying to mask.

I had to say something to hide my sudden shyness. I pointed to the stout trunks of the trees, the strange knives-like blades atop bare branches. "Why are those called dragon trees?"

"Some species ooze a sort of red resin that has been used as a pigment since ancient time. They call this resin dragon blood."

"How peculiar."

"Surprisingly, these trees are in the same botanical family as asparagus." He lowered his head and laughed softly. "That is all I remember. I am still learning."

We walked next to each other in silence. I felt Khaled's presence next to me so violently that I had to control the shaking of my hands. The trees, the garden, the entire city of Algiers, even the war disappeared, and all I could sense was his body only feet from mine and the abyss that was the short space that separated us.

"Here we can be seen speaking to each other in daylight," he said once we were out of earshot of the old man on the bench.

"Are you actually a garden guide?" I asked.

"For a few hours a day."

"How many professions do you have? When do you ever sleep?"

"I constantly sleep," he smiled. "Usually as I work."

I laughed, "Is that what it is when I see you close your eyes in between taking orders?" He smiled, but I regretted saying this. I did not mean to let him know I spent time observing him. It seemed that around Khaled I had difficulty controlling what I said and did. "You know, I'm not worried about anyone seeing us speak," I said defiantly.

"I worry," he said.

I followed him onto a tiny path, barely a path at all, through a bamboo forest. He offered me his hand, which I took avidly. He guided me through thick vegetation, but I saw nothing; all I felt was my hand in his. We emerged out of the thickness of the bamboo forest into a small clearing the size of a very small room at the base of four tall eucalyptus trees.

"I discovered this place," Khaled said. "I come here when I need to think." The tiny clearing had a sharp menthol odor. The sun filtered through the canopy. Above, the tops of the eucalyptus swayed. A strong wind had picked up, but at the base of the trees, the air was still, and the sounds were muffled like inside a cocoon. Khaled stopped and turned to look at me. He was inches from me. I wanted him to touch me. He whispered, "All I want is to hold you in my arms."

"I want to be in your arms." I nearly begged.

My back pressed against the smooth, white bark of the eucalyptus's trunk, I let him kiss me. His kisses were nothing like what I had experienced before. I could feel them in every atom of my being. "I can't stop thinking about you," he murmured between kisses.

"Neither can I," I said.

He held me in his arms, and I surrendered to his kiss. I understood what should have been obvious from the moment I had first seen Khaled at Café Djurdjura: I would not be resisting him. There was no resistance possible.

All of a sudden, he stopped himself and stepped back from me. "I have to leave now," he said. I looked at him, confused. "If I stay longer, someone will notice that I am not at work." I was still breathless, thrilled. He caressed my cheek. "You stay here for a few minutes after I go so that no one sees us together." And he left.

I managed to make my way across the Jardin d'Essai and back to the trolley station. On the way back home, sitting on the hard leather of the trolley seat, my body swaying with the street car's meanderings, all sense of caution and reason had gone out the door. This was irrepressible. And right. I just wanted more of it; whatever "it" was I could not even name.

As I stepped out of the trolley, a violent gust of wind ruffled my hair. A corrosive mistral wind had appeared in a matter of an hour, frigid and unyielding. It pushed the tops of palms trees with increasing force. I shivered as I walked, and just after I crossed rue Michelet, I stopped, overwhelmed by a sense of catastrophe. Khaled had not made plans for us to meet again! He had not asked me! Doubt hit me with an almost physical force. I walked home against the wind, struggling to put one foot in front of the other.

That night, I lay awake on top of my blanket, replaying our encounter, the wonderfulness of being with him, the kisses, the sense of melting into one with another human being. But I was also gripped with doubt, and fear, and dejection. What if after kissing me, Khaled had lost respect or interest? What if, after kissing me, he had decided he did not like me after all?

The following day, I ran out of the apartment as soon as my father was out of the house. I was unthinking. I did not care if I was about to embarrass myself. I needed to see Khaled again. I took the trolley in the direction of the garden.

I walked around the park for an hour before I finally spotted him. He was guiding a group of older French women. I was quite far away, but I knew that he saw me. I went to wait in the clearing below the eucalyptus trees. There, I waited for fifteen minutes, out of my mind with anticipation and worry.

When he appeared, he advanced toward me as if pulled by my body's gravitational force and took me in his arms.

"You came," he said.

"Did you want me to?"

"I did not dare hope. But this is dangerous for you. Much too dangerous."

"I am not afraid," I whispered, kissing him.

The third day we met again. And again, the following day, and the next days after that.

Khaled could steal only a few minutes away from work before someone might notice his absence. Sometimes five minutes, sometimes ten, rarely more. Each day, I waited for him below the eucalyptus trees, my pulse racing. I burned with impatience, but at the same time, I could have waited in the small clearing all day with a mind devoid of other thoughts. Things that were ever-present sources of anxiety, the war, the oppression of the Jews, the terrible news from Europe, Father's well-being, Mother's bizarre descent into something that resembled insanity, now had recessed to the very back of my consciousness. I had always scoffed at the notion of love. It had seemed to me an invention, something silly girls and poets convinced themselves of, but that was merely self-delusion: an affectation. But now, I knew.

I wanted to be with Khaled more than I had ever desired anything. I knew nothing of him. But I knew his scent, his touch, the eagerness of his lips, the feel of his perfect, smooth, golden skin. And that was all that mattered to me.

Khaled had a system to meet without raising suspicion. I would make my way along the paths of the garden and eventually sit on a bench and read. I even took notes about plants as though I had an interest in botany. As soon as Khaled and I saw each other from a distance, we gave ourselves twenty minutes before meeting in the clearing, which I now referred to as our clearing. Our room.

We never had much time together. We would lie down on a blanket that we hid under thorny bushes covered with fragrant white flowers: Carissa macrocarpa, as Khaled called them. The shrub's flowers and the pungent scent of eucalyptus perfumed our encounters. Between kisses, and in our ten-minute increments, I got to learn about him.

Khaled was reluctant to talk about himself. His chin propped up on his hand, his elbow on the blanket, he spoke while studying my face, as though he was trying to unlock a mystery. I lay on my back on the blanket, my eyes lifted toward him. I too detailed his jaw, his skin, his beautiful eyelids, his brown pupils, the corners of his lips, upturned in a permanent half-smile that balanced the seriousness of his eyes. Above us, the silvery leaves of the eucalyptus canopy rustled in the wind against the bright blue sky.

"I am the eldest," he said. "We are twelve children. I have mostly sisters. My two brothers are five and three."

"What are your parents like?"

A shadow floated across Khaled's eyes. "My father is dead. I am the man in my family."

"You can't possibly be the head of a family of fourteen!"

He shrugged, "who else would be? I have no choice."

"What happened to your father?"

I had the sense that this was not a question he wanted to answer, but that he forced himself to for me. His face turned hard. "They took everything from him," he said. "They imprisoned him; they tortured him to make him talk about crimes he had not committed. Then they released him to die when he was too sick to recover."

"Who did this?" I said, outraged.

"It is in the past," he said, but the bitterness in his tone expressed the opposite.

"Tell me. Who?"

Khaled looked away. "Your people."

"My people?"

"The French," he said. His tone held anger and contempt.

"Those whom you call my people don't see me as one of them."

"Because you are Jewish?"

"How do you know that?"

"Those boys you are with," he said.

I wanted to move away from the topic of religion. I wanted to look for common ground between us, not for what could separate us even more. "How can you support so many, especially with the war?"

"Everyone in my family works, but I earn the most. Often, I sleep on the pier to be assured a morning's work mending nets after the fishing boats arrive at dawn. Afterward, I go to the sea to bathe, if I have time I go to the public bath. Then I take the trolley to work at the Jardin d'Essai. Before they fired me, I took the trolley to Café Djurdjura and worked until closing, sometimes until two in the morning."

"You sleep just a few hours a night?"

"I sleep in the trolleys too. The drivers know my family. They wake me up when I get where I need to be."

"This is much too hard," I said.

He had a bitter laugh. "When the French send me to war, I will be well prepared for it."

"How old are you?" I said, horrified at the thought.

"Eighteen soon."

"They won't give Muslims the French nationality, but they expect you to die for them?"

Khaled peered into my eyes with a burning intensity, as though he was recognizing something he had been hoping to find there.

"My father believed I needed an education as the first-born son," Khaled said. "My friends did not have to go to school, so I fought against it. But now I can see he was right. I was lucky to go to school until I was fifteen."

"But then you stopped?"

"My father was gone. It was my responsibility to earn money. For years at the garden, they only gave me chores: raking, weeding, watering." He shook his head. "I was the Arab, the nobody. Now they have fired the Jewish tour guides, and my education finally became useful."

He looked at me, and thinking perhaps that he had been insensitive toward Jews, he bent toward my face and kissed my eyelid gently. "I showed the boss that I had learned everything about the garden, and that I could read and write in French and Arabic and speak some English, and Italian, and German from working at the café. So, he hired me." He laughed softly to himself, as though this was impossible to believe. "They like me here. They trust me. My supervisor wants me to apply for a position as master groundskeeper. If I am accepted, it will pay better than all the other work I have combined. It would be a real career."

"When will you know?"

"I have to pass their tests. I borrow books from the library, and I am learning botany and biology the best I can. I need to know the names of plants in Latin, their genus, their common name. I have to recognize plants and label them, know how they will thrive, and in which part of the garden." The way Khaled spoke of plants, I could tell he was passionate about this work. And a horticulturist was a respectable profession. Already I hoped that Khaled would impress my father. "Part of it is observing, you know. And there are so many plants and families of plants. Less now with the war, but we receive samples and seeds from different nations all the time. And then we study them in the greenhouse; we grow seedlings, we propagate, we find ways to fertilize them and ways to make the soil better."

I sat up. "I can help you study," I said.

"I can manage," he said, visibly irked. "I don't need help."

"Is it because I'm a woman? You can't accept help from a woman?"

He beamed, and his face lit up. "I have angered you," he said.

"What is so funny?"

He caressed my face with his finger and then traced the contour of my lips. "What are you?" he asked.

"What am I?"

"Are you one of the bewitching Sirens of the tales? You have every power over me."

"I wish I were that magical," I said, laughing.

Khaled's eyes were so expressive, even as his face remained brooding. He began to speak as if lost in a reverie. "After I saw your family that first day at the pier, when I carried your bags, I did not see you again for months, and I did not know where I would find you, but I knew that I would one day."

"You were one of the very first people I saw in Algiers. Did you understand that we were being smuggled into the country?"

"I did not know what to think. But I saw that your family was worn out and afraid that morning. But not you. I knew that moment that you were not like other women."

"Not like Muslim women?"

"Not like any woman." He moved his face to kiss me, and I dissolved in his arms, buried my face in his neck and inhaled his scent.

"I would dream about you," he whispered in my ear. "I searched for you in the streets. I knew I should forget about you. I lied to myself; I told myself I wanted to see you just one more time, to see if the feeling would be there again, and that would be enough. And then one day you appeared at Café Djurdjura. I knew then that it was fate and that Allah wanted this."

I caressed his forearms. I wanted to be skin against skin, but that was out of the question. The risks we were taking were already enormous. We were hiding in the deep recesses of a public park. But if Khaled had discovered this secret place, others could stumble upon it too. For two young people to be found intertwined on a blanket, even fully clothed, was seen as indecent. But I was a French girl, Jewish, and he was an Algerian Arab, a Muslim, and those further transgressions might be enough to put us both in jail. At the very least, he would certainly be fired from work.

A week later, I asked Fernand to meet me on the pier, a public enough setting where we did not have to worry about the police asking us why we were there.

Now that pleasure boats had restricted access to the sea, the pier felt abandoned. I walked toward Fernand, who stood on the dock, smoking. He turned toward me and did not smile. His gray suit and hat aged him. In the nearly two years since we first met, we had stopped dressing like children and made every effort to look older than we were, but Fernand genuinely seemed aged, his flippancy now an affectation rather than genuine playfulness. The airs of his privileged youth seemed to have vanished, and in their place was an air of cold, calculating determination. This edge, this bitterness, was what war and injustice did to people.

I had declined meeting Fernand at the hotel for several weeks now, and he was perceptive enough to know that I was here to break up with him. "Are we to remain friends?" he asked before I could say anything.

"I'd like that very much," I answered. The truth was, friends were hard to come by, especially when you were Jewish, and I was not about to dispense with one if it could be helped.

"It is probably for the best, in the business we're in," Fernand said, "Better to keep the sentiments out of it."

I laughed. "I doubt that there were ever sentiments between us."

"Speak for yourself," Fernand said.

"Fernand, don't turn things around. You're the one with the fiancée."

"I am in love with you, sweetheart, and you know it," he said. "How could I not be? But you're a tough nut to crack."

"How so?"

"You don't need me. You don't seem to need anyone."

"That's not true," I said.

"A man wants to know he is loved and needed. It's never quite felt like that between us."

"Perhaps not," I admitted.

"I can't blame you for breaking up with me, darling. But if there is someone else, you better be clever about it. Choose someone who won't endanger you."

"I have no idea what you're talking about," I said. But I worried that Fernand knew exactly what he was saying, that he might be referring to Khaled, that he knew about us somehow.

He looked around, lit another cigarette, and hesitated. "This is as good a time as any to ask you something. Let's walk" he said. We walked past the moored boats, many of them in disrepair now that money was scarce, and war had shifted priorities. There was no wind, and the Mediterranean Sea was flat as oil. Buoys made dull clanging sounds as they knocked against each other. Above us, seagulls circled, cawing piercingly. "You have been useful," he began. "Your translations are precise. You don't need things explained to you: you get it. You're discreet."

"Thank you," I said warily. With Fernand, there always seemed to be a layering of motives.

"Don't thank me yet. What I'm about to ask you is something you should think twice about. We've been eyeing you for a bigger role. We're looking for…." He hesitated. "A woman's touch. A woman with your particular attributes."

"Which are?"

"There is this fellow, this German officer, in a post here in Algiers. We've been trailing the guy for months. We know his comings and goings. Some of our men have even been placed to be his bodyguards. But we need to know more about him. We need someone to get closer."

"How would that involve me?"

Fernand gazed at the horizon. "We think you might have the right kind of finesse."

"You want me to seduce a Boche?"

"Something like that."

Seducing a German officer: I let the concept sink in. "You might be overestimating my powers of persuasion," I said.

Fernand offered me a cigarette. "How could he resist a gal like you?"

I put the cigarette to my lips, and Fernand lit it. "If I'm as fetching as you seem to think, won't your Boche find it a little suspect that I would be interested in him?"

Fernand gave me one of his crooked smiles. "Darling, never underestimate the idiocy of men. We never doubt those kinds of things. He won't believe his luck and will promptly convince himself that his power and his uniform make him irresistible."

"Men can't all be that conceited."

Fernand lit his cigarette and inhaled. "For the time being, all you need to do is gain his trust."

"You mean his lust?" Fernand's response was to chuckle softly. "Don't ask me to go to bed with a German," I said. "I'm not that patriotic."

Fernand flashed that crooked smile. "We want you not to go to bed with him. As a matter of fact, we want you to resist him. We want his balls blue and his dick in a knot so that he won't be able to think."

"What is the goal?"

"No goal yet. Just thinking ahead in broad strokes. This is espionage, Marceline, infiltrate: inspire trust, all that swell stuff. Any little thing you learn might end up being of interest. How the fellow likes his lamb chops cooked. What's his favorite brand of pomade?"

"What kind of man is he?" I asked. I must have looked more worried than I wanted to appear.

Fernand shrugged it off. "Love, he's no match for you."

"Won't he be put off by the fact that I'm a Jew?"

Fernand brushed away that pesky detail with a swat of the hand. "No need to get into that. You don't look Jewish; your last name doesn't sound Jewish; there is no mention of it on your papers."

"Who is the 'we' you keep referring to? Is there really a 'we,' or is it just you?"

Fernand answered with one of his trademark questions. "You don't think I cooked this up all by my lonesome, darling?"

It dawned on me that what Fernand was asking me to do was much more dangerous than scribbling translations by the light of a candle. If caught, my false identity might be revealed, as well as that of my entire family. "I don't know about this, Fernand."

"We need a gal for this job, and you're the top choice. The clock's ticking, and we need an answer. Think about it, Marceline; the possibilities." He cocked his head and smiled. "The Wehrmacht, fooled. The outcome of the war, tilted in our favor. And at the center of it all, a beautiful Jewess."

I laughed. "Well, of course, if you put it in those terms, how could a vain girl like me resist?"

"I know that if you choose to do this, it will have nothing to do with your ego," Fernand said.

"This entire war has everything to do with ego, starting with Hitler's, De Gaulle's, Churchill's, Roosevelt's, and down to the lowliest clerk in the Vichy administration, and ultimately down to you and me."

That night at home, no one said a word as we sat around dinner. Sandra had produced yet another depressing tagine made with canned vegetables. She had waited in lines for hours, but when it was her turn, there had been no meat or fresh vegetables left, and Father did not want her to encourage the black market. As Mother, already too thin, picked at her food without appetite, and as Father held the week-old newspaper, he was reading in one hand and ate with the other, my mind floated between Khaled, Fernand, and the Boche. We all looked up in surprise when Gustave's voice broke the silence. "I've inquired about enrolling into the Chantiers de la Jeunesse," he said.

We looked at him, incredulous. The Chantiers were a sore subject. Now that the French army had been dismantled, the Pétain regime had thought of creating a sort of military service without the military. Parents would enroll their sons in training camps where for months they were made to rise before dawn, "fortify" themselves with cold morning showers, work on their musculature, and perform "character building" activities. No one would subject themselves to this by choice, or so we thought. My father lifted the palms of his hands in incomprehension. "Why?"

"I want to do something," Gustave said proudly. "I'm seventeen."

My mother patted him on the arm. "Tss, tss, don't be silly now."

Gustave's face closed. "How is that silly?"

Mother used her most patient tone. "People pay bribes to prevent their sons from being subjected to something as strenuous as it is pointless. And besides, hiking for miles carrying bags filled with stones, digging useless trenches, and cutting down perfectly good trees like a regular lumberjack: I'm afraid it might not be in your disposition, darling."

After months of our mother hardly speaking or getting out of bed, the sudden burst of motherly wisdom did not sit well with Gustave. His face reddened. He made a point to ignore her and turned to our father. "The French army is gone, and anyway they didn't want Jews. The administration won't hire Jews. The schools won't teach Jews." Gustave gave me an accusatory look. "The Resistance wants Jews but for some reason is rejecting me."

"Shhh," my father said urgently, "we should never speak of this."

"I can't wait to see you in a Jeunesse uniform," I laughed. "A bouffant pair of pants, a knee-length cape like Zorro, a cravat and a beret that looks virile on no one."

"Many suspect there's a darker design behind the whole enterprise," my father said. "They say that the Chantiers de Jeunesse's purpose was never good health and exercise, or moral fortitude for that matter, but to build the youth into better slaves to dig up German mines and repair German railways."

"That's only a rumor," Gustave protested. "The Vichy government—"

Father interrupted him. "Any organization whatsoever created by the Vichy government we should mistrust."

Sensing rising tension, Mother made a small overture. "Well, I'm sure our Gustave would enjoy the camaraderie."

Gustave turned to her savagely. "No doubt you would applaud any opportunity to have me sent away."

"But," Mother protested feebly, "quite the opposite...."

Red-faced, Gustave stood up from the table, his fists in his pockets. "I know what I'm doing," Gustave said.

"No, you do not," said my father, who was turning as pale as Gustave was red. "What I want from you is that you do nothing risky. Don't act rashly, stay home, be safe."

Gustave's voice rose. "I'm not a child!"

"You are *our* child."

"You can't expect me to stay passive. I have nothing to do."

"There is plenty to do!" Father said. "You don't need school to study. Read books; they are free at the library. Volunteer with Jewish charities; help Sandra find better food for us."

"What's the glory in that?" Gustave snapped. "When men are dying for their countries every day?"

Now Father was raising his voice too. "And so you want to die with the lot of them? What will your death bring to this world? How will it improve it?"

"I am not afraid to die," Gustave announced.

My father sat stiffly at the table, full of contained rage. He spoke to both of us. "War may seem to be all glory and big sentiments in your overheated spirits. But war is a wretched thing! A wretched, wretched thing that tears your soul apart."

"Anyway, the age to join the Chantiers is twenty, so you're too young," I said.

Gustave turned to me. "One can request a derogation to go earlier if they wish."

"We'll see about that," my father growled.

Khaled and I saw each other every day except on the weekends, when the garden and streets were more crowded. I also spent time with Fernand, André, Émile, and Béatrice as we wasted entire afternoons at café tables nursing a single drink, usually syrup and water. Even when the others were out of earshot, Fernand did not mention the German mission. When I asked, he said that things were shaping up and to be ready for a day trip on a moment's notice. But nothing was happening, and so I forgot about it. I was so immersed in my love for Khaled that I couldn't give thought to much else. My entire days were governed by plotting my next escape so that I could run to the garden and see him.

When we were together, Khaled and I were starved for each other's physical presence, even if we had met just the day before. We wanted to learn about each other's thoughts and dreams, looking for common desires, for proof that we were on the same path. Our moments together were too brief. There was the ever-present risk of being discovered, compounded with the logistics of his work. He could not leave his post for very long, and so I spent a good deal more time in our secret clearing alone waiting for him than I spent with him. I was mad with craving for him. But being with him was a mix of agony and pleasure. I wanted his kisses, yes, but I wanted more. As inflamed as our kisses were, Khaled had impressive self-control and remained in every way a gentleman. It would have been inconceivable for me to be as forward as I wanted to be for fear of pushing him away. The frustration we felt expressed itself in arguments. We argued almost from day one, not as adversaries but as two passionate people bringing forth our differences and daring each other to meet halfway.

"I don't care about consequences," I told him one day as we lay down on our blanket. "I am not ashamed of being with you."

Khaled kissed my hair and said, "You do not care about consequences because you have never suffered any."

I pouted. "You sound like my brother."

"Your brother is wise."

"My brother would advise me against seeing you."

"And here again it would be wisdom." Khaled sighed deeply. "I am the crazier of us both. You refuse to imagine the consequences if we are discovered, whereas I know the consequences, and yet it does not stop me."

"And so, what if you are fired from this job. You are educated, intelligent. My father is a foreigner too. He managed. You could blend in if you tried. There is no stopping what you could do. You could become a lawyer, a banker, anything you wish—"

Khaled stared at me mockingly. "Blend in? Your culture is not something I aspire to blend into."

"Why not?"

He shook his head in amused disbelief. "This is the arrogance of the French mindset."

"What are you talking about?"

"I would like you to truly see my people, Marceline. See them when they are not serving the French. Our culture is ancient and beautiful. Or was, until it became one of servitude to the French colonizers."

"Haven't the French helped by—"

"Do you imagine my people want to be under French rule any more than the French want to be under German rule?"

"It isn't the same at all," I said, indignant.

Khaled spoke in a calm voice, but I could feel the rage behind the words. "Do you believe that we welcome happily the injustice done to us? Do you think we are glad that our land was stolen from us, our civilization upended? Do you think we want to be ruled by Catholics?"

"But look at all the positive things the French have brought to North Africa."

He shook his head in dismay. "Name one."

"The architecture, the buildings!"

"Where only the French and the Jews can afford to live?"

"How about museums? Gardens like this one, the education system, medicine?"

"We had our own. We don't want to be French, Marceline. Nothing about it appeals to us – not the way of thinking, not the way of conduct, not the principles, not the customs, not the clothing, not the food, not the music, not the medicine, not the religion, not the industrialization. We have our way of doing things, and we prefer it. Is that so hard to imagine?"

"But civilization!"

"Ha. That word. Here it comes! You call yourself civilized and us barbaric because it serves your purpose not to understand us. We are civilized. We have a civilization! You people have bastardized the word. And your education is not freely given to all. Do you know why that is?"

"No."

"Arab children don't get educated so that we can remain slaves to the ruling class, less than human."

"And why would the French want your people to be less than human?"

"That way you can do everything with us that pleases you. You can tell yourself that our rights and needs are less than your own. You can tell yourself that we can't be educated. You can convince yourself that we do not have the same emotions as you. Human emotions."

"I didn't mean to offend you," I said. "It's only that I see you as different from other Muslim men."

"I don't believe I am any different. I don't aspire to be."

"Usually Arab men aren't as ambitious as you are." As I said this, I already knew that I sounded bigoted.

"Most of us work incredibly hard and still live in near misery. And if we don't work, it's only because there is no work to be had. If we aren't educated, it's because your people have made it nearly impossible to be. We are starving. Families have to put their children to work as soon as they are old enough. No one can afford to have children spend their day in school until they're twenty."

I should have apologized at that point, but I continued. "You seem to aspire to something greater."

Khaled was angry. "My people aspire to greatness just as much as anyone. And we are a great people already, not some lesser class." He spoke with fury. "Do you have any idea of what it's like to be a Muslim in Algeria? Do you know how vulnerable my countrymen feel? In the span of one hundred years, we have gone from a flourishing, vibrant culture to becoming nothing in our own land."

"I was only asking a question."

"The police are French. The laws that rule us are made in France. The politicians who run this town are French people with no sensibility to our land or our culture and no understanding or respect for it. And yet French education is denied to us. The entire justice system is slanted against us. For people like me, there is danger at every turn. I could be arrested just for walking in the street having committed no other crime than to exist. And if I were arrested, what would become of my mother? And my brothers and sisters? It pleases you to see my people as inferior and think of me as the exception. But I am not different than they are. I am who I am because of my poverty, because of my religion, because of the last hundred years of injustice toward my brothers."

"Don't put me into the same bag as the people you loathe," I said. "Remember that I am Jewish. I am their victim as well. So don't be angry with me."

"You have done nothing, it is true, yet your thinking is corrupted. You see the world in terms of classes, and you don't want your thoughts rearranged."

I put my head against his chest, wanting to be forgiven. I knew he was right, but it was not in my nature to back down in a disagreement. "Still, though. You believe your country was better before, but you've never known Algeria without the French. How do you know that it wasn't worse?"

He took me in his arms and said, "Well, maybe the French will learn to feel German one day."

"Never!"

"Your children might. If they have never known it any other way."

"Perhaps Christian children would. Being Jewish, my future children's chance of integration would be nil."

"Then you know how we feel. The French and the Germans have similar ancestry, a similar faith. Assimilation is possible. But Arabs were seen as inferior by the French colonizer one hundred years ago, and today is no different. And that is how they see the Jews now. Meanwhile, Jews and Arabs look down at each other and neither Jews nor Arabs consider marrying each other."

"You don't know that for a fact."

"Ask your parents how they feel about it."

"My mother is not a good example," I said. "To her, no one will be good enough for me. Unless I marry a Baron."

"Who is this Baron?" he said, glowering.

I laughed, "Oh, any baron will do. Even an ugly one three times my age. My mother is not picky in that regard."

"Why not a prince?" he asked. He was laughing now, and I was relieved.

"That's what I say!" I put my arms around his neck. "I already have my prince."

We lay side by side and looked up at the swaying treetops and cloudless sky, holding hands. After a while, he said, "We are here, you and me, in our clearing. And the shade of these trees is for both of us, and the birds sing for both of us. In front of nature, in front of God, we are the same. But in the world of men, things are different. In the world of men, I could never be one of your people, and you could not become one of mine."

"Why are you saying that?"

"I am reminding myself. Sometimes I want to forget."

"First, it's not true. We can be what we want."

"No, we cannot. Look around."

"The world changes faster than we can imagine. That's what my father always says."

"It changes for the worse."

"Not always," I said, not believing it as I said it. "Sometimes the world changes for the better."

Fernand came to me the following day. Instructions, he said, would come at a moment's notice, but I needed to set up a pretext to be gone for the day so I could take a train to nearby Oran sometime that week. "Dress to look attractive but respectable, the kind of girl you introduce to your parents," he had said.

I told my family that I was spending the day with Béatrice. We'd be looking through town for things that were hard to come by: good soap, nail polish, ointments, shampoo. My parents were too preoccupied with their own lives to pay much attention.

Three days later, I was on a crowded train to Oran. At the station, the day before, Fernand had handed me a third-class ticket for Oran, and a first-class ticket for the way back to Algiers. I was to have my 'chance' encounter with the Boche on the way back.

When I entered the third-class car, the Arab men, women, and children around me, pressed shoulder to shoulder, turned silent. I sat in a wooden seat by a window. The air was hot and sticky. I was ridiculously overdressed in my pearls, my small hat tilted to the right, and the gray flannel A-line skirt and belted jacket stolen out of Mother's closet and re-cut, re-sewed and re-purposed by Sandra at my insistence. As crowded as the car was, with many people having to stand most of the way, no one even attempted to sit next to me.

When the train began to move, conversations resumed. I observed the women in their white cloaks and headscarves. Many had children in their laps, and at their feet were bags of belongings. The women spoke to each other but not to the men. The men's faces were profoundly sun-weathered. The adults did not look at me. Only the children observed me by turning around in their seats, although when I smiled at them, they did not smile back. In fact, many of the children looked at me with defiant hostility.

I thought of the Boche, of the mission, a mission I had no doubt would fail. I was an attractive young woman, but I knew nothing of what might seduce a man. And besides, I hated the Germans. Every last one of them. How could my demeanor not show it? To me, there was no such thing as a decent German, no matter how friendly they pretended to be. I saw them as a monolithic block of evil warmongers, and I'd sooner see all Boches dead than have to change my opinion about even a single one of them. As the train bumped along, I tried to keep my mind on the mission ahead, but the angry stares of the children unsettled me. Was that hatred I read in their eyes? I thought of what Khaled had told me, and it dawned on me that I was their invader. I was *their* Boche. Whatever politeness or friendliness I had experienced on their part, and accepted as my due, must have been no more sincere than the obsequiousness most of us adopted in dealing with the Germans. I hated our invaders with all my might. And as I sat stiffer in my seat among these people, Khaled's people, I had the sickening feeling that they felt the same about me.

****

I had boarded the nine-a.m. train for Oran and arrived there a few hours later with no idea what was about to unfold. I could not imagine the stakes being high, perhaps because Fernand and I seemed little more than children.

But when the train arrived in Oran, and I saw Fernand through the window, I had a sinking feeling. He had his hands in his coat pocket and his hat pulled down over his forehead. He looked tense, dark, unsmiling, and very much like an adult. I understood in an instant that this was not a game, and if it was, it was the kind that could cost us our lives.

He helped me down the steps and spoke fast, under his breath. "You'll be boarding in two hours. He's already on the train, coming from Tlemcen. We know which car he's in, and we've arranged for you to get a seat there." He handed me a first-class ticket to Algiers.

"I don't know the first thing about him."

"It's better that way. So nothing can slip by accident. We don't know why he's in Algeria. We know he's an engineer. Did he pull favors to get himself a cushiony assignment in Algiers away from combat, or did Hitler send him? Why would Hitler send engineers to Algiers? These are all things we want you to find out."

"How could I? Fernand, this is ridiculous!"

"Just relax. For now, just be yourself. We simply want you to meet and hope for sparks."

"And afterward?"

"Get close to him."

"You know there will be limits as to how close I am willing to get."

Fernand was irritated. "Either you do this, or you don't. I vouched for you. I told people you were the right gal for the job."

"I, yes. I am. I'll do it. But what if the Boche isn't interested in me?"

Fernand dismissed the possibility entirely. "You'll have him eating out of the palm of your hand in no time. One thing, though…."

"Yes?"

"We have friends on the train, watching over you. In case things turn sour."

"I need protection?" I said, stiffening as I scanned the platform.

"Don't look," Fernand urged, but already I had spotted at various distances from us a burly boy on a bench smoking a cigarette, his hat firmly screwed on to mask his eyes, and another young man with his face buried in a newspaper. A third one was conspicuously staring at his cuticles. All three were very young; one of them did not look a day over sixteen. All made brief eye contact with me and then looked away. "They'll be boarding when you do," Fernand said. "You're in no danger; this is just an insurance policy. Remember, you're just a pretty girl boarding a train. If anyone wants to see your papers when you get into his car, let them see them and don't sweat it. He's got bodyguards, but this is not an occupied zone. They have no jurisdiction."

Air got caught in my lungs, and I forgot to breathe for a moment. Was there still a way to back out of this? But the excuses I could think of felt weak. *Just a girl boarding a train*, I repeated to myself. "What's his name?" I asked in what I hoped to sound like a self-assured voice. "Where in Germany is he from?"

"It's better for you to know nothing about him. Let him tell you all this. You're a student. You're a good girl. You have a nice mom and nice dad, a darling little brother. Don't say anything else for now. We'll come up with a solid cover; we'll even sign you up for school if he takes the bait."

I frowned. "So what do I do exactly? Talk to him? Introduce myself? Strike up a conversation?"

"Marceline, you're supposed to make him fall in love with you."

With these words, Fernand retrieved a package wrapped in brown paper out of his coat pocket, pushed it into my hands, turned around, and left.

I stood rigid, alone on the platform. What was I holding? The package was a bit heavy and rectangular, like a book perhaps, but with a small bulge in the center. To my left and my right, the young men were nowhere to be seen. I tried to control my growing panic. I could leave right now. Throw the package in the trash. Take the next train. Go home and forget about the delusion that had brought me here in the first place. But almost immediately, the train entered the station, and when it stopped, I was facing the first-class cars. People came down from the train; others went up the steps and disappeared inside. And for a moment, I stood as if frozen. I looked at the steps. There was no time to think. I took a breath, stood straighter, and climbed aboard.

Inside the first-class car, it was all polished brass and woodwork, as luxurious as the third class had been sparse. Plush green velvet covered the seats. The windows were open to let in the breeze, and it smelled of powdery women's perfume. Each compartment was composed of two rows of three seats that faced each other. The train was full, and each seat was taken, with more people standing in the corridors. Looking at the number above each sliding glass door, I walked to the number of the compartment marked on my ticket.

Two men with square jaws stood in front of the compartment as if guarding the door. I did not doubt that they were police or military. I heard them speak in French. Through the glass, I saw the German officer who sat by the window. The only two other people in the compartment were an old husband and wife. Three seats were left open, the one by the window across from him, and the two seats for his bodyguards, who seemed intent on remaining in the corridor. Right then I lost my nerve, what little I had, and walked right past the compartment. My rookie escorts, if they had not already scampered away, were no match for these men.

Suddenly, the train shook and rumbled. Almost immediately after, it began to move out of the station. I was deep into this now. What else could I do at this point but sit in my assigned seat? I did not have to say a single word. I could sit there and wait for the train to take me to Algiers. I would tell Fernand that the Boche had not even looked at me. Maybe he didn't like women after all.

I headed for the bathroom, my heart beating along with the rhythm of the accelerating train, my fingers gripping the package.

In the bathroom, I opened the package. No gun or bomb, thank goodness. In fact, I wanted to laugh when I saw a school textbook and a tube of contraband lipstick. Chanel! I opened the tube. The intoxicating scent, the sight of bright red plunged me back into the world of before, the world of small luxuries and vanities, the world where people did not fear for their lives. With a surprisingly steady hand I applied the lipstick and smiled at my reflection. Fernand, that scalawag, knew what he was doing. The lipstick changed my look from teenage girl to a captivating cross between a studious young woman and budding femme fatale – or so I hoped!

I exited the bathroom, walking past two of my escorts, who must have climbed on the train behind me. It was nice to know I wasn't alone. I walked toward my compartment with flutters in my stomach. The guards didn't move away from the door as I stopped in front of the compartment. "My seat is in here I believe," I told them.

"Show us your ticket," one of the men said, "and your papers."

I presented the men my ticket and papers, ready to dart away, wishing they would deny me entry. They must not have seen me as too big of a threat because they barely glanced at them before letting me inside the compartment.

The German man I was supposed to seduce rose and saluted me with gallantry. He was not the portly, balding, heinous Nazi I had pictured, but an intellectual-looking young man in his early thirties, acne still haunting his face. I smiled with what I hoped to be sufficient coyness and sat across from him.

The older couple nodded at me, then ignored me. The wife occupied herself with crossword puzzles. The husband promptly fell asleep. In the corridor, the bodyguards stood by a pulled window smoking, throwing their butts out into the dry landscape every so often.

The train ride from Oran to Algiers would take five whole hours. I had no idea what to do next. For fifteen interminable minutes, I stared out the window, seeing nothing, trying to look normal, but not remembering what normal was supposed to look like. I felt the German soldier's gaze on me but could not be sure. Once the pounding of my heart subsided, I took out Fernand's book from my purse. It was an engineering textbook. I pretended to read for a few minutes, but it might just as well have been written in Japanese. I scrunched up my face and soon closed the book with a sigh.

"Forgive my impudence, Mademoiselle," he said, unable to resist such serendipity, "but are you pursuing engineering studies?" He spoke an accented but polished French.

I blinked, appeared hesitant to speak and said, "Architecture, as a matter of fact." Instinctively I had changed the pitch of my voice to sound younger, and I guess stupider. "To be honest, I understand none of it."

"It is a fascinating field, and so useful especially in our times," he said.

I pouted, "How will I become an architect's secretary if I cannot understand all the geometry."

"Oh, but you must not get discouraged," he said, his eyes glimmering with earnestness. "The architect bothers with all this; you only need to learn to support him in his work."

"I just started my classes, and I obviously know nothing yet," I said. "I'm not even certain that this is what I want to do."

"It's a matter of discovering your aptitudes. I am an engineer myself," he said.

I batted my eyelashes. "Did you always know you had aptitudes?" I asked.

We conversed for the rest of the trip. I was keenly aware of the men standing guard on the other side of the glass door. They would glance at me every so often, not with suspicion, but with amusement, perhaps contempt. The German's thrill to speak to me was almost painful to watch. I measured my every word and tried to appear reticent. I had to. He was, after all, the occupier, and any other behavior on my part would have been suspect or else a show of poor respectability. I told him I had visited an aunt in Oran for the day and was going back home in Algiers. I said as little as I could about myself. I was a student. I had a brother. My father was in the import business. He said he was from Heidelberg, describing it as a small paradise. I acted pleasantly and listened with feigned interest to his exposé on the thrills of engineering. What I found trickiest was to act demure. The things women must do and say to appear unthreatening to men are harder to master than one would think.

By the end of the journey, as the train rolled into Algiers, we still had not exchanged names. One thing was clear to me: he had to pursue me, not the other way around. He liked me; this much was obvious, but he was no ladies' man, and I wondered if he would muster the courage to ask me out. Because yes, it was a game indeed. And I wanted to win.

He gave me his hand to help me out of the train and offered to give me a ride home. I declined. No well-bred young French woman would enter the car of a stranger alone. He walked me to the taxi station and introduced himself at last. "*Oberleutnant* Dietfried Von Becker," he said. Here I was, a nineteen-year-old Jewish girl with a fake identity, flirting with a Senior Lieutenant of the Wehrmacht. He offered me his hand to shake. "I – had a lovely time making your acquaintance, Mademoiselle—"

"Marceline Dupont," I said, shaking his hand, but he took it instead and reddened as he pressed his lips to my glove with cringeworthy eagerness. He was just being a shy, awkward boy, courting a girl. He was German, and he was the enemy, but I felt that there was nothing monstrous about poor Dietfried. "It was lovely to speak to you too," I said, smiling for added encouragement. To this, he responded by opening his mouth and closing it without uttering a sound. He held the door to the taxi for me, and I entered slowly to give him more time. If he let me go now, that was it, the so-called mission was a failure, but Dietfried made no move.

"Au revoir, Mademoiselle Dupont," he said.

"You can call me Marceline," I said as pleasantly as I could, though inside I was fuming about his ineptitude. Because now I *wanted* this. It had been the highest of highs, and in the last few hours I had discovered one thing about myself: I definitely had the nerve. The door was shut. The taxi began moving. I was furious. This fool's golden opportunity was missed, and my exciting career as a spy over before it started. But just as the car moved a few meters, there was an urgent rap at the glass. I ordered the driver to stop and rolled down the window.

"I was wondering," Dietfried said, red in the face. "I am new to Algiers. I don't know anyone in the city, and I … well, you were so kind. I was wondering if you could recommend…." He tried to think of something to add. "Good local restaurants."

"There are many excellent ones. Now, of course, with the restrictions, things have changed. I guess I could write down addresses for you. I don't know them by heart."

"Perhaps I could telephone you some time," he suggested. "Or you could telephone me?"

"Well, I'm not sure how…."

"I apologize, I often forget that not everyone has a personal telephone."

Although Father had a Bakelite telephone installed at the apartment the month of our arrival, I pretended to be impressed. "A personal telephone? I suppose that if you gave me your details, I could call you from a phone box."

"Please do!" Emboldened, he tore a piece of paper out of a notepad in his coat pocket and handed me his number. "Thank you, so very much!" He added ridiculously, "I shall be standing next to the telephone day and night waiting for your call." He tried to make it sound like a wisecrack, but both of us knew he meant it.

"I will call you tomorrow," I said.

As the taxi drove me away from Dietfried, I felt exhilarated with power.

I asked the taxi to drop me off on rue Michelet, and I walked on clouds the rest of the way. When I arrived in front of my family's apartment building, Fernand was leaning against the entrance door, waiting for me.

"I better sign up for school," I said, beaming.

"You talked to him?"

"We practically have a date," I said.

Fernand whistled admiringly. "Good girl," he said. "I knew you'd be great at this. We're going to build you a cover solid as bedrock, I promise."

"You better," I said. "Now I better run upstairs. I'm late for dinner."

When I entered the apartment, Sandra, who was coming out of the kitchen, gave me a forewarning look. Mother, Father, and Gustave were already sitting at the dinner table. "I'm sorry I'm late," I chirped, sliding in my chair. My father didn't look at me, but Gustave's thrilled expression told me I was in trouble. Mother lifted her face mournfully and stared through me with vacant eyes. Since her diagnosis of anhedonia, the cocktail of medicine prescribed by our doctor made her agitated to the point of paranoia during the day and useless by dinnertime. Apparently, the Benzedrine had worn off, and the Barbital she took for sleeping had kicked in. Throughout dinner, the only sounds were the clicking of forks on plates. I would have preferred punishments and admonitions than the strained silence that weighed on me through dinner. Before Sandra bought our mint teas, Mother rose from the table and walked to her room like a somnambulist.

As soon as she had left the room my father said, "I did not want to upset your mother, but now I want an explanation about why you were out in the streets until that hour."

"I was spending the day with Béatrice."

"To go where?"

"We were looking for shampoo."

"Until past dinner time? And where is that shampoo?"

I said the first lie that came to my mind. "We didn't find any, so we decided to visit the Jardin d'Essai," I said. "And then we got held up."

My father would have none of this. "Held up by whom? Bandits?"

"We were just … our trolley broke down, and we had to wait for them to repair it."

Father crossed his arms. "And if I were to call Béatrice's house, her mother would attest to this?"

I looked at him with innocence. "Yes," I said.

"Only I already called," he said, clearly furious. "She said Béatrice stayed home and neither of them saw you all day."

I took the offensive. "I am nineteen. You have no right to spy on me!"

"I have every right!" my father snapped. He was yelling at me but silently, so as not to upset Mother, and the result was almost comical.

"Baba was not spying," Gustave said, taking it upon himself to defend my father. "He was worried."

"Stay out of this, Gustave!" I said. "Baba doesn't need an interpreter."

"You think you can get away with everything," Gustave said.

"I don't want to hear that you have any more involvement with those factions," my father said.

I looked askance at Gustave. "I thought you said never to speak of It in front of him." 'It' was the Resistance, the word that must not be pronounced at home. Gustave looked at me with hatred.

"Those people don't know what they're doing," my father continued. "They're mere children playing with your life."

My father's statement rocked my confidence for a moment. Did he know something I didn't? But the German officer was real. The intelligence about the train, the plan, none of this had been child's play. What if Fernand was mistaken about my father's involvement in the Resistance? If my dad was part of the Resistance, would he try to stop Gustave and me from getting involved in something he believed in strongly enough to risk his safety? If the Resistance was too dangerous for us, wasn't it also too dangerous for him? In a split second, I decided to feign the innocence of the wrongly accused. "I'm late for dinner. When has it ever happened before? Never. And now you're reading me the riot act?"

Gustave chimed in, "If they stop you after curfew and they ask to see your identity papers, you put Baba and all of us at risk."

"Don't be a hypocrite, Gustave," I said. "You do plenty to put us at risk, sniffing in affairs that do not concern you, knocking at every door to join the … group."

My father stood up from the table. He looked at Gustave, his rage barely contained. "I forbade you to go near Géo Gras!"

My father's tone, his outrage, struck me as ridiculously unfair, especially if he was indeed knee-deep in the Resistance.

"If Gustave wants to be heroic, then let him embarrass himself," I said.

"I have every right to help our cause," Gustave snapped.

In one tremendous bang that had Gustave and me jumping up in shock, my father slammed both fists against the table, toppling wine glasses, and sending the salt shaker onto the floor. "Enough! Both of you!" He stood there, red-faced, beside himself with fury, he who was usually so soft-spoken and measured. He shouted, "I'll tell you how you can help our cause! By remaining alive! You want allegiance to something, both of you? Have allegiance to me!" Sandra hurried into the room and looked at him with surprise and pain. Perhaps my father realized then that he was shouting. He lowered his voice, but the fury was palpable in his every word. "Focus on your family. Keep yourself alive! Pointless bravado will never make you a hero. It will make you a dead person." Staring at Gustave, he said, "You want to be heroic? I'll give you a mission: watch your foolish sister's every move and make sure she stays out of trouble."

I jumped to my feet, enraged. "If Gustave puts his nose in my affairs, I will kill him with my bare hands."

My father, at his wit's end, said, "If Gustave doesn't stop you, I will. Starting with forbidding you to take a single step out of this apartment." He looked at Sandra, who was standing stiffly by the door, and he seemed to have an epiphany. "In fact, I am implementing some changes starting immediately."

My father told me to make space in my bedroom for Sandra's things. "Now you will share a room with Sandra," he said in a tone that didn't tolerate contradictions.

"Baba! Why on earth?"

"That way, you won't get any ideas about going out at night."

As he said this, Sandra, looking apologetic, was entering my room with a bag, blankets, and pillows. Following behind was Gustave, dragging her mattress.

I sat on a chair looking falsely contrite. I was not worried about Sandra sharing my room, but it was better if they believed they had won the battle.

After they had left my room, I watched Sandra put her bed together. "You won't say a word about me to anyone, will you?" I asked her.

Sandra looked at me. Her eyes were kind, but she looked torn. "Your father has told me to look over you," she said.

"Whose side are you on?" I said. "You know he has no reason to fear for my safety. So, I have a boyfriend, big deal. You've covered for me before, and this is no different. I'll have you know that I plan to continue to do as I see fit."

"If you do things your father and mother do not like, I must tell them," she said.

"Do you really want to be the bearer of bad news to poor Mother?"

Sandra gave me a pleading look. "Please, Marceline, do not go out at night. It is all I ask."

I put my arm around her. "Let's you and I come to an agreement. You let me do what I want during the day, and I promise to stay home at night."

She did not agree nor disagree, as was her habit.

Prudently I waited for things to settle, and I did not return to see Khaled for three days. On the fourth day, I told Mother and Sandra that I was going to study at the library with Béatrice – my usual excuse – and jumped on the trolley in the direction of the Jardin d'Essai. Just in case Gustave had taken my father's ridiculous orders to heart, I devised a convoluted way to get to the garden, taking four different trolleys and buses, looking behind me to make sure he was not following. I told myself I ought to be more careful. But I was high with euphoria and denial. I was giddy; this was April 15th, the one-month anniversary of our first meeting at the clearing. I was carrying a basket, a picnic lunch that I had managed to sneak out of the house, with real cheese Sandra had found at the market and homemade bread.

There was a new balminess to the air. Khaled and I lay on our blanket, ate our cheese and bread, and kissed. Khaled had been more of a gentleman than all the boys I had met until now. He had not even attempted anything other than a kiss. I could tell this was not out of shyness on his part, but a choice. We were talking about this and that. I lied to him about the reason I had not been able to come and told him that I had been visiting Oran with my family.

"There are many beautiful mosques in Oran," he said. "Have you visited them?"

"I did not know that was allowed."

"Mosques are for everyone."

The subject of our respective religions was one we carefully avoided. I told myself I didn't want to dwell on it, and that it didn't matter, but really, I was worried about the topic. "Do you spend a lot of time in mosques?" I asked tentatively.

"I rarely have the time," he said.

"And so … you're not very religious?"

"I don't need to be in a certain place to feel Muslim," Khaled answered. "Islam is who I am, how I see the world. Islam is everywhere. It inhabits everything."

"Same for me," I said, relieved. "I'm not practicing, but I know down in my bones that I am Jewish. But thousands of years of beliefs and traditions only define me up to a point. I would not want to be narrowed down to some clichés if I were Christian or Muslim either. Why do people want so terribly to belong to a group? Does that reassure them? It does not reassure me! Is people's sense of identity so tenuous that they crumble if they don't classify themselves and align themselves with one religion or another?"

Khaled looked at me with an amused expression. "You are speaking of the political," he said. "I am speaking of the mystical."

"The what?"

"My connection to Allah."

Khaled had a connection to Allah? I did not have a connection to Adonai or anything of the sort. "Do you ever feel that you might be betraying your religion when you are with me?" I asked.

"No," he said thoughtfully. "Not yet."

"Religion is not significant to French Jews," I said, not even knowing whether it was true. "We mostly had to brush our religion aside. To be French, you know."

"So why do you spend all your time with other Jews?"

"Who else will have us?" I said dryly. "Muslims hate us, Christians hate us. I'm not ashamed of being Jewish if that is what you are asking."

He smiled. He had seen the anger rise in me. He seemed attuned to my emotions and could discern what I was feeling even before I could. He moved strands of my hair between his fingers. "Why would I think that?"

"Judaism is nothing like people depict it," I said. "We are not how the world sees us!"

"Is your faith strong?"

I deflected the question. "Religions bring people further from spirituality, not closer. Immoral men invented religions so that they could rule over the moral ones."

"Even so, humans need God to fill the sense of void we all feel inside. It is a void that nothing else can fill."

"I have faith in men," I said. "I know, it seems unlikely at the moment. But I believe that if a single evil man can alter the course of things and destroy the world, a single good man – or maybe a woman – can repair it."

"Like Jesus?"

"Like Tikkun Olam."

"Who is that?"

"It's not a person; it's an idea. It's not about the heavenly afterlife for us Jews. Tikkun Olam means to repair the world; it's the positive impact we can have in the here and now that matters. Not that I've had much personal success with this."

He looked at me tenderly. "You need to do nothing other than walk on this Earth to make it better," he said.

We lay on our backs, our hands intertwined, watching clouds move briskly in the azure sky between the treetops. Already, it was time to go. How long had we been together? No more than fifteen minutes. It felt like an instant. It felt like a lifetime.

Khaled left the clearing. I waited ten minutes and left too. I walked down the alleys toward the exit in the dizzying state my encounters with Khaled always left me, but today, I also felt uneasy. Per Fernand's instructions, I was to telephone Dietfried that afternoon.

It had been four days since our meeting on the train, and I had had time to think about the mission. If it came about that Nazi Germany swallowed all of Europe, my father's plan was to flee. He spoke of going deeper into Africa, all the way to South Africa if need be. Me, I wanted justice. I wanted to win the war. I wanted to crush them all. I wanted Hitler and all his generals, the anti-Semites, the racists, the bigots, the cowards, the crooks, everyone in the Vichy government, the haters, the monsters of this world vanquished. I wanted them to suffer. I wanted to see corpses and skulls riddled with bullet holes. I would fire those bullets myself if I had to. I wasn't naïve. I knew that I was about to engage in something I would not be able to control. I also knew that I would disappoint people I loved if they saw me with a German officer. My family and Khaled would be devastated to learn that I was spying for the Resistance, but even more so if they thought that I was fraternizing with the enemy, and I would not be able to justify myself without revealing my mission. The thing was, neither my father nor Khaled would take too well to the news that I spent time with a Nazi, whatever the noble reason for it.

I passed the central pond and walked in the shade of the cypress trees. Was I effectively becoming a spy? This would mean paying closer attention to details beyond my narrow field of vision. In the last few years, we had learned to suspect everything and everyone; we made sure not to speak when we could be heard. Now I needed to become even more vigilant. For one, I needed to be certain that no one followed me. I needed to watch people better in case suspicious faces sprang up in too many places. Also, I was too visible, too young, too well-dressed. I needed to dress down, put a shawl over my hair, blend in.

Rather than follow the main path toward the exit, I veered left to the area that cut through a patch of dense strelitzia. As a mental exercise, I tried to archive in my mind all the smells, sights, and sounds around me.

But some smells, sights, and sounds must have escaped me because as I came through the strelitzia and stepped into the alley, I suddenly found myself face to face with my brother! He appeared as shocked to see me as I was to see him. "What are you doing here?" I shrieked.

He had his hand on his bicycle. There was sweat on his forehead, as though he had been riding up a hill. His shorts revealed strong calves from the incredible amount of bicycle riding he did up and down the streets of Algiers, as though he were training for the Tour de France. "Same as you," he said. But the real answer came in the redness of his face and the guilt in his eyes.

"You were following me!"

Gustave tried to sound casual, "Stop thinking you are so special that I would care what you do."

How long had he been following me? No, it was impossible. Not after the circuitous route I took to get here. And then I remembered: the day I had gone to Oran I told my father that I had been visiting the Jardin d'Essai. Either this was a coincidence, and my brother had wanted to visit it as well, or Gustave had come here looking for me. The second option was most likely the correct one, or he would not be here, looking guilty. Anger rose through my body. "Oh, but you care," I said, furious. "You're obsessed with me in fact."

Gustave shoved his hands in his pocket to look unconcerned. Using the tone of a mature man he said, "It's not safe for a girl to roam the city the way you do. You should be appreciative that I keep an eye on you."

I stepped toward him menacingly. "I don't need defending; I'm not a damsel in distress like in a stupid book. Get that notion out of your head. If anyone needs defending, it's you, no matter how many push-ups you can do."

He scoffed at this with an arrogance I wanted to slap off his face. "Why would I need defending?"

"I've been defending you since you were six years old, stupid," I said, spitting out my words. "It's always been like that. You can't get anyone to like you or trust you. People want to beat you up. If it weren't for me, the men of Géo Gras would have given you a beating already."

He seemed taken aback by my meanness. He stuttered, "You – You're – conniving, you – use people. You care about no one but yourself."

"And you're nothing but a wimpy baby with bulging muscles and a scraggly mustache!"

Now his eyes were red, as though he might very well cry. "You don't help Mother at all!" he exclaimed.

I was puzzled by this lame accusation. "Mother needs to take care of herself," I said. "She's the parent and not the other way around. You take care of Mother if you're so inclined, only you despise her more than I do."

Gustave stood taller and said haughtily, "Father does not know half of the ways in which you are degrading yourself, and I am the one you should thank for that."

I wondered if he was referring to the time he saw me leave the Hotel de Paris after seeing Fernand, or if he knew about Khaled, or if he had seen me step out of a train with a German officer. Just what was the extent of his spying on me?

Siblings fight. It's innocent at first. But parents often dismiss children's rivalries. My parents noticed nothing out of the ordinary in the increasing fighting between my brother and me, or if they did, they did not act. "Like oil and water," they would say. "Like nitro and glycerin, those two," as my father used to joke before the war. Parents say those kinds of things. They might refuse to take sides, or are reluctant to take on the role of mediator, or are too preoccupied with their own concerns. Perhaps they see one child as the victim and the other the aggressor, or they consciously or unconsciously favor one child over the other. The result is the same. Over the years, the resentment between the children grows. The original offense, now forgotten, is never digested. The differences become intractable. At times, it can come to the point when siblings turn on each other as viciously as rival countries at war.

My father made a terrible mistake by empowering Gustave with the responsibility of watching over me. Between my mother's illness and my father's relative absence, I had gotten a taste of freedom at a dangerous time. I thought that I needed no one's help and that no one should get in my way. Also, I was in love. Like the fox that chews his own paw to get out of a trap, I would have done anything to see Khaled.

As I faced Gustave, I wondered if he saw me disappear into the clearing and reappear from it. Did he know what Khaled looked like? Had he seen him at Café Djurdjura? Would he put two and two together if he spotted Khaled working in the garden? I hated and dreaded him immensely at that moment. I watched Gustave's uneasy smirk. And I did not see his loneliness, his self-doubt, his desire to gain my father's approval and closeness. I ignored the fact that perhaps he too was grasping at straws in this disintegrating world. I only saw that he was getting in my way, and so I attacked. Not with bombs, bullets, knives, or fists. I struck him with what I had in my possession: anger and words. In the heat of rage, I said things I would come to regret for the rest of my life. "You are the one degrading yourself by following me around," I said. "It's sick! Positively sick! Father would be embarrassed if he knew how obsessed you are with me. He'd be more ashamed of you than he already is. Yes, he is ashamed of you! He thinks you're weak. He told me so himself. Return to Mother or crumble and die for all I care but get away from me!"

Gustave blanched. His body seemed to collapse on itself. He looked at me with an expression of incomprehension and pain that I will never forget. He opened his mouth to say something, but instead, he stumbled back a few steps, turned around without a word, climbed on his bicycle, and left.

I watched my brother's silhouette recede on the dirt path. In my anger, I had forgotten that inside the body of a young man still resided the soul of an anxious child, bullied and rejected, a child who wanted to be loved – my little brother. My stomach tightened, but it was too late. The damage to our relationship was done.

That night, Gustave stayed in his room, and Mother in hers. Father did not return until the next morning. Sandra and I ate in the kitchen in silence. I told myself to suck it up. The times had no use for my crisis of conscience. France needed me.

****

Upon my return from the Jardin d'Essai, I entered a phone booth and called my German prey. It all worked exceedingly well. I gave Dietfried the names of local restaurants. He said he wished to know the city more. He did not know anyone in town, he said, and did not know where to go, and what a shame that was when the city was so rich in history. Would I serve as his guide? Dietfried sounded educated, soft-spoken, and excessively polite. He was also German and the enemy, a fact I had to keep remembering. After feigned hesitation, I agreed to give him a tour of the Great Mosque of Algiers. I scheduled that visit for two weeks later, per Fernand's instructions, to give Dietfried time to simmer and give Fernand time to iron out in his plan.

****

I met Fernand at El Bahdja, a café on a tiny street off rue d'Isly. The place was nearly empty aside from a group of old men who drank coffee and spoke in Arabic. I sat down at the wobbly table across from Fernand. The table was sticky, so I kept my hands on my lap.

"Are you hungry?" he asked.

"Just a mint tea for me."

Fernand ordered two mint teas. The plaintive voice of El Hadj M'Hamed El Anka played over the radio, and as my eyes became accustomed to the dim light and my nostrils to the pungent odors of spices and pipe tobacco, I relaxed in my chair. These days it had become easier to breathe among Muslims, away from the eyes of Europeans. The owner, a small man whose fez absorbed the profuse sweat on his brow, set his tray down on our table and poured scalding tea in our glasses. The aroma of mint and sugar spiraled up between us.

Fernand, who clearly understood the male's psyche better than I did, began to map out my artificial romance with Dietfried. "You let him take the lead," he said. "Men need to feel they are the ones doing the chase. The more demure and morally above reproach the woman is, the more compelling the conquest. Men want to take women to bed, but it's the chase that excites them. Don't believe for a second that he is an idiot. He'll spot your deceptions from a mile away. But he'll be powerless against self-deception. Pursue him, and he'll smell a rat. Resist him, and he'll manage to convince himself that he can make you fall in love with him. You'll see. Here is something," Fernand said as he placed a thick book in my hands. "The

Architecture of Algiers. You'd better learn a thing or two about the city you're supposed to know so well."

"Listen," I said, "there's an issue with my brother. He might be following me."

Fernand took a drag of his menthol cigarette and narrowed his eyes. "Is that a fact?" he smiled a dangerous smile. "I'll have a couple of our guys trail him," he said. "If he gets too close, we'll scare him away. We'll just take him off course, that little weasel."

Scare him away? I should have told Fernand nothing. I took a sip of my tea trying to act unshaken. The Arab men were still talking. Two French men entered and then exited. The café must have had a bit too much couleur locale for them. A pale man in his fifties wearing a worn fedora and a crumpled suit walked in and went to sit at the table next to us when so many other tables were available. He looked at me with uncomfortable insistence. Fernand sipped his tea and ignored him. I suddenly wondered if there wasn't something oily about Fernand. I had known him for a while now, but was I an apt judge of his character? Could I trust him? The man in the fedora ordered something and looked at me again. His face was deeply marked. He was not Arabic. Maybe Greek or Armenian. Something about him felt familiar; maybe I had seen him before. "My brother is harmless," I said. "He's only doing what my father asked him to do. My family wants to protect me. They don't even know what from."

Fernand's face hardened. "The sooner they face the fact that you are not a kid anymore, the better for you and them. In this business, you can't worry about bruising the feelings of your family members."

I stared him down. "I'll handle them," I said.

"Just make sure all your protégés stay away from our business."

My protégés? "And what business is that?"

"The business of saving the world, sweetie," Fernand said.

The fedora-wearing man got up from his chair, and on his way past me, he smiled with big white teeth and lifted his fedora to salute me. Did we know each other from somewhere? Did he work at one of the local markets maybe? Did he live near our street? Or was he just being courteous? Just in case, I smiled back. The next moment, the man was gone from the café and from my mind.

Back at home, I sat on the couch and leafed through Fernand's architecture book without much fervor. My thoughts were so much on Khaled it's a miracle I retained anything at all. Sandra walked in, carrying things for her sewing. She smiled the way she always did.

"That's it!" I said, beaming.

"What?" she asked.

"I saw a man this morning! A stranger. But he looked so familiar, I thought perhaps I knew him, but now I know why."

"Why?" she said, smiling at my excitement.

"He had your eyes! In fact, he looked a lot like you. He even smiled like you. He looked so much like you that he could pass as your brother." Sandra at that moment must have tripped. All the fabric she held in her arms fell to the floor. She stared down at the strewn clothes like she was about to cry. I kneeled to help her gather her things, but Sandra just stood there. "Are you all right?" I asked. "You don't look well."

"I don't have a brother," she snapped. She snatched the fabric out of my hands and left the room.

****

When the day came to meet Dietfried, I wasn't feeling the trepidations the situation warranted. Algiers, in a short time, had become my turf. Fernand had repeated to me that I was doing nothing grave, only meeting a man and reporting to him afterward. "Don't ask him a single question about what he does or why he is here. You are only trying to gain his trust," he had said.

I met Dietfried at the foot of the Great Mosque. "Thank you for meeting me, Marceline," he said, offering me his arm.

I mentally consulted the rulebook for Jewish girls pretending to be Christian, cross-checked it with the spy rulebook, neither of which existed, and paused only briefly before putting my gloved hand on a Nazi uniform. "The entire pleasure is mine," I said.

Only when we entered the mosque's grounds did I realize my absolute foolishness. I had no idea where we were or what to say, and I was supposed to be the guide, an architecture student! I scrambled through memories of things I had glanced at in Fernand's book. What were those domes called? What about those turrets, those markings? I had not the faintest idea how to go from one part of the mosque to the other. Why had I not rehearsed this or at least visited the place before? My only preparation had been experimenting with various hairstyles and running up and down Algiers with Sandra looking for the appropriate belt for the outfit I had planned. I banked on the hope that coming here had only been Dietfried's excuse to see me and that he would not ask questions.

"So, Marceline," he said. "What can you teach me about this famed mosque?"

In an unexpected surge of clarity that could only be attributed to alchemy in the brain brought upon by a surge in adrenalin I recited, "It is known as Djama'a al-Kebir. Its oldest parts are nearly nine hundred centuries old."

"And what is this?" he asked, pointing to a mezzanine above the entrance.

"This is the … sedda." I said, surprising myself again. "That's where the muezzin calls the men to prayer."

We entered the rectangular courtyard and walked along the arcade gallery. We entered a vast prayer hall supported by large pillars. Would more of the information I had read in Fernand's book magically come back to me? I recognized the row of alcoves with Moorish arches and exclaimed in relief, "Those are the naves. They are all perpendicular to the qiblah."

"What is a qiblah?"

What was a qiblah? "That is the – the direction of the Kaaba in Mecca. The direction people must look when they pray!" … Or something like that. It sounded right. Hopefully, Dietfried was as ignorant on the matter as he professed to be.

As our footsteps echoed on the tiled floor, we both stopped speaking. The majestic austerity of the place commanded silence. I wondered why I had not visited mosques in the past. Djama'a al-Kebir was pared down except for the few carvings of stylized plants and the occasional mosaic; its design was sober, which was very different from all the temples and churches I had visited in my life. We walked through the marble columns and down the central path, and I felt the palpable weight of centuries of faith in each stone, each mosaic, each pillar. For a moment, I forgot whom I was walking next to or why I was here. Khaled had spoken about the sense of wonderment he felt before God. Now I pictured him here, removing his shoes and kneeling among a hundred other men.

For an hour, we walked through the mosque. I soon realized that I could have said just about anything, Dietfried was hardly paying attention to the content of my words. I could make grotesque errors; he did not mind. Better yet, he loved it. I was a pretty French woman, and nothing more was expected of me. As Fernand instructed, I remained charming but cold. Polite but hesitant. And the more aloof I pretended to be, the more smitten Dietfried appeared to be. By the time I told him I had to leave, he was begging me to show him more of the city.

My entire first interaction with Dietfried was a lesson I would forever owe to Fernand. It offered me a glimpse into the power of women over men, opening the door for skills that would shape my career and my life.

****

"He never once asked me if I was Jewish," I told Fernand when we met afterward at El Bahdja, which would become our meeting place.

Fernand shrugged, "Those things rarely come up in polite conversations. Just like men wouldn't ask ladies if they have the crabs."

"A comparison in poor taste," I said.

"Your identity papers make no mention of it. If he asks, deny it," Fernand said. A skinny adolescent came to take our orders. Even in the darkness of the café and the haze of pipe smoke, I could see that the boy's neck was smudged with grime. "Are you hungry, darling?" Fernand asked me.

I considered the boy's dirty fingernails. "No," I said. Fernand ordered a café au lait and mbesses, a sweet cake Algerians liked to eat for breakfast. "What if the Boche has me investigated?"

"What crime have you committed, sweetheart?"

"Is it beyond the scope of a German officer to obtain intelligence on someone? I don't want to put my family at risk."

A busboy set coffee, the cake, and a small dish of honey on the table. Fernand dipped pieces of the cake in the honey. "Ersatz flour, watered-down coffee. Even the honey has been mixed with agave syrup," he sighed.

I felt wary. Fernand and I were on the same side against a terrible enemy. He trusted me with a mission; perhaps it was time I made an effort to trust him as well. "There is something you need to know about my family," I said. "We're here under a false identity. My father's a foreigner. We left France under less than pristine conditions. If his real identity is revealed, he could be deported or imprisoned. The police have been searching for him in Paris and the South of France."

Fernand smiled in a way to indicate that none of this was news to him. "Here you are just another family among many," he said. "The police have better things to investigate. Your father is a prudent man. Your mother is emotionally unpredictable, but she does not go out of the house much. As for your brother, he has no friends in Algiers, so that puts him at low risk of indiscretions."

A flutter of anguish ran through me. "You know a lot about my family."

"Enough for us to decide to trust you with all this."

"Who is us?" I asked. "Émile? André? What about Béatrice? Is she part of the 'us'?"

"Béatrice isn't as dumb as you think," Fernand said. "So continue to be discreet around her. But we have enough dirt on the girl should she become a nuisance."

My hair rose on the nape of my neck. How long before my family turned into a nuisance in someone's eyes? "Don't mingle in my family's affairs, Fernand, if you want to keep our friendship."

Fernand dabbed the corners of his mouth and pushed the plate of cake toward me. "Would you finish this," he said. "Algerians consider it a sacrilege to throw out bread, and I have enough enemies as it is." He sat back in his chair and observed me, his expression between amusement and menace. "We're at war, darling. Friendship is irrelevant to what we're trying to accomplish."

Before the war, Dietfried had been a civil servant, of undistinguished physique and meek personality who throughout his life must have failed to impress his professors, his superiors, and women. But here in Algiers, he was impressive. In his carefully pressed Wehrmacht uniform, he represented the Third Reich no less. All eyes, albeit filled with hostility, converged in his direction. He did not yet fully embody his newfound prestige. At times, he assumed an air of self-confidence, but he did this the way a second-rate actor in a theater performance might. The rest of the time, he reverted to what I suspected to be his natural ordinariness, his natural dullness. In the few weeks since I had met him, a sparse mustache had sprouted above his upper lip. He was clearly unused to the sensation of hair under his nose, so he petted it constantly as he spoke. Dietfried appeared to be without malice. Like everyone else, his life and his future had been taken off course by the war. He hadn't chosen this military life. His engineering education, and the fact that he spoke French well had resulted, through an agreement with Vichy, in an appointment as part of a small German military contingent on Algerian soil. Were it not for the accent I was conditioned to despise and the dreadful uniform he wore on most of our outings, I could have forgotten that he took orders from a madman, hell-bent on conquering the world. Under different circumstances, I might have given Dietfried charitable pointers: use less cologne, stand up straight, listen to your date rather than to yourself, and above all, keep your hands off your mustache. But I was supposed to find him irresistible, so I bit my tongue.

Just as I had avoided the topic with Khaled, Dietfried made no mention of religion. Perhaps he had decided that it did not matter. Perhaps he was afraid of insulting me by asking. Or perhaps, as Fernand said, infatuation was a blinder that prevented him from seeing what he did not want to see. Because Dietfried was infatuated with me; this much was clear. He did not try to kiss me, but he was awkward in my presence, which revealed plenty. He was intelligent enough to know that his nationality worked against him, so he did not declare himself and rather attempted to woo me.

To act as though I liked Dietfried, to pretend to be someone I wasn't, turned out to be surprisingly more relaxing than being myself. Unthreatening girls don't try hard to say smart things. They let the men do all the talking. Their opinions agree with whoever is in front of them. They don't take offense. They are apolitical. Béatrice was my inspiration: I would remain steadfastly passive. I would say the occasional naiveté and watch Dietfried glow in his superiority. I giggled. I had contempt for the person I pretended to be, but Dietfried seemed to like her very much.

We carefully avoided the topic of war, and this was no small feat when it permeated every instant of our lives, nearly every thought in our minds, and every fear in our hearts. Instead, he spoke about life before the war: his life in Heidelberg, his studies, his family. We discussed travel, food, nature, fashion, sporting events. Conversing with Dietfried was tedious, humorless, but I made sure to chortle at the appropriate times. With anyone else, at any other time, I would have demanded that interesting things be discussed. I'd have said something provocative to spice things up. Or more likely I would have called it a day. Dietfried was terribly dull. But spies must be chameleons in more ways than one. It is not only about the way you dress and speak. It involves becoming a reflection of the emotions and interests of the person facing you. My dates with Dietfried taught me that there was much to gain by listening, a skill I hadn't cared to develop. It also taught me patience. I burned to ask about his role in Algiers, but Fernand had warned me against questioning him. Useful intelligence would come from Dietfried relaxing his guard, from his boasting.

I let Dietfried think he was in charge. I let him decide where to meet, what new part of Algiers to visit, which park, which museums, which streets. From there, Fernand would mastermind the entire date. He would tell me about the area in question ahead of time, and once there, I acted as though I was familiar with the place, when in fact Dietfried and I were discovering it at the same time. This required gumption, improvisation, cockiness, and fearlessness. The complexity of what I was doing was exhilarating, but I had to act reserved and a little bland.

Dietfried went from trying too hard to acting aloof in the hope of making me want him. He reeked of shyness and insecurity. I watched him get frustrated with himself as I continued to play hard to get. Meanwhile, Fernand continued to be the puppet master. Part of me could not help but feel sorry for Dietfried. As much as I enjoyed the challenge, I was not particularly fond of mental cruelty. It is difficult to completely hate someone you learn to know. I found myself thinking he was not such a horrible fellow. He was educated, soft-spoken, and excessively polite. He was also German and the enemy, a fact I had to keep remembering.

On one of our outings, we visited the Algiers zoo. We leaned over the parapet that separated us from an enclosure where two polar foxes played. The animals were beautiful; their fur was stark white against their incongruous desert settings. "How did a fox from the North Pole end up trapped in Algiers?" I said.

"I often wonder the same thing about myself," Dietfried quipped.

"Do you think those two were born in captivity?"

"I hope for them that they were," he said. "If they've never known freedom, they can't imagine it."

For a while, we watched the foxes play, then curl upon themselves and begin to groom each other with quick licks of their pink tongues. As I watched the foxes, I wondered if tricking Dietfried into falling in love with me was amoral.

He cleared his throat and asked, "Forgive me for asking Marceline, but do you have a boyfriend?"

"I do," I told him. Dietfried's face fell so blatantly I had to suppress a smile. "He's a law student at the University of Algiers."

"Are the two of you serious?"

Fernand had prepared me for this. Expressing a mixture of commitment and doubts was the best way to keep Dietfried at bay and interested. "More importantly," I said, "my family approves of his family."

"That is not the strongest of endorsements."

"French men in North Africa have conservative ideas about women," I said. "Not unlike Muslim men, as a matter of fact. They want women in the house, and they disapprove of higher education for them."

"How illogical," Dietfried said. "Any thinking man would realize how much more enriching it is for his sons when the woman who cares for them is well educated." He looked at me guilelessly. Women, to him, were merely a means to the breeding and upbringing of Aryan sons.

"I hear that the restrictions might force the closing of the zoo," I said. "What will become of the animals?"

"Likely, a couple of white fox stoles are soon to appear on the black market," he chuckled and added, "and somewhere in Algiers, a Jew will just get a bit richer." When he said this, my smile was sincere.

It was a smile of gratitude for jolting me out of complacency. When one got to know him, Dietfried turned out to be easy to despise after all.

****

I had a double life now – a triple, a quadruple life. There was my role as a sister and daughter where I felt childish and aggravated. There were my outings with Dietfried where I pretended to be a regular girl while all my senses were on alert. There was my work with Fernand where I watched my steps and acted more mature and sophisticated than I was. And then there were the few stolen minutes with Khaled where I felt I could be myself, except that I kept my Resistance activities secret from him. I wasn't naïve enough to hope that he would understand or accept what I was doing. Knowing how Khaled felt about France, how could he make sense of my dedication to a country that had turned vicious against people of my religion?

Everything, even my challenging hours with Dietfried, felt insipid compared to my time with Khaled. It wasn't just that I was drunk on our emotional connection. I was drunk on our chaste physical contacts. We kissed feverishly, but it was never enough – not enough time, not enough kisses, and not enough to fill my physical hunger for him.

Over time, I told Khaled about my life in Paris. I described our family's powerlessness as we witnessed the inexorable rise of anti-Semitism. I told him how in the span of a few short years the entire nation had turned against the Jews. Every day was cause for disbelief. It was not only that the people in power used baffling false logic and lies, but it was also the eagerness with which the population embraced them. The nation had become insane before our very eyes. The more absurd a lie, the more it gained ground, the more readily people embraced it. I admitted how insidious hatred was. The propaganda was so successful that it made even the Jews feel different about themselves. It was soul-crushing to see Jews portrayed as vile and disgusting, but what crushed my soul the most was the disgust I had felt. I thought Jews stood out too much, should have blended in more. I thought my brother stood out the most.

It was with Khaled that I could articulate for the first time that Mother and I had wanted Gustave sent away, not because, like Father, we were worried about his safety, but in retrospect because of how Jewish he looked. Mother and I had wanted Gustave away because with him around it was more difficult to pass as Aryan when we walked in the streets. I told Khaled how I had even been ashamed of my father for being too foreign, how I had felt that it reflected negatively on Mother and me.

"You were a child," Khaled said.

"I was a child, but I still feel terrible guilt about it."

"Tell them how you feel. The truth makes things lighter to bear."

"What purpose would this serve? I don't want them to know I was ashamed of them."

I told Khaled about my mother's disintegration and my rage at her. I told him how much I adored my father, but how he appeared absent most of the time, even when he was physically present. How for a while he had seemed to favor me, and, although I could see how unjust my family had been toward Gustave, how jealous I was when my father had become close to Gustave in Cannes. I told Khaled about Sandra, who had raised us and who loved us, but who might be fired at any time because I had manipulated her into closing her eyes to my escapades. "My brother resents me for good reasons," I said. "My father is disappointed in me, my mother knows she cannot count on me, and I'm betraying our loving nanny."

"You can always ask God for forgiveness," Khaled said as he twirled a strand of my hair and brought it to his lips.

"It is hard to believe in God when one looks at humanity," I said.

"Of course. That would be looking for God in the wrong places."

"Where should I look?"

"Me, I look at the trees and the sea. I look into your eyes." Saying so, he let his hand hover just above my belly. I wanted to scream for him to touch me, but what if too much forwardness on my part drove him away?

His hand hovered for a long minute. Finally, he removed it. "I want to respect you," he said finally.

"Touch me," I implored.

Slowly he lowered his hand and slipped it under my blouse. He let his palm rest softly on my belly as I tried to catch my breath. "I am afraid of what my body wants to do," he said.

There was one thing Khaled needed to know about me. Immediately. "The truth makes things lighter to bear," he had said. I did not want to be apologetic. In my heart of hearts, I did not care what society thought. I had made a conscious decision to have no regrets and no shame about this. Regrets and shame were the opposite of freedom, and I wanted to be free. But this was a conservative world, and his culture was even more traditional. I composed myself. I made sure to speak calmly and clearly so that he would have no doubts about it. "I am not a virgin," I said.

Disbelief at first and then confusion and grief washed over his face. Slowly, as slowly as he had placed it there, he removed his hand from my belly and rolled onto his back. "I have to go now to report to my desk," he said. "It is late."

I forced myself to say, "Fernand was my lover, but I broke it off."

He got up from the blanket and gave me his hand to help me up. He was not looking at me. He folded the blanket and placed it neatly in its place under the thorny bush. I brushed my skirt and flattened my hair with the palm of my hands and placed myself in front of him so that he would be forced to look at me. "I am in love with you," I said.

"You are?" he said, dumbfounded.

I tried hard to repress tears of frustration. I was angry. I had wanted him to forgive me immediately, and now I felt his distance, his disgust perhaps. "Why is this so incredible?"

"I'm in love with you," he said as if surprised to have a name for his feelings.

"Well then, I don't want you to be in love with a fiction of me."

He rubbed his face with the palm of his hands, overwhelmed. "What are we going to do?" he asked.

"Continue to meet here whenever we can," I said firmly. Inside, I was shaking.

Khaled put on his uniform jacket and looked in the direction of the maze of bamboo that led out of the clearing. "If I don't leave now, I will lose my work."

My throat tightened tears seemed a very real possibility. "Will you see me again, or will you not?" I said. "Look at me! Is what I told you so distressing that you can't even look at me?"

He took my face gently between his hands and gazed into my eyes with sadness. "There is nothing you or anyone can do or say that will stop me from seeing you," he said.

On May 29th, a German ordinance ordered the Jews in France's occupied zone to wear a Star of David patch sewn on their clothes. We were past outrage and received the news with despondency. That month, I met Dietfried twice. Twice I walked around Algiers on his arm, with me smiling and chatting and appearing to have a swell time. We met in places where my family would not usually venture, but I was more worried about their disappointment than I was afraid for myself.

"You were right," Fernand told me in late May. "Your brother was seen following you."

I was immediately enraged. "How often?" I said.

"Often enough."

"Does he know about the Boche?"

"Not sure. He follows you when you leave home. But once you get on a trolley, he can't climb on the same one without you seeing him, so he stops there."

"Which means your men are surveilling me?"

Fernand smiled charmingly. "Only to keep you safe, in case the Boche gets funny ideas."

"How much am I being followed?"

"When you are with the Boche." He looked at me, an ironic smile in his eyes. "Why should we follow you for any other reasons?"

I felt hot suddenly. If Gustave was following me, and Fernand's men were following Gustave, who knew about my visits to the Jardin d'Essai? "I don't need your protection," I said.

Fernand ignored my comment. "We've also seen your brother on his bicycle, trying to keep up with the trolley you were on. Our guys had to stand in his way a couple of times to slow him down."

Now I wasn't sure if I was more infuriated with Gustave or with Fernand. "How did you stand in his way? You did not intimidate my brother, did you?"

"We put an automobile in his way a couple of times. Once we stopped him to check his papers."

"Why don't you give my brother a job trailing people other than me?" I said. "He's obviously gotten good at it."

"Give him a role with the Resistance you mean? In my cell?"

My father would never forgive me if he knew I had anything to do with Gustave becoming part of the Resistance. A solution presented itself to me brilliant in its simplicity. "He keeps mentioning the Chantiers de la Jeunesse. He wants to join, but he is too young."

Fernand tapped his forehead with the palm of his hand. "The fool. Why not Hitler's Youth while he's at it?"

"They accept younger people on a voluntary basis. He applied for a derogation but was turned down. Could you pull strings? Could you get them to accept his application? That ought to keep him busy."

Fernand must have read my thoughts. "What does your father think of this?"

"The Chantiers de la Jeunesse is a more benign occupation than Resistance work I should think."

"I'll make it happen, sweetheart," Fernand said. "Anything else?"

The lack of adornment in my relationship with Fernand, in its many incarnations, suited me. Just like we had never complicated our sex life with talk of feelings, our work together was not burdened by sensitivities. There was something I needed off my chest, and I took this opportunity. "Yes," I said. "Quit calling me sweet names. Treat me with respect."

Fernand smiled. "The sweet names are how I express affection. Choosing you for a mission is to show you respect."

"I'm not doing any of this to impress you. You realize that?"

"You impress me nonetheless, sweetheart. And I don't believe you're the kind of gal who needs praise to operate."

****

A few days later, Gustave came home brandishing his approval letter and stamped paperwork. "Screening starts Monday!" he said excitedly.

"What screening?" Father asked.

"The Chantiers de la Jeunesse! My derogation came through. But I need to pass the health test first."

"Hmm …" my father said. Judging from the expression of dismay on his face, I got the sense he was the one who had maneuvered to get Gustave's application rejected.

"What does the screening entail?" Mother asked.

Gustave gave a nonchalant shrug. "Talks about morality and the virtues of work, family, homeland, and further brainwashing, I suppose," he said. "The screening lasts three days. It's in town."

"This is nonsense. Gustave, you are not going!" my father said.

Gustave raised his voice. "I was accepted! I can't turn it down now."

"Then you must fail the screening."

Gustave's face turned crimson. "And be humiliated?"

"He might fail without even trying to," I said to egg him on.

Father glowered at me, and Gustave looked at me with hatred.

"Maybe," Mother said, "it is not such a terrible place for children."

"I'm not a child!" Gustave bellowed.

"What about the S.T.O?" my father said. A rumor was gaining momentum that Vichy was drafting agreements with the Nazis to create the S.T.O. or Service du Travail Obligatoire. Forced labor for young French men to work in Germany in exchange for freeing our prisoners of war. Many suspected that the Chantiers de la Jeunesse might be a secret training ground for forced laborers.

"The Maréchal would never allow it," Mother said.

"Mother! Your Maréchal is who sold us out to the Boches," I said. "Can't you understand anything?"

My father just shook his head in exasperation and left the room.

That Monday, Gustave reported to the Chantiers de la Jeunesse office. While my father further schemed to extricate him from it, I was free to move around the city without the fear of running into my brother, or so I believed.

Gustave, I would learn later, never went to the Chantiers de la Jeunesse. He was only using it as an excuse to be gone day or night without my parents asking about his whereabouts. What he did for those three days, and during the ensuing weeks, I would find out later. He too was being trained. But neither one of us knew of the other's missions – until we did.

The following day, I waited in the clearing for Khaled to arrive, but he didn't. After we had spotted each other in the garden, it wasn't rare for him to join me twenty minutes later, sometimes half an hour. Forty-five minutes, once, when his boss had asked him to guide a visitor. That day, I waited in mental agony for an hour. Each minute that passed cemented the fear that my truth had been irreconcilable with his faith, his culture, his pride. I had been with men. I wasn't a virgin.

When I heard the familiar rustling of leaves, I turned and stood there, rather than run into his arms. He walked toward me and took me in his. "The boss had me trim dead flowers off the hydrangea bushes. I worked as fast as I could."

We spread our blanket and lay side by side. We kissed. I was tremendously relieved at first and then unnerved. It was as though nothing had been said.

We began to talk about the future. This was something we did, despite the war, despite all that separated us, despite how improbable the chance of a future together.

"When the war is over. we can rent a house in the South of France for an entire summer," I said. "And I want to take you to Paris," I said. "We'll bring a picnic to the Parc de Bagatelle." Khaled smiled at this. Those notions were as alien to him as a trip to the moon. He described the Kasbah where he lived. "I want you to see it with your own eyes," he said. "It cannot be described with words. It is a city, and it is a home. Imagine it like a house with many rooms, filled with one family so large that you cannot know everyone, and yet they all take care of you. A house with a hundred kitchens where women cook a hundred meals, hundreds of fountains and balconies, a thousand windows, with streets and steps and shops and mothers, fathers, and children all living together, supporting one another."

"People say it's dangerous."

"Only when the French police arrive to arrest our brothers or search streets and houses looking for someone." He shook his head, angry. "It used to be that if someone wanted to hide in the Kasbah, he could never be found. But now they use spies and informants. Brothers turn on each other. They are corrupting our way of being."

"The police?"

"The French. All people want is to live in peace in the Kasbah, live their life, be happy."

"What about the women?" I asked tentatively. "They can't be that happy?"

He raised an eyebrow. "Why would they not be?"

"Don't they feel … subjugated?"

I immediately saw the hurt on his face. "You have the wrong idea about Muslims," he said. "This is why I want you to come to the Kasbah. I want you to see for yourself how our women are well cared for and respected."

"But not free."

Khaled sat up and looked at me intently. "No one is free in this world, Marceline. Men or women. Even when we move without restraints, even if there aren't wars or jails, we aren't free. We all have duties."

"Duties?"

Khaled searched for the right words, or else he hesitated to reveal his beliefs. "In my culture, it's our duty to have children," he said. "Our duty to keep things holy, to care for our families and our elders in the faith and tradition."

"And people follow this blindly?"

"These rules, these duties, they were developed over thousands of years. They exist because they are our cement. They are the means by which we can all experience order and joy."

"Laws get in the way of freedom," I said, "with new laws added every day. We don't have a choice about laws, or about wars. Religion is an added ball and chain, but at least we can refuse that burden, walk away, be free."

Khaled got up and began pacing. "Freedom is not what men crave most," he said. "They crave heroism, and purpose, and God, and family. They will happily sacrifice their freedom and their lives in the name of something greater."

I leaned back on my elbows. "Men," I said. "It's always about the men."

Khaled kneeled next to me on the blanket. "Women have the same desire to be part of a whole that is greater than them." The way he looked at me as he said this, I wondered for a moment if it was possible that Khaled knew about my Resistance work. But what he said next was more worrisome. "It is not about me, or what I want," he said, distraught. "I want you. You must know this. It's about my people, my faith. I would never betray either."

"What are you saying?"

"I am saying that I am in love with you," he said, peering into my eyes.

"So why do you sound like you are breaking up with me?" I said stiffly.

"I am part of a community, Marceline. You must understand this. My family depends on me to behave within the rules of the community. That is the way I bring them honor."

"So?"

"Things are expected of me. How I worship … who I … marry, it's all part of it."

I felt a pang of nausea. "Who is even speaking about marriage?" I said.

"Things aren't simple. The truth is, my family, my people, they – it's expected of me to keep things holy and to…." He paused and looked away and added, "Marry within my religion."

I stood up in a huff and dusted my skirt. "And I'm unholy!"

He took my hands. "I love you just as you are," he said.

"What makes me unholy?" I said, furious. "Is it that I'm Jewish or that I'm not a virgin?"

"No … but … neither. It's just that—"

"I'm not damaged goods, Khaled! Being with me is a privilege. A privilege! If you feel otherwise, I have no desire to be with you!"

We stood in the clearing, facing each other like enemies.

"We are slaves to our upbringings," he said. "I am a slave to mine, as you are a slave to yours."

"Can't you see those notions are inventions? Lies repeated!"

"But there is a solution," he said.

I crossed my arms and faced him. "Is there now?"

"Would you convert to Islam?" he asked. His face was grave, his eyes hopeful.

"In which case, you might be willing to overlook my lack of virginity?"

He brightened. "I would."

I eyed him with something that must have resembled hatred. "What possesses you to think I would consider converting? Why don't you try and convert to Judaism instead?"

"It would make no difference to you," he said softly. "You don't even believe in God."

My face was flushed, and it took everything I had not to shout. "I believe in nothing! I don't believe in God or marriage! I don't even believe in being indignant about what you just said. It's just so ridiculous I will ignore it!"

"Please do not be angry," Khaled implored. He tried to take my hands, but I shook free of him. "I'm only looking for solutions."

"You use the word marriage as though it's the most heavenly thing. I despise the institution!"

"And yet you must marry someday."

"Of course not. Can't you see the world is upside down? The old rules no longer apply."

"There are reasons for humanity to have evolved the way it did," Khaled said. "The same in every religion, with a man as the head of the family and the woman at its heart, under one faith. It has evolved that way because it is the glue of civilizations."

"And here I am, bringing civilization to its knees!" I was trying not to cry. How was it possible to lose control so fast and so irrevocably? Why was it that I could not love Fernand with whom everything was easy, and instead had to fall in love with Khaled with whom everything was impossible? "No man will own me," I said.

Khaled looked at me unflinchingly. "I don't want to own you any more than I want to own the moon or the sun. I love you, and I want to be with you and hold you in my heart. All I want is for us to be together. I know you would love living in the Kasbah. I am certain of it! The women in the Kasbah—"

I interrupted, full of venom. "You have no idea what hides under those veils, behind those lowered gazes. Muslim women are watching European women, and do you know what they think? They don't congratulate themselves on how holy they are. They yearn to become like us! Before long, they will rebel against the veil and everything it represents. Muslim men will have no choice but to adapt. You would do well to change the way you think because, like it or not, you soon will be left in the dust, without a single woman to own."

Khaled's eyes were thunderous. He was insulted, yet he tried to use reason, and as he spoke, the width of our cultural divide widened, and my heart broke a little more. "It has nothing to do with ownership!" he said. "What European women are doing is an experiment, and we have no idea of the outcome. Traditions evolve over thousands of years. Like plants, species evolve slowly to adapt to variations in their environment. But take a plant and transplant it without giving it time to adapt, and it will most certainly perish. The changes in women you are speaking of are happening too fast. The human species is not ready for it."

"So be it then!" I said. I added dramatically, "The human species is not ready for me!" I grabbed the blanket and shook it off. Khaled watched me, his expression clouded with disappointment. I threw the folded blanket on the ground and added, "Your rules are all in your imagination. You are, in fact, free to do as you wish. I feel sorry for how trapped you are by your conventions. I have nothing but pity for narrow-mindedness. And I don't even care that I am a whore in your eyes."

The expression on Khaled's face went from anger to indignation. "Why would you say this?"

"Admit what this is really about: I slept with a man, and now you see me with disgust!"

Khaled stepped toward me and murmured, "What you did or didn't do changes nothing in my eyes. You are the most sacred thing on which I have ever laid eyes. The most precious. The rarest. I am powerless before you. But I can't promise what I cannot give. I am not a free man and will never be."

I tasted tears in my throat before I felt them in my eyes. "Did you hear me ask for anything?"

"I am the one asking. I want a future with you!"

We were still standing in front of each other, but our anger was gone, and all that was left was the desolation we felt. The truth was I wasn't free of the burden of family expectations either. I knew how one's place in society, whether because of race, religion, or class, could cling to your skin like a personal prison. "Why can't we just live now?" I said. I was sobbing now.

"These stolen moments, they are not enough. They will never be enough," he said.

"You have to go back to work," I said. "They will see you are missing. You've been absent too long."

"Will you come back?" he asked.

"What's the point, Khaled? We can't be together, and you know this. We both know this."

Khaled grabbed my arms and pressed me against him. "You will come back. Tell me you will!"

I melted against him, and all vestige of anger vanished from me. "I will come to the Kasbah," I said. "I want to see it. Just tell me when and how."

He took my hand, brought it to his lips, and kissed the inside of my wrist lightly.

****

With July came unfathomable news. The French government had orchestrated a massive raid and arrested over ten thousand Parisian Jews, a large proportion of them foreign or, just like my father, stateless. Those without children had been sent to an encampment in Drancy, but families were being held captive inside the Vélodrome d'Hiver, an enclosed bicycle stadium in the fifteenth arrondissement, with little indication that anyone in the government knew what to do with them.

A few years ago, our father had dragged us to the Vel' d'Hiv to watch a bicycle competition. The stadium had a glass ceiling. The day was hot, and the temperature inside had been too sweltering to bear. Mother had complained, so we had left. We put ourselves in the shoes of those families awaiting their fate, and they were all that was on our minds. Over the next few days, we held our breath as accounts of what was taking place inside the Vélodrome d'Hiver grew unimaginable. Men, women, children, babies, grandmothers, and grandfathers were parked there like beasts without food, water, or latrines. There were rumors of horrors that defied the imagination, rumors of suicide, filth, and death, of people trying to escape and being shot on the spot.

"It's not possible," my mother kept mumbling as she walked around the apartment in a Benzedrine-induced state of agitation.

"Do you think it's true, Baba?" Gustave dared to ask.

"Of course not," my father said, which cheered me up. This was one more rumor to discount. You could not trust the official news channels, but neither should we rely on word of mouth. But when my mother left the room, my father spoke to Gustave and me. "I do not need your mother be troubled any more than she already is. We need to hide the truth from her."

"They can't let people die of thirst?" I exclaimed. "Surely someone will intervene. How could the Parisians let their next-door neighbors be taken away and killed?"

My father did not look at us as he said, "The average French person is trying to survive under the occupation. Acts of righteousness might save a few, but even a handful of evil people placed in a position of control is enough to annihilate all decency." He shook his head. "It is the nature of the most aggressive and heartless humans to spread terror and control the decent, peaceful ones. It has been the case throughout the ages. In my days, I have seen these kinds of things happen. There will never be enough jails for all the people they hate."

"What do you mean, Baba?"

My father hesitated. "It isn't incarceration they want to achieve, but annihilation. In my youth, they walked people from entire villages in the desert until they died."

I felt ill. "They cannot be killing Jewish families on purpose, Baba!" I thought of other rumors, of starvation, of poisonous gas, and prayed that my father would reassure us.

"Persecutions of Jews have happened throughout history," he said. "You are old enough to hear this. You must be attentive, on guard, always. Jews, Communists, homosexuals: those are the people Hitler is after. He has plainly said so. To think he does not mean to exterminate us all makes us just as delusional as he is."

We let the thought sink in. The world did not only hate us: it was putting a system in place to eradicate us. "Is that why so many Jews are staying in Paris, Baba? You think they're delusional?" Gustave asked.

"Many foreigners and refugees have no friends or family in Paris to hide them. They have no money and no means to flee. Maybe they left their countries because of persecutions there, not thinking that France would become just as bad. They might be trapped in France even if they wanted to leave."

Gustave said out loud what we both thought. "If you had not taken us away from Paris, we too would be gathered at the Vel' d'Hiv."

My father did not answer, but in his eyes was unbearable sadness.

"What will happen to us if they find us here in Algiers?" Gustave asked.

"We're in the unoccupied zone, and our false identity is holding," our father said. He paused, weighing whether we should hear the truth. "But do not think for a moment that we are out of danger. The Vichy government seems intent on developing its own policies against Jews, regardless of what Hitler wants. If Vichy has jurisdiction over non-occupied territories, Jews are in danger here as well."

"So, what shall we do?"

"Don't dismiss rumors, err on the side of caution, plan and prepare for every eventuality. And as sad as it is to say, expect the worst from people."

"French colonies in India, Cameroun, Tchad, and New Caledonia have rejected Vichy and are following De Gaulle," I said. "North Africa might still break politically from Vichy."

My father shook his head. "I don't think that will happen."

A sense of entrapment and fear rose in me, and anger too. "And why not?"

"We are too close to France. If it were going to happen, it would have happened by now."

"That was my last hope," I said, sitting down on the couch and placing my forehead in my hands. Gustave stood at the door, pale and stiff, the way he looked when he was upset. My father looked from Gustave to me. He seemed to hesitate. In a voice barely above a whisper, he said, "You must take heart. There is hope, my loves. There is … I can't give you details, but there are plans in the works. The Allied forces … Things are looking up. The fighting in Egypt is giving Rommel a hard time. If we can drive him out of Egypt, the Allies might attempt something."

His words hovered over us, powerful enough to hold our spirits aloft. Gustave did not cross-examine him, and neither did I. We could not risk discovering that our father was only trying to raise our spirits. For my part, I needed to be buoyed by this. I wanted to be reassured. And in this way, I wasn't so different from those dying inside the Vélodrome d'Hiver because they had hoped for the best until it was too late.

The events at the Vel' d'Hiv devastated us psychologically. Sleeping was difficult. We had nightmares. It was hard, at times, to find a reason to get out of bed in the morning. We cataloged in our minds those we knew who might now be dead. We obsessed about what might have happened to us had we stayed in Paris. Despair and fear gripped us without warning from one moment to the next, and we walked in a daze, searching for ways we could reconcile our sense of right and wrong with what had happened at the Vel' d'Hiv and might happen to us.

My early involvement in the Resistance had been a little girl's game I played; now I glimpsed the significance of my actions. I ached to extract something useful out of Dietfried. The couple of dull walks by the seaside when Dietfried never discussed his work tested my patience. But Fernand continued to warn me against asking questions. "Play it smooth, sweetheart," he would say. "No need to put him on guard. We want him to trust you." But I suddenly felt in a terrible hurry, one that bordered on desperation.

Finally, Fernand let me accept to have lunch with Dietfried. We met at Le Neuilly, a classic French brasserie renowned for its rich patrons and its apparent immunity from shortages in the kitchen.

Dietfried rose to greet me and helped me to my chair. In the gleaming restaurant, filled with mirrors and polished brass, the atmosphere was jolly, perfumed, chatty. A pianist played a lively tune. Everything about the place was meant to make you forget the war. I glanced across the hectic, crowded room and saw that I wasn't the only pretty girl being treated to a fancy meal by a powerful man. I despised the sight of those women with their little out-of-fashion hats, bad rouge, and cheap nylons, who cooed and simpered odiously as Germans in uniforms laughed drunkenly. But then I realized that, to the uninformed eye, I was no different. I was just another girl, fraternizing with the enemy in exchange for a full belly and perhaps more.

Dietfried ordered lamb chops, and I ordered roast chicken and potatoes au gratin. As the war progressed, the meals that Sandra managed to prepare for us increasingly lacked fat and protein. I was always hungry. My stomach churned in anticipation, and I had trouble paying attention to Dietfried's ramblings. When the food arrived on our plates, steaming and delicious-looking, I had to compose myself not to devour the content of my plate, trough-like. With every bite came the nearly physical sensation that my blood was replenishing itself. Dietfried ordered German beers, cold and foamy, and I told him that it was the most delectable beer I had ever tasted, and he blushed as though the quality of German beer was evidence of his own merit. As was his habit, Dietfried pondered on and seemed perfectly happy with my lack of opinion and the fact that I had nothing to say about myself. But the beer loosened my guard, and it occurred to me that Dietfried was always available, no matter what time of the day I said I could meet. "Don't you ever have to work?" I asked, forgetting that I was not supposed to ask him how he spent his time in Algiers.

"I mostly work at night," he said.

"In that case, shouldn't you be sleeping now?" I asked.

Dietfried seemed to swell with importance and casually said, "I'm a communication specialist, but it turns out there are very few communications to be had. Perhaps one per night, if that much. Mostly, I wait and read. I have been in Algiers for three months and have done little more than read and re-read every book in the library."

The information was critical. I laughed to appear tipsy and to kill the subject before it raised suspicion. "That makes no sense to me whatsoever," I said, giggling.

"How about we catch a movie after lunch," he asked.

Both of us were aware of the only benefit of being in a movie theater in the middle of the afternoon. I pretended not to understand. "Oh, but Dietfried, do you not realize that being seen at the movies with a man would be terrible for my reputation? What would my parents say if they found out?"

Dietfried reddened. "I … of course not … that would be improper."

"Quite improper!" I assured him.

When I returned home, Fernand, dressed in a brown suit and matching hat, was already waiting for me inside the apartment building's entrance. He was standing near the mailboxes, next to the dark space below the staircases where people left baby carriages and bicycles. If someone we knew appeared, he could retreat in the shadow and not be seen, and I would pretend to open my mailbox.

"Anything new?" he asked.

"It depends," I said. We were speaking just above a whisper, halting our conversation when we heard a door close or footsteps in the staircase. Seeing those girls at the restaurant, and judging them and hating them the way I had, I sensed that I might not be indestructible. It was not a matter of how people might judge me; I needed to shield myself. "If Algiers ever becomes independent from Vichy and Germany, how will I be protected?"

"What have you heard?" Fernand asked.

"Nothing. But here I am, parading around Algiers with Dietfried. I want to make sure that more than one person knows what I am actually doing with him."

"It's Dietfried now?" he said. "How sweet of you to call him by his Christian name."

"What name do you want me to use? Goebbels and Himmler were taken already."

"Never forget he's the enemy, Marceline."

"I don't need a reminder," I said icily. A man entered the building and nodded hello. We nodded back. He pushed the button to the elevator. Fernand lit a cigarette. The man entered the elevator, the door closed behind him, and the elevator went up. "What if we win the war?" I said. "What if we lose? People won't be likely to forget that they saw me at the side of a Boche."

"I will vouch for you. I will tell everyone about your involvement."

"What if you get killed?"

Fernand pretended to shudder. "That's so very morbid of you!"

"I have intelligence. You either want it, or you don't. Give me guarantees."

"You are getting touchy, darling."

I crossed my arms. "I am getting tired of the condescending."

"Me? Condescending?"

"I'm doing a job. I work for you – under your orders. I need a guarantee that I will be safe when this is over. If you cannot offer me one, then I won't be wasting another minute with this."

"All right," Fernand said. He drew from his cigarette, crushed it on the stone floor, and exhaled a cloud of smoke. "Your code name is Brantôme."

"I beg your pardon?"

"Your involvement as Brantôme is being documented. That information is then encrypted and sent to London. When the time comes, if you're ever questioned or doubted by one of us, all you'll need to do is bring up your code name. Is that enough of a guarantee?"

"I have a spy name?"

He smiled thinly. "You do."

I was Brantôme. I liked that. "How is it that I'm the last one to find out my own code name?" I asked.

"What is the intelligence you spoke of?" Fernand asked impatiently.

"Dietfried is a communication specialist. He told me so today. He broadcasts at night apparently, sleeps during the day."

Fernand stiffened. "From his house?"

"Wherever he is at night. He didn't say."

"That is why his house is so well guarded!" Fernand beamed. "Our patience and efforts are paying off."

"Are they?"

"The Germans are in constant communication with Berlin from Algiers, though we don't know exactly how. We didn't know who was transmitting or from where. The man is a fool to tell you this."

"Unless it's a deliberate red herring. A trap."

Fernand dismissed the notion. He was excited. "Finding where they are communicating from was like searching for a needle in a haystack. But now we can check it out, look for an antenna. Wherever he works from, there should be encryption tools, things of that nature. That's why they have an engineer seemingly twiddling his thumbs all day long in Algiers. He works at night! It makes perfect sense." Fernand clapped his hands. "By the looks of it, your small fry turns out to be a much bigger fish!"

Upon my return to the apartment, Gustave was brooding again.

"Why are you here?" I said. He ignored me, went into his room, and slammed his door. "Why is he upset this time?" I asked Sandra, who was hurrying about the living room, emptying Mother's ashtrays and fluffing throw pillows.

"He is sad," she told me.

Mother emerged from her room, wrapped in her white silk kimono, a long ivory cigarette holder at her fingertips. She was perfumed and made up for the first time in weeks. Benzedrine was quite extraordinary, indeed. When she took it, you'd forget she had been down in the dumps, barely able to use a comb or a toothbrush thirty minutes before.

"You look nice, Mother," I said. "Are you and Baba going somewhere special for your anniversary?"

She took a puff of her cigarette. "Wouldn't you know your father has surprised me with a night at the opera no less," she said, tapping the cigarette to drop the ashes and missing the ashtray.

"Well, you look pretty," I said.

She turned in front of the mirror, pleased, and patted her coiffed hair. "You think so?" she said in the breezy tone she used when her system was soaked with the new wonder drug the doctor had prescribed. "I hardly know what to wear. What a bother not to be able to buy anything new. And my good clothes are nowhere to be found."

"You probably left them in Cannes," I said, knowing full well that I had coaxed Sandra into taking many of them apart to make new, more fashionable clothes for me.

I had noticed lately that the new medication made Mother forgetful and sometimes suspicious. "I brought them here," she said sotto voce, "but someone stole them." She emphasized the word 'someone.'

"Who would steal your clothes, Mother?"

"That one," she said, pointing to Sandra without even trying to be discreet about it. "She steals."

I felt bad for Sandra. "What would Sandra do with your clothes? She wears the same things all the time."

"She sells them on the black market and buys meat for herself."

I sighed. "You're being absurd, Mother. Sandra is more honest than everyone in this family put together. When are you and Baba leaving for the opera?"

"He's picking me up in an hour." She looked at herself in her mirror. "I've lost so much weight," she sighed. "Everything hangs on me like a rag." Her shoulders slumped. "I don't even know that I want to go out anymore."

"Here," I said, guiding her by the elbow to her room. "Let's find you something lovely to wear."

There was no way I was letting Mother stay home. Not after all the maneuvering my plan had entailed. I had convinced Father to make an effort for Mother on their anniversary. I had bought the opera tickets. Tonight, I was meeting Khaled at the Kasbah. Nothing short of the arrival of De Gaulle himself that evening would prevent my parents from being out of my way.

Thankfully, I coaxed Mother out of her mood. Father was on time to sweep her up before she changed her mind, they left for the opera, and I was free, save from the unscheduled presence of my pesky brother. But unlike me, Gustave was allowed to go out after dinner as long as he stayed in the neighborhood and returned before curfew, and in the warm months, he usually went. He was seventeen, and this exotic city was filled with excitement for a boy his age.

Once it was only Sandra and me in the apartment, I told her, "I'm going too."

"You aren't allowed," she said looking upset.

"I'll be out for an hour or so."

"Marceline, you cannot leave in the evening!" Sandra said imploringly. It was true that now that we shared a room, she could no longer look the other way.

"It's not even night yet, not even close."

"I'll go with you," she said.

"Oh, don't be a grump," I said cheerfully. "It's barely six o'clock. Curfew won't be for hours." Before she had time to protest, I kissed her on the cheek. "Don't worry," I told her, "I'm like a cat who always lands on her feet."

In the stairwell, I took out of a tote the long tunic and headscarf I had taken from Sandra's shelf without her knowing and put them over my clothes. I clutched the headcovering around my neck with one hand the way Muslim women did, and I stepped out of the apartment building dressed like the Arab women of Algiers who worked as maids in the French neighborhoods.

Outside, the city's walls still radiated the day's heat. As I made my way toward the Muslim parts of the city, I kept my eyes low. Dressing up like a Muslim woman had been Khaled's idea. The length of the djellaba hampered my steps, and the veil and headscarf diminished my vision, yet moving through the city unnoticed was exhilarating. French men, the rude ones who usually whistled and said things to me as I walked by, and the well-mannered ones who eyed me and tipped their hats, now went right past me as if I were invisible. Policemen who usually harassed me under the guise of protecting young French women ignored me entirely.

I arrived at the foot of the Kasbah. The mysterious city inside a city, against which everyone had warned me, stood before me, oversized and foreboding like the entrance of a treacherous maze. Dozens of people came in and out. Some men dressed like Khaled did, in the western style, with pants and button-down shirts. Many wore burnouses and kaftans, turbans, and fezzes. Women were wrapped head to toe in white tunics and shawls. Only their eyes, strikingly lined with kohl, their hands, painted with intricate henna patterns, and their ankles and feet were visible. The Arab men did not display the subservient demeanor they usually adopted in my part of town. Here they looked dominant, intimidating. My stomach tightened. Perhaps I would do well to turn back. But then I saw Khaled.

He sat on a low wall, waiting for me to notice him. When we made eye contact, he did not smile. He hopped down and moved his head to signify I should follow him.

My heart thumped with anticipation as I followed him through the wide entrance. As instructed, I left several feet of distance between us as we walked.

Because I was with Khaled, I felt safe. At no point did it occur to me that I might be followed. At no point did I notice that all the way to the Kasbah, someone had been watching me.

I had never tried to imagine what the Kasbah was like on the inside. From a distance, it resembled a stack of whitewashed, squat constructions, one atop the other, that clung to the flank of the Bourzareah Mountain. I had not imagined the people who live there. The sinuous, narrow streets and staircases concealed a bustling world of sounds, sights, and smells. We entered the souk, the market, and walked past dozens of coffee shops, some as tiny as an opening in a wall, where groups of men sat at flimsy tables, smoked the hookah, and drank coffee. Shops appeared to sprout out of doors and windows. There were weavers, potters, bakers, pipe makers, tailors, and carpet sellers. Men, women, and children moved through the streets carrying goods, baskets, and live ducks and chickens or pulling a goat or a donkey. The scent of spices, roasted coffee beans, grilled food, and trash was overpowering. The women wore white, the men white and shades of earthy colors. French people were few, aside from the many French policemen patrolling in pairs, and I did not see any French women. Hordes of little boys, some as young as five, their little faces ferocious, moved stealthily through the streets like small armies.

Every twenty steps or so, Khaled looked over his shoulder and smiled at me with his eyes, and mine smiled back. I followed him up a hundred stone steps and deeper inside the Kasbah, away from the souk, where the jumble of streets turned less chaotic. The architecture, far from being primitive as I had assumed, was perfectly designed to keep the heat at bay; because the walls were tall and the streets narrow, the sun rarely reached the streets. Houses had tiny, rectangular or dome-shaped windows. A few had small wooden balconies held up by haphazard pillars. I looked up at the blindingly white walls where the sun reached. Above our heads, laundry hung like flags on clotheslines that went between windows from one side of the street to the other.

The steps that crisscrossed the Kasbah seemed to serve as extensions of people's houses. Entire families sat on the steps, playing cards, speaking, eating, playing reed flutes, smoking, laughing. Everywhere dogs and children ran free, and cats who were perched up high witnessed the scenes with half-closed eyes. From every corner came the smell of tagines and grilled fish. The houses themselves kept the sun out and their mysteries in.

Under my veil, it was a new experience to observe and not be seen. I felt perfectly safe and decided I had been ridiculous. The Kasbah was not dangerous. It was a place where people coexisted peacefully in a throbbing, vibrant life. Khaled walked ahead of me, turning every so often to smile as we went up several narrow, serpentine streets and through a labyrinth of passages, steep stairs, alcoves, courtyards, and alleys. We walked past more playing children, and soon there were few sounds aside from those of our footsteps and faint music coming from somewhere.

We passed palaces with ornate doors and whitewashed walls with mosaic and wood details. We passed a hammam. We walked in front of a minuscule mosque. We walked past wooden doors and walls ornate with mosaic tiles. I was out of breath from climbing. Khaled stopped, leaned against a wall, and looked into the distance as he waited for me to catch my breath. I turned and discovered the Kasbah from above. Overlooking the immense blue sea and the azure sky was a layering of rectangular terraces that reflected the sun. From where I was, I could see people on those terraces, women pinning laundry out to dry and children playing. The higher we went, the quieter it was. Somewhere, someone played the lute, and a plaintive Arabic melody became more pronounced as we climbed. There were fewer people in the streets and soon almost no one. Khaled spoke for the first time. "Kasbah means citadel," he said. "But it's not fortified; all the gates are open. It's just a medina."

"What's a medina?"

"An Islamic city where people live the way of our ancestors. But a medina is open, whereas the Kasbah was built like a fortress. The pirate Barberousse erected it, they say."

"I was worried that someone here would notice that I'm an outsider," I said.

He smiled. "They noticed."

"How would you know?"

He laughed. "Because everyone I saw pretended not to know me."

"How could they tell?"

He pointed to my feet. "Did you see your shoes?"

I looked down at my leather shoes. The Muslim women wore babouches, or sandals or went barefoot.

"My shoes gave me away?"

"And the way you move, the way you walk: anyone who paid attention knew that you were not one of us. The Kasbah is full of gossips, but it's also very discreet. You would not be the first French woman, or French man, smuggled in."

"What would have happened if I had dressed normally?"

"Normally? You think women wearing trousers and pointy brassieres is normal to the people here?"

"I guess not."

"You dressed in a way that did not stir anyone. The idea was to be left alone, and that's what happened."

We entered through a small wooden door and found ourselves at the center of a vast bright courtyard filled with plants and the crisp bubbling sound of water dripping into a faded mosaic fountain. Light came from above, diffused through a wide opening. The house was built on three levels with balconies overlooking the courtyard. On the floor of the lowest balcony, a young child sat, his hands clasping the wrought iron bars, his skinny bare legs and dirty feet dangling toward the courtyard. He looked down at us. A veiled woman scooped him up and disappeared.

"This is where I live," Khaled said.

"Is this your family?"

"Many families live in this house." He took me to the area his family occupied, a large room with low benches and a hexagonal table. Rugs hung on the white-washed walls; the floor was covered in red tiles and sheepskins. The next room was a tiny kitchen where a stew cooked in a pot on a cast-iron stove. Khaled smelled the contents of the pot. "Eggplant," he said.

"Is someone here?"

"My mother or my aunt. But they must have seen you and chosen to leave us alone."

"Where are the bedrooms?"

He pointed to sheepskins on the floor. "We sleep here, and here," he said. He pointed at the floor of the balcony. "Sometimes here; it depends on the temperature." He smiled. "When it is cold, it's all bodies on the sheepskin at night."

We left Khaled's house, returned to the streets, and continued up the steps. My legs were sore from all the climbing. We reached the highest point of the Kasbah and emerged onto a large terrace. The sun was low in the sky. I realized that I would never be home before curfew. I did not say anything.

I was dying to remove my veil and for the breeze to cool my skin. What was it like for young girls the day they donned the veil for the first time? Did they suffer, or did it become as natural to them as it was for a French woman to wear a brassiere, hose, and heels?

From where we stood, we could see the entire Bay of Algiers, shimmering in the setting light. On the terrace, someone had planted a lush vegetable garden in pots; dirt had to have been painstakingly brought here, pound by pound. There were cherry tomato vines that crawled up bamboo posts, and cilantro and mint tufts bursting out of clay pots. I picked a mint leaf and brought it to my nose as we walked around the terrace.

"You planted this?" I asked.

"Many help care for it. I want to show you my favorite place. Come." We walked on a wide ledge until we reached a stone parapet. We sat, out of sight, our backs resting against a wall, and watched the Kasbah cascading below and the darkening sea and sky on the horizon. In the distance, a dog barked. The sound of a radio playing Arabic music escaped from a nearby window. I removed my veil and lifted my hair to refresh my neck. Khaled kissed my neck, and I did not dare move. He put his arm around me, and we kissed. I rested my head on his shoulder, bursting with happiness, and longing, and love. For a long time, we didn't speak. Then he said, "I look for solutions, and I find none."

Cool air arrived from the sea, competing with the Sahara dry air, and the wind ruffled palm trees below. The sky went from blue to purple, and a few stars lit up. "I think something will happen soon," I said.

"In the war?"

"I think the fighting will come here soon, either from the air, or from Rommel's armies in the desert, or from the sea."

"What will that change for us?"

"If we defeat Hitler, then maybe Jews will be able to return to France. You could come with me."

"Do you know how people from the Maghreb live in France? They are packed into shantytowns. They have no rights. They live a life of misery to earn a few francs they can send to their families who also live in poverty here. All this, compliments of your beautiful colonial empire." He said those last two words with contempt.

"But if you came to France, you'd live like us. You'd live *with* us! Most assuredly, my father could give you work. His business was good before the war."

"It is not so simple, Marceline. When this war ends, our struggle will continue."

"What struggle?"

He looked at me and spoke gravely. "The time will soon come when my people will fight for their independence from the French," he said.

"Another war, you mean?"

"It's inevitable. And if your people and my people become enemies, you might come to hate me."

"I will never hate you," I said, kissing him. "For one, my people aren't the French, but the Jews. Jews and Arabs have no reason to ever be at war. Besides, I'm certain that the French and the Arabs can find peaceful ways of resolving their differences."

"Tell me about a time in history when peaceful solutions were chosen over fighting and destruction?"

We were silent. The wind had died down. Soon my parents would return from the opera. I needed to leave at once. But I did not move. I wanted to continue to feel the warmth of Khaled's body next to mine.

"I have some happy news," he said. "They hired me as a full-time groundskeeper at the Jardin d'Essai."

"Khaled," I said, throwing my arms around his neck, "your dream has come true!"

"That used to be my dream," Khaled said with sadness.

"What changed?"

"Now I have a new dream," he said, searching into my eyes. "But this one is unattainable." Up in the sky, the stars began to come out. Behind us, the warmth of the desert brought with it the plaintive howls of coyotes. "I think about you day and night," he said.

"Then kiss me," I said. "Hold me in your arms."

We kissed; our breathing became heavier. Khaled pulled away. "Even here we have to be careful."

"I don't care what people think!"

"It's not what they'll think that I fear," Khaled responded somberly. "It's what they'll do. I better take you back. It is nearly dark."

I put my head covering back on, and we rapidly made our way down through the maze of streets and stairs. We got out of the Kasbah through the same door I had entered. "I will walk you to your street, or as far as I can," he said.

"If you do this, you will have to return after curfew."

"I will take the risk."

The clock was ticking. People were rushing to be home before dark, and we hurried our step. A block away from the Kasbah, we walked under a small bridge. The bridge was only a few yards long. Under it was cool, damp, and dark. Khaled said, "Remove your djellaba and veil. Once on the other side, I will follow you at a distance."

"Why change clothes now?"

"During the day, you don't want to be a French woman in the Muslim quarter, but at night it is better not to be an Arab woman in the French quarter." I quickly took the tunic off. Now I was in my cardigan and skirt. In the dark, Khaled's eyes gleamed. I moved to kiss him, but he stood rigidly. "Too dangerous if we are found," he murmured.

"It's not fair," I said.

"We took risks. But I am happy you saw the Kasbah."

"Thank you for showing it to me."

"If you come again, I could bring you to a place that is more private." He hesitated. "A friend's room somewhere. Would you want that?"

"There is nothing I want more," I murmured.

We were interrupted by the sounds of rapid footsteps. Many footsteps. People running.

"Shhh. Don't make a sound," Khaled murmured. He took my hand, and we pressed ourselves against the damp walls of the tunnel, holding our breath.

The footsteps stopped a few yards away from us. From the darkness that concealed us, we saw what was happening on the other side of the bridge, which we only perceived as silhouettes. They were boys, some of them only children. They were holding someone who was trying to scream. They threw the person to the ground and began to beat him with merciless savagery. There were voices in Arabic, the sounds of someone being struck repetitively screaming in pain, and then a weak call for help in French. "À l'aide!"

"Stay here!" Khaled ordered. "Don't move." Before I could say a thing, Khaled had run out from under the bridge and shouted, "Stop," followed by a few words in Arabic. The boys froze up. All noise stopped. Khaled said more things I could not understand. They looked at Khaled, and, perhaps recognizing him, all at once, like a flock of birds that gets startled, moved as one and scattered away.

Instantaneously, the street turned silent. The human shape on the ground was motionless but let out a moan. Khaled leaned over him. I stepped out of the shadow. "We need to call the police, and a doctor," he said.

When I bent over the body, I gasped. "Gustave!" I cried out.

My brother lay on the ground, his face covered in blood. It was too dark to know how badly injured he might be. "Gustave" I called. "Gustave! Can you hear me?" I told Khaled. "It's my brother!"

"We're both in bad trouble now," was the first thing Gustave mumbled before a wave of nausea overtook him and he turned to the side to vomit.

"Why is your brother here?" Khaled asked.

"He's been following me everywhere," I admitted.

"Sit with him. I'll call for help."

After a few minutes, Khaled returned, accompanied by two French policemen who had been doing their rounds. If they were so close, how had they not heard what was going on? By now, it was dark out. I sensed that they had heard the commotion but chosen not to get involved until Khaled asked for help.

"What happened here?" one of the policemen demanded to know.

My lies came out swiftly. "My brother and I were walking back home, and a group of young boys assaulted him." I pointed to Khaled. "This boy here made them run away."

"Do you know the assailant?" the policeman asked Khaled.

The other policeman observed me with suspicion. "They attacked your brother but left you alone?"

"What were the two of you doing near the Kasbah after curfew?" the first policeman asked.

I remembered who I was. I was a French citizen, and they were the police. "What does it matter?" I shouted. "My brother needs to be taken to the hospital immediately!" Gustave was getting to his feet by the time the ambulance arrived. I turned to look at Khaled just as one of the policemen handcuffed him. Khaled was not speaking, not resisting. "Why are you handcuffing him? What has he done? Where are you taking him?"

"It's police business, Mademoiselle."

"This is a mistake! I just told you he's the one who saved my brother! You have no grounds to arrest him."

"We have to conduct an investigation, and he might know the attackers. If he has nothing to reproach himself, he will give us their names and be released."

Khaled and I exchanged looks. We both knew that any kind of resistance would make the problem worse. One of the policemen pushed him forward. Khaled tripped slightly. To my horror, the policeman struck him on the back of his head.

"Why are you hitting him?" I cried out. "Don't hurt him!"

Khaled looked down, expressionless.

"You and your brother should know better than break curfew," the policeman said. "How can I reach your parents?"

I had no choice but to give the police the information. One of the policemen walked to a police telephone set up in the street, and we waited.

Two vehicles arrived. One was a police car, the other an ambulance. A nurse in white uniform and the ambulance driver, with the help of one of the policemen, helped Gustave into the back of the ambulance, and the nurse went in with him and began to tend to his wounds.

I climbed in the front seat next to the driver, a mournful-looking older Algerian man. As we drove off in the night, the ambulance's headlight briefly shone on Khaled, still handcuffed, being pushed into the police car.

"Why are they taking him?" I shouted. "He is the one who saved my brother from being killed! He's a hero."

The driver shook his head slowly. "He's an Arab," he said. He turned on the siren. I could hardly think straight between my sobs and the piercing noise that rattled my brain. How could my brother be so stupid and so fixated on me? Why had he followed me to the Kasbah? What did he know? Did he understand that I was meeting Khaled? Had he realized that Khaled had saved him? I turned to see my brother, who was being tended to by the nurse. I urgently needed to tell him the version of the story I had given the police, but the presence of the nurse and the terrible noise made communicating with Gustave impossible.

I was in the hospital's waiting room when my parents arrived, dressed in their opera clothes: my father in a tuxedo and Mother in her fur and pearls. First, the police spoke to my father while my mother rushed to Gustave's room, brushing past me without looking at me.

My father came to me and, reassured that I was unhurt, asked me to stay in the hallway while he went to see Gustave.

Twenty minutes later, my father came out of the room, livid. He took me aside into a hallway so that we would not be heard. "Gustave needs stitches. Three of his ribs are broken, as is his nose," he said. "But what your brother told me about what happened has nothing to do with what you told the police."

"Baba, you need to call the commissariat!" I cried. "The boy who saved Gustave was taken there!"

"Saved? Your brother was savagely attacked. He does not look saved to me! He will probably require surgery to fix his nose."

"Gustave would have been much worse; in fact, he could have been killed had the boy not intervened when he did."

"The police will find out what actually happened and not some lie you concocted," he said. "You told the police that you and your brother were just walking together after curfew, that you were attacked, and that a boy who was just passing by intervened."

"That's it. That's what happened. Had it not been for this stranger—"

"Gustave said that he saw you leave the apartment, that he followed you, and that he saw you enter the Kasbah right before curfew. He said he waited at the foot of the Kasbah for two hours until you came back with a boy. By then it was dark and after curfew. He then followed the two of you until a group of boys attacked him."

I had no choice but to tell my father the truth. "It's true. I was meeting a boy there." My father's face turned red. "But we did nothing, Baba!" I quickly said. "I swear it to you! He just wanted to show me the Kasbah."

"Who is this boy you will take such ridiculous risks for?"

"He was just – showing me the Kasbah. What harm is there in that?"

My father put a hand up to stop me. "We will stick to the version you told the police," was all he said.

Gustave was kept under observation in a crowded hall full of hospitalized patients and their families. We were advised that he should not fall asleep, as he might have a concussion. My mother and father, still in their opera attire, fretted over him, my father intent on Gustave drinking water, and my mother crying the entire time and panicking and calling the nurses each time Gustave appeared to doze off. I sat in a chair, furious at the spectacle our family was.

Dawn came. We were all exhausted. My father paid for a private room, and Gustave was transferred to it. In the private room, Father, Mother, and I slumped into chairs, thankful to be alone at last. Gustave looked terrible. Both of his eyes were swollen shut, his nose was cut and misshaped, and it seemed that at least one of his teeth was missing.

"This country is a terrible, lawless place," my mother said. "Look what those savages did to my son. His beautiful face is ruined!"

"Right now, Algeria isn't any more lawless than everywhere else in Europe," I pointed out.

"And his face is not ruined," my father said. "Nothing is ruined. He will heal."

"I don't mind a few scars," Gustave said.

"He will look more rugged," I said.

Now that it was just the four of us, my mother, whose eyes were red from crying, turned to me. "So Gustave was following you. What I fail to understand is why you were out at that hour."

"She was meeting a boy," my father sighed.

"A boy? At night? Oh my!" Mother screeched. "What kind of boy?"

"Is he one of those Jewish students?" my father asked.

I widened my eyes. "How do you know about them?" I said. My father just shrugged in exasperation.

"What Jewish students?" Mother bellowed.

"He's a local boy," I said, bracing myself.

"What does she mean by *local*?" my mother asked my father in complete incomprehension.

My father shrugged toward me and said, "Ask your daughter."

"Ask her? When she's been telling us nothing but lies?"

"He's a Muslim boy, Mother," I said defiantly. "He's the one who stopped the attackers."

An icy silence fell upon the room. We heard a mumble come from Gustave's bed. "I've been trying to keep an eye on her," he said. "Like you asked me to."

"You weren't supposed to risk your life," my father said.

"I thought I'd tell her to stop and she would. I just needed proof."

I was furious that they felt entitled to talk about me as though I was not in the room. "Proof? This is not a criminal investigation!" I said.

"Enough!" my father snapped.

"Tell me you did not actually enter the Kasbah," Mother said.

"It's a perfectly safe place. Lovely in fact." I admitted, "And I was dressed like a Muslim woman."

"Oh my," Mother said again. "But why with this … Arab?"

"His name is Khaled," I said defiantly. "And I'm in love with him!"

Mother slumped in her chair and began fanning herself. "I will die right this minute," she said. "How did you procure yourself those clothes?"

"I took them from Sandra."

Mother went quiet, as she suddenly understood something. Fury passed through her eyes like a maelstrom. "Sandra gave you the clothes! And she let you out, didn't she? How could you have gotten out of a room you share otherwise?"

"It was only going to be for a few hours. If Gustave had not—"

"This is all her fault!" Mother erupted. "She has ruined your reputation, and she's caused Gustave to be nearly killed!"

"Sandra had no idea," I lied, trying to look innocent.

My mother turned to my father and growled between clenched teeth, enunciating each word. "I want that woman out of my house by morning."

I could deny all I wanted; this was the last bit of news Mother needed in her case against Sandra, and there was nothing any of us would be able to do or say to protect her now. Father and Gustave seemed crushed. I lowered my head.

Father, in an empty voice, briefed Gustave on the official version of the story he should give the police: Gustave and I were together, walking, we got lost, he was attacked, Khaled was a stranger passing by, a good Samaritan who stopped the assailants.

Gustave remained at the hospital overnight and Mother, Father, and I returned to the apartment where Sandra was wringing her hands. My father reassured her about Gustave. Mother refused to look at Sandra and stormed into her room, slamming the door behind her. My father called Sandra into the kitchen and closed the door behind them. They stayed there for a long time, with me pacing on the other side of the door. I will never know what he said to her, but when she came out, her eyes were red. Heartbreakingly, my father looked to have been crying too. It dawned on me that the night had set in motion events beyond my control, and I blamed Gustave for that.

Sandra went to the bedroom we shared. Wordlessly, she began to gather her few possessions and set them out on top of her bed. I helped her fold her clothes, crying. "I thought that if anyone found out, I would be the one to get into trouble. I never thought I would get you fired. I don't want you to go. Where will you live?"

"Your father will drive me to a hotel for now, and then I will see."

"Sandra?"

"Yes?"

"I'm so sorry."

Sandra shook her head. "I knew what you were doing. I let you. I endangered you and Gustave. Your mother is right."

"You couldn't stop me. You tried."

"I could have. I did not want to."

"But why?"

She inspected me with her wide-set, unflinching eyes. "You have a wild spirit and no fear. I wish I had no fear."

"That's not true. I'm afraid for you now."

Sandra had a small, sad smile and said, "Tell me about this boy."

"He is a wonderful person, and smart too." As I spoke, a dam broke inside me. I burst with happiness just to be able to tell Sandra about Khaled. I told her everything: who he was, where we met, how handsome he was, and also how there was no future for us because of our races, our religions, and our places in society. "He works all the time. He supports his entire family. He wants to make something of himself, and I know he will. I know it!"

She beamed at me. "You respect him."

"Oh, Sandra, I love him!" I said, and then I broke down in tears because neither of my parents had wanted to know anything about him.

"Does he feel the same toward you?"

"He does!"

Sandra sat on the bed next to me and caressed my hair. "I too fell in love once," she murmured. "Just like you and this boy, the boy I loved was from a different religion, a different world from mine. We could not be together. To do so was to risk our lives. Still, we ran away together. But then there was the fire. The city was destroyed. So many died. The great fire of Smyrna tore us apart. We were separated."

"How long did it take for you to forget him?"

She took my hands. "I have never forgotten him."

"Was there ever another man after him?" I regretted asking. With her appearance, finding love again would be nearly impossible.

As though she could read my thoughts, Sandra said, "One great love is more than many people will ever experience."

An hour later, Sandra was gone from our lives.

She visited Gustave at the hospital, and then Father took her to a hotel. He paid for a month in advance and gave her money for her expenses. He told us this and said that he would help find her a new position.

Mother had her replaced the same week by a local woman, a wrinkled old thing with no personality. In truth, Gustave and I had long outgrown the need for a nanny. The circumstances of the war had made it difficult for my big-hearted father to leave Sandra behind in Paris or Cannes, postponing the inevitable. It had made little sense to keep her for as long as we had, especially as Mother had made her into the focus of her unhappiness. I felt certain that Sandra would soon find a family with young children she could take care of. She was so wonderful with children.

Through August and September 1942, I saw Sandra a couple more times. I visited her at her hotel once. She looked resigned. Another time I met her by accident at the market, and we walked through the aisles together and chatted. She was distraught, I could tell. I asked if she had money. She said that my father had been generous. I asked her what her plans were; she said she'd be just fine and not to worry about her. But there was something else, ominous, dark. Or do I only think this in retrospect? Because I have since wondered if her troubles were already brewing that day, below the surface.

When we parted, she hugged me tightly and told me that I was a wonderful, intelligent girl, that I was brave but that it did not mean I should be reckless, and that she was proud of me. Were those parting words? Did she know what was about to happen? She also said she was sorry for the pain she had caused. She uttered not a word of bitterness or resentment toward Mother or Father for leaving her in the dust after her devotion to us.

****

Marceline looked at Cassandra. She now looked back at her early forties, the age her niece was, as her infancy. Everything before that had been a wash.

Vanity. Selfishness. She had made so many mistakes. She had saved the day a couple of times, but who remembered?

The tea in their cups was cold. Marceline felt drained. She had not gotten around to what she wanted her niece to know. She could not. Not today. She would first need to find the strength.

Cassandra sat upright, riveted, expectant. She was going to disappoint her. "This was the last time I ever saw Sandra," she told Cassandra. "When we heard from her again it was a whole month later and through the police."

"What happened?" Cassandra exclaimed.

"It was all very mysterious, as you shall see. But I'm quite exhausted. Perhaps we can continue tomorrow."

"Yes, or course. I understand," Cassandra assured her, although her expression told a different story.

"You wait till you reach my age, ma chère," Marceline said. "Aging is not for the weak, as you'll one day find out."

"It's only that I'm leaving Paris soon."

"I will try to remain alive a few more days then. So as not to inconvenience you."

Cassandra looked aghast. "Oh, but not at all!"

"Come tomorrow. It will be lovely weather I am told. We'll have tea in the garden."

"But tell me first, what about Khaled?"

"Khaled?"

"How long did he stay in jail?"

"That's part of a much longer conversation," Marceline said.

After Cassandra had left, Marceline turned to Laure. "Do you think she looks like me at all?"

"It's in the eyes, that unusual color."

"But she doesn't have my strength I don't think. She's more of a delicate flower, like her father."

"Few people have your strength, Madame," Laure answered.

CHAPTER 3

The Man Who Made Pasta

Cassie stepped out of Marceline's house enveloped in a cottony feeling of unreality. She walked on the cobblestone pavement, surprised at the song of birds, at the fact that it was spring in Paris and not Algiers of the 1940s. In Cité des Fleurs, only faint, distant street noises hinted at the twenty-first century. The façades of hotels particuliers peeked from above metal gates, just as they had since their construction a hundred years before. Her cowboy boots hit the uneven pavement in rhythmic sounds that brought her back to here and now. These cobblestones had once been trampled on by horses and carriages. They had been under the wheels of the very first automobiles. They had absorbed the blood of soldiers, résistants, and Jews during the Second World War. In the sixties, revolutionary students had unearthed them to use as projectiles against the police. In Paris, to ignore history was impossible. Every wall, every clock, every statue and building reminded you of it. In the mere twenty years between 1918 and 1938, Europe had ended the supposed "war to end all wars," seen unparalleled growth and progress, revealed in the wild optimism of the années folles, only to embark on the most destructive conflict in human history. How precarious was the balance of things? Economic chaos had been the fertile terrain for anger and xenophobia to fester until the world was ripe for exploitation by the kind of leaders that thrived on divisiveness and fear.

Across the Seine, in the fifteenth arrondissement near Métro Bir-Hakeim, a plaque acknowledged the ignominy that had taken place at the Vel' d'Hiv seventy years before. French citizens beyond reproach, policemen, war heroes, politicians, had taken it upon themselves to round Paris's Jewish families and gather them under the glass dome on a sweltering July day. At what point was it decided to let them die by the hundreds from heat and dehydration? Was it the plan? Or had something gone awry? After allowing that carnage to take place, these upstanding citizens had left the Jews to die and had returned to their wives, children, or grandchildren in time for dinner. It was unfathomable because you wanted to believe in decency, in moral courage. You wanted to believe that mankind was good. But history told a different story. Mankind was awful. And without peace-minded leaders keeping our worst nature in check, it had repeatedly all gone to hell.

Cassie thought of fate, of prescience. Which was it that had compelled her grandfather to run away rather than stay in Paris? Her family had narrowly escaped the fate of other Jews so that Cassie could be conceived. So that she could have two beautiful children. How dare she resent her childhood? How dare she brood with ennui and disenchantment while she lived in safety and abundance? Her father had endured so much yet had chosen to hide his childhood's suffering from his daughters. But this too, she thought, had an impact. In a single generation of deliberate amnesia, all lessons had been lost.

Cassie turned onto Avenue de Clichy with its cars, mopeds, people carrying groceries, children in strollers, pregnant women, honking, whistles, métro vibrating below ground, and smell of baked bread and rotisserie chicken. The arrival of sunshine had transformed the city, altering the sounds and smells, brightening the stone façade of buildings, shifting moods. Because the Parisians were liberated from their umbrellas and raincoats, their eyes met, as if to acknowledge the arrival of springtime.

Maybe she could redeem herself. It was going to be up to her. If she was unable to define herself outside her unrequited love for her father, or for Peter, it was her own fault. She needed to take note, to remind herself of her singular existence at this moment. All around, beautiful things were happening: miracles, moments of grace. In the same hospital where her father languished, babies were born. In studios and apartments across the city, artists created, people kissed under street lamps, men and women made love in bedrooms.

Hervé, she thought. His skin, his lips on her. She hurried her steps, embarrassed by that flash of lust. Only days ago, she was certain that she was done with all this. Sex, desire, those silly things, she never thought about. Or only in those occasional dreams that baffled her. And now she was hurrying through Paris, her heart racing as she thought of a man.

Careful, her mind whispered to her heart. Careful. But those were just words, barely a flutter.

****

When Cassie entered the hospital's waiting room, Odile was alone. She had a book on her lap but was not reading. She sat on the edge of her seat, leaning forward as if she wanted as little of her butt as possible to touch the plastic chair. Her hair was pulled back by a severe little headband that gave her the look of a girl who was never given the authorization to play. Odile had always been uptight, self-righteous. Part of Cassie felt sorry for the perpetual imaginary burden Odile carried. But mostly she felt annoyed. There had always been a rivalry between them. They saw the world and everything in it very differently; their brains were not wired the same way, but was this enough to explain why they were at each other's throat? The antagonism between Gustave and Marceline seemed like a big, sad waste, something that needed repair. And yet, she moved through life not giving a moment of thought to the waste of her relationship with her own sister.

Odile looked up from her book and said in a hollow voice, "The antibiotics aren't working."

"What does that mean?"

"They're putting him on dialysis. Something to do with his kidneys." Odile's eyes flooded. "What if Papa doesn't get better?"

Cassie had the vision of her father in that hospital bed in Algiers, after the gang beat him up. She patted Odile on the shoulder. "The dialysis will help. The doctors know what they're doing. Right?"

Odile stiffened in her chair. "Is that a question or an affirmation?"

"Quit thinking that everything I say is an affront."

"You're the one who keeps questioning the treatment."

Cassie closed her eyes, already exhausted after one minute with Odile. "I really wasn't," she said. "At least not this time."

"How long do you plan on staying in Paris?" Odile asked in a tone of reproach.

"My return ticket is for Wednesday."

"So, you're going to leave?"

"What else can I do?"

Odile had a small laugh. "What can you do besides leave me alone to deal with all this, as you always do?"

This wasn't a new argument. Odile took care of their parent's finances; she did their taxes, blah, blah, blah. They called her when they could not fix something in the house. She scheduled their doctors' appointments. When they needed new glasses, when they went to the dentist, it was Odile who took them. In return, Odile got to play the act of the long-suffering victim. "Are you kidding?" Cassie snapped. "First you don't tell me that Papa is having surgery, then you block me from seeing him."

Odile shrugged. "You don't get it, and you never will."

"You're the one who doesn't get it. You've made it so that I can be of no help at all."

"I'm not asking you to help Papa," Odile said coldly. "Even the doctors can't seem to do that! I'm asking you to help me and Maman."

Cassie took a breath before responding. She was not the selfish, irresponsible person Odile was making her out to be, but it was true that Odile's willingness to sacrifice herself allowed for Cassie to be in another country and live her life, a fact that was never far from either of their minds. "I'm here now," she sighed. "What is it you want me to do?"

"You need to help our family instead of running away from home like you always do."

"The United States is my home. It's been my home for the last twenty years. If anything, I'm running away from there to be here."

"You know very well what I'm saying."

"I don't."

"Every time there is an issue, you're all high and mighty. You act so wronged by us. Or whatever guilt trip you're into, whatever story you tell yourself. But this is not the time and place, Cassie. This is a crisis. We have to stick together."

"Is that what you call casting me away from his room?"

"And here you go again! You keep making it about you! I need to protect him. The doctors agreed. I *don't* know why Papa gets agitated when he sees you. I'm not saying that it's your fault, but the result is the same."

"Oh, I get it. It's not about me, and that's because it's about you! Always. *Your* fear, *your* worry. How about the possibility that I might need to be in that room with Papa just as much as you do?"

Odile thought for a moment. "To be frank, no. I don't think you need to be in the room as much as I do. You said it yourself: your home is elsewhere. You washed your hands of him a long time ago."

In the wave of hurt and outrage, Cassie was rapidly succumbing to an old feeling, something in her soul was being torn open, and she had to steady herself. "You think you have a monopoly on loving Papa? I could love him plenty too if only he'd let me." Cassie tried to take in air, but her lungs seemed reduced to useless pockets. She studied the scratches on her hand, still fresh from the gardening she had done the day before coming to Paris. The scratches felt grounding. Whatever this awful moment was, it was temporary. There was normality to return to, elsewhere.

"I'm sorry that things were so difficult between you and Papa," Odile said. "But it was not my doing. The two of you created this. I was in the middle."

"What was I guilty of, Odile?" Cassie asked in a small voice. "Why was he so irked by me? What did I do that rubbed him the wrong way?"

Odile looked away. "Things would have worked themselves out over time. The two of you hit a rough patch, and you left the country. You just picked up and left. How were things going to ever improve between you after that?"

"You know this was not new. He was like this with me from the time I was a kid."

"Why didn't you try to fix things?"

"I tried everything!" Cassie cried out. "But he shut me out! Moving away didn't create the problem. I moved away for self-preservation! When I finally realized that I would never be loved by him. And this after killing myself trying to accomplish that since I was little!"

"You were always trying to be perfect and being so competitive."

Cassie spoke without a breath. "Yes, I tried too hard! And yes, I was desperate! But every movement I made, everything I said and did, it all seemed to annoy him. And you? You could do no wrong."

"Don't be melodramatic."

Cassie looked straight into Odile's eyes, her fury daring her sister to look away. "Are you telling me that he never said negative things about me behind my back? That, in fact, he said loving things about me when I didn't know it? Please tell me that I'm imagining all this because I'll want to believe you. I would desperately want to believe you!"

Odile stared at Cassie. "Why get into all this now? Papa's antibiotics aren't working. He needs dialysis, and you just want to talk about the past."

Cassie looked at her feet. "You're right. It's just … so many emotions. I don't know how to feel right now."

Odile sighed. "Look, I didn't know why Papa was like that with you back then," she said. "I still don't know."

Cassie felt a deep silence sweep through her. And then, a sensation of brightness, as though all the lights in the room turned on at once. It was real! It had happened! Odile was confirming it. And yes, she was devastated by this truth, but it was the truth she needed to hear. "Thank you for acknowledging this," she muttered.

Odile rubbed her face with the palms of her hands. "I mean … I thought I knew why he was like that with you, like part of him could not stand you." She was speaking to Cassie but mostly to herself. "It was the way you were, and all, you know … bossy, annoying, superior."

"Superior?"

"But the way he saw you maybe colored the way I perceived you. It's hard to tell. It's … I don't know. Messed up." Odile was crying now. Why was she crying? Was it remorse, sadness, self-pity, or the simple fact that their dad was very sick? Cassie was thankful for her sister's tears because she was not able to shed her own. Something in her was blocked. Or perhaps it was that if she began crying, she might never stop.

"All those years, being told it was all in my imagination."

"I'm sorry. I feel like a piece of shit for telling you this. I don't want you to be mad at Papa. Or Papa to be mad at me for telling you."

"It helps actually."

"I feel really bad about it."

"But why superior? I was insecure my entire childhood."

"Well, like when you think you know better than the doctors what to do about Papa."

"I don't think I know better. I just ask questions."

"Same difference," Odile said with a shrug.

"It's not the same! I—"

Cassie stopped herself. What was the point? The way Odile perceived her was too ingrained to change in a day. Instead, she said, "I need you to put me back on the visitors' list so I can be in Papa's room with you guys."

Odile wrung her hands. "I want to, Cassie. I really want to. But I can't take the chance of Papa having another episode. For the moment, he's calm. If he sees you and goes ballistic, they'll go back to sedating him, and you know that it would make his recovery that much more difficult." Odile looked at her feet. "I'm sorry, Cassie."

Cassie was stunned. "Does Papa even realize that I came all the way here just to support him? Did you even tell him?"

Odile spoke uneasily. "What if he sees you and gets into another fit and has a heart attack or something? I'm sorry, but I'd rather insult your pride than take that chance."

Cassie drew a quick breath to control her mounting anger. "My pride?" she exclaimed. "How can you live with the thought that I'm outside his room and not allowed in? How can you sleep at night after you treat your own sister like a frigging leper?"

"I *don't* sleep at night!" Odile whined.

A childhood urge made her want to throw herself at Odile and pull on her hair, the way they used to when they fought as kids. The adult part of her told her that she had better walk away. Trembling with fury, Cassie looked at Odile. "I will come back later or call to see how he is. I guess for now it's better if I just go, or I'm going to lose my shit."

As she left the room, she heard Odile whimper, "I'm sorry. I really am."

Cassie's boot heels clapped down the hospital corridors, her anger fresh and raw. She needed to bite someone's head off right this minute! She charged toward the ICU's reception desk where Mademoiselle Pinçon huddled with the usual weary group of nurses and interns. "I want an appointment, and I want it now," she told Pinçon. "If your Chief of Services doesn't meet me, I'll escalate the hell out of this!" she said.

"More than you already have?" Pinçon said tonelessly.

"I'm writing day-by-day accounts of our interactions. He'd better meet with me before I post them all over social media with the name of this hospital front and center!"

The nurses averted their eyes, but Pinçon looked at her, or through her, with a calculated mix of hostility and boredom. "You can always try eight a.m. tomorrow."

Cassie had not expected Pinçon to cave, and so she doubled down, improvising, "I have videos! Damning pieces of evidence!" Pinçon gave her an uninterested look. "If he doesn't meet me tomorrow at eight a.m., this hospital's ineptitude will go more viral than any of the germs this place is rampant with!"

"I will pass this on, Madame," Pinçon said.

"Eight a.m. sharp! I'll be here. You better count on it," Cassie yelled before turning around with a flourish and leaving the hospital.

Back in her hotel room, Cassie drew a bath and slipped into the hot water. She floated there for a long time, incapable of aligning two thoughts. It all came in a jumble: Hervé, Odile, Albano, her dad and mom, Sabine, Marceline, Lucienne, her children. And then back to Hervé and their night. Hervé and his hands, his…. Be careful, she reminded herself.

She felt numb, curiously detached from Odile's admission of what she had suspected for years. She wasn't destroyed. Would she feel destroyed later, when the numbness went away? It was one thing that her father "could not stand her" as an adult. She could see why: she had opposed him, she had contradicted him, she had cross-examined him. Eventually, she had married an American and permanently left France. But the confirmation of what she had suspected, felt in her bones rather, that he did not like her even as a child, that was too much to process.

She floated in her warm bath, thinking, trying to make the jigsaw pieces of her childhood fit together. Her dad had not been openly hostile. Things that happened were subtle: a slow and steady neglect of her dreams, a failure to notice her talents, a pruning of her self-esteem. The shaping had been bonsai-like. Imperceptible almost. And just like a bonsai, things looked healthy on the outside, but something was off. She had been shaped by him, by the way he looked at her, or rather did not look at her. His indistinct animosity toward her was a poison that had tasted almost like parental love. How he seemed never to see her, never to hear her. His pointed interest in her sisters. The way he delighted in them but looked away when Cassie was trying so hard to do well. It was not aggression; it was pointed neglect. Had he beat her, or screamed at her, she would have been sure. But he was quiet and sneaky about it, and because she was a child and could find no fault in him, she could only hate herself.

She thought of Albano, her grandfather who had instinctively known to take his family away from danger when so many other Jews had stayed behind. In a way, she had done the same. Without understanding the magnitude of the danger or the nature of the enemy, she had packed her things and left. She had moved to the United States, latched on to Peter, not knowing herself at all, but fighting tooth and nail for survival. She had fought to reclaim the lost parts of herself. Only she had gone about it the wrong way. Instead of sitting with her sadness, she had discovered anger. Instead of going deep, she had gone wayward.

Now, maybe, things could start to make sense. She would have to sit with the sadness, at some point. For the moment, it was relief she felt. She was thankful to Odile for validating her experience. She felt relief that perhaps she was not a bitter ingrate, but justifiably heartbroken.

She took her hands out of the water and examined her pruned fingers. Five years after removing her wedding ring, her finger still showed an indentation. Peter had served as her emotional punching bag. That's why he had left her, wasn't it? But she could not quiet the nagging suspicion that this wasn't the whole story. Something about Peter and Jessica's tale of how they had met smelled fishy. She knew that, had always known that, but healthy self-preservation had dictated that she should not confront him about it. As with her dad, she had blamed herself for the failure of the relationship rather than blame the man she loved. One day she would need the courage to look deeper. But not yet. Not now.

An hour later, she heard Hervé's motorcycle in the street below, and she ran down the stairs, making herself forget Peter, Marceline, Odile, her father, and even, temporarily, her children.

They drove on rue La Mouzaïa, and Hervé made a turn into a narrow cobblestone alley with small two-storied square houses on each side. Clematis and wisteria in full blue bloom were tangled in gates and climbing façades. A fat orange cat, stretched out on the cobblestones as if determined to soak up every remaining ray of the setting sun, moved begrudgingly to make way for them. Hervé stopped in front of a small gate and turned off the engine. They climbed off the motorcycle. He opened the gate and walked his bike into a tiny courtyard. "This is home," he said.

"What is this area called?" Cassie said as she removed her helmet. "It doesn't feel like Paris at all."

"This is the La Mouzaïa neighborhood. For a Parisienne, you don't know your city very well."

"My family was like a sect, I told you. We weren't encouraged to expand our horizons."

"Well, there are 250 houses in the neighborhood along alleys like this one. The houses were built in the late eighteen hundreds as housing for the quarry workmen who worked at mining the gypsum underground. Below it's all quarry tunnels and galleries. That's why the neighborhood was never demolished. The ground is not strong enough to build up the way they did with those atrocious buildings all around." Hervé took the mail out of the box and opened the front door. He turned on the light. Inside, it smelled of wood fire and books. The living room was furnished with old things: a battered brown leather sofa, mismatched wooden chairs, frayed rugs, a fireplace filled with the remnants of a fire. There were two electric guitars in a corner. There were shelves filled with vinyl records and books. The wide beams on the ceiling were sprinkled with cobwebs. "This place looks like you," Cassie said.

"I saw you look at that cobweb."

"I meant it as a compliment."

"My ex took all the good stuff," Hervé said. "And the cleaning supplies."

"She didn't take the house?"

"She kept our house in the Lubéron," he said, leaving the mail on an atrocious coffee table covered with glass, set atop a rusty oil can bedazzled with broken mirror pieces.

"You could not convince her to take this table," Cassie asked.

"This was my brother's first attempt at building furniture. He was twelve years old. He's a talented wood crafter now. He makes all sorts of magnificent things. I kept it because it's funny-looking." He leafed through the mail and brandished a motorcycle magazine. "Again, that crap?" he exclaimed. The back cover had a garish advertisement for *Women in Black, Part Two.* Hervé turned the magazine over, to show Cassie the photograph of all the *Women in Black, Part Two*'s cast members in full costume. "I give up," he said, and he tossed the magazine into the fireplace.

"What's your beef with that movie?" she asked, defensively. "It's harmless."

"I don't find stupidity harmless."

"Hollywood writers are actually pretty smart."

"Even more worrisome if intelligent people are deliberately fine-tuning this crap." He took her coat, removed his leather jacket, and tossed them on a chair.

She sank on the couch. The leather was supple and warm under her fingers. She saw no sign of a television. "What's so wrong with a little mindless entertainment once in a while?"

"The word entertainment itself is the danger," Hervé said. "People absorb the output of creative people and forget to produce anything of their own." There was a scratching sound coming from the front door. Hervé went to open it, and the orange cat she had seen in the street walked in, looking put-upon. "I know," he told the cat. "You're hungry. I know, I know."

From the couch, she watched Hervé enter the kitchen and look in the cupboard for a can of cat food. The cat began purring loudly, throwing himself at Hervé's legs.

"What's his name?"

"I don't know. He adopted me, not the other way around. I call him Le Chat." He crouched and scratched the cat's head. "I understand human's desire to escape their thoughts. We're terrified to contemplate the deep questions: morality, mortality, life's meaning, the universe."

Cassie rubbed her temples. "I'm not sure I want to ponder all of that either."

"But isn't this precisely what you're doing now with your aunt?"

"I thought I was pondering my family history."

"It's all too enormous. We think we might implode with despair if we so much as think about deeper questions. But humans are existential creatures. What you call harmless entertainment yanks us in every direction except inward, and inward is the only place where we'll find any peace."

"So, the problem is the cure?"

"You bet it is. Look at people jab at their telephones and computers, desperate for a distraction. Look at them pack into movie theaters to cram down fake emotions, fake relationships, fake dialogues, cramming a fake world down into their starving psyches. People will never find meaning from the passive absorption of vapid Hollywood crap."

"Where would we find it then? Religion?"

"It will come from the opposite of distraction. The ability to sit with one's thoughts, the ability to make things, to create, to move, to get excited about ideas, to dream up something better, to earn a living doing honest work."

"But you hate your job, you said."

"My true work starts when the job ends. My work is to pay close attention to small things, to the process of things."

"What is this process you keep talking about?"

"Maybe there is a better word for it." Hervé came to sit on the couch next to her. The golden light that came through the window shone on his face. "It's about finding mundane things beautiful," he said. "Then it all becomes simpler. Here, I'll show you." She followed him into the kitchen. "Have a seat," he said. He washed his hands at the small enamel sink. The kitchen was tiny, crooked, with a chipped, old-mosaic floor, an antique buffet, a small range, and an old refrigerator. The walls were lined with shelves covered with a disparate assortment of plates, glasses, pots, and pans. "Bon, so here we are," he said. "We are making pasta, yes? But why? It's a waste of time, correct? I can buy a box of decent dry pasta for two euros. I can leave it in the cupboard for a year, ten years; it will not go bad. When I want to eat, I toss it into a pot of boiling water, and it's done. How convenient! What an impressive shelf-life! These are the yardsticks these days."

He went to the shelves. "But look: here is a bowl, and here is flour and sea salt, and good olive oil." He went to the small refrigerator. "And here are eggs. And what we get out of those four ingredients is an adventure." He moved through the small kitchen naturally, each gesture relaxed and precise. He clipped herbs from a planter in the windowsill: mint, parsley, coriander leaves. "Smell this," he said, putting the herbs near her nostrils. "It's for later." He returned to the table and dropped flour onto it. "So, first, you use good, honest flour, none of that refined stuff that looks like crack and is just about as nutritious. Then you make a well. And then you break the eggs into the well, add a little olive oil." He did this, cracking the eggs with one hand with a flourish. He winked at her. "See that? I hope you are impressed. I practiced for so long that by the end, live chicks were coming out of the shells."

"Duly impressed," she said. She peered at the bright yolks in the white flour well. "Why can't you put the whole thing into a bowl?"

"Drama. Danger. If you put this in a bowl, it won't get all over the kitchen, and getting dirty is part of the tradition." He rolled his sleeves up. His hands dove into the flour. Soon he was whisking the egg in the center, folding in the flour, and then going at it with his hands until his fingers were coated with sticky goop. "Can you add a handful of flour please?" She did, and he began pushing and pressing the dough with his palms until it came together into a ball, shiny and smooth. He spread a thin coat of flour on the table and set the dough on the flour. "And now we wait," he said.

"For how long?"

"Long enough for a glass of wine." He poured her a glass of Bordeaux and plucked the fresh mint, parsley, and coriander leaves off their stems. The combined aroma of all three herbs bounced through the kitchen as he crushed leaves between his fingers. He had beautiful hands, masculine and wide.

"What will you do with these?" she asked. "Are they for a sauce? What do you call it?"

"Bah, no name. I just mix in what I have. Sometimes I add ground pistachios or almonds." He took a head of garlic and with a well-calibrated drop of a fist, separated the head into cloves. He took the cloves between his palms and rubbed them together to detach the skins until each clove lay bare on the kitchen table. He placed the peeled garlic into an antiquated, eighties-looking blender, added olive oil, salt, and pepper, and then added the leaves. The air filled with the aroma of garlic and mint.

"I like your kitchen. It reminds me of my hotel room."

"The old doors creek, the handles wobble, the plumbing is mercurial. I can't find the origin of that mildew smell. But the house has personality. The whole neighborhood does. It's bucolic. Cats roam like sentinels. How many Parisians can boast to have bird nests on their windowsills?" He took out a rolling pin, flattened the dough, flapped it over, rolled it thinner, adding speckles of flour onto the dough, and repeated the motion until the dough was very thin. He folded the sheet of dough lightly, and with a knife, cut thin strands of dough the width of fettuccine. The strands were uneven, but he did not seem to care. "Mix those up with a little flour, so they don't stick to each other."

As Cassie tossed flour on the strands of pasta, she felt the resistance of the dough between her fingers, pliable and soft but also resilient. She dipped her hands in the flour, tossed the pasta until each strand separated. There was flour on every inch of the table and a good deal dusted the floor. Soon there was a jumbled pile of blond pasta in the center of the table, each strand self-contained and perfect, like individual small beings. "Et voila," Hervé said, opening both palms toward the result of their effort. "And here is my point. Was this convenient? Of course not. I have boxes in the cupboard. Was it important? Not either. Was it urgent? No. These might not even taste better. But it was beautiful making those, wasn't it?"

Cassie smiled at the mound of pasta. "It was."

"That, my dear, is what I call The Process."

She noticed in herself a sort of softening. Her guard had been up, and now it was down, and that was all right with her. The kitchen smelled of mint and coriander and garlic. The cat sat on the countertop, his eyes half-closed. Hervé had flour in his hair. She smiled. "I get it," she said.

"Good. Now we wait."

"How long do we wait this time?"

He washed his hands, wiped them on his jeans, came to her, and took her chin between his fingers. "As long as we want." He guided her toward the leather couch. He went to the fireplace and placed branches around a log. He scratched a match and tore the magazine apart, crumpled the pages, and lit them on fire. The Woman in Black was set ablaze. He returned to the couch, sat beside her, and began to kiss her neck.

Night had fallen. Cassie had moved to the table Hervé had set outside in the tiny garden. He went into the kitchen while she picked at olives and cubes of goat cheese. Candles flickered on the table. A record played a French song she did not recognize. Wisteria blooms cascaded down from the fence that surrounded the patio.

What she wasn't telling Hervé came to the surface of her consciousness accompanied by the vaguest of ill-feelings. She brushed her uneasiness aside. For now, she'd continue to circumnavigate any mention of the United States or the ticking clock of her return ticket. A romance. At her age. Possibly for the first time in her life. Because to marry your first boyfriend at nineteen on account of being preggers with twins wasn't the definition of romance.

She was amazed to see how, once deprived of a computer and cell phone and taken out of her natural habitat, her life in Los Angeles had receded into a ghostly fog. A week ago, she agonized over what she should donate to the Salvation Army. This had been the extent of her rebellion; the only way she could attempt to let go of Peter was to reject that job he had given her as curator of all the broken things he was attached to but did not want in his own house. Her new reality included different broken things, not just in her past, but in her father's and grandfather's past. She was the product of suffering she hadn't known about: fear, war, rage, jealousy, resentment, self-loathing. And there were the broken things she knew about but had ignored: her relationship with Odile, her children's bond, which was falling apart, Peter and Jessica's relationship and their lies, and Sabine's heart.

She was brought back to her presence inside Hervé's house as he walked into the patio holding a steaming bowl of pasta in one hand and a smaller bowl of sauce in the other. "Are you cold?" he asked. Not waiting for an answer, he returned inside to fetch a blanket. He wrapped it around her, and she felt immense well-being. He sat down next to her, served the pasta on two plates, spooned the sauce over it, and shaved parmesan over the plates. "On mange," he said.

She took a bite. "My God, it's too good!"

"They say that raw garlic should not be eaten in polite company, but I have chocolate cake for dessert. Chocolate cancels out the garlic; that's a scientific fact."

Soon enough Cassie would pop out of this temporary madness and return to her reasonable self. But not yet. Now, the moment was hers. Hervé served her more Bordeaux, and they ate dinner in the purple glow of the moon as it shined through the wisteria.

****

The shrill ring of the telephone awakened her the following morning. Cassie looked at her watch. It was eight in the morning. Hervé flailed around the bed, feeling with his arms for the telephone on the bedside table. "Yes?" he grumbled, sitting up in bed. His hair stood up on his head; he was wearing a threadbare V-neck undershirt and nothing else, and the stubble on his face was salt and pepper. He was gorgeous.

"There is nothing I can do," he told the person on the telephone. "Better yet, there is nothing I want to do. What? No! Then tell her to stop harassing us. I deal with logistics and flow charts, not people, and you know this. That was the deal I made for as long as I'm in this … purgatory." Hervé ruffled his hair. "Find an excuse. Tell her I'm in meetings all day. Diplomatically, of course. Tell her I'm in a meeting all week. I don't care." Apparently, the person on the telephone was insisting. He put his hand on Cassie's bare shoulder and caressed the side of her body. "Then tell her I'm on a safari to kill baby pandas," he said while smiling at Cassie. "You might as well since she's obviously made me out to be the devil."

He hung up the phone and rolled over in bed to face Cassie. "And you want me to get a cell phone?"

"Headaches at work?"

"Not for much longer. As soon as I can, I'm taking the first plane to Africa to help people with real problems."

Cassie felt the moment tarnished. What had she been imagining? She was leaving. He was leaving. "I'll take a shower," she said.

"I'll make you breakfast."

They took showers, had a quick breakfast, and hopped on Hervé's bike. He dropped her off at the hotel and zoomed off to work. At her hotel, the old man saw her and disappeared behind the reception's counter. After a few "attendez, attendez," he handed Cassie a small flat package. "It came this morning, special delivery," he said in a tone of utter puzzlement, and then looked at her questioningly, as though she owed it to him to open it right there and solve the mystery.

She went up the stairs to her room and opened the box. It was a tablet and a wireless keyboard, compliments of Peter. Not quite the computer he had mentioned, but he must have paid a small fortune to make this happen regardless. Amazing how simple things became once Peter wanted something.

The sleek tablet, all deceptive minimalism and advanced technology, was a thing of beauty, and yet she felt curiously turned off by it. It made her think of shackles and wastefulness or whatever was the opposite of making pasta from scratch.

She put the tablet in her bag, grabbed her coat, and ran down the stairs. In the phone booth, she dialed Peter collect. "I got your package," she told him. "But I can't leave early."

"But I bought a ticket!"

"Peter! I never agreed to this. I need these few days in Paris."

On the line, there was silence. Peter said, "We're in a very tight spot. What you French people would call a case of force majeure. I realize the timing sucks. I totally empathize."

She stiffened, shocked by the arrogance of his certainty. "Do you?"

"Wasn't I the one who wanted you to go to Paris? I insisted, in fact. I had to drag you to the airport."

"You were right, though. I needed to be here."

"I'm sorry, honey, but I can't let you stay longer, unfortunately. Our name is at stake here."

Now she was angry. She felt it inside her belly like a ping-pong size ball of fire. "My name is not at stake."

"What?"

"You're the A-list writer. You're the one getting the big bucks. I have no name at stake at all."

"Goodness, Cassandra," Peter said, his eye-roll practically audible, "the rehashing, again?"

"I—"

"Besides, you said your dad was unconscious. So, he might not even realize that you left."

"Peter!" she shouted. "I'm not doing it! I'm not rushing to the airport just to please you."

"Same old, same old. Don't turn petty, Cassie."

"When I want something, it's pettiness. When you want something, it's ambition."

"It's always the same thing with you. You start being difficult for no reason. Just because you're in a mood."

"This isn't a mood!"

"Yeah, it's a mood. You have a good thing going, and you sabotage it."

"What the hell are you talking about?"

"You ruined our marriage with all this, and you know it."

"If you're making it about the marriage, is it possible that you were neglecting me, that you were taking me for granted? That you were using me?"

"That's fantasyland, Cassie, and you know it. I was devoted to you. I was quite literally the perfect husband."

She thought for a moment. "Really? So, what about Jessica?"

Peter paused a beat too many before asking, "What about her?"

"You leaped out of the marriage and into her arms." She raised her voice. "Not my definition of devotion."

"You kicked me out!" Peter said, outraged. "You wanted the separation, not me, remember? You brought the whole thing upon yourself. I was heartbroken. I was vulnerable. I looked for a place to stay. I happened to meet her when I was house-hunting."

Cassie knew the story by heart, explained and repeated since their separation like a screenplay rewritten too many times until only the words remained, constricted, incongruous, ill-fitting in the new narrative. She said, "It's just too neat a story, Peter."

Now, Peter was shouting. "I have a contract with the studio!"

"And my father is in the hospital!" she shouted back. She hung up thunderously. She stayed in the booth for a minute, catching her breath. She must have been as red as the surrounding velvet. She got up to leave, but something stopped her. She inhaled deeply and made a credit card call to Alex's cell phone. It rang numerous times. She wanted to hang up but made herself continue. A moment later, Alex was on the line. When she heard her baby, she had to fight back tears. She steadied herself. "Alex, it's Mom," she said. "How are you doing, my love?"

"Mom? Are you back in L.A.?" Alex asked. "I don't recognize the number. I'm walking into class now. Can we talk later?"

"Do you have a minute? I'm calling from Paris."

"My roaming charges are going to be crazy."

"Put it on my tab. How are things in New York?"

"What's wrong?" Alex said. "Is French Grandpa okay?"

"He has a nasty lung infection that's resisting antibiotics. But I'm not calling you about that. It's just that … I'm spending time with my parents and my sisters, and, well, something has been on my mind as I deal with them. Honey, I just … I've been thinking about what you have been saying all these years about your sister."

"Yeah?" he said. He sounded hesitant, like someone who knows no good could come out of broaching this particular topic.

"You were right, my love," she said. "I didn't want to hear it, but it was the truth."

"What was?"

"Sometimes one kid is kind of the squeaky wheel that gets the oil, and we didn't treat you and your sister with equality. We lowered our expectations with Jeanne."

"That's what I've been saying for years!"

"I convinced myself that you were pushing yourself because you wanted to."

"I do want to push myself. But it's just so—"

"Unjust?"

"Yes."

"We found excuses for Jeanne. Not because we thought she deserved them. Only because we were weak."

"Weak with parental love for her." There was thick acerbity in Alex's tone.

"Maybe by denying that there was an imbalance I was hoping that the two of you would get along. But it created the opposite. It drew a wedge between you two. The fact is, she's been terribly lazy and we have been indulgent toward her."

Alex was quiet for a moment, as though he was processing it all. "Well, good. Okay. That's the truth. Mom, I'm outside the classroom. I have a midterm starting in, like, one minute."

"Honey, I have just one other quick thing."

"What?"

"When you were five or six years old, you know, when Dad wanted us all to move, and he kept looking at houses. He would take you and Jeanne, and you'd see houses, and then the three of you would try to convince me to look at them, but I never did. Remember?"

"I guess."

Cassie hesitated. "I mean this was a long, long time ago, but … do you happen to remember seeing house after house? This went on for a year at least. Some of the houses you really liked."

"I remember," Alex said, impatient now.

"You do?"

Alex waited to answer this time, as though he too was bracing himself for her question. "Yes," he said at last.

"Do you have memories about the real estate agent?"

Silence. Then, "Yep."

"Do you remember what he or she looked like?"

"Of course, I remember, Mom." He was upset now.

"It was Jessica, wasn't it?"

"Yes."

"You're certain of this? You were so young."

"I am. It's not like we met her just once. We saw her every time."

"But you never told me."

"Told you what?"

"You didn't tell me, later, when Dad and she … I mean…."

"I thought you knew. I mean, what am I going to say? I was just a kid."

Her heart was beating hard in her chest. "Well. Thank you, love. That's all I wanted to ask you. Water under the bridge; no worries. I was just curious. Are you, um, still happy at Columbia?"

"Reasonably so."

"Are your roommates clean?"

"That they are not."

"Alex?"

"Yes."

"You were right about your sister."

"Got it … got it. Thanks, Mom. It means a lot. I got to go now; class is starting."

"I love you."

"Me too. Bye, Mom."

Cassie hung up. She felt dizzy. The red velvet around her looked about to swallow her. She rattled the door manically, and when it opened, she sprang out of the booth, out of the hotel lobby, and into rue de Seine. Only then did she try breathing. Outside, she hurried to the taxi station. A car was there, and she jumped inside. "Cité des Fleurs, s'il vous plaît."

"What is that?"

"A street. Seventeenth arrondissement."

"Never heard of it," the cab driver said.

"Off Avenue de Clichy, corner of rue Guy Môquet."

"Never heard of it," he repeated.

"Trust me," she said. "It's there."

It had all been at the tip of her consciousness, refusing to be formulated. Could it be that she had known all along? But yes, she *knew*. How could she not have? But she had wanted to believe his lie. Peter had deceived her, and she had let him deceive her.

The car careened through Boulevard de la Chapelle. Cassie saw nothing. She was sweating. She was nauseous. There was a sudden, sharp pain low in her belly like a mean knot. "Stop!" she said. "Stop the car now!" The driver did not slow down; he frowned at her in the rearview mirror, but as soon as he saw how green her face was, he stopped abruptly enough to embed deep skid marks on the asphalt. She just had enough time to open the door and move her hair from her face before throwing up.

The cab let her out near rue de la Jonquière. She entered the first café and washed her face in the bathroom. She ordered a Perrier and downed it in an instant. She felt better. She felt cleaned somehow. Lighter. Unencumbered by the sense of guilt she had carried for years.

At Marceline's door, Armelle, the stepdaughter, had her arms crossed over her chest and a tight smile on her lips. She stood in the door, making no attempt to invite Cassie inside. "It is only that, there's been plans made," Armelle said. "And, well it seems as though Mother has been quite upside down about things. You are here after she's been estranged from her brother all those years. At her age, stirring things can be upsetting."

"She wants to talk to me. I'm only interested in the family's story," Cassie said. "My family story."

"And I'm only mindful of her health."

In a Marceline-like display of straightforwardness, Cassie said, "Do you want me to camp on your front lawn until Marceline finds out that you keep getting between us?"

"No, but of course," Armelle said. "I'm only mindful of her needs." She sighed. "Mother is in the gazebo. Go around the house down the path."

CHAPTER 4

Operation Torch

Why did they have to make the print so tiny? Marceline wondered. Only old people read the newspaper anymore, so wouldn't it make sense to enlarge the type?

Under the gazebo, she looked up from the magnifying glass she held over her copy of *Le Monde* and watched Cassandra walk toward her. The girl looked annoyed. What an open book she was, so unlike Gustave.

"What now?" Marceline asked.

"Your step-daughter," Cassandra said as she plopped down on the empty chair across from hers. "She's starting to get on my nerves,"

"Ha! And on mine."

Marceline contemplated her niece: no compulsory hellos, no niceties, and no waste of time. What a relief it was to interact with a straightforward person. She decidedly liked the girl.

"Why does she make it difficult for me to speak to you?" Cassandra asked. "She has all those excuses. You're tired; you're ill, you're upset about the past, blah, blah, blah. If you didn't want to talk about all this you would tell me, wouldn't you?"

"Don't mind her, ma chère."

Cassandra settled in her chair, put her purse down, removed her coat and took out her notepad. She looked up at the gazebo. "This is so nice," she said. "Everything in Paris is so pretty all of a sudden."

"Paris in the springtime," Marceline said, already bored with the weather talk. "Nothing quite like it."

"The thing I still can't understand," Cassie said, "is what you might have done to deserve my father's hatred."

Now, that was more like it. "Getting right down to it, aren't you?" Marceline said.

"So far, I see that you were annoyed with each other, but what siblings aren't? My sister Odile and I are at each other's throat most of the time, but we are still sisters. We have a rocky relationship, but it's a relationship. And my children. They aren't talking to each other right now. But that's temporary. It's salvageable."

"Until it isn't," Marceline said.

Cassandra looked at her, distraught. "It is salvageable," she insisted.

"Today I'll tell you what happened, and then you can decide if I am worthy of your father's hatred, or not. Where did I leave things?"

"My father was beaten, and Khaled went to jail," Cassandra said.

Marceline was going to tell Cassandra everything. Let her decide if anything at all between Gustave and her could have been salvaged.

****

Days after Gustave's beating, Khaled had yet not been released. I was mad with anguish and guilt. I asked my father how much longer he thought the French police would detain him. Khaled may have refused to identify any of Gustave's assailants, my father explained, and they could hold him until he did.

"They still won't say where they put him?" I asked my father.

"No, and it worries me," my father said. "Despite how upset we are about what happened to Gustave, to the police it's nothing. I cannot imagine why they would even bother making this into a big investigation. This is strange." He looked at me with suspicion. "Are you sure there isn't more to the story?"

I thought of Khaled's family, and the job at the garden he would now certainly lose. All because of my stupid brother. "He's just a nice boy who works very hard to support his family. He stays out of trouble."

"Apparently not enough."

"Oh, Baba, we have to free him!"

"There are limits to what I can do without drawing attention to our family."

"But this is so unfair!"

"It would not be the first time an innocent man is detained," my father said. "Listen, I will do everything in my power to help this young man because he saved Gustave, not because I approve of your fling."

Together with my father, we visited every past employer of Khaled I could think of: at the fishing mole, at the Jardin d'Essai, and at Café Djurdjura. We collected letters attesting to his hard work and to his character. I wrote daily letters to him but had nowhere to send them. I cried, and I raged, over Sandra being fired and Father not standing up for her, over Mother for being so unjust, over Khaled, and mostly over myself. I was inconsolable and at the same time angrier than ever at my brother, who was the reason Khaled was imprisoned in the first place.

Gustave and I avoided each other. When we found ourselves in the same room, we yelled at each other. It was awful between us. We blamed each other for getting Sandra fired, and we both profoundly resented Mother, who declared herself inconsolable about my actions and extremely distraught about the state of Gustave's nose, which she felt should be fixed immediately to look, as she put it, less aquiline and more French. For weeks, I was essentially on house arrest. I could spend time with Béatrice, either at my house or hers. But I was not allowed so much as to go down to the mailbox.

By now Mother's mood swings, her anger at Father, her obsession with me, and her fretting over Gustave had taken their toll. We each had our reasons to shut her out. We all began to retreat to our own corner of the house. The new maid would bring food to our rooms on trays and take them away later. We did not talk to each other. I would have liked to speak to my father, but he was never home. He was acting very strange. He was gone all day, and some nights he did not even come home at all and would reappear in the morning without any explanation given.

I lasted three weeks before disobeying. I decided that I would wait for Gustave and my father to leave the apartment and then go to Mother. I would tell her I was at my wit's end, that I was repentant, that I needed oxygen and sunshine. I knew that she would not resist my cajoling and begging for long. At first, I only asked to wait in the breadline in place of the new maid, insisting and crying, or throwing a tantrum until Mother relented. Little by little, I regained my freedom of movement. In the end, my mother was preoccupied with her ailments and angry at Father for always being gone, and she did not put up much of a fight.

I saw Dietfried three more times throughout September and early October: a walk on the beach, a visit to a local church, lunch once. His interest for me grew in direct proportion to my lack of availability.

And then, everything happened.

It was mid-October when Fernand passed me a note through our usual florist. It was brief: I needed to find a way to be out the following night and this time probably until morning.

Béatrice and I had no qualms about covering for each other when we wanted to spend the night with our lovers. She agreed to lie for me.

Where was Fernand taking me? I did not question his motive. I would have done anything. I wanted to help our cause, but mostly I felt powerless about Khaled, and it drove me crazy. Two months had passed since the Kasbah attack, and he was still in an undisclosed jail somewhere.

I begged my father to let me sleep at Béatrice's home. I told him that I had been a model citizen, that I recognized the error of my ways, and please let me do it. He relented, and I returned a message to Fernand via the florist telling him that I would be there. All was set.

"You're back with Fernand then?" Béatrice asked.

"I guess I must be," I told her.

"Does it mean I can be back with Émile, then?" she asked.

"Béatrice, you don't need my permission."

The following evening, I packed my night bag as though heading for Béatrice's apartment, but instead I went in the direction of rue Joinville. Fernand's instruction was to wait at the corner of rue d'Isly and rue Joinville, where a green Peugeot 202 would pick me up. The days were shortening considerably. The evening was windy. The chill of fall could be felt, and I wished I had worn something warmer. The date was October 21, 1942.

At the precise time it was supposed to arrive, a dusty Peugeot 202 came to a stop in front of me. A man came out to open my door. I stepped inside. Immediately, the car bolted through Algiers's empty streets.

I had expected Fernand to be there, but the two men in the car were French men I had never seen before. The driver, his fedora deep over his eyes and one arm out the window, could have been one of the men who had watched over me on the train where I first met Dietfried, but I could not be sure. He intermittently peeked at me in his review mirror. The other man, angry-looking, sat in the passenger seat, smoking. Neither said a word to me.

"Where's Fernand?" I asked.

"No names!" the man in the passenger seat ordered.

We drove through the dusk alongside windswept palm trees and the darkening sea, leaving the city. I became anxious. My thoughts went to my father. He spent all his energy trying to keep us safe; what would he think of me now? I was in a situation I could not control, zooming away from the city close to curfew, in an automobile driven by unknown men. I had no idea whether I was going to be part of a Resistance mission or about to be raped and bludgeoned to death.

We drove for a long time. The wind made the car sway at times, and the driver tightened his hands on the wheel. Night fell. The police stopped us twice for violating curfew. Each time, they took one look at the driver and let us go.

We had driven for about an hour when we stopped next to a parked automobile. A thin, nervous man got out of it and entered our car. He sat next to me in back, tilted his hat as a form of introduction, and offered me a cigarette. He looked at me intensely, measuring me. Satisfied, he asked in a clipped tone, "They say you can translate French to English and back to French?"

I relaxed. This was no plot to murder me. "I can," I said.

"There's a meeting tonight. We need you to translate what is being said so that people can understand each other."

"I can translate writing. I'm not sure I'm fast enough to translate as people speak."

The man's face hardened. "The meeting is now. We have no one else. Can you do it, yes or no?"

"Are they British? American?"

"No questions," he said.

"I can do it," I told him.

As we drove, it occurred to me that for Fernand's recommendation to have placed me in this place and time, he must have been more influential within the Resistance than he had let on. After another thirty minutes of driving in the dark, I saw a sign for the small seaport town of Cherchell. Minutes later, the driver slowed down and turned off the headlights. This was a nearly moonless night, and suddenly all was dark. I could make out the silhouette, pale against the black of the sea, of an isolated beach house. The automobile left the paved road and drove on a dirt path. The driver rolled down his window and guided himself by putting his head out the window and watching the edges of the path.

We stopped in front of an iron gate. After a minute, men with guns emerged. They aimed flashlights at our faces. The gate was opened for us, and we went through.

Half a dozen vehicles were already parked in front of the house. Silent, armed men stood all around, some by the windows and doors, some on the roof. We stepped out of the automobile, and a strong sea wind ruffled my hair. No one spoke. I heard car doors opening and closing, footsteps on the pebble path, nearby waves crashing on the beach. Someone took my arm and guided me toward the house.

We entered the farmhouse and went through an entryway decorated without frills, in a mixture of Arab and European styles. We walked into a large room. About twenty French men were waiting there, sitting on chairs and couches, smoking, playing cards. Some were old, but I was surprised at how many of them looked my age or younger. All eyes converged on me. I was immensely relieved to see Émile's face, but he averted his eyes. I understood it was best to pretend not to know him.

"Who's she?" someone asked.

"This is no place for a woman," another man said.

An angry old man in a beret and woolen pullover waved his finger at me menacingly. "You better keep your mouth shut! I don't want to hear a peep. It's an order, you hear?"

I decided to respect the "order" by staring him down and not answering.

"She's the translator, dummy," a man said. "How good will it do if she can't speak?" There were laughs, and the man with the beret turned back to me. "Then keep your mouth shut after the meeting."

"Calm down, Pierrot," someone said.

I found a chair in a corner and sat there. We all waited wordlessly for a good hour. The air grew thick with smoke and tension.

Through the window, I saw people sending light signals toward the sea. As the room filled with smoke and the smell of men, some could not resist talking, and I garnered whatever understanding of the situation I could. There was a submarine at sea, and we were waiting for its occupants to make their way onto rafts and come ashore on the beach. The sea was rough, and things weren't happening as smoothly as hoped. They had been waiting for two hours, and still, there was no sign of the rafts.

"Merde," the grumpy one with the beret said. "They better arrive before sunrise, or this meeting is over before it started."

"Why a submarine of the Royal Navy?" someone asked. "I thought they would be Americans."

"You've been brainwashed to think the Brits are your enemies and Vichy your friends," someone said.

"But in Mers El Kebir—"

"Forget Mers El Kebir!"

Finally, we heard the news that four dinghies had pulled onto the beach.

In the room, everyone sat straighter, conversations stopped, men forgot to light their cigarettes. But when the door opened, only three people were asked to go into another room, and I was one of them.

We were in a small, windowless room. In the center was a farm table on top of which was a large map of the area. The only light came from a lamp placed on the table. Two men walked out of the shadow. I was told to memorize their names as I would need to introduce them to our visitors. They were Henri d'Astier de la Vigerie, whom I later learned had been sent to Algiers to head the Resistance, and Colonel Jousse and Général Mast, the two who were dressed in civilian clothing. The men who had entered with me were Bernard Karsenty and José Aboulker. I had never met them, but I knew them by reputation. They were Jewish, and they were at the heart of Algiers's Resistance, a Resistance composed of a ragtag group of Jews, many of them barely old enough to drive.

Minutes later, the back door to the outside was opened, and several men in British and American uniforms were led into the room. They were drenched. Someone hurried to give them towels. Those uniforms, albeit pitifully wet, were the most exhilarating sight. As far as I was concerned, the Allies had arrived, even if only a handful of them. Hope was here. We had not been abandoned.

A British officer communicated with the submarine via an object that resembled a long metal shoebox with antennas. It was my first time laying eyes on a walkie-talkie.

The meeting began, with me translating as the men introduced themselves. There was Robert Murphy, an American diplomat, and General Wayne Clark, who spoke directly for General Eisenhower. The general was in a foul mood after that difficult entry onto French territory. My mouth was dry; my heart beat fast. The smallest mistake on my part could mean disaster. Lives would be at stake. Perhaps even the fate of Algeria. But after months translating newspapers for Fernand, I had become well versed in the vernacular of war in both languages, and my time with Dietfried had prepared me for thinking on my feet. The French men spoke in French, the Anglo-Saxons in English, and with adrenaline helping, I translated.

When more maps of North Africa were laid out on the table, I gasped at the scope of the operation. Here, in this ordinary house, on this extraordinary night, they were preparing no less than the invasion of North Africa with a simultaneous landing in Morocco, Tunisia, and Algeria! We had been descending into what seemed like a bottomless abyss, and suddenly, everything was possible! For a long time, the men went back and forth as I translated. They discussed the towns that should be part of the strategy, listed which Vichy officials might join our side, and who were suspected to remain at Pétain's beck and call. Questions emerged as to who would lead Algeria once Vichy's people were taken down, but no one seemed preoccupied with this. These were military men, who thought in terms of maneuvers and movement of troops, not politics. What the military men wanted to know was the quality of the Resistance infrastructure already in place to facilitate the invasion.

"We have about eight hundred men here in Algiers, and we've identified and infiltrated most strategic posts," Karsenty said.

"Are all your men Jewish?"

"About two-thirds of them are."

The men from the submarine, seemingly reassured by this information, nodded approvingly.

"But we need weapons," de la Vigerie said. "Ours are obsolete, and we have too few, barely enough for four hundred men."

"Weapons will be sent ahead of time."

"How?"

"We'll find a beach for a night drop," Murphy said.

"We will need several months to organize."

"The landing will take place before the bad winter weather," General Clark said.

"Before winter? General, with all due respect! We are almost at the end of October. There is no way to—"

General Clark exploded. "My submarines might be submersible, but my men are not!" We can't wait for the sea to get even rougher than it is now. "The landing must happen in the next few weeks or not at all."

"Our men are ready," Karsenty said. "Cells are already in place."

"How will you neutralize those who might attack us as we land?"

"We have a plan set in place. We are prepared," Colonel Jousse responded.

"Can you give us a date?" Karsenty asked.

"The date will be given to you shortly beforehand to avoid leaks," Murphy said. "Just be ready."

Two hours later, the Anglo-Saxons climbed back in their dinghies, returned to their submarine, and we were left to ponder what had just taken place. Colonel Jousse and Général Mast discussed things with de la Vigerie, Karsenty, and Aboulker. I was not needed anymore, but they did not ask me to leave. I played it cool and professional, but I was thrilled. An Allied invasion was about to take place, and its success was in the hands of very few people, most of them Jews!

When they had thoroughly discussed all of the details, with me doing my best to translate, we returned to the main room where the rest of the men waited. "It's happening," Karsenty simply told the crowd of men. "The first order of business is to identify hotspots throughout Algiers, but I think we know where they are, don't we? Police commissariats throughout the city, the army headquarters, the naval office, all telecommunication centers, and the places of residence of individuals favorable to the Vichy regime. We're setting up teams. The day of the invasion we are to neutralize those hotspots long enough to create chaos, and then we will hold down the fort until the Allied forces arrive."

"For how long?" a voice called.

"A few hours at most."

A voice in the room asked, "Will we have enough weapons?"

"They are sending them." Général Mast said. "They'll be dropped off on an agreed-upon beach beforehand."

A murmur of approval swept through the room.

"Do we have enough men?"

"We're not putting together an army," Colonel Joust said. "Our mission is not to fight, although there may be fighting. Our purpose is to neutralize the hotspots. It will be night. We'll be taking everyone by surprise. The challenge will not be in the number of men, but in the accuracy and orchestration."

Someone dared ask the question on everyone's lips. "When, Boss?"

Karsenty hesitated. Mast answered, "Before winter."

In the room, there was a roar of voices. Fear and excitement swept through this motley crew of men. Everyone was speaking at once.

"The point is," Aboulker said, "Free France and the Allies are entrusting us with a mission of utmost importance. The Allies will be landing, whether we are ready or not. The lines of communications must be under our control. The army and the police cannot get alerted, so they won't have time to mobilize. The Wehrmacht must be prevented from knowing about the arrival of troops, for as long as we can make that happen. And if we fail to do our work, we'll have the blood of French, British, Canadian, and American soldiers on our hands. Our actions can be the difference between success and failure for the entire landing operation."

After that, no one asked another question, and many points floated in my mind, unresolved. General Clark and Robert Murphy had revealed too little for my comfort. Had they not been excessively vague about the arrival of the weapons? How could such a massive operation not have a set date? And did they truly not have a man in mind to run the next government after they toppled the existing one? Like a good little soldier, I swallowed my doubts and did not share my worries with anyone.

I found out later that my suspicions were correct. Only a few in the room had been privy to the truth: the Allies knew precisely what the next government would look like. The invasion date had long been set. Roosevelt had given the order of attack. Ships and submarines were already designated for combat. Over one hundred thousand well-trained soldiers were waiting. The invasion was set for November 8th. Barely three weeks away.

What I did not suspect, but what I hoped with all my heart, was about to come true. The British-American invasion of North Africa, code name

Operation Torch, would turn out to be World War II's first successful Allied landing on French territory. And for all my modern ideas about the role of women, it never occurred to me that I was about to be propelled straight into the fire of battle.

The men shook hands, people left. Someone noticed that I was still in the room. "You did a swell job, sweetheart," the grumpy old guy who had hated me on principle said. "La demoiselle needs to be taken back home."

"I'll take her," Émile said.

Minutes later, we were in Émile's car. "Wasn't this just incredible?" he murmured.

"Incredible," I echoed.

"And you were right there in the room with those generals! After we win this, you'll have to tell me how it all went down."

Dawn was breaking through the morning fog. We had missed a night's sleep, but I could not have felt more awake. "You were swell; they said so," Émile continued. "You know you can't discuss what just took place." He hesitated. "Not even with your boyfriend."

"Don't insult me, Émile," I told him. "And besides, Fernand and I are only friends these days."

Émile was quiet for a moment. Then he said reluctantly, "I meant, your new boyfriend. You're going out with that Muslim chap from the café, aren't you?"

I felt a sharp sense of danger. "Who told you this?"

"Algiers is nothing but a spy nest these days," he said, philosophically.

I watched Émile's profile in the darkness of the car. "Does Fernand know about this?"

Émile, who laughed at everything, wasn't smiling. "If he does, it's not because I told him."

"Fernand doesn't need to know who I choose to see."

"The thing is," Émile said, "I'm not in the habit of keeping secrets from Fernand. He was a brother to me long before you came along."

"Well, I don't report everything to my brother. Far from it."

Émile, who has no hard edges to him, no meanness, and no anger, said, "But why did you have to go out with the *one* chap Fernand despises so much?"

"What does he have against him anyway?"

"He doesn't show Fernand respect."

"Baloney! Khaled didn't show Fernand respect because he doesn't owe him respect! You all think that he should stay in his place because he's an Arab? Because Monsieur Fernand believes himself superior? Anyway, my boyfriend, as you call him, was put in jail for no good reason. They won't let him out or give him a trial, and I'm going half mad about it."

"Maybe…." Émile paused. "Maybe it would be easier if you broke it off."

"Easier for whom?"

"For everyone," he said as he pulled in front of Béatrice's apartment building. He did not look at me when he added. "Easier for your chap, too."

Too much had happened in the last twelve hours to make sense of his words. I was drained. "Can you find out where they have him locked up? Even my father cannot find out where he is."

Émile considered this. "I'll see what I can find out," he said.

He dropped me off in front of Béatrice's apartment building. I walked the few blocks from there to my house just as the streets of Algiers awakened. Sidewalk sweepers and trash collectors said hello to me as I mulled over Émile's cryptic words. Easier for your chap, he had said. What had he meant by that? Now that exhaustion was replacing excitement, I began to feel nervous. What would happen to Fernand, Émile, and André if the landing failed? Did they not risk jail, or worse? What about my father? Would he be involved in the invasion?

The following day, Fernand and I sat in the darkness of the Pathé Cinéma. It was a matinée. We were alone in the theater. The reel of *Film Actualité* was about to start. A nasally voiced announcer extolled the merits of esprit national and patriotism over visuals of Maréchal Pétain parading through a near hysteric crowd, holding babies, and receiving flower bouquets from little girls. We sat lower in our chairs. "They were impressed with your aplomb," Fernand said. "You didn't blink, love. And they took notice."

"How much do you know about last night?"

"As much as I need to. So, say, how's your Germanic romance going?"

I sighed, "He is growing much too adoring for my comfort."

"Learned anything new?"

"The thing is, Fernand, I'm running out of reasons not to be kissed by him. I don't know how long I can keep him wanting."

A couple walked past us as they went down the cinema's aisle and settled in the front row seats. Another couple went to sit in the far back. On the screen, a cartoon depicted a grotesque-looking Jewish man, with a nose the shape of a banana and paw-like hands, bleating into a microphone. "Ici Londre. Les français parlent aux français. London here, the French speak to the French," the man said in an unctuous voice that mocked London and De Gaulle. The propaganda was at work, linking the Jews, which they had so successfully turned into a source of disgust, with the Allied forces.

"There is no harm in throwing your adoring Boche a bone," Fernand said. On the screen, Mickey Mouse, Popeye, and Donald Duck flew planes that dropped bombs on French farmhouses.

"What do you mean?"

"A little kiss has never harmed anyone."

"Who do you take me for?"

He shrugged, "Come on now, princess, haven't you kissed worse frogs?"

Émile's comment rang in my ears. It would be easier if you broke it off, he had said. Easier for your chap. I tried to contain the alarm in my voice as

I dropped all pretenses. "Do you have anything to do with Khaled being stuck in jail?"

"Khaled who?" Fernand asked lightly.

"Were you involved with those kids who attacked my brother?"

"The Kasbah is a place for savages. It's not my fault that he and you chose to venture there."

"How come you know about all this?"

"Algiers is a small town."

"How long have you known about Khaled and me?"

"Questions, questions, so many questions," he said. Fernand's eyes shone with the screen's reflection of soldiers in Nazi uniforms lifting their boots in menacing unison. "Here is one I'd like you to answer: what if I told you that your Casanova is the enemy?"

"An enemy of whom? He's not a Vichy sympathizer. He's not a Nazi."

"He's an enemy of French Algerians, of which I happen to be the very embodiment. If he and his little group figure they're going to get their country back to themselves, they got another thing coming."

"Is this all because of me?"

"As lovely as you are, I'm not the jealous kind. All that matters to me is the mission. I know where my interests lie, and they're better served in keeping you happy than in provoking your ire. Although I am just a bit insulted you would prefer an illiterate over me."

"Khaled is perfectly educated, I'll have you know. And if his people aren't, it's because the French won't let them in their schools."

Fernand stared at me coldly. "I see his counter-information techniques are effective."

"If I learn you had something to do with what happened to Gustave, or to Khaled—"

"You'll learn no such thing," Fernand said.

"Then tell me you're innocent."

"I am. But let me tell you something: no one likes the idea of one of our girls fraternizing with Arabs."

"I'm not one of your girls!"

"You're French. You're Jewish. You're one of us. The best thing you can do is forget about him. I'm sure he'll be left alone much sooner than if the two of you persist."

I felt a chill down my spine. Émile had been right. "Are you threatening us?"

"I'm only appealing to your common sense."

I stared at the screen, my heart pounding with fury. Also, I was ashamed. I had been ridiculous, thinking myself smart when everyone around me, my brother, Fernand, Émile, and who knows who else, had known about Khaled all along. My brother was hurt, and Khaled was in jail, and I had no one to blame but myself. And even worse, I had every reason to believe that Fernand might have orchestrated the beating.

"So, what do you say?" Fernand said playfully pursing his lips as if to blow a kiss, "Just einen kleinen kuss for our horny German friend?"

"I won't let those Nazi lips touch mine. And besides, Dietfried repulses me physically."

Fernand laughed silently in the darkness. "So which is your main objection about our friend Dietfried? That he's our mortal enemy, or that he's not as cute as your Arab?"

Before I knew it, I had slapped Fernand across the face. This made such a noise that the sparse moviegoers jeered and whistled. "What have you done now?" one man snickered, and the handful of people in the theater laughed.

Fernand rubbed his burning cheek and smiled as if this has been only a game. "Listen," he said. "There's something I need you to do if you'll get off your high horse."

"You're in no position to expect a favor."

"Not for me, honey. For France."

I crossed my arms. I hated Fernand at that moment and could have murdered him on the spot, but if he had a mission for me in the scope of the one from the night before, I wanted in. "What is it?"

"Not here," Fernand said.

We left the cinema before the start of the film and came out into the street. We walked down to the pier, away from undesirable ears. "My cell was assigned a mission for the big night," Fernand said. "We're in charge of shutting down the communication between Algiers and Hitler."

I looked at him, afraid of what I was understanding. "You're going to shut Dietfried down?"

We sat on a bench that faced the sea. The sky was gray and low. Powerful silver waves crashed against the jetty. "Here are our facts," Fernand said. "He may or may not be their transmission guy, but he's our best bet. All intelligence points to him. We found his antenna, and it's a nice big one, powerful enough to transmit to Germany and beyond. We think that he set up a full transmission facility at his house. The phone lines will be down on the big night, but he could still communicate with the Reich via Morse code, radio transmission, and so forth. We can't have that happen. We can't have the Boshes coordinate anything. They must be kept in the dark as long as possible. At least as long as it will take for our forces to subdue the rest of the town and let the Allies take over."

"What are you going to do? Destroy his facility?"

"That's the tricky part. Hitler expects an Allied offense in North Africa, but he doesn't know when. As long as he receives reassuring news from your Dietfried, he'll think all is dandy for the time being. So, we can't take him down before the attack starts or it would raise a red flag. We have to do it the night of."

"What does this have to do with me?"

"We know how many armed guards circle the perimeter of his house day and night. Some of his guards are with us. If we go in with force, all he'd have to do is lock himself in and send a message about being under attack, which alone will alert Germany that something's the matter."

"So, what are you going to do?"

"Take him from the inside." Fernand lit a cigarette and offered me one. "With God's help." He smiled his beguiling smile. "And a little help from you as well."

"Me?"

I could tell he was hesitant to speak. "On the night of the operation, we want you to get invited inside his house."

"And do what?"

There was a long silence. At last Fernand said, "We need you to neutralize him from the inside before he has a chance to send a message."

"Neutralize him?" I repeated. I burst into laughter. "Have you gone raving mad?"

"Not in the slightest."

I thought of the Cherchell night, the dozens of men armed to the teeth, the American and British officers, the secrecy. "How am I to neutralize him? Will a stern word or two suffice? Or do you envision something more radical, such as chopping him into pieces with a machete? I don't even know how to use a gun, and anyway, his guards would search me for weapons when I come in."

Fernand was serious now, his tone more pressing. "When we get the green light, you find a way to spend the night with him. He can't abandon his night post, so logically he would think of inviting you over to his house."

"All right, let's imagine that's possible. Then what?"

"Then it's phase two."

"And what might that be?"

"I'll let you know when we get closer to the day."

I looked at Fernand. His face revealed nothing. "Please tell me there is a plan," I said.

"There is a plan," he answered. "A solid one."

"How am I going to see Dietfried at night when I am even forbidden to leave my house during the day?"

Fernand snickered. "Can anyone forbid you to do anything? You found a way to be here now. Find an excuse."

After Fernand and I had parted, I did not mull over the risks too carefully, or I would have turned down the mission. For a few days, I was only concerned with setting up a situation that would lead to Dietfried inviting me over to his house on a moment's notice. Did I need to become his girlfriend? The thought repulsed me physically and morally. And anyway, he might want to meet in a hotel room, which would defeat the purpose. An idea came to me. But first, I needed to set the stage.

One morning, I volunteered to wait in the bread line. Once in the street, I walked to the nearest telephone booth and called Dietfried. We met the next day for a walk along the seafront.

That day, in addition to the fragile feminine persona I had fabricated for Dietfried, I added distracted looks, forlorn gazing toward the horizon, and the occasional sigh and nervous chew of my fingernails. At first, Dietfried was busy pontificating on the merits of industrial sea fishing, and it took him a while to notice that his usually rapt audience was being inattentive. "Dear Marceline, you seem out of sorts," he asked at last.

"Nothing I want to bore you with."

"Please tell me."

"My fiancé has been acting overly possessive." I lowered my eyes and added, "And he's not always a gentleman."

Dietfried frowned. "Has he disrespected you?"

"It's just that … he's not taking too well to my showing you the city."

"You told him about me?" he said, unsure if he should be pleased about this or not.

"When he found that I spent time with you, he went into a fit. I told him there was no harm in showing you the city. You and I are doing nothing wrong, but he's quite old-fashioned. And jealous I'm afraid."

Dietfried took the reins of the situation and patted my hand in a fatherly way. "Are you certain it would be a good idea to marry someone so unreasonable?"

"If there cannot be trust between us, and if he's going to have those fits of rage…." I let my voice trail off and added, "You are right. He is unreasonable. And his anger scares me. Oh, I'm sorry Dietfried to burden you with my story. It's only that I have so few friends to confide in, and my parents have their minds set on us marrying and refuse to hear me out."

"Oh, Marceline, I understand. Just know that I am here for you. Day or night, you absolutely must know that you can count on me."

I blinked away imaginary tears. "Do you mean this? Oh, Dietfried, I'm so glad to have you as a friend!"

One thing I had told Dietfried was true. Now that Khaled was in prison, I truly had no one to confide in. Khaled's imprisonment, the terrifying news from the war, the impending Allied invasion, and my mother's behavior were for me to shoulder alone. And if that was not enough, even my father had started to behave erratically.

He had come home the day before, staggering, his face pale and distraught. Since then, he had not left the apartment. He spent hours smoking on the balcony, looking down into the street as if he were awaiting impending doom. He wasn't speaking and barely ate. He explained that he was feeling ill, but to me, he looked confused and scared. If my father knew that Algiers was inching closer to an Allied operation, I hoped that his mood wasn't an indication that things weren't going well.

The following day, Émile came through. I found him at the foot of my building, waiting for me. "I know where they locked him up," he said, not naming Khaled.

"Where?"

"I will tell you as long as you promise not to do anything reckless."

"I only want to send him a letter," I told him.

"He's on the outskirt of town in a suburb east of Algiers," Émile relented. "It's called the Maison Carrée prison. It's not a high-security prison. They put petty thieves there, people awaiting trials."

"Are visitors allowed?"

Émile looked upset. "You said you only wanted to send a letter!"

"You said it's not high security, and that they allow visitors."

"Don't do something foolish, Marceline."

I didn't know if I would be allowed to see him, but I knew I had to give it a try. Khaled needed to know that my feelings were unchanged. He needed to know that at least one person was doing all she could to help him. "There is nothing illegal or even suspicious about a young woman visiting a person who had saved her brother's life," I said.

I thought of a plan. To go this far out of town, I would have to be gone for several hours, perhaps half a day. It was one thing to slip away when only my mother was home, and another to pull the wool over my father's eyes. I decided to dispense with parental authorization and deal with the consequences later. The tension at home was tremendous. Father and Mother were barely on speaking terms ever since Sandra had gone. With a little luck, they would continue to be too preoccupied with their issues to ask each other where I was.

The following day, I went to the Agha train station and bought a ticket in the direction of Maison Carrée. Through the short, bumpy train ride, I sat oblivious to the scenery and the other passengers. It was a hot day, rendered bearable by the speed of the train and the open windows. When we approached the Maison Carrée train station, I noticed that the people on the train were getting up from their seats to close all the windows. An awful stench rose through the wagon, coming from outside. I asked the French woman who sat next to me what was happening. She explained that years of pollution had transformed the river into a cesspool of industrial and animal waste. "One gets used to it, eventually," she said.

When we arrived at the station, I made my way to the center of town where a livestock market was in full swing. I walked across the plaza and my nose stung from the odor of animals combined with the sulfurous smell of the river. I asked for directions to the police station and hurried past the live donkeys and geese, past the rabbits and horses, and past the food stalls, the barrels full of olives, the mounds of dried figs and garbanzo beans, the citrus fruits on mats, the wine barrels. There was a clear racial divide in the market. In the aisles, French shoppers carried shopping bags and opened their wallets. Inside the stalls, Arab men and women, often shoeless, worked at selling their goods. Ever since the onset of restrictions, food prices had gone up exponentially, and the Arab population's buying power had shrunk to nothing. Many depended on their chicken coops and vegetable gardens to eat. But even for the city folks, food was getting difficult to come by. It was everybody's daily struggle to get our hands on fresh milk, eggs, or butter. Desperation grew at the thought that the bulk of the goods sold in the market would make its way to the kitchens of the rich and powerful of the city and to the restaurants that catered to them.

I entered a large, square building with too many windows, too much direct sunlight, and no ventilation. The architecture was ill-suited for the climate; the glass panes magnified the sun and trapped it along with the stench of the market. A half dozen French policemen in uniform and bureaucrats in suits moved about importantly. Meanwhile, no less than a hundred Arab grandmothers, mothers, wives, and daughters sat on rows of seats set around the room, under signs bearing numbers, or stood in various lines where bored French clerks stamped papers without making eye contact. Behind their desks, the French policemen eyed the younger women, elbowed each other, and snickered. I felt the burn of their disrespect for the women who covered their faces as much as possible. Everyone shone with sweat, but the Arab women seemed resigned and waited placidly for their turn. Where were the Arab men, I wondered? As far as I could tell, I was the only European woman in the room.

I waited in line at the information desk for an hour, struggling to breathe. My clothes were too tight, the stench and heat untenable, but I stood firm and stared straight ahead. The French men's eyes were on me now, their bestiality barely in check. I could feel the corruption of the place on my skin. This, I could tell, was not a place where one wanted to show weakness.

As I got closer to my turn at the desk, I could hear what was said. An old Arab man clearly out of his depth stood by the clerk and interpreted questions and requests. It was always the same story. The woman was here to see a father, a husband, a brother, a son. She was usually told that the man she wanted to see was in isolation, awaiting trial, and that visitors were denied to him. The woman would then beg and cry and be told that nothing could be done. I watched with rising anger as the dismissed women left the building, their despair palpable. I also noticed that on occasion, one of the women was given a number. She would then head for a smaller waiting room and sit there. This was the room where I wanted to be sent.

When it was my turn at the front of the line, I presented my identity papers to the clerk. "I'm looking for someone who might be incarcerated here," I said. "Could you look it up? His name is Khaled."

The clerk, a dull man with a drooping mustache, eyed my papers, lifted his face, and spoke patronizingly. "Every other convict here is named Khaled, Mademoiselle. What would be the last name?"

"I – I don't know his last name," I admitted.

"I'm not a miracle worker, Mademoiselle. There is nothing I can—"

I was not about to be sent away. "Could someone here help me look for it. I have the date of the arrest and the location. Perhaps in your files there would be…."

Already bored with me, the clerk gave me a small card with a number printed on it. "Wait there," he said, pointing to the waiting room. "Your number will be called."

Inside this new waiting room, a dozen women sat, stoic, while their children sat around them, playing in silence. This was a windowless room, and the air inside was stale, suffocating. A ceiling fan labored above us but did little else than blend odors of heat, sweat, and the smells of the animal market. The women, who would never have been caught looking at any of the men, made no effort to hide their curiosity about me. I must have looked out of sorts because the woman on the chair next to mine offered me water from a gourd in her basket, which I accepted with gratitude.

It was another hour before my number was called. I was directed to a room where a bespectacled French man in his sixties without a hair on his skull sat at a metal desk. "Sit please," he said. For what felt like an eternity, he purposely ignored me as he laboriously contemplated, and then stamped, documents one by one from a pile of papers scattered in front of him. I watched him select the stamp he wanted, press it into the proper color ink pad, lift the stamp to see if it was inked properly, stamp the document, and repeat the process with the next document. I wondered if he acted this rudely with everyone. "It's the Sirocco," he said at last with a defeated sigh.

"I beg your pardon?"

"The damn wind dries everything in sight," he said. "Those inkpads are useless after mere days. How do they expect me to do my work?" He took a handkerchief from his waistcoat pocket, wiped his brow, and rather pleasantly said, "Pardon the odor. It's the same horror every Friday. Brings in the flies too." To illustrate, he grabbed a fly swatter and whacked it on an unsuspecting fly on his desk, then meticulously moved the dead fly between two pieces of blotting paper and tipped it onto the waste bin. At long last, he put the form request and my open identity card in front of him. He looked at them, then at me, then back at them. "So," he said, "this individual you are looking for, this Khaled, you have no last name?"

"I was told he is kept here."

"Surely you must have a birth date?"

"I do not."

"An address, then? Name of relatives."

"I can only give you the date of the arrest, and the circumstances," I said, realizing how little I knew about the man I loved. To me, he was just Khaled. Had his last name not come up, or had he told me, and I had paid no attention? Perhaps because it was an Arabic name, I had found it hard to remember.

The bureaucrat stared across the room at the metal filing cabinet as though it would be beyond his physical ability to get to it. He seemed to measure what would take the least effort, giving me what I wanted or opposing my request, and appeared to decide on the former. Reluctantly, he shuffled toward the cabinet, leafed through the files, chose one, returned to his desk, sat down heavily, and again wiped his brow. The file was inexplicably thick. He opened it and with unbearable slowness proceeded to read it page by page, licking his thumb copiously before turning each page. At last, he took out a document and handed it to me. "Is this the individual you are looking for?"

My heart leaped. It was a photograph of Khaled. His face was closed, stubborn, his eyes dull, and because of that expression, he hardly looked like the version of him that I knew. "It's him," I said in the calmest, most indifferent tone I could manage.

The bureaucrat closed the file and looked at me askance. "And what would a young French lady want with a known radical Algerian nationalist?"

I was taken aback but continued to act nonplussed. "He saved my brother and me from a brutal aggression."

"I see," the man said.

"And he's still being detained in error while the perpetrators got to run away."

"The only reason those perpetrators, as you call them, got to run away is that this man pretends not to know who they are." He tapped at the file with his index finger, taking his time to observe me. "This is a very thick file, Mademoiselle. And most of what's in it has nothing to do with your story."

"There must be an error. He's an upstanding citizen."

He squinted. "How well acquainted are you with this man?"

"I am not. But his action toward my brother speaks for itself," I said haughtily. "His past employers have vouched for him. That's probably why your file is as thick as it is."

"Indeed, there seems to be no shortage of people willing to vouch for him. This only confirms our belief that he is a man of importance."

"Of importance to what? He defended us, that's all!" I said, furious.

"Maybe so, but for now he is awaiting trial."

"Trial for what? What is his crime?"

"That is for the jury and judge to decide."

"That's a complete travesty!"

"Mademoiselle," he said in an exhausted tone, "why don't you simply tell me what you want from me."

"I – I want to visit him."

He seemed genuinely surprised. "But what for?"

"I want to thank him in person, quite naturally. As well as bring him every reassurance that my family will testify in his defense during his trial."

"In these difficult times, we have to proceed swiftly so as not to congest the system." He continued to observe me, his words saying one thing, his expressed another. "I would love to help, but I am not sure how."

I clenched my teeth. "I must be misinformed then," I said. "I was told that you had the authority."

The man smiled unctuously and gave his tone layers of significance. "I do have a range of authority," he said.

At last, I understood. I took my wallet out of my purse; I was prepared for this. I knew of the system worked. "I would be happy to contribute to the commissariats' widow fund," I said, taking a hundred-franc bill out of my purse.

"Your generosity is much appreciated," the bureaucrat said, snatching the bills from between my fingers. "I am glad we could come to such a mutually satisfactory agreement."

An hour later, I was one of perhaps a dozen women sitting in a row of makeshift booths inside a long, gray room separated in its center by metal bars. Desks and chairs were set against the bars and on each desk were two sets of metal partitions for privacy. I couldn't see the other women's faces or those of the men they were here to visit, but I could hear the voices, the guttural melody of spoken Arabic and the muffled sobs.

I sat facing the metal bars and waited, my stomach in a knot. My skull ached from dehydration. I fought to push away the loop of fear that moved from my head to my belly and back. By coming here, I could no longer live in the delusion that Khaled's case was following a process that resembled justice. This was clearly a place where the local authorities parked people they intended to forget. Vichy was a parasite that corrupted all decency. The worst of human nature had been dormant, but Hitler had given it the fertile ground to find new vigor and blossom. The basest instincts of men now had the perfect terrain to wander unchecked. I held on tight to my memories of the Cherchell night, the sight of those American uniforms.

A door on the inmate side periodically opened, and a guard entered the room pushing a chained inmate. The inmate was always an Arab, pale, weakened, defeated-looking. What were they doing to those men? My anxiety rose as I waited for Khaled.

Suddenly, he was in the room. My chest tightened. He, already thin, had lost a tremendous amount of weight. His hands were handcuffed together at the waist. He was unshaven, pale, with dark circles under his eyes. There were bruises on his face, a deep cut to his lower lip, and his expression matched the one on the photograph; hardened, dull. He squinted as though his eyes were not accustomed to the light and I had a chance to compose myself.

The moment he saw me, he froze, made a gesture to leave the room. The guard had to push him in my direction and then push down on his shoulder until he sat on the chair that faced mine. He hooked Khaled's handcuffs to the metal bars that separated us. "You have ten minutes," he said and went to stand against the wall.

"Why are you here?" Khaled said. He was whispering, but his tone was full of fury.

I had expected loving words and effusions, and so I had to fight the onslaught of tears. "How are you?" I asked. "Are they treating you well? I am doing all I can to get you out of here. As is my father."

"You should not be here," he said coldly. "Leave. Return to Algiers."

I saw in his eyes a kind of despair and buried rage that had not been there before.

"What are those cuts and bruises? What is happening?"

He whispered urgently, "You must not act like you care about me. And you cannot cry. Not when they are watching us." He was right. I was a fool. I took a deep breath and swallowed up the emotions that risked betraying me. Once I had composed my face, Khaled could relax. "I have been thinking of you night and day," he said softly. "How is your brother?"

"He is free, and you're not," I said between my teeth. "Why are you injured?" I demanded to know. "Who is hurting you?"

"Institutionalized cruelty," he said, shaking his head.

"I will get you out of here. You know I will."

"I need to ask you something," he said, looking at his hands. "People say they have seen you around town with a German officer."

I could not help but smile. Khaled was jealous. The guard was ten feet away. I came closer to the bars and put my chin in my hands so that the guard could not read my lips. "You have to trust me," I said. "Things are happening soon that will change everything. Before long, this government could topple, and they'll have to set you free."

"You are working with the Germans?" he asked, shocked.

"Quite the opposite."

He stared at me with a burning intensity. "Are you in love with a German man?"

"It's nothing like that. But I did hide things from you," I admitted. "I only wanted to protect you. I spend time with him to get information, that's all. I despise him. I promise."

"You are spying?"

"But don't worry; he's not dangerous."

"Everyone in Algiers is dangerous. You are naïve if you think otherwise."

"I am protected."

"Whoever it is that gave you this assignment cannot protect you or will only protect you as long as it doesn't endanger them. I know how these things work."

I stiffened, defensive. "Do you?"

"You should stop at once. Stay out of this, Marceline. They only care to get what they want and are using you."

"I work for the French Resistance."

He shook his head angrily. "Why have allegiance to a country that betrays both Jews and Muslims?"

"Vichy is not France," I said. "If we can get rid of Vichy and Hitler, then things will get back to normal."

"Who is making you do this? Is it Fernand?"

"No one is making me do anything. I chose to do this." Khaled clenched his jaw. My chest tightened. I was done discussing this with him. I would not get his approval. "My father has come to see all your past employers and asked them for letters of recommendation," I said. "We are mounting a defense for you."

"You must tell your father to stop," Khaled whispered.

I blinked at him in incomprehension. "Why?"

He lowered his eyes. "I have not told you all the truth about me either. There are men in this prison who think the way I do. Algiers might one day be liberated from Vichy, but it will not help *my* people. New French men will take the place of the present ones, and those will enforce the same policies against the Arabs that have been going on for a hundred years. Removing the Germans will change nothing for us."

"Some French politicians believe in equality for the Algerians. Including the right to vote. After the war, they will fight for it."

"That's not enough, Marceline," he said, shaking his head. "There is a man imprisoned here. I cannot tell you his name. He's a visionary man. He's been condemned to sixteen years in jail. He's the first one who had the courage to demand the independence of the Algerian nation. Every government has asked him to collaborate with them because they need his power, but he's rejected them all. He is intransigent about our right to sovereignty. For our people, he is ready to spend his life in prison. And with each day, he refuses to negotiate, and for each day he spends in prison, his prestige grows. People in the streets are gaining hope."

"What does it have to do with you?"

"I have worked for this man. The police knew that immediately upon arresting me."

"What work are you talking about?"

"We are learning to shape the future of our country. And I've decided the only way for me to learn from this great mind is to stay here."

"Here?"

"In this prison."

I was horrified. "Have you been indoctrinated?"

Khaled smiled at my outrage just as I had smiled at his jealousy, and for the first time since I got there, I saw that the man I love was intact. "Not any more than you have been. Can't you see we are the same, you and I? Each of us fighting for what we believe."

"It's not the same. France was invaded! We are fighting to get our country back—"

"It *is* the same, Marceline," he interrupted softly.

"What about your work? What about your mother, your brothers, and sisters, the Kasbah? What about us?"

"This man is a hero. His ideas will make it possible to have a future for my people."

I felt chilled to the core. "How will your family survive with you in jail?" I said.

"They are being helped by people on the outside, now that I have joined the cause."

I looked deep into his eyes. "Where does this leave you and me?"

"You are the woman I love," Khaled whispered. "That is all I know. It is simple, and nothing can change that. But when the revolution comes in Algeria and my people fight to retake our ancestral land, we will be in opposition to the French. When that time comes, which side will you be on?"

"The only side I can be on!" I said, irate. "The side of France Libre! Anything else would be to betray my country."

"But what if France Libre become Algeria's enemy?" he asked. "A whole lot can happen in a war. The heroes of today can become the traitors of tomorrow."

"Time's up!" the guard said. In a few steps, he had his hand on Khaled's shoulder and was unlocking his chains from the bar. Khaled and I could only lock eyes for a few instants as he was jerked up to his feet, his wrists were handcuffed together, and he was pushed out of the room.

I sat in stunned silence. There had been no chance to say goodbye, no time for a promise, or for words of love. I stood up, shaken, and left the room. I left the jail. I left the police station, with the stench and the heat, and took a train back home in a state of shock. The Allied operation had to succeed. Vichy had to be annihilated. Because with each passing day he spent in this jail, the forces from within would have a pull on Khaled that I would be increasingly powerless to influence.

I took the train back in a state of rage. I hated that prison. I hated what Khaled had told me. I hated that he had put a seed of doubt in my mind about my mission, and I hated that he was dismissing my country. I walked home from the train station at dusk sullied by the experience in too many ways to count.

I walked into the apartment where Gustave, my father, and my mother waited for me. At first, they seemed relieved to see me in one piece, but at the same moment, they were ready to pounce. Mother was agitated. Gustave sat on the couch, ostensibly leafing through an old book but not about to miss a moment of the cross-examination about to begin. My father only sat slumped in an armchair.

"Marceline, I don't know what you think you're doing but this time you've gone too far," Mother said.

"What have I done?" I said coolly as I took off my jacket.

"You've gone to the prison to see that boy," my father said. So much for secrecy. How did they know all this? My father seemed to have no energy left in him. I did not know if he was seething, or exhausted, or perhaps heartbroken because of me.

"Let me guess," I said, "Gustave was following me again?"

"Guess again," Gustave said. His bruises had healed except for some swelling around the nose and a yellowish hue around his eyes. "Why do I care what you do anyway."

"A friend saw you at the prison and made a phone call to Uncle Moshe," my father said. His voice softened. "Ma petite, you have to trust me to help this boy through proper channels. Through influential people we know. We must do this without attracting attention to ourselves. The situation is complex and getting more so every day."

"The situation with Khaled?"

"The situation with … everything," Father said. "I am working on getting this boy out of prison. Please don't let your stubbornness make it impossible. Apparently, there are people in Algiers who intend to keep him there. He has affiliated himself with a dangerous extremist."

"How are his ideals any different from ours?" I said. "He believes in returning Algeria to the Algerians, just like we want France back for us. But in his case, it's called extremism?"

My father shook his head wearily and was about to say something but my mother, vibrating with indignation, said, "Are you aware of the reputation you are acquiring for yourself?"

"I'm speaking of politics, and once again you worry about my virtue?"

"Just don't talk about politics," my father said. "It's as simple as that."

Mother said, "What if people learn that you are involved with a … Muslim, for goodness sake?"

"What people?"

"The – the good people," she stammered.

"Wake up, Mother! The old world is gone! How can you expect me to live by rules and values that no one heeds or respects? Look no further than those good people you speak of, and explain to me what it is they are doing to the Jews? Doesn't that shake your sense of values just a bit? And women are changing too. They're in factories building weapons, and even in the Resistance, using those weapons."

"A woman's role has never been in battle. You're being completely irrational," my mother screeched.

"Women are fighting this war every bit as much as the men. The only reason they're not piloting airplanes and submarines is that men won't let them."

Mother ignored my cris de coeur and pulled out all the stops. "You're taking advantage of my illness to run around town with god knows who!"

"Illness? Oh, please! You've acted like a victim ever since you set foot in Algiers."

My father raised his voice. "Marceline, I'm warning you!"

Mother plopped down on the couch looking crushed.

I softened my voice and added, "I'm made of stronger stuff than you are, Mother."

"How would you know what you are made of?" my father asked with exasperation. "You haven't been tested. What if you discover that you are, in fact, made of flesh and blood? As fragile and vulnerable as everyone else?"

I shrugged, "I shall cross that bridge when I get to it."

"How can I blame my children," my father mumbled, so low that I wasn't sure if he was speaking to us or to himself. "I have created them this way. I had a dream of a life for them that would be free of fear. I coddled them so that they would not have to witness the ugly things I have seen. I should have prepared them better. I should have taught them fear, instead of that dangerous sense of invincibility and entitlement they have."

Gustave chimed in, "She's been sheltered and pampered her entire life. She thinks she can do anything she wants."

"Like you haven't been coddled," I said.

Gustave gave me a murderous look. "I was sent away if you remember."

"Not this again," I said. "Everyone goes to boarding school, you dunce. It's not a punishment."

"Not everyone goes," he said. "You didn't."

"Blame Mother and Father! They're the ones who sent you and kept me at home. And you've resented me ever since."

"Enough, the two of you!" my father roared. "The point is, you must stop all of this at once, Marceline! The visits to the jail, the translations, the nonsense with the Resistance. You're not helping anything, and you're endangering us all."

"I'm trying to save us!" I said. "I am not about to sit in a room behind closed shutters and hold Mother's hand. If I must perish, then I want to do it fighting for our country!"

"I have heard this kind of rhetoric my whole life," my father said, shaking his head in disgust. "And for what? Death and destruction and despair. Patriotism is a poisonous beverage, my daughter. Soon enough you'll have your own children, and you'll understand that everything your mother and I are trying to do is to keep you safe. I took you and Gustave out of France to escape danger, and you both are throwing yourself toward it. We sent Gustave to boarding school for his safety. We want you to marry the right kind of man who will provide for you and protect you and for Gustave to find a nice young woman who will love him and care for him. You'll one day understand what governs mankind. It's not fear for ourselves, but fear for our children."

"Who in their right mind would want to bring up children in this world?" I said.

"You'll have children someday. You will see."

"I won't. Nor do I intend to live in the shadow of a self-important Frenchman. I have no desire to model myself to society's expectations of what it is to be a proper wife. I've spent the last nineteen years learning to be polite, believe me, and I found no joy in it nor reward."

"Perhaps I am the one who has been wrongheaded," my father said. Was he addressing me, Gustave, my mother, himself? "Perhaps I am trying to do something that is impossible, keeping those I love safe. People have their paths to take, the course of their own lives to follow."

I'm not sure what my father meant when he said this, but Gustave became incensed. "So, that's it? You agree with her? You wouldn't let me join the Chantiers de la Jeunesse, but you'll let her do whatever she likes? This is what she does. She lies, and she manipulates. She puts thoughts in people's heads. She's the most two-faced—"

"Who asked for your opinion, Gustave?" I shouted. "Can't you see you don't matter? Don't you see you're a non-entity? You're nothing but a weak little boy."

Without warning, Gustave threw himself at me, head first, like a bull, and struck me with his head in the solar plexus. I fell to the ground gasping for air.

"Marceline! Gustave! Stop this!" my father shouted, grabbing Gustave by his shirt collar and pulling him off me.

Gustave retreated to one corner of the room. He was red-faced, breathing hard, and beside himself with rage. My back was against the opposite wall. I sat on the floor and tried to catch my breath. My entire chest hurt. Mother wrung her hands, muttering, "Oh my God, oh my God."

"What's the matter with you?" Father shouted at Gustave. "You cannot hit your sister! You cannot hit a woman, any woman. Ever!"

"She's no woman! She's a beast," Gustave screamed. "She's the worst human being. Everyone in this family thinks she is great. You refuse to see her as she truly is."

"She is your sister."

"I hate her!"

"I forbid you to say this," my father said, not in anger, but in deep sadness. "I forbid you to think this. We are family."

"I hate her, hate her, hate her!" Gustave screamed, tears flowing from his eyes. Mother, her fingers shaking, opened her pillbox. I got to my feet, resolved never to speak to my brother again. Gustave stood at the other side of the room, panting.

"I cannot make this family listen to reason against their will," my father said, defeated. "I cannot tell you who to choose to love or to hate. You won't hear my advice. You refuse to learn from my experiences. I cannot try to make you happy if you constantly do the opposite of what I ask. I cannot make you think of the future when all you think about is the present or the past. God is my witness that I have tried." He walked out onto the balcony and leaned over the handrail. He seemed to gaze at the horizon, the sea in the distance, the myriad of tiny boats. I could see him from the back. He had both hands on the handrail, and his back shook lightly. Was he crying?

Mother closed her pillbox, sank onto the couch, and closed her eyes. I got up, flattened my hair, and smoothed my clothes with my hand, thinking of what I could tell Gustave to destroy him, but I worried about upsetting my father even more. Gustave, red-eyed and still breathing hard in his corner of the room, seemed about to consider jumping at my throat again.

Suddenly there was a tremendous knock at the door that jolted us all to the core. We all looked in the direction of the front door and at one another. This was entirely out of the ordinary. Visitors needed to buzz downstairs to be let in. No one ever knocked on the door.

There was a second knock, just as forceful.

My father took a moment on the balcony as if to gather himself for the inevitable, as though he knew who was at the door, which, of course, he could not have. He left the balcony and headed toward the door. There he took a deep breath and opened it.

On our doorstep was a policeman in uniform accompanied by a man in a dark suit. They presented their badges. The man in the suit was a police detective who introduced himself as Detective Poitras of the Algiers police. Could he please take a few minutes to speak with us? "I have a few routine questions," he said, adding that he wanted to speak to the whole family. The word routine, if it was meant to calm us down, had the opposite effect. For years now, routine identity checks, routine vehicle stops, and routine questioning were precisely what sent entire families into trains and off to deportation or forced labor camps all over Europe. My mouth turned dry; my legs were heavy. I shot a look at Mother. Would she be able to pull herself together for this?

We invited the detective and the policeman to sit. The detective sat in one of the armchairs. The policeman declined to sit and stood by the living room door, looking at nothing. We offered them mint tea and almond cookies, and the detective accepted a glass of water. Gustave went to fetch the glass of water and placed it in on the coffee table in front of the detective who drank avidly.

Detective Poitras was a Frenchman in his mid-forties. His skin was pale, as though the Algerian sun had never touched his skin. He had a thin body, a narrow face, and eyes that seemed to take in everything at once. He peered from my mother to Gustave, to me, to my father, and back to me. Could he sense that he was arriving in the middle of chaos? Mother was jittery. Gustave was red in the face, and I was probably still disheveled from our fight. Only Father was composed, at least on the outside. But I knew his calm was an act, his air of surprise and innocence a complete fabrication. To me, he looked terrified. He spoke slowly and made an effort to lessen his accent. Did he think that his identity had been revealed and he was about to be apprehended? Perhaps we all would be arrested today.

Father sat on the couch beside Mother, Gustave sat on the second armchair, and I on the arm of the couch, next to Mother. We were all guilty. We had false identities, fake names. Mother was guilty of sending her maid to buys things on the black market. Gustave was guilty of roaming the streets after curfew. I was in the Resistance, and until evidence to the contrary, so was my father.

Then Poitras's eyes rested on me, and I thought he was here for me, that he knew of my involvement in … something.

"We are investigating a homicide," Poitras finally said. We all gasped at him in surprise. The sensation of relief was physical. Whatever the reason Poitras was in our living room, it obviously had nothing to do with us. "We believe that your maid was involved," he continued. We all looked up at the new maid, a gray person devoid of age or personality as she brought a bowl of olives and set it on the table, oblivious to the fact that we were speaking about her. "Your name is Xandra, isn't it?" Poitras asked her. The maid looked at him blankly.

"Oh, so not that one?" Mother exclaimed shrilly, pointing to the new maid. "You must be speaking of our past employee. Her name was Sandra with an S. A homicide, you say? Are you saying that she was murdered?" Mother had taken her calming pill, but it had not yet taken effect. She was still on edge from the fight, and I worried she would become glib and say something idiotic.

Poitras said, "Not murdered, no. She is the suspect."

"The suspect?" Gustave and I echoed. The notion was so outlandish that I let out a laugh and all eyes were on me.

"I do not see what is amusing about this," Poitras said.

"It's just impossible," I said.

"You must have the wrong address," Gustave said.

Poitras looked at his note. "Sandra-Xandra, whatever her actual name might be, is being investigated for murder. You are listed as the employer."

"Well, yes, but she was fired," Mother said. "Over a month ago. I certainly cannot fathom this."

I realized that we were doing all the talking and that my father was silent. Poitras told us that a man had been found dead in her hotel room and that Sandra had vanished.

"I can think of a dozen theories why she had no involvement in this!" I said.

"With all due respect, Mademoiselle, we are not interested in your theories. Only in what you know." He turned to my parents, "How long was she working for you?"

"Two years," was the answer my father gave. These were my dad's first words since the policemen arrived. I could see now that the entire time he had listened to the detective, he had prepared his lies. He needed to lie about when Sandra had started to work for us to avoid being asked about the time before we arrived in Algiers. She was Armenian, he said. He had no idea how long she had lived in Algiers before working for us. She had resided in a maid's room on the fifth floor. We had to let go of her recently.

"Why did you terminate her employment?" Poitras asked.

"My wife no longer felt comfortable with her."

Mother, Gustave, and I listened carefully, taking cues from my father. He told the detective how Sandra had been expected to watch me and instead had allowed me to go out at night. He told him about the ensuing attack at the Kasbah. About her subsequent firing. I admired my father's smooth lie and the way he incorporated the truth that the police already knew or could verify. The inspector looked at me with amusement.

"Breaking curfew, the Kasbah at night, or in daytime for that matter. It seems that your children are quite disorderly."

I clenched my teeth at being dismissed as a mere child. *The government you work for is about to be toppled,* I thought, *and you'll have this disorderly child to thank for it.*

"I can assure you, Detective, that we are keeping them on a tight leash now," my father said, which was ironic considering that I had just been caught in the flagrant act of disorderliness of taking a train to a nearby jail to see a boy I loved.

"Smart of you. Especially in these times," the detective said. He turned to me and added, "Mademoiselle, if I may, as a police detective, I see all kinds of terrible things happening to young French women who take the chance of walking freely in the streets. Especially at night." He said this in a way that felt more threatening than protective. "The police cannot be everywhere. Prevention is the best defense." I nodded obediently. His gaze had been fixed on my chest the entire time. "You mention that you were not comfortable with your maid," he asked my mother. "You no longer trusted her with your children. Do you believe her capable of murder?"

My mother answered with a shrug. "She is certainly careless, but I doubt she is dangerous."

"Could you give us a physical description?" Poitras said as he took a small black notebook and a fountain pen from his pants pocket.

"Black eyes, I think," my mother answered. "About four foot nine. But all that people see is that scar on half her face. Trust me, she will not be missing for long. She has the kind of physical description one cannot alter. You shall find her easily."

Unable to contain myself I said, "Mother, Sandra is innocent, evidently!"

Poitras asked, "Would each of you tell me when you last saw her?"

"At the market," I said. "About three weeks ago. I ran into her, and we spoke for a few minutes. Then we went our separate ways."

"I have not seen her since the night my poor boy was nearly beaten to death due to her irresponsible behavior," Mother said.

"I saw her last at the hospital the night I was attacked. My parents had just fired her. She came to say goodbye to me," Gustave said, lowering his eyes.

My father said, "I know nothing past the time when I brought her to that hotel."

"Besides the man who was murdered, there was another man," the detective said. "He might have lived with her, but his name was not on the register. People saw him come and go. No one has a good description. And you know how they all dress the same, those Muslims. Medium built. No beard. That's all I have. Have you any idea who he might be? He was her lover, most likely. We think it might have been a lover's quarrel. Some sort of romantic triangle."

Mother and I scoffed in unison.

"Is this so difficult to imagine?" Poitras asked.

"It most certainly is," Mother said. Her medication was taking effect, I saw, from a slight glazing of the eyes. She had stopped fretting, and she looked sleepy when she said, "The notion of two men willing to kill each other over her is simply ludicrous."

"Besides, Sandra is a devout member of Armenian Apostolic Church," I said. "She is a quiet person, very religious, conservative. Hardly the type who would generate intrigue, or a lover's dispute, let alone a crime of passion."

Poitras smiled as though I was the cutest thing he'd seen in days. "A feisty daughter you have here, Dear Monsieur," he told my father. "Keep her on a tight leash indeed." I stared him down. He turned to my mother. "Would you concur with this?"

"Her … proclivities were not of interest to me," my mother said. I recognized the now familiar slowing of her speech, like a light that first flickers before slowly dimming. Her pill was taking effect. "If she did have a lover, I would be the last one informed." She added, "She was indeed quite … religious. She's an … assiduous churchgoer."

"Are you Christian?" the detective asked, addressing my father.

If my blood weren't already boiling, it would have turned to ice. My father's response came, unflappable. "We are Catholic," he said.

"Ah, yes," the detective said, but it was clear that he did not believe him for a second. He jotted something down on his pad. "I better put 'rectify this' in your file."

"We have a file?"

Poitras answered in a syrupy tone, "This is 1942, Monsieur. *Everyone* has a file."

"Who is this man who died?" my father asked.

"I was going to ask you the same question. Do you have any idea about this? We cannot identify him. He was possibly a vagrant."

"How did he die?"

"He was stabbed."

The notion was so preposterous that I relaxed. "Sandra is incapable of anger, let alone that sort of violence," I said.

"The woman you know and the woman she is might be two very different people," Poitras said. "All we know are the facts: a man found himself in her room, invited or not. She is the one who stabbed him. We are certain of this."

"How can you be?" I asked.

"She took the time to wipe on her dress the blood that had been on her hands and then change out of her bloodied clothes, fold them, place the weapon back into its case, and the case in a drawer. Not only did she kill, but she did so with a chilling amount of cold blood."

"Could it have been in self-defense?" I asked.

"If it were, she would have had no reason to run away."

"Innocent people are put in jail every day," I said, with an arrogance I regretted when my father silenced me with one look.

"Detective Poitras," my father said, "is it possible that someone stabbed the man and that Sandra ran way because she was afraid for her life?"

"This is an excellent question, which she will be at liberty to answer when we find her." He turned to my mother to say something and froze. We all watched Mother in embarrassment. She had dozed off on the couch. Disconcerted, but polite enough not to call attention to my mother's bizarre behavior, Poitras turned to my father. "Please do not leave town. We might have more questions as the investigation progresses."

"We won't," Father assured him.

After the policemen had left, Gustave and I bombarded my father with questions. "What do you think happened, Baba?" "Do you think it's really Sandra they're talking about?"

My father did not want to discuss any of this. "Gustave, you are grounded for a week for hitting your sister," he said. "Marceline, if I hear that you've gone anywhere near that jail, I will hire a bodyguard to camp outside your door, and you will spend the rest of the year looking at the street from your balcony."

"But, Baba," Gustave and I protested in unison.

"Can't you see that this city is terribly dangerous, and about to become more so? Did you not hear this policeman? Did you not see what happened to your friend and now to Sandra? Innocent people are being accused of crimes, and there is nothing we can do to help them." With this he added, "I'm going to work," and he left the apartment, slamming the door.

Mother was jerked out of her stupor by the sound of the door. She adjusted her clothes. "Where has that nice man gone?" she mumbled, presumably referring to the detective.

****

On November 6th, 1942, less than three weeks after the Cherchell meeting, I received a message from Fernand to meet at café El Bahdja. I sneered at Gustave, who was still grounded for hitting me, and left the apartment.

Café El Bahdja was a deserted, grimy place which had become our default meeting spot. There we could speak without being heard, although we coded most of what we talked about. Fernand and I sat at a back table.

He ordered olives and anisette for us both. He lit a cigarette, exhaled and whispered. "It's happening," he said.

The hair on the back of my neck prickled. "When?"

"Tomorrow night."

I was knocked down by the news. "But they said before winter!"

"Tomorrow night," he repeated.

"How can we be ready?"

"We're ready." He added grimly, "That's the good news."

"What else?" I asked, trying to mask the trembling of my hand as I put the cigarette he offered me between my lips.

Fernand leaned toward me to light my cigarette. "The package arrived at the wrong beach and sank."

I knew what Fernand meant. What he referred to as the package was the delivery of weapons promised by the Americans. I felt a hollowness in the pit of my belly. "How then—"

"We will manage with what we have."

"It will never work without the package."

"We have a trick up our sleeve. If the plan works, we will barely need the package at all."

"How?" I asked.

"Not here."

Fernand paid the bill, and we walked in the streets of Algiers until we knew we were entirely out of earshot and he could explain the plan. "At the start of Pétain's administration, the Algiers government put a system in place in the eventuality of an attack or a coup. It's designed to relieve the police of their function or assist them in the case of an attack. That system is valid for the mairie, the commissariat de police, the houses of commanding officers, the Nineteenth Corps headquarters, the arsenal, Radio Algiers, and telephone switchboards. Let's say the city is under attack, a special force comes in with specially signed papers, and takes control in order to protect it." Fernand smiled and crushed his cigarette on the pavement. "What will happen is this: we are turning the emergency procedure created to protect the city from an invasion into a way to facilitate an invasion."

"How?"

Despite Fernand's tension, his excitement was communicative as he spoke. "Our men will arrive in the middle of the night dressed in the uniforms of reservist officers and present ordres de mission stating that they are the emergency force set in place to take over."

"How in the world will you get your hands on those orders of mission?"

"The two officers you saw at the Cherchell meeting, do you remember them?"

"Colonel Jousse and Général Mast?"

"They are above suspicion from Vichy. In an exquisite twist of irony, it is those two that Vichy has put in charge of signing the orders of mission."

"So, the orders will be perfectly authentic?"

"Isn't it a thing of beauty? Tomorrow evening, our men will dress as reservists. At midnight, with orders and weapons in hand, they'll knock at all the strategic points and take them over. Not a drop of blood shed. In fact, the people in place will feel protected by us the entire time." He laughed softly. "From there it will be a perfect lockdown. No command will be given or received. Without the police, or a mayor, or any way to get directives from Vichy, no one will know how to react once they realize we're in the middle of an Allied invasion. They won't know if Vichy is for it or against it. They won't know if they should consider the landing an act of liberation or an act of war."

"What if someone suspects the orders to be fake?"

"The phone lines will be cut off precisely at midnight, so they won't be able to reach anyone to verify. They'll have an easy choice to make: either disobey written orders and risk their career or go along with them. And don't forget that even if they work for Vichy, they are French above all. It will be easier to let themselves be relieved of their duty. The alternative would require a sense of initiative most bureaucrats don't possess."

"A perfect plan … if they buy it."

"If they don't, we will be armed. Once inside, it will be easy to neutralize any resisting bureaucrats. And remember, they are pencil-pushers. Not trained or armed, the way we are. The crucial part is to cut communications. We're counting on confusion and the effect of surprise. With the phone lines down, it will be chaos. The only ones in Algiers with any sense of what's happening will be our men. As all this is happening, other cells will be at work throughout the rest of the city, gaining control of access in and out of the Algiers by taking over bridges and roads." Fernand inhaled deeply from a new cigarette, exhaled, and inspected me with half-closed eyes. "And then, there is you."

"Me."

"Early tomorrow evening you will call your Boche, tell him you need to see him, some sort of emergency. Can you do that?"

"I have a plan. I think it will work."

"That-a-girl."

"What happens then?"

"Tomorrow night, you are the one who will prevent your Boche from contacting the Wehrmacht."

Fernand's commanding tone nearly knocked me out of my chair. "But I can't – how would I?"

I took a measure of Fernand's cold expression. No matter how much he professed to care about me, he was willing to sacrifice me for this mission. "This is crucial, Marceline. The Resistance's single advantage is the element of surprise. If the Boche rings the alarm bell, Berlin will alert the Afrika Kopf. Rommel's troops are already at the Tunisian border. The Italians in the Syrian airbase could deploy their air force. Our job is to prevent the Nazis from making their move a moment too soon. We must stop this Boche from sending or receiving messages, and you're our ticket in. There is no one else." I looked at Fernand, speechless.

"Two possibilities," he continued. "You can lure him out of his house, and we'll kidnap him, or you have to subdue him from inside the house."

I was speechless for a moment. This sounded more like fiction than any sort of reality. "Why not simply kidnap him now?"

"Because they would put someone else in his place. Someone who has no reason to let you close. And his kidnapping alone would be a warning sign to the Germans."

"Oh my gosh, Fernand, how could I possibly do any of this?"

"If you follow the plan, the poor fellow will never know what happened to him."

"What *will* happen to him?" I asked.

Fernand took my hand and placed in my palm two large capsules. "A terrific night's sleep," he said.

I stared down at the capsules and felt the fear like a punch in my gut and understood a whole lot at once. I understood what Fernand was asking me to do. I understood that everything had felt like a game to me up to that point and that my father had been right: I had been in denial about the gravity of it all.

I also understood that I was far too deep into this to refuse.

****

I spent the following day in a state of abject panic that I made every effort to conceal from my parents. Fernand had not given me the mission because of skill or talent, but because the German officer I was assigned to had turned out to be more valuable than expected. As the only person with a connection to Dietfried, I was all the Resistance had. I had no doubt in my mind that I would fail, and the weight of this responsibility was too much to bear. But everything was happening the following night, and there was little time to ponder the risks for myself or my family.

On November 7th, 1942, the eve of the planned Allied landing, I told Mother that I was spending the night at Béatrice's. It was easier to get out of Béatrice's place than to leave my own apartment in the middle of the night. As we had done many times, Béatrice helped me get out of her apartment without her parents seeing, and then she went to her room and closed the door so that her parents thought that I was with her.

I went down the steps of her building shoes in hands. In the street, I walked to the end of the block and entered the wooden telephone box. The phone rang and rang. With each ring, I desperately wanted to hang up.

When Dietfried picked up the telephone, he seemed astounded to hear my voice. "I hope I have not awakened you," I said. I did not have to pretend to be distraught. I was.

"Of course not; is everything all right?"

"You said I could call you anytime and I…." I changed the pitch of my voice and made a sound as though I was muffling tears. "It's just that I didn't know who else to call."

"Marceline, calm down, I urge you," Dietfried said in a commanding but soothing voice. "Tell me what's the matter?"

"I just needed to hear a friend's voice, that's all," I said, sounding, I hoped, pitiful.

"Please tell me what's going on!"

"It's my fiancé." I broke into false sobs. "You were right about him. He's not a gentleman. He got so upset that I was spending time with you. He had a terrible anger fit. He's nothing but a jealous, irate boy."

The thought of my imaginary fiancé being jealous of him opened a door inside Dietfried's subconscious. "Has he hurt you?" he asked, and from his tone, I could tell he was already feeling a sense of proprietorship toward me.

"I'll be all right."

Chivalrous Dietfried took control. "Marceline, has he put his hands on you?"

"It was awful. I don't know what he will do next. I ran away."

"Are you safe from him right now? Where are you?"

"I am near my apartment, but he is standing in front of the entrance. I'm afraid to go home. My family is away, and he knows this. I'm scared, Dietfried. I'm scared that he will force his way into my apartment."

"Can't you call the police?"

"The police?" I repeated. I had not thought of the police. In a flash of creativity, I improvised. "He is a policeman himself. That's his work. That's why I cannot call the police."

"Marceline, just tell me how I can help."

"Could you, would you come down here?" I asked in a small voice.

Fernand had told me that the chances of Dietfried accepting this were slim, but it was worth a shot. If he came, Fernand's men would kidnap him as planned, long enough for Dietfried to be unable to transmit a signal. There was a silence on the line. Finally, Dietfried said, "I am sorry Marceline. I absolutely cannot leave my house at this hour. For reasons I cannot explain just yet."

"I completely understand," I said. Part of me hoped that he would leave it at that. But a stronger urge pushed me to succeed. If I did not find a way to see him tonight, the entire mission might fail.

"We're in a state of alert," Dietfried hurried to add. "Rumors. Absolutely nothing you must concern yourself with, but I cannot go anywhere. It would be tantamount to abandoning my post."

"I should never have bothered you," I said, breathlessly.

There was more silence on the line. Dietfried was processing this. "I do have an idea!" he said at last. "Perhaps you would like to come over here."

My heart beat faster. "Come where, Dietfried?"

“My house. There is a guest room. You’ll be safe until morning when your parents return. Would you like that?”

“Do you really think so?”

“Yes, definitely. Just tell me where to send my chauffeur.”

I could still turn back. I could still say no. But a process had been set in motion, and I was no longer an individual but a crucial cog in a terrifying machine. “I would like that very much,” I said.

We planned for his chauffeur to pick me up at the corner of rue d’Isly and rue Joinville. Next, I dialed Fernand’s telephone number. “The dove flies to the nest,” I said when I heard his voice, and I hung up.

From the phone box, I dashed to the courtyard of our apartment building. Father’s car was parked in its regular spot, as was my bicycle and Gustave’s. Curfew time was approaching.

I pedaled away through the emptying streets. My breath was heavy, my heart pounding. The tires made whooshing sounds on the pavement. Night fell, and lampposts lit up one by one. By now, I thought, the Allies must already be positioned a short distance from the shore. Soon enough, a boat, or a submarine, or an ally carrying M1 carbines would be spotted. A bridge would explode. There would be an exchange of gunfire. Everyone in the city would be alerted. Hopefully, by then it would no longer matter. A few hundred Jews bearing obsolete weapons would have wreaked havoc on all communication systems and rendered the police force useless. I pedaled frantically.

I hid the bicycle out of sight just as Dietfried’s driver pulled into the street. The chauffeur came around and opened the door for me. He was a French man, burly and violent-looking. Although he worked for the enemy, the contempt on his face displayed how he felt about a young French woman on a nighttime rendezvous with a German officer.

I sat in the back, and the automobile made its way out of the center of Algiers. I thought of what Fernand had told me would happen tonight. At this moment, our men, young and old, prepared or not, were taking their weapons out of hiding, donning reservists’ uniforms, badges, and armbands, scurrying around the city with their precious ordres de mission. At the city’s edge, others were placing explosives under bridges and getting ready to block roads. Everywhere, our men were preparing to shut down phone lines. And I was about to face Dietfried.

So much could go wrong. An alarm could ring too soon. The local Vichy forces could know in advance of the Resistance’s subterfuge, and orders would be given to open fire on our liberators. If I could not stop Dietfried from sounding the alarm in Germany, the entire landing operation might be compromised. If the Nazis found out about the landing before we had Algiers under our control, they could move to mobilize their forces in and around North Africa.

And then, there was the ignominious possibility that the Allies had changed their mind, for whatever reason, without notifying us and that our group was heading towards a suicide mission.

Of all the doubts that assailed me as the automobile headed toward Dietfried's house, it had not occurred to me that my inexperience, my hubris, my stupidity, and my sense on invincibility were matched only by my brother's.

Gustave too had been given a mission that night. He too was out past curfew. He too was about to risk his life. And with this, the fate of my family was sealed.

It was a fifteen-minute drive to the outskirts of town before Dietfried's driver pulled in front of his house.

Armed guards opened the gate, and we drove into the courtyard. In the night, I could only see the outline of the house and the date palms that framed it. It was a two-story house, painted white and surrounded by a wall and a garden. I looked up at the windows; all the shutters were closed.

There were guards everywhere, dark silhouettes against the night. I counted about ten. Fernand had explained to me that the security provided for Dietfried, compliments of Vichy, was composed of Frenchmen, each outfitted with a Wehrmacht Karabiner. Some of those men were secretly with the Resistance and on our side. Some of them were not. I could not tell who was with whom, and it felt as though it was just me, surrounded by enemies.

And then I saw him: Gustave, my brother, standing guard by one of the palm trees.

He was wearing a dark turtleneck, and there was a leather strap across his chest, holding a Karabiner.

Gustave, my brother, impossibly, was one of Dietfried's guards!

My legs went limp, my mouth dry. Our eyes met briefly and widened in horror at the sight of each other. Immediately, we both looked away. I felt ill.

Outside the front door, one of the guards searched me with deliberate roughness, groping my breasts as the others looked me up and down, sneering. To them, I was nothing but a French tramp about to spend the night with a Nazi. I wondered if Gustave had seen this. I felt ashamed.

At that moment, Dietfried stepped out of the house, greeting me effusively as though I were a guest at a cocktail party. "Dear Marceline, please do come in," he said. He took me inside the house. Inside, I collapsed into his arms, and I did not have to pretend.

"I am so glad you are here and safe," Dietfried said once we were inside. Instead of his usual uniform, he was wearing casual pants and a shirt unbuttoned at the neck.

I let him guide me into the living room. I don't know what he was saying. All I could think about was Gustave. What was my brother doing here? I felt rage and panic all at once. How could my brother be guarding a Boche unless he worked for the French Algerian government – in other words, for Vichy? But Fernand had said some of the guards were in the Resistance. For sure, Gustave had to be on our side! Either way, the implications of his presence here were too dire to fathom. If my brother was with the enemy, he might be shot to death tonight. If he was one of us, Dietfried's Vichy guards might shoot him. Whichever it was, Gustave was in terrible danger.

"Are you quite all right?" Dietfried asked. I thought I might throw up. I'm certain I now looked as distraught as I had earlier pretended to be.

"You have a lot of guards," I told him.

He smiled apologetically. "It does seem overkill, doesn't it? Nothing ever happens in Algiers." He looked at my worried face and added quickly, "I mean, in your case something *did* happen, my darling. It's terrible, this unfortunate aggression by your fiancé. Do you not prefer being surrounded by armed guards at this moment?"

I smiled weakly. "I guess I do."

"No harm can come to you as long as you are with me."

The living room was a well-furnished space with high ceilings, crown molding, comfortable sofas, and expensive furniture. This was someone's home, requisitioned, just as our house in Paris had been. I thought of our home, swarming with Nazis, who slept in our beds, took baths in our tubs, ate out of Mother's delicate Limoges china.

In the fireplace, someone had started a fire. A bottle of Bordeaux and two wine glasses were set on the coffee table. The setting was transparent as to Dietfried's intentions. Here I was, allegedly terrified and upset, and he was about to take the opportunity to try and seduce me. "Please do sit and relax," he said mellifluously. "You must be exhausted after the evening you've had." He pointed to the wine. "Please relax. Do sit down on the couch; yes, right here. A glass of wine will strengthen you."

"Thank you, Dietfried, for being so attentive," I said as I sat on the too-soft couch. It was a good thing that I was supposed to be afraid and upset because now I truly was. I thought of my father, of what he had said about his fear that something might happen to either of us. And now both his children were in great danger and might even die on the same night.

Dietfried sat on the sofa too close to me. He poured wine into one of the glasses and offered it to me. I was about to take a sip when I saw that he had not filled his own glass. "Aren't you going to have wine?" I asked.

"I'm very much on duty at the moment," he said.

But Dietfried needed to drink something right now. Had to or else none of the plan would work! "Perhaps its best that I don't drink either," I said, jumping to my feet and walking agitatedly around the room as though I was suddenly able to realize that I was a proper young lady in a compromising situation.

Dietfried must have seen that he could make no headway with me unless he found a way to calm me down. "A glass of wine would help your nerves," he pleaded.

"Oh, a glass of water will do," I said, uptight.

"I will drink with you," he sighed. "But only if you promise to sit down and relax." He poured a glass for himself and raised it. "To our friendship," he said.

We drank, and he listened to me with rapt attention, leaning ever closer as I fed him a tale of domestic abuse and womanly distress. I cried too. Not because of my lies, but because of Gustave, because of my dad, because I might not see morning come, and I was too young to die. Dietfried, perhaps noticing that it gave him courage, filled both our glasses again.

My opportunity was here. I had to seize it. "Dietfried," I said. "Do you mind? All this wine on an empty stomach. Would you have anything to eat?"

He jumped up. "Forgive me. I'm an appalling host. I shall fetch something to eat at once!"

He disappeared into the nearby kitchen. I heard dishes clang and cupboard doors being opened and shut. Everything happened in an instant: I reached into my purse, took the capsules Fernand had given me, opened one, and dropped its powdery contents into Dietfried's wine. I watched the glass in horror: the whole thing had begun to fizz violently. I added the content of the second capsule, and it fizzed some more. An instant later, the wine was still, and I could breathe. I marveled that my fingers had been steady enough to carry this out.

Another moment and Dietfried was back with a plate of olives, cheese, and bread. He sat next to me, urgency on his face, as though his time in the kitchen had resulted in renewed determination. He offered me my glass.

"Let's have some food first, shall we?" I said, thinking that the taste of the cheese might mask any odd taste in the wine.

We ate our cheese and bread. Mine had the feel of quicksand in my mouth. "Have I told you about my childhood holidays in Rügen, off the Pomeranian coast?" he asked. "It is in the Baltic Sea."

He had. "Tell me about it," I said.

He embarked on one of his soliloquies. I heard nothing. I only watched his lips move and tracked the glass as it went from his hand to his mouth. I also noticed something: as Dietfried spoke, his eyes kept veering toward a narrow wooden door to our right. A bedroom? Was this where his equipment was set up? My attention kept returning to the fireplace mantle where an imposing marble clock indicated that it was already past ten at night. Where was Gustave right now? Where were Fernand and his men? Would Fernand recognize Gustave and make sure no one shot at him?

Dietfried did not seem to notice anything strange with the taste of the wine, but neither did he seem affected by it. Doubt gripped me. What if the product failed to work? Or what if Fernand had lied to me and it was, in fact, poison and Dietfried was about to drop dead? What if there was no Allied landing, and I was found in this room with a corpse?

Dietfried downed the rest of his glass to muster the courage to do something. He took my hand in his. "Dear Marceline, I am so glad you came here tonight. You are so … You are, lovely and…." He blinked twice and looked at me with puzzlement. I watched him intently, my hand stiff in his. Dietfried looked confused as he went on with his courtship. "You are so…." He leaned toward me as if to kiss me. I leaned away from him, and he made a nosedive into the throw pillow. He pushed himself up, shook his head, and leaned in again to kiss me. I got up from the couch. He looked confused and got up. He staggered toward me, flailing his arms. I took a step back. "Dear Marceline," he said, grasping for my dress. "That pig fiancé of yours … does not deserve…." His speech slurred. He squinted with great effort and passed his hand over his face. He was sweating, shaking his head. I went to stand by the window and looked through the spaces between the wooden shutters. I wanted to see signs of our men, signs of Gustave, but all I saw was the night. Dietfried set out to pursue me, but at a snail's pace. He got close. I stepped away. He followed me around the room, stumbling, his shoulders slumped, still not realizing that he had been drugged. "You were correct," he mumbled. "One mustn't have wine on an empty stomach." The marble clock on the mantle marked fifteen minutes past ten. I heard something at last: a commotion coming from outside. There were shouts. An instant later a gunshot tore through the night, then another one and a third and a fourth in rapid succession. Gustave! Where was he? My heart began to beat violently in my chest. Dietfried stumbled to the window. "Was ist das?" he exclaimed drunkenly just as a machine gun roared into the night.

"Move away from the window," I yelled. We both ducked. Our faces were inches from each other, and he looked at me. I looked at him, expecting him to fall face first, but he did not.

An expression between disappointment and disbelief passed across his sweaty face. "*You* did this?" he said, stricken.

As gunshots and men's voices pierced the night, Dietfried and I, in unison, looked at the narrow door to the right of the room, confirming my intuition that something important such as his radio equipment was in that room.

Dietfried and I moved at the same moment, me jumping up, him stumbling to his feet. I got to the door to the room first, but he pushed me out of the way, hard. I was thrown against the wall, and I fell to the ground. The honeymoon was over. My blood laced with adrenaline. I got to my feet. Dietfried was at the door, but his cottony fingers did not obey him. He fumbled with the key. Had the door been opened, he would have gotten inside the room and locked himself in, but he had kept the door locked. While he failed miserably in the simple task of inserting a key into a keyhole, I bolted to the mantle, grabbed the heavy marble clock as though it were no heavier than a loaf of bread, rushed toward him, lifted the clock above his head, and brought it down on his skull with all my strength.

I thought I heard the breaking of bones. Dietfried looked at me in shock. He wavered, and his body just tilted forward. His eyes wide, he collapsed to the floor with a loud thump.

He lay on the rug, motionless. There was a large bloody gash on the side of his head.

I could hear more gunshots outside. Tears began to stream down my face. All I could think of at that moment was Gustave. I imagined him dead, my father and mother heartbroken for life.

I kneeled next to Dietfried, not knowing if he was alive or dead, and took the key from his clenched fingers. I stepped over his body, unlocked the door, entered the room, and locked myself inside as the sounds of gunshots continued to tear through the night.

In the room were a metal desk, rolled-up maps, and more maps taped to the walls. There were folders and documents everywhere, shelving, office furniture, a typewriter. On a table set against the wall were all kinds of wires and equipment, a microphone, something that looked like a Morse code machine. Fernand had told me what to do if I found myself in this exact situation: damage as much as I could, as fast as I could. My heart thumped. I hurried around the room pulling wires and smashing things to the ground. Gunshots continued outside, dozens at first, and then fewer. As I broke things, my mind raced. What if Fernand's men were outnumbered? What if they failed? I had, by some miracle, managed to take Dietfried down, but would I live past the hour?

Outside the window, I heard someone shout, "We're all brothers. An Allied landing is underway. Allied ships have entered the port!" Was the man bluffing? No matter; it sounded convincing to me. "Surrender!" the man shouted. "We don't want bloodshed. The Allies are at the city's door. Do the right thing and join us!" From that point on, there were no more gunshots.

Holding on to the hope that Gustave was either with us or had surrendered, I darted around the room, grabbing and shoving maps and documents into an empty briefcase. My focus kept returning to a bizarre-looking typewriter, which had a keyboard, but also a strange pull board and small rotors. Next to it was a wooden case with a handle that fastened perfectly over it. I packed it together and waited.

For many interminable minutes, I stood with my ear to the door, the briefcase in one hand, the wooden case in the other. I heard no sound, no voice, no stirring. Dietfried was unconscious on the other side of the door. The men were no longer firing. There was no sign of Fernand. I set the wooden case on the floor and turned the key ever so slowly. I cracked the door open.

I leaped backward. Dietfried was standing in the middle of the room, blood running down his face, looking like a rage-filled wounded animal. He snarled and rushed forward. "Hure!" he roared. I had just enough reflex to slam the door inches from his nose, turn the key, and lock myself inside. I leaned against the door, breathing hard. I stepped away from the door just in time: in an instant, there was a deafening series of explosions and the wood of the door burst in several places. Sweet, attentive, love-struck Dietfried had found himself a gun and was shooting at me through the door!

I took cover under the metal desk. There was nothing else I could do. Dietfried shot again, and again, each conflagration making a bigger gash into the wooden door. I curled on myself and held my breath.

The sound of a different weapon blasted on the other side of the door, and then silence. A moment later I heard a voice.

"Marceline? Are you in there?" It was Gustave's voice! "Are you all right?" he asked.

"I'm in here," I said feebly from under the desk. I looked at the door. The wood was riddled with large gashes.

"It's safe now," Gustave said. "Are you wounded?" I got up and went to open what was left of the door just as Gustave pushed it open. He was pale, disheveled, the Karabiner by his side. I was shaking so violently I could barely stand. "Did we win?"

"I *think* so," Gustave said.

"What side are you on?" I asked.

"He's on our side!" said a voice. It was Fernand who was entering the room. He looked just as scared as Gustave and me. "Did you stop the Boche from sending a signal?" he asked.

"I can't believe I did, but yes." My knees buckled unexpectedly from under me, and Fernand caught me.

He, Gustave, and I walked out of the room. I clutched Fernand's arm as we walked past Dietfried's body sprawled on the Persian rug. He lay on his back, his eyes open, a bullet wound to the heart. "He's dead. He's really dead," Gustave said, overwhelmed.

"Did you shoot him?" I asked Gustave. He just nodded.

As I looked at Dietfried's body, I had the strong sense that it was I, not Gustave or Fernand, who was responsible for his death. Dietfried was dead because he had trusted me.

"We need to get you back home," Fernand said. He took the briefcase from my hand and pointed to the wooden case. "What is this?"

"I haven't the faintest idea," I said, wiping my eyes with my sleeve. "Maybe we should leave it behind."

Fernand picked it up. "I'll take it," he said.

Outside, Dietfried's guards had been rounded up in the dark. They were kneeling in the dirt, their hands atop their heads, as a half dozen of our men stood around them. Gustave went to join them. I climbed into an automobile, and Fernand took the wheel. "What about my brother?" I asked.

"He's part of another cell."

"Are we leaving him behind?"

"He will come back with his team, when their mission is complete, as per their instructions."

We drove off into the night. I was trembling, but I did not know if it was because of the cold, or the shock of it all. Fernand lit a cigarette and offered me one.

"What will happen to the guards?" I asked.

"They're prisoners for now," Fernand said.

"Have the Allied forces arrived?"

"They'll be here," he assured me. "Soon they'll be landing."

"But you don't know for sure?"

"The Brits, the Yankees, the Canadians," he said with forced cheer. "You'll see."

"Who recruited him?" I asked.

"Who?" Fernand said.

"You know very well who."

"I did," Fernand said.

"Why Gustave!" I exclaimed. "He's only seventeen years old. He knows nothing!"

"He knows enough. We needed all the bodies we could get."

I was livid. "I asked you to do the opposite! I asked you to keep him safe!"

"Not at all. You asked me to make sure he left you alone. This was the best way I could think of to keep him from trailing you so you could do your mission. That kid was tenacious about following you. So I had to give him something to do."

"Did he know I would be here tonight?"

"Even I didn't know that he'd be there tonight. We are in different units," Fernand said.

"So my brother saved my life," I said.

"He shot the Boche. He did what he had to do. We all did." And in his tone, I sensed that he felt entitled to get some credit for what Gustave had done.

We arrived in downtown Algiers and still nothing. There was hardly any moon and no light in any of the windows of the houses or apartments we drove past. The streets were so quiet it seemed hardly possible that anything out of the ordinary was taking place at all. I found the courage to ask. "Why is no one in the streets?"

"We've done our part," Fernand said. "We better hurry home. If things fall to shit, we'll need to act as though we were home the whole time."

"But should the streets be this quiet?" I asked again. Fernand did not respond. My spirit sank. I thought of Dietfried, his love for Heidelberg, his quiet manners — at least until he began shooting at me through that door –

and I hoped that his death wasn't for nothing. I closed my eyes and sank into my seat, drained of all energy.

We reached the heart of the city, and there still was no signs of activity. I wanted to hear sirens, gunshots, tanks rolling in, but the only car on the road was ours.

Fernand understood something. "It's too quiet!" he said excitedly. "Where are the police? The place should be swarming with them looking to apprehend people after curfew."

A buzz spread through my body. "Do you think we have the police on lockdown?"

"Something is happening for sure," Fernand said, beaming.

At that moment, a massive explosion tore through the night, so powerful that it rattled the car. The sky above the sea illuminated like fireworks. Fernand pushed on the brakes abruptly. We looked at each other, hopeful, excited. "What was that?" I said.

"That," we found out later, was the Vichy forces shooting a canon at two U.S. destroyers that had arrived in the port.

Within minutes, it was mayhem in the city. All around, windows of apartment buildings lit up like a Christmas tree. Forgetting all about curfew, entire families, awakened by the noise, stepped out onto their balconies, squinting at the dark sea. Men and women, having noticed that no phone lines functioned, descended, frazzled, into the streets to ask what was happening.

Fernand started up the car. We passed the commissariat, where a crowd had congregated in search of information. The same scenario was taking place in front of the préfecture. Once we arrived at the foot of my apartment building, I jumped out of the car. Fernand smiled at me and drove away into the night.

I ran up the stairs, opened the door to our apartment, and found Mother in her bathrobe and curlers standing in the middle of the living room. "There are explosions!" she said, frantic.

"I heard."

"Did you just come back from Béatrice's in the middle of the night?"

"Yes," I lied.

Her voice shrill, she asked, "Where are Gustave and your father?"

My eyes widened. "Baba isn't home?"

"Nor is Gustave. Would I be asking if they were?" Mother whimpered. "I'm all by myself in this horrible apartment, in this horrible country, and something scary is happening in the city! On top of it, our telephone is out of order. Alban must not have paid the bill. Oh, look!" she exclaimed. She pointed outside.

We rushed to the balcony. On the darkened balconies around and below us and in the building across the street were the pale silhouettes of people in their pajamas craning their necks to see what might be happening. In the street below, dozens of men stood conversing in hushed voices. Suddenly an explosion, distant but powerful, startled us all and briefly illuminated the street. The men who had been standing in the street ran for cover. "It's the Nazis," my mother shouted hysterically. "They are coming for us!"

I gripped Mother by her shoulder and steadied her. "Mother!" I whispered, "it's the opposite! We're being liberated!"

She gave me a confused look. "Liberated from what?"

At that moment, the front door opened and Gustave appeared. Seeing me, he looked relieved. "You're back," he said.

"Goodness gracious, Gustave! You're safe!" Mother sobbed. "Where were you?"

"I was on a mission for the Resistance," he said.

"I would not be trumpeting that quite yet," I said.

"Well, you should be glad I was."

"What an idiot! Do you realize how dangerous this was?"

"Do *you*?" he asked, furious.

"I did, as a matter of fact," I said.

"What is happening out there?" Mother interrupted. "Things are blowing up all over the place. And the telephone isn't working."

"If I hadn't been there, we wouldn't be having this conversation," Gustave said. "You'd be dead."

"If you hadn't been there, Fernand would have been, and I'd still be fine."

"You're a monster, do you know that!" Gustave shouted. "You can't even say a simple thank you!"

"I don't understand what you two are talking about," our mother cried out. "Where is Alban?"

"Do you know how terrified I was when I saw you?" I shouted back at Gustave. "I thought you were on the Vichy side. I thought our men were going to kill you!"

"I was placed there by my cell. That was my mission. That's where I was all the time you thought I was doing stupid team-building exercises at the Jeunesse. As if I would ever join those idiots."

"But where is Alban now?" my mother said.

"I was trying to complete my mission and subdue a *German officer*, and I could hardly concentrate because I was terrified that you might get killed."

"Your mission—"

"WHERE IS ALBAN?" Mother suddenly shouted at the top of her lungs.

I turned to Gustave. "Do you know where Baba went?"

Gustave looked dumbfounded. "He's not home?"

"He must have heard the commotion and gone into the street to look for you," Mother told Gustave.

"Why would he be looking for me and not Marceline?" Gustave asked.

"Because he knew that Marceline was at Béatrice's house. All I know is that I jumped out of bed when I heard the explosion, and no one was home."

Mother slumped onto a chair and spoke in a ghostly voice. "I know that your father is involved in this nonsense."

"Baba is in the Resistance too?" Gustave asked. It was obvious from his tone and expression that he had no idea.

A new succession of explosions shook the walls of the apartment. The chandelier swayed. "We're being bombed!" Mother shouted. "We must go down to the cellar at once!"

"They're blowing up bridges, Mother," I said. "The Allies are landing. And Jews are leading the Resistance!"

"Oh my God. Where is Alban?" my mother said, whimpering.

As the sun rose, we learned that the Resistance's ploy had been a success. Our men had walked into every government building and agency, presented the official paperwork saying that they were assigned to take control, and they took over. The landing and subsequent occupation of Algeria by the Allied forces took place with a minimum of fighting or casualties. While the commissariat, the préfecture, the Grande Poste, the telephone company, and most public buildings were under the control of our men, the landing progressed unhindered. As it turned out, though, our men didn't get help from the Allied forces until much later than expected. The sea was rough, and it took many more hours before the American and British forces could land on beaches and enter ports and march into the city. For hours, our men had stood their ground until the soldiers arrived, without being certain that they would arrive at all.

Throughout the day, elements of the French police and the French army continued to shoot at the Allied forces and members of the Resistance, but that effort quickly ended.

By five p.m., all of Algiers was perched on apartment balconies, witnessing the arrival of the American soldiers in open cars sporting the American flag. It was a sight to behold! Gustave, Mother, and I, along with thousands of the residents of Algiers, descended into the street. The sight of the American flag was just the happiest thing to see. It represented the hope of an entire nation, an entire continent. Still today I get goosebumps remembering those young soldiers, so brave and so thrilled as they let us kiss and hug them.

But as the American jeeps were driving under our balcony, Father still hadn't returned.

There was tremendous confusion following the invasion. The telephone lines were still down, the police force was under arrest, all local government officials were under military guard, and there was no place to inquire about anything. At first, we were able to soothe ourselves. We reasoned that if Father had been captured, since he was a Resistance operative on the winning side, he soon would be released. But by sundown, our optimism of the afternoon had turned to anguish. Once the Allies had the ceasefire secured, and Father still wasn't back, we began to fear the worst. Between my fear for Baba, the loss of sleep, the trauma of narrowly escaping being shot, and the persistent memory of Dietfried's dead eyes, I unleashed my bottled-up emotions onto Gustave. "Baba went looking for you," I told him. "Why did you have to get involved?" I very much believed that it was Gustave's fault. Perhaps I *needed* to believe this. I needed to believe that it was he, not I, who might have put my father at risk.

It took five days for the Allied forces and the local authorities to decide who in Algiers should now be in charge. Everyone, from the police to the local army, was afraid to counter Vichy's orders. After all, no one knew for sure if the Allies would keep their hold on North Africa, and everyone in Europe still believed Hitler unstoppable.

Mother, Gustave, and I spent two days frantically searching for my father. Once the telephone lines were restored, Uncle Moshe, Fernand, André, Émile, and our family made dozens of phone calls. We knocked on every door; we asked everyone we knew. In those few days, I completely ceased to think of Khaled.

On the sixth day after the landing, there was a rap at our apartment door. Gustave, Mother, and I rushed to open it, but it was not Baba. Two men stood glumly on our front step, hats in hands, and asked to speak to Mother in private. Full of dread, Gustave and I stepped away, as she let the men into the living room. Gustave and I were behind the door, holding our breath. We heard Mother let out a muffled cry like the moan of an animal. We rushed in. Mother was hunched over, a hand over her mouth as if she was about to vomit. One of the men stopped her from falling and helped her to a chair. The sight of her was enough for me to know the worst had happened. I hung on to the doorframe, too stunned to react. Mother buried her face in her hands; her shoulders shook violently. Gustave's face was white, frozen in distress.

The taller of the two men turned to us. "It was an explosion," he said.

"We found this," the other man said opening a cloth from which he extracted the blackened remnants of two objects. We recognized them immediately: they were my father's wallet and his hat. I stared at them unable to speak. "Close that!" Mother ordered. The man wrapped the hat and wallet back into the cloth and set them on the dining room table.

"We are very sorry," one of the men said. "His remains are at the morgue. We are required to ask you to identify the body. Unfortunately, the explosion was followed by a fire so…." He paused, then changed his mind about completing his sentence. Instead, he said, "Please accept our condolences."

And then they left us to our grief. On the table were Father's scorched belongings and a piece of paper telling us how to get in touch with the mortuary.

****

Under the gazebo, a large cloud passed in front of the sun. Marceline felt a bit of a chill.

"But it wasn't him in the end. Right?" Cassandra asked her.

Marceline looked at Cassandra and then looked away. The young woman who sat across from her did not resemble Gustave one bit, but Marceline had to be mindful that she was his daughter indeed. She mustn't get carried away by resentment. The girl loved her father and whatever fiction of himself he had given her. She would try to be fair. She took a small breath and said, "We did have confirmation of my beloved father's terrible, useless death the next morning."

Cassandra let her pen fall on the table. "Baba was killed?" she exclaimed. "That can't be!"

Marceline tried to compose herself by taking a sip of her tea, but emotion overtook her, and her hands trembled violently. She set her teacup in the saucer. "Forgive me," she said. "Even after all these years."

"What happened?" Cassandra asked, her eyes clouded with tears.

Marceline composed herself and took a sip from her cup.

"Uncle Moshe accompanied us to the mortuary. He was the one who identified my father's remains. We could not do it. We were told his body had been scorched. It was beyond our strength to look at him. After we left the morgue, I began to weep and could not stop for days.

"Through Uncle Moshe, we learned what had happened. My father was indeed the leader of a Resistance cell in charge of destroying a bridge. Something had gone wrong. The bridge was set to explode at three a.m. with the others, but there was a misunderstanding, and it was blown up an hour too soon when my father was still too close to it. Moshe told us that no one could explain why our father was there in the first place. The explosives had long been installed; someone else oversaw the detonation. Our father should have been safe at home. Had he wanted to make sure that things went smoothly, Uncle Moshe wondered? We would never know Baba's reasons, he said.

"We did not have the desire to tell Uncle Moshe that Mother, Gustave, and I knew the reason. We knew all too well why my father was at the bridge: he had been looking for Gustave. Not finding Gustave at home on the night of the invasion, my father must have worried. He had headed to the one place he knew for a fact was set to explode. He had wanted to make sure that Gustave wasn't there. He had wanted to protect him."

Marceline stopped speaking. If she said any more, she might be unable to contain her tears. Laure offered a welcome diversion by appearing through the door that led from the kitchen to the backyard and headed for the gazebo under which they sat, carrying a three-tiered silver tray filled with tea sandwiches. She set the tray on the table and gave Marceline a quick look to make sure she was all right. Marceline nodded at her to tell her she was. The top two levels of the tray were filled with pastel-colored macarons, the bottom one with small sandwiches. "I've always thought cucumber sandwiches to be a culinary aberration," Marceline said with forced gaiety. "Whoever thought of putting a slice of a tasteless vegetable between two slices of plain bread and calling it a delicacy?"

"I guess," Cassandra said. Marceline appreciated how the young woman had listened attentively and quietly, taking notes like a studious child. She was a good listener. Nothing was quite so annoying as being interrupted when trying to tell a story. Now Cassandra was very still as if processing what she had just learned required complete immobility.

"It's lovely weather, isn't it?" Marceline said to break the uncomfortable stillness of the moment. "I'm told this should be an exceptional year for climbing roses."

"I can only imagine what it will be like in your garden when all these roses start to bloom. Your gardener is a magician."

"My gardener?" Marceline repeated. She sighed deeply and nibbled on a pale green macaron. "I hardly ever see them in bloom. I prefer to spend the warmer months away from Paris. I go to my country house. I am heading there soon, in fact."

"And so, my dad blames you for the death of your father," Cassandra said. "He has blamed you all this time. That's why he hates you so much,"

Marceline nodded, "That's correct."

"And you've blamed him?"

Marceline pondered the moral obligation to describe the facts not as she had perceived them, but for the first time perhaps, as they were. "Also correct," she admitted.

"What happened to you after all this? How could the three of you manage?"

"It was all a blur," Marceline said. "We buried my father just as the entire city was in a state of jubilation. It was so surreal. Algiers was free. Jews were safe, at least in Algeria. This was precisely what my father had dreamed of, hoped and fought for, but he was not here to enjoy it. We were in shock and too devastated to experience relief at being liberated. Soon thereafter, things turned erratic at home. Mother immediately suffered a mental breakdown. She was hospitalized for months. I guess you could say that her falling apart was years in the making. As strained as her relationship with my father was, she was utterly lost without him."

"You did not want to return to Paris then?"

"Remember that this was only November 1942. Paris and France would not be liberated for another three years. While our mother was hospitalized, Gustave and I lived together in the Algiers apartment without exchanging a word. We blamed each other for everything that had happened, and neither of us was willing to support the other one in grief. It was all quite ugly."

"And you were children, orphans, and left to yourself at a time of war."

"Not children. I was nineteen, and your father was seventeen."

"My twins just turned eighteen," Cassandra said. "Trust me: they are babies."

"In times of war, you become an adult much faster."

"Did you ever find out why the bridge exploded early?"

"A death in wartime becomes part of the statistics. My father's death, the explosion, Sandra's vanishing act, the circumstance of the murder of which she was accused: none of that was ever examined. In the months following Operation Torch, the Algiers government officials and the city's entire administration resembled a barnyard full of donkeys and headless chickens running amok, and those of us in the Resistance kept a low profile. There was no investigation."

"I wonder why I never heard of Operation Torch before. Shouldn't it be as famous as D-day?"

"History is conveniently murky on those few days in November 1942. There is some mention of the patriotic stance of the French of Algiers who bravely defied Hitler and Vichy and sided with the Allied forces. What they never talk about is the handful of Jews who held those alleged patriots at gunpoint so that they would not shoot at the Allies."

"But without all of you, the landing might not have been possible!"

"The truth needed to be altered into a narrative that would make the new government shine in a better light."

"What do you mean?"

"Deals were made. Someone had to govern Algiers after all. The government officials had been humiliated by the deception that had tricked everyone into inaction on that fateful night. So, after all was sorted out between the Allies and the local authorities – the Commissaire, the Préfect, all the military and police personnel, the very people who had been subdued by our men so that they would not shoot at the Allies – they all recovered their original posts. Only now they were on *our* side. Enemies just a few days before now shook hands and began to work together against the Wehrmacht."

"You mean that the police and the local government took credit for the success of the invasion?"

Marceline could not repress a laugh, which was more of an expression of disgust. "It was better for morale that they portray themselves as part of the Resistance, from the first hour. History must rewrite itself in more palatable bites. I made peace with that, eventually. Although at the time, the injustice was hard to swallow. In war and in life, you have to be pragmatic."

"What about you? You must have received a medal?"

"Don't be absurd."

"A recognition of some sort?"

"To this day, my involvement in Operation Torch was never revealed. In the end, it was more useful that I stay undercover."

"Why?"

"Because it was only the start of my Resistance work."

"And so, my father did save your life."

"He did shoot Dietfried. But if he hadn't, Fernand was right behind him and would have shot him…." Marceline paused. This was all so ridiculous: hanging on to a narrative, being right at all costs. And for what, for whom? "Yes," she admitted, "Gustave did indeed save my life."

"Was Sandra ever found?"

"I'll never know if she died, if she was caught, or if she found a way to leave the country. And I don't know if she ever found out that my father was killed."

"What about the boys?"

"Fernand, Émile, and André enrolled in the Seventh Battalion of the Corps Francs d'Afrique. Shortly after that, Gustave was old enough to enroll as well, and he did."

"And you?"

"I spent the rest of the war in Algiers, taking care of Mother and working for the Office of Strategic Services."

"The OSS? Really?" Cassie exclaimed. "So you were an actual spy!"

"When the OSS was dissolved and turned into the CIA after 1945, I was promptly recruited by the French intelligence. First, the Direction Générale des Services Spéciaux and then, the Service de Contre-Espionnage. In the years that followed the Second World War, there was an urgent need for someone with my demonstrated experience and skills. Where one war theoretically ends, another quagmire begins. There was the Algerian war, the cold war, and so forth. My work through the years will remain classified until long after I'm gone."

"So, no medal."

Marceline laughed. "No, no medal."

"To devote yourself to your country like you did: I don't think most people would be so brave."

"Call it what you want," Marceline said. "I only did what I had to do."

Marceline was tempted to tell Cassandra the truth of how she had felt at the time. She who had dreamed of independence, who had wanted to feel all grown up, was suddenly propelled into a forced adulthood. Nothing had prepared her for the loneliness and despair it entailed. Her father was dead, her mother had become unglued, her brother and all her friends had joined the army, and Khaled was transferred to an undisclosed jail somewhere deep in Algeria. There was no one left to bicker with, no one left to give a purpose to her life, no one left to love or care for her. She was perfectly alone when the OSS recruited her.

"Eventually, once the Germans were defeated and the war ended, things were reabsorbed."

"Reabsorbed?" Cassandra asked.

"I can't say that things returned to the way they were. How could they? The entire world was adrift in trauma: seventy million civilian and military deaths, an entire generation lost. There were trials, to restore the beloved illusion that justice prevailed, and to provide the human psyche with clear villains and heroes. In actuality, most of us had had no choice but to turn into a bit of both. As for the few Jews who had managed to outlive the carnage, everything had been stolen, so everything needed to be rebuilt from the ground up. Jewish students were able to resume their studies. Jewish teachers, bureaucrats, and lawyers were reinstated. And everyone was anxious to pretend that life was back to normal and that nothing like this could ever happen again."

"Selective memory loss must be a way to heal," Cassandra suggested.

"Especially for the perpetrators," Marceline said. "Returning to Paris was a surrealist moment. Imagine humanity's worst instincts being given free rein for nearly ten years and then everyone hurrying to forget. They call it rebuilding, but I call it reabsorbing. The hatred, the bloodlust, the anti-Semitism all shoved back into the psyche and muffled, silenced, at least temporarily."

Cassandra smiled. "Permanently, I hope."

Marceline contemplated the crushed macaron on her plate. "You must be more of an optimist than I am," she said.

****

Under the gazebo, Cassie nibbled at her cucumber sandwich, found herself incapable of swallowing, and set it down. Had her dad wanted his daughters to know the truth, he would have told it ages ago. Odile was right in the end: by learning something her father had wanted to keep secret, Cassie was betraying him. The question remained, why had silence been easier for him? He could have spun the story to his advantage and made Marceline the villain. With his silence, he had taken the high road and protected Marceline – if pretending not to have a sister could be considered the high road. Could his silence reveal that he outwardly blamed Marceline for his father's death but inwardly believed himself responsible? And if he felt guilt, how much of that did he carry around with him?

Cassie did see a commonality between Marceline and Gustave: neither seemed big on feeling their emotions. They found different ways not to feel: where Marceline acted out, Gustave became aloof, where Marceline deployed sarcasm, Gustave retreated in silence. She wondered if those mechanisms weren't two sides of the same coin.

The old gardener appeared in the backyard dragging a tall wooden ladder. He propped the ladder against the stone wall that surrounded the garden and, a heavy metal trimmer in hand, climbed it methodically, one step at a time, resting a moment between each step. Once at the top, he began to clip bare remnants of Boston ivy that climbed the walls. The clippers made a little rusty sound with each cut.

"At what point were you able to return to Paris?" Cassie asked Marceline.

"Mother and I stayed in Algiers through the end of the war," Marceline said. "She in her pension, a euphemism for the private mental institution where her doctors and I had placed her, and me alone in the dreadful apartment where everything reminded me of my father. As much as I hated to, I visited Mother every day. I had to; there would have been no one else. While Gustave was in the army, he communicated with us less and less. The mail service was terrible, and the relationship was strained, to say the least. I resented Gustave for not being there for Mother. I think part of him felt vindicated by her internment. She wrote him a letter incensed about having been 'put away,' in a mental hospital, to which he responded that now she knew how he had felt when she did the same to him. We stopped communicating after that."

"And what about Khaled?" Cassie asked.

Marceline wistfully looked out on the garden, at the old gardener up on his ladder. "They sent him to an internment camp where he stayed for the remainder of the war," she said. "A place deep in Algeria where there could be no visitors. With Father gone, there was no one to testify in his favor, and no one would take me seriously. After years of enduring typhus, semi-starvation, and mistreatment in jail, Khaled was freed, eventually. But his time in imprisonment had hardened him." Marceline had a little laugh. "Nothing quite like putting an idealist in jail to turn him into an extremist."

"An extremist?"

"When we had our meetings in the clearing, Khaled still believed in a peaceful resolution to his country's independence. But there was no peace to be had. There always seems to be so little peace to go around, have you noticed? It's exhausting. He became part of the FLN while in prison. Because, as you know, Algeria's troubles did not end with World War II. Quite the opposite. In fact, in 1945, at the same time when people all over the world celebrated the unconditional surrender of the Nazis, there was in Algeria a pro-independence protest in the town of Setif that turned into a bloodbath. The next twenty years or so remain a dark phase of our respective countries' histories. Just as Khaled had predicted, he and I found ourselves on opposite sides of the conflict. As an undercover agent for the French forces, I was on the side of France, a country that had just emerged from the ruins of war determined to hang on to its remaining colonies. Khaled became a leader of the Algerian independence movement. This made any sort of romance life-threatening for both of us."

"What did you both do?"

"We risked our lives. I was heartbroken on more than one occasion. But that's a much longer story."

Cassie had the urge to ask Marceline how she had recovered from her heartbreak, and how long it had taken her, but she decided against it. Marceline had lost Khaled to war and geopolitical conflicts, whereas Cassie's heartbreak over Peter could only be attributed to her own stupidity. "Did your mother get better?" she asked.

"She did, eventually," Marceline said. "And as soon as she was back on her feet, which was a full year later, I moved in with Béatrice."

"Your mother was well enough to live by herself?"

"It was ruthless of me to leave Mother to fend for herself, alone in Algiers. I realize that. Eventually, I made it up to her."

"How so?"

"By marrying well."

"Really?" Cassie interjected. "But what about Khaled?"

"You seem disappointed?"

"I was hoping that love would conquer all, I guess."

"In love, it's often a matter of the risks you're willing to take. And at that time, there were a great many barriers between Khaled and me."

Cassie thought of Hervé, of all the reasons she felt she needed to nip the relationship in the bud. But did it not also all boil down to her unwillingness to take risks? Was it really about the logistics of living in different countries or rather about the logistics of risking a broken heart?

Marceline took a blanket from the chair next to her and set it on her lap. "After the war ended, Mother returned to Paris. Because our house had been used as a Nazi habitation, it was in good shape, although everything not bolted to the walls was stolen. The house was an empty shell with only the walls, the roof, and the plumbing remaining. The silver, the bedding, the artwork, the furniture had vanished, to say nothing of Mother's precious things passed down through the years. Uncle Moshe helped us retrieve our money hidden in Swiss banks. We fixed up the house, bought what we needed, and went on with our lives. Gustave never lived in the house again."

"And then you married."

"Not immediately, far from it. Not until fifteen years later, in 1960, after I had traveled the world and lived life to the fullest, and arguably the most precarious. One day I will tell you about those years if you're interested. The point is, I was in my forties when I began to aspire to a more conventional life. I also felt that I owed Mother a bit of happiness, and nothing could delight her more than my joining that elusive and exclusive segment of the French elite."

"Nobility?" Cassie said.

"It was, after all, her dearest dream. A common friend introduced me to Victor de Pontieur, a wealthy man who happened to be a count, or rather a count who happened to be a wealthy man. He courted me aggressively, and

I went along with it. Mother was over the moon. Poor Victor wasn't happy with me for long. I made a terrible wife. I traveled constantly for the French secret services, but he could never know about my whereabouts for classified reasons. I had no desire to give him children. The man was left to take mistresses and attend society salons without me."

"What about my dad? Where was he during those years?"

"Gustave traveled the world as well, and we crossed paths on a few occasions. We only knew of his comings and goings through Uncle Moshe, who was aware that we were estranged and did everything he could to serve as a liaison and repair our relationship. But how could he, when he never knew what was at the root of it all?"

"Where did my father travel?"

"He never told you?"

"No."

"I don't know much. Once, he was stranded in Patagonia."

"Patagonia? My father was in Patagonia?"

"Allegedly. He had not given signs of life for years but remembered he had a family only long enough to demand money. We did not send any. So, he wrote us a letter riddled with insults, the kind of diatribe best suited for the wastebasket. We did not hear from him for another five years. Uncle Moshe undoubtedly extended him a lifeline each time he acted irresponsibly." Marceline must have seen Cassie scrunch up her nose. "I apologize," she said. "I forget he is your father."

"My dad is many things, but never irresponsible," Cassie said defensively. "He worked all his life to provide. He never bailed on us," she said, omitting to mention her resentment over his bailing on her emotionally. "Do you know what he was doing all the years between the end of the war and meeting my mother?"

"I honestly have no clue. If Uncle Moshe were still alive, he would tell you everything, but unfortunately, he passed away years ago."

"Did you and my father communicate much at all over the years?"

"There was no real conversation. But I did invite him to my two weddings."

"You had two weddings?"

"Count Victor de Pontieur was my first husband. That lasted a few years. And your father didn't attend that one. Then I married the Count de Bécasel D'Alompe."

"Both were counts?"

"When you are a part of certain circles you tend to meet the same kind of fellows. To my surprise, Gustave came to the second wedding. Although I'm sure his presence had less to do with making peace with Mother or me and more to do with showing off his pretty wife, a Parisian twenty years his junior and gentile as could be."

"My mom," Cassie said. "She mentioned meeting you at your wedding."

"Your father was very proud of her; this much was obvious."

"How about his name change? Do you think it was to reject his Judaism?"

"I can hardly blame him if that was the case. What had Judaism ever done for us? It certainly never helped us. We weren't religious, so why burden ourselves with five thousand years of alienation and suffering? The difference between your father and me is that I was never ashamed of being Jewish and never attempted to hide it."

"Maybe by not telling his daughters he wanted to protect us. In case something terrible happened again. To the Jews I mean."

"Whomever and whatever people choose to reject of their past is their mysterious business. I won't entertain any guesses about my brother's motivations. You will have to ask him. We received birth announcements when you and your sisters were born, but that was the extent of our communication. I suspect your mother is the one who sent the announcements and possibly without your father's knowledge. I responded with a card and proper silver-engraved baby cups, as was the custom at the time. I hardly know what else was expected of me.

"In later years, as Mother got older and became ill, I particularly resented Gustave's callousness toward her. For my part, once I was past the initial blinders of youth, I wanted my mother to be happy. And one of the things preventing that happiness was the absence of her son and grandchildren. I know, too little too late, but people can change. That was a moot point; your father wanted nothing to do with her. That cruelty sealed my opinion of him. Mother might not have been the warmest of mothers, to say the least, but the years had been hard on her, and she suffered greatly from Gustave's rejection and from being forbidden to know the only grandchildren she had."

In a flash, Cassie shuttered to imagine what life would be like if either of her children decided they wanted to have nothing to do with her or if they had children, but she wasn't allowed to know them. It would destroy her. "It would have been so good to know you both," she said, betraying her father again by siding with Marceline.

"When Mother passed away in 1972," Marceline continued, "Gustave did not come the funeral. Your mother and you and your sisters did not either. I figured you all chose not to attend."

"My sister and I were little girls then."

"That's true," Marceline said.

"And we never knew of her death. We didn't know she was still alive to start with."

"I realize this now." Marceline shook her head. "One thing you might have learned by now about the people in your family is that we know how to keep a secret. But this, the idea that your father would tell you absolutely nothing, about your roots, about his past, about his mother, his father, and sister. It defies reason."

"Did you see my father after that?"

"A few times. Once was shortly after Mother's passing. And again during the lawsuit."

"A lawsuit?"

"There was the matter of the will. Eventually, I bought out his share of this house."

"When was that?"

"1974."

"I was ten years old," Cassie noted. It was at this time that her parents had moved to their present apartment. They had bought nicer clothes, gone on more expensive vacations. It had never occurred to her that her father had inherited money.

"The house was all the wealth Mother had. I could afford to buy back his share of it because by then I had married Bécasel D'Alompe, who had money."

"Armelle and Jean-Bernard's father?"

"He was a widower. Those two were adolescent when we married. He died this year, and now those two worry that their fortune and mine will be plunged into new uncertainty with my refusal to give them power of attorney. Not to mention the pesky fact that new relatives are coming into my life."

"New relatives?"

Marceline peered at Cassie. "Well, you for one."

Cassie had an epiphany. "So that's what they're worried about?"

Marceline giggled. "You bet."

"I have no interest in your money. I hope you can reassure them."

"Why do so when watching them twitch and sweat is so much more entertaining?"

Cassie looked out at the beautiful garden. Her father had spent his boyhood in this lovely place, and then it was robbed from him by war, the Holocaust, and family hatred. "Did you love him?" she asked Marceline.

"Who?"

"Your new husband?"

"I was fond of both my husbands, but Khaled remains the love of my life."

"And yet you married them and not Khaled."

"Marriage is a matter of practicality. Love is something else entirely."

"How French of you," Cassie said.

Fifteen yards from them, the old North African gardener laboriously moved the ladder toward the portico, slowly climbed to the top, and, unfurling string, began to attach roses to the pillar. Cassie pointed to him and frowned. "Isn't this a bit dangerous for someone his age?"

Marceline smiled. "I've never been able to stop him from doing anything he wanted to do."

As though he had heard them, the old gardener waved at them. Marceline smiled and gave a wave back.

"I brought a little something for you," Cassie said. She foraged inside her tote bag, took out the tablet Peter had just sent, and set it on the table among teacups and plates of macarons.

Marceline adjusted her glasses and looked at it with interest. "What is this thing?"

"It's a tablet. But mostly you can use it as an e-reader."

"An e-what?"

"Like a tiny flat computer that can do all sorts of things. You turn it on like this," Cassie said, demonstrating. "You can use it as a camera, if you like, and take pictures with it. But the best part is that you can read books on it. You can increase the size of the letters. You'll never again need a magnifying glass to read. You can have your favorite books and newspaper subscriptions in it. It's quite easy to use; you flip through pages by moving your finger, like this, and it even remembers what page you're on."

"How do books appear in this thing?"

"You download them."

"Download?"

"It comes in via … the airwaves or something, and then it pops right into the tablet, somehow."

Cassie spent the next hour connecting the tablet to the Wi-Fi, downloading books, apps, and games, and teaching Marceline who sponged it all up with the excitement of a child, saying little ohs and ahs when something appeared on the screen. Laure took notes about passwords and account numbers and helped set it all up.

"How much longer will you be in Paris?" Marceline asked.

"Three more days."

"I'm off to my house in the Loire Valley. I won't return to Paris until summer when everyone goes on holiday. Paris is so much more pleasant without Parisians cluttering it up. Oh! I nearly forgot. I have something for you as well." Marceline called for Laure who appeared from inside the house. She whispered something in her ear. Laure returned inside the house and came back to the gazebo a few minutes later carrying something wrapped in black fabric and put it in Marceline's hands. The old lady untied the strings of what appeared to be a felt pouch and reached inside. "Tadah!" she exclaimed. In her hands was the twin of her father's finial.

Cassie was incredulous. "For me? No…."

"Quick take it before I accidentally drop the dang thing."

Cassie took it, moved it at arm's length into the light. "Yep. It looks exactly the same. Amazing."

"Bring it back to America when you go. Or give it to Gustave. I'll let you decide."

"I can't accept this," Cassie said. "It's too valuable."

Marceline shrugged. "Its greatest value lies in its meaning."

Cassie held the finial awkwardly. She thought of her father and felt her chest constrict. "I don't know why I am getting so emotional about this."

"Your father wanted it. That's what made it valuable in my eyes. Even as far as a week ago I'd sooner have thrown it down the Seine River than give it to him. But now that I know you, telling you his story, well … It's allowed me to think differently. You are right; we were children. And we were coping the best we could. I did reckless things, but I never meant harm, and I realize now, neither did Gustave." She shook her head as if she were chasing away painful thoughts. "I doubt Gustave would accept an apology from me. Not after all these years. But he can appreciate this, as my acknowledgment to the wreckage of it all."

"Your step-children won't object to your giving this to me?"

"It's just one more knick-knack to them. To be sold at auction as soon as I croak."

"You have to stop saying things like that!"

"Fine. I'll write a letter to go with it, so you have proof that it's now yours." She turned to Laure. "Type up the letter Laure, will you? Blah, blah, blah, sound of mind and spirit, all that jazz. You as witness, and I'll sign it."

"I've meant to ask you," Cassie said. "How did you and my father come in possession of the finials if the Nazis stole everything?"

"It's a strange story actually. It was Uncle Moshe. Moshe had them all along. We had no idea. For years, he kept them. We had assumed they had been stolen. He should have returned them to us when he retrieved the rest of our fortune from the Swiss account, but for some reason, he kept them without telling us. As a memento of my father perhaps. Who knows? Or because it was a Jewish artifact he was attached to. Uncle Moshe did things in mysterious ways. He was a man of many secrets. Quite an extraordinary person, in fact, at a time when being a homosexual and a Jew was no small feat of survival.

"After our father's passing, after the war, and even as Gustave and I made up our minds never to set eyes on one another, Uncle Moshe kept in touch with us both. He always had a camera with him. Later it would be a Polaroid camera. He would take me to lunch and ask every detail of my life and insist on taking my portrait. I think he did the same with your father. It was as though he was making a record of our lives. I never knew what he did with all of that. One of his chief concerns remained that Gustave and I should make up. It was his obsession. When he died, he left the entirety of his considerable fortune to Jewish causes. Gustave and I were at the reading of the will, and you can imagine our dismay when we learned that he had left us merely the twin finials, that they, in fact, had been in his possession the entire time. The will stipulated this very annoying thing: that Gustave and I would each get one. I think in Uncle Moshe's mind, the idea of splitting the pair was so intolerable that Gustave and I would have no choice but to make up and come to an agreement about who should keep both. Suddenly Gustave remembered he was Jewish, that old rascal. The male son. The Kohen. He used this as an argument that he should have them both. Well, you can imagine that this did not sit well with me. I told him that I was the firstborn and therefore I ought to be the Kohanim. In the end, we each kept one."

"But why did my dad say that you *stole* the second one from him? You split them equitably. That's not stealing."

Marceline chuckled. "Well, I *did* steal it from him. I was a brat about it, I'll admit. After Mother had become sick, Gustave did not once visit or offer to help. As I mentioned, once she passed, we both inherited the house. Again, something needed to be split in two, but this time it was something impossible to split unless we sold it and shared the money. Gustave immediately said he wanted to sell the house. Of course, he would; I lived in it, and he had not since 1939. He wanted to see me lose the house. Think of it: a house that had been in our family for three generations, and he thought nothing of letting strangers have it. Eventually, I bought out his share of the house, for well over its value I might add. Part of the deal we made, which he insisted on, was that he should sell me his half and he would get both finials in return. I agreed to it all, but I never gave him my finial. I kept it."

"Why?"

"Out of spite, just as he had been spiteful about selling the house, or not visiting Mother. He started a lawsuit over that stupid finial. I turned vicious and countersued. I was the one who had taken care of Mother until her death, while he had done nothing! He did not have my means, so he eventually gave up on the lawsuit."

Cassie contemplated the small crown-looking object, turning it in her hands. "And now after all this chaos, you want me to have it. Are you certain of this?"

"You know, what infuriated me the most about my brother? It was his unrelenting refusal to forgive." Marceline sighed and brought her shawl tighter over her shoulders. "Only as I spoke to you have I come to the realization that I might be guilty of precisely the same thing."

Cassie decided not to make another comment. Marceline's confession, her repentance, was more than her father had ever expressed, and that was enough. She caressed the finial as though it were a magic lantern. "It is beautiful, thank you."

"So," Marceline said pointing to the tablet "can you play games on this thing?"

"Absolutely. Card games, crossword puzzles, memory games. What kind of game do you want? Sudoku?"

"No, not that game. The other one."

"Chess?"

"No, that funny one."

"Scrabble?"

"There is the word bird in it."

Cassie scratched her head. "Not Angry Birds?"

"That's right," Marceline clucked approvingly. "I want to – how do you say? – *download* angry bird."

CHAPTER 5

Holy Grail

Cassie walked onto rue de Clichy, and the honking of cars and roar of jackhammers brought her back into the 21st century. She hurried past bar-tabacs, salons de coiffures, fleuristes, and boulangeries. There was heavy construction in the street, something to do with the sewer system. Men in orange vests and helmets disappeared into deep trenches dug into the pavement and emerged from manholes like the inhabitants of a parallel civilization happening underground. Each time she heard the roar of a motorcycle, the nape of her hair tingled ridiculously, and she found herself mentally in bed with Hervé. The noise of jackhammers intensified, and the ground shook under her feet. She cut through a thick cloud of dust and walked a few more blocks before it was calm again. She was on a quiet street somewhere in the seventeenth arrondissement. A small park had sprouted before her like a tiny oasis of calm, and she entered it. She walked on the dirt path feeling the sun on her face. She sat on a bench. There were candy-colored houses on an impasse that looked down at a small playground where a young dad helped his daughter navigate the monkey bars, while his other daughter went down the slide, arms first, shouting, "Attention!"

She should come here with Hervé, she thought, and then kicked herself for thinking that. She removed her coat and took the finial out of her tote bag. A romantic, superstitious part of her told her that the spirit of her grandfather had wanted her to have it. She had worn her grandfather's coat, hadn't she? She had miraculously found Marceline and learned her family's story all without much effort, and she now was in possession of his finial. *Are you here with me, Albano*? She mentally asked the finial.

What was she supposed to do with this thing? It was a funny little object. It looked exactly like the one in her parent's apartment. It was the same weight, hollow in the center, like a small crown made of silver, with some gold parts. There were tiny bells that did not make much of a sound. As she moved it between her fingers, she wondered why, of all things, it had been worth hiding and saving.

On closer inspection, there was one thing that was different: the engraved inscription inside. Instead of the address of the bank that was engraved inside her dad's finial, in Marceline's finial was a series of numbers and letters.

454B5743589112A.

What did that mean?

She had just enough time to get to rue Bonaparte, where she was meeting Sabine for lunch. Maybe her sister would have some ideas about what all those numbers might mean.

She hurried toward Place de Clichy and down the steps to the métro. Thirty minutes later, she emerged onto the street at Métro Saint Germain des Prés. There were cars and people, the latter seemingly being dragged on leashes by their cell phones. But the architecture, the cafés, and the restaurants, even the cobblestones she stepped on, must not have changed much since 1942. Cassie walked past the Deux Magots terrace, filled with people basking in the spring sun. Back in 1942, the terrace must have crawled with Nazis. Parisians, their army now powerless, their leaders having betrayed them, lacked everything. The country's riches were being pillaged. All the food produced was sent to feed the German army while Parisians, ration tickets in hand, waited in hours-long lines for a few eggs or a liter of milk. On the other side of the street, inside Église de Saint Germain des Prés, women must have prayed for the safety of an imprisoned son or the return of a husband forced to work in a German factory. If there were Jews left in Paris in 1942, they would not be there for long, unless they had found a way to hide. Had her grandfather not left for the South of France, and then for Algeria, would her family have survived the rounding up of Jews? Cassie had the sense that she owed her grandfather her life in more ways than one.

At the corners of rue Jacob and rue Bonaparte, she spotted Sabine, who was waiting for her. They kissed twice on both cheeks. "Where do you want to eat," Sabine asked.

They walked in front of Ladurée and pressed their faces to the window, detailing the macaron arrangements. "How about an all-dessert meal," Cassie said. "It's the new thing, I'm told."

"Don't you start with the subversion," Sabine said.

It was just warm enough to eat outside. They sat on the terrace of the Pré aux Clercs and studied their menus. Their waiter appeared. "Bonjour, Mesdemoiselles," he said.

"Bonjour," Sabine and Cassie said in unison.

"What will it be for the petite demoiselles?" he asked.

"I want this," Cassie said, pointing to the foie gras and fig jam platter, cautiously adding, "s'il vous plaît."

"Excellent choice," he said.

"Eight hundred calories," Sabine noted. "I'll have the Pré aux Clercs salade, s'il vous plaît, Monsieur."

"What's in it?" Cassie asked.

Sabine read: "Lettuce, smoked salmon, avocado, poached egg, crème fraîche, and blinis. I think my calorie count beats yours."

"Merci, Mesdemoiselles," the waiter said.

"Merci, Monsieur," Cassie and Sabine answered.

"I can't believe the amount of time and energy French people spend saying hello, please, and goodbye," Cassie said as soon as he left. "I had forgotten that. I mean, get to business already! Jeez. Right?"

"Eh?" Sabine said.

"Practically years of our lives spent in politeness and niceties. And to think that French people are supposed to be the rude ones!"

Sabine shook her head in incomprehension. "You are so weird," she said.

"I spent the morning with Marceline," Cassie said. "It was pretty incredible. I've got the whole story now. Straight out of a World War II espionage novel. She told me why she and Papa hate each other, and you won't believe it: all this time, Papa, among other things, has been blaming her for their father's death."

Sabine looked stunned. "His father's death? Our grandfather?"

"And Marceline blames him!" They were interrupted by the arrival of their lunch. Cassie spread foie gras onto toasted bread, took a big bite and moaned with pleasure. "I haven't had this in forever. Foie gras is cruelty to animals in California," she said with a full mouth.

"I'm pretty sure it's cruelty to animal everywhere," Sabine pointed out.

As they ate, Cassie told Sabine all about Operation Torch, their father and Marceline's involvement in it, and their grandfather's tragic death.

"That's flat-out incredible," Sabine said. "If you believe Marceline's story."

"Why wouldn't I?" Cassie asked.

"She could be senile."

"Marceline is more with it than both of us put together."

"Still, you'd think she single-handedly freed Europe from the Nazis," Sabine said. "You don't think she could be exaggerating?"

"She does downplay Papa's role in saving her life. She told me the facts, but I certainly interpret them differently. I mean Papa was a badass hero, and she won't give him that. At seventeen, being undercover in the Resistance, killing a Nazi to save her life! And then he never bragged about it. If you ask me, that's the most heroic part of the whole thing: him keeping his mouth shut. He did not try to make himself look good. And you know what? He might have been an annoyance to Marceline, but he never gave up on trying to protect her, and he never told his parents about what he knew."

Sabine shook her head. "The strangest part is to reconcile this past with the person he is now. Have you ever met someone more risk-averse than Papa?"

"And yet he did all this. And he was barely older than my twins are now."

"I think that his memories and all his emotions of the time had to be pushed back inside. Swallowed and never digested. Maybe he is risk-averse and uncommunicative because he lived with PTSD his whole life," Sabine said.

"Imagine Papa growing up in the shadow of a sister like Marceline, where he could do nothing right," Cassie said. "The one memory he sure hung on to was his rage and resentment against her. And the best way to not change his mind was to make sure never to see her. That way, his perception could not be challenged."

"Also," Sabine pointed out, "there is no risk of us meeting Marceline and maybe liking her."

"I couldn't help but see parallels with the way Papa raised us. He had an idea of how I was and how Odile was, and that was pretty much set in stone. In the end, Odile and I fought because there was not enough love from Papa to go around."

"Papa's not that bad. He never was violent, never was without a job; he didn't drink or chase women."

"Okay," Cassie said. "He was not a serial killer. That doesn't mean he didn't neglect me as a child. I loved him so much growing up, but it was a desperate, unrequited sort of love. Trying to jump through flaming hoops, and missing, and getting burned, time and again. And it's not just me that suffered from that. You weren't showered with attention either."

"Not all fathers are warm and fuzzy," Sabine said.

Cassie was stunned by Sabine's neutrality. Their father had been emotionally absent with her too. Did she truly feel no anger about it?

"At least one person was pretty perfect: our grandfather. At least according to Marceline. It's sad that we did not get to meet him. Had it not been for him, our bloodline would have probably ended in Auschwitz or Drancy."

"There must have been more to him than perfection," Sabine said. "Why else was his family so messed up? I mean, his wife was a wreck, his son broke ties with them, his daughter is a complete bitch."

"Marceline doesn't strike me as a bitch, just very sure of herself."

"Or a narcissist who played spy games," Sabine said.

"If she hadn't played those spy games, it might have changed the course of history."

"Hmmm … let's not get carried away."

"I like Marceline," Cassie said. "In fact, I like her a lot. She doesn't sugarcoat things; she is forthright. I wish she and Papa had not been so stubborn. We could have grown up with an extended family: a grandmother, an aunt. We could have had gatherings in that big house, birthdays parties, Christmases together."

"Christmas?" Sabine said.

"So, okay, maybe not Christmas. Maybe we'd feel Jewish, instead of nothing. It might be nice to have some religious upbringing, don't you think? It would have given us something to lean on when we were sad or scared."

"Like prayer?"

"Like a set of rules and traditions to hang on to when the emotional seas are rough."

"I guess I could have used that," Sabine said.

"Well, now we know what happened between them. It had to be something big for a relationship between siblings to sour to this extent. Although, on second thought, I'm not sure it takes that much," Cassie said, rolling her eyes. "Try spending five minutes in a room with Odile and me."

"You and Odile don't hate each other like that," Sabine said. "Not to the point of telling your children that the other doesn't exist."

"It pretty much felt like hatred, growing up. You were younger. You were not in the thick of it."

Sabine looked out onto the street. "Two angry, uncommunicative parents, two big sisters at war. Having to take sides." Sabine forced a smile. "And after you left, there was nothing at home but suppressed emotions."

Cassie was genuinely surprised. "You never acted upset back when I lived at home."

"I'm more like Papa," Sabine said. "I internalize."

They ordered espressos and the bill and Cassie said, "You want to see something cool?" She unzipped her tote bag and, still keeping it inside the bag, she uncovered Marceline's finial. Sabine's eyes widened. "How did you get that from Papa and Maman's house? They're going to be furious!"

Cassie beamed. "It's not theirs. It's Marceline's! It's the twin of the one we have. Papa was right: there was a second one. And it had been stolen. By her!"

"You stole it back from her?"

"I'm not that brave. Marceline gave it to me. Returned it to our family, to be specific."

"Why?"

"She seemed to feel magnanimous suddenly."

"Maybe you could have a second career as a snake charmer," Sabine said, setting the bag on her lap to see the finial better while still keeping it inside the bag. She turned it around in her hands. "I don't know why I'm trying to hide it. It looks like some trinket bought for three euros at a flea market."

"I know. I feel the same way. We've been brainwashed to think it's a mythical object."

"Papa's going to freak out when he sees it," Sabine said, laughing. Her laugh was communicative, or maybe it was the relief Cassie felt hearing her laugh. It was good to see her sister capable of lightness.

"So, you think I should bring it to him?"

"Hell yes!" Sabine said. "And complete the mission. Return the finial to its rightful owner. The Kahobib, or kohasomething."

Had this been the United States, and had Sabine been one of her American friends, Cassie would have told her how happy she was to have lunch together, and how wonderful it felt to connect with her. But this was France, and Sabine was her sister. She had to be careful not to scare her away with her puppy-like American enthusiasm. "I wish we could have lunch more often," she said tentatively. "Get to know each other more."

"That should be no problem at all since you only live five thousand miles away," Sabine said. "And speaking of long-distance relationships, have you seen that man again?"

Cassie felt herself blush. "Hervé? Oh, yeah!"

"What is he like?"

"He's a character."

"Like Peter?"

"Peter is a character?"

Sabine shrugged. "I never understood your passion for him."

"What don't you like about him?"

"He's … I don't know. Oily."

"Peter is oily?"

"I don't know. Slippery. Not trustworthy. It's hard to put into words."

"Hervé is peculiar in his own way. He rides a vintage motorcycle. He cooks. He's always philosophizing about one thing or another. He doesn't believe in cell phones."

"He's a typical French contrarian. Nothing peculiar about that."

"I guess the peculiar part is how handsome he is." Cassie hesitated "Shouldn't he be interested in a more suitable woman?"

"You're not suitable?" Sabine looked surprised.

"I might have my own brand of sexiness. But it's not that Barbie doll look."

"Newsflash," Sabine interrupted, "little girls are the ones who like Barbie. Boys hate them. Unless they can tie them to rockets and shoot them up in the air."

"There is that other small detail. I – ahem. I still haven't told him that I live in the U.S."

"Are you serious?"

"I was afraid he'd run away. I kept postponing."

"That's a disaster in the making."

"I didn't want to jeopardize the first fun thing that had happened to me in, what … a lifetime? Should I deny myself this moment? Out of high moral principles?"

"Don't ask me," Sabine shrugged. "I've made nothing but reasonable choices my entire life."

"I was the picture-perfect, selfless, bake-sale, little league kind of mother, and now my kids are gone, and I have little to show for it. I stayed in a marriage that wasn't working for either of us out of principle, and Peter moved on from me without batting an eyelash. I let myself work in his shadow because I was too principled to demand proper credit, and now I don't have a career to my name. I could have done with fewer principles and a bit more self-worth."

"Why did you ever give Peter so much power?"

"I kept waiting for him to tell me that I was good at what I did. I was waiting for his encouragement, his authorization to shine, I guess."

"Like with Papa?"

Cassie looked at Sabine dumbfounded. "Yes. Just like with Papa!"

"Ha!" Sabine said. "Full circle."

"Yep. Crawling for crumbs of acceptance and love. Peter leaving me was the ultimate rejection, after all those years trying to impress him by being deserving and selfless. But at the same time, I was overbearing and constantly furious at him. And I *did* kick him out in the end."

As she said this, Cassie realized that, in fact, she knew what she needed to know, about herself, about Peter, about Jessica. She would not be able to return to the lies to which she was a willing accomplice – deception and self-deception. She had been so afraid of losing Peter's approval that she had been willing to bury all her suspicions. The doubt had been there, and it had slowly poisoned her. That's why she had been so overbearing and furious.

"And then this Hervé character drops from the sky," Sabine said.

Cassie shook her head. "It's nothing. It's just a sex thing. He plans on traveling the world, and my life is in L.A."

Sabine raised an eyebrow. "Except you've fallen in love with him."

Cassie paused. Stunned. "I didn't – whether I did or not is immaterial. I don't believe someone can fall in love with *me*."

"You and I are in the same boat," Sabine said sadly. "Feeling hopelessly unlovable."

"I'm sorry. I keep whining about myself when you've just gone through this momentous heartache."

"My life veered off the path," Sabine said. "I don't know what the next chapter is. I keep thinking about the chapter that was not written."

"You know what you should do?" Cassie said. "You should come to California."

"For a vacation?"

"American men would be lining the streets to meet your cute tush and your exotic French accent. Take a leave of absence from work. Come stay in Los Angeles for a few months."

Sabine sighed. "That sounds perfectly unreasonable."

"Has being reasonable made either of us happy?"

"It's made us feel safe."

"But has it actually *made* us safe?"

"I see your point," Sabine said. And in her eyes, Cassie thought she could detect the birth of an embryonic sense of possibilities.

****

Thrilled with the content of her bag, Cassie walked down rue Bonaparte toward the Seine. Odile might well be the favorite daughter, but Cassie was the one bringing back the frigging family's Holy Grail!

She veered right and walked up onto the Pont des Arts to cross the Seine. The bridge was replete with tourists and couples in love. Cassie stopped walking and leaned against the banister. A péniche glided under the bridge. The people on the open platform waved to the people up on the bridge, so she waved back. It made her think of her dad, the way he was always hunched over a table, carving little sailboats out of balsa wood. Now she understood his hobby for what it was: a retreat to his childhood, to before the war, to a time when his dad was alive, to a time when being Jewish wasn't a death sentence, when he did not yet hate his mother, Marceline, and himself.

She looked out on the water. On the left bank was the dome of the Beaux Arts School, on the other side of the river, the Louvre. The Seine, wide and shimmering, curved through the city, reflecting the monuments and the sky. A few riverboats moved lazily along. She felt a flutter inside her chest. She took notice of how she felt. She felt different. Nothing had changed, really: she still had no husband, her kids had grown up, her mother and father all but shunned her. But she did not feel lonely or sad. It was a strange feeling, that realization that she did not, at that moment, feel lonely. Could the finials, now reconnected, magically erase her dad's hurt and self-blame and everything that trickled down from that? Her own hurt? Her own self-blame?

What had taken place in Algiers, the death of Albano, the guilt over it, the mutual blame, had set the course of all their life. Because of one ugly secret, no one in her family knew where they came from, where they belonged, or how they fit into the narrative of history. Shame was unconsciously taken from one generation to the next, festering into a cesspool of neurosis.

She could see now how the familiar hollowness in her chest, that usual, unnamed emptiness she filled with drama, and frantic activity, had in fact been loneliness. Coming to Paris and meeting Marceline gave her the unexplained sensation that her life had just been jump-started. For the first time in a very long time, things felt possible. She had been trapped inside a tunnel and had not even known to look for a light at the end. And suddenly, she was on the outside, in broad daylight, in the most beautiful city in the world.

****

Later, she faced the entrance to the hospital. Having stepped on Odile's fragile toes and crossed her mother's line in the sand, she knew that she would not be getting their permission to enter her dad's hospital room. So what she decided to do was go there anyway. But how, without being stopped by them or the staff? Her eight-a.m. appointment with the Chief of Services had slipped her mind, and this would not help her already tenuous credibility.

But if nineteen-year-old Marceline could be brave enough to visit the man she loved in an Algerian prison in 1942, Cassie decided to give this a shot. The worse thing that could happen to her was humiliation. Focusing on the finial in the bag, her golden ticket, she took a deep inhalation and pushed through the hospital gate.

The waiting room was densely packed. There were at least ten people in line at the reception. Miraculously, the dreaded Pinçon was not at the desk. Her heart beating a little too fast for a grown woman, Cassie crept from person to person, hiding behind them. She moved fast, and she hoped stealthily. In thirty seconds, she was at the double doors that led to the patient area. She ducked and pushed the doors open. Once on the other side, she zoomed to the changing room. Inside, visitors were fumbling with their paper outfits. She rolled her hair up into a bun, removed her coat, expertly put on a paper gown and boots, and even helped a woman figure out which way of the gown was up. She then tied a paper mask over her face, waited for a group of visitors to go out, and went out with them.

She headed toward her father's room unmolested. Amazing how much easier things were when you dispensed with authorizations!

Inside her father's hospital room, the light was dim. She had half-expected her mother and Odile to be there, but her dad was alone in the quiet room, with only the beeping of the monitors for company. The sight of him broke her heart. He lay on his cot, his arms covered in taped IVs and tubes that connected him to bags of liquid and machines. His eyes were open, and he stared at the ceiling, blinking rapidly. He had the panicked expression of a man who dreams that he is the victim of a scientific experiment and awakens to discover it is not a dream.

She approached tentatively. "Papa, it's me," she whispered. He turned his face toward her and blinked some more. She slowly put down her paper mask so he could see her face. To her relief, he looked surprised, not angry. The beeps of the machines remained steady. She relaxed. "You breathe without an oxygen mask now. Fantastic!" she said. Her father looked at her haggardly. Again, she was struck by his growing beard. Dignity was a fragile thing, as skin-deep as a shave. All her life, she had desperately tried to impress her father. Was she still trying now? But the man on the cot was no longer just the father who kept her at a distance, but the suffering boy, the teenager, trying to survive a war, the young man whose father had been killed perhaps because of him. In his eyes, she saw a whole lifetime of fear, injustice, sadness, and rage, the veneer of distance between him and his emotions about to crack.

Cassie's composure plummeted. There was a floodgate of tears, stuck somewhere between her heart and her throat, and she was not sure how long the dam would hold. "I brought you a surprise," she said with forced cheer. "You won't believe this, but I got my hands on the second finial! Look!" She unzipped her bag, took it out, and held it out. Her father's eyes widened at the finial. Finally, he opened his mouth and mumbled something unintelligible.

She came closer to him to listen. "What, Papa? What did you say?"

"That bitch," he said laboriously, as though he were giving painful birth to each syllable. "She … stole it."

"But I got it back, Papa! You have both finials now. They're both yours. Isn't that amazing?"

"She … she wants to steal it."

"Not anymore," she said, using the soothing-but-firm tone of a kindergarten teacher. "See, one is safe at home, and the other one is right here." He closed his eyes. She did not know if this was in acquiescence or exhaustion. "I got it back for you. I did. Are you happy?"

"You," he said, his eyes closed.

Cassie felt herself dissolve. It was the first time he acknowledged her presence since she arrived in Paris. "Me?"

"You always … fall back on your feet."

She smiled, shaken, and tapped his hand gently, "I didn't, Papa. Not really. Not any more than anyone else."

"You're … ruthless."

Cassie's smile faded. "That's not the way I am. You have the wrong idea about me. I'm … I'm really nice … usually."

"I saved your life."

"Wh-what?"

"I shot the Boche …" he said laboriously. "The bridge … It's not my fault."

Cassie brought her hand to her mouth. Her throat constricted. He still thought she was Marceline! She fought back her tears, but it was a battle she was rapidly losing. She wanted him to see *her*. She wanted him to accept *her,* to love *her*. But in his eyes, had she ever existed without the shadow of Marceline tainting everything? She wiped the tears that pooled in her eyes. The only way he would be able to make peace with her would be to make peace with Marceline. And so, although when every bit of her wanted to contradict him and remind him of who she really was, she whispered, "You're right, Gustave. You saved me."

"I wanted to … protect you," her dad said. "Baba asked me to."

Cassie crushed an angry tear on her cheek. "You were heroic. I was reckless. Baba's death was an accident. But it's really all my fault for being selfish."

Her father nodded weakly. "That's what I've been trying to tell you, and Mother," he murmured.

"Mother knows that you are not to blame. She … she's proud of you. For your bravery. We all are."

He smiled tiredly. Cassie took his hand. "I want us to love each other, Gustave, just like when we were little. We used to be good friends, remember? Can you forgive me now?"

"Ah, yes," he mumbled. He seemed peaceful now, as though a weight had been lifted. He closed his eyes.

Cassie was weeping silently. She had a thought. "And … do you remember Cassie?" she asked. "Your daughter?" She felt sickened by what she was trying to do. "She loves you very much, too." Suddenly her father opened his eyes wide, his face washed with panic. He raised his arm, pulling all manner of tubes and IV. His pulse shot up. A loud alarm began to ring shrilly. "Shh … Papa," Cassie said, frantically. "Calm down … shh … it's me!"

"Go away!" he roared.

Cassie looked back at the door. In a minute, someone would walk in. "But look! I brought you the second finial," she said urgently, showing it to him in a last-ditch effort to soothe him. "I got it back for you!" Gustave was waving his arms spastically, pulling tubes and wires with them. His IV pulled out; blood began to spill. She held the finial in one hand, and with the other, she held his arm down. "It's okay, Papa; it's okay," she said, feeling mounting panic. He was hollering now, out of pain or rage she did not know.

The alarm blared. There were hurried footsteps in the hallway. A moment later two nurses were inside the room, tending to him and pushing her out of the way. "I can't believe this!" one said, as she added a syringe of fluid into his IV bag while the other nurse held him down, "You're not supposed to be in here." She shouted, "Security!" Cassie cradled the finial and watched powerlessly as the nurses struggled to restrain Gustave's jerking movement and to reattach him to his IV. One of the nurses turned her head to look at her. "You better leave!" she said. The other one shouted again, "Security!"

Cassie shuffled backward toward the door. "I'm leaving," she said, just as Mademoiselle Pinçon entered the room. In righteous indignation, she looked even more horrible. "Yes, you certainly are leaving!" she blurted out. "You have no place being here. Look what you did!"

Cassie's panic transformed into fury. "You're the one who has no place here. I'm his daughter! What have you done to him? Poke and probe at him like a lab rat. It's monstrous! And all these drugs you're giving him: they're making him crazy. He doesn't know where he is! He doesn't even know who I am!"

"Leave! Security!" Pinçon shouted.

"Bye, Papa! I love you!" Cassie said. Still cradling the finial, she turned back to look at her dad one last time. She saw him turn his head away from her, but through the tears that blurred her vision, she could not be sure.

At the door, she bumped into two interns, geeky young men but tall and strong nonetheless.

"That one!" Pinçon told them. "She's a big problem. Make sure she is under control."

Pinçon had not finished her sentence when the interns had their hands on her. They tried to each hold one of Cassie's arms, but she curled over the finial to protect it. "Take your hands off me!" she yelled. They continued jerking at her arms. "You better not break this. It's a museum piece. You'll have to pay for it, you hear me?"

"Ma'am, stay calm."

"I'll follow you. Stop trying to hold me! I'm warning you – if this thing falls…."

"If you calm down, we won't call the gendarmerie."

"I'll calm down when you stop grabbing me!"

They let go. Cassie straightened, and, clenching her teeth through tears and fury, she carried the finial like a baby as she walked, now accompanied by four interns, past the people at the reception desk.

At that very moment, Odile and Raymonde were entering the reception and stopped in their tracks in shock. "Goodness gracious. What have you done?" Raymonde said. Her eyes dropped to the finial. "Did you steal it from the apartment?"

"Come off it, Maman! That's not your damn finial. This one's mine!"

"Yours?"

"Please follow us, Ma'am," said one of the interns.

"It was given to me," Cassie told her mom.

"By whom?" Raymonde mumbled.

"By … myself! Since Papa thinks I'm Marceline, apparently."

"You're not making any sense," Odile said.

"No one in this family makes sense!" Cassie shouted.

"We have patients here. You need to stop yelling!" Pinçon hissed.

"Please, Mesdames, we need to sort this out," an intern said. He turned to Cassie. "Madame, if you would please follow us without creating more chaos."

"Follow you where?" Cassie asked.

"To sort this out with the Chief of Services."

Cassie shook her head in disbelief. "You have got to be kidding me!"

"Do you want us to come along?" Odile asked limply.

"Oh no," Cassie said savagely. "This is too good!" She turned to Pinçon, whose mouth looked reduced to a thin downward line. "I would be delighted to meet the Chief of Services at long last!"

They arrived at a large wooden door, and Pinçon knocked. "Come in," said a male voice. They opened the door, and all pushed in, two interns, followed by Cassie, followed by three more interns, followed by Pinçon.

They were in a large, bright room lined with wooden bookshelves heavy with medical reference volumes.

"What is this?" asked the man in the suit who sat at the desk by the window.

It took Cassie several seconds to compute inside her brain what she was seeing. "What are you doing here?" she exclaimed.

Hervé looked up at her in incomprehension and got up from his chair. "Cassie, what's going on? Why are you here?" He pointed to the finial. "What is that thing?" He pointed to the interns and asked them. "Why are all of you here?"

"I don't get it," Cassie said. "What are you doing at the hospital?"

Hervé shrugged, "Working, what else?"

She shook her head. "That can't be."

"What?"

"You can't be the Chief of Services of the ICU," Cassie said, her brain buzzing to reconcile the mess this was. "I've been trying to see you for days!"

Hervé looked utterly confused. "You saw me this morning."

Pinçon looked from Hervé to Cassie and blinked. "Should we call the gendarmerie?" she asked meekly, suddenly not too sure of where this was headed.

"The gendarmerie? Why in the world would you?" Hervé said.

"My lord!" Cassie said.

"This is the cra – the lady who's been wreaking havoc for days," Pinçon explained.

Hervé widened his eyes. "You? You're the crazy American?"

Cassie now understood the incomprehensible. "I must be," she said. It was all coming back to her. He was a doctor. He had a suspended license. He was now stuck in purgatory doing bureaucratic functions. That was the reason he came to the Jument Bleue where they had met. It was close to his work because the hospital *was* where he worked! What an idiot she had been! The phone call from the office this morning when they were in bed: it was *her* they were talking about! All along, it had been *her* that Hervé was avoiding and ditching. The Neanderthal who so rudely refused to see her had been Hervé.

"But how can you be American?" Hervé said. He was standing in front of her now, looking at her with profound confusion. "I don't understand any of this."

"Do we cancel the gendarmerie then?" one of the interns asked thickly.

"Of course, cancel the gendarmerie!" Hervé shouted. "Everyone out of my office! Now!"

Pinçon scampered out of the room. One of the interns took Cassie by the shoulder. "Please follow us, Ma'am."

"Not her!" Hervé said.

"She could be dangerous."

"She's NOT dangerous!" Hervé bellowed.

The door closed behind the mayhem with a hollow thud.

Now Hervé and Cassie were face to face, each trying to process what was happening. Cassie was the first one to speak. "How could you be the asshole who has been giving me the run around for days?"

"I told you I was terrible at this job. I'm a physician. I don't know how to babysit loonies."

"Such as myself?" she said, livid. "Loonies who are sick with worries and are not getting the least bit of humane treatment from this crappy hospital? All I asked for were honest answers and some humanity. Instead, I got contempt and red tape."

"You made up that you were American? Why?"

"Well, I did not make that up. It's the truth."

"You're obviously French; what are you talking about?"

Cassie rolled her eyes. "I am French. It's just that I live in California. I've lived there for the last twenty years."

"What? You live in Paris and—"

She decided to rip the bandage, interrupting him. "My return ticket to the U.S. is on Wednesday."

"You're leaving?"

"Wednesday," she repeated, speaking slowly so that he understood. "Because I live in the U.S. Not here."

"This Wednesday? The Wednesday three days from now?" he asked.

"She nodded." Yes.

"But I made you fresh pasta!"

"I just … I didn't think there was any need to … I had no idea where this was heading."

"You must be joking!" Hervé exclaimed. "Where could this ever go if your ticket back is Wednesday!"

"I told you my situation was complicated," Cassie said. "You're the one who said, oh no, no, no, this thing between us, was, AND I QUOTE: 'an uncomplicated thing.'"

"Well, it's complicated now," Hervé said angrily. "Why didn't you tell me your father was dying?"

Cassie received the news like a punch in the solar plexus. "My father is *dying*?"

Hervé backtracked too late. "I … hmm. I need to consult the file."

"My father is dying?" she said, realizing how obvious this was for the very first time.

"He's in kidney failure, Cassie," Hervé admitted. "And the antibiotics aren't making a dent in his pneumonia."

Her father was dying. This might have been the last time she would ever speak to him, and he had not once acknowledged her. "Let me uncomplicate things for you," she said. "You're the big heartless a-hole who made it impossible for me to be at my father's deathbed. How about that?"

"And *you* lied through your teeth and played with my heart."

"Heart? Oh, perfect! Now you're the wronged party? How convenient! Yesterday you were all penis, and today you have a heart?"

"So, what other lies did you tell me?" Hervé said spitefully. "Are you in fact happily married to some American imbecile?"

"Well, you know that movie you despise, that film that embodies all that's wrong with humanity? That piece of garbage that's a disgrace to mankind?"

"What about it?"

"Well, I'm the one who wrote it!"

"Why am I not surprised?"

Cassie looked at him. There was nothing left to say. She turned around, walked to the door, opened it, and slammed it shut as hard as she could before leaving.

She ran out of the hospital, and Hervé did nothing to stop her.

****

She glanced at her watch. It was 4:20 p.m.

She had a hunch to follow and only about forty minutes to do so.

She grabbed her tote bag with both arms and ran down rue de Maubeuge and then down rue du Faubourg Poissoniere, where she hopped on the métro.

She was standing shoulder to shoulder with dozens of zoned-out commuters as the subway weaved through the underbelly of the city. Thoughts of her father, of Hervé, of Peter, of Marceline, of her sister, her mother, the hospital and the finial senselessly crackled through her mind like popcorn. Nothing made sense and everything did, like disparate, unconnected elements that were also mysteriously linked. She was disappointed. She was heartbroken. She was a mess. She kept glancing at her watch. The bank would be closing at five.

She emerged at Métro Chaussée D'Antin, ran in the direction of the Galeries Lafayette and crossed the street. She was the last person let into the Société Générale before a guard closed the door.

The only change in the twenty years since she had last been at the bank was the thickness of computers. The beautiful art deco glass roof above and the patina of the wood counters looked exactly as they did when she was a teenager. She waited in line, tapping the heel of her red boot against the mosaic of the flooring. When it was her turn, she slammed a piece of paper in front of the teller: 454B5743589112A. The number engraved on Marceline's finial.

The teller typed in the number on his keyboard. "Would you like to access your safety deposit box now?"

Goosebumps rose from her legs up to her neck. "Yes, I want to open it," she said, breathless.

"May I see the key?" he asked.

Cassie's smile turned rigid. "The key?"

"The box can only be opened with your key."

"I don't have it."

"Ah then, Madame, you'll need to bring it tomorrow. Unfortunately, we are closing for the day." Already, the teller was picking up things on his desk.

"What if I, hmm, lost it?" Cassie asked. "Can't you break the safe open or something?"

"That is not how this goes," the teller said with the lack of patience of someone who is five minutes away from going home. "Unless you have the password. If the key was lost."

"I have neither."

"In that case, there is nothing we can do. Not without a notary and an attorney." He pushed in front of her a form she'd need to fill out. "The process takes six to twelve months."

Cassie looked around her at the beautiful building, and up at the dome-shaped glass ceiling. She muttered, "I can't believe how stupid I am."

"I beg your pardon?"

Cassie sighed, shook her head dejectedly, "Nothing. Thank you for your help."

Perhaps the teller felt sorry for her at that moment. "All our keys have the bank's monogram, B. S. G., Banque Société Générale," he said helpfully. "But this is an account in the old vault. It would be an old-fashioned looking key like they made in the old days."

****

At the reception of her hotel was an envelope from Peter waiting for her. It contained a first class return ticket to Los Angeles, leaving three hours later.

It took her no more than fifteen minutes. She wrapped the finial with as many clothes as she could fit in her bag. She shoved the rest of her clothes into the broken suitcase, including the lingerie she had bought with Hervé in mind, and set the whole thing by the wastebasket. She grabbed Jessica's four little packages from the mantelpiece and slipped them inside a plastic Monoprix bag. She looked down at her feet. Those red cowboy boots were never really her, only some optimistic fictionalized version of her that was rapidly disintegrating. She placed the boots on top of the broken suitcase near the wastebasket and slipped on the Uggs.

She came down the stairs with only her tote and her purse, paid her bill, told the old man at the reception that everything she had left in the room was trash, and took a taxi to Charles de Gaulle airport.

CHAPTER 6

Two Boys from Smyrna

When he was a small boy, Albano had wandered alone on Mount Pagus. It was 1910. A month earlier, his entire family had perished in the cholera pandemic, and now he was an eight-year-old orphan raised in the Jewish quarter of Smyrna by his Uncle Jacob and Aunt Sadie. The heaviness in his heart had grown impossible to bear, especially when he first woke up in the morning and found himself in a strange house, sharing a room with sleeping cousins indifferent to him.

That morning, he had awakened before dawn, crept out of the bedroom, left his uncle and aunt's house, and carefully opened the wooden door and closed it behind him. In the Jewish quarter, everyone was asleep. Above, the moon was bright and cast long shadows as he set out on the dirt path that led outside of town. He had left the Jewish quarter without plans. He had not even truly meant to run away.

For a long time, he wandered in the mountain guided by the light of the setting moon. All was quiet; the birds hadn't awakened yet. Even the crickets were asleep. Only the occasional calls of coyotes bounced around the empty mountains, distant at first, and then very near. Under his bare feet were rough pebbles and dirt. The air was dewy and smelled of wild sage.

The sun was rising, and the sky had turned pink when Albano arrived near the top of the mountain. From where he was, he could see his way back to the Jewish quarter, to the place that wasn't his home.

Something moved. Albano stopped, startled. A moment later, a rabbit scurried near his feet. He watched it disappear into the bushes at the foot of a tall rock formation. The rabbit must have its nest in the bushes, he thought. He also thought that if he were to find a baby rabbit, perhaps he could bring it back with him and Aunt Sadie would let him keep it as a pet. His mother would have. But Aunt Sadie was mean, and it wasn't easy to keep a rabbit in a crowded home.

Albano squatted to look between the bushes at the foot of the boulder where the rabbit had disappeared. He moved thorny bushes out of the way and discovered an opening in the rocks. Curious, he went on his hands and knees and crept inside.

What he found on the other side of the opening took his breath away. He was inside a large cave! Just enough light came in from the rising sun through a crack between the rocks for him to see how large the cave was. It was a true castle! It was at least twenty steps across in all directions and tall enough for Albano to stand and still have about ten feet above him. Inside, the ray of sunshine bounced against the smooth rocks and made the walls of the cave shimmer like gold. The air smelled of wet earth and fungi. The only sound, echoing eerily, was a trickle of water. When he found the water stream and put his hand in it, it was cold and clear as diamonds.

That day, Albano curled upon the cave's dirt and allowed himself to sob with grief, but also with relief because for the moment he felt protected by God.

****

It was thirty-two years since the discovery of the cave but Albano, now almost forty years old, remembered that day vividly. He remembered his joy, his relief, the feeling that God had guided him there. The cave would become the center of his life. It was the place where he would hide the finials passed down from his dying father and the money that he and Hagop earned selling newspapers on the quays of Smyrna. The cave was the place where he had protected Hagop and then lost him. The cave was the hidden temple where he and Xandra had loved each other, where they had stayed in hiding as her belly grew with their child.

Today, the secret room where Albano was hiding felt more like a coffin than a castle. It was narrow and windowless, concealed between two walls. It smelled of mildew and old papers. The room was equipped with everything a man in hiding could need: running water, a toilet, shelves lined with food provisions. This was the room where he and Moshe put friends who needed a few days of safety, and today it was Albano's turn to use it. This room was like a coffin also because today was the burial of his old life. He could still change his mind, as long as he was inside the secret room. But once the decision was made, it would be a death of sorts. Or rather a rebirth.

Outside, the Allies had begun the invasion of North Africa. Their success or failure would decide his fate.

Albano listened and heard not a sound.

Years of planning, and, as Moshe liked to call this, "constructive pessimism," had led to this moment. This day. After two years spent in Algiers and working tirelessly to help finance the Resistance effort, Albano was proud of his involvement. Their operation guaranteed a financial lifeline to Jewish groups in North Africa and elsewhere, as well as that of many Resistance cells in occupied France. But Albano's involvement in all this ended today. Freedom would come, he hoped, as a result of tonight's Allied invasion by sea and air – freedom for his family and freedom for the French people of Algeria. But for him, it would lead to freedom of a different kind, one he dreaded and feared, but one he was choosing.

No one was making him do this terrible thing.

One did not have children to possess them, Albano reasoned, but to eventually release them into the world. And whether the world was ready for them or not, his children seemed ready for the world. When they were little, Albano had been able to keep his brood around him. But now, Marceline and Gustave were young adults, and the war had changed them. This city had changed them. Lucienne was incapable of parenting; she had become like a child herself. Marceline and Gustave were wayward and unruly, as futile to try and contain as a running spring. They wanted to risk their lives for their ideals, and there was nothing he could do about it. If the invasion turned out to be a success, the city would be freed, and his family would no longer need his protection from the Nazis. If the invasion was a success, they would be safe.

Xandra had tried to open his eyes. She had demonstrated the courage he lacked. Ultimately, she had been the one to commit the unthinkable act instead of him. But ultimately, they were only peons. It was all the will of God.

The tiny, coffin-like room was built to be soundproof. If the fight had already started, Albano had no way of knowing. If there were gunshots, explosions, men and women screaming, children crying, those noises did not reach his ears. This also meant that no sounds inside the room could be heard from outside. Albano sat on the cot, and, just like he had as a child, thirty years before, he began to weep, over Lucienne, over Marceline, and Gustave, and Hagop, and Moshe, and Xandra, and over what he was about to do.

****

Nine months earlier: March 1942

As was his daily habit since he and the family had come to Algiers, Albano had washed, dressed, and walked down rue Michelet to get his coffee and newspaper before the rest of the family awakened. He had always loved being up at daybreak, a leftover habit from his years selling newspapers on Smyrna's quayside. Algiers was a beautiful city, which seemed to have gotten the essence of two cultures right. It was like Paris, but with the sunshine. It was like Africa, but with European architecture. The seaside even had the feel of Smyrna. As he walked down the streets, he wondered if he should worry Xandra with the upsetting news he had recently learned: according to Moshe, Hagop was no longer in Nice. Not only that; they had no idea where he was.

As he walked through the streets of Algiers, he thought of how, at first, he had been pleased with the swiftness with which his children had accommodated to their new life in North Africa. But now, be it due to their adolescent moods, or their endless conflicts with one another, he was appalled by their poor judgment. Marceline slipped away every chance she got and spent time with boys. The whole translation business he had managed to thwart, but even if he were to ground Marceline for a week, on the eighth day, she'd head straight into the next mischief. And there was Gustave's obsession with joining the Resistance or the Chantiers de la Jeunesse. The children were on edge, disobedient, lashing out at each other over the merest slights. True, Lucienne's condition helped nothing. And how could Marceline and Gustave not want out of the apartment when he himself could not bear to be anywhere near her?

And now they were all turning against Xandra, she who selflessly served them without expecting, or receiving, an ounce of appreciation or recognition. From Lucienne, he expected this, but the children? He had overindulged them, and so he could only blame himself now that they were spoiled. Just last week he had believed the children would remain on Xandra's side, and he had been devastated to discover that they weren't. He had hoped to enroll Marceline in an intervention, as she was still her mother's favorite. "Your mother keeps telling me to fire Sandra," he had told Marceline. "I hope you can make her listen to reason."

"All the same," Marceline had said, "I can see how Mother feels."

"What do you mean?"

"Mother has been in a state, and maybe not having Sandra around would be best."

Albano had looked at Marceline with incomprehension. "Fire Sandra? Is this what you're asking of me? You agree with your mother?"

"You can't impose her on Mother for the rest of time," Marceline had said. "If she's so miserable with Sandra, why keep her?"

"But wouldn't you miss Sandra?" Albano asked, aghast.

Marceline answered in a paternalistic tone that surely had no place in the mouth of a child. "Baba, we really don't need her. At least, Gustave and I don't. Not as a nanny. And Mother doesn't want her as a maid. What are we to do when Mother is adamant about it? Choose Sandra over her?"

"But Sandra is like a member of this family."

Marceline frowned prettily. "With all due respect, she is not."

"We're the only family she has!"

"I'm not saying leave her destitute. We can find her another family to work for. I'm just thinking about Mother."

Albano saw Marceline for the callous, selfish girl she was. "If you were truly concerned with your mother's well-being," he said, "perhaps you would not lie to her again and again and put her through so much grief!"

"I'm sorry, Baba."

"I'm sure your brother feels very differently about Sandra," he said defensively.

Marceline shrugged. "I think he would agree." She patted Albano on the back, and her touch felt like an electric shock finding its way all the way down to his bone. "Sandra's time has passed, Baba," she said. "It really has. We're nearly grown."

Albano, full of righteous indignation, marched into Gustave's room. Surely Gustave, for whom Xandra was more of a mother than Lucienne had ever been, who knew she had believed in him from the moment she set eyes on him, and believed in him still to this day when he did nothing much but grumble and resent the entire family, would want Xandra to remain. Gustave, at least, would be on her side. "Your sister and mother want to let go of Sandra," Albano told him upon entering his bedroom. "What do you think about this?"

"I'm a man," Gustave answered without lifting his head from the train set he was working on. "I don't need a nanny."

Albano was in disbelief at first, and then he felt angry. "And so, you think I should let Sandra go?" he said, raising his voice. "In the middle of a war? In a country she hardly knows?"

Gustave shrugged. "I didn't say that. I just said I don't need a nanny. It's not my decision. You can keep her if you want to."

"It's not about what I want!" Albano exclaimed. "It's about – about…." Albano was so distraught that suddenly he could not describe what any of this was about. It was about his eternal love for and devotion to Xandra. He could hardly expect his children to share his feelings.

"You're the one who keeps saying we need to save money," Gustave said.

Albano was disgusted. Disgusted with his wife, with his children, disgusted with himself. What would he tell Xandra now? He would not tell her that the children she loved as though they were her own were ready to dispose of her like a spent item. Xandra had done nothing but take care of them, and this was all the appreciation they had for her? Did they not realize her selflessness? Her sacrifices?

And in truth, how could they?

They had been deceived for over ten years. And yet, to think that Xandra mattered so little to them! They would have shown more loyalty to a pet. Or perhaps children grew up, and their love for their family needed to dull for them to move on with their lives. One day, they would feel the same way about him. Perhaps it had happened already.

****

Albano sat down at the terrace of Le Beaugrenelle, a nice café-brasserie that looked in every way like the kind one could find in Paris. He sat at his usual table. Pierre, the terrace's waiter, was an older man, grumpy and arrogant with Arab customers, obsequious with French ones. With Albano, he wasn't sure how to feel and alternated between the two. For a few moments, he and Albano talked about the weather, careful to avoid the topic of politics because spying eyes and ears were everywhere in Algiers. Albano knew how to be careful and how to appear ordinary. Even those at the highest echelons of the local Resistance must not know what he did. The system had been set in place long before France had entered the war. The money, channeled through England, came from all over the world, especially

America. He and Moshe had experienced war as civilians before, and so they had understood that setting up escape routes, developing connections, and designing systems to channel money was best done before a war, not in the middle of it when communication became extremely difficult. They knew that communication was often intercepted, which in turn risked the money ending up in the hands of the enemy, not to mention the risk of lives. They had found a way to bypass communication. Their contacts could expect airdrops at irregular intervals on dates prearranged and memorized far in advance. The contacts didn't know each other and had no knowledge of other drops or other dates. No one in Algiers, or elsewhere, knew how the money to finance the Resistance was channeled, not even those in the Resistance.

Pierre brought his usual coffee and croissant, and Albano told himself that next time he would get toast instead. Small pleasures were becoming too much of a luxury. He drank his coffee and ate his croissant and forced himself to concentrate on the newspaper, which was mostly Pétain propaganda and contained no truth whatsoever about the war. His mind kept returning to Hagop's disappearance from Nice. Half of France was occupied by the Nazis, so he doubted that Hagop would have the stupidity to head north toward Paris. If he did not get the idea of heading south, and perhaps crossing the Mediterranean and going to North Africa, there was no reason to worry. And even if he did, North Africa was a vast place. For Hagop to look for them in Algiers would be like looking for a needle in a haystack. Still, he and Moshe had hired people to inquire about his whereabouts and were hoping to find more information soon.

Albano folded his paper, paid, and left. He needed to do something about Marceline, he thought, as he walked back to the apartment. His daughter's latest transgression was the last straw. He had lost his temper the night before when she had arrived well after curfew, her mouth full of lies, professing that she had been at her friend Béatrice's home when he knew for a fact that she was not. What had she been doing, and with whom? This had turned into a family fight. The children took the opportunity to turn on each other like scorpions, and Lucienne had swallowed more pills to numb herself. At some point, Albano had slammed his fists on the table, thus acting like a child himself. Was it the right thing to do to give Gustave the mission to keep an eye on Marceline, he wondered? But what else could he do? He could not have eyes everywhere. It would make Gustave feel like a man while keeping Marceline out of trouble, God helping. He was aware that this decision might exacerbate their mutual resentment.

The living situation in Algiers suited no one. The small apartment had only three bedrooms. Marceline and Gustave each had their own, which meant that Albano had to go back to sharing a bedroom with Lucienne, while Xandra lived in a maid's room on the top floor of the building.

In Algiers, he and Xandra had no privacy. During the day, she worked in the apartment. But Lucienne, who lived in terror of the city and its inhabitants, was always home. Visiting Xandra up in her room was out of the question. It was not done to go up to the servant's floor where only women lived. The corridors and back stairs that led to the maid's rooms were always filled with women, and his comings and goings would spur a wave of gossip that might find its way to his family's ears. Albano felt terrible about this. In Paris, even in Cannes, Xandra had had her own room in the house. But here, the apartment was too small. He loathed how the worlds of servants and masters were kept separate. In the morning the servants, most of them Muslim women, went to work in the French people's apartments, and at night, they went back up, like things taken out of a cabinet to be used and then placed back inside when one was done with them.

Albano had never seen Xandra's bedroom in all the months they had lived in Algiers. He and Xandra had had only brief moments of true privacy in the last two years. They had to content themselves with a few words exchanged in the kitchen, a smile, a furtive kiss, a quick squeeze of the hand. Maybe once a month, they saw each other at Moshe's. But Moshe's Algiers apartment served as a hub of Resistance activities. It was more often than not crowded with men and thus hardly a suitable place for a lovers' rendezvous. Lovers. If that's what they were. They loved each other; that much they knew. And they lusted for each other – at least he did for her. But Xandra had never wavered on her resolve to refuse intimacy. He was a married man, and she was a pious Christian woman. Ever since she had materialized in Paris twelve years ago, that was that.

Albano walked back on rue Michelet toward his apartment building, looking up at row after row of windows. Behind those windows, housewives put water to boil on stoves. Businessmen shaved in their bathroom mirrors. Students prepared for school. Lovers had a last embrace. Mothers combed their daughters' hair. As a boy, when he and Hagop sold newspapers on Smyrna's quayside, Albano always liked to imagine how people lived behind their windows and doors. Back then, he believed that those who had wealth were by essence happy. He had been wrong about this and many other things.

He entered the building and walked up the stairs to his apartment thinking of Xandra, his beloved, so close and yet so out of his reach. He craved to speak to her, to hold her in his arms. He missed her. Life was a disjointed whirl of activities, full of urgencies and risks, without a moment to pause or think, and, at the same time, cloaked in wretched loneliness. Without quite knowing what he was doing, he found himself passing the floor to his apartment and continuing up toward the fifth floor and the maids' living quarters. A moment later, he was searching for her door in the mildew-smelling corridor. He found it and knocked softly.

Xandra opened after a few moments and widened her eyes. "You know people will talk," she whispered, taking him by the arm and pulling him inside.

As soon as he was in her room, he took her in his arms, and they held each other without speaking.

"What is happening with Marceline?" he asked finally. "Where did she go yesterday?"

Xandra's face closed, the way it did when she had decided not to speak about something. The strain of the last two years was even affecting Xandra, although they never discussed it. Xandra, his anchor in life, his bastion of certainty, was impatient at times. Little things she said and did. A new stubbornness. Sometimes she seemed to be on the children's, or even Lucienne's, side more than she was on his. "I don't know where she went," she said.

"Do you think she was with a boy?"

"It was probably for a boy," Xandra said. Albano contemplated his beloved. She was wearing a nightdress made of thick white cotton. Her braid was undone. Her hair, lustrous and black, fell on her shoulders.

"Marceline is with men, and it doesn't make you upset?"

Xandra looked at him meaningfully, not letting him pretend that he was ignorant of this. "You know this has happened before."

"I cannot understand my own daughter," he said, distraught. "How can one have so much intelligence on the one hand and so little brain on the other?" He looked around the room for a place to sit, but there was no chair in the pared-down room. He had been told the room was furnished. Where, then was the furniture? All he saw was a thin mat set on the bare floor and three rattan trunks; one at the foot of the bed and one on either side. There was the small rug he had given her for a birthday. There was her Jesus on the cross above her mat. She had pinned postcards of Paris to the wall and draped bright shawls on a string that ran from one corner of the room to the other, and this gave the place a warm feel, but there was no dresser, no desk, no chair, no lighting except for an antiquated oil lamp set atop a lace handkerchief. And there was no chimney either, so where would the heating come from?

He felt a wave of unease. In Paris, Xandra had a beautiful room. In Cannes, she had a pretty room with her own bathroom. Now she lived as she had in the cave, no better. And alone. All those hours, alone. For two years, she had served them during the day and been alone in this terrible room at night. And not once had she complained. "Maybe if Marceline becomes pregnant, she can marry," Albano said absurdly. He leaned against the wall self-consciously. Xandra was sitting down on her mattress, looking up at him. "Lucienne will not like that very much," he continued, "but at least she would be a married woman."

Xandra answered nothing and looked at him strangely, as though she had the capacity of seeing straight into his soul. "What do you think of those Jewish boys?" he asked. "You would not want her to become a widow. They are taking risks, spending their time at Géo Gras."

"*You* take risks," Xandra pointed out.

"Moshe and I started something, and now the Resistance counts on us to organize the finances. If I were to quit now, a large part of the Resistance funding would stop flowing." As Albano spoke, he became aware that he was looking for an excuse, a reason why he had been unaware of Xandra's living conditions. He had been working for the Resistance. And this was true. He was under a great deal of stress; this was also true. "I take these risks for Marceline and Gustave, for their future. And all they do is attract trouble."

"They are a young man and a young woman in a world at war," Xandra said. "They are idealistic. Could your family ever stop you from doing what you wanted, what you needed to do? My family could not stop me. Not even my brother could stop me."

Albano rubbed his eyes, confused, and blurted out, "This room is terrible, Xandra! Why did you not tell me? I would have brought in decent furniture. A mattress worth sleeping on!"

Xandra smiled. "The happiest days of my life were spent on a straw mat in a cave."

"Where is the bathroom?"

"At the end of the hall. There is a toilet."

"You and the other maids share a toilet?"

"Have you forgotten the time when no house had one?" she said, smiling. "And we had to walk to the terrible bathhouse to wash? I go to the hammam. It's a beautiful one."

The idea and the solution to two problems sprang into Albano's mind unexpectedly. "You will come to live in the apartment!" he exclaimed. "And you will share a room with Marceline. I will tell Lucienne that it is so that you can keep an eye on her. She will have no choice but to accept this, she who is so worried about Marceline's honor." He beamed. "Yes, this is perfect!"

Xandra crossed her arms and shook her head. "Albano, do not make me Marceline's jailor."

"Your presence will dissuade her, that's all. You'll tell me about her goings on, and everyone will be much better off."

Xandra pinched her lips stubbornly. "I will not be her jailor or your spy. Marceline is like a daughter to me. I will not betray her trust."

"But it's not for this reason," he implored. "It is an excuse. The real reason is that I need you to be comfortable." He gestured at the room. "Not living here. Not like this. And yes, I need Marceline to be safe. It will serve two purposes."

"What is safe, Albano?" Xandra asked softly. "Is safety to remain alive, but not taste life at all? Marceline will not bear to be deprived of freedom when the world is turning to dust and rubble. Not her. Not your daughter."

"If she works for the Resistance, I have to stop her."

"But what about the work she does?" Xandra asked.

"What do you mean?"

"How about its importance?"

Albano looked at her in incomprehension. "How could a nineteen-year-old girl influence the outcome of the war?"

"Not a girl," Xandra insisted. "A woman. Look at her: fierce, intelligent, full of passion. Who is to say what she can or cannot accomplish?"

Albano was astounded. "Tell me you do not approve of all the things she does?"

Xandra answered with that air of stubbornness he knew not to contradict. "I think my own thoughts, Albano."

Albano wanted to tell Xandra that she was defending a selfish girl who was entirely unwilling to fight for her. "The children are taking you for granted," he said. "You deserved children who consider you their mother, not their maid."

Xandra laughed. "Every mother wants this; few obtain it."

"And you are Lucienne's equal, and she should treat you as such."

Xandra dismissed the improbable notion with a shrug. "Even those who Lucienne considers her equal, she doesn't treat as such."

Albano paced the few feet between the door and the window, frustrated that he was getting nowhere. "Still," he said, "you are more of a loving mother and caretaker than Lucienne ever was and ever will be, but you receive none of the credit. You deserve to be in the light. You should not be here, forgotten, but in my life, as my wife!"

"Albano, you are my man, and I am your woman," Xandra said tenderly.

"In almost every way but the one that matters most," Albano said in a tone more bitter than he had intended. Xandra frowned as she did every time he alluded to the fact that she refused physical intimacy in the name of his marriage's sanctity. "I have put you in an impossible situation," he added quickly so that she would know that he was resigned to this. "I've asked you to do something, and you accepted. It was a terrible pact. A terrible request."

Xandra got up from her mat, walked up to him, and touched his cheek softly. "But it has made me happy, Albano. Do you remember when we sold pastries together in the Levantine quarter? It seemed impossible that we could ever be together, you a Jewish boy and me an Armenian girl. I have loved taking care of your home and your children. It did not matter to me if this was not our home and our children. It nearly felt as if it was. Lucienne is the one who suffers the most. To love a man who loves another is the cruelest of fates."

"I have kept my pledge to Lucienne," Albano said. "But what about my pledge to you?"

"What pledge to me have you not kept? You took care of me; you gave me your support; you made me feel beautiful when the rest of the world saw me as a monster. You took me into your life when no one else would. You have kept me safe and adored."

"I also promised you a beautiful house, and look how you live."

Xandra peered at him. Albano looked away. "What is it?" she asked.

"What is what?" he answered.

Xandra crossed her arms and scrutinized his face. "Something else is upsetting you," she said. It was a statement, not a question. "Albano, speak to me."

"It's only that … I received some news. I did not want to bother you with it until I had some answers. We received a call from the custodian of Hagop's apartment in Nice." Xandra stiffened perceptibly. Albano paused, gathering himself so as not to betray his emotion. "Hagop is not living in the apartment anymore."

Xandra brought her hand to her neck as she took a quick breath. "Where did he go?" she murmured.

"The custodian cleaned the apartment weekly, but for the last few weeks, nothing was dirty. His clothes were gone, too. She did not think much of it because her wages were paid for the whole month. She thought he had gone on a trip. When he did not return at the end of the month, she called to inquire about him."

"A month," Xandra said. Her face had turned pale. She sat back down on the mattress, and Albano sat next to her. "Could something have happened to him?" she wondered.

They looked at each other with the same thought, but neither dared express it. Could Hagop be looking for them?

"The bank account in Nice where I left him money has been emptied," Albano admitted.

"Was it a lot of money?"

"Enough to live for about a year if he paced himself. Maybe he was tired of France. He never liked it much."

"You were too generous," she said.

"Look, he does not know where we are. He has no idea. I never told him a thing about Algeria. There is no cause for alarm. The custodian only had the telephone number of a trusted friend of Moshe's in Paris. That's who she called, and the friend then called Moshe."

Xandra did not say anything. She walked to the rattan trunk at the foot of her mat, crouched next to it, and opened it. She took out a folded piece of cloth and put it on the mat, stood up, and stepped away from it as if it contained a live snake. "I have this," she said.

"What is it?"

"Look."

Albano unfolded the cloth. Inside was a leather sheath, and Albano immediately knew what it contained. He slid the seven-inch blade out halfway and quickly slid it back into the sheath and dropped it on the mat. "Xandra! what is this?"

"In case my brother finds us," she said.

"He'd have to look for us in the whole world, so there is nothing to worry about." He was staring at the knife, unable to touch it or take his eyes away from it. "Where did you get this?" he said, his voice shriller than he intended.

"I bought it."

"But why?"

"For my protection."

"From what?"

"Things happen to women who are alone."

"Xandra! Now you tell me this? This horrible room, and now I learn you do not feel safe here? That you are scared? This is one more reason not to be in this room another minute." Xandra did not respond. She carefully folded the cloth over the knife and put it back into the trunk. "And what would you do with this knife?" Albano asked. "You would not know what to do!"

She answered with an impatience that betrayed her anguish. "Who do you think butchers the meat on your plate or empties out those fish you and Gustave insist on scooping out of the sea? I know how to use a knife, Albano."

Albano stopped her anger by taking her hand. As always, the contact soothed them both. "Hagop might just as easily have emptied his account and drunk himself to death," he said softly. "He is self-destructive."

"He is destructive," she said, voicing her anger without hesitation. Unlike Albano, Xandra did not feel ambivalent toward Hagop.

"Even if he were to find us, he would not want to harm us. Not physically."

"He has in the past."

"How so?"

"He pushed me and beat me, remember?"

"Oh, yes."

"You have to go, Albano." She got up from the bed and nudged him toward the door. "You have stayed here too long already. People will gossip."

"Let me take you in my arms before I go," he said, coming close to her.

She let him, and as he held her, she softened. "A single kiss," he begged.

When Albano returned to the apartment and walked into the living room, the curtains were down, as Lucienne preferred it, and so he did not see her right away. What he saw first was a thin serpent of grey smoke rising from the embers in the ashtray. Lucienne was sitting at the dining room table in the dark. She brought the cigarette to her lips. After almost two decades of marriage, Albano knew what to read in Lucienne's apparent self-assured composure. Her rigidity had never been much more than a wall to keep fear at bay. She fought fiercely about every small thing, and he accommodated her, but that was because they both knew that the important decisions would be up to him. With Lucienne, it was better not to express doubt. If he left her any room to decide what she wanted, she filled that space with an anxiousness that distressed them both. Ever since he had been proven right about leaving Paris, and then leaving France for Algiers, she had been relieved to defer to him on most decisions.

Albano pulled up a chair and sat across from Lucienne. He dreaded speaking to her. He dreaded her reactions, her emotions, her accusations. "I decided it is best that Sandra shares a bedroom with Marceline," he said. Lucienne remained wordless and motionless for a long moment. In the dim light, he could only make out the outline of her face and the red tip of her cigarette. Finally, she reached into her pocket and produced the tiny silver box that contained her pills, swallowed one, and took a quick sip of water from a glass. "Our daughter doesn't obey us," Albano continued. "She is childish and reckless and puts us all in danger. With Sandra sharing her room, she won't be able to run out into the streets when we're asleep."

Lucienne continued to sit, very erect and tense. She exhaled a puff of smoke. "I am not sleeping under the same roof as that woman," she calmly said.

Albano had expected complaints, not opposition. He was immediately furious. "What difference does it make to you where she sleeps? She slept under our roof in Paris and Cannes."

"That was before," Lucienne said.

Albano did not ask what she meant for fear that she would tell him. Ever since they had left Cannes and come to Algiers, bringing Xandra, Lucienne suspected something that was never discussed. "She is here during the day doing all the work, cooking our meals, cleaning our home," he said.

"Oh yes, Saint Sandra, saving us all," Lucienne said bitterly.

Albano had no other option for Xandra. He could hardly afford this apartment and was in no position to get her a place. But the horrid room upstairs would not do, especially when the Hagop situation was not under control. And besides, what he said about wanting to protect Marceline was the truth. "Do you want our daughter to get hurt?" he said, more aggressively than Lucienne deserved. "Or abducted? Is this what you want?"

"I'll be the one sharing a room with Marceline," Lucienne said, her voice quivering. She was about to cry. Perhaps she was crying already, but Albano could not see her eyes in the dark.

"You are drugged most of the time. You don't even see when people go in and out of the apartment during the day, let alone at night." He was shocked by his meanness. But this also was the truth.

"Those are medications I must take so as not to lose my mind in this wretched place!" Lucienne said. A month ago, this was the point where she would have started to scream and bawl, but her medication dulled everything, even sadness and rage.

"All the same," Albano said.

The pill Lucienne had just swallowed was taking effect. Her speech slowed. "Why can't Marceline and Gustave share a room?" she asked sluggishly.

"They resent each other enough as it is."

Lucienne got up slowly, dropped her cigarette in the ashtray and ambled to her room, her gait uncertain. "The day will come when I can no longer bear this," she murmured so softly that it wasn't clear if she had meant to say this out loud. "I will simply jump off this balcony."

"Lucienne! Must you resort to this every time?"

She stopped, steadying her body by pressing a palm on the wall, and without turning or speaking any louder, she said, "When I am found dead on the pavement five floors below, you will have yourself and her to blame."

"If you throw yourself off the balcony," Albano said. "The only person who can ever be blamed for it will be *you*."

The next day, to his daughter's savage indignation, Xandra moved into Marceline's bedroom.

All through the month, Lucienne refused to speak to Xandra or look at her. April was otherwise uneventful until one day when, upon returning to the apartment from Moshe's place, Albano found Xandra looking pale and distraught waiting for him by the front door. With her eyes, she signified to him that they needed to talk later. Albano immediately assumed that Lucienne had done or said some mean thing to her. But she and the children did not seem particularly out of sorts.

When they needed to speak about something, Albano and Xandra would arrange to bump into each other in the stairwell or on the street. A couple of minutes were usually sufficient to exchange a few words. That day, though, Xandra appeared so distraught that Albano just walked into the kitchen to see what might be the matter. She was washing the dishes, and when she saw him, she immediately said in Armenian, in a murmuring, pressing voice full of anguish, "Something has happened! Marceline came to me today. She thought nothing of it, but she said that she saw a man in town. A man who she says looked so much like me that he could be my brother!"

Albano felt dread fall upon him like a heavy cloak. "That's … simply not possible," he said.

"He is here, in Algiers, Albano," Xandra insisted. "He found us!"

At first, Albano found nothing to respond. Then he mumbled, "We left no trace."

"We must have."

"We have to be logical about this," he said, his confidence waning as he spoke. "How would he have found us when the French police couldn't?"

"My brother has his ways. He is clever."

"Even if he knew where we are, which he cannot possibly, how would he have managed to leave France in the middle of this war, come all the way to Algiers, and find us?"

"But what if he did?"

"Marceline saw a man who looked a bit like you. That means nothing."

Just as he said this, Marceline walked into the kitchen asking in that haughty, breezy tone that made her sound both detached and amused, like a femme fatale in one of those motion picture films she loved, "What's all the mystery?"

Xandra turned away toward the sink to hide her distress, and she plunged her hands into the sudsy dishwater.

"Not much," Albano answered as he left the kitchen.

That night, Albano lay rigidly in bed as the rising moon cast growing shadows on the ceiling, the dresser, the lamp, slowly creeping down the wall like ghostly figures. In the distance, the sound of an Arabic melody entered the room through the open window. In her bed, not four feet from his, Lucienne softly snored while the woman he wanted slept in Marceline's room on the other side of the apartment, out of reach of his embrace and his love.

In the morning, he would speak to Uncle Moshe. He was perhaps making too much of this. Moshe would be able to reassure him. Moshe would tell him it must be a coincidence. A look alike. A man in Algiers may or may not have had a family resemblance with Xandra. Or Marceline could have just made up the whole thing to make herself sound interesting. The chance of Hagop being in Algiers was minuscule. But as Albano struggled to find sleep, an alternate thought intruded, a thought impossible to quiet. If it was indeed Hagop that Marceline had seen, then it could only mean one thing: if Hagop was in Algiers, it was not by accident. He had looked for them and taken risks to track them down. This would mean he was even more obsessed and desperate than Albano had feared. This would mean that an undoubtedly deranged, possibly dangerous man had been following his daughter.

The following day, Moshe was not as reassuring as Albano had hoped. "Still though," Moshe said, "it might have nothing to do with you. He might have chosen to come here because Algiers has the feel of Smyrna. The pier, the town, the people, the climate. People know this. This is why many come here."

"Emptying his bank account? Leaving a paid-for apartment? Suddenly finding himself in my daughter's path? No, Moshe, I have come to understand that Hagop leaves nothing to chance."

"We have to find him," Moshe said.

"And then what?"

"And then give him what he wants."

Albano shook his head. "Over the years, I have given him my help, my friendship; he wanted none of it."

"Every man wants something."

"He wants my demise, Moshe," Albano said. "I'm afraid he wants that and only that."

Through May and June, Moshe and Albano deployed considerable resources and contacts looking for Hagop throughout Algeria and found no trace of him. No one had recorded his arrival by boat or plane. No one in the Armenian community had seen him or heard from him. As time went on, Albano relaxed. Had Hagop been in Algiers, they would have found him by now. Hagop perhaps had feared the volatile situation in France's free zone and decided, because of his immigrant status, to return to Syria, or to make his way to Italy or Spain, or any of the Greek islands.

One morning in late July, Albano awakened at dawn after a dismal night's sleep. The news from France was so distressing it was a miracle he had slept at all. He got up, washed, and dressed, careful to let Lucienne sleep, and came down the stairs of his apartment building. He stepped onto the street and walked past the city's workers and merchants, hard at work as they prepared the city for the rest of its inhabitants. He had always enjoyed walking through the streets as the city awakened, but these last few months, stepping away from the apartment felt like an escape; as though he were running for his life. He could barely stand to be home at all. They were all reeling from the terrible news from Paris, and there was nothing he could tell his children to reassure them. There were terrible rumors about the conditions in the Vel' d'Hiv, of families without food, water, or sanitation, of people shot for trying to escape, rumors of filth, of death by dehydration, of little children and old people expiring under the glass dome, when the temperature inside had risen to a deadly level in the summer heat. No, it could not be true. No French government would carry out a horror of that sort. Even Pétain's terrible government could not allow such a thing to happen.

Albano felt powerless. All he could do at this point was to continue to channel money to the Resistance, continue to hope that what the Resistance was saying was true: that they would soon see an Allied push into North Africa.

He headed for Le Beaugrenelle for his morning coffee, walking past housewives throwing soapy water at the curb, grocers arranging meager produce in neat piles, young men carrying burlap bags. The smell of freshly baked bread wafted out of the bakeries' basements. A baker and his apprentice, covered in flour and slick with sweat, took a break and shared a cigarette. Already, sleepy-faced children as young as five waited in the bread line. Today again, because of the shortages, the city would run out of bread before noon.

He thought of his happy times in Smyrna when, his pockets heavy with newspaper money, he would wait for Xandra at the street corner and help with her route to distribute pastries to the Levantine families. Where were the Levantines now? What was their country? Did their wealth and connections spare them from the worst?

Albano stopped at the newsstand just as it opened, and took the first newspaper on the pile. He arrived at Café Beaugrenelle just as Pierre, the terrace server, brought the last of the tables and chairs out.

"Just how warm do you think it will be?" Albano asked Pierre.

"At this time of the year, there is enough heat stored in the city's walls that it never quite cools down at night," Pierre responded gruffly, as though Albano were to be held personally responsible for this. "What will you have today?"

"Black coffee and toast, thank you, Pierre," Albano answered.

"No more butter; we used the last of it yesterday," Pierre said. "Only margarine. And now we have to charge extra for jam."

"I will do without," Albano said.

He leafed through the newspaper, a pointless act he insisted on out of habit rather than with expectation to gain any real insight from a news agency that continued to portray the British, Canadians, and Americans as the enemy. German and Italian armies were now at Egypt's border, he read. Hitler was closing in on him and his family. He scrutinized the pages for mentions of the accusation emanating from the BBC that over six hundred thousand Jews had been killed throughout Europe. No mention either of the other terrible rumor: the alleged convoys that moved Jews imprisoned in Drancy and Pithiviers to Dachau, a German internment camp with conditions so dire that many did not survive.

He leafed through the pages hoping for insight on the Vel' d'Hiv events. Rumor was that the roundup of Jewish families had not been ordered by the Nazis, but that it had been desired, planned, and implemented by Vichy. The most pessimistic people, even those who spoke of a deliberate act of genocide, of plans of mass extermination of the Jewish people – although most did not want to believe such a thing was possible – did not believe the French government capable of taking it upon itself to surpass the Nazis in zeal. But Albano had seen enough in his life not to discount the insanity of men. Through the centuries, insanity periodically seemed to grip men, irrespective of their race, their country, or their religion. Yes, one could point the finger to a single leader, Hitler, Mussolini. But nothing could happen without the participation of men. Humans, with their violent, hateful nature, would always find justification to follow their basest instincts. Give humanity evil leaders, and men eagerly followed.

He had been careful to keep the news surrounding the Vélodrome d'Hiver events from Lucienne. Her psyche was too fragile, he felt. But rumors found their way through the cracks underneath doors; rumors traveled in the wind. He feared Lucienne would panic and try to telephone or write acquaintances in Paris, even though he kept explaining to her that people could listen in on phone conversations or open mail and that for a few Algerian francs anyone could turn into a spy. But Lucienne had trouble remembering. His children, too, refused to face the situation, moving through this treacherous time, this foreign country, as though it were all a game. They did not realize that in the game of war there were no rules and no decency. Innocents weren't spared. Pity did not exist. Civilians suffered the most. Justice did not prevail. He had never told them what he knew, what he had seen in Smyrna, what people had done to each other. In his heart, Gustave and Marceline were children, and he could not bear to burden them with such horrors.

Pierre brought his coffee and set it on the table. Albano did not ask for sugar, partly because Pierre seemed in a sour mood. He might as well get used to being without sugar, he thought. He returned to the newspaper. The sports events had been reduced to nothing. No Tour de France this year. No rugby championship. No soccer World Cup. Only horse races, but he had scant interest in that. Absorbed in his paper, he did not notice the man standing next to him.

"Pardon me, Monsieur," the man said in French. "Is this chair available?"

In the same instant, Albano's mind split into two. Part of his mind wondered why a stranger would ask to take his chair when the terrace was nearly empty. The second part of his mind was seized with a hollow sense of panic as he recognized the man's voice. He lifted his face and opened his mouth, but the only thing he found to say was, "Hagop!"

As stunned as if he had come face to face with a ghost, Albano watched Hagop sit across from him. Hagop's face was filled with such joy and mirth that for an instant Albano felt joy too, a fleeting emotion immediately replaced with dread.

Hagop was in Algiers. Hagop had found him.

"Are you happy to see me, old friend?" Hagop asked in a pleasant, jovial tone. "Oh, but how could you be, when you took such care to lose me?"

In shock, unable to speak, Albano took in Hagop's appearance. His face was gaunt, his cheeks hollow. His suit was dirty and tattered and torn at the knees and elbows. This was the suit of a man who had been sleeping in the streets. But what gave Albano the most anguish was the absence of his dentures. It wasn't only that without teeth Hagop looked twenty years older, it was the insanity, the drunkenness, the loss of control that would bring a man to lose an item so indispensable to self-esteem, physical comfort, and social belonging. Without his dentures, Hagop nearly gave an impression of helpless benevolence. But all it would take for rapaciousness to return to his face was a set of expensive false teeth. Albano tried to slow his breathing. He needed to appear calm. Whatever emotion he expressed, Hagop would find a way to use against him. "How did you find me?" he asked in the most even-quelled way he could.

"I always knew where you were," Hagop chuckled. He was speaking in Armenian now. "You thought you had lost me, didn't you? But you cannot, dear friend, no matter how hard you try." Hagop smiled with the open satisfaction of a man who has patiently hunted his prey and caught it.

Albano decided to appeal to Hagop's vanity to learn more. "It must have been difficult. How did you manage?"

"You told me where you would be yourself!" Hagop snapped with triumph. "That first day in Nice, when I came off the boat. That day you told me where your uncle was." Seeing Albano's confusion, he beamed. "You do not remember, do you? You told me that pig lived in Algiers." He said the word pig without anger, as though it was a natural way to refer to Uncle Moshe. "You told me this, and then you forgot. But I was paying attention! You underestimated me because my body was weak." He smiled sheepishly and lowered his voice, as though he were retelling a detective story. "But all the while, my mind was sharp. Already, back then in Nice, and even before, when you thought I was lower than dirt in Aleppo, you were already caught in my net like an unsuspecting sardine." He laughed out loud at the image.

Albano was baffled by his own folly. "I told you this?" In the warm feelings of that day in Nice when he had welcomed Hagop from the boat, he must not have thought it necessary to hide anything. In his excitement and trust, he must have said too much. He had no recollection of this.

"Of course, you were too busy thinking what a wonderful benefactor you would be to me." Hagop paused and thought. "You were too preoccupied with buying my affection. You had not started with all your lies quite yet. You forgot that you were speaking to your old friend, Hagop, the man who listens, and thinks, and forgets nothing."

Albano felt the warmth of the rising sun on him, harsh already. At the terrace tables around them, six or seven people were ordering breakfast, opening their newspapers, the waiter and busboys moving from one to the other with efficiency. "Why are you here?" Albano asked. He tried not to sound accusatory.

Hagop looked at him with amusement. "The money was running out, so I decided to go where the money was."

Was this what it was about? "Money has run out here as well," Albano said through tight lips.

Hagop laughed, too loudly. "Of course, it didn't. Not for a Jew it hasn't! Jews have a way with survival. Or rather what Jews call survival, which is more akin to thriving at the expense of others." He was saying the word Jew loudly, and the man at the next table peered at them.

Albano looked out into the street where the first of the automobiles were beginning to appear. Only expensive cars and taxis could function through the rationing and rising costs of gas. "Why did you not stay in Nice?" he asked. "You had a good life there?"

"A good life where your best friend and your own sister run away from you under cover of night?" Hagop was not bothering to smile now. Perhaps the excitement of the hunt had waned and what remained was cold anger.

"We were running from the Nazi threat," Albano protested without conviction.

"But you left me to face it alone?"

"I am sorry," Albano said, looking down at the pavement. He meant this. And yet faced with the same choice today, he would do the exact same thing. As he watched Hagop and listened to him, Albano was furious with himself. Had he interpreted the facts correctly, had he taken Marceline's words and Xandra's intuition seriously, he could have taken them all out of Algiers and moved to Oran or Casablanca. He would not be right here, apologizing to and agreeing with Hagop. Because what else to do when facing a crazed man but agree, to gain time? There was no doubt in his mind now, and perhaps he was admitting this to himself for the first time, that for whatever reason, because of whatever seed of madness having sprouted over time, or due to whatever terrible torments he had witnessed and endured, Hagop had become insane. And his insanity was now single-mindedly powered by an obsession with him. "How long have you been in Algiers?" Albano asked with feigned casualty so that Hagop would not know that Marceline had seen him. "And how did you find me in this big city?"

"It took no time at all," Hagop said, his voice thick with contempt. "My dear friend, you are nothing if not predictable. Waking up early, sitting at café terraces the moment they open, your coffee, a single cube of sugar, your dear French newspaper, your little habits of comfort." He added meanly, "Don't forget, I know you better than your own wife does. I only had to walk around the French areas until I found you. I am a very patient man. Patient and discreet." He added with a smirk. "Invisible even to my own sister."

If Albano had any notion that Hagop did not know that Xandra was in Algiers, that hope vanished. He felt the beating of his pulse rise to his temples. As the sun now lit the buildings, heat oozed out of the walls. Hagop had been following him for weeks, perhaps months. He knew where he lived. He had followed Marceline and most likely Xandra, Gustave, and Lucienne as well. And yes, he was excellent at it if even Moshe's men had not been able to spot him. Albano realized his stupidity. The teeth! He should have mentioned to Moshe's men that the individual they were looking for might have no teeth.

"But I am tired now, I must admit," Hagop said, lighting a rolled-up cigarette and sitting back in his café chair. "I cannot keep up with some of you. Your daughter is all over town." He made a sound of disapproval through his teeth. "Tt, tt, a free spirit that one. Marches to the beat of her own drum, much like her papa."

Despite himself, Albano could not help but react. "I forbid you to intimidate my children or even cross their paths!"

Hagop feigned surprise. He displayed emotions like a second-rate actor, the seething anger and the threat leaking through each word he uttered. "I never saw you this emotional about Xandra, but make a single light comment about your daughter, or that boy of yours, the forlorn one. What does he have to be so upset about, your boy, I wonder? A life of nothing but privilege, yet he is always moping, always keeps to himself. He could use a friend is all, a real man in his life whom he could look up to. And that wife of yours? Does she still not know about Xandra, a mistress in her own house? Perhaps that could explain how sad she looks. That is the look of a woman betrayed."

"I am warning you," Albano growled.

Hagop stared at him defiantly and said in an innocent voice. "Warning me of what? What is it I am to fear? Being abandoned in the middle of a war? Well, that was done to me already, and I am not the worse for wear."

"I could cause you harm," Albano said, regretting his empty threat immediately, showing his cards when he still knew nothing of Hagop's plan.

Hagop answered, his words dripping with sarcasm. "It must be true that I am nothing and you are a powerful man. It is not as though I could reveal to the Vichy police that you are a foreign Jew, here in Algiers living under a false name."

Albano came closer to him, whispered in the hope that Hagop would start doing the same. "You are just as much an illegal immigrant in a country that doesn't welcome you as I am."

"Only you are a Jew." Hagop let the word hover between them. In his mouth, it sounded like a disease, a deformity. "And as such you are doubly unwelcome." As he spoke, Hagop's face twitched and contorted into peculiar emotions, one replacing the other in rapid succession with no rhyme or reason. The face of a madman. "And you are rich. With money stashed away somewhere, that could undoubtedly be appropriated by the authorities. As to me? What have I to fear? I am nothing to them – a vagrant, a drunkard. They think of me as one of those Arabs, so far below them. Oh, I loathe imagining what they would do to you. Arrest you? Almost certainly they would, wouldn't they?" He feigned outrage. "That's what they do to Jews these days." Now he was shaking his head with affected pity. "And would that not be a great shame? To think that a single word from me and suddenly there is no one left to protect this charming and unsuspecting family of yours, the two children … the two wives." Now Hagop made a show of acting as though he were speaking to himself. "How long before they are destitute and lost? It would only be natural for them to want the support of the next strong man. Certainly, as your closest friend, it would be my responsibility to take over for you. Your flock, your sheep. Yes, I would do this for you. I would. All they need is a shepherd, and the responsibility would fall to me in the name of our friendship."

Albano's mind flooded with savage thoughts. Murder. That would be the only sure way to get rid of Hagop. Move. Leave the country. Blind him. Cut off his tongue. Maybe Moshe knew people who could do this. "Leave my family alone," he said. "I am warning you!"

"Do not get upset, Albano. You know I am being facetious."

"What is it you want?" Albano asked icily.

"What do I want?" Hagop sighed, and for a moment he was sincere. "It is the same thing I always wanted. Peace. But my demons will not allow for it. I cannot sleep. And when I am awake, my mind is cruel to me. It goes to and fro, to and fro, incessantly. Only wine allows me some respite."

"I can get you wine."

Hagop immediately gestured to the waiter and ordered a pitcher of wine in perfect Arabic, making it clear to Albano that he could easily pass as Algerian if he wished. "I was wondering when you would offer me something to drink." He sat back in his chair, looked around, looked up. "Sunshine at long last!" he exclaimed. When the waiter brought the wine, he said with a wink, "Sunshine in the sky, and now sunshine in my glass. What more could a man ask for?" He brought the wine to his lips and drank avidly, emptying his glass.

"If it is money you want, I will help you the best I can," Albano said.

In an instant, Hagop's expression changed to sour. "Money, money. It was always about the money to you Albano, wasn't it?" He raised his voice. "Yes, I was robbed that day when I left the cave with the satchel! Will you always hate me for it?"

"Of course, I don't," Albano said. "You've twisted everything in your mind."

Hagop wasn't listening; he had turned sullen and melancholy. "Years of hard work we did, selling those newspapers. We were filled with schemes and dreams for a wonderful future you and I, weren't we?"

"We were indeed."

"Do you remember that day on Smyrna's quayside, when you sold your first newspaper? You were shaking like a leaf. You were a weakling. You reminded me of the way your son looks, wide-eyed, eager, ignorant. And look at you now. Powerful. Rich. Only one of us got to fulfill those beautiful dreams."

"I'm not—"

"Because that never affected you, did it, that our hard-earned money went straight into the coffers of the Turkish police?" He added so loudly that people nearby turned to look at them. "Bringing wealth to my tormentors."

Albano could not believe this. "Can't you remember how I begged you not to leave the cave?"

But, as if all the reminiscing had burst a dam in Hagop's psyche, he could no longer restrain himself. Now he was sitting forward as if ready to throw himself at Albano. His face was red; he was nearly shouting, thank goodness in Armenian so that the people on the terrace did not understand what he was saying. "Had you not done the filthy things you did with my sister, the money would have remained in the cave and me with it! The gendarmes would not have arrested me. I would not have been robbed, and beaten, and taken to a slow death across the Syrian Desert!"

Pierre came to their table. "Messieurs, a little calm please, or I will ask that you take this elsewhere."

Hagop gathered himself quickly – too quickly, as though yet another man had entered his body. He smiled at the waiter and answered sweetly in very good French. "I am sorry, I was only telling my friend the plot of a motion picture film I saw." Pierre left, and Hagop continued in a wistful, whispering tone. "Who knows, had all this not happened, I might have a good life by now. The money would have helped me start an honest business. I am thinking a bakery. It was in my blood. It would have honored the memory of my father. Although I never much liked all the shelling he gave me to do, that bastard. I would have a wife perhaps, children, grandchildren."

It was hot now, uncomfortably so. Albano looked at his watch. Gustave and Marceline must be awake by now. Lucienne would rise later, usually around eleven. The terrace had filled up. In the street, people were going about their morning amidst the clanking of trolleys. The beggars had found their spots in the shade. The shoe shiner had set up his stand. The street sellers had displayed their merchandise in neat piles.

Albano would walk to Moshe's and see what could be done about leaving the country. How long would it take to pack what they had? "I can give you enough to be comfortable," he told Hagop. "You would not have to work."

Hagop seemed to consider this. "My needs are humble: a place to sleep, a few francs a day for a meal, perhaps a few bottles of wine. A new suit I would need so that I do not get arrested. What would help are identity papers, a doctor's letter explaining that I cannot enlist."

"I will get you all this," Albano lied.

Hagop called the waiter and ordered another pitcher of wine. "I like this city," he said. "The people are friendly. The climate reminds me of the old country. Yes. I could be at peace here with your generosity."

"As long as you stay away from my family and Xandra."

"You deny me the joy of seeing my own sister?"

"She is afraid of you."

Hagop had a sinister smile. "As well she should be."

Albano felt a terrible sadness drape over him. Hagop's reasoning and restraint, the ability to see things in shades of gray, were gone, his capacity to view the world from another person's standpoint washed away. Hagop had survived by clutching to notions of injustice and revenge, and he had made Albano the center of his paranoia. Trying to appeal to his reason would be a futile pursuit, and yet he tried one last time. "Please, believe me, Hagop. I never meant to hurt you or disrespect you."

"Oh, but you have," Hagop growled. "You did; you did both those things. And you know it."

"What can I do to repair the harm you feel I did to you?"

"Start by returning my sister to me."

Albano stared him down. Hagop had shown his cards, and now he had no choice but to reveal his. "Xandra is not your thing to have," he said. "Or mine. I do not own her that I can return her, as you say." He reached into his pocket, took out his wallet, and retrieved a few hundred-franc notes. "This is all I have with me. I will help you with money, but that is all I am willing to do. If you go anywhere near Xandra or any member of my family, I will do what I have to do to protect them." Hagop pocketed the money without a word. There was a cold light in his eyes. Anger, detachment, and maybe something else Albano could not read that gave him a chill. "Tell me, where are you staying?" Albano asked. "When can we see each other again to discuss details?"

At that moment, a trolley stopped a few meters from the terrace in a screech of metal on metal. A bell clanged, and a dozen people stepped out, French men in suits, Arab women carrying baskets, children in school uniforms. The trolley emptied, and new people pushed their ways inside. Just as the trolley was about to leave, Hagop got up from his chair and without another word made ten steps toward it and hopped onto the platform as casually as if he had done this his entire life. An instant later, he was gone.

Albano expected Hagop to return to the café the next day. He did not. The rest of July was a string of restless days and sleepless nights as Hagop stopped giving signs of life. Albano returned to the same café at the same time every day, but Hagop did not come. He could not find it in himself to tell Xandra that first day. He thought he would tell her the next day, once he knew how things were evolving. But day after day, Hagop did not turn up, and Albano postponed telling Xandra. This continued throughout August, with the secret he kept from Xandra turning into a festering sore, less the lie by omission it originally was and more a sign of his own cowardice and powerlessness.

The men he and Moshe hired to find Hagop learned that he had been seen among the homeless of the city, but that he had since disappeared. This could mean that Hagop was no longer in Algiers, but it also could be that he had found refuge in the Kasbah. If he were there, they would never find him. Despite the scrutiny of the French police, political refugees from every country, deserters of every army, criminals, madmen, people without identification, nationality, or religion could become invisible in the Kasbah. Hagop looked like many other men of indistinct race and age. His pale, olive skin could turn dark when exposed to the sun. Like Albano, Hagop spoke half a dozen languages, all of them with an indeterminate accent. He could blend into the crowds of the Kasbah as easily as a rattlesnake among desert rocks. When he realized this, Albano found it even more difficult to tell Xandra that her brother not only was here but that he had lost track of him.

And then, in late August, on the night of the twentieth anniversary of his marriage, everything that had kept Albano up at night was legitimized.

The last two anniversary dates had come and gone unacknowledged by him or Lucienne, but Marceline had coaxed him into making an effort. She had suggested that he should get opera tickets for the evening. This kind of tender attention was very much unlike Marceline, but instead of being suspicious, fool that he was, Albano had been touched by her thoughtfulness and congratulated himself on the change in her now that Xandra shared a room with her and on how fine and thoughtful a daughter she was turning out to be.

While they were at the opera, Marceline had escaped to meet up with a boy. Gustave, taking to heart his mission to keep an eye on her, a mission Albano himself had senselessly assigned, had followed her all the way to the foot of the Kasbah where he had been attacked and brutally beaten by a group of kids. The hospital had called them at the apartment. Xandra had answered the telephone and managed to reach them at the opera house. He and Lucienne had rushed to the hospital where the details of Marceline's preposterous story had been revealed to them: the manipulation of the opera tickets, Marceline dressed as an Arab woman, Gustave following Marceline all the way to the Kasbah, the Muslim young man Marceline was meeting, the assailants stopped just in time by the young man who was unjustly taken to jail while the assailants disappeared into the night.

As he sat by Gustave's hospital bed, Albano's heart felt as though it would burst with sadness at the sight of his boy hurt so badly. Also, from the moment he heard the attack had taken place near the Kasbah, he knew with certainty what had happened. And what had happened was far graver than his children's mischief and ill-conceived strategy. This was not a random attack. Hagop, he knew it, was at the root of this! Hagop had orchestrated this. Hagop had hired the group of kids who had done this to his boy.

They left Gustave to spend the night at the hospital. In the taxi back to the apartment he, Lucienne, and Marceline did not exchange a word. When they got home, Xandra, her eyes red from crying, was waiting for them by the door. "Gustave will be alright," he told her, as Xandra wept with relief.

"You!" Lucienne screamed, pointing her index finger inches from Xandra's face. "What business do you have crying? You are the one who did this! You were supposed to watch my daughter. She was your responsibility! You let Marceline leave, and you caused Gustave to be harmed. He could have died, and it would be your fault!" Xandra put her face in her hands. "Pack your things!" Lucienne shouted. "I want you out of the house this minute!"

"But, Lucienne!" Albano protested.

"She is not spending another night here. I don't care if she sleeps in the gutter."

Xandra sobbed. Albano looked from Lucienne to Xandra, and his heart broke in tinier pieces still. He said, "Lucienne, please don't be this way."

"This way?" Lucienne shouted. "I tell you what way I am. I will jump off this balcony! That is the way I am!"

"Mother!" Marceline said, trying to take her arm. But Lucienne shook herself free. Her eyes were red, her skin pale and blotchy.

"You have poisoned this family!" Lucienne shouted at Xandra.

"Mother, it's not Xandra's fault, it's my fault," Marceline implored.

But Lucienne would not stop. "I will kill myself, Alban! I will throw myself down five stories if she is not out of here in an hour! Then it will be clear. You will have made your choice." Lucienne ran to her room and slammed the door.

"Come," Albano told Xandra, and they went into the kitchen, leaving Marceline on the other side of the door.

"She is right," Xandra sobbed. "I saw Marceline leave. I said nothing."

"It is only one person's fault, and I will get to the bottom of it. There was nothing any of us could have done."

"What do you mean?"

"For now, all I know is that Lucienne is mad enough to endanger herself or draw even more attention to us than this episode already has."

"Do you think she would jump?"

"It's not her I want to protect," he admitted. "It's you."

"What do you mean?"

"Pack your things, and I will take you to a hotel. We'll leave in one hour. I will take you to a hotel, so he won't know where you are. Lucienne will think it is because she fired you."

"He? Who do you mean?"

"There is something I need to tell you. But not now. Now you need to pack your things, and we will go."

"Albano, I think Lucienne will never let me back in."

"Maybe it is for the best."

"But the children? How will I see the children?"

"You can see the children."

In a small voice, she said, "When I'm gone from their lives, will they ever think of looking for me?"

Albano's heart sank. "It will change nothing," he assured her. But he didn't believe his own words.

Xandra shook her head, dabbed her eyes, and in a tone that was clear-headed and without a trace of bitterness said, "The children don't need me anymore."

It was past midnight when Albano and Xandra arrived at the hotel. He asked for a room and paid for a week in advance. The manager asked him to write down his name and address and sign the register, then he took his money without looking at either of them and retreated to his office. Albano held the pen above the page, wondering what name to give, and then decided to write down his own first and last name.

This was in no way the kind of expensive hotel he could have afforded before the war, and there was no bellman to help with the luggage, no elevator. Albano grabbed Xandra's bags and walked up the three sets of stairs with Xandra following a few steps behind. The stairwell smelled of tobacco and strong detergent, masking the odors of human filth. Until he found something better, Albano felt Xandra would be safe here and comfortable. But this was not home. She was losing her home and the only family she had. She was being fired from her own family, by her own family. Thank God, she did not know how the children felt. They did not deserve her. He did not deserve her.

Albano opened the door to the hotel room. It was modest but clean, and the wallpaper and bedspread appeared to be in good condition. Xandra went from the bedroom to the bathroom, turning on lights, inspecting. "This is good," she said with her usual pragmatism.

Albano placed the bags atop the dresser, and Xandra began to take her things out, placing them inside the drawers. He saw her hold the cloth that contained the knife and said nothing when she placed it in the drawer of the nightstand. He admired her lovely silhouette, the thick braid of her hair. Xandra owned so few things that they took up hardly any room inside the dresser. "Your daughter is in love," she said as she folded the last of her shawls and placed them in the drawer.

Albano shrugged, "She knows all too well she can't be with a Muslim."

Xandra faced him. "If she loves him, she should be with him."

Albano frowned, confused. "But her life would be too difficult."

"A loveless life is more difficult."

"Lucienne wants so much more for her."

"So much more than love?" Xandra asked with a smile. "What else of importance is there?"

Albano went to sit at the single chair that faced a tiny desk. At least this was a room with real furniture. He tried to take in what her life would be in this room. She, so industrious, would have nothing to do. The most important part was to hide her from Hagop. Again, he felt that terrible guilt in his belly. He needed to tell Xandra the truth. "Marceline has a bright future for herself after the war," he said. "She cannot throw her opportunities away."

"There was no future for us, and yet we are together," Xandra said as she took out something white folded between sheets of thin paper.

"Do you know if she is promiscuous with this boy?"

"I would think yes, but I don't know."

Albano sighed, discouraged, but not finding himself angry or surprised. "How long have you known this?"

"Women are changing, along with the world," Xandra said. "They are doing what they please, not caring about who will judge them."

"You sound like Marceline."

"Modern women want to follow their hearts and do not care about notions of decency invented by men."

"It does not scandalize you?"

She smiled. "What scandalizes me has changed."

He could not help but tease her. "Hmmm. I so wish this was true."

Xandra gave him that playful smile she used just with him, which had the power to lift him out of just about any mood.

She went into the bathroom. Albano stood up from the chair and patted the bed. It was a good bed. Not too soft, not too firm. He wondered about the kinds of things he might need to buy to make the room more comfortable. In the bathroom, there was the clanging of glass jars as Xandra placed her things on the shelf above the sink: the one oil she used for her hair, her soap, all elements that contributed to the alchemy of Xandra, the scent Albano equated with love mixed in with unrequited lust. And suddenly he felt embarrassed. Or shy. Yes, shy was more like it. It was only the two of them in this hotel room, past midnight, Xandra in that bathroom, and Albano standing by the bed. "This room is only until I find an apartment," he called. "Something with a nice window and a balcony." The water was running; he was not sure that she had heard him. After all that had happened today, would it be insensitive to try to kiss her, he wondered? No, of course, he must not. Not with the war, and Gustave in the hospital, and Lucienne's morbidity, and Xandra being fired, and his daughter on a nightly rendezvous with a Muslim in the most dangerous part of town. Kissing was out of the question in such circumstances, regardless of how amorous he might suddenly feel.

His thoughts came to a halt when he saw that Xandra was standing by the bathroom door, smiling at him. Her hair, now unbraided, floated down alongside her body. She had changed into a thin white gown that left her shoulders, neck, and arms bare. She looked like a sumptuous goddess. "You look … extraordinary," he said. His throat constricted suddenly. It was all too much. This desire felt as wild as it had been when he was a young man, and she was a young woman, and they had lived together in the cave.

Defying any possible scenario his imagination could have conjured up, Xandra came to stand right in front of him, took his hand, and placed it on her belly and said, "I am worried, Albano."

His hand on her, he felt her warmth through the thin gown. Her hair. Her body. So close to his. "You … you are worried?"

"About letting you see my body."

"I … I'm not worried about that," he stuttered, suddenly understanding that something had shifted.

"I am burned."

"I am in love with you and your burns!"

Xandra laughed, "You cannot love my burns."

"I love them!" he exclaimed. "I love all of them!" And to illustrate this, he began to kiss her burned hand and kiss every inch of her burned arm, all the way to the side of her neck and burned cheek.

"But I am more worried that there will not be a tomorrow," Xandra murmured, taking his head between her hands and placing it against her chest. She kissed the top of his hair. "The world is collapsing around us, and I don't want to be afraid of the same things anymore."

And so, Albano, trying to absorb it all, took her wonderful, warm body in his arms. When they began to make love, it was as though no time had passed since the cave at all.

Afterward, they stayed in bed, their bodies entwined. Albano held Xandra in his arms, not moving for fear of breaking the spell. But after a while, he could not wait any longer. "I have not been truthful with you. Please forgive me. I was only trying to spare you this until I knew what to do but … there is something I must tell you."

"Hagop is in Algiers," Xandra said.

"How did you know?"

"You did not believe it, but I knew it was him from the moment Marceline told me about the man she saw. I have been expecting this. And then you were tormented the last few weeks. So, I knew."

"I was only trying not to frighten you."

"I know."

"He came to me at the end of July," Albano said, sitting up in bed. "He had lost his teeth; he looked bedraggled like he had been sleeping in the streets. He was emotional, but not in any kind of normal way." Albano hesitated. "He looked deranged, Xandra."

"Did he say how he found us?"

"It was because of my carelessness," he admitted. "I guess I had told him that Uncle Moshe was in Algiers when I first saw him in Nice. I don't even remember saying this to him."

"You could not have known the future."

"Moshe and I hired men to look for him, and when they did not find him, part of me wanted to believe he wasn't here. But even now that I have seen him and I know for a fact that he is in town, our men can't find him. He is somewhere in the city, my darling."

"Did he say what he wants?"

Albano sank back on the pillow, and turning toward Xandra so their faces nearly touched, he said, "I think he was involved in what happened to Gustave."

Xandra blinked, fright and anger washing over her face at the same moment. "How?" she asked.

"The police said that this felt like an organized attack. These kinds of things don't usually happen otherwise, they said. Gustave was ambushed at that bridge. This was a planned attack. Someone paid those boys."

"Hagop did this?" Xandra said in a hollow voice.

"Who else would wish my family harm? Hagop knows where we live. It's possible he followed Gustave all the way from our apartment to the Kasbah. While Gustave waited at the foot of the Kasbah, Hagop hired a mob of boys and paid them."

"Do you believe him so full of hatred?"

"Full of hatred or insane."

"To hurt an innocent boy like Gustave. That pig!" Xandra's face was hard with anger.

"We were lucky because the young man who was with Marceline knew those kids, and the kids knew him. The moment he intervened, they ran away, when they could have easily overpowered all three of them."

"The Muslim boy Marceline loves?"

"Without him, Marceline could have been hurt as well. And Gustave could have been hurt even worse."

"If you are correct about this, Hagop must be stopped."

"Even if we knew where he is, how would we stop him? I cannot call the police on him, even if I have proof, because he knows too much about us. And where would I even find him? I don't think he has papers or even an identity card. Already he can blend into this city so well that even you and I cannot recognize him when he follows us. No, the only way is to reason with him. Appease him. Give him whatever money I have. Keep him drunk. I don't know."

"And what if he cannot be appeased?"

"That is one of the reasons I think it is better you are here instead of the apartment. It is for you I fear the most. That's why I did not fight Lucienne when she fired you. I want you in this hotel. For the time being, you are safest here."

****

Through the end of summer and early fall, as Gustave's cuts and broken bones healed, and Lucienne sank deeper into her depression, and Marceline was forbidden to leave the apartment, Albano and Xandra spent entire, wonderful afternoons together as lovers.

As the weather cooled and found its way through the wooden shutters into the hotel room, they ate in bed, took baths, rediscovered each other's bodies, and forgot the world. His love for Xandra burst out of him. He could not have enough of her presence, of her touch, of her scent, of her body. Now the apartment did not feel like home to Albano, but like work that he must return to each day, going through the motions until he could run back to Xandra. He felt differently about his family. Seeing Gustave's bruised face, he should have felt sadness for his son, but instead, he felt annoyed by his fragility. The emotion he felt with Marceline was no longer pride and amazement but resentment at her impulsiveness, her unwarranted sense of superiority over them all, and her indifference toward Xandra. As for Lucienne, he should have felt compassion, but instead, he felt impatience and irritation.

When Albano wasn't with Xandra, he worried about her safety. He was terrified that Hagop would follow him and find the hotel. He took the utmost care not to be followed. Walking back and forth between the hotel and the apartment, he took long, circuitous routes, stopping at shops and cafés along the way, checking behind him every few meters. He took an hour to get there when the hotel was ten minutes away. He wore a disguise. He wrapped himself in a burnous to walk to and from the hotel. He would leave the apartment, find a café's bathroom to change into, and walk to the hotel dressed as an Arab man. He made sure to have his hood covering his eyes, which he knew to be his most distinct feature. On the way back, he would do the same in reverse. If Hagop could disappear into an Algerian crowd, so could he.

Perhaps it was a ridiculous disguise, one that might fool only the French for whom everyone with Semitic features looked the same. But would it fool Hagop for long? And was Hagop even still in Algiers? For all he knew, he had left the country. Moshe's men had not ceased sifting through the city, but Hagop had not given any sign of life since that morning in July, over three months ago. As time went on without any sign of him, Albano found himself wondering if he had not imagined Hagop's involvement in the beating. Perhaps he had overestimated Hagop's desire to harm them or his ability to do so. Could the attack on Gustave have been a random act of hatred by a random group of kids? Hagop had no connections, had little money, and had to avoid the police for fear of being thrown in jail for not having papers. If he had wanted something from him, money or favors, would he not have come to him by now?

One afternoon in late October, Albano left the apartment and made his convoluted route to the hotel, stopping at a café to change into his burnous. Once at the hotel, he walked past the clerk who never paid him any attention, across the tiny, dark lobby and up to Xandra's room, and as usual, he knocked at her door.

Xandra did not open. He knocked again. After knocking several times and wondering what was wrong, he heard the door unlock and saw it open. Xandra now stood at the door with unusual stillness. She did not open it all the way. Her face was taut. Immediately he read in her eyes a command not to enter. He put his hand on the door, expecting Xandra to let him in, but she made a barrier with her body, and so he nearly had to push past her to enter the room. "What is happening?" he asked.

What he saw inside took the air out of his lungs.

Hagop was sitting on Xandra's bed, his back resting against the pillow, one leg casually crossed over the other, his shoes on. He was dressed elegantly, in loose breeches and a white shirt. In his hand was a gun aimed at them.

"It is me!" Hagop said jovially. "*I* am what is happening!" Albano looked from Hagop to the gun in his hand to Xandra, who remained absolutely still as if she was crossing paths with a scorpion. "My sister and I were waiting for you." Hagop waved the gun loosely. "You," he told Xandra, signaling to a spot on the floor beneath the window to the left side of the bed, "sit by me." Xandra obediently went to the bed and sat on the floor. Now she crouched below the window in the narrow space between the wall and the bed, and her face was at the level of the mattress. She looked up at Albano. She was afraid, but calm, her eyes deliberately without expression.

"What do you want from us?" Albano said when he was able to make a sound. He was standing between the door and the bed as Hagop sat on the bed, his legs extended, his back propped by a pillow as if he were waiting to be served breakfast in bed.

"Why are you so hostile?" Hagop said with a honeyed voice. "I am just a brother visiting his sister."

"Then put down that thing."

Hagop waved the gun as though it was a toy, making big arm gestures as he spoke. "This, you mean? I bought it with the last of the money you gave me. A man cannot be too prudent in this treacherous city."

From the cadence of his speech, the way he bobbed his head slowly, Albano thought that perhaps Hagop was drunk. But it could just as well be an act. When it is coiled, and still as stone, the rattlesnake is still an instant away from striking. "What is it you want from us?"

"What a hospitable man you are; thank you for asking, brother. Do you have wine here? I am parched. And food?" He turned to Xandra and said harshly, "Have you any food, woman?"

Xandra looked at Albano, who nodded to indicate it was best to oblige. "I have some food in there," she said softly, pointing to the drawer of the bedside table, the drawer that held the knife. Albano's stomach dropped. He held his breath as Xandra foraged through the drawer, and breathed again when she only retrieved small packages wrapped in paper. She unwrapped them. One contained dried fruit, the other one, bread. She set those on a tray, which she placed on the bed. Hagop held the gun loosely in his hand, as though he had forgotten it was even there. With his other hand, he picked at the food. He laughed. "Look at me, reclining and dining like an Ottoman prince." He turned to Xandra. "You, sit back down." Xandra returned to crouch on the floor to his left of the bed. Why was she crouching and not sitting Albano wondered briefly?

Albano stood by the door, motionless, his head still covered by the woolen hood. There was no air in the room, and yet the sweat that poured down his neck felt like ice. Was the gun loaded? Hagop loved being dramatic.

Whatever it was Hagop wanted, he was in no hurry to tell them. He was enjoying himself or at least wanted to give that impression. "Was this food for the two of you?" he cooed. "You know what this room reminds me of? It reminds me of the cave, that cozy little love nest you had made for yourselves, where you waited for me to have my back turned so that you could do your filth." He said this last word with rage and then tore at the bread with his teeth, savagely. Because now the teeth were back, white and gleaming. That day at the café, the gummy mouth, the hollowed-out cheeks, that air of indigence and weakness, it all had been another game of manipulation.

But then, in the stifling heat, as Xandra crouched by the bed, and Hagop made big smacking chewing sounds, Albano could not wait anymore. "Did you have something to do with my boy being attacked?" he said.

Hagop gave him a hurt look. "Come on now; why would I do such an evil thing to a boy?"

"So, you know about it?"

"How could have I orchestrated such a thing? Does it not seem too complicated for someone like me?" He shook his head in self-admiration. "That would be the work of a mastermind." He popped a nut in his mouth with unmasked contentment. "Imagine my surprise when I saw your boy by his bicycle at the foot of the Kasbah. I had not planned on anything. And here he was, waiting and waiting, that stupid boy. Asking for it, really. A scraggly boy. A Jew among Muslims. I waited and watched him, and then night fell, and he was still there! I could hardly believe he would be so foolish, and for what? To protect his sister? Is that what he was trying to do? Is that why he was there? Because that boy would not know how to protect himself if a kitten wanted to scratch him."

Xandra and Albano briefly looked at each other. "It was you. I was right. You paid those boys to beat my son?" Albano only asked.

Hagop smiled modestly, as though he were being recognized for a remarkable deed and was too humble to accept praise. Anger rushed to the tips of Albano's fingers, a wild tingling. His neck throbbed with the desire to pounce. Albano, attuned to Xandra's emotions, felt in her a surge of anger and desperation that matched his. Her eyes burned with such an intense fire that he wondered if she might be about to be sick. He felt like he was about to be sick. Xandra's head was inches away from the gun. It would be madness for Albano to make the slightest move. "If someone had not interfered, my son might have been beaten to death!" Albano said between clenched teeth. "Is that what you wanted?"

Albano's anger only resulted in Hagop sitting upright in bed and pushing the tip of the gun to Xandra's face. Albano and Xandra froze. Hagop was pale now, his smile gone. "I never pretended to be a good man. That's the difference between you and me, Albano. When I commit a crime, I might lie about it so as not to get into trouble, but I do not lie to myself. I believe this makes me a better man in fact. A more honorable one."

His eyes on the gun, Albano hoped to appeal to Hagop's reason and asked softly, "A boy of seventeen who did nothing to you? A child. If you wanted to hurt me, why did you attack him?"

"Think about this, my brother. If I were to kill you, it would be the end of your suffering. Whereas if I hurt those you love, your suffering would only increase." Xandra and Albano exchanged a look. Filled with melodrama and bitterness for his circumstances, Hagop added, "I thought for a long time that I was the one who should die. It would serve no justice, but perhaps then my suffering would stop." Hagop, deeply moved by his own words, forgot to aim the gun at Xandra. As soon as the metal no longer touched her skin, Albano relaxed, and he could think again. Hagop's eyes filled with tears of self-pity. "Easier said than done. Though I might wish for death at times, it simply won't happen on its own. This old body won't quit. And it has needs, this body," he said, thumping his heart with his fist. "It has *wants*. No, it is my soul that is tormenting me. An obsession. Yes. You could call it that." Hagop's voice broke. "Oh, my brother, why do I love you so and hate you so? Why are you to me crueler than any Turkish jailor?"

Albano blinked, trying to take in the absurdity of the accusation, the profession of love, the quick succession of bizarre emotions. "You know I am not trying to be cruel—"

"You are!" Hagop shouted. "By your mere existence, you are. Your handsome face, your wealth, your good fortune at every turn. And then, luring my sister into a life of servitude and sin! And she is too mesmerized by you to even rebel." He shook his head. "She is under your spell, Albano, as I am. But to her it is pleasurable, and to me, it is relentless torture."

Xandra looked at Albano intently. Something electric passed between them, the meaning of which he did not decipher. She was telling him something – a warning. "I will give you whatever money I have," Albano said. "There is money in the apartment. I have diamonds. Not many, but I still have a few. Please put down this thing."

"Good!" Hagop snickered. "I want all of it. All of it, you hear me? Your diamonds, your gold. Let your family live under bridges and sleep on beaches. How about that for a change?"

"Anything you want. Now please, let Xandra go."

"You go fetch the money first," Hagop said impatiently. He pointed to the door with his gun. "What are you waiting for? Go! Hustle up!"

"Xandra will go to my apartment," Albano said hurriedly. "She knows where to find it. She'll get the money and bring it back here." This was a lie. There was little money at the apartment, and the diamonds were at Moshe's. But once Xandra was out of the hotel room, Albano would pounce on Hagop. He would punch him, grab the gun, and throw it out the window; from there he would find a way to overpower Hagop. "Keep me here as hostage," he added, "while Xandra goes to get all the money."

"No! Not that!" Hagop loudly whined like a toddler on the verge of a tantrum. "You go, and she will be my hostage." Saying so, Hagop leaped at Xandra, grabbed her by her hair, and shoved the gun hard into the flesh of her neck.

"I will go. Please don't hurt her," Albano murmured.

Hagop only yanked Xandra's hair harder, brought her head closer to his, and smiled like a demon.

Had Hagop been less self-admiring, he might have noticed Xandra's sudden pallor, the combustion in her eyes, the grip of her hand even as she, like a prey who knows that resisting is futile, appeared to go limp under his touch. She looked as though a thousand springs had wound up at once inside her body.

Albano read the message in Xandra's eyes. She was telling Albano what to do. She was telling him to go.

Now that Xandra had given him that command, Albano knew he would go and fetch every bit of fortune he had left and that he would trade it for Xandra. He would imperil his family, render them destitute, all to rescue her.

But had Albano not been so afraid for Xandra, he would have remembered that a woman capable of surviving a stillbirth, a fire, and the destruction of a city all on her own, a woman who was unrelenting as she searched for him, a woman who endured years of another woman's contempt and raised that woman's children nonetheless, a woman who would resist his sexual advances until she reconciled them with her sense of right and wrong might not need rescuing. Such a woman was in fact formidable. But at that moment, Albano did not remember this, or perhaps he did not know what she was capable of. Because when a situation calls for fight or flight, there is no telling which constitution will choose which. Sometimes the strong man will run, and the quiet woman will be the one to coil and strike.

One moment later, Albano was in the hallway and had his ear against the door. Now that Xandra and Hagop were inside and he was outside, the thought of walking away even for an instant when Xandra was in a room with a madman waving a gun was beyond his strength. Hagop might try to rape her. He might decide to make good on his threat to hurt her in order to hurt him. Albano placed his ear on the door and listened in, his pulse beating hard against his temple. The hallway was empty. It was cooler there than inside the room and very dark. He could not budge, as though both his feet were nailed to the floor. He listened. He heard Hagop's order. "Give me more food, woman."

Albano sensed in his bones what was about to happen, and yet his reason rejected the idea: the knife.

He heard something. He did not know what he heard. Rustling. Gurgling. Sighing. All very strange noises that he probably imagined because it was all very quiet at the same time. This was followed by a minute of complete silence when he heard only the sound of his heartbeat. And then there were footsteps. The door cracked open, and it was Xandra opening for him. "Albano," she murmured.

"I didn't go yet."

"Come inside," she said.

That's when he saw the blood on her dress. "Xandra!"

"It's not my blood," she whispered as she pulled him inside and shut the door behind them. What he saw, Albano could not believe. He fell to his knees with shock. Hagop was on the bed. His eyes were open. Blood came down in a slow rivulet along the left side of his chest; the gun handle rested in his open palm. There was a knife planted in his heart. Xandra was pale and still as a tree. "There was no other choice," she said.

If Hagop had a chance to fire it, he had not taken it. It seemed to have happened in an instant, in silence, without a struggle. "What have we done?" Albano said in a voice barely above a murmur.

"I did this," Xandra said calmly. "Not you."

"But how … how did this happen?"

"He asked me for more food, and so I went to the drawer and took the knife. I was so scared, Albano. But I was more afraid of him than I was of killing him. And so, I did it."

"By God, Xandra! How could you? How did you?"

"The blade went in," she said, not believing it herself. "It just did, between his ribs, into his heart. He had no time to do anything. Or else he didn't choose to fight me." She paused and looked up at Albano.

"Mon Dieu," he whispered.

"I had thought about it before," Xandra said. "Where to strike. Between the ribs. Into the heart."

In disbelief, Albano echoed, "Into the heart."

On the bed, Hagop, dressed in white against the white sheet and the white wall, the small crucifix just above him, had his dead eyes fixed on nothing. He looked as though he were enacting a scene in a Caravaggio painting. The only sign of life in the scene was the expanding crimson blotch on his chest and the mattress. It struck Albano how Hagop's face, his body, gave a feeling of relaxation, as though the demon that possessed him had drained out of him and what was left was a lovely sense of peace.

As though she could read his thoughts, Xandra said, "It was fast, but in his eyes, as he expired, I could see that my brother welcomed death." Xandra went to Hagop and, placing her palm gently on his face, closed his eyes shut. She said a prayer and, looking at the crucifix above the bed, signed herself. Albano felt a profound hollowness in him. He felt confusion, paralysis, but no sadness. Just relief, for now. No matter the future, they were freed from Hagop.

"We will go to the police together," Albano said. "We'll say he attacked you and so I stabbed him in self-defense."

"I did this," Xandra said, turning to him. "I am unhurt, and he is dead. No one screamed. No one called for help. I am a murderess now."

Albano looked at Hagop's body, and the immensity of what had just taken place hit him at last. He turned frantic. "We'll topple furniture! We'll tear your dress so that it looks like an attack! You'll scream, and then people from the other rooms will come, and I will tell them I came in and defended you. We can move his body to the floor. Some of your hair could be in his hands … They will fetch the police and—"

Xandra was perfectly calm. "No police," she said. "You saw what they do to innocent people like this boy who helped Gustave. We will leave the body where it is. In a few days, it will start smelling. This gives me time to run away. You make sure that no one sees you leave, and you return to the apartment. The only time people saw you here in regular clothes is when you first brought me. But there is an explanation for that. You were helping me move in. The other times you came dressed as an Arab man. If the police come to you, tell them you have not seen me since you dropped me off."

"Uncle Moshe will help us hide you."

"I cannot hide anywhere in this city. Everyone in this hotel saw my scars."

"Then Moshe can smuggle us out of the country."

"Us?"

"To Greece, or Corsica, or Cyprus."

"Wherever I go, you cannot come with me, or people will assume you are guilty. No, you must stay."

"I'm not letting you run away to some strange country while I stay in Algiers."

"If I go to jail, you won't be with me there either. And if you are crazy enough to accept the blame, then you will be sent to prison, and your family and I will be without you."

"I don't … I can't—"

"Listen to me," she said imperiously. "I did this because someone had to, and I didn't want it to be you. I did this so that you would not go to prison."

"I don't know that I could have killed him. I don't think I would have been capable."

She caressed his cheek, lovingly. "I know," she said.

****

Albano stood on the balcony looking at another balcony on the building on the opposite side of the street where a middle-aged French woman in incongruous pearls and curlers was tending to chickens in a cage. She took their eggs and gave them something to eat. In wartime, people did what they had to do.

He was trying to calm down. Inside the apartment, Lucienne had just taken one of her pills for nerves, and Gustave and Marceline were on separate ends of the living room, red in the face and disheveled. There had been another fight. This time, Gustave had thrown himself at his sister, and Albano had to jump in to separate them. It was as though the war outside also raged in their heart. Rather than rally against a common threat, they mistook the enemy for each other.

The Allied invasion was imminent. An American general had arrived via submarine and conversed with top-ranking Resistance organizers. Now they all waited for the date. In a matter of weeks, perhaps days, the Allied forces would attempt to take the country. Marceline did not know how dangerous the times were, but regardless, she had once again disobeyed and lied. She had taken a train to the Agha prison to see that Muslim boy. Someone he knew had spotted her and called Albano right away.

If Albano could not do the simple thing of helping his children be reasonable, what hope was there? He raised his eyes to the implacably blue sky. Xandra, he asked the sky, do you feel as lost without me as I am without you?

He wished it would be more of a comfort to him to know that Xandra was safe, protected by friends of Moshe. It was only three days since Hagop's death, three days since she had taken the boat to Portugal. A lifetime. An eternity. Portugal was for the moment neutral in the war, and he and Moshe had Jewish friends there, taking refuge. The same fishing boat that had brought Albano and his family from Nice to Algiers was always moored at an Algiers fishing dock, ready to smuggle people in or out of the country at a moment's notice, in case the Allied invasion failed, or if things got too dangerous in Algeria. Xandra had been whisked onto the boat and out of the country in a matter of hours. Three days without Xandra, and already Albano could not bear the distance between them. One moment he had been on his way to spend an afternoon with the woman he loved, and the next moment she was gone, possibly forever.

Since Hagop's death, Albano had hardly left the apartment. He was waiting for a telephone call from Xandra, although Moshe had told her not to make contact for now. But mostly Albano needed to be present when the police came knocking at their door.

Because the police would come; of this he was certain. He had signed the registry the day he had checked Xandra into the hotel. He had disguised himself, made sure to cover his tracks, but the police would link Xandra to his family sooner or later. He wished he could warn Lucienne and the children, explain to them what had happened, tell them that the police would invariably come, and what story they should all stick to. But it occurred to him that real ignorance was preferable to a feigned one.

What had happened replayed in his mind without mercy: Hagop on Xandra's bed, the knife in his chest; he, haggard and reeling, stepping out of the hotel in broad daylight dressed as an Arab man, hiding his face, and then melting into the noon crowd. He had walked in circles in the city, hiding in entryways every few blocks to make sure no one followed him. After an hour, he had entered a public urinal and stepped out looking once again like a Frenchman in a white shirt and wool pants. He had tossed his djellaba and burnous on a pile of trash and had climbed on the first bus. From there he had taken a second bus and a third. He had sat on garden benches and pretended to look at merchandise at the outdoor market. He had sat at cafés. He had had conversations with people in the street so that there would be a trace of his whereabouts that day. Two hours later, he had, at last, walked to Moshe's apartment and told him everything.

Meanwhile, Xandra, following their plan, had waited in the hotel room, steps from her brother's dead body. She had removed her bloody clothes, packed a few possessions, and waited for nightfall. At night, she had wrapped herself in black and walked to the fishing dock where Moshe's boat awaited her.

Albano had not seen Xandra off as he had promised her. Moshe had not let him, insisting that he needed an alibi and must at once rush back home and make sure everyone saw him there. The police would have a hard time figuring out the exact time of death, but he could not risk being away for another minute; neither could he be seen at the fishing dock. There were spies everywhere, and they could not take the chance of divulging their escape strategy.

He and Xandra had not said goodbye. They had not made a single plan for the future.

Across the street, the chickens on the neighbor's balcony pecked and fought for the food. It was only a matter of another day, two at the most, before the stench of Hagop's decomposing corpse would find its way below Xandra's hotel room door and through the open window, and the process of alerting the authorities would be set in motion. Perhaps Hagop's body was already found, and the police were on their way.

Albano was trying to come up with a plan to see Xandra, but he could not think straight. When had his plans ever made a positive difference? Over the course of his life, how much control did he have over fate? Every encounter, every action of his life had led to Hagop's body rotting ignominiously in that hotel room. Everything that had happened to him and everything that was about to happen now seemed inevitable: Smyrna, Uncle Moshe, Hagop, Xandra, the baby, the fire, the rescue, France, Lucienne … his children. Even his children had not been shaped by him. They were creatures firmly planted in this mad century and had been shaped, no, distorted, by the world's xenophobia, anti-Semitism, Hitler, the war, as well as the years of abundance and entitlement before the war. Albano had been a fool to think he had power in any of this. Their story, and his story, had long been written by God, who writes every story. Each time Albano had attempted something, each time he had believed himself in control, he had had as much influence over his existence as a bit of straw tumbled by the wind, and God had laughed.

An evil man wanted to conquer the world and destroy his race. His beloved friend had become demented. His wife was suicidal. His children risked their lives and tore each other apart. The woman he loved was a murderer. The police would come any moment to arrest him for the crime. And he had a decision to make, a decision that did not involve a futile attempt at controlling other people's destiny, only his own.

"Tell me, God. What should I do?" he asked the sky.

There was a sound like a flag flapping in the wind, a wide shadow came across the sky, and a powerful gust of air ruffled his hair. He jumped back, startled. A massive pelican had appeared, flown straight at him, and nearly touched him with his wing, and now, with a few more beatings of its dinosaur-like wings, it hovered above him a few feet away. The vision was so extraordinary that Albano opened his mouth to call the family. But before he could utter a single sound, the bird soared above the building and, in an instant, disappeared.

"Did you see that?" he called out to his family inside. But no one heard him.

Had God meant to speak to him alone?

His anger at Marceline and Gustave vanished. Air entered his lungs for what seemed to be the first time in days. Yes, Marceline was lying again. Of course, she was. She lied because she was pulled by her fate, unconscious of it, as they all were. His children, like him, were nothing more than cogs in the gears of life. Who was Albano to decide what they should do or not do, whom they should see, what they should say, where they should go, whom they must love when God's grand design was all that counted?

Albano looked down at the street. A police automobile had come abruptly to a stop in front of the building. Two men, one in police uniform, the other in civilian clothes, hopped out and hurried inside. Albano felt the dread of being caught. He had only a few minutes to regain his composure before they knocked at the front the door.

He turned on his feet and entered the living room. His eyes adjusted to the dim light. Gustave and Marceline were just as he had left them, each on opposite sides of the living room like boxers ready for their next round. Lucienne was fanning herself, looking absent or overwhelmed.

The knock at the door was so loud that they all jumped, even him.

His mouth dry and palms wet, Albano walked across the apartment and went to open the door.

On the doorstep was the policeman in uniform accompanied by the man in a suit and hat. But instead of handcuffing him, they removed their hats and asked if they could come inside, and Albano understood that they were not here to arrest him. This was an investigation.

The detective sat in one of the armchairs. The policeman stood. Both had thick mustaches. Someone offered them water. Albano put all of his concentration into appearing normal.

A man had been murdered in Xandra's hotel room, the detective explained. Xandra was nowhere to be found and thus was their prime suspect. The hotel records showed that Albano had paid for her room a month in advance. What exactly was the nature of their acquaintance with the suspect?

Albano did his best to match his family's reaction and painted his face into an expression of dismay. He hoped the children and Lucienne paid attention to the lies he was about to give the detective. They all needed to corroborate to keep the secret of their identity intact. It would not take much for an overzealous cop to start digging into their past and find inconsistencies. Xandra was Armenian, he told the detective. They did not know where she was born or how long she had lived in Algeria. She had answered an advertisement and had worked for them for two years. She had lived in a maid's room upstairs. From there, Albano went on with the truth. She had moved into the apartment to sleep in her daughter's room. But their daughter had run out at night, had broken curfew to see a boy, and Xandra had been fired for letting her. Albano went on to describe the attack at the Kasbah. There was a police report; the detective could look this up. That same night, Albano explained, he had taken Xandra to the hotel, paid for a month in advance, and given her a sum equivalent to a month's wages, and they had not heard from her since.

The children were shocked and swore of Xandra's innocence, although her disappearance wasn't anything they could explain to the police. Even Lucienne admitted that Xandra was incapable of murder. More things were said. Marceline was arrogant and feisty. Albano meant to tell her off, but he thought that perhaps it would be better, more authentic, if he appeared to be a weak father.

"A man was seen visiting her hotel room," the detective said, squinting and looking at each one of them slowly as he spoke, his eyes always lingering on Marceline.

"The man who died?" Albano asked.

"Another man. An Arab. Or most likely a Kabyle. Light eyes." There was no clear description, the detective went on to say. "He came and went at various hours. We assume he was her lover. He too was not seen since the murder, so he might be an accomplice, if not the murderer himself. Is it possible that the murder was rooted in a lover's dispute?"

They all shrugged off the notion of Xandra being caught in a love triangle. Had the police come just a few minutes earlier, Lucienne would have been strident, but now all she could manage was a weak pique at Albano. "Her sexual proclivities were not of interest to me," she said.

Marceline interjected, "Mother! Sandra lived with us. When would she have the time? Or the opportunity?"

To this, Lucienne agreed cryptically. "If she did have a lover, I suppose I would be the last one informed."

"What about you?" The detective asked, turning to Albano. His gaze was attentive, measuring.

"Me?"

"Do you have any idea who the dead man might be? And why he was killed? Do you have any theories of what might have happened?"

Albano had no time to come up with a plausible theory that might satisfy the man. What would an innocent person answer? "Perhaps he was wounded and found his way into the hotel, and into her room … somehow."

The detective scoffed at this. "Monsieur, with all due respect, the man was found with a knife planted in his heart. Not exactly the kind of wound that allows much meandering."

Lucienne put a hand to her mouth. "Goodness."

"What I will say with certainty is that we can all vouch for Sandra's character," Albano told the detective. He wondered if he seemed to care too much. Xandra was supposed to be nothing more to him than an employee he fired. The detective had a few more questions and Marceline said a few insolent things that nevertheless made it apparent that she knew nothing. From the corner of his eye, Albano noticed that Lucienne was dozing off. "We are glad to assist you in any way we can," he said at last as the detective got up to leave.

"Very well; I will leave you to your day." The detective turned to Lucienne. "Au revoir, Madame." He looked taken aback when he saw that Lucienne, although still sitting upright had her eyes closed, her chin, down and her mouth slightly ajar. He turned to Marceline, polished his mustache with a coquettish turn of the finger and said, "Mademoiselle." With this, he planted his hat back on his head and left, followed by the policeman. But just as the door was about to close behind them, he spun on his feet to look at them, his gaze steady on Marceline, Lucienne, Gustave, and finally Albano, and said, "Please do not leave town in the eventuality we need to call you in for further questioning."

That afternoon, Albano went to Moshe's to tell him about the police visit.

"You were not identified! This is fabulous news," Uncle Moshe said. "And there is nothing they can do about Xandra. Under normal conditions, the International Criminal Police would seek her out, and because of her physical description, they would rapidly apprehend her. But now the communication between countries is difficult at best. The world has more pressing issues than the fate of a woman of no consequence murdering a nameless man for undetermined reasons in a second-rate Algiers hotel room."

"They might still decide to arrest me. I am right at their fingertips. If they see that our papers are false, they will have grounds to, even if they cannot link me to the death."

"Once the Allies are here, Algiers will no longer be ruled by Vichy," Moshe said. "It is only a matter of days."

"If the Allied invasion is successful, how long do you think before Xandra can return to Algiers?"

Uncle Moshe raised an eyebrow and shook his head. "Albano, she did kill her brother. There is a warrant for her arrest. You must understand that she can never come back to Algeria."

Albano felt no hesitation. "If that is the case, I have made my decision. I will meet her in Portugal."

"You want to move there, the whole family?"

Albano thought for a long moment, wondering how he could explain this to Uncle Moshe. "I've decided," he said, "to do something that may shock you."

"Shock me?"

"My wife hasn't been a wife to me, or I a husband to her, in years," he began. "Lucienne is ill. In fact, my love for Xandra is precisely what is ailing her. My children are grown, or nearly, and they are set on doing whatever they please."

Moshe frowned. "What are you saying?"

"I will leave the money for them. All of it. After the war, you can help them recover our assets in Swiss banks."

Moshe looked shocked. "You want to run away with Xandra?"

Albano took a quick breath and nodded. "I have made my choice," he said.

Moshe crossed his arms. He was a smart, cool-headed man who found solutions to the most difficult problems. But now Moshe was shaking his head. "If you run away, it will make you guilty in the eyes of the police."

"Let the police think whatever they want."

"But what would your family think, Albano. Could you live with that?"

"I would write a letter explaining about Hagop."

"I can understand you would leave Lucienne, but to abandon your children—"

"What about Xandra? How can I abandon her?" Albano erupted. "The children have had me. They've received my time, my energy, and love, and care. They've had their turn. Whereas Xandra continued to get nothing!"

"They would think you didn't love them. Is that something you can live with?"

"But I do. I love them so very much! Even Lucienne, I want her to have a good life. I want them to be happy." He looked at his uncle imploringly. "But I need Xandra. I need her, and she needs me, more than I need my children and more than they need me at this point in their life." At once, the absurdity of his logic beset him. "But if the children see that I chose Xandra over them, it would destroy everything they believe to be true about me, or about her. They would know I have lied to them all these years. They would hate me for what we did to Lucienne."

"If you disappear," Uncle Moshe said, "the police will think that you were the one who murdered Hagop or that you were Xandra's accomplice. When this happens, the government is likely to confiscate the money you have."

"They would have no grounds."

"How long before they learn that you are Jewish? They would find any loophole in the law. If they succeed, how would your family cope? How would they survive? Not only that, but it would draw attention to your identity and your family's. And they would surely put their nose in all your activities, which might lead them to me and what we're trying to do here."

Albano slumped in his chair, as discouraged as he'd ever felt. "There is no solution," he said.

"Are you certain that you are willing to run away with Xandra?"

"Yes," Albano said.

"Even if that means you might become permanently estranged from your children?"

Albano stayed quiet for a minute, and then he said, "If they can be safe and protected without me, my answer is yes. But I can see how that is not possible. If I run away, they will be vulnerable. There is no solution to this."

"Actually, there might be one." Moshe hesitated. "One you will not like."

"What is it?"

Moshe got up from his chair and began pacing the room. "Let's speak from the standpoint of pure practicality. Imagine that you are dead."

"Dead?" Albano echoed.

"Imagine you died. The murder investigation against you would stop. Your family would be left alone."

"Yes," Albano shrugged. "But I am not dead."

"Lucienne and the children would have enough money to last in Algiers if they continued to live conservatively. When the war ends, provided Hitler is defeated, which will happen now that he had the fatal arrogance to turn on the Soviet Union, you know my certainty on this, Lucienne would gain access to the money in Switzerland. Eventually, the house in Paris might even be returned to her as well."

"But I am not dead and—" Albano interrupted himself, suddenly struck by the understanding of what Uncle Moshe was saying. They looked at each other. The solution appeared to him vividly. When people died, their loved ones moved on. "I believed that Xandra was dead," he muttered.

"And when you set fire to the boat off the coast of Cannes, no one questioned that you had all perished."

"And people went on with their lives," Albano said. The boat had burned down, they were missing, and there had been no further discussion on the matter, no investigation. People without fame came and went unnoticed in this life, especially in times of war. Uncle Moshe was right. If Albano died, it would mark the end of the police investigating him.

All he needed to do was to pretend to die.

Numbed by this realization, Albano looked at his hands. There would be very little time to prepare. In a matter of days, the Allied troops would be at Algiers's door. The dawn of the day after the Allied invasion might see Algeria free from the Nazi threat and Pétain's government, and Lucienne, Marceline, and Gustave would be safe in liberated French territory. "Only it matters to me that I see my children," Albano said in a fog. "How could I not be in their lives?"

"If they imprison you for murder, you will not be in their lives either," Moshe said. "They are old enough to start their own lives. Perhaps even without you. You said so yourself."

"In fact, they already have," Albano said. If they believed him dead, Marceline and Gustave would be devastated. They would mourn him, and they would grieve. But in a few weeks, a few months, a year, they would start anew. In Moshe's plan, their memory of him would remain intact. They would not feel betrayed. They would not once doubt he loved them. From a practical standpoint, it worked too: at the end of the war, they would inherit the assets hidden in Swiss banks. It would be a terrible betrayal, but they would never know about it. "Either I betray them and live without them," Albano said. "Or I betray Xandra and live without her,"

"What betrayal?" Moshe said impatiently. "You would be ensuring their safety and future, while sacrificing yourself." Moshe paced faster, talked faster. Albano could see all sides of Moshe at work: the big-hearted man, the warrior who already was planning the logistics of Albano's escape, and at the same time, the rug salesman, convincing himself as he tried to convince Albano. "You are the reason your children and wife weren't in Paris when the monsters rounded up our people in the Vel' d'Hiv. You are the reason they weren't trapped in the South of France when they started imprisoning

Jews there. You are the reason there will be a considerable amount of money waiting for them at war's end. They will remember you as the man who gave them their life through his quick-thinking, his decisiveness. What is better? Tell me. Is it better for your children and their children and grandchildren to think of you dead but heroic or rotting in jail for the murder of a vagrant?"

"But the lie…."

"So now you owe them the truth? Isn't it too late for this, Albano? Ask yourself: would their lives be improved by the knowledge that their father ran away and abandoned them for the woman they thought of as their nanny?"

Albano was thinking in even broader strokes. If he was gone, the children would have no choice but to turn into adults, and it was about time. They would have to care for Lucienne. Marceline would have to stop endangering herself. His daughter had a good head on her shoulders when it came to getting things done. And Gustave would become head of the family, and it would give him a function and a purpose. As the new head of the household, Gustave might be allowed to stay away from combat. This alone could guarantee his safety. "The children would have to grow up and stick together," he said.

Moshe stopped pacing and softened his voice. "Moreover, your love for Xandra would remain a secret from all, and so their respect for you both would be intact. Those are all things that matter to you."

"Although," Albano said, "this would be leaving Lucienne in her most fragile moment."

Moshe shrugged. "Lucienne can remarry if she finds a man foolish enough to have her."

"I asked Xandra to sacrifice everything for my children," Albano murmured. "And she has." He could see it now; it was his turn to make a sacrifice for Xandra, even though she would never ask him to – *because* she would never ask him to. He thought of his beloved, alone and exiled. He imagined himself with her, free, starting a life somewhere in Portugal, in Greece, in Palestine perhaps. "But I would never see my children again," Albano said numbly.

Moshe placed his fleshy palm on his heart. "You will always know what is happening to them, as long as I live. On my honor, I will do this for you."

"They will marry; they will have children." Albano's voice broke into a strangled sob. "Grandchildren I will never know."

Moshe sat down heavily on a chair. His forehead was moist with sweat. "You must do what you think is right," he said. "I have given you the wrong advice before." They both knew that Moshe's plan was no loss to him. Moshe never liked Lucienne. He would get to see Gustave and Marceline whenever he wanted.

"Every advice you gave me served God's purpose," Albano said. "I never could reconcile my beliefs and my actions, my heart, and my reason. Each time I do one thing, it brings a result that seems worse than the original problem. I suffered when I thought I had lost Xandra, and then when I found her, I suffered even more. And now I am about to suffer in yet a new way." His throat constricted; his decision was made. "I want to do this for Xandra," he said. "I want to start anew with her. That is what I want."

Moshe smiled sadly. "God knows the saintly woman has earned it."

Albano had seen his uncle do this time and again, the way he set aside emotional components, including fear, and came up with a plan. "The day of the Allied operation will be mayhem," Moshe said. "That's the day to do it. We'll manufacture your death and whisk you out of the country."

"How?" Albano asked.

Moshe blurted out ideas as they came to him. "An event. An explosion. A fire. A mission where you set up explosives … somewhere. And something goes wrong. We produce charred remains. I know someone at the morgue. We get a body and burn it beyond recognition. And then we place it where you would have been. You, dead as a Resistance hero, which by the way you are. Your reputation preserved, beyond reproach."

"What if the Allied operation fails? My family would be left in Algiers to fend for themselves. I simply won't do this to them."

"Then we hide you in the chamber for a few days, and we watch what happens," Moshe said.

"The chamber," Albano repeated. That musky room where they had hidden countless people already. Food, water, a windowless, soundproof place hidden from sight to take refuge in for a few days.

"If the landing fails, you can always reappear a few days later," Moshe continued, "saying that you were trapped somewhere. But if the landing is successful, and your family is safe, then you head off to Portugal. We will get you and Xandra a new identity as husband and wife."

"As husband and wife," Albano echoed, mesmerized by the sound of it. They would no longer have to hide their love. They would not have to lie. And at the same time, they would be hiding forever – lying forever.

"I will help your family in every way they need," Moshe said, his hand on Albano's shoulder. "I will be the liaison. You will know of their whereabouts. I will tell you everything. One day you could come back to them if you chose to, and explain why you did this."

"Fake my death only to reappear years later? What kind of man would do this?"

"A man who, through a dark twist of fate, has found himself in an impossible predicament," Moshe said, indignant that Albano would entertain any other thought. "A generous man. A loving man. A man willing to sacrifice himself."

The simplicity of Uncle Moshe's solution, its finality, were as if an almighty giant hammer of judgment had descended from the sky onto Albano's head. Like a death sentence, and at the same time, like salvation. Albano was overwhelmed. This was not a road that could be walked back in the opposite direction. But suddenly, more than anything, he longed for his life to take this new turn. "I promised Xandra that when the children grew up, she and I would be together," he said. "Now the children are grown. Marceline might be headstrong, but she also has real strength."

"More than most men I know."

"As for Gustave, my presence is almost an impediment to his becoming himself. Lucienne deserves her freedom as well. Maybe she will get a chance to remarry."

"Without the embarrassment of a divorce," Moshe noted.

Albano closed his eyes. He had heard of a place, a small Greek island, where people had dug an entire city out of the mountain. A place with nothing to do but rest one's eyes on blue sky, blue sea, and walls painted in white lime. A place where, when the war was over, a man and a woman could live a simple life in peace.

When he looked up at Uncle Moshe, his face was pale, and he was shivering, but his eyes were dry.

"And so, it is yes?" Moshe asked gravely.

"It is yes," Albano answered.

****

November 8, 1942

Inside the secret chamber, Albano listened in for the sounds of gunfire, but he heard nothing. Back at the apartment, his children and his wife were asleep when he had gotten out of bed and left this life with nothing other than the clothes on his back. He had walked to Uncle Moshe's place, making sure no one saw him. He had left his family for the last time without being able to say good-bye, or ask for forgiveness.

Had the Allied forces already entered the Algerian sea? From inside this room, he had no way to know. Had the invasion begun? Would it be successful? The Resistance was in place. Outside, people might already be risking their lives for freedom while he stayed in hiding.

If the invasion failed, he would return home to his family.

If it was a success, he would take the fishing boat to Portugal and be reunited with Xandra.

At the bridge, which was set to explode in just a few minutes, two of Moshe's men had taken a corpse of bulk similar to Albano's from the morgue. That corpse would be set in flames at the time of the explosion. Albano's wallet, his hat, and his handkerchief would be left nearby, proof that the unrecognizably scorched body was, in fact, his.

His family would have a good life – a life without him. He wiped his tears; there would be many more. He would never hold his children again. He would never again see them or meet his grandchildren.

And then he felt a flutter of happiness. Xandra. Soon he might be with her again. She would know that he was choosing her over them this time. Their life, which had been interrupted by fate twenty years before, would begin again. A fire had stolen their future, and now another fire would return it to them.

CHAPTER 7

The Curator of Broken Things

On the plane to Los Angeles, Cassie had a dream. Her father was in it. In the dream, she was the mother, and he was the child. She held his hand firmly. They wanted to cross a street with cars zooming in front of them. On the other side of the street was an island with white houses built on a cliff. Suddenly the boy let go of her hand and leaped to the other side of the street. She woke up.

****

At the airport, Peter was the first person she saw after she passed through security. It was a different Peter she faced. Or else she was the one who had changed. "How is your father," he asked.

"Like you care now?"

"Don't make me out to be a monster because I asked you to come home early," Peter said.

"You're not the reason I came early," she said. "And I don't want to talk about my father."

"Oh boy, I sense a mood," Peter said.

They were on the 405 freeway. The Porsche smelled of Jessica's perfume. Thin palm trees reached for the hazy blue sky. The anchors to Cassie's life had become unmoored. Now it was her life in Los Angeles that felt unreal. Would her time in Paris recede just as easily? Would memories of Hervé, the hospital, her dad, and Marceline fade until they had no more corporeality than a dream?

Peter asked, "Have you had a chance to—"

"Work on the screenplay? No."

"I sent you a tablet at great expense."

"About that tablet …"

"You broke it!"

"I gave it to someone."

"What?" Peter yelped.

"To my aunt. I needed a parting gift."

"For God's sake, Cassie, it cost six hundred bucks!"

"Six hundred dollars for you is like six dollars to a normal person," she said. They did not speak again until they were driving up Laurel Canyon, when Cassie said, "I can't work until I get some rest. Can you come back in a couple of hours?"

Peter dropped her off at her house. She let herself in. Everything was exactly as it was eight days ago when she had received that phone call from Sabine. It might as well have been eight years ago. She could hardly remember the person she was then. The cardboard boxes intended for the Salvation Army were still stacked near the front door, awaiting pickup. They were still overflowing with Peter's and the kids' bric-a-brac: an old tennis racket, beach towels, bad art, that frame with the broken glass and a key mounted against velvet, a pair of ice skates used once. Before leaving for Paris, she knew she needed a change, but spring cleaning had been as far as her imagination stretched. That's what she did: she swallowed feelings; she reacted to trivial things but let the big ones slide. She had bickered with Peter when what mattered lay dormant like hidden abscesses.

If Paris had been on the fence about deciding between winter and spring, here in Los Angeles, it was summer. When wasn't it summer in Los Angeles? The sleek architectural kitchen in which she never cooked basked in natural light. Outside the bay windows, the mountain was peppered with multi-million-dollar houses with infinity pools, and indoor-outdoor kitchens with sandstone countertops and flower arrangements dropped off twice weekly, and maids that picked up dirt before it could hit the floors. Sabine would get a kick out of that. But for Cassie, the charm had waned.

Part of her longed for her ignorance of a week ago, before Paris, before Hervé, before Marceline, when her defenses had worked pretty well for the job of living her existence. How she saw her life, how she saw her marriage, how she saw her family, and how she saw herself: all of that was gone. What would replace it? She tried not to think about Hervé, but thoughts of him were creeping in through the back door, and each time they did, her throat constricted. Disappointment. In him. In herself.

She sat on the couch, curled up on her side, rested her cheek on a throw pillow, and sank into a deep sleep.

Two hours later, the sound of a key opening the front door awakened her. "Look what Santa brought!" Peter said in a thundering voice. Peter had never once respected her sleep. He plopped down on the couch heavily, sitting on her foot.

"Ouch!" she yelped. She sat up, her head in a fog.

"It is Christmas in April, yes, it is!" he exclaimed, unpacking a laptop. "Here it is! A brand new 15-inch, complete with screenwriting software! I know a guy, don't thank me." Cassie grunted and put a throw pillow over her face. "Wake up sleepy head," he continued. "We're open for business!" Cassie rubbed her eyes. Every molecule in her brain told her to get back to sleep. She dragged her feet to the kitchen sink and splashed cold water on her face. She prepared coffee on automatic pilot, a confused part of her wondering how it could be so bright out when, in her brain, it was the middle of the night.

Later, they sat across each other facing their respective laptops, the same way they always did, and she dipped her lips in her coffee. "Do you have fresh Oreos," Peter asked. "Those from last week must be stale."

"That's the beauty of processed food, Peter," Cassie grumbled. "It can't go stale because it was never food to begin with."

They opened a shared document. Peter was in a chatty mood. He went on, and on, and ON: about the screenplay, about Jessica, about the baby. He moved his arms, his eyebrows, his mouth. It all felt like gibberish. She wanted silence. She could not focus on what he was saying or on the page in front of her. She looked at Peter and his moving mouth and suddenly had the vision of herself hurling the content of her mug across the table to make him SHUT UP. Instead, she focused on the page in front of her. Her mind was blank. Across from her, Peter was chatting happily and typing up useless sentences, pretending to work. Really, he was doing as he always did: he was waiting for her to do the thinking. But the only thinking she was capable of was that she did not want him to be there. She did not want to hear about the producer, the film, Jessica, or their stupid baby.

"Chop, chop. You're off your game, Cassie," he said.

"Why don't you come up with an idea for a change?" She put her hands in her lap as they turned into fists. *Peter was a user and a manipulating jerk, and she did not want to hear another word from his lying mouth.*

She drank her coffee, typed a few words, erased them. The coffee was starting to work. Or was it really the coffee? Her skin buzzed. She erased a sentence Peter had just written, then a whole paragraph. Seeing what she was doing, he looked up at her. "What are you doing? You're not supposed to do that. That's not how it works!"

"No, you're right. How it works is that you write crap, and I try to make you think it's gold and change it anyway. This goes faster."

"I can see that France awakened the bitch within," Peter said. He looked good in his V-neck T-shirt. Not Hervé-good, but handsome nonetheless. She realized that she was feeling this without the usual pinch of wistfulness.

Things did have a way to work out for Peter, didn't they?

Don't, she told herself. But she could tell it was too late. Peter looked at her, handsome and unperturbed while everything in her life was going to shit. "There is something I've meant to ask you," she said, grabbing the empty coffee mugs from the table. She went to the sink and turned on the faucet.

"Go ahead, sweetie," he said, closing his laptop and stretching lazily on the chair.

"I'd like you to answer truthfully," she said. She rinsed the mug, her back turned to Peter, gathering strength.

"O-kay," he said, separating the syllables to indicate his misgivings about any conversation that might require truth.

She needed to look at him, or he would find ways to elude her. Elude her. That's what she had allowed him to do for too long. Courage. She breathed in, filled her lungs, turned around, leaned against the sink, wiping her hands on a cloth to appear casual. "When did it really start?" she asked in the most detached tone she could muster.

"Start what?" he asked. He unpeeled the top of the Oreo package, took out a cookie, and put it into his mouth.

"With Jessica," she said. "When did the two of you start your thing?"

Peter stopped chewing, then started again, slower, as though the cookie had turned to sand in his mouth. "What thing?"

"You didn't meet her after we separated," she calmly said. "You met earlier. Much earlier."

Peter swallowed but did not reach for a second cookie. "I'm not sure what you're talking about."

She stayed at the sink. She needed to lean against it for support because what she was about to do demanded more courage than she thought herself capable of, and at the same time, it required her to be sneaky. Very sneaky. Peter-sneaky. "You and I have a good relationship," she said. "We work well together. I've grown to appreciate Jessica. We're all a big family now." He was staring at her, making his face expressionless. It took everything she had to appear conciliatory. "We're grown-ups. I'm just curious, that's all. I think it's time to come clean. Put this all behind us."

"We met when I said we met," Peter said. Now he was sitting upright in his chair, everything about his posture and his tone on guard.

She returned to the kitchen table and sat down close to him, like a trusted old friend, and leaned toward him. Too much depended on her calm. She could not back down. If she did not get the truth from him now, she never would. "The twins remember Jessica showing you houses when they were five years old."

He looked surprised. "They said that?"

"You met Jessica twelve years ago. You know that; the twins know that; Jessica knows that, and I know that." She added, honey in her voice, "Don't you think for the sake of our relationship you owe me to verbalize it?" She patted him on the arm and said sweetly, "Don't worry. I won't get mad." She pushed the box of Oreos soothingly toward him. He looked at her hand and at the box of Oreos, took a cookie, and put it in his mouth.

"I was looking for houses, and you didn't want to come," he said. "And there she was. She showed me a couple of houses. The children were there. I was not trying to do anything behind your back." He added, accusatorily, "you were invited to be part of this. I asked you a hundred times, but you refused to entertain the idea."

"I didn't come along, and there she was," Cassie said. She made herself sound motherly.

"And there she was," he repeated, as though things from there were self-explanatory.

"And after a while, you continued house hunting, but you didn't bring the kids anymore."

"They got tired of it; you know kids."

"And you started an affair."

He shook his head, "Cassie…."

"I'm way past this, Peter." She said this with a smile and so casually that she should have been offered an Academy Award on the spot. "Come on. Just tell me. Get it off your chest. You'll feel better."

Peter was uneasy about the whole thing. "I was extremely devoted to you."

"It's okay," she said, magnanimously. "A man is only a man."

He looked relieved. "I've wanted to tell you this so many times. But I did not see the point in hurting you."

"But that affair. It went on for a while, didn't it?"

"Yes," he said, shrugging. For the very first time in forever, Peter's eyes were telling the truth.

"For years if I'm correct."

"You promise you won't get mad?" Peter said guilelessly.

"Honey, I already know. I just need to hear it from you." She was lying. Still now, and even though she should have known, she did not know. She had not wanted to know. And now she needed to know as though her life depended on it. Had Peter looked at her at that moment, he would have sensed the hairline fractures in her tone, the cracking varnish of her composure. Instead, he peered into the box of Oreos, hunting for the perfect one.

"Twelve years ago. Yeah, that sounds about right. Yes. What can I say; we fell in love."

Cassie drew a silent, sharp breath. "So, in all fairness to me, wouldn't you say that the affair was the reason you were not into me anymore?"

"I was into you," he assured her. "I loved you both. Each in your own way."

Cassie let that sentence float between her ears. It was vague and amorphous and unsettling. "On the one hand, I was the mother of your children, but on the other hand, Jessica was hot."

"You were hot too," he said, chivalrously.

"Wasn't it hard on Jessica, that you wouldn't leave me? I mean, she was in her prime; she probably wanted children quite badly and, well, to be the other woman must not have been easy. How long did she have to wait until you finally left me? Let's see; the kids were five. We divorced when they were thirteen, so that's what? Seven years? Eight?"

"It was hard for her. And don't think Jess didn't feel guilty. She felt real shitty about it. You know how she's got this huge heart."

"Poor thing," Cassie said, her jaw clenched to the breaking point. "And then I decided to take time apart, and so you jumped at it. You moved out, and 'officially' met her for the first time."

"It was your decision to separate," Peter said, defensively, but at the same time dully, like an automaton that repeats itself one time too many. "I wanted to stay married for the kids. And you better believe that Jessica was pressuring me to leave you. But then you wanted to separate, and the children were older by then, so it happened, organically."

"Except…." Cassie had to pause. The image of Marceline came to her, and it stopped her from dissolving into tears. "Except, the only reason I mentioned a separation was that you didn't love me anymore."

"Unconsciously, you gave me my freedom," Peter said. Even this was a concept he must have repeated to himself.

"It's interesting how the subconscious works," she said. She was silent for a moment. "Eight years. Wow. That's quite something," she murmured to herself. "You had a mistress for eight years out of our twelve-year marriage."

"I'm sorry, Cass," Peter said. She could tell that he meant it.

"You know what's funny about it?" she said, "It's that if you add up the years and include the overlapping, Jessica's was with you longer than I was when we divorced."

"I didn't do the math," he said, irritated now.

"You know what's even funnier?"

"What?"

Her voice changed pitch. "What's funny is how the two of you can look me in the eye, invite me for dinner, invite me to your wedding even – and I came! And how she brown-noses me constantly. And how you use me, day after day, after day, to further your career. Of course, you didn't want to lose me. I would have stopped writing for you!"

"Writing with me," he corrected.

She took this in the solar plexus. Still, in the middle of this, he maintained the alternate reality, the brainwash. This was enough to send her to the other side. She was yelling now. "Oh, this was so perfect for you! You had me, the unsuspecting idiot, raising your children, working like a horse in the shadow, making your career possible. This is not something you would want to fuck up even for an unforgettable piece of ass like Jessica!"

"You said you would not get mad!"

"Well, I fucking lied!" she screamed.

"She was in love with me!" he screamed back.

"So was I!" she said, tears erupting from her eyes. "I was in love with you. I was in love with you from the day we met until long after our divorce. I'm probably still in love with you now!"

He bent his head and shook it with real sadness. "But I'm in love with her," he said. He had tears in his eyes, the big oaf. "I'm so sorry, Cassie. I do adore you. I care about you. You are a friend, very dear to me. And I have the utmost respect for you as the wonderful, selfless mother of my children. I never wanted to hurt you. Not then, not now."

Cassie felt something collapse in her. It was over. She knew the truth. She had to let go not only of the fantasy that she could get him back but of the hope that he had loved her.

Tough. To be tough was a quality, not a flaw, Marceline had said. This was where the courage part started. Cassie needed to learn to live without clinging to the hope of her father's love, and she needed to learn to live without Peter's. The very fabric of her soul had been shaped by cultivating those illusions. She did not even know how to live without the hope. "I'll have to live with this," she murmured.

"Can you forgive me? Cassie! You have to forgive me."

"I can forgive you for loving her. I even can forgive you for not loving me." As she said this, she knew it was the truth or that it would become the truth one day. She inhaled deeply and added coldly, "But I can't forgive you for the deception."

"Cassie, come on…."

She spoke slowly. "You say I'm your dear friend, but to you, I am nothing but a means to an end."

"How can you say such a thing?"

"It's not your friendship with me you're trying to protect. It's your ass."

"Cassie, you know that's not true."

"But I'm done with this."

"With what?"

"With all of it. For one, I'm done doing any kind of writing for you, or with you."

She saw a flash of anger on Peter's face, but he controlled it. "But, Cassie," he said. "Work is an entirely separate issue."

"All those years you denied me the credit I deserved. You knew my weaknesses. You banked on the fact that I would allow myself to be hidden from sight."

Now the anger in him was here too, bare and unbridled. "Here we go again. If it is writing credit that you want, you can get the credit. I can't believe you would be so egotistical."

"I'm egotistical?"

He was in attack mode. "Your ego needs feeding. Is that what it comes down to? Your name on a billboard? Sad, really."

"But when your name is on a billboard, that's not egotistical? Screwing a woman behind my back for years, that's not egotistical? Keeping your wife silent and unloved, that's not egotistical?"

"I'm done with this argument. It goes nowhere when you get hysterical."

"When you're angry, it's righteous, and when I am, it's hysterical. You know what, here is the good news. You won't have to put up with any more hysterics. I swear to you right now that I will never write another line for you. With or without credit."

"That's nonsense," Peter said. Somehow, at that moment, buried deep in the recess of her heart, she longed for him to tell her that she was wrong, that he loved her best, that his continued relationship with her was with no strings attached. But instead, he said, "You *have* to work for me. Per our contract!"

She looked at him and burst into laughter. She tilted her head back and laughed for a long time, freely, and without anger, while he stared at her, puzzled and furious. This fell so short of the declaration of love she had longed for. But perhaps, it was better. This was the truth she needed to hear. He did not love her, had not in over twelve years, if ever, and he was not about to start loving her now. But he *needed* her. He needed her for her skills, which meant she *had* skills. It was an admission of the importance of her work, the validation of her talent. "Consider this a breach of contract," she said, and with those words, she was drained of any residue of hope, expectation, or illusion. She was free of him.

At that moment, the front door opened. It was Jessica letting herself in. Waltzing in without even knocking first, as though it were her right, as though she were welcome to do so since, after all, Cassie had allowed her to steal her husband's heart and had let her insert herself into every moment of her children's life.

When Jessica walked into the kitchen, did she not see Cassie's and Peter's pale faces and shining eyes, the clenched jaws and fists? "Hi, you guys!" she chirped. She was dressed for horseback riding, lithe and tight in her close-fitting pants and tall black boots.

"Oh, Jessica," Cassie said, "I brought you a little something back from Paris." She caught the warning glance Peter gave Jessica, which only served to fuel her energy. She marched to her tote bag, marched back to face Jessica, pulled put the Monoprix plastic bag, and shook its contents out onto the floor. Out came all four of Jessica's exquisitely wrapped packages. They landed with small thuds, dusting the wood floor with glitter. With Jessica watching in mute shock, Cassie, with four sharp blows, stomped once on each with all the force she could muster. The packages burst in quick succession. Bam. Bam. Bam. Bam. In one fell swoop, Cassie kneeled, scooped up the mess of broken packages, put them back into the Monoprix bag, and thrust it into Jessica's hands. "My father, mother, and sisters thank you warmly and ask you to stay the hell away from them from now on," Cassie said.

In an instant, Jessica and Peter were out the door.

Cassie stood in the middle of the room panting. She felt a wave of relief beyond any kind she thought possible. From there, she ran to the couch, grabbed a throw pillow, and buried her sobs in it.

An hour later, she called Sabine. In her rush to get out of Paris, she had not told her sisters that she was leaving. "It's me," she said when Sabine picked up.

Sabine sounded frantic. "Cassie, where have you been? We've been trying to reach you. They said you checked out of the hotel. Are you staying with that guy?"

"I'm so sorry; I should have found the time to tell you. No, no more of that guy. He was just a fluke. Peter needed me for work, and well, after the circus at the hospital, and Mom, and Odile, and well, I was disgusted. Exhausted. Fed up with all of them, so I went home."

"Home … *where*?" Sabine moaned.

"Back in Los Angeles. I took the night flight."

Sabine had a sharp inhalation "Oh no, Cassie."

"What?"

"It's Papa…." She left her sentence hanging, perhaps counting on Cassie to fill in the blanks.

"What?"

"He didn't make it, Cassie. Papa passed away during the night."

Cassie felt the room swirl around her. Her knees buckled. "That's not possible! I *saw* him! Just hours ago." On the line, Sabine was silent. "He was awake," Cassie insisted. "He spoke to me. I just … don't understand."

"Can you come back?" Sabine said in a tiny voice.

"I'll be on the next plane out."

"Can you stay with me this time?" Sabine asked pitifully. "I don't want to be alone."

"I'll head straight for the airport. Just hang on for a little while."

After hanging up the phone, Cassie realized that none of her limbs worked. Her legs were limp. She sat on the first chair she found. This could not be! She and her father were not finished yet! He still needed to tell her what she needed to hear to feel whole! She waited for a feeling of reality to reenter her body. What did this mean? What just happened? *You didn't tell me your father was dying*, Hervé had said. And yet after hearing him say this, Cassie had left the country. Just how delusional had she been? Just how incapable was she of seeing things as they were? Maybe her mother was right: she was a liar. And the person she lied to the most was herself.

She sat on the couch wondering what to do next. She was numb. She needed a bag, a suitcase of some sort to shove in some clothes into. She looked at the pile for the Salvation Army. Was there something there she could use?

Something about the boxes piled near the door was at the tip of her consciousness and at the same time vague and urgent. What had Peter said before she left for France? It was something about her dad. What was it? What were they talking about? They were arguing about the kids. No, not about the kids: about the things she wanted to throw away. "Alex found that key, and your father said he could have it," Peter had said. "Alex put it in a frame because he liked the look of it."

A key?

Cassie flew to the pile of boxes. "Please, please, please," she repeated. She found it immediately: a small gilded frame, cracked glass, and, behind the glass, a key mounted on black velvet. This key was an object she had known her entire life! First, growing up, it had been in a drawer in the kitchen among batteries, chopsticks, and flashlights. One day, when he was perhaps six years old, and they were in France visiting her parents, Alex had found it. It looked cool to him. Her father said he could have it. Not only that: it was the very same key that Marceline had amongst the trinkets and pendants she wore around her neck. Keys to the safety deposit box had been in their possession the entire time! Marceline wore one around her neck, and Cassie had nearly thrown hers away!

She broke the glass hastily and turned it over between her fingers. It was heavy for its size. Engraved in the metal were three letters. B. S. G., Banque Société Générale.

She called Air France and made a plane reservation for that same night.

After that, she called Odile and her mother.

When she was done with that, she called Marceline.

CHAPTER 8

The Vault

Cassie slept on the plane for eleven hours straight. When she landed at Charles de Gaulle Airport, she had to explain to the border officer why she had flown out of Paris, to the United States, and back in under forty-eight hours. "My father passed away," she told the stranger, and for the first time since she learned the news, she burst into tears.

"Please take me to the Societé Générale Bank on Boulevard Haussmann," she told the taxi driver.

At the bank, she tapped her foot on the mosaic floor as she waited in line at the circular counter in the center of the room. When it was her turn, she presented the account number and the key.

She was taken to the entrance of a vault guarded by a metal sculpture of entwined snakes, and then to a massive, circular, esoteric-looking metal door, all gleaming steel and copper, like a giant wheel that made her think of the entrance to the Nautilus. Inside the vault, she was taken to the third underground level via a small elevator. Finally, she was in the room that contained the safety deposit box. The room was covered wall to wall with built-in metal cabinets. The clerk unlocked one of the cabinet doors and slid it open, revealing a series of small drawers. He verified the number one more time and let her insert the key. He pulled the drawer out from the casing and set it on one of the several small copper desks that had sides built in opaque glass for privacy. Cassie sat down at the desk, took a deep breath, and opened the box.

It fell open like a ripe fruit.

Inside were two envelopes and five photographs.

Three of the pictures, yellowed in places and brittle, were black and white. Two of them were color. On each photograph was the same smiling couple. Each photo appeared to be of the couple in a different decade: in their forties, in their fifties, sixties, seventies, and eighties. The background was always the same: the sea with islands in the distance. In the back, of each photo always the same mention, Oia Santorini, and a date: 1945, 1952, 1963, 1974, 1985. Cassie recognized the man instantly. She had only seen a photo of him once when she was five or six, but it was him without the shadow of a doubt: handsome, like a silent movie star, well-aligned teeth, an aura of gentleness, and on the color photographs, that peculiar golden eye color they shared. This was Albano, her grandfather. But how could it be? The math didn't work. How could there be photos of him in the fifties, or eighties, when he had died in 1942 at the age of forty?

The woman beside him was very short, petite, with long black hair in the early portraits, which became gray, then white in subsequent photos. Her eyes were grave, dark, and beautiful. Cassie took a closer look. On the right half of the woman's face, below her eye, alongside her temple and her cheek, and down her neck, there seemed to be some sort of disfiguration, as though her skin had melted terribly.

Cassie felt a chill run through her body.

Sandra, the nanny?

Astonished, she turned the photos, looking at them from every angle, trying to understand with her eyes what her heart already knew.

She took out the first letter, unfolded it. It was addressed to Uncle Moshe and signed by her grandfather.

Oia Santorini, Greece, December 1977

Dear Uncle Moshe,

Xandra and I cherished every word of your last letter. On the picture of Gustave's family, baby Cassandra looks like Marceline at the same age, don't you agree? And little Odile looks so serious! Xandra and I think she takes most after her father. Will Gustave and Raymonde have a third child you think? As always, your letters and photograph fill us with utter joy.

The wind knocked out of her, Cassie stopped reading. Albano's letter was written several months after her birth and twenty years after he was supposed to have died. And he knew her name. And Odile's. And her mom's!

Xandra and I continue our happy life as troglodytes. This year, Paco took the reign of the family construction business, and I am thankful for the rest this allows me. We just celebrated my seventy-fifth birthday, and it is taxing to walk up and down the steep, uneven alleys of the city even if the donkeys are the ones doing all the carrying. Now I let Paco handle the physical work, and I oversee the stucco. I like to think that Oia Santorini keeps getting more beautiful every day, partly thanks to our work. Paco, always the attentive son, took it upon himself to dig deeper into the hillside and expand our bedroom to one side. This gave us a window. Now Xandra and I can watch sunrises from our bed! Since my last letter, Paco and his wife welcomed a second child. His name is Alyes, and he is the apple of our eyes.

Our joy can never be cloudless. Alyes, like his sister Eva, will never know that they have French cousins about their ages. Just as Paco will never know of Gustave and Marceline, or that they are his half-brother and a half-sister. The constant weight in my heart is the punishment I must suffer.

Some nights, it feels as though the only thing alive in the universe is my own mind, filled with regret and guilt. This year will mark thirty years since Operation Torch; thirty years since Xandra and I left Algiers. When I lay awake at night, I focus on my children's good lives. That Gustave and Marceline have become so close is perhaps my greatest comfort. Will you soon send the picture you promised of both their families together?

Xandra had a wonderful idea: You must celebrate your 90th birthday here in Oia. They have direct flights from Paris, and I promise that once you are off the airplane, all you would have to do is drink ouzo, eat Xandra's pastries, and rest your eyes on our incomparable sunsets.

Here is a photograph of Xandra and me that Paco took recently. She and I have aged, I know. But we're still as much in love as when we were children.

Please come and visit us. Xandra and I miss you very much.

Yours,

Albano.

Cassie read the letter again and scrutinized the pictures until the fog in her mind cleared up and the understanding burst through, but slowly, almost painfully, with a mixture of pain and joy, like a birth.

She opened the second letter. It was signed by Uncle Moshe.

Paris, July 2nd, 1987

Dearest Gustave and Marceline,

If you are reading this letter, it means that I am gone from this earth. It also means that you were able to piece together the riddle that led to the safety deposit box.

I am the one who had the finials engraved, one with the code to the vault box, the other with the bank's address, just as I am the one who gave you the two keys without telling you what they were for but to keep them because you might one day find out. The rest was up to you, or rather, up to God. I am leaving things up to fate. I could not make myself the arbitrator of what you should know, so I have created this riddle. If you are reading this letter today, it means that God wants you to know your father's secret.

Today, I must inform you of the truth. Your father, Albano, was not killed during Operation Torch. He did not die at 39 in the explosion of a bridge in Algiers. He died a month ago, at the age of 85, after a long, peaceful existence spent in Greece with the love of his life.

In 1942, under my advice and with my help, we staged Albano's death. A few days later, once Algiers was liberated and he knew the two of you and your mother would be safe, he fled to Portugal where he was reunited with Xandra, the woman you know as Sandra, the caretaker of your childhood.

"Oh my God," Cassie said out loud. She settled her breath and read on.

There is more to the story than Xandra appearing into your life when you were children. In truth, she and Albano knew each other long before you were born, and long before he ever married your mother. They met in 1913 in Smyrna when they were children, and fell in love then. Theirs was not an ordinary infatuation, but the kind of deep love one should only dream to experience in a lifetime. However, it was a dangerous and forbidden love between two people of different religions at a very precarious time and place in history. They had no choice but to conceal their love. When Smyrna burned to the ground in 1922,

Xandra and Albano were accidentally separated, and for years believed the other one dead. When you were five and seven years old, in 1930, eight years after the fire, Xandra was found alive. But by then, your father had started over in Paris and was married to Lucienne.

Xandra was a very principled and deeply religious woman. She never thought to break up your father's marriage, which was sacred in her eyes. She agreed to live at your house and take care of you on the condition that their secret love remained a chaste one. Perhaps it was madness on Albano's part to have Xandra join your family as your nanny, but what is a man to do who loves and wants to protect two families?

In 1942, when you lived in Algiers, Xandra was accused of killing a man. We believed the police would soon apprehend Albano as an accomplice. At the time you were seventeen and nineteen, and Albano had to make a choice. The circumstances of the man's death are not important. What is important is that your father and Xandra, had they not left the country, would have been arrested and surely accused of his murder. There would have been a trial, and your family's identities would have been revealed, putting you all at terrible risk. Staging Albano's death solved all the problems. By then you were adults, or nearly. At the time, it seemed the only solution. Operation Torch, I told him, was just the diversion he needed. He knew what this sacrifice entailed. He would thereafter live in hiding and would never again see his children. There was little time for him to make this terrible choice. The police had already begun their investigation.

The night of the Allied invasion of North Africa, we met at the bridge that was set to explode. My men set up the explosion. Albano's hat and some of his clothes and personal belongings were put on a corpse, while Albano escaped by car and was taken to a boat, and eventually abroad where Xandra awaited him. If you remember, I was the one who identified the body so you would not have to.

Over the many years, your father was never out of touch with your lives. Each time I visited you, I took photographs, as you might remember. I reported everything to Albano and gave him your photographs. I told him all the happy news. He knew that the money hidden away in Switzerland had allowed Lucienne to return to her family home and to live in material comfort. He learned about Marceline's life as a modern woman, about Gustave's three beautiful daughters. But I could never tell him the entire truth. How could I have told Albano that his children's rivalry had hardened into hatred? I could not do this to him. Over the years, I did all within my power to help the two of you reconcile, but you never ceased to be inexplicably thick-headed and full of bitterness toward each other.

As I write this letter, I am 97 years old. Xandra and Albano should have outlived me, but it seems that few people do. It was Albano's deepest wish that Gustave and Marceline have a close relationship. He died believing this was the case. I am at peace with the fact that I lied to him, and I don't regret my actions which allowed for Albano and Xandra to be together at last. For 42 years, they lived in peace on the island of Oia Santorini. Their miracle was that Xandra, who had been told that she could not have children, became pregnant soon after leaving Algiers. Paco was born. They had two grandchildren by the time Xandra passed away abruptly at age 85.

When this happened, Albano buried his beloved. After that, he did something he had attempted to do sixty years before in Smyrna when he thought he could not live without her; he swam out to sea and let the waves take him.

Yours truly,
Moshe

Cassie put down the letter, disconcerted to find herself at a small desk inside a bank vault. Everything Marceline had told her over the last few days was turning on its head. The locations and events from Marceline's account matched: Paris, Cannes, Algiers, Xandra as a murder suspect, Operation Torch, the bridge explosion. But the story was something else entirely.

She looked at the photos of Albano and Xandra. They stood, their bodies tight next to each other, he with his arm around her waist, or draped over her shoulders. They smiled radiantly in their adoration for each other.

What they had done was unforgivable. They may or may not have been involved in a murder and wanted to run away, but Albano had pretended to be dead and abandoned his children and wife! He had conducted a love affair with the nanny for nearly the entirety of his marriage to Lucienne.

And yet, after listening to Marceline's side of the story for the last few days, part of Cassie understood Albano. She rooted for him. She also understood, as she was reading the letter, that she would never tell Marceline any of this. And had her dad been alive today, she would not have told him either. Her head spun with the ramifications, the altered course of so many lives and Gustave and Marceline burdened with shame and guilt they did not deserve, and entrenched in resentment that had no legitimacy. But it would be a terrible thing for Marceline to learn that Albano had abandoned and betrayed them, and so she would say nothing.

She put the envelopes and the photographs back in the box, closed it, and rang for the clerk to return the box to the vault.

Outside the bank, she hopped in a taxi and headed for the Montparnasse cemetery.

The taxi stopped outside the cemetery gate just as Marceline's limo pulled up. The chauffeur came out and walked around to open Marceline's door. The old lady looked regal but frail in a structured black coat and hat. Cassie came to greet her.

"I wish I could have met your family on a less somber occasion," Marceline said.

"We're all very thankful that you're letting my dad be buried in the family sepulcher."

"Why would Gustave not be? This is where he belongs. Our mother is here, as well as her father and mother and her two brothers. Sadly, Father's remains were buried in Algiers."

"We' re happy that you came," Cassie said, in case her mother and sisters omitted to say it. She saw that Maurice had walked around the car to open the door to another passenger. To her surprise, Marceline's gardener emerged from the car. Why on earth would he come to her father's funeral? The old man was dressed to the nines and stood, light on his feet and distinguished in his suit. His hair was bright white and contrasted handsomely with his tanned skin. His kind eyes smiled at Cassie, and he came to her and took her hand in his. "I am sorry for your loss," he said in his North African accent.

"Thank you. My name is Cassandra, by the way," she said. "I'm afraid I don't know your name."

"Don't be absurd," Marceline said, as she clutched the old gardener's arm.

Cassie widened her eyes, understanding. "You can't be … are you …?"

"I'm Khaled," the man said, shaking Cassie's hand.

"I thought you were—"

"The gardener?" Khaled asked.

Marceline laughed. "Evidently not! He's my lover."

Khaled smiled playfully and said, "I tend to all Marceline's gardens."

"Well, that's rich!" Marceline exclaimed. "How was it not evident? I've been yapping away about him for days as he was right in front of us."

"I never made the connection," Cassie said, astounded at her blind spots.

Marceline shrugged with irritation, "I thought it was quite obvious."

"I asked if you and Khaled ever married," Cassie said, "and you said no, so I assumed—"

"I did not think you would be so provincial as to assume that marriage is the only way to have a relationship," Marceline said.

"So, you two did have a happy ending!"

"What ending?" Marceline said. "There is no ending in sight as far as I am concerned."

Khaled took Cassie's hand in his again. "I met your father just once."

"When you saved his life."

"He was a gentle young man," Khaled said.

"Thank you."

"Have you written my biography yet?" Marceline asked her as they walked inside.

"It's only been a few days," Cassie said, flustered. "It will take months. Years."

"You better get started soon, then."

"How did you and Khaled get together at last?" Cassie asked.

"Well, there was the Second World War. And then there was the Algerian war," Khaled said. Minus his ladder and crumpled trousers, and in his well-cut suit, Khaled was a regal, handsome man. And now that Marceline stood by him, putting her hand on his arm, his identity was, as Marceline had said, obvious.

"It's a very long story," Marceline said. "I will tell you about it someday. It's ripe with drama. You'll love it. In fact, I think you should write it."

Cassie could not help herself; she was beaming. "As long as in the end love conquers all," she said.

"Did you give Gustave the finial?" Marceline asked.

"I tried."

"You failed, you mean?"

"He was delirious at the time. Or hostile towards me. Or you; I will never know. He still had you and me mixed up."

"He rejected the finial?"

"I don't even know if he saw it." Cassie thought of stopping there but then decided that if one person would understand, it was Marceline. His rage at them was one thing they had in common. "I think he resented me until the end. I could never impress him quite in the way I hoped, even when I brought him the finial. I was naïve about ever gaining his approval. I guess I can say that I tried, so that might be worth something." Cassie took a deep breath. In the hospital room, in the middle of the mayhem, she had told her dad that she loved him. She was convinced now that he had turned away on purpose, that he knew it was she who was in the room, and that he had held back his affection until the end. But she would never know for certain, and it was better that way.

"Perhaps," Marceline said, "what you are naïve about is not whether he could not approve of you or not, but why."

"What do you mean?"

"It was not because he found you inadequate, darling, but because he found you impressive."

"Impressive? Me?"

"Well, yes," Marceline said. "It scared him. It made him feel insignificant. Wasn't that his reason for hating me all along? He made a sort of amalgam between us two, for whatever reason I don't know. But believe me when I say that he wasn't upset that you weren't good enough. He worried about how remarkable you might turn out to be. He worried about your potential. With all due respect to your departed father, he seems to have made every effort to suppress in you any sort of ambition of greatness."

"But why?" Cassie exclaimed.

"For fear that you would turn into me."

She faced Marceline, blinking. What if her aunt was right? Yes, it was very possible that her father had wanted, consciously or not, to smother Cassie's *spark*. What if the parts of herself Cassie had smothered to please her dad – and later to please everyone else – were, as Marceline pointed out, her *best* qualities? He had called her annoying when she was excited, arrogant when she showed determination, a know-it-all when she was passionate, bossy when she was confident. She had, over the years, learned that creativity, ambition, the desire to shine were somehow shameful and better left hidden from sight. He had redrawn the map of who she was, who she could dare aspire to be. And now came the curious concept that those traits weren't flaws but gifts – attributes that should not be squashed but fostered and nurtured.

It was as though her dad's fixation on Marceline had compelled him to repair a perceived injustice through his daughters. She had played the role of

Marceline, and Odile the role of Gustave. Only in this new scenario, Gustave came out on top, and Marceline was the one whom everyone dismissed.

Perhaps, in the end, Cassie had not failed her dad by missing some kind of mark. It was he who had failed her. Perhaps she wasn't unlovable, but rather he had failed at loving her.

****

Before the service started, Cassie introduced Marceline and Khaled to Sabine, Odile, and her mother. Odile's face and eyes were swelled up as though she had been crying for days. Raymonde was curiously dry-eyed. Perhaps it would hit her later. "I am very sorry for your loss," Marceline told her sisters and her mother. "Thank you for including me. Gustave and I may not have seen eye to eye, but we share the same blood."

"Thank you for letting my dad be part of the sepulcher," Odile said. "It means so much to be in such a beautiful place. To think that he belongs here is heartwarming. To all of us." She stopped herself to blow her nose. "I'm not sure why, but it feels as though burying him here honors him. It makes him belong somewhere special."

"We have four generations buried here," Marceline said. "Do you know that your father comes from a great Parisian family. Gustave belongs here. And so will you, one day." She added with a Machiavellian smile. "I am told that you did not know that Gustave was Jewish?"

"Well … we…." Odile stuttered. "He was not religious. Not at all."

"One can be Jewish without religion. Gustave was Jewish as a fact of history, not as a matter of choice. I'd love to explain to you how that works sometime."

They were interrupted by the start of the service. The room was much too large. There were Raymonde and Sabine, Odile, her husband and children, Marceline and Khaled, a few neighbors and old co-workers, several of Raymonde's friends. In all, about twenty people. Not enough to fill two rows of chairs. Odile had decorated a table with photographs of her father with her children and a few other photos of the family. There were no photos of Cassie's children, as though they had been erased from existence. There were flowers people brought, but in the vast room, they looked meager, insufficient. Odile gave a tearful eulogy. Neither her mother nor Sabine volunteered to talk. And so, without having planned what she would say, Cassie went up to the pulpit.

"When I was on the plane coming here, I scribbled a few thoughts," Cassie said. "It was not meant to be read out loud, but … I guess why not. Here it goes:

"We're all the product of our family's dynamic, which is bred from the generation before us, and that generation is filled with the issues and neuroses of the generation before that. In a way, we are fools to believe that we choose our lives." She paused, unsure. "Here is what this means to me: my dad tried his very best throughout his life while carrying the weight of his difficult childhood. He tried not to burden his family with it, but it was there … under the surface. I loved him very much. I tried to show this to him in every way that I could. I'm thankful that I got to do that because to love someone and express it fills the heart. I'd rather experience unrequited love than feel no love at all."

Across the room, Odile's face turned red, and Marceline nodded approvingly.

Later, when they emerged from the sepulcher into mid-day light, Cassie looked up, stunned. Standing in a black suit outside the sepulcher, holding an oversized funeral wreath covered in white gladiolus, was Hervé.

"Who is this?" Sabine whispered in her ear.

"That," Cassie said in disbelief, "is Prince Charming."

On unsteady legs and her heart thundering in her chest, Cassie walked toward him. In his suit and coat, Hervé looked incredible.

She took him aside. "How did you know about today?" she asked.

"I work at the hospital, remember," he said.

Steady your cardiac rhythm, she thought. "It's nice of you to come," she said.

"I never knew your last name, where you live exactly, or where to reach you," Hervé said. "I'm sorry to intrude in your family circumstance, but this was my only chance to catch you."

"Listen," she said. "Can we talk later?"

"When and where?"

"Later," she said evasively. "Somewhere. Not here. I mean this is not the time or place. At a café later, maybe?"

He shook his head. "Not a chance. You'll never show up."

"Why would I not show up?"

"Because you're afraid of me."

"I am not!"

"Afraid of what I represent."

"And what do you represent?"

"The future," he said.

She thought about this. "Can you stick around?" she asked.

Hervé followed her into a small reception room. Sabine grinned at her, and Cassie grinned back. A cold buffet had been set in the center of the room and Cassie watched the surreal spectacle of universes colliding: Marceline speaking to Hervé, her mother speaking to Khaled, Hervé speaking to Odile. Cassie thought of Albano and Xandra, how their secret had held separate universes intact. She felt Xandra's and Albano's presence with her, hovering, looking down at them.

At one point, Hervé cornered her near a window and said, "You look very pretty today."

"What are you talking about?" Cassie said. "I'm at my worst; I'm jetlagged beyond recognition, my dad just died, my ex-husband and his wife are … the point is, I look and feel like crap."

"Your worst is better than ninety-nine percent of the population's best," he said, and she giggled like a school girl.

It seemed that the whole room was looking at them with curiosity, except for Odile, who looked about to combust with anger. "I don't know what I am, at the moment," Cassie said. "A basket case, I think. I really can't focus on this right now."

"Understood," Hervé said. "I'll make myself discreet."

"Fat chance," she said.

She walked toward Odile. "I can see that you have a bug up your butt," she said. "What now?"

"What the hell was that?" Odile asked angrily.

"He's a friend. What, I'm not allowed to bring a friend?"

"I'm talking about what you said in there. About neuroses. You had to attack Papa one last time? At his funeral!"

"Really? Are you going to do that thing right now?"

"What thing?"

"That thing you do where you suffer more than me?"

"I *am* suffering more than you!" Odile cried out. "Here you are with your new boyfriend, and your little clique of new relatives, and I didn't see you shedding a tear. Instead, you do this bogus eulogy, like salt in the wound, blaming Papa."

"That was me trying to provide him with extenuating circumstances."

"For heaven sake!"

"Look, Odile. You can live in your bubble all you want, but I can't. Papa grew up as a Jewish kid in Paris at one of the most openly anti-Semitic times in history. He and his family ran for their lives, literally, to avoid being killed in the Holocaust. He then proceeded to legally change his last name, marry a non-Jew, cuts all ties with his family, raised his daughters Catholic, and never tell them about his past. He swore Maman to secrecy, as though being Jewish were either a terrible crime, a terrible shame, or both, and you don't think it had an impact? And then there is everything that happened that even Papa didn't know about."

"Like what?"

"His family had secrets, just like ours, and those secrets had secrets. All that is passed down as neurosis. That's what the eulogy was about."

Odile sighed. "You are exhausting, you know. For just this once, on the day of his funeral, could you have not stirred things up?"

"My whole life I tried to please Papa, but it was impossible. Just this week, I understood why for the first time. I could not please him because I reminded him of Marceline. There was nothing I could have done. I was marked from the start."

"How long do you plan on blaming him? Whatever he did to you, when you were a kid, you're more than happy to do it to yourself now."

"What are you talking about?"

"You're subconsciously finishing the job Papa started: beating yourself up for some masochistic reason."

"How so?"

"In your marriage. You did the same thing you accuse Papa of doing. You accused your ex of squashing your ambition and talent when, in fact, you're doing this to yourself."

"You have no idea of what you're talking about. You know precisely ZERO about my marriage or my work."

"It's so much easier to resent someone else and be the victim."

"You're such a BIG bitch, Odile!"

Cassie left Odile planted there and rushed to the bathroom. She avoided looking at herself in the mirror and splashed cold water on her face. Reverberating with outrage, she dug into her purse and found her lipstick. With a trembling hand, she applied the lipstick, hating herself and everyone with whom she had ever come into contact.

But when she finally looked into her own eyes in the mirror, she saw: Odile was absolutely right!

Why risk making the man you love insecure with your talent and ambition? She had muffled her soul and spirit in the hope of pleasing her dad and her husband, and in the process of making herself smaller and unthreatening, she had lost herself completely. She had spent a lifetime pretending to be someone she was not, to devastating results. Her last-ditch effort at self-preservation had been to move to the United States, but there she had re-created the same pattern with Peter, offering him a reduced version of herself and then waiting for his seal of approval. She had kept herself in the shadows, made herself small and angry but unthreatening to his ego. Success, strength, those were not safe paths. Anytime she sensed she risked being impressive, as Marceline had said, she squashed it in the bud for fear that it would make her unlovable.

That was the reason she had let Peter take the credit for her work. How could she not end up resenting him? How could she not push him away? How could she not drive him to fall in love with someone else?

What would she look like today had her genuine talents and traits been valued by her father? What would it be like to be more like Marceline? What would freedom feel like?

She walked out of the bathroom and to the cloakroom and asked for her travel bag. She reentered the reception room and headed toward Odile. "Here," she said. "This belongs to you." She opened her bag, uncovered the finial, and put it in Odile's hand. "You have the pair now."

"Me?" Odile said, stunned. "Marceline gave it to you. Why me?"

"Because Papa would have wanted you to have them."

"Why?"

"You are the person in the world he loved most," Cassie said. She said this without anger or bitterness. She said it because it was the truth.

Odile eyes flooded with tears. "Are you sure you want me to keep both?"

"They were always meant to be a pair, to be whole. And I think that you're right. You are suffering more than I am today. For you, Dad's loss is brand new. Me, I've had a lifetime of practice losing him."

When she was speaking with Odile, Cassie saw Sabine shoot her a look. They met a few minutes later by a window overlooking the cemetery. "What was that all about," Sabine said. "You're giving Odile *the finial*?"

"I don't want to be mad at Odile anymore," Cassie said. "Gustave and Marceline hated each other, and look at the results."

"Not to change the subject," Sabine said, "but Hervé is a frigging dreamboat."

Cassie laughed. "I know! Right?"

Sabine twirled a strand of her hair between her fingers, hesitant. "Do you know what you said about me taking a leave of absence from my job? I think maybe it's a good idea. Being elsewhere for a while might help me digest everything. I need to jumpstart my thoughts in a new direction. My doctor said he would prescribe a few months off. Does your offer stand about California?"

"Absolutely! When?"

"Soon."

"Fabulous! Although there is this one thing I need to do. One place I need to go. I can't explain. Sorry if I sound overly mysterious."

"Speaking of mysterious, who is this man with Marceline, the old guy with the white hair?"

Cassie repressed a laugh. The day should have felt somber, but it was all so slapstick and out of body. "He's Marceline's lover," she said. "Her lover with gardening benefits."

****

When everyone had left, Cassie and Hervé walked to a nearby café on rue de la Gaité. They sat across from each other at the corner table. The place smelled of espresso and croque monsieur. Outside, it had begun to rain. It felt right to be there; it was their environment: she and Hervé in a Parisian café, sharing a small table.

"I have your boots by the way," Hervé said. "Your red boots; you forgot them at the hotel."

"How in the world?"

"I went to look for you. They told me you had checked out and forgotten your stuff. I said I'd return them to you."

"I had left them there on purpose. They're not really me."

"They're exactly you: hot-blooded and American."

"Is that how you see me?"

"Isn't that how you are?"

"I don't know what I am. The version of me I've stuck to my whole life is changing by the minute."

"You convinced me to make a change in my life," Hervé said. "I'm quitting my job. You were right. It was bad for the soul."

"What will you do now?"

"I'd like to go back to traveling, and to actual medicine. Doctors without Borders, something like that. I'm a few months away from recovering my license."

"Well, I'm glad for you. Congrats," she said coolly. "And thank you for coming. It was very considerate." She took hold of her purse.

Hervé put his hand on hers. "What's the big hurry? Do you have a better place to be? A plane to catch? Other love interests to push away?"

"I do have a plane to catch. Eventually."

"Why didn't you tell me where you lived?" he asked.

"Why didn't you tell me you worked at the hospital?"

"I thought I had. Looking back on it, where I worked must not have come up in the conversation."

"Okay," she conceded. "I guess that's possible."

"I was not trying to hide anything, but I'm pretty confident that you were. Why didn't you say anything about your dad being in the hospital? You told me everything else you were going through."

"I was looking for all kinds of reasons why it wouldn't work between you and me," she admitted. "I didn't want to be hurt. I didn't want to be disappointed."

"So you hurt me and disappointed me."

"That's because I didn't think anything would come of us. We had one date and then another. I knew I was leaving. But mostly, I think I was afraid of rejection if you knew I'd be gone a week later."

"Look, I don't collect women. I don't chase them looking for a boost to my ego. I'm just as afraid as you are to get my heart broken."

"You told me you were planning on traveling," she said accusatorily. "You said, and I quote, this was just a fun thing between us. By the second date, I thought that if I told you where I lived, you would see I had been deceptive. I thought … well, I thought I'd be gone before we'd have time to start to like each other."

"The first moment I saw you steal my table at La Jument Bleue, the harm was done," Hervé said. "I already liked you very much."

"You liked me for the time being. But it would have been temporary."

"Everything is temporary!" Hervé said. "I don't know the future. I might drop dead. You might drop dead."

"That's not exactly reassuring."

"I'm willing to take a chance with you."

She looked at him in amazement. "Take your chances with a liar who writes crappy movies?"

He smiled. "Who also happens to be sexy, and smart, and fun."

"My children are in college in the U.S., and I have a house there. In Paris, I have nothing. I can't put all my eggs in the same basket. I've been burned before."

"I have now experienced it."

"What?"

"The burn."

"Well, that's not me," Cassie said. "At least not usually. I am usually dreadfully reliable. I am the most boringly reliable person you will ever meet. When I make a commitment to someone, I stick to it. Believe me, I'm still trying to untangle myself from my relationship to my ex-husband, and he's been with another woman for twelve years, most of it when he was still married to me. That's why I lied to you. I needed to protect myself from my forever mentality."

"I can't commit to forever. No one honest can do that."

"And I'm afraid of temporary, so there you go. What if I gave myself to you, heart and soul, and then you tired of me? I'm afraid that there would be nothing left of me after I gave it all to you. Do you understand how terrifying that is? Not to mention how much pressure's put on you? And there is something else you need to know about me."

"Another big secret?"

"The biggest secret of them all."

"What is it?"

"I'm not tough."

"What?"

"That's the crippling narrative. That's how my family sees me. *Cassie is tough. She falls back on her feet.* You don't know how many times I heard that said about me. So, I act tough. I act as though I don't need anyone. I act as though things don't bother me. I act as though it doesn't matter to me if my kids forget my birthday, or if the man I love doesn't know my favorite flower, or if my mother doesn't call me to see how I'm doing. I might look as though all I need to be happy is to dispense love and care and remember other people's favorite flowers, and birthdays, and call them and anticipate their needs. But it's all an act. I need to feel known; I yearn for someone to anticipate my needs. I want to be the object of small kindnesses as much as the next person."

"That seems perfectly reasonable. I agree to all conditions."

"You what?"

He reached across the table for her hand. "Where do I sign up?"

"Well … I don't even know how to get started."

"With me?"

"With anything."

"How about we take it a moment at a time?" Hervé said, squeezing her hand.

Cassie looked at Hervé. "How do you do that?"

"You start with a good espresso machine – the crappy kind. And then you put good espresso coffee in it. And water. Then you pour it, and you take the sugar and the milk. None of that fat-free nonsense. And good bread, and good butter. And while the coffee is brewing, I take you in my arms and hold you very tight." He got up from his chair and came to sit beside her. "Like this." He took her in his arms. "And we have one good breakfast, and then we make love."

"Not love first?"

"Either way will be fine. But you can only be in one place at a time because if all you do is fret about the next moment, you miss out on this one."

CHAPTER 9

Epilogue

Oia Santorini, Greece. 2013

Barefoot and in a white cotton bathrobe, Cassie stepped out onto the terrace of the hotel room.

How easy it was for her to side with her grandfather for this terrible thing he had done. He had done it for love. He had lied and deceived and abandoned his family, and yet all she could think of is that he had not had a choice. This was a case of momentous double standard, to take the side of the adulterer. Because, in her own story of hidden love, she had played the role of Lucienne, the unloved, betrayed wife.

Love was love, and you didn't get to choose who you fell in love with. With luck, you fell in love with a person who loved you back. But what were the probabilities of that perfect synchronicity? She could see now that Peter, like Albano, had had a difficult choice to make. His choice to lie to her to preserve the family intact was messed up but had intrinsic value.

Falling in love, was, as it turned out, a free fall. It *happened* to you. It knocked you off course and transformed you. It made you act and think profoundly out of character. It made you throw caution to the wind. Now that she understood this, she could start to forgive Peter.

Everything she wanted to become was at her fingertips. She was done altering herself in the hope of being loved. With a little moxie, she could, at last, harness the power she had always suppressed. She could wear red cowboy boots or feathery boas and no bra. She could become a field nurse, climb high peaks, write epic novels, dabble in espionage, or be someone's lover. She could laugh too loud and have lipstick on her teeth and drink champagne for breakfast. She could sell the Godforsaken house and its spiral staircase leading to a narrower and narrower version of herself. She could dwell in hotels around the world and never set foot in another kitchen or lift another laundry basket. She could let the wind decide where she should live next.

She stepped out onto the terrace and into the bright morning. Oia Santorini was indeed one of the most beautiful places in the world. An entire city dug out from a hillside, all gleaming white-washed walls and dome-shaped roofs painted blue, and as a backdrop, the Mediterranean. Hervé, in a bathing suit and barefoot, was reading the paper at the table. Breakfast had been set under an umbrella. He folded the newspaper and looked at her. "What a vision you are," he said. "Are you nervous?"

"Terrified."

"All right then," Hervé said, folding his newspaper. "Let's go meet those Greek cousins of yours."

The end of The Curator of Broken Things Trilogy.

******

A note by the author:

Dear reader, I hope you enjoyed reading The Curator of Broken Things Trilogy. Since this is the first edition of this book, you might have detected typos and errors and I apologize for those. It was quite a labor of love for me and I am continuously seeking to improve the book with corrections from my readers, so if you detected issues, or just to say hello, don't hesitate to send me an email at ***corinegantz@live.com****. I love to hear from my readers.*

I hope you will kindly leave a review, or attribute 'stars' on Amazon or where you purchased the book. This will help nudge the series toward greater visibility.

You can also sign up for my newsletter at ***www.corinegantz.com*** *to received updates and promotions.*

Thank you so much for coming along for the ride!

Corine Gantz

ACKNOWLEDGEMENTS

Thank you to my first readers, Joanna Kamburoff, Katherine Kohler, Catie Jarvis, Peggy Schmouder, and Betsey Parlatore, for kindly and carefully sifting through versions of the books when they were still a mess. Thank you to Isabelle Bryer, Jan Schafer for their keen eye for post-publishing typos (no doubt saving me from mortal embarrassment by detecting that my characters at one point 'circled the *glove*'). I am incredibly thankful to Donald Berman, a man with the soul of a writer, for his precision in English *and* French and for his support for the novels. Most of all, thank you to my husband Joe for his tireless editing, his honesty, his intuition, his kindness, his ebullient optimism, and for not wavering in his belief in me in the past 30 years.

ABOUT THE AUTHOR

Corine Gantz was born in France where she spent the first twenty years of her life. She studied Contemporary Art at the Sorbonne and worked in advertising and marketing in Paris, San Francisco, and Los Angeles. Her first novel, *Hidden in Paris*, was published in 2011 and has been translated in nine languages. She is the mother of two sons and lives near Los Angeles with her husband.

Email her:
corinegantz@live.com

Visit her website:
www.corinegantz.com

For information, email:
corinegantz@live.com
www.corinegantz.com

The Curator of Broken Things Trilogy

Carpenter Hill Publishing

ISBN: 978-0-9834366-9-0

Proofreading and copyediting by Don Berman
donaldberman@hotmail.com

Cover illustrations by David Navas

Made in the USA
Middletown, DE
25 April 2022

64711359R00456